The Infinite Cycles of Qeauríyx

Awakenings

M. J. Sales

b15138173

THE INFINITE CYCLES OF QEAURÍYX

AWAKENINGS

Dedication

For my Dad (Michael) who introduced me to Tolkien, Asimov, and countless literary, religious, philosophical, musical, and historical conversations...

&

For my Ma (Juanita) who typed my stories at her job, listened to me read Howe and Cleary stories when I was a kid, and encouraged my compassion, star-gazing, and weirdness...

&

For the baby my wife and I lost... Mommy and Daddy will always love you...

CONTENTS

Qeauríyx West

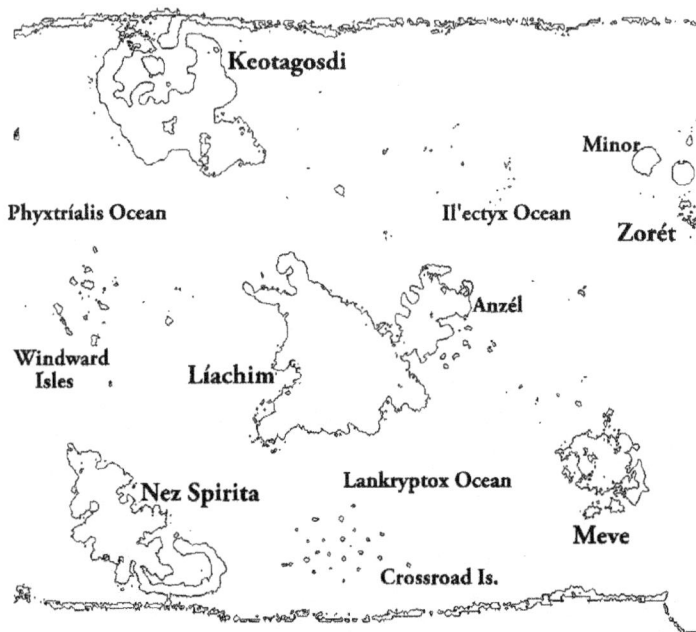

Keotagosdi

Minor

Phyxtríalis Ocean

Il'ectyx Ocean

Zorét

Anzél

Windward
Isles

Líachim

Nez Spirita

Lankryptox Ocean

Meve

Crossroad Is.

Qeauríyx East

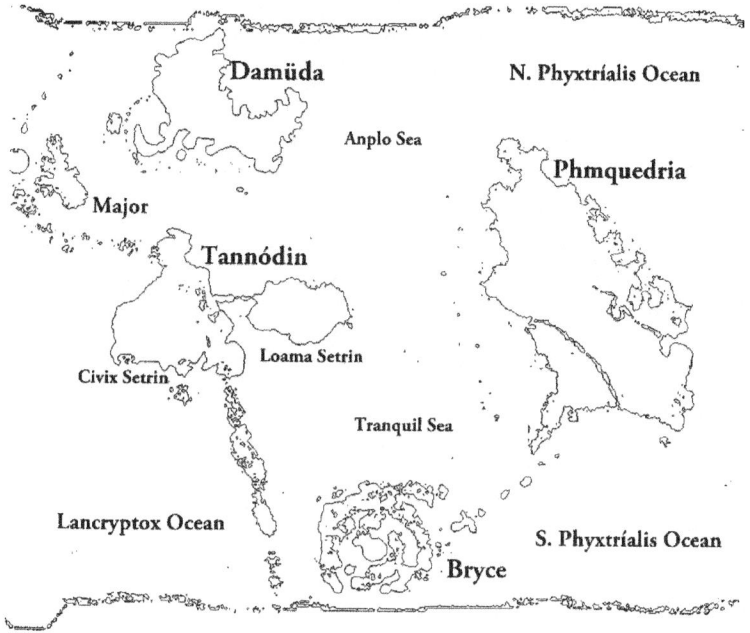

Map by. M. J. Sales

CHARACTERS, CONTINENTS, AND MISCELLANY

Characters

Anámn Klyphaju'an Matriester (Kinesis)
Neztríanis Phyxtríalis (Temperature)
Kaz Vincallous Fierce/Van Fénüra (Vicious)
Kaz Késhal Supreme (Pre-Eminent)
Lo'Marc P'tan (General Maximum)
A'reznu Feolenz (Old Flint)
Reníz Bläno (Violent Fist)
Galís
Timura
Brenko Zó'ethys
Lénü'íque Jínwa
Tarían
Kéma'fém
Bíoske
Syla
Jennó
Malchían
Nísyx Tekil
Rydín
Wapla
Alzhexph ju Xaníz
Héthyx
Kaimero
Hamin
Captain Säkno
Haptian Spiax
Isürus Tekil
Crína Tekil
Phesiana Phyxtríalis
Phenicia Supreme
Hafir
Namí
Van
Zotham
Huyé

Continents and Islands

Bryce
Phmquedria (Mining, Shipping, Lumber, and Business Districts)
Líachim
Anzél (now part of Líachim)
Keotagosdi
Nez Spirita (Windhorse Peninsula, Infinite Circle, Bitzroy Plains, N.
Country)
Tannódin (Civix Setrin and Loama Setrin)
Zorét (Major and Minor; Edaw Peak; Cometstone Island)
Damüda
Meve
Windward Isles
Crossroad Islands

Global Initiative Armed Forces

Blue Rapier
White Scythe
The Eradicate (Espionage, Protectorate, Wind)
The Interror [Damüda]

The Keep (Témoic Government)

The Principle
The Den
The Enclave
The Adjudicate
The Orators

Major Bodies of Water

Il'ectyx Ocean
Phyxtríalis Ocean
Lancryptox Ocean (The Infinite Deep)
Ocean of Mirror (Anplo and Tranquil Seas; Glacier Bay)

Durations of a Cycle

Kazíz
Myaíz
Ízdak
Gamíz
Fürníz
Namíz
Opíz
Ízneko
Janíz
Tsahíz

Days of a Week

Kazlé
Myalé
Daklé
Gamlé
Fürnlé
Namlé
Oplé
Nekolé

PROLOGUE

I pray they are ready. We pray they are ready. The que is fatigued.

Would that I was the last of my kind—that my daughters and sons would escape the forthcoming wrath! We are weary. The resistance is near its end. I cannot recall a time when we were not oppressed. I cannot recall a time when my ancestors screamed so despairingly in my aching knees. The cartilage is worn; the time is now. They must be ready. The Cycle is near completion.

Qeauríyx twists and turns like a knot, binding us closer to our own extinction and eternal life. Finitude and the Infinite rub closely here. The Great Drift was evidence of that. How many millennia, how many centuries, did the continents shift and plow into one another? How many earthquakes and cyclones and eruptions placed us on the path of annihilation? What truly exists in the innermost parts of this planet? Yet, ten thousand cycles ago, the First Sczyphamek stopped the Drift and gave us a chance to live. But a chance to live is but a chance to die.

Two hundred and forty one cycles ago, the Sczyphamek, who happened as Imperial, launched Global Initiative. She was the first Elemental warrior to appear on our planet in over fifteen hundred cycles. Imperial marshaled her homeland, the continent of Tannódin, and its steadfast ally, Damüda. With the full brunt of her military, continental, and Elemental might, she made war upon the continents of Phmquedria and Nez Spirita. It was the beginning of our end. How many have died since then? I do not recall.

To what end?

Some bastards say the end is the beginning. Damn them and their misbegotten sayings. On a planet like Qeauríyx, platitudes reveal and conceal too much. Platitudes bastardize this place. And that's why I can't stand bastards—religious, political, economic, military, and cultural bastards.

Damn them.

All they want to do is justify this madness. Justify and conceal our deaths so that others can live. So that others can live we must die. I can't stand bastards who rationalize death so easily. Platitudes lie like the people who make them. Laws are as malleable and brittle as the flesh that is bent and broken by the blunt trauma of energy weapons, the mundane, and life itself. Do platitudes consider injustice, loss, and finitude? Myanálas. They're all myanála. Even the Nameless One...

I pray they are ready. The cartilage is torn; the time is late. They must be ready. The Cycle is at hand.

Phmquedria fell into slavery. Nez Spirita fell into subjugation and extermination. Only a remnant of Nez Spiritan resistance remains. After those two lands fell, the Windward Isles and Bryce were soon defeated. Keotagosdi and Líachim are the last continents free of Tannódin'é rule. But Sczyphamek Imperial's granddaughter, Késhal, will soon march against them. She too is a Sczyphamek, as is her consort, Vincallous.

May the Nameless One have mercy have mercy on his qanín...

I pray they are ready... We pray they are ready. Our time has not yet come.

Chapter One: The One-Ember Fire

5 Ízdak, 241 OGI

He smelled the mines.

Liquids, solids, and gases.

Shit, grains, dirt, trash, piss, water, mineral particulates, and putrid effervescences.

A potpourri of wretchedness.

But the stink of the mines reigned unparallel.

The slave barracks were almost floating amidst the deluge of warm rain. No one could enter the mines that day, not even the slaves. Arrhythmic roars of thunder smacked against the dreary sky. The atmosphere shuddered.

The rainy season commenced earlier than expected, and Phmquedrian[1] storms had a habit of lingering.

During Phmquedria's rainy season, precipitation was as mundane as urine. Stock, routine, conventional, ordinary. Repetitive synonyms. But some of the worst oppressions and pains were generic and dull. Many who suffered the mundane rejoiced at the blessed occasion of extraordinary suffering.

If anything symbolized a continent built upon the ubiquitous liquidity of slave labor, it was the rainy season. Water was a universal solvent. With enough persistence, pressure, condensation, and patient violence, water would erode any surface. And given enough cycles, slavery abraded and diluted personhood and community. Even if one survived the effacing, irrevocable and irrecoverable scars would linger.

Under the onslaught of the mundane, the membrane of resistance inevitably became permeable.

So with weary eyes, Anámn[2] knew that even in this rainy torment, this soaking *gynix*,[3] someone would come and hoist him out the hole. This was slavery after all. His death, like his life, was under the ownership of

---

[1] Phmquedrian (fîm k[w]eh dree ahn)
[2] Anámn (uh-na*h*mn)
[3] Gynix (gih-niks)

1

another.

Throughout the past twelve hours, many slaves stopped by to witness the spectacle. The pit was only used for special acts of disobedience.

Then again, perhaps, and maybe… the pit was more than "spectacle." Maybe the dump was more than the meeting of actors, spectators, staging, and props. Perhaps life was more than slave-masters, slaves, and Phmquedrian slavery.

In the sump, predetermined meanings warred with one another: domination, resistance, or absurdity? When one was inescapably waist deep in a community's waste, critical analysis and lucid implications warred with the narcotic of hopelessness.

But Anámn still smelled the mines.

The pit materialized excessive cruelty out of vacuous meaning. As such, the abyss siphoned the entirety of Phmquedrian slavery unto Anámn.

The flailing bodies that hung there; the precarious system of exploitation it performed there; the fascination and repulsion between slave and slave-master—all these happenings made the pit an instantiation of the oppression-filled saga that was Global Initiative. These concomitant acts made the pit an instantiation of the prosperity-filled saga that was Global Initiative. These realities made the pit an instantiation of a kind of resistance that would never yield to the barbarity that was Global Initiative.

Or maybe Anámn was a worthless piece of kíma[4] on display for the world to see.

Even in their infinitude, the possibilities were few and far between.

Small wonder that even in the abyss, he smelled the mines.

The void was placed in the middle of the eastern slave barracks. Most slaves in Anámn's community passed by the hole throughout the day. However, few, if any, belonging to his community-in-chains, showed overt signs of compassion. Just the subtle head nod of understanding. The quiet clenched fist that said "don't give up." Or the head shake that signified what all slaves knew: "That's a damn shame."

Others were not so compassionate. There was the "if I don't look at the hole, then it doesn't exist" scamper. The subtle smiles of those who didn't care for Anámn in the first place were also in great variety. And then there were the overt signs of hate. Like those who urinated in the pit and on him.

Anámn's appropriate anger soon turned into ineluctable helplessness then finally into cynical insightfulness.

They were the same.

The compassionate and the hateful—Anámn watched and studied their thankfulness, *thankfulness that they did not have to suffer his punishment.* Indeed, a community, no matter its constitution, always hated *and* prized its scapegoat. Witnessed since childhood, affirmed in tales of fantasy, and pressed under Anámn's excrement-filled toenails lay a conclusion

---

[4] Kíma (kee-mah)

unblemished by communal whitewash.

During their lifetime, scapegoats were bereft of sympathy. Only after death could a scapegoat be remembered with compassion and lamentation.

Perhaps if his mother or sister's presence circulated about him, Anámn would have been able to remember what true compassion felt like. Senselessness, death, and injury… There was no need for their recollection. They were as near and visceral as the grime on his skin, the refuse groping his eyelashes. His depression and scars, his blood and tear-soaked life had coalesced into resignation and bitterness, with the occasional and primordial will to revenge.

A scapegoat's lot was retribution and redemptive suffering. There were no other possibilities.

Kíma.

Anámn was muddy and naked. But public humiliation was a gratifying change compared to the monotonous scourging he normally received. He could get sick from this. Infected… Perhaps gravely ill. Maybe even die. And truthfully, he welcomed it.

His death would make his community happy and apprehensive. They would celebrate his demise, yet worry that one of them might soon become the next surrogate scapegoat. Communal and colonial violence was a macabre cyclical carnival. Would that a community could resurrect their scapegoats, just to kill them again!

Anámn hoped he would die once and never return. He did not wish for an eternal home of bliss. He did not crave reincarnation. He cared not for a better future. He just wanted his pain and his life to end. That was salvation enough.

But, the slave knew better. Héthyx,[5] his overseer, would beat and torture any slave, but he only killed one on special occasions. And it was clear to everyone in Euhilv[6] and even to Anámn himself that a slave's existence, like the rainy season and slavery, was not extraordinary. He was a mere victim of history.

The water was already up to his shoulders, for he had been standing in the hole for the past six hours, and there were still four hours of daylight remaining. The water had cooled, but it was mixed with dirt—good, Phmquedrian dirt—that turned into good Phmquedrian mud. Black as tar and heavy as a témo,[7] the muddy soup made his brown, raw sienna complexion darken like a winter night with new moons.

He reeked of mineral deposits, feces, and urine because the hole also contained runoff from the barrack's dismal sewage system. After vomiting for the first few hours, he finally adapted to the rank smell and hellacious tactile onslaught of granular waste and excrement. However, the repetitive

---

[5] Héthyx (Hey-thiks)
[6] Euhilv (yoo-hilv)
[7] Témo (tey-moh)

raindrops splashing upon his bald head became excruciating.

With every splatter of stool, with every splash of water, with every piece of unknown matter clinging to his lips, his despairing hope grew. Anámn longed; he prayed that he would drown in a pool of shit before Héthyx returned.

Suicide was not an option. Every slave understood that.

To commit suicide was the most grievous offense in the Euhilv slave metropolis. Those who took their own lives would take the three next closest of kin with them, after the survived were sufficiently tortured. If none were present, random murder would be the recompense. The same fate awaited those who attempted to run away. It was a rule the elder ju Xaníz[8] instituted after the Euhilv slave rebellion almost one hundred and seventy five cycles ago.

It worked then, and it worked now.

Slavery allowed for personhood to be used in the most perverse ways. On the one hand, those few slaves who ran away or committed suicide demanded equality and justice, and they were willing to die and have others killed for the precious treasure of subjectivity. On the other hand, personhood also demanded that one consider one's children and friends, the bonds of affection and family. To escape sure death and extermination and negotiate the meantime was also a moment of personhood. And the Euhilv slave municipality banked on both personhoods to destroy personhood. The murder provision, the desire for freedom, the instinct to survive, and the bonds of kinship fostered demoralization.

Most slaves did not commit suicide or run away. Slavery was still better than death. Their choice had nothing to do with resignation. The specter of the Great Drift was too near for any inhabitant of the planet to quickly discard life at the expense of survival. There was little to no telling if a worse existence awaited the slaves of the Euhilv mining district after death. Living on Qeauríyx[9] granted the living this one truism: situations could always grow more disastrous, even after death.

Anámn contemplated suicide on a number of occasions, but the thought of his sister and his short list of friends kept him from acting on it. Now he no longer cared. The fear of "worse" was now heresy to him.

He was a victim. He was property; he was chattel. He was a "thing." And it was lunacy for a "thing" to have the fear of "worse." His existence testified to the truth, and those heretics who believed that something could be worse than his experience were proclaimed *anathema*.

"*Staxis!*" Anámn cursed and moaned. "Staxis…" He was losing consciousness; he hoped for the last time.

"Hmmph. I know you have not learned your lesson nor will you repent under false pretense. However, I do not want to be the one to tell Master

---

[8] Ju Xaníz (joo zan-*ees*)
[9] Qeauríyx (kay-awr-*ee*-iks)

Alzhexph[10] that I killed his bastard of a son... As if he would even care..."

The overseer. It was Héthyx. Anámn hated the man's inflection, his cadence, his high vocabulary, his delightful use of wordplay in the midst of misery and woe.

"Héthyx... go to Qalfocx,"[11] Anámn replied groggily.

"Damned Phmmy." The overseer's chuckle brimmed over with spite. Beating the rain off his cloak, Héthyx motioned to one of his personal slaves to hold his umbrella, which was large enough to protect three persons from the rain. "Beyond a sliver of doubt, you embody the term 'stubborn bastard.' But what can I expect? All of you Phmquedrian swine are animals.

"Boys, get him out of that kíma."

Anámn said nothing as Héthyx's servants pulled him up from the hole. Anámn's hands were bound in front of his abdomen by a rope, which was linked to a pulley at the top of the hole. Héthyx held the counterweight with gloved hands.

Anámn's vision was blurry. He barely made out the figures of the overseer and his henchmen; indeed, the shapes of the men appeared apparitional.

Creak by creak, the pulley squeaked and raised the slave from the deep. Anámn's body dangled in the air, and without the mud and waste to cover him, he became quite cold in the wind. The overseer dropped the counterweight and Anámn's weak, naked body plunged to the ground.

"Get up." Héthyx kicked Anámn in the stomach, knocking the wind out of his body.

Anámn, too weak to scream, let out a muted shriek. Gasping for breath, he fell unconscious.

"Miscreant," Héthyx muttered. "How typical."

***

He awakened in a bed with the familiar stench of the mines prying into his nostrils and the sound of fire in the background. The rain had stopped, but his countenance was the picture of the gray, dim sky, unceasing in its torrential monotony.

Anámn was tired. Regaining full consciousness, he felt the presence of a familiar aura. As the smell of the mines dissipated into normalcy, a new, more personal scent filled his surroundings. He was in the old one's shack; the aroma of food mingled with his fragrance was unmistakable. The elder's hovel was the only edifice in the eastern slave district that smelled halfway pleasant and amicable.

---

[10] Alzhexph (al-zheksf)
[11] Qalfocx (kal-foks)

Anámn found himself clothed in his normal rags, yet he was clean. It must have been the mystic's doing. The youth arose from the bed, scratched his bald head, and gazed out the small window in the front of the shack. Although narrow, the window revealed more than Anámn desired.

It was morning, and he heard the enormous current of the Kamo River to the southeast, cresting and swashing due to the rains. The sound of Phmquedrian accents littered the atmosphere. Walking towards the makeshift windowpane, the young slave gazed towards the north, and saw *the* mountain. It was nameless, and Tannódin[12] would have it no other way. The only thing valuable in that pile of rock was the ore and slave labor that kept the insatiable war machine well fed.

Deceived he was not. He was still in Euhilv. How unfortunate.

His head felt heavy and the pain of his abdomen evinced the lingering of Héthyx's boot.

"Malchían,"[13] moaned the still groggy Anámn, "how long was I out?"

"An interesting question." Malchían sat in a shadowy corner. Anámn strained his eyes to make out the elder's silhouette. "Perhaps the question is, 'how long have you been submerged?'"

Malchían was always full of double meanings, and Anámn did not feel like engaging the old man in a game of riddles. The day had been torturous enough. So, he ignored Malchían's statement and asked another question. "How'd I get here? The last thing I remember was Héthyx..."

"I brought you here. The rain cleaned you. The rain... And *that*." The old man's arm and fingers emerged from the shadows and pointed to a stick with a large soiled rag wrapped around it. A small barrel of soapy water sat next to the stick. Anámn sensed Malchían's gaze shift away from the shadows and towards him. "What did you do this time?"

Anámn offered no reply. He felt no need to answer the old one's question. It might as well have been a rhetorical exercise. His existence was reason enough to suffer his fate.

Malchían disregarded Anámn's silence. "It was time to help you out of the hole. You have been in the chasm for too long..." Scooping some food out of a pot over the fire, he stared beyond Anámn and smiled. "Here. Take some."

The young man was quite hungry. Meat and bread, and some of Malchían's heralded sauce—it was a delicacy that few slaves had been honored to share. Ravenous, Anámn swooped upon the meal with unrestraint.

The venerable sage stood up from his penitent crouch, and Anámn's famished eyes gazed upon him as if the moment was their first encounter. Malchían's dark brown face was covered with grayish white hair that extended to the top of his head. His facial hair was short and frazzled, and

---

[12] Tannódin (Tan-n*oh*-din)
[13] Malchían (mal-k*ee*-ahn)

his goatee was enunciated by a triangular junction with his sideburns at the bottom of his chin. The man's eyes were a reflective black, the kind of eyes that saw everything, yet revealed nothing. His mouth always possessed a peculiar half-smirk, and Malchían's bushy eyebrows accentuated his face with reverence. His voice rang with a melodious and methodical high-pitch inflection, which became deep and mysterious at a moment's notice.

He was an elderly man of medium height and smaller than average frame, and he wore a dark yellow robe, even while working in the mines. In fact, Anámn had never seen Malchían without his robe. Stranger than that custom, the cloak did not become dirty in the mines. It remained spotless, despite the most strenuous of labor. The old man also carried a cane of extraordinary height made of Blackwood, and they traveled together like friends of old. Many a slave attempted stealing the staff in the past, yet none succeeded. Reportedly, the cane was so heavy that two strong Phmquedrian slaves could not lift it. Stranger than that fact, his feet were always uncovered, even in the mines. Though the slaves were poorly cared for, the ore from the quarry was so abrasive that all slaves were given boots to wear. Malchían wore them, and though his feet were gnashed daily by stone, shovel, and pickaxe, he walked tirelessly on them every day.

The bond-sage had lived in the village for an unknown span of time. No one recalled his emergence within the Euhilv slave camp, not even ju Xaníz. His presence was so *seamless* that no one questioned his origins. Cycles ago, conflicting stories surfaced about strange acts of magic that Malchían conjured, although nothing had been substantiated.

Slaves throughout Euhilv flocked to him in mass and believed him to be great religious and mystical teacher. Two hundred and forty-one cycles of Global Initiative had all but erased the collective memory of many Phmquedrians. Seeking knowledge and identity, many slaves sought out the elder's expertise.

Malchían recounted myths, legends, and history long forgotten by the people, and through his efforts, he was able to pass on a vast cultural deposit to future generations. Ju Xaníz forbade slaves to read (although there were secret literacy meetings), but the elder appeared to have a genuine knowledge of the sacred Fragments of the Auría,[14] especially the Fragment of Justice. Massaging his sideburns, he recited and exhorted upon the sacred writings and performed healings and rituals among the people. If called upon, he would also mediate disputes, but the man with the yellow robe shunned overt leadership roles within the community. Rather, Malchían concerned himself with teaching the community his knowledge and learning from them.

Ju Xaníz coveted his departure, natural or otherwise, but he knew that Malchían's assassination would incite a revolt, the kind of debacle his grandfather faced cycles ago. And Tannódin was unforgiving when its war

---

[14] Auría (awr-*ee*-uh)

machine supplies were late. Not to mention, the slaves had developed a good morale in the past ten cycles, but ju Xaníz suspected that something subversive was underneath their demeanor…

No one had seen Malchían angry, except on one occasion. Anámn tried to destroy one of his father's most beloved trinkets: an elyandir[15] sword passed down through the generations. Anámn believed the act would force his father to confront him personally. But before he could demolish the priceless antique, he was caught stealing the sword by Héthyx and nearly killed for his actions.

When Malchían discovered that Anámn took such a reckless course, he became infuriated, as if the young man had stolen his Blackwood cane. Malchían raised his voice for the first time. Anámn remembered the scolding almost word for word. The old man muttered under his breath about the young man's brash ignorance, claiming it would cause the ruin of them all. Anámn was confused. He knew that he had not put the slave community in danger.

But ever since that incident, the elder shunned many of his roles in the community in order to keep a close eye on the youth known as Anámn Klyphaju'an Matriester. Malchían's withdrawal was not without consequence. Many slaves hated Anámn for limiting Malchían's presence in the community. Others were jealous of their relationship. Based on Anámn's lineage and Malchían's withdrawal, the slave was left with very few friends.

"What day is it, Anámn?" the medicine man asked.

"Oplé, I think," Anámn wiped his mouth after taking in the last of his meal. "Like it matters though. Every day on Qeauríyx happens the same way."

Malchían shook his head and grunted humorously, confirming and disagreeing with Anámn's statement. "Let's take a walk to the running water. We can't work in the mines today anyway. The seasonal rains may soon quit falling, and my journey here is almost done."

"Done?" the son of ju Xaníz stood up and looked at Malchían. His eyes demanded an answer.

"Follow me," Malchían replied and left out of the abode.

***

Malchían led Anámn to the southern outskirts of Euhilv, near the River Kamo.[16] It was a lush environment, a testimony of Phmquedria's brilliance. Due to the rain, the yarké trees were a luxuriant green and the river crested and thrashed about, filling the surrounding forest with the sound of its current. The clouds were breaking, and the blue-green sky peered ever so

---

[15] Elyandir (el-ih-ahn-deer)
[16] Kamo (kah-moh)

slightly through the gray.

Near the river's banks, the old man hunched over, leaned on his cane, grasped the wet ground in his dry hands, muttered a few inaudible words, and reclined on the base of a tall evergreen. Malchían seemed lost in space and time, as if the mines did not exist, as if Phmquedria itself was displaced in epoch and location long ago before recorded memory. The elder's eyes shone of a past omitted: Phmquedria was a desperate land weakly clinging to its storied reminiscence. His yellow cloak complimented his demeanor, appearing like a linen mural of the continent's history and struggle.

Phmquedria, a continent recognized by its flourishing jungles and hills in its midsection and vivacious forests at its northern and southern ends, gave rise to people who paced themselves to the syncopations of life. Ancestral tradition spoke of The One with No Name's generosity to the continent. The Nameless One granted Phmquedria a great supply of resources, rivers, and life. The only desolate area was the auspicious Valley of the Ancestors, which lay between the Noble and Sternpain Mountains. Those two ranges, stringing from Corsound to the south to Portal in the northwest, were the spine of Phmquedria and provided most of the landmass with water and minerals.

After its imperial advance, Tannódin split the continent into five districts: the shipping district in the extreme northwest; the lumber district in the north-central; the farming district, located on the Tranquil Coast, west of the Noble Mountains; the business/industrial district, in the southeast; and, the mining borough, which lay in the continent's midsection. Euhilv was the capital of that province, and ju Xaníz was the ruler over the entire continent.

In the early cycles of the Great Drift, Nez Spirita[17] and Phmquedria were sister-lands. Phmquedria was close to the equator of Qeauríyx and enjoyed the warmth and rain that came along with its planetary position. During the Drift's cycles, Phmquedria drifted clockwise and towards the northwest, eventually finding its shores proximate to Tannódin. At the Great Drift's end, the two continents were three thousand lengths apart, a reachable distance by sea vessel. This distance would prove pivotal in the cycles leading into Global Initiative.

The yarké[18] trees witnessed it all: Phmquedria's rise, glory, decline, and servitude. The clans quarreled too easily.

The elder sniffed the bark of the tree and tore off a wood chip.

"Thank you my old friend," the elderly Malchían said to the tree with a tone so gracious that it pierced the very heart of Anámn.

The leaves of the tree rustled though no wind prevailed. Malchían took the bark from the everbloom and combined it with the dirt from the ground. He closed his eyes and spat onto the earthen mixture, and it

---

[17] Nez Spirita (nez spir-i-tuh)
[18] Yarké (yar-key)

became consumed by a purplish blue flame, which flickered and pulsated to a measured tempo. Though possessing a single ember, the violet fire blazed with measured intensity.

Anámn was astonished. He heard stories about the old man's powers, but no one in his generation had seen them. In fact, most considered Malchían's abilities to be tall tales.

The river slowed to a solemn, steady flow, and the animals of the field stopped their activity and stared. Sparks emerged from the one-ember fire. Malchían opened his eyes and gazed into Anámn's.

"Look at me." The old one's voice was soft yet commanding.

Instinctively, Anámn felt the urge to shy away. He felt ashamed and insignificant. His eyes tarried towards the river, but the elder's presence exerted a gravity he was unable to withstand.

"Kinesis," Malchían said. "Kinesis, look at me."

Anámn was unsure, but somehow he knew that Malchían was speaking *his* name. He gazed into the old one's eyes with fear and caution.

"Hold out your right hand." A smile emerged from the elder's white beard. "Do not be afraid."

With ongoing reservation, the young slave outstretched his hand, unable to grasp what was happening. His body felt strange, and sensations beyond his reckoning pressed against his flesh. His mind wandered into an unknown place. He felt it *happening* in his heart.

"You sense it Kinesis," Malchían said. "But you must see it. You must touch it. You must *hear* it."

Malchían's voice faded out of Anámn's range of senses, and the son of ju Xaníz started to hear the sound of raw ambient kinetic energy all around him. He heard it, but he could not explain what he heard. He felt the motion of his blood moving through his veins, the river running downstream, the old tree gathering the sun's energy, and the rainwater seeping into the dirt. But no enlightenment accompanied the feelings. Potential energy hailed at every turn: a leaf hung precariously on a branch, an insect was about to flap its wings. Without the comprehension or words to explain it, he tasted potential and kinetic energy drawing nigh unto him; it was sensational, yet numbing. His breathing became erratic.

"Calm down," he felt Malchían say.

He actually *felt* the kinetic movement of the air molecules, which was caused by vibration.

"Open your eyes…"

Anámn did not realize he closed them. He glanced at his right hand. A dark green aura fluctuated around it. Humming and pulsating, the aura released a force that lifted dust and leaves around Anámn.

"By the One!" he exclaimed. "Kíma! What is this? What's happening to me?"

The aura slivered up his arm and began to emanate from his entire body. Focusing upon his right arm and then gazing beyond it, he noticed the aura causing ambient distortion. His surroundings appeared like a picture shaken at a rapid pace. The distance grew obscure.

"You are beginning to remember that you are asleep," the old man replied. "Breathe easy Anámn…"

Anámn took a deep breath and sighed. While exhaling, the half-sleep youth lost himself in the energy. Perceiving Malchían, he gasped.

"Y- you…" Anámn gasped, terrified by what he saw: pure inexhaustible energy. "You are… You can't be…"

"I am and am not who you think I am," Malchían paused. "The One Who Has No Name…"

Anámn became unsettled. The energy around him gathered to his left hand, manifesting itself as an orange-green anomaly. The energy crackled and hissed.

"Calm down," the old man repeated.

The elder's words were unheeded. Anámn became frightened by the sight of himself, and losing his self-control, he released the energy in the direction of the river. Matriester was sure the river water would be scattered in a rancorous fashion.

He was mistaken.

First, the water steamed; then, the river reversed direction with incredible speed. Droplets of water rose in the air and dispersed at such a rate that the droplets pierced holes clean through the bark of the old trees nearby, resembling a concentrated discharge of an energy weapon.

The event concluded in seconds, and yet Anámn saw and felt everything. It was as if Qeauríyx had slowed its spin. Anámn stood in awe of his newfound ability. Minutes later, the river returned to its normal pace, and the only remaining evidence of the incident was the wafting steam and the holes in the trees.

The young man surveyed his hands and body. The aura that once engulfed him had now dissipated. Trying to regain his composure, Anámn sat down and watched the one-ember fire. The conflagration burned away all of his anticipation.

He could not return to the slave camp. At least, not yet…

The old man sat across from him with a wary spirit.

CHAPTER TWO: THE GREAT MOTHER

1 Myaíz, 241 OGI
Kazlé

The cold wind intruded into her hut without warning. She pulled the covers over her head but that ill-conceived strategy was soon made apparent because her copper feet were no longer insulated. Her toes protested. This happened every morning, and she still was not used to it.

It was particularly cold that morning in Hopha.[1] In fact, the entire continent of Nez Spirita was experiencing unseasonably cool autumn weather. Those in the village interpreted it as a sign of things to come. Her feet cringed at that meteorological portent.

The young woman pulled her cloak off the chair next to her bed and sat up. Her long, black hair, which covered her face, had slipped out of the braids she wove the night before. Tying her hair back into a tail, she let out a sigh loud enough to let the Great Mother know she was awake. She yawned and wrapped the tan shawl around her body.

She stood up and stretched out her slender, yet toned arms. Her right arm popped as it did every daybreak. She rotated her arm gracefully and dropped it to her side, leaving her to gaze at her left hand, which felt warm considering the temperature.

Maybe after twenty-six cycles, I am finally getting used to the cold mornings, she thought to herself and examined her reflection in a small mirror next to her bed.

She slipped on her favorite pair of animal skin pants, dark brown, with a hint of blue, loose in the waist and legs, and took her belt off the wall and tied it around her waist. Then she placed some rinse in her mouth, walked outside her hut and spit it out. No sooner than the rinse met the ground, a familiar voice called to her in a timeless Nez Spiritan accent.

"Neztríanis,"[2] the voice reverberated, "you are late."

"I am sorry, mother."

She felt like she said that every morning, to the Great Mother of Hopha, Phesiana Phyxtríalis,[3] who was the leader of a large tribe of

---

[1] Hopha (hoh-fuh)
[2] Neztríanis (nez-tr*ee*-ahn-is)
[3] Phesiana Phyxtríalis (feh-zee-an-uh fiks-tr*ee*-ahl-is)

Spiritans in southeastern Nez Spirita. And with such responsibility Neztríanis still wondered why Phesiana took her in twenty-three cycles ago.

Neztríanis greeted the woman who was not just *the* Great Mother, but also *her* mother. A familiar trepidation crept into her heart. The heaviness returned. She had kept it at bay for fifteen days—a new record. But records were meant to be broken.

"Nez," the venerated woman said, "you must let that feeling go or you will never lead our people."

The daughter avoided eye contact and stared at the ground. "Yes, Mamisí[4], I am trying."

"*Mamisí...* You still call me that after all these cycles." Phesiana smiled then scanned the horizon. "Let us go. It is almost dawn, and we must arrive at the Sacred Space in time."

Stepping out of her hut, Neztríanis touched the ground underneath her feet and between her toes. *Her feet.* Somehow, she forgot her boots. Her feet were not as cold as they were when she awoke. She ran back into the hut to retrieve her footwear.

That is quite strange, she thought, as she placed the boots on her feet and emerged from her abode.

Noticing her expression, the Great Mother asked, "What is wrong?"

"Nothing. I have not perceived the cold this morning as I normally do. I forgot my boots because my feet did not feel cold. I am probably getting used to the weather... finally."

Wrapped in a periwinkle shawl, Phesiana's wrinkled and majestic reddish brown face gave no reply, although she glimpsed at her daughter cryptically. The closest expression appeared to be sadness. But instead of continuing the conversation, the Great Mother started towards the Sacred Space and beckoned her daughter to follow.

They sauntered for quite some time, and no words were exchanged between the two women. Like them, the woods were mute. Not an insect sung, not an animal moved. The wilderness was in deep slumber. The forest was so quiet, one could hear waves from the Bay of Hero washing onshore some two lengths away. Neztríanis perceived the breathing of her mother. Phesiana's breaths coincided with the waves' rhythm.

While scratching her forehead, the young woman noticed her left arm was wet. She wiped off the moisture, and realized that it was not the morning dew, but sweat.

Maybe I am passing into an illness.

Her mind wandered into routine reflection as she followed her mother's footsteps. For nearly two weeks, she successfully avoided the forthcoming thoughts, but now the daily, morning ritual of unspoken, angst-ridden questions would recommence.

---

[4] Mamisí (mah-mih-*see*)

How could she lead Hopha after the passing of her mother? Why should she? Tannódin had conquered most of Nez Spirita, save the holdout at Lozé. The peoples of the Windhorse Peninsula signed a non-aggression pact with the House of Kaz after the Solemn War, which, as the cycles continued, all but relinquished their freedom outside of their villages. Hopha, along with Hero and Nextu, were the last three remaining tribes of the old days of glory, when Nez Spirita's Nine Houses of Peace enjoyed two millennia of stability. Point Sank, though located on the Peninsula's terminus, was the first House to fall in the Solemn War. Therefore, Hopha, like Nextu and Hero, was surrounded by imperial power. Their freedom to self-determine was all but eroded.

What did leadership mean when one was already defeated? And why *pray* to the elders and The One with No Name? They did not save them from Global Initiative. While pondering these matters, she heard the distinct sound of a traveling herd of wild Spiritan windhorses, galloping towards the Hopha range to the west.

"Do you hear the strides of those windhorses?" Phesiana asked. Her mother's ability to ask pointed and relevant questions made Neztríanis wonder if Phesiana possessed telepathy. "Those horses can run about as fast as a railcrusier and are used for transportation to this day. However, they were not always so fast. The Great Drift caused all of us, every inhabitant of this planet, to evolve. It is the ability to evolve and change that the One with No Name knew we would need." She paused and beheld her daughter with discerning eyes.

Neztríanis had suffered this tale countless times, but on this occasion, her mother's delivery was unlike any the daughter previously encountered. Or maybe it was because her disillusionment felt somewhat new that the daughter heard the words differently.

Something was different.

Phesiana continued, "Even though Nez Spirita was the only continent that remained unmoved during the Drift, we constantly faced volcanic eruptions and earthquakes. Despite those harsh conditions, we survived and thrived. We learned, as did everyone else on Qeauríyx, how to grow food in such terrible circumstances." The Great Mother picked up some fallen leaves, smelled them and continued walking. "The windhorses, in turn, grew strong and fast. They had to, in order to live on.

"We, my young daughter, must understand the beauty of Creation. Not just the creation of our kind, but of all life and silent happenings. Our creation, our evolution, the mystery of our appearance—they point us toward something."

Neztríanis beheld her mother with hopeful yet downhearted eyes. She prayed that unlike other times, she would actually believe Phesiana's answer to her forthcoming question: "What, Great Mother? *Where* do they lead us?"

"They lead us to the truth that circumstances need not have the last say, nor must we surrender ourselves to our surroundings. We can and will evolve by the power of the Nameless One and our own."

Hopeful, yet unconvinced (as usual), Neztríanis bowed her head in reticence. "Great Mother…"

"Nez," Phesiana interrupted, "I know you wonder everyday why I took you in even though you were an orphan. I have no children, and I could have chosen any child from a prominent family in Hopha to succeed me like the Great Ancestors before me…"

Neztríanis was unable to stop her head from shaking in anger, shame, and frustration. Melancholy, like always, filled her qanín.[5] It was not as if she was ungrateful to the Great Mother. But no matter how many cycles passed, Neztríanis could not help but be angst-ridden. No matter how many times Phesiana fed her, clothed her, and told Neztríanis that she loved her, the daughter of Hopha could not bring herself to completely believe someone who refused to answer the most obvious question there was to ask.

Did Phesiana know her parents? And if she did, why hadn't she told her the reason they abandoned their daughter? And even if both of her parents died when she was young, did she truly have no extended family in Hopha?

Yes, the Great Mother chose Neztríanis, a village orphan, to succeed her. But Phesiana never told her about her lineage or her place of birth.

The Great Mother adroitly perceived her daughter's silent frustration. "You happened as a Nez Spiritan. You are of Hopha. You are my daughter and I love you with my entire qanín. Though I have not always made the best decisions, I always believed that you would make a wonderful Great Mother. One day, you will face the legacy of your parents. But the circumstances of your birth do not completely control who you are or what you do.

"Your burden will be difficult. I've mourned for your future as much as your past. I had to push you…"

The daughter of Hopha grew more disconsolate and interrupted her mother. "What are you saying? You speak in misdirection and riddles."

Phesiana stopped and eyed her daughter directly. Her face was nondescript but there was substance behind the old woman's countenance. Something was different.

"Neztríanis… The leaders of Tannódin, the Malevolent Sczyphameks[6] who happened as Pre-Eminent and Vicious, will stop at nothing until Global Initiative is fully implemented. Their actions betray their thinking and feeling. Relationships and life are fundamentally based upon antagonism in their eyes. They believe domination is the sole option for our kind. And while you are unable to stop them alone, you may be able to

---

[5] Qanín (k[w]ah-n*ee*n)
[6] Sczyphamek (Tzahy-fuh- meck)

with some help."

That was different.

"What are you speaking of? It cannot be me!" Neztríanis was terrified. Her exclamation perceived the seriousness of her mother. "I am not strong enough to stand against the Sczyphameks. Phenplyacin[7] is proof that no one can. And they say Pre-Eminent is stronger than Vicious! How can I lead anyone?" All of her fears spilled to the surface, and she felt engulfed, excoriated, and heavy-laden by their breadth, depth, and weight.

Phesiana resumed her walk and pressed her daughter to follow. "Neztríanis, I have prayed and meditated for you, long before you entered my household. You are insecure now, but when you gain strength, you must encourage and lead your brothers and sisters."

Neztríanis had no rejoinder. She hoped her mother would turn around and assure her that she was being playful. Instead, the Great Mother continued her stride towards their destination. She spoke nothing to her daughter for twenty minutes, which felt like hours of neglect to the disaffected young woman.

Suddenly, the old woman halted. They were at the Sacred Space.

"You have been raised in the ways of the Auría, and though unbeknownst to you, two elements were present in you since birth."

The daughter of Hopha shook her head. "I do not understand."

"Yes. Yes, you do. Neztríanis, look at your hands. It has already begun."

How had Neztríanis become so unaware of her own body? The woman noticed that her right hand was giving off a frozen mist, creating a fog; her left hand was hot, causing the air around it to become unsettled. An orange-white aura moved up her feet and legs. The grass beneath her froze and cracked against her weight. As the aura ascended the daughter's body, she noticed her mother chanting the words she had studied and meditated upon her entire life:

"Fá'atoño má.[8] Fá'atoño má. Fá'atoño má."

Neztríanis chanted with Phesiana to calm herself; and while chanting, the aura consumed her. Her hands gave off a cold heat, and she heard the voice of the elements in her heart, mind, body, and spirit: her entire *qanín*.

She emitted a powerful energy around her, so much so that the herd of windhorses stopped running, and the water near the shore of the bay four lengths away swirled a bit. The animals of the wilderness awoke, and Neztríanis drifted into liminality. Time and space became amorphous to her. She saw visions of the past and of things yet unseen.

At once, she understood that she was evolving into a Sczyphamek. Her breathing slowed. The aura, which had once engulfed her, slowly retreated

---

[7] Phenplyacin (fin-plahy-uh-sin)
[8] Fá'atoño má (*fah*-uh-tohn-yoh m*ah*)

into her body. The forest grew quiet once more. The sun was rising, the moon, recoiling. Listening to her heartbeat, the daughter of Hopha inhaled and smelled the fresh air of the forest, surveyed her hands, torso, and legs, and felt neither hot nor cold.

She sensed a strange force in the direction of her mother.

"Who are you, Mamisí?"

"I am more or less of whom you think I am."

Neztríanis entered into a position of reverence. She knew better than most that the One with No Name was everywhere and nowhere, something yet nothing, Inexhaustible meaning and mystery.

"You are truly a perceptive woman. I can tell I raised you. I have passed all of my experience and knowledge on to you, as my Great Mother did with me. I made sure that you studied the duplicate Fragments of the Auría. You know the history of Qeauríyx, the Sczyphameks, and the Sundry Elemental. Your faith is strong in spite of your fear. But a time will come when you must move beyond reservation. You must learn to sow what you gathered."

"Yes, Great Nameless Mother," the young woman said in obedience. "What must I do?"

Phesiana answered, "A Sczyphamek's full capacity must be Awakened in order to claim the said title. Awakening is evolutionary and revelatory. Only through constant prayer, meditation, and action is this possible. You can develop your abilities, if you continue down this path…

"So, you must leave now and go to Pike Metropolis. You are urgently needed there. Kaz Vincallous Fierce, or Sczyphamek Vicious as many know him, has formed a covert party to recover the Auría from the ruins of the Hidden Tabernacle. You must retrieve the Auría and take it to Sunrise Mountain in the North Country past the Bitzroy Plains and the Crag Mountains. This is your destined choice."

Neztríanis blinked. Obedience gave way to reality. And "reality" was Global Initiative and the Sczyphamek who happened as Vicious. Reality was fear, death, and impotence. Neztríanis struggled to regain her composure.

"I have doubted in the past, but how will I find what so many have failed to find? The Auría has been missing for more than ten thousand cycles, since the end of the Drift. And during the Ancient Orality, it appeared on every continent at one point or another. How can we be sure the book is in the Hidden Tabernacle? And even if the Auría is there, no one knows the temple's location. And if I retrieve it, the journey to Sunrise Mountain is almost a three thousand-length trek. I have not ventured farther than Nextu. The Bitzroy Plains is filled with White Scythe and Blue Rapier. And that is before the—" Neztríanis stopped speaking when she caught sight of her mother's countenance.

Phesiana's eyes sizzled, her nostrils flared, and her mouth erupted in the flames of parental correction. "You always give up so easily, despite your competitive nature. You know that your gaze determines your steps."

"Mamisí..." Neztríanis whined the term of endearment before she could stop herself.

"Do *not* Mamisí me," the old woman replied through clenched teeth. "You *must* have confidence. I believe in you. There is no one I trust more, and only you can survive in the North Country."

The women spoke nothing for a few minutes as Neztríanis tried to adjust to a newfound heaviness.

"What is my name?" Neztríanis asked Phesiana.

"Temperature," Phesiana responded.

They fell silent once more. Neztríanis chanted and conjured heat in her right hand.

"What way should I take?" she asked.

"Forever full of questions that contain double meanings... Cross over the hills of Hopha and follow the Xarkim[9] River to the outskirts of Pike Metropolis. At this point take what way seems best to you. A Sczyphamek cannot sense one who has not fully Awakened unless in extreme proximity. Neztríanis, I do not need to say what is common sense, but I am your mother so I will say it anyway. Temperature, until you master your powers, stay clear of all Sczyphameks."

The young woman nodded and looked towards the foothills of Hopha. She traveled beyond them just once in her life, sixteen cycles ago, when she and the Great Mother journeyed to Nextu to meet the new head of the village. They rode the windhorses leisurely, so it took twenty-four days to get there. When she crossed the foothills this time, she would not be returning for quite some time.

The Auría is the life of this planet, she thought. *In the wrong qanín it will destroy this entire world. I happened as a Sczyphamek... I... I cannot allow them to retrieve the Auría.*

"Do you know where the temple is located, Great Mother?" the daughter of Hopha asked.

"The visions were hard to decipher, but I believe that temple's entrance is somewhere near Mount Xarkim."

"Mt. Xarkim..." Neztríanis' voice trailed. "*Kíma.*"

"*What did you say?*"

"Nothing." Neztríanis laughed awkwardly. Her mother despised cursing more than she despised excuses born of premeditated surrender.

"Do not be troubled, Nez. Tannódin is probably a cycle away from recovering the Auría. They do not know which mountain houses the entrance. And although Kaz Vincallous Fierce is here in Nez Spirita, he is also attending to other matters, namely Lozé and some other secret mission involving the témos. I do not know the full extent of the latter, but I doubt it is good."

---

[9] Xarkim (zar-kim)

The Great Mother sighed, gently stroked the trunk of a tree, and returned her attention to her daughter. "What I am trying to say is that the Auría does not enjoy his complete, undivided attention... at least, not yet. While you must move deliberately, do not rush blindly into action. Learn about and dialogue with your new powers."

Neztríanis nodded. She did not want to know how the Great Mother received such covert information. Obtaining that intelligence probably broke the conditions of the treaty her people signed cycles ago.

"How will you explain this to the village?" the daughter of Hopha inquired.

"I will say that you started your rite of passage to take my place. And I will also tell others that you ran away; those two stories should spark many rumors..."

"Rumors?"

"Tannódin knows who you are. There is no doubt. You are next in line to succeed me. But because of the treaty, their presence here is minimal. Still, I am sure they will find out that you are no longer with us. As long as the reasons are trivial in their eyes, they should not grow suspicious. And even though these are lies, they are not far from the truth are they, daughter?"

Ashamed, Neztríanis looked away. The young woman did *not* want to lead the village, and running away from that responsibility crossed her mind on *numerous* occasions. But the gravity of this newfound task superseded any of her fears. Even though she did not want to, she had to go.

The sun rose beyond the horizon and set itself on the back of the sky, casting uneven shadows over the mother and daughter. With love and appreciation, Neztríanis gazed upon Phesiana, for what felt like the last time. She beheld humble majesty colored in mahogany, crowned with elegant black hair, wrapped in a sparkling blue shawl, standing amongst the land to which she had dedicated her life.

"You have given me so much," she said to her mother as tears slipped down her cheeks. "I will miss you. I will miss this place."

"I know," came the warm reply. "I will miss you as well." The regal woman walked over to Nez and embraced her. "Remember your faith and your actions."

"Yes Great Mother."

Phesiana entered a hut next to the Sacred Space and brought out an enormous shoulderpack of supplies. The shoulderpack was so stuffed that some of the contents spilled to the ground. "This will be enough."

Neztríanis wiped her teary eyes and giggled. "You will always be my Mamisí. How long have you planned this?"

"Oh, not long," the woman responded and chuckled as well. Their laughter subsided, and the elderly woman sighed and placed her hand on her daughter's forehead, which was a Nez Spiritan sign of affection.

"Before you go, let us eat together, my daughter." While preparing breakfast, the Nez Spiritan women sang, prayed, and chanted the sections of the Fragments of the Auría, the hymns of the forest, and the history of the village. With her newfound abilities, Neztríanis created a fire, and the mother and daughter ate and gave thanks. The meal was timeless; yet it moved with purposeful tempo, a foreshadowing symbol of her upcoming journey.

Being somewhat conscious of her powers, Neztríanis stood up, chanted, concentrated, and extinguished the fire by creating a cold mist to cover the kindling. She smiled to herself, beginning to feel more confident about her journey.

"I have always been proud of you Neztríanis," Phesiana said, "but there is much you still must learn. Sczyphameks are gifted with increased speed and strength though in varying degrees, and all are able to fly. You must master these techniques as well, while cultivating your unique powers. And remember: to master is to surrender, because no servant is greater than its master..."

"And no master is greater than its servant. Because all are the same," Nez completed the saying she was reared upon. The woman approached her elder, embraced her, and kissed her forehead and cheeks. "Goodbye, Mamisí."

"Goodbye, my wonderful daughter."

CHAPTER THREE: KNOWING THE WORDS

She felt almost weightless. Neztríanis raced westward through the flat, grassy outskirts of Hopha towards the hills. Her velocity matched a young windhorse. She grinned to herself and felt a sensation previously unknown. Testing her top speed, Neztríanis pushed herself harder and headed towards a pack of adult windhorses. She tried to keep up with the herd but quickly grew short of breath and hunched over, holding her sides.

Following the trail of field particulates, the daughter of Hopha faced the village in amazement. She traveled six lengths in ten minutes. Though hardly alive in her new powers, she accomplished a feat, which just a day before was an impossibility. Her studies rang true: the onset of a Sczyphamek's power was sudden, and normally, a mediator was present.

"By the Nameless One," she said aloud, panting, "that was fun."

Catching her wind, she turned to the Hopha foothills. On the other side of the hills, lay the mouth of the great Xarkim River. The river's source was its namesake, Mount Xarkim, the immense mountain of central Nez Spirita. Crossing over the small Hopha Range to the west would put her in Hero's Valley, the westernmost terrain of the Windhorse Peninsula. On the far side of the basin lay the Ryphaz Mountains; traversing them would take her northwest, into Nextu Forest. Like the Hero's Valley, Nextu Forest was largely uninhabited by people, except for the Nextu village on the northwestern edge of the vibrant woodland, which was filled with Yarnínga[1] trees.

Because of the distance between Nextu and Hopha the uninhabited land between them, and Hopha's proscription on railcruiser travel, a journey to Nextu was rare. For those who lived in Hopha, travel was usually restricted to Hero and the outskirts of Point Sank. The eastern half of the Windhorse Peninsula was full of small villages, trading outposts, and places of recreation. This fact, plus freedom from Tannódin'é interference, made travel outside of the peninsula inadvisable.

Though the largest, Nextu was the most isolated of the remaining Houses of Peace. The sprawling village was occupied by other Nez Spiritan clans and boasted a population of several hundred thousand. Nextu was about eleven hundred lengths away from Hopha, a three-week journey on a

---

[1] Yarnínga (yar-neen-guh)

21

windhorse, due to the terrain. The daughter of Hopha reasoned that if she kept the same pace on foot, she would be making good time.

After Nextu, her next major stop would be Pike Metropolis, a journey of about four hundred lengths. She had not visited Pike nor did she know anyone there. But her studies granted her exceptional knowledge of Nez Spiritan geography and topography. She recalled that nine sizable mountains encircled the conurbation. All nine crags were all over twelve thousand feet, which only granted five passes leading into the city. The largest of the mountains was the twenty-seven thousand foot Mount Xarkim.

The city itself housed too many people to count. The metropolitan area stretched to the mountains with skyrises forming a line of structures underneath the gaze of natural, rocky splendor. Three mountain ranges met around the city to form what Nez Spiritans called the "Infinite Circle." The southwest range was called the Nextu Range since it was adjacent to the Nextu forest. The eastern range was named the Limestone Mountains, while the final range to the northwest was called the Gemansu[2] Range. Besides this information, Neztríanis' only other recollections of the great city were the tales reported by travelers stopping in Hopha. They spoke of its technological genius with awe. The Triple Skyrises, the rail system, and the airlift port were supposedly beyond anyone's reckoning.

Neztríanis had never seen an airlift up close, but a Tannódin'é railcruiser line ran through Hopha and the entire Windhorse Peninsula. Those in her village decided they would continue to live as they had for centuries, to protest against Global Initiative. The protest was not against technology per se, but what the technology represented: the destruction and death of so many of her ancestors during the Solemn War.

Soon, other, larger apprehensions began to loom in her thoughts. Pike Metropolis teemed with soldiers from Tannódin and its ally, Damüda.[3] How could she go to a city she knew nothing about, successfully navigate through it, without drawing attention to herself? Was that a concern worth having since so many people dwelled in the city? Would she actually stick out? She would be noticed by her accent and dress, but did that matter? She simply did not know what to expect.

Neztríanis could afford to make no blunders. The stakes were too high. That being the case, in all likelihood she was probably going to need some help. Asking for assistance was a gamble, but Neztríanis was no fool. As an inhabitant of Qeauríyx, it was an indisputable fact that no one lived without help and that nothing important was ever achieved by oneself.

Neztríanis did not need to wonder why Tannódin was searching for the Auría. It was the holiest of all books on Qeauríyx, and only a few fragments remained. It was said that to those who were able to unlock its

---

[2] Gemansu (geh-muhn-soo)
[3] Damüda (dah-myoo-duh)

words and secrets, great power and understanding would be granted to them. In the wrong hands, the results would be disastrous. No one quite understood its origins, but Nez Spiritans believed it to be connected to Qeauríyx, the One with No Name, and the ancestors.

During the Ancient Orality and cycles of the Drift, the book would appear in temples and houses on every continent, but never in the same way. With each instantiation in time and space, the manuscript invariably varied. At the Drift's end, the Auría was believed to be housed and lost in one of the nine continents great places of worship. And the number of possible tabernacles totaled twenty-seven.

It seemed unlikely to impossible that Tannódin knew the exact location. Even the Mystics of the Auría were uncertain, and their number was dwindling by the day. Oral tradition approximated the location of the Hidden Tabernacle to be near one of the nine major mountains of the Infinite Circle. According to legend, the doors of the temple were destroyed during the Great Drift's end, due to the destructive force that resulted in the creation of the Infinite Circle.

Neztríanis held an overwhelming advantage. Even with Tannódin's technology, it would still take them many durations to search the entire area, granting her time to develop her powers as she made her fateful journey towards Pike. Even an elite Sczyphamek would not be able to sense the entrance without much meditation and prayer. Neztríanis possessed another great boon: neither Sczyphameks Pre-Eminent nor Vicious knew of her or her mission.

Even though Vincallous was in Nez Spirita, she learned through the Great Mother, newsprints (which she obtained unbeknownst to her mother), and rumor that he was preparing his troops to strike against the city of Lozé. Her mother also mentioned something about the témos. Nez Spirita was the closest continent to the Crossroad Islands, the home of the témos. Témos were known throughout Qeauríyx as winged felines of justice who had fought against Malevolent Sczyphameks for ages. Their species was near extinction, and Neztríanis was sure Sczyphameks Pre-Eminent and Vicious would see to it that their number was completely erased from the memory of Qeauríyx.

These two tasks would predispose Vincallous and give her some time to develop her powers without the need of rushing off to a conflict she could hardly win. Yes, what was the point of retrieving the Auría if she was unable to defeat Vicious? She was no match for him unless she Awakened, and even then, she might require more training. Yet, confronting Vincallous Fierce as an unawakened Sczyphamek was certain suicide. Still, she needed to prepare herself for an eventual confrontation.

Her journey was long, arduous and risky. Because they both were in Nez Spirita, encountering Vicious before she was ready was an actual possibility. Walking towards the foothills of Hopha, Neztríanis shuddered in horror at that thought and tried to refocus her attention and confidence by chanting and praying to the ancestors and the Nameless One. Her pace picked up to a full stride, and as she glanced over her shoulder, the village's form became lost in the horizon.

***

The tent atop a verdant mound was quiet; only the crisp breeze made a sound. The morning was clear and bright; those in Lozé would remember the forthcoming days. His breathing was methodical; the ground trembled softly beneath his feet. His brown hair flapped in the wind, and his darkened, fair face fashioned a countenance of sheer defiance, daring the planet to take retribution for his actions. He smiled, confident that that day had not yet arrived.

The sword and sheath fastened upon his back generated a distinct red glow, which pulsated and caused small tremors and his brown cape to flutter. As the force picked up speed, his countenance grew aggressive; his nostrils flared and his light armor glistened as the aura radiated and filled his tent. He fastened his boots with dispatch and dusted off his trousers.

Kneeling down and whispering in a heavy voice, he chanted: *"Fá'atoño má. Fá'atoño má. Dé'wa.[4] Keh mányx phen da pet…?"*[5]

He repeated the phrase for many moments, and suddenly stopped. "Yes, my old friends," the man said to the elements dwelling inside of him, "it has been here too many cycles. I feel the resilience in the earth. The wretches of Lozé are stubborn and insolent. Their stench has fostered the asinine hope that Global Initiative will fail."

The ground underneath him shook, and he scratched his beard. "They are *weak*. And the weak shall inherit disaster. The strong shall inherit nothing. *We make our fortune*, do we not? Yes… yes, *we* do… while the meek pray for the remains…"

He stopped for a moment and a flash of discontent entered into his spirit. He pushed an intermittent though recurring thought away. "Lose my nerve? Van… Vincallous Fierce does not lose his nerve…"

He felt footsteps and powered down, as to not alert his troops. Even though twenty cycles had passed, he had not reestablished a trustworthy relationship with his soldiers. Phenplyacin caused an institutional fear from conscript to command officer. Only the Eradicate remained completely unaffected in their trust, but that was due to Violent Fist.

"Potentate Vicious," a voice called out.

"Yes," the response came quickly, "what is it General P'tan?"

"Sir, we are ready to deploy on your command," replied Lo'Marc P'tan,[6]

---

[4] Dé'wa (dey-wah)

[5] Keh mányx phen da pet (k[i]h mahn-icks fin duh pet)

[6] Lo'Marc P'tan (loh-mahrk pih-tahn)

the commanding general of the elite military branch called White Scythe, as he entered the Sczyphamek's enclave.

"What is the final count of the soldiers?" asked Vicious.

"We've seventy thousand ready to depart and another ten thousand in reserve in Pike Metropolis. We will leave the last sixty-five thousand here, in the plains of Bitzroy. We also have fifteen thousand of Commandant's Feolenz's Blue Rapier in support."

"Exceptional," the Sczyphamek responded with a smile. "General, I am here as an observer. Conduct your attack as you see fit. I embrace your command. After all, I trained you myself in the art of military technique."

"Thank you Potentate." The honored general saluted with masterful arrogance. "We should arrive in Lozé in three days, and when we arrive, they will suffer the meaning of anguish and pang. *I will fragment that city into irreparable pieces.*"

***

Anámn jogged southeast down the banks of the Kamo River, towards the town of the river's namesake. He tried to fly, but managed only to levitate for a few seconds. Malchían told him that it took some time for a Sczyphamek's abilities to develop, so Anámn had to keep practicing.

His thoughts were disparate, consumed with many ideas. But he kept returning to his father. He finally possessed the power to do what he dreamed: killing his father. Anámn believed that if his father died, the slave metropolis would be no more and he would obtain revenge for what ju Xaníz did to his mother.

"That bastard is mine," Anámn said to himself and ignored the obvious irony of that statement.

Inexplicably, the element inside of him seemed distant. He did not understand why he was unable to generate his aura again.

At Anámn's current pace, his half-sister, Nísyx Tekil, was just two days away. He needed to move with greater dispatch. His mind wandered again, and he wondered about the meaning of his journey. Malchían gave him no specific directions or objectives, only to travel to see his sister. The old man also mentioned something about an "Awakening," but it made very little sense to Anámn. Though illiterate, the young slave had memorized many sayings of the ancestors and verses from the Fragments, but he never gave much thought to them. Gradually, Malchían's last words to him began to resound in his remembrance...

"Remember Anámn," he said pensively, as the one-ember fire receded. "There are many paths to truth. But some paths are not for everyone. One man's nectar is another woman's damnation. Do not forget this. You must learn how to believe and how to rise above your situation, if this is to succeed." Muttering, he continued, "You will both need to grow, but in different ways."

"What did you say?"

Malchían ignored Anámn's question. "'*Fá'atoño má.*' Do you know these words?"

"Yeah. I've chanted once or twice in the past. And I hear you chanting those words all the time."

The old man with the staff shook his head. "I asked what you *know*, not what you *chanted* or *heard*. Chanting... Hmmph.

"Many people hear and think they know, but they know nothing. It's like a person who thinks that just because they hear someone singing, they know how to sing."

He paused and placed his left hand on Anámn's shoulder. "Hearing is only one part of knowing, and knowing is only one part of doing. You must master all three and more."

Scouring Anámn with serious eyes, Malchían forced the slave to reciprocate the gravity of the moment. "The phrase is from the Ancient Tongue. 'Fá' means 'will;' that is your action or your practice. 'Toño' means 'faith.' This is not just to believe or trust something, but being committed to something beyond oneself. 'Mányx' or 'má,' for short, means 'to embrace.' This is more than you holding an object. Indeed, you must let it hold you. It must permeate, bind, and subsume your qanín..."

Although Anámn did not fully understand what Malchían's lecture, he knew it was of grave importance. Malchían closed his eyes and pondered how he should proceed. He chose his words carefully.

"The most cunning and perceptive Sczyphameks, whether they were Benevolent or Malevolent, or even somewhere in between—Apathetic, they were reckoned—they embraced their faith and practice. Yet they also embraced something more. This step challenges one mentally and physically.

"You see, a Malevolent Sczyphamek believes and is embraced just as much as a Benevolent. Idolatry is still belief, and it causes people to do anything if they truly believe in it. Truthfully, most Malevolent Sczyphameks do not see themselves as 'evil.' Even apathy is a belief, and its effects are just as reverberating. You must train your mind, body, spirit and Elemental in relation to each other. There is no difference between them, and yet, they are distinct and important. This will allow you to heighten your Elemental..."

"My 'Elemental'?" Anámn asked, trying to grasp all that Malchían spoke.

"Your Elemental... This is where your ability comes from. Elementals are tied to the planet, to the universe, and to the One with No Name. You have a portion of the Sundry Elemental inside of you. It has a qanín of its own; the greatest Sczyphameks are those whose qanín can coexist with their Elemental, to the point that there is no difference between them. *They do and are the same.* Various methods are used to create this harmony; you must find yours. Listen to your Elemental, Anámn. It will help you discover and develop your kinetic powers."

"'*Kinetic*...'" he repeated, unsure of the word's meaning. "Sounds like the name you called me... 'Kinesis.'"

"They are related."

"Well, what does 'kinetic' mean?"

"Energy. Power."

Anámn's eyes sparked in anticipation.

"Don't mistake meaning as reality..." Malchían warned. "Kinetic energy is predicated upon potential energy."

"*What's that?*" Anámn asked, even more bewildered than before.

Picking a rock up off the ground, the elder explained, "Do you see this stone in between my fingers?"

"Yeah."

"Holding this stone represents potential energy. And if I drop this stone, it will fall to the ground. Kinetic energy is this 'falling to the ground.'"

Malchían let the stone go and it fell to the ground.

Anámn observed the stone, blinked, then gazed at Malchían. "I don't get it."

"I will not explain this again." Malchían's face grew stern and his body language indicated he would not accept Anámn's ignorance. "When I asked you to come out here, did you have to?"

"No," Anámn responded.

"That is correct. You might have stayed in my abode. Or you could have gone back to sleep. You possessed the potential to do many things."

"But when I came out here, I *acted*, right?" he asked with insight. "I turned that potential into action."

"Correct. Just like the stone. I can throw the stone, or set it back down, or toss it to myself. Each action will have a different result and requires a different amount of energy to accomplish it. But the potential energy for any of these choices directly influences the kinetic result. Your Elemental is tied to this phenomenon."

Though doubtful of "phenomenon's" meaning, Anámn somewhat understood the elder's teaching.

"How do you know all this stuff? And how'd you know I was a Sczyphamek, with this kind of power?"

The old man sniffed and smiled, unwilling to answer. "None of that will mean a thing if you do not understand." Rubbing his hand against a tree, he concluded, "'Fá'atoño má.' It can be dismantled into its parts, but its whole is greater than the parts that comprise it. Knowing what the words mean will not reveal the true content of the phrase. You must *know* the phrase itself. Work hard and meditate on this Kinesis."

"I will Malchían." A confident smile graced Anámn's face. "So, when are you gonna train me?"

Malchían burst into laughter to the point of weeping. "Train you?! Me? Have you noticed I am an old man?"

"Yeah. But you're an old man who carries a cane that three slaves can't carry."

The man with the yellow robe grunted in affirmation and at the youth's erratic perceptiveness. "Anámn, you still have a lot to learn. Appearances deceive, and I do not train anyone. You have a great obstacle, and I will not see you again until you confront it. When that will be is your choice."

Anámn was disappointed, but Malchían tapped his cane caringly on the young man's shoulder. *It was heavy.*

"I will tell you this. You should go see your sister in Kamo. Your father will allow any slave twenty-four days of rest or travel per cycle."

"Oh yeah. I forgot. How nice of him. That should make up for this kíma of a life."

"Stop…" Malchían shook his head as if he was going to say something more, but thought better. "These three weeks are all you need. With your new powers, you should make it to Kamo in two days or three."

It was Anámn's turn to laugh. "How am I supposed to do that, Malchían? Kamo's almost four reaches away from here. Even if I can travel faster with these powers, there's no way I can make it there in three days."

Malchían smiled through his beard and stuck his right hand in his cloak. It reemerged with a slip of paper. "I thought you might need this."

"What's this?"

"Power." The old man smirked. "It is a railcruiser ticket to Kamo."

"A train?"

"Yes. One's power is never confined to self-reliance alone."

It was another one of Malchían's double meanings. Anámn ignored the proverb and asked, "How'd you get a ticket?"

"Do not worry about that. You can pick the train up in Skylark, about forty lengths downstream. Your newfound speed should allow you to get there in a day. I hear the railcruiser can travel over 200 hundred lengths an hour. Should be an interesting trip."

"*An interesting trip on my feet.* You know that railcruiser is segregated. Slaves are only allowed on one car, and there are no seats."

"Should give you some time to work on your powers of endurance."

Anámn smacked his lips together and sighed in displeasure.

"Negativity can become a self-fulfilling prophecy," Malchían retorted.

Their conversations were always like this. They resembled a game whose objectives were to nuance, ignore, and circumvent one's own teammate, as if one's comrade was actually one's opponent.

"Well, I better get going then," the son of ju Xaníz attempted to end the banter. "Thanks for the ticket and the help." Reviewing the conversation in his mind, Anámn sought to confirm his conclusion. "So if I chant a lot, I'll become stronger, right? I mean, I know I gotta believe too…"

Malchían groaned in agitation. "Anámn Matriester, Do not feel as if you must master all of your abilities at once. Let them come to you. Use the time on the railcruiser to speak to your Elemental and meditate. Do not let your heart, mind, and body become so easily distracted."

"Yeah... I won't Malchían...Well... least I'll get to see Nísyx."

He had not seen his sister in cycles. If anything, the trip should bring him some much-needed happiness.

"Remember," the old man said with dramatic syncopation, "Fá'atoño má."

"But what about..." Anámn stopped his sentence as he witnessed Malchían fade out of space and into a tree.

"You must know the words," the elder's voice echoed in Anámn's thoughts.

"Qalfocx..." the young one murmured to himself as he traveled down the riverside to Skylark, in recollection. "I've gotta 'know the words...' Fá'atoño má..."

When he spoke the phrase, he felt the element inside of him draw nearer, but just as quickly, it retreated into a seemingly hidden place. Anámn repeated the phrase again, but felt no response from the element.

"Why even choose me if you won't come when I call you," he grumbled against his Elemental.

He continued to work on levitation and could almost sustain himself, but he struggled to conjure any velocity. Focusing with closed eyes, he picked up a great deal of momentum, but he was so intent on moving that he did not notice a tree directly ahead of him. He was too close to swerve completely out of the way, so Anámn braced for the oncoming collision. His body shattered the tree with such force that the top half splintered into many pieces, causing a loud snapping sound that echoed throughout the woods.

Anámn's body somersaulted through the air and hit the ground with extreme impact. He had just enough time to be thankful that he was alive when the remaining trunk of the tree fell on his legs.

"Arrghh!" he yelled. "Staxis!"

The base of the tree was directly on top of his lower trunk. Although the pain was excruciating, Anámn could not believe that he was not dead or severely injured. He tried to move the trunk with sheer strength, and almost succeeded, but the tree was too heavy and crashed down on him again.

He uttered a most virulent squeal. Tears of agony welled in his eyes. He was in danger of losing consciousness, perhaps his life. The slave camp no longer mattered; his father no longer entered into his thoughts; he was furious and scared for his life. In extreme panic, he pleaded with the element inside of him.

"Fá'atoño má! Fá'atoño má!" He chanted with great emotion and instigated the element inside of him. "Fá'atoño má!"

The green aura returned ferociously, producing the long repressed rage and desperation of its host. The aura brushed all debris aside with effortless ease. Drawing in kinetic and potential energy at an alarming tempo, so much so that random flashes of energy destroyed nearby branches, leaving smoke and ashes in its wake, the young man continued to gather uncontrolled, unbridled power into his body. With his left hand, he harnessed the unfettered distortion of unrefined potential energy, and smashed it into the trunk, causing an explosion that obliterated the tree, catapulted him off the ground, and sent a shockwave throughout the proximity, bending trees and frightening the animals. He landed one length away near the bank of the river, gasped, and fell unconscious.

***

Nightfall would be upon her soon. Neztríanis had cleared the Hopha range and traversed nearly a third of Hero's Valley in seven days. At her current pace, Nextu was seventeen days away, matching the clip of a traveling windhorse. Although she was astounded, that feat was only the beginning of her powers, and she still posed no threat to Vicious or Pre-Eminent. As she took in the rays of the descending sun, she realized that she had not partaken a full meal since breakfast with her mother six days ago. Her only sustenance had been water from various streams and berries and nuts from the forest.

Finding a clear area, she made a campsite. She picked up fallen branches from the surrounding Yarnínga trees for kindling and washed her face in a nearby branch of the Xarkim River.

Hero's Valley was a breathtaking masterpiece, a witness to the creativity of the One with No Name. The eldest Yarnínga trees fashioned their distinct blue-orange leaves. As the moon shone upon them, the trees glowed and filled the surrounding area with tree light. Although taller than most women, she felt like a small insect next to the wondrous trees. While marveling at their luminescence, Neztríanis made a fire. The crackle of the embers were like a percussionist, complementing the audible melodies of the insects and animals.

She took her shoes off, felt the grass beneath her feet and smelled the brisk air. Loosening the belt around her waist and removing her cloak, the Nez Spiritan let her rich, black hair down and sat in front of the fire. The young woman massaged her slender, yet round face, near her temples, and ran her fingers through her tangled hair. Next, she retrieved a detailed map Nez Spirita from her shoulderpack. But upon studying it, her vision grew blurry and her brown eyes felt heavy. She was exhausted.

Rummaging through her supply bag, a jar of water surfaced, although Neztríanis was searching for a collection of verses from the Fragments. Taking in some water made her realize that she was quite hungry. She took out some dried, smoked meat from her waist pouch and ate. Her arms were exposed, and the daughter of Hopha reached towards her elegant and muscular legs and scratched her left calf. Smiling, she remembered the men of the village ogling over her legs, but never audibly flirting because of the Great Mother.

Neztríanis felt a melancholy liveliness. She sensed the warmth of the earth, the heat of the trees, and the sunlight reflected by the moons. The element of heat within her appeared to be requesting her attention. Nervous, she ignored the petition by clearing a place to sleep and took out a blanket from her shoulderpack although she needed no cover, thanks to her abilities. Gazing upon the stars and growing astonished by their number, Neztríanis realized, in all her cycles, she never paid much attention to the celestial heavens. The sky burst at the seams with stellar activity.

The element of heat still sought an audience, and trying to appease it, Neztríanis concentrated on one of the stars and began to chant, trying to feel the distinct heat from the star. At once, she felt heat from every star almost to the point of incineration, and being terrifyingly overwhelmed, she hastily discontinued the exercise. Her eyes were wide, wild, and aghast. She forced herself to think of something else in order to move beyond an altogether alien feeling.

Nervousness and fear beset the xenophobic Sczyphamek. *Maybe later, when I learn more control*, she thought.

She hoped that by attempting to use her powers of heat, she would assuage the advances of the fiery element, but to no avail. Although she knew not why, Neztríanis was quite afraid.

Her mind moved to the teachings of the ancestors and the Great Drift, and she recalled the origins of the planet. In a time long before Recorded Memory, even prior to the Ancient Orality, Qeauríyx was a world most inhospitable. Consumed by volcanic eruptions and cosmic showers, the planet's surface was little more than lava and ash. That was until the One with No Name traveled the solar currents in order to examine Creation. Perhaps by chance or by fate, the Nameless One was drawn to the erratic planet, and being so moved, the spirit channeled its energy and breathed a healing mist upon the globe. An atmosphere developed, causing a subsequent torrential downpour that lasted many cycles.

The land reemerged above the water, at a place called "the Epicenter," at an astonishing rate, giving rise to the continents of the planet: Tannódin, Phmquedria, Líachim,[7] Keotagosdi,[8] Zorét,[9] Nez Spirita, Damüda, Anzél,[10] Meve and Bryce.[11] Soon, plants and creatures materialized out of the dirt, the dust of the air, along with the waters of the deep. The Nameless One

---

[7] Líachim (*lee*-uh-khim)
[8] Keotagosdi (keh-oh-tuh-gahs-dee)
[9] Zorét (tsawr-*eht*)
[10] Anzél (ahn-s*ehl*)
[11] Bryce (brahys)

was both a part of and beyond the rebirth of Qeauríyx.

As the land developed, the creatures also evolved alongside the planet. Yet, something lingered in Qeauríyx; an aggression could not remain silent. The planet itself struggled along with the One with No Name, but the chaos of its history persisted. The Great Drift became the ultimate expression of this hostility.

Neztríanis observed the fire and tried to sleep, but the dirt, the air and the clouds filled her thoughts. *The land... Que...* The planet spoke to her through the elements inside of her. The fiery Elemental pressed for her attention and made her uneasy.

"Fá'atoño má... Fá'atoño má..." she felt herself say. Disembodied, her mouth uttered unknown words from the Ancient Tongue. The element of heat was guiding her. "Mona fla renzgé ná[12]... Fá'atoño mona..."

Her flesh grew cold, then extremely hot. Her hands erupted in blue flame and her body followed suit. Somehow, neither she nor her clothes were consumed. Her aura picked up potency with each emanation of blue flame. The orange-white aura that consumed her earlier turned dark orange.

Neztríanis was horrified, aware that she was losing control of her powers. She felt afloat and began to understand what was happening to her. She was drifting into the consciousness of the planet. The aggression and pain of its past and the uncertain hope of its future were thrown upon her, stoning her mind with conflicting thoughts.

"Stop..." she moaned. " Please..."

No.

Qeauríyx was upon her, and it would not retreat. Her breathing was heavy and her body near eruption. In the midst of the confusion, she heard the element of heat inside her, repeating words of the Ancient Tongue in a sweet, destructive melody.

Moved with great emotion and sadness she sang, *"Mona fla renzgé ná... Mona fla renzgé ná..."*

The trees around her were set ablaze, engulfed in the blue flame, but they did not burn. Neither her clothes nor skin was consumed.

Tears rolled down her cheeks, and they grew cold and frosty while she continued to sing, as she unknowingly levitated amongst the trees. The conflict of Qeauríyx was deep and endless, but throughout the sorrow, she felt an unrelenting longing; it felt cold, rigid, like a glacier melting over millennia. Her tears became like snowflakes, and she heard another voice responding to the element of heat; this voice was responded in song as well.

"Zí mányx que rai[13]..." she sang in response. *"Mona fla renzgé ná. Zí mányx*

---

[12] Mona fla renzgé ná (moh-nah flah rins-*gey* n*ah*)

[13] Zí mányx que rai (tzee mah-nicks k[w]*ey* rahy)

que rai…"

The aura that was previously dark orange, regained its natural orange-white color. The mixture of heat and cold created a tumultuous storm that sent down a fiery ice amongst the forest. The trees were still engulfed in blue flame but the temperature dropped so rapidly that the trees did not catch fire.

Neztríanis had little dominion over her powers. Qeauríyx was trying to reclaim what it felt was its own possession. Remembering that the elements were tied to the planet, Neztríanis realized that she was fighting for the right to be joined with them. She sang louder as lightning flashed, and the embattled atmosphere continued to rain down incendiary precipitation. This was no Awakening; this was a life and death struggle, much like the Great Drift.

The tempest continued to grow, and Neztríanis tried to calm herself, while maintaining her connection to the emotion of the planet. An ice-sphere emerged from her aura and covered the area in glacial frost. She kept singing, and eventually she matched the tempo and key of the planet's harmonic dissonance. She sang in long tones, *"Zí mányx que rai,"* and in shorter tones, *"Mona fla renzgé ná."*

Eventually, the weather subsided, and Neztríanis found herself completely alone, high above the ground.

The planet had accepted her petition, and Neztríanis had learned new melodies and incantations to augment her abilities. The elements dwelling inside her were almost drained and needed rest. So did she, but as the young Sczyphamek floated down elegantly to her campsite, she found it covered in ice. Although utterly spent, Neztríanis would not let the surrounding forest remain despoiled. Kneeling in a reverential position, she channeled small waves of heat throughout the encampment, and thawed the frozen trees, at which point she laid on the ground and fell fast asleep.

CHAPTER FOUR: A BLADE OF DESTRUCTION
AND ITS WIELDER

Gamlé

On the fourth day of Myaíz, in the two hundred and forty-first cycle after the dawn of Global Initiative, White Scythe engaged the last military stronghold of anti-imperial rebels in Lozé, Nez Spirita. Lozé, a city on the Phyxtríalis shore of central Nez Spirita, was about four hundred and fifty lengths west of Pike Metropolis and had been a hotbed of Nez Spiritan pride for centuries.

Nez Spirita fell to Tannódin and Damüda in eighty-fifth cycle of Global Initiative (85 OGI) in the conflict known as the Solemn War. When the war concluded, the august city of Zívento,[1] the Nez Spiritan haven, found itself demolished. The first empress of Tannódin and founder of Global Initiative, Sczyphamek Imperial, ordered a new city, Pike Metropolis, to be built on its ruins near Mount Xarkim. She also directed a mass campaign to exploit and appropriate the natural resources found within the continent, as well as the religious and mystical affluence of the indigenous. She exterminated many indigenous Nez Spiritans in the process through unrelenting labor and murder, so much so that she was pressed to send Phmquedrian slave labor to the land.

Nez Spiritans were a people of strong will and did not fully assimilate within Global Initiative. Generation upon generation of Nez Spiritans violently revolted against the rule of Tannódin and Damüda. And the city of Lozé became a municipality that always maintained a high level of resistance despite the fact that, at present, the overwhelming majority of Nez Spirita was either occupied by Tannódin or had signed non-aggression pacts with them.

When Imperial's granddaughter, Sczyphamek Pre-Eminent, came to power in 221 OGI, crushing the insurrectionists of Lozé was a key strategy in her long-term Nez Spiritan agenda. First, she allowed the non-violent,

---

[1] Zívento (tzee-vin-toh)

anti-technology "protest" of many Nez Spiritan villages as a diplomatic concession. Then, Pre-Eminent began to isolate Lozé from the rest of the continent through embargoes and sanctions. After twenty cycles of isolation, many Nez Spiritans left Lozé as refugees due to a lack of basic necessities. Once the city emptied of most of its civilian population, Pre-Eminent made her move. She dispatched White Scythe to the area and asked her consort, Sczyphamek Vicious, to oversee the defeat of the centuries-old insurgency. Vicious obliged and ordered Lo'Marc P'tan to ready his troops for battle.

P'tan, a native of Loama Setrin, the agricultural landmass of Tannódin, captured the attention of Sczyphamek Vicious during his days as a young soldier in Blue Rapier. The perceptive Sczyphamek ascertained an innate military gift within the grunt. Personally training him, Kaz Vincallous instilled in P'tan a sense of ruthlessness that few had seen since Vicious himself. Lo'Marc possessed a brilliant military mind and deeply empathized with those under his command. Likewise, he possessed powerful charisma. With fervor, efficiency, and firm resolve, his soldiers followed him without hesitation. P'tan was White Scythe's Eighty-Fourth General Maximum and had never lost an engagement nor left the field of battle to the enemy. He was the perfect choice to lead White Scythe, or rather, that choice was up to the mystical blade itself.

White Scythe was the oldest and second most elite military chamber of Tannódin's imperial engine. The armed force had existed over four millennia and was directly implicated in Tannódin's rise to power. Initially formed by mercenaries on the desert island of Zorét Major, their leader wielded a mystical scythe that absorbed the life force of those it smote. The sickle-shaped weapon glimmered an eerie white, an almost opaque kind of brilliance. Few energy weapons managed to harm it. And throughout the Cycles, the scythe even managed to kill a few Sczyphameks.

As cycles progressed, the blade became increasingly harder to wield, and only the most trained qaníns were able to control its power. White Scythe consumed lesser folk with an undeniable bloodlust that craved carnage and ultimately killed the wielder. But to those who were able to master it, the scythe granted a military might so awesome that when the Thirty-First General Maximum held the blade, he was able to conquer southern Damüda.

The Thirty First's daughter also possessed great skill and completed her father's conquest by completely surmounting Damüda 2600 cycles before Global Initiative (2600 BGI). During this era, the second generation of Benevolent Sczyphameks arose, those of great justice, and fought against White Scythe. The decisive battles took place at The Gate and at Pruphane in northern and southeastern Damüda respectively. The Thirty-Third General Maximum was killed at Pruphane, and the entire continent fell into a feudal system for centuries to come. The blade was not destroyed, although it was severely injured. Unbeknownst to the Benevolents, it was smuggled back to Zorét Major, where the line of General Maximums was broken for one thousand cycles, until an opportune time presented itself.

That opportunity emerged during the Bitter War, fifteen hundred cycles BGI in the lonely Agosti Tundra of Keotagosdi. It was a forty-day battle involving every Sczyphamek on Qeauríyx. For the first time in the planet's history, all Sczyphameks, Benevolent, Apathetic, and Malevolent—a number of about eighty—participated in a gruesome conflict that eradicated the entire Sczyphamek population.

Word of the Elemental bloodshed reached the ears of White Scythe. The blade waited patiently; its wounds had healed. After the Bitter War left all the Elemental warriors dead, White Scythe moved into action. One cycle later, a new General Maximum was selected, and the blade, which had not been grasped in a millennium, possessed an unquenchable bloodlust.

Gathering their full strength, the mercenaries of White Scythe sailed to Tannódin, and made war upon the land. In those days, Tannódin was an agrarian society, without a strong centralized government or military and did not foresee the attack. The Thirty Fourth General Maximum maimed, smote, and consumed five hundred lives on the initial day of war, granting the blade incredible power. Cities, villages, and houses submitted to White Scythe as it marched across Civix Setrin, the western isle of the two-landmass continent, and into Loama Setrin, the eastern landmass. During the occupation, Tannódin was transformed through militarism, innovation, and industrialization. The continent became the first technologically advanced land on Qeauríyx. Viewing the blade's imperial advance as the beginning of time, the indigenous of Tannódin forgot and/or discarded their history before White Scythe and assumed the superior identity of a Tannódin'é.

As the Tannódin'é grew in strength and technology, they proclaimed Tannódin the "premier" continent of Qeauríyx, and Civix Setrin became the standard of such a claim. By 600 BGI, the majority western landmass was transformed into a sprawling metropolis. About this period, the mystical blade grew discriminatory towards its wielder, instantly crippling or killing those unworthy of its power. Future General Maximums were required to undergo rigorous scrutiny and preparation.

By the time of Global Initiative, White Scythe was a full-fledged military chamber with a complete chain of command. White Scythe was constituted by elite soldiers removed from the ranks of Blue Rapier, the main body of armed forces for Global Initiative. Trained in the Skill of the Scythe, members of General Maximum's force were excellent close-quarter combat soldiers and uniquely gifted in tactical onslaught. Lo'Marc P'tan was believed to be one of the greatest proprietors of the mystical weapon, wielding it with unparalleled grace and speed.

Although Blue Rapier normally handled these types of engagements, Pre-Eminent desired a special display of power and destruction wreaked upon the combatants of Lozé. Lozé presented Pre-Eminent with a unique challenge. Although the overwhelming majority of Nez Spirita posed no serious threat to her order, Lozé signified an incessant defiance of her generational authority.

Tannódin was a light to Qeauríyx, but much of Qeauríyx did not see or rejected its luminescence. Pre-Eminent was convinced that her actions were justified. She *must* bring what was in darkness to light. She was anointed with the powers of an elite Sczyphamek, and what was the point of power if one did not use it? Bred in the tradition of Tannódin'é Néwan, Kaz Késhal[2] Supreme believed her course of action to be in line with the First Sczyphamek's Great Extinguishing. In her eyes, she was continuing the First's mission to unite the planet.

Once Késhal's plan, passed down through the generations, succeeded; she would usher in a new, platinum era that would be to the benefit of all Qeauríyx. Lozé, and Nez Spirita for that matter, although located near the heart of the Auría, turned their backs upon this truth. They of all people should have recognized her hallowed task. Somehow, their centuries old insolence had created an institutional, vainglorious insanity among them. She needed to convince them, murderously it seemed, that they were wrong.

White Scythe seemed an apropos answer.

On the day of battle, Lo' Marc P'tan stood before the eastern mountain pass that led into Lozé and fastened his eyes upon his troops. White Scythe, the military chamber, was now comprised of soldiers from Zorét, Tannódin, Damüda, and Bryce. The General Maximum amassed five of his twelve divisions for the battle. Each division consisted of fourteen thousand troops, commanded by a Secondary, one of P'tan's sub-generals.

The Sczyphamek called Vicious stood behind the General Maximum, while five Secondaries strafed his left and right flank.

P'tan turned around and smiled at his mentor. The frequent repetition of the forthcoming question had become ritual. "Potentate, may I ask that you amplify my voice, so that I can address the Second Military Chamber of Global Initiative, the brave men and women of White Scythe?"

Kaz Vincallous nodded. His red aura burst forth and encompassed the mass of soldiers. A hush fell over the crowd, and they lent their ears to the pronouncement of their leader by way of Vicious' Elemental.

Lo'Marc spoke these words:

"You. This has always been about you. *Your families. Your homelands. Your hopes and aspirations.* Global Initiative is for you, and you are its cutting edge."

The General Maximum reached for the scythe, which rested on his back, drew it forth and proclaimed, "You are the cutting edge of White Scythe. You're my strength. You are the strength of Global Initiative.

---

[2] Késhal (key-shawl)

"For over two centuries, the men and women of Blue Rapier shed their blood in order to tame this archaic land and make it suitable for the cultivation of our times. And for the past twenty cycles, the Eradicate has seeded this land, here and there, carrying out clandestine and diplomatic missions for the sake of the harvest.

"My friends. My comrades. Brothers and sisters… The two chambers did their jobs. And many lost life and appendage to accomplish their objectives. Their sacrifice has made *this* time possible.

"It's harvest time. It is time for the harvest. And White Scythe will separate the good crop from the bad. We know well that this blade shall usher in a horizon from which no one can hide. And we will cut down to cinders that which does not produce the fruit we desire.

"You're too wise to be persuaded by our adversaries. You are too ironclad to be softened by their futility.

"We gave them opportunities to withdraw. We offered them treaties. We offered them peace. We offered them non-aggression pacts. We offered them relocation. We offered them life. And now they will submit to our final offer: *War and condemnation.*"

Lo'Marc raised the blade, and White Scythe and its Wielder were consumed in an off-white, nearly opaque haze.

"Your Potentate is here. I am here. The Secondaries are here. You are here, brothers and sisters of Qeauríyx.

"Don't be deceived by the ignorance of our foe. They possess the desire to fight, and we will crush their desire. They possess the desire to live in disrespect of our time-honored traditions and divinely-inspired purpose. And we will crush their disrespect. They possess the hope that they are on the side of the Nameless One and their ancestors—ancestors who are neither alive nor helpful. We will crush their heresy and their pagan beliefs. Rightfully, they shall become dispossessed.

"War is not moral. Nor can it happen justly. Though some may enter into its bowels with righteous intentions, all become soiled in its brutality and will inevitably compromise. War is violent and its aim is victory and superiority. Let no one deceive you. While most armies champion rules of engagement and protocol for dealing with civilians, those protocols and rules will be set aside in the interest of victory if need be.

"Rulers of the past would lie to you. They'd try to conceal what White Scythe has revealed for Cycles. They'd try to make you feel better by rationalizing the injury, pain, and death.

"But our battles are above limp rationality. Our battles are above petty emotion. Our battles are the consummation of past victories that move unceasingly into the future. Our battles are stained with the blood of progress. The cosmos, Qeauríyx, and the que selected us for this task. And these Nez Spiritans of Lozé mock us as much as they mock the truth to which they refuse to submit. History is written by the winners, and life will do whatever it takes to win.

"Global Initiative is superior; therefore its morals are superior. Global Initiative keeps winning; therefore its protocols are reliable. And when our leaders—when Kaz Késhal and Vincallous—realize the errors of prior protocols and acts, they have the power to change... because their power flows from the Nameless One's Power and not from morals, rationality, or divine interpretation.

"They, like we, have a lifeline to power. We happen as Power! And *this* Scythe and *this* General Maximum and *my* cutting edge—all of you—we will teach those in Lozé of their folly. We will instruct them in ways of war. We will teach them that the wages of their disobedience is death.

"The Sczyphamek who happened as Vicious will not participate in this conflict. Nor should he. Global Initiative is yours, just as much as it is his. He will observe the power of our tactics, the power of our resolve, the power of our chamber, and the power of our cutting edge.

"We are here to eradicate the qaníns of the Nez Spiritan resistance and we will not stop until every heart, mind, spirit, and body is consumed by this blade and rent asunder by our cutting edge. White Scythe happens as onslaught, aggression, and precision.

"Now, who will bleed with me? Will Bryce bleed with me? Will Tannódin bleed with me? Will Damüda bleed with me? Will Zorét bleed with me? Are you my cutting edge? Are you still the Blossoming Comet?"

The men and women of White Scythe erupted in thunderous shouts and passionate exhortations. Soon the cacophony coalesced into a powerful refrain of call and response. The General Maximum and his Secondaries led, while the remainder of the troops became a choir of mass destruction.

"Bleed!"

"Bleed!"

"We are the cutting edge!"

"Cutting edge!"

"Blossoming comet!"

"White Comet!"

"Comet! Comet! Power! Bleed! Bleed!"

"Comet! Comet! Power. Bleed! Bleed!"

The General Maximum faced his mentor with a determined countenance. Lo'Marc placed the Scythe in its holster, which strafed his back, and bowed.

Kaz Vincallous nodded. His red aura retreated, and a hush fell over the crowd. The troops strained their ears, and the sound reached the very rear of their guard: "Attack."

The citizens of Lozé foresaw this day. They had long opposed Tannódin and ferociously defended the city's borders when any imperial contingent stepped foot within a twenty length radius of the city. Making due preparations, the resistance army of men and women stockpiled many energy weapons and created a war plan for such an occasion. Although no one had managed a glimmer of success against a major assault from Tannódin and Damüda, Lozé would not surrender. The memory of Nez Spirita's exploitation could not be rinsed away by the promises of prosperity preached by the ministers of Global Initiative. Their ancestors were killed in the planting of its seeds, and they did not want its savory fruit.

Propaganda circulated throughout Qeauríyx, brandishing the revolutionaries as insolent extremists. Many in the distant corners of the planet were sympathetic to the plight of the Nez Spiritans, but those lands had imperial tribulations of their own. Nevertheless, when news of the impending conflict spread across Qeauríyx, many warriors from afar flocked to the city. The leaders of Lozé hoped the legendary Brenko would arrive and coordinate the city's defense, but no one had seen or heard from him in quite some time. He belonged to the worldwide resistance group called Miska Kea,[3] a once powerful and ingenious bloc of indiscriminate men, women and a few témos that was all but wiped out at the battle of Phenplyacin.

After that ignominious defeat, no group dared a planet-wide, coordinated offensive against the house of Kaz; therefore, most conflicts were local in scope and nature. Presently, Global Initiative had two major concerns: Zotham, the prefect of Aphaz and the de facto representative of the entire continent of Líachim, and the persistent citizens of Keotagosdi, the remote northwestern continent in the far reaches of the Il'ectyx[4] Ocean.

When word reached the ears of the rebels in Lozé that White Scythe was approaching, they were fraught with expectant alarm but also emboldened with gritty determination. Brenko,[5] the great military tactician, had apparently abandoned them at their greatest point of need. The leadership of the city was focused on a council of three: Rydín,[6] the city prefect; Syla, a woman of military genius; and Wapla, the religious leader of the community. Syla, a Nez Spiritan survivor of Phenplyacin, tried to contact Brenko, through underground channels. She hoped that her old comrade would join her in the resistance; however, when she failed to hear from him she fashioned her own defense for the city.

Rydín ordered all remaining non-combatants out of the area and charged them to travel to Nextu or sail as far as Aphaz, so that they might to seek protection from the oncoming battle. Rydín gave the evacuation order eight durations before the fighting commenced. Those who stayed faced certain extermination. Tannódin sent him a stern warning. If Lozé

---

[2] Miska Kea: (mee-skah key-uh)
[4] Il'ectyx (il-ek-tiks)
[5] Brenko (brangk-oh)
[6] Rydín (rahy-deen)

did not desist in its "insurrection," the punishment rendered would be pitiless.

Five durations before the conflict, Syla ordered that Lozé be placed on internment; no one entered and no one left. This was to ensure the secrecy of her battle plan. During those one hundred and sixty days, the remaining inhabitants were repeatedly drilled on their roles in the defense of the city.

On the day of the battle, Wapla, a devout Nez Spiritan, who had resisted Tannódin his entire life, gathered the remaining warriors—men, women, and children—into a great assembly.

"My friends," the old mystic said, "the time has arrived for us to truly stand for what we believe. When our ancestors arose from the ground, in this land, so many cycles ago, they were entrusted to make it a land worthy of the Nameless One. Generations passed, and through the help of our Great Mothers and Fathers, and all creaturely hosts, we learned the way of the Auría.

"We were not perfect, and we made mistakes along the way. Some of them were horrific and egregious. And for them, we must and still repent even to this day. Yet we toiled on. Because with all our hearts, most Nez Spiritans believe that the Nameless One hopes we would cherish balance, seek peace, and love this cosmos.

"We had the opportunity to make technological leaps, but out of personal experience, we chose to take our time. From the North Country to the ends of the Windhorse Peninsula, our ancestors from the Nine Houses of Peace took measured steps in order to preserve our balance with the land and with all life. Because of those efforts, our continent was without war for two thousand cycles.

"Our mothers and fathers recognized that technology is as old as language and the walking staff, and that is why it must be dealt with judiciously. It is not a matter of comfort. It is not a matter of conservatism. It is not a matter of backwardness. It is a matter of modesty and respect and truth.

"Technology gives us the ability to grasp ever so closely a kind of power normally reserved for the Divine Happenings. Wielding this kind of power causes issues to arise within our species. We happened as nel'asmív.[7] And as we happen, we often wield it destructively towards each other and the land that we love.

"The windhorse is our brother and sister. The windhorse has testified to our misuse of technology. Yet we know that misuse does not mean that we cannot use technology for the benefit of all. In Nez Spirita's own time, we would have created sustainable ways of interacting with our creaturely brothers and sisters and the land we love so well.

---

[7] Nel'asmív (neyl-ahs-m*ee*v)

"We do not feel like we are better than anyone, but neither are we inferior. We have our ways; let others have theirs. We have birthed children with other continental brothers and sisters. Although rare, some of us have traveled and settled in other lands. We have never turned away those from other continents who come to Nez Spirita in peace.

"The Tannódin'é came, proclaiming peace, technology and 'assistance'."

"But we did not ask for Tannódin's assistance. We possessed no want for their technology. And we certainly did not need their peace.

"But they came anyway. They came with energy rifles. They came with empty treaties and promises. They came with pollution. They came with technologies that leveled cities in a few days, even though our cities took centuries to build. On top of the ashes of those same cities, they rebuilt in cycles what took us centuries to build and refine. The Tannódin'é and Damüdans claim this feat to be proof of their ingenuity and superiority.

"They hardened their hearts, choked their spirits, beat their chests, and championed their minds, though their qaníns were dim. They shut their ears to call of the stone, the land, and the Yarnínga trees. They did not understand how dirt, wood, and rock were our predecessors. They mistook the windhorse's bellow of caution and pain to be an irrational cry from some wild beast. And because they cared not to understand, we were left with no choice. Though we are spirits of peace, we had to fight.

"They tried to breed us out. Some of us were enslaved. Many of us were slaughtered. All of us went hungry. Our physical weapons were 'archaic' indeed, but our spiritual, mental, and emotional resolve was advanced. Unlike our Phmquedrian kindred, Sczyphamek Imperial took no immediate hold on us. They tried to break us, and indeed seven Houses of Peace fell to their persuasion, but two Houses in the Peninsula remain intact.

"Undoubtedly, this war changed us. The energy rifles you grip now are proof of that. Yet in the heart of every Nez Spiritan lies the pathway of justice, balance, and peace. As long as one Nez Spiritan carries that flame, the fire will not die, for our qaníns prove to be ample kindling, the Nameless One be praised.

"Although the Tannódin'é proclaim themselves in continuation of faith, their methods betray their belief. They speak of luxury, and luxury they possess: the luxury of destroying anyone who stands against them. They speak of development. Develop they do, at the expense of us. Yes… We too have *developed.* We have developed *their* luxury, which breeds *our* death. They speak of the One with No Name, as if we are all the Nameless Spirit's children. Maybe we are, but it is clear to them that the majority of Qeauríyx are illegitimate offspring, and they are the *true, divine offspring.* That offense we cannot allow…

"Regardless of their disposition or how shrewdly and convincingly they conceal it: Domination is their means and their end.

"Today may be the last for us all. If this is the day that we return to the ground, the dust of the air, and the waters from whence we came, know this: we are a testimony for all of those who have come before and will come after us. We do not fight to dominate. We do not fight out of pride, nor do we fight for honor; we fight only because we must. We must fight against any power that uses the sacred for destruction and manipulation. Let us pray…"

Wapla was unable to supplicate; his petition was interrupted by the rumbling rhythm of heavy machinery in the distance and the syncopation of seventy thousand White Scythe soldiers marching and breathing in tempo, with their leader conducting the orchestra of cataclysm to a heightened crescendo.

Hearing the cadence of their foes, Wapla muttered, "It appears that White Scythe is upon us."

The cadence of war imprinted itself on the minds of all those who were about to partake in destruction, causing both sides to fall into the historical consciousness of the planet. For a moment, time stopped and space constricted. This momentous sliver revealed thousands of cycles, thousands of deaths, thousands of tragedies… From the rise of White Scythe to the destruction of Nez Spirita, Qeauríyx would not allow those involved in the battle to escape time and space through self-deception or propaganda.

Most inhabitants of Qeauríyx recognized the planet could share its memory at any time. Indeed, one's consciousness could merge with Qeauríyx's sentience. Although the planet and its creatures were distinct, they were intimately interconnected. The historical weight of the moment pressed upon the qaníns of all those involved in the oncoming battle. Lozé became another location for Qeauríyx to purposefully manifest itself, and not even a Sczyphamek could shake its presence. All parties randomly walked into this fate; and now, there was no turning back. Whenever such moments happened on Qeauríyx, the planet had a penchant for brandishing the participants with the foreknowledge of temporal and spatial inescapability. Indeed, the past was irrevocably connected to the present and future. Of all people, Lo'Marc P'tan and Wapla knew this.

Indeed, the battle of Lozé was a continuation of a process started by White Scythe before Lo'Marc was born; he had to obey the call of the blade. It *thirsted* for this day, craving the qanín of those who would dare oppose it… The path of bloodshed marked a road throughout the cycles, and White Scythe was there, in the majority of battles, growing stronger and more insatiable. The cause of Tannódin to unite the planet under one banner was an appropriate means to that end, *if* indeed that was the blade's desired "end." Currently, however, Global Initiative and White Scythe certainly appeared to share the same fate.

Indeed, the battle of Lozé was a continuation of a process started by Nez Spiritans long before Wapla was born. He had to obey the call of the

Nameless One, the land, and the windhorse. They gave him life and companionship. They strengthened the qaníns of those who dared to oppose White Scythe. The path of resistance and technological judiciousness was there in the majority of battles with Global Initiative. And Nez Spirita was there, in the majority of battles, growing weaker and more emaciated. The cause to stand up for one's homeland and way of life was a noble end, and the end of the rebellion was nearly all but certain.

White Scythe and all those inside Lozé surfaced from the suffocating waters of the past, and breathed the insidious air of the present.

Facing the crowd, Wapla smiled pensively. "Brothers and sisters, this will not be a glorious battle; for no war is glorious, just violent. May the Nameless One protect us all, and if we should fall today, know that there is a day when the House of Kaz will face what we face today…"

Raising his voice and filled with great emotion, he exhorted, "Come! Let us make them aware of our resolve. For Nez Spirita, and for all Qeauríyx! Let them come, and let them understand that we will not bow down gracefully; we will not run or cower! Now, rise men, women, and children of justice. Rise!"

The room erupted in shouts and applause, to such an extent that their faint echoes of resistance reached the ears of those marching against the doomed city.

There were no illusions; the battle was sure to be deadly and costly for both parties.

Syla calmed the crowd down and spoke in a matter-of-fact tone. "To your posts."

***

Standing atop a mechanized vehicle of destruction, the General Maximum bade his troops to attack. After crossing a large field at the city's outskirts, Lo'Marc ordered twenty thousand of his White Scythe troops to engage Lozé from the southeast, another twenty thousand to flank their northeastern border, while the last thirty thousand would directly attack the main entrance to the city from the east. Lozé itself was about eight lengths east of the Phyxtríalis Ocean.

Since Blue Rapier's Navy was deployed elsewhere, a beach attack was out of the question. There was no sufficient way to surround Lozé. The topography of the coastline was too craggy to the north, and Lozé was encapsulated by small mountains and foothills to the east and south as well. Lo'Marc's plan was to drive the rebels to the beach, where they would have little cover from White Scythe's potent artillery. Sczyphamek Vicious hovered in the sky, observed the battle from an aerial perspective, and watched his protégé unleash his strategy.

Syla foresaw the plan Lo'Marc would employ. The battle of Lozé was not a battle hedged in trickery and misdirection. It was a battle of will and opposable forces. The first side to crack would be the one who lost. Therefore, Syla engineered a strategy to ambush and bottleneck White Scythe. Although murderous, Global Initiative employed standard rules of engagement. They did not believe in fighting a faceless war. The imperial behemoth desired their enemy to behold their power with fear and trembling. A worthy empire did not hide behind its long-range ordinance. Indeed, White Scythe's preliminary volley was merely a warning of impending doom rather than actual combat.

Beneath the surface of the city lay underground tunnels built centuries prior. A cycle before the conflict, the inhabitants of Lozé began to reinforce and restore the tunnels at key junctions. Syla predicted that White Scythe would enter into the metropolis at its eastern entrances. Once the elites fully embedded themselves within the city limits, she would give the command for the underground troops to emerge and attack them from behind. Thirty thousand rebels fortified the center of the city, and ten thousand hid underground at various junctions. No one from the outside knew Syla's tactical deployment because of the lockdown placed on Lozé.

Syla ordered small legions to incite and draw White Scythe into Lozé by attacking them three to five lengths outside the city gates, then retreating back towards the town, all the while maintaining a steady barrage from their antiquated, combustible cannons and Automatic Energy Assault Rifles.[8] She needed the violent deception to last at least two to four hours, so that it would appear the insurrectionists were trying to keep White Scythe out of the city.

The rebels found success with this strategy and kept the war machine at bay for five hours. Lo'Marc grew restless, wanting to impress his mentor, Vincallous. Despite the General Maximum's impatience, he possessed too much military acumen to underestimate his foe. He understood the rebels had not yet shown their full hand. Lo'Marc's troops had only suffered minor casualties, but if they did not make headway within the next few hours, a stalemate would develop into the night.

Soon, White Scythe moved within a length of the city. On cue, the rebels armed underground land mines and explosives that were planted twenty days prior under the cover of darkness. Immediately, a tank to the right and two to the left of the General Maximum exploded, sending shrapnel everywhere and cutting random holes in the ranks of White Scythe. Lo'Marc was surprised; their intelligence did not suggest that the field was mined. Then again, the Eradicate were unable to carry out firsthand espionage of the area for three durations. Nor were they able to assess the rebel's war strategy due to Lozé's self-imposed internment.

---

[8] Automatic Energy Assault Rifles abbrev. AEAR

It also appeared that Vicious was indeed keeping his end of their agreement. Lo'Marc asked Vincallous not to participate in the battle in any way. With his powers, the Sczyphamek probably sensed the traps long before the first blast. Yet, when Lo'Marc gazed up at Vincallous, the General Maximum swore that surprise and disgruntlement was etched upon the Sczyphamek's face.

P'tan shook his head while thinking to himself. *Was Vicious unaware of the mines too? No. That's impossible. Keep to the task, Lo'Marc.*

Through radio communication, the General Maximum ordered his troops to halt. He would not allow the needless decimation of his soldiers by a minefield. Lo'Marc commanded the tank operators to reverse half a length and to change their regular ordinance to a specialized "cascade shell." Haptian Spiax,[9] a paramount scientist for Tannódin, developed the munition. Although a brilliant biochemical alchemist, he was also a talented inventor of mechanized weaponry. The cascade shell was just one of his many contributions to the armed forces of Tannódin and Damüda. After the initial detonation, a chain reaction ignited smaller concussive blasts, which would canvass the surrounding area along with sizzling projectiles. The last twelve tanks complied, and the rest of White Scythe took cover behind the heavy machinery.

"Excellently played," Vincallous commented, moving away from the apex of the battlefield.

When Syla saw that the tanks were no longer moving towards the city, she called all of her decoy legions back into the city, but it was too late.

The salvo was maddening, and the entire field sparked in bright light and fire. Dirt ejected into the air, raining down on all the combatants. The ground shook, knocking those in the city off their feet. The minefield was virtually destroyed, along with many combatants from Lozé who remained close to the city's outskirts.

The inhabitants of Lozé were down to their last plan. Fortunately for the rebels, the blast created craters so wide, the mechanized vehicles would be unable to enter into the city, only the foot soldiers. After receiving reports declaring the minefield incapacitated, the General Maximum commanded his forces into the city.

When White Scythe entered into Lozé, everything went as Syla predicted. The troops were ambushed at the three eastern junctures of the city, in the midst of buildings and alleys. Syla hoped that urban warfare would slow White Scythe down, because most of their battles were fought in open areas. She prayed that in the midst of the confusion, her adversaries would fire upon each other, or at the very least become disoriented.

---

[9] Haptian Spiax (hahp-tee-ahn spee-aks)

The General Maximum was among his troops at the southeast. Before long, a stalemate ensued with White Scythe caught in the middle. Although the rebel center was a half a length in front of them, the imperial troops could advance no further; the suppression bursts were too great. And when White Scythe tried to take cover in structures behind them, the rebels who remained hidden under the city ambushed them. The General Maximum inwardly smiled at this strategic move, for he was trained to never lose respect for his enemy. He recognized that his opponent was a tactical genius, and the Scythe titillated in the agreement.

As the deadlock continued, Lo'Marc completely analyzed Syla's strategy, and within a half hour he developed a counterattack. Through radio wave communication, the General Maximum ordered five thousand of his troops at each skirmish to break formation and flank the center of the rebel line. By engaging the rebels at numerous angles, the General Maximum forced them to thin out their center, which weakened their overall firepower. He also ordered five thousand imperialists at each skirmish to guard their rear with cover fire. Next, he ordered the tanks on the outskirts of the city to switch to a pressure shell and aim their cannons at an angle that would place the explosive at the center of the city. The pressure shells were capable of traveling greater distances than the regular shells because they were only filled with excessively pressurized air, which upon detonation, could cut through metal and concrete.

Once his troops successfully positioned themselves and readied their ordinance, he ordered the remaining troops fighting the center to charge the power cells on their weapons, and discharge seventy-five percent of their cells in a concentrated burst simultaneously towards the center. This was a remorseless and risky move; for when the troops and tanks fired upon the rebels, the synchronized energy beams and shells decimated all matter that stood in their way.

The sound was incredible, and the reverberation even caused Vicious to brace himself in the air. The area fell silent, filled with smoke.

It was time.

He fastened his helmet and reached towards his back. His left hand took hold of it, and the scythe awoke from its daydream ready to inflict permanent slumber. Those under his command instinctively backed away, as soon as they heard the distinctive low, repetitive hum: the Metronome of Death.

As the ashen mist cleared, sounds of coughs, moans, and agony filled what was left of the debris-filled center. A square length area was flattened and demolished. Those rebels to the southeast who survived had no time to regroup. A calm shadow moved within the smoke. It vaguely emerged, holding an opaque weapon that gleamed with power.

The wielder wore a shiny, ominous off-white mask of death, which reflected the translucent glare of the weapon. His fluttering white cape slithered in the shadows. In desperate fear, some fired at the object, but the smoke made it impossible to acquire adequate aim. It was still relatively quiet, but soon half-uttered screams filled the area.

Syla, who was knocked momentarily unconscious by the destructive volley, emerged from the rubble and heard the sound of her brothers and sisters dying most horrific deaths. Instinctively, she reached to her back, only to remember that she gave it up long ago. She wished she had not parted with it.

Syla, she thought to herself, *don't think about that now. That memory is death.*

Coughing uncontrollably, bruised, and bloody, she picked up two nearby rifles.

A distinct sound hummed, violently vibrating the air. Few had survived to describe it: A whistling cacophony that spoke lamentation and woe.

It's the mystical blade, Syla reasoned. *It has to be.*

Flesh ripped with little friction. Every execution brought the weapon into greater view, for the glimmer of bloodlust multiplied. The rod of the scythe was long and pure white, with streaks of black appearing randomly. Its base bore a shiny knob, made of dark blue cometstone, one of the rarest jewels found on the planet. The blade itself appeared to be made of a luminous metal, a metal unknown to Syla. She was unable to make out the color of the blade. The opaqueness of the gleam drowned out any spectral analysis. The illumination could only be approximated as "white." The blade seemed like it would disappear into oblivion yet somehow its luster was undeniable.

Three face-to-face skirmishes broke out at the three junctions. The combatants of Lozé at the northeast, eastern, and southeast had to contend with White Scythe, the military wing. Yet those to the southeast, near Syla's immediate position, also had to deal with the blade and its Wielder.

A few rebels discharged their firearms at the glistening weapon and its immediate adjacency. Astoundingly, every shot was deflected or absorbed by the scythe or dodged by the Wielder. Some lost their wits and charged into the dissipating billow, screaming and firing aimlessly, only to take their last breaths.

The men and women of White Scythe took aim upon the remainder who ran away from the Wielder.

His metal boots were as light and flexible as the wind, and his steps were as quick as flashes of lightning. The taps of his boots danced in rhythm with his sparkling partner of death. As the haze almost lifted, Syla saw his dark gray armored short jacket, outlined in white, and the Tannódin'é insignia inscribed on it. His left hand was gloveless, but he wore a gray forearm guard. His right hand was covered with a charred brown metal gauntlet traversing his forearm that depicted a battle from time immemorial. A chain hung around his neck, and it seemed to move in concert with the scythe. His pants matched his coat, and his light metal boots, sharp as an assassin's dagger, emerged from the bottom. His cape was wet from the blood of the rebels, and his entire wardrobe seemed anachronistic.

But that was the *lie*. His garb was not out of place. His outfit, the blade, and their symbolic and actual violence *belonged* in Lozé. They exemplified the cycles of Qeauríyx and the imperial advance of Tannódin and Damüda. It made Syla all the madder. The General Maximum wore archaic clothes into battle and his vestments were deemed exemplary. However, Tannódin and Damüda castigated Nez Spiritan's ways as backwards and archaic.

Syla held one, slippery chance to kill the General Maximum. She cycled the power cells on her AEARs to full discharge and waited for the eventual confrontation.

Confrontation came swiftly. As soon as Lo'Marc heard the sound of her weapons gathering strength, he turned around, faced Syla, and belligerently swiped the air with his blade. Instantly, the remaining dust withdrew. His menacing off-white helmet stared through her.

She was terrified, but Syla was determined to administer murderous retribution. Her body was calm. She had seen and lived through worse. She strapped one rifle across her back and fixed the other upon his position.

"Make it count." His voice sounded eerie and chilling behind the mask, and although Syla did not see his face underneath it, she knew he was smiling. Without hesitation, he ran and somersaulted in the air.

Syla waited for the opportune moment. Testing her patience, Lo'Marc sought to provoke the daughter of Nez Spirita into thoughtless action. He grotesquely dispatched her few remaining living comrades in front of her eyes. Many sparred valiantly with the General, but they were injured and/or no match for his skill. Heads were lost. Appendages, ripped. Qaníns, masticated. Entrails, punctured and removed. Bodies, quartered. Skin, flayed. Death reeked. In two minutes, the General Maximum killed twenty soldiers.

Syla did not look away. In those murderous yet precious moments, the woman proficiently analyzed the Wielder's fighting stance, style, and preferences and the hum of White Scythe. P'tan was clueless to her real identity. Otherwise, he would have killed her at his first opportunity.

Her friends-in-arms did not plead for her help. They knew, as well as Syla, that if she fired upon him, he would dodge and bludgeon her. Lo'Marc had not yet committed to a compromising attack. And based on her assessment, a close range shot gave her the best chance of success.

Although she tried to suppress the urge, her regret of parting with her sword reemerged. She would have held her own against him if she still held...

Stop it, she thought. *Stop it, Syla. It is too late for regrets. My punishment is coming to an end.*

In the background, Syla witnessed a host of White Scythe standing at attention and watching their leader show his remarkable scytheplay. They dared not interrupt the General Maximum's melee. In the far distance, she looked upon the rebels, her comrades, who ambushed the Tannódin'é soldiers. They were fighting to the last against a significant contingent. The eastern rebel flank appeared completely annihilated. Syla beheld no energy bursts from either side's firearms. Concussive blasts and explosions of light consumed the northeastern section of town. Rydín and Wapla were part of that skirmish.

There was very little possibility that any of them would survive. Even if she managed to kill the General Maximum, his soldiers would unleash their remaining ordinance upon her. This thing—her death—was certain.

She did not believe Brenko when they last spoke fifteen cycles ago. He told her that he was done fighting. She laughed in his face and slapped the tears off his cheeks for saying such a thing. Clearly, he was not lying.

Brenko, you damn coward, she thought to herself. *Bíoske, you're still wrong...*

The dead were splayed all around Syla and throughout Lozé. Casualties mounted on both sides, but the outcome was inevitable. Ensanguined corpses slept on the rubble and drooled streams of blood, but the rebels' claret was by far the greatest source of flow. Syla pushed her loss and rage to the back of her mind. Those passions, though righteous, would cloud her judgment.

Soon, the Eighty-Fourth General Maximum finished the last of the nearby insurrectionists and once again turned his attention to Syla.

"Exceptional," he said. "You possess a great military mind and forbearance. Any attack on me would have been pointless..."

Syla was quiet. Talking was a distraction. Her final mission was to take him down or die trying.

Lo'Marc strafed to the left and right at incredible speeds, but Syla ignored her eyes and listened for the blade. And within the blink of an eye, the scythe wielder disappeared and reemerged behind her, just as Syla suspected. Still, this was not the deathblow. He was too pompous to kill her from behind.

Syla did not flinch. Her finger itched on the trigger.

Seamlessly, the General Maximum reappeared to her left. She heard the blade's signature whir and ducked, just dodging a horizontal blow to the head. Yet, the General's recovery was swift, and he twirled the scythe vertically, gnashing at the ground, breaking rubble. Syla rolled out of the way with mercurial speed, and seeing an opportunity, she fired at close range. The General Maximum *just* evaded the blast, and as he glanced at his opponent, Syla's sights fixed directly upon him with her second weapon.

He was in her line of fire. He could not avoid it. The blast was savage and blinding and hurled Syla backward. Regaining her focus, she dropped her head in bitter disbelief.

Although his arm bled profusely, the Wielder survived. Somehow, he managed a defense with the scythe even though her execution was flawless.

Lo'Marc sucked air in pain. "Staxis!" he exclaimed and glared at his opponent. "That was impressive, woman, but not good enough." The General Maximum clenched the blade tightly, and White Scythe scintillated with power and whistled and hummed a most violent tune: the void of Qeauríyx.

"Finally…" she mumbled. "Kíma…Just get it over with."

Chapter Five: Obfuscation/Clarification

They had been in the same conversation for the past five hours, and Anámn's patience finally failed him.

By the time he awoke from his "encounter" with the tree, it was nightfall. He raced throughout the night to make it to Skylark in time. His pants were torn at the knees. His body was sore from running for nearly five hours at full speed. And he was already in pain from the explosion. Lucky for Anámn, his powers aided him in healing.

It was bad enough that he almost missed the train. But, this... this is what he rushed to? Those damn fools kept arguing nonstop.

The train was full but not packed. There was just enough room for everyone to sit down. Anámn even managed to get about seven hours of sleep before they woke him.

They were Phmquedrian slaves, but something was unusual about them. Their countenances were too jovial, their clothes, too clean.

One was tall and a bit older than Anámn, with a black cloak wrapped around his body. His glistening shoes were also black, and they were exquisite compared to the makeshift feet coverings the slaves from Euhilv wore. This observation alone proved the two men were not from the Mine District of Phmquedria. The tall one flaunted neatly kempt hair, which was shocking to Anámn's neglected qanín. Each follicle was groomed with intimate detail and collectively cut and shaped into an almost perfect sphere.

The tall one's companion was short, stocky, and middle-aged. His hair was balding and gray, and his beard was the same color, although it was trimmed as gracefully as his partner's hair. He wore a burnt maroon jacket and pants set, and the creases on his pants were as sharp as razors. Anámn felt an instinctive contempt for their malapropos vestments. Didn't they understand that this train was for slaves? Why were they dressing like Tannódin'é?

"I'm telling you Hamin," the tall man said.[1] "Ancestor worship isn't true to the Auría. Tannódin's been real clear on that."

---

[1] Hamin (hah-min)

"Kaimero," the other said.[2] "There you go again. Always talking what Master Flan says. Why don't you just let him do the talking? He sounds more educated than you anyway."

Both laughed at that statement. Although their dialects sounded quite lowbrow, intermittent spurts of high grammar and vocabulary speckled their playful bickering. Anámn did not understand everything they said, but their intonation irked him to no end.

"Well, that's true," Kaimero joked. "After all, we are just some lowly Phmquedrians who don't know any better. It's just too bad that you really don't, Hamin."

"Will you all *please* shut up," Anámn interjected with disgust. "This Qalfocx of a trip is bad enough without both of you keeping everybody awake. Kíma."

"Hey…" the short man said to the tall one with interest. "What do we have here? An ill-tempered Phmmy?"

"*What did you call me?*" Anámn stood up and spat out indignantly. The word "Phmmy" was a derogatory name given to Phmquedrians by the Tannódin'é and Damüdans.

"Don't be like that to the young man, Hamin." The tall one put his hand over his partner's mouth, in order to ease the tension. "Young man, what's your name?"

"You don't know me," Anámn sneered. "Don't be talking to me like you know me, and you need to tell your friend over there to shut his damn mouth."

"Yeah," the old man muttered in condescension. "Definitely one of them Euhilv Phmquedrians."

"Hamin, be quiet now," Kaimero urged his friend to restrain himself.

"He is the one who stuck his nose in our business. We said nothing to him," Hamin replied, switching out of his Phmquedrian dialect to a more Tannódin'é inflection. "It was not as if he asked us politely. So I simply spoke his language; it seems he understood it quite well."

Anámn cut his eyes at the old man and was about to lunge towards him, but he restrained himself. Kamo was a long way off, and if a fight broke out he would be kicked off the railcruiser, although he knew this was one fight he could win.

"Is there a problem back there, ah?" a Damüdan guard asked, opening the door to the slave car.

"No," Kaimero replied courteously. "We're just joking with each other."

"Keep it that way," the man said, "or all three of you will be walking to Kamo." At that, he shut the door, and stood guard on the other side, making sure no Phmquedrian would travel into the free cars.

---

[2] Kaimero (kahy-meh-roh)

The train jostled on the tracks, while Hamin shook his head and said politely, "Young man, I apologize. I lost my wits just now. Though I do not understand why our conversation was so bothersome."

There was that switch talk again.

"Everybody on this railcruiser is trying to sleep." The slave from Euhilv matched Hamin's changed tone. "Y'all are keeping me and everyone else up."

"Who's up?" Kaimero asked, surveying the slave car. They were indeed the only ones awake.

"Well, you're keeping *me* up."

Hamin and Kaimero smiled at each other and then at Anámn.

"Young man, what is your name?" Kaimero asked.

"Anámn. And I take it that your names are Kaimero and Hamin, huh?" The two men nodded.

"What did you mean about me being one of them 'Euhilv Phmquedrians,' Hamin?" Anámn asked calmly.

"You all have very interesting temperaments," the middle-aged man replied. "It's impossible to read what you are thinking."

"Heh…" Anámn replied, somewhat amused. "Where are you from?"

The younger half of the duo spoke up. "We are from Prosephyr,[3] in the northern country."

Anámn smiled. "Oh, that explains it. You all are some of them *northern* Phmquedrians. It figures."

All three of them laughed.

"I don't know what you all are talking about anyway. It's not like it makes a difference about what we believe, whether its ancestor worship or not."

Now Hamin and Kaimero appeared amused, prompting Anámn to continue.

"I mean, who cares? Phmquedria is Qalfocx, whether you believe in the ancestors or not. Y'all's argument isn't really helping anybody, *at least not any Phmquedrians*. You're talking like a Tannódin'é."

"And?" Kaimero prodded.

"*And* Tannódin hasn't done anything for us, except cause us grief. If I were you, I would stop wasting time talking like a Tannódin'é or even caring about what they think; they're wrong anyway." Anámn stopped and folded his arms, believing he just put the two intellectuals in their place and silenced the matter altogether.

Hamin summarized, "So what you're saying is that Tannódin is wrong and Phmquedria is right?"

"Yeah."

Kaimero frowned. "Young brother, that doesn't seem a bit too simple to you?"

---

[3] Prosephyr (proh-sih-feer)

"I mean, don't get me wrong. Phmquedrians act wrong, but that's because Tannódin messed up how they think. I ain't trying to start anything, but you all prove my point. You all are caught up in Tannódin'é ideas. Some of the other slaves I know are the same. If it weren't for Tannódin though, none of you would even think this way. So yeah, there are some 'bad' Phmquedrians, but it's Tannódin's fault."

Hamin shook his head. "Do you know any history, Anámn?"

"Why? What's the point? I know what I see," he retorted, angry that the duo did not accept his argument.

Hamin, although perceiving Anámn's discontent, continued in a soft, reflective tone, "No, I am afraid that you do not know. Your argument is faulty; you are using myanála[4] to present your arguments."

"Mya-what? Mya... Nawla... Mynawla?" Anámn stumbled. "There y'all go using that high talk again."

"Myanála," Kaimero corrected. "It means 'two points' in the Ancient Tongue. Phmquedrian thinkers used this term long ago to describe the type of argument you are giving. It's when a person places two things on opposite ends, like 'good' and 'evil.'"

"Yeah," Anámn said intuitively. "I get it. So?"

"There is a problem." The duo said in unison.

"What?"

"You assume that you can objectively judge good and evil, or that reality exists only on these two poles," Hamin said. "You just rendered the basis of your assessment futile, or in your vernacular, 'you dealing in double talk.' Nobody clean in history, Anámn. Nobody."

"Qeauríyx is more complicated than you give it credit for," Kaimero added and placed his hands in his cloak. "That is why you must know what has happened in order to try to fix the problems."

"And how's that working out?" Anámn raised his voice, virtually ignoring the brunt of Kaimero's statement. "Pretty good I'm sure. Who's your master? I bet he treats y'all real good doesn't he?"

The intellectual slaves of Prosephyr let their antagonist's anger burn against them.

"Quiet, huh? Don't worry about too many beatings? Get to eat real nice? All you had to do is think like Master."

Kaimero's patience wore thin. He shook his head and grumbled in displeasure. "Anámn, you're crossing the line. You don't know us either."

"I know you talk like this old man in my village. He's always talking about 'knowing and thinking' when what Phmquedria needs is action."

"No," Hamin sighed. "Phmquedria needs all three."

"All I know is that if the Seven Elders of Phmquedria were still in charge there would be action, and we wouldn't be in this gynix."

---

[4] Myanála (mahy-uh-*nah*-luh)

"You think the Elders would have saved us?" Hamin asked.

"Yeah."

Both of them nervously frowned to themselves.

"Anámn," Kaimero hesitated. "Anámn, the Elders are partly responsible for this slavery."

The young man almost lost his nerve and nearly charged at his continental brother. Kaimero's declaration was blasphemy to his ears. The Elders of Phmquedria represented a pristine history of flawless grace and wonder for many Phmquedrians. In the midst of their harsh servitude, the Elders provided them a hope of what their people were and what they might one day attain once again.

"You Phmmys've lost your kímaz minds." The hothead Sczyphamek threw his hands in the air. "Staxis. Your master got both of you to believe whatever he wants."

"Master Flan isn't like most Tannódin'é," Hamin countered.

"'Master Flan ain't like mos' Tannódin'é,'" Anámn mocked and changed his voice to a subservient, spineless slave. "Staxis, you keep proving my point..."

Kaimero, with searing eyes and a stern tone, responded, "Anámn, I would strike you where you stand, if your arrogant ignorance hadn't already done so."

Hamin, noticing his partner's displeasure, became the mediator and sought to calm the two young men. "Master Flan is not actually our master. He purchased us from our former master in the lumberyards of Prosephyr and then set us free.

"He's a historiographer from Tannódin. He offered us a choice: learn about Phmquedrian history by traveling with him or do whatever suited us. We chose to learn. He taught us how to read and write, and yes, sometimes the Tannódin'é bastard is quite oblivious to his own bias, but he continues to realize this as well."

Anámn started to open his mouth, but Kaimero cut him off, "No Anámn, that does not excuse Tannódin from its role in our history, and Hamin and I both realize we are the lucky ones. But, to believe that all Tannódin'é are the cause of this Qalfocx or that all of Phmquedria was blameless is ridiculous."

Anámn began to speak again, but Hamin interjected. "You're guilty of the same haughty narrow-mindedness you accuse the Tannódin'é of possessing."

Although Anámn did not believe, understand, or trust everything that was being said to him, Hamin's statement made him take pause.

"Do you think men are superior to women?" Hamin asked Anámn.

"No. Not even the Tannódin'é believe that. Nobody on Qeauríyx does."

"Of course we don't," Kaimero added. "Nor do we believe that women are superior to men. And you know why?"

"*Yeah,*" Anámn said with self-congratulation. "Anything that survived the Great Drift has proven its worth and right to be here."

"That's right," Hamin agreed. "If it weren't for everyone and everything working together, none of us would have made it here. There was no time for petty differences during the Drift; it was survival."

"You're right." Anámn scratched his baldhead. "And that's what I been trying to tell you. That's what makes Tannódin so unforgiveable. They're the ones who changed things."

"Maybe," Kaimero replied. "But that doesn't make us perfect. Remember, even you said this. No one is superior or inferior to anyone else. We all are the same. We all are capable of love and treachery."

Anámn's Elemental shifted at those words, causing him to become uncomfortable.

"Is something wrong?" Hamin asked.

"No," Anámn trailed off, wondering what his Elemental was doing.

Hamin seized Anámn's pause as an opportunity to teach the son of ju Xaníz. "As you know, Phmquedria was once made of a confederation of seven states. One hundred and fifty cycles before Global Initiative, when Damüda and Tannódin appeared to be gathering strength for military incursions, the Elders, under the advisement of the témos, decided to draw up a non-aggression pact with their closest neighboring continents."

"That's right," Anámn said. "And Tannódin and Damüda broke that treaty."

"Yes and no," Kaimero responded. "For one hundred and forty-five cycles did that treaty hold, until the reign of Sczyphamek Imperial."

All three paused. The name alone was enough to evoke dread and malice.

"Kímaz Imperial," Kaimero cursed.

Hamin nodded. "Secretly, a strong minority of Elders in some of the clans desired to join forces with Tannódin. They believed Phmquedria lagged behind their continental neighbors in terms of technology and economy. Such a lag, they felt, would lead them to decline and eventually ruin. Other supporters of Tannódin just wanted power for their clans. But, there remained over half who wanted nothing to do with the House of Kaz."

Anámn listened intently. The way Hamin told the story was compelling; it reminded him of Malchían.

Seeing the youth was drawn into his historical tale, the old man spoke on, "Fighting soon broke out between the seven states of Phmquedria, plunging the entire continent into civil war and a brutal stalemate for six cycles. You may not know this Anámn, but Imperial only had one power of the Sundry Elemental."

"What?"

"A form of telepathic mind control."

Anámn was silent at first, but then stated, "So she was the one who controlled the elders and—"

Hamin put his hand up. "No, her powers couldn't have worked that way. If they did, Nez Spirita couldn't have put up such a resistant fight."

Anámn was quieted. Thinking and linking things historically was challenging to the youth.

"Only a weakened mind was truly subject to her power," Kaimero supplemented. "When Phmquedria broke out into civil war, Imperial offered her services to end the dispute. Our ancestor's minds were in a fragmented malaise due to the war, and because some wanted Imperial here in the first place, they accepted her offer.

"They were deceived of course. Once Imperial gained a foothold in our land, she never let go, and she installed her husband as the governor. Those Phmquedrians who believed that they had a share in Global Initiative soon found out that their ambitions would be betrayed."

"Betrayed?"

Hamin became upset and solemn. "Before the war commenced, Imperial offered to arm some of the Phmquedrians with technologically advanced weaponry, and they—we accepted."

Anámn shuddered. His people would do that?

"So you see, Tannódin is even fouler than you once thought, and Phmquedria is not as guiltless as you believed," Kaimero said. "I know it is hard to fathom. Hamin and I were the same way when we found out, but we've seen evidence that this took place."

"Evidence your master provided," Anámn matched their vocabulary and delivery once again. He had heard Héthyx and his father speak enough to know how to play language games. With enough flourish and power, the most magnificent and biting words could signify lies and nothing.

"Don't be foolish, young man," Hamin said.

"Don't believe everything you hear," Anámn countered. His sigh was the definition of exasperation. "I should've kept my mouth shut. At least then I would've heard kíma instead of lies."

The train decelerated and a distorted voice crackled from the one, barely-functioning speaker in the slave car. "We are entering into the town of Gumos. Kamo is two-hundred lengths away. We should arrive in two and a half hours."

None of the Phmquedrians moved or acknowledged the announcement, neither did they awake during Anámn, Kaimero, and Hamin's conversation.

"I'm going back over here and going to sleep," Anámn declared.

Kaimero and Hamin looked at Anámn with sorrowful countenances. Instead of concluding or continuing their original conversation, they somberly sat on the floor and spoke nothing. Occasionally, Anámn gazed over at them during the next hour. As the train neared Kamo, it stopped on the tracks to let another train pass. The railcruiser fell silent, and the calm of the slave car was excruciating to Anámn. Mumbling to himself, he stood up and knocked on the door to the free car.

"I want to get off here, while the train is stopped," he told the Damüdan guard.

"Whatever," the guard responded. "But we are still thirty lengths away from Kamo."

"I'll be alright."

"Like I care, Phmmy."

Anámn shook his head at the guard and glanced victoriously at Kaimero and Hamin. The prejudiced guard proved his point. The duo looked on, and grunted a sign of "no." The guard opened the side door, and Anámn jumped out of the railcruiser and into the jungle where the River Kamo lay. When he went deep enough into the trees, he found the river.

Its current was rapid and its width was enormous. No one would be traveling it until the rainy season ended. Anámn gazed downstream and followed the current, running at a swift pace.

***

Three days had passed since her encounter with Qeauríyx. She wanted to resume travel the next morning, but she was too exhausted. Never had she felt so terribly spent in her life. Therefore, Neztríanis rested for a few days before she continued her journey. She could not move very far, so she spent time reading a copy of the Fragments her mother placed in her shoulderpack. There was a poem, translated from the Ancient Tongue, which was her favorite. In her village, the verse was sung with such a sweet melody.

Our Qanín can only exist in Your grasp
We shall not fear.
Like a newborn held by the Great Mothers and Fathers
We are comforted.
Loving Mystery, graciously breathe
Breathe on us throughout the cycles.

The daughter of Hopha was strengthened inwardly by these words. Physically, Neztríanis was just strong enough to crawl to a nearby offshoot of the Xarkim River in order to collect water for her jug.

The second day, she tried to stand, but her feet and calves were gelatinous, and she tumbled to her knees. Lying on her back, she thought about the meaning of her altercation with Qeauríyx. Did Pre-Eminent or Vicious experience a similar process? Although she was versed in the Fragments of the Auría, there was much about Sczyphameks that remained a mystery. And there was no report that the Elemental warriors confronted the planet early in their walk.

Sipping some water and eating a few berries, Neztríanis meditated upon her display of power during the planetary confrontation. Somehow, her Elemental conjured incendiary ice. And the flame that consumed her was completely blue, which signified a more refined heat. Finally, she engulfed the surrounding trees in a spherical sheet of ice. These feats were entirely her Elemental's doing. Neztríanis had very little control over her powers during the confrontation.

The daughter of Hopha disdained losing, powerlessness, and the feeling of ineptitude. Neztríanis vowed that at the return of her strength, she would learn how to master every technique, especially the ice sphere.

Upon awaking the third day, she was reinvigorated and ready to resume her journey. With matted hair and a crusty mouth, the restless Sczyphamek recalled the phrase that seemed to incite her element of cold: "Zí mányx que rai." Adept in the Ancient Tongue, she began to translate the phrase.

"Zí?" meant "extremely frigid." Could Zí double for both her power and the name of her Elemental? "Qe" and "Ke" translated into "world" or "planet." In fact, "Qeauríyx" approximately meant "the world happening as the Auría." "Que" was a slight variation of "qe/ke" and symbolized the earth and land of Qeauríyx. At this point in her life "mányx" needed no explanation. She was reared upon the sacred chant, "Fá'atoño má," for as long as she remembered. The word "rai" was unknown to Neztríanis, and she was unsure of the relationship it implied. Perhaps "rai" was the name of her Elemental and not "Zí."

"Is your name Rai or Zí?" Neztríanis asked aloud. "Or something else?"

No response.

Although she did not know her Elemental's name, she gathered the rough meaning of the phrase, "Zí mányx que rai." The phrase had something to do with allowing herself and her frigid Elemental to permeate one another, drawing upon the power of Qeauríyx and the One with No Name.

After washing up and eating breakfast, the daughter of Hopha resumed her journey and walked for a few hours. She did not feel winded so the young Sczyphamek decided to recreate the wave of ice that extended from her body. She chanted "Zí mányx que rai," and although her element of frigidity granted her audience, she could do nothing more than release streams of cold air from her hands and body.

The next day, she felt more energized. Neztríanis chanted with great faith and power, but with little understanding. Believing she could will the ice sphere into happening, Nez's method was based on pure coercion. At once, the trees frosted over, the grass cracked, branches fractured, as a freezing wind whirred. The wind gradually picked up force and created a small blizzard-like condition. The daughter of Hopha released the gathering algidity, but the energy expelled chaotically. Sharp icicles plunged into, buckled, and felled many Yarninga trees.

Neztríanis was a Nez Spiritan cut from the cloth of tradition and equilibrium. She felt no amusement in her powers. She needlessly damaged an ecosystem that did no wrong to her. Ashamed, the Sczyphamek fell upon her knees and repented, petitioning the Nameless One, her ancestors, and the Yarníngas for mercy.

Uninhibited power was not the answer.

Breaking from her Elemental experiment, Neztríanis exercised with increased fortitude. Life in Hopha made her unaccustomed to continuous exercise. She needed to build up her endurance. She climbed trees and jumped from limb to limb and also ran at full speed at least once every two hours. Whenever she encountered a fallen tree trunk, she attempted to lift it over her head. She enjoyed moderate success with that feat. Though out of all of her "common" powers as a Sczyphamek, flying was undoubtedly the hardest. Circumventing gravity was absolutely excruciating.

On the third day of her resumed journey, she awoke with cirrus clouds overhead. As a child, Neztríanis enjoyed cloud gazing, imagining them to be different people, animals, and shapes. Her mother used to comment to her that although clouds were made of water vapor and ice, they inspired visions, signs, and wonders.

Neztríanis yawned, but her mouth soon grew into a smile. "That is it!"

A cloud's shape was contingent upon many phenomena; however, in most cases, its composition remained the same. Clouds were made of water in the form of ice and water vapor and other particulates. Whenever Neztríanis created ice, she was actually condensing water by freezing it. And since ice was made of water, ice took the shape of that which contained it. In order to accomplish the ice sphere, the Sczyphamek needed to focus her frigid Elemental in such a way that it forged a sphere of water vapor cooled well below freezing.

Nervousness and doubt crept into her heart. A technique like that required strong belief, stamina, and creativity. After eating some breakfast, consisting of more berries and nuts—a meal she was beginning to loathe—the daughter of Hopha searched for a clear area in the forest that would allow her to test her hypothesis and face her unease.

Her route placed her in the central forest of lower Hero's Valley. It was early autumn. The leaves were changing color, and most of the fruit trees were losing their drupe. After this oncoming span of training, Neztríanis could only stop once more before she made it to Nextu. Even if her powers protected her from the Windhorse Peninsula's harsh winters, food would grow scarce. She had to reach Nextu by the end of the duration. It was already the second week of Myaíz, the second duration.[5] Ízdak, the third duration, would soon be at hand, and foliage decreased rapidly

---

[5] A cycle on Qeauríyx spans ten durations, called "íz" in the Ancient Tongue. There are exactly three hundred and twenty days per cycle. Each íz is exactly four weeks, and a week consists of eight days.

towards the end of that duration. By the time Gamíz arrived, most trees were bereft of fruit and leaves, and the animals of the forest either migrated or entered hibernation.

If Neztríanis was lucky, she would arrive in Pike Metropolis before the winter exerted itself. The Infinite Circle would be impossible to search, especially the areas beyond the tree lines. Even a Sczyphamek would have trouble surviving there. Her mother was correct; if Tannódin did not find the Auría by the middle of Ízdak, their search would definitely be suspended. Since the agents of Global Initiative did not know the location to the temple, it seemed that this subjunctive statement would be concretized. Her enemies may not be able to search, *but Neztríanis could.* Temperature's Elemental was a saving grace, but even she had no idea how long she would last in the upper elevations of Mount Xarkim in the winter. All things considered, the Sczyphamek decided to stop for about five days in order to try to master the ice hemisphere technique.

Neztríanis continued to travel about half a day. She was about forty lengths from the southern shore of Hero's Valley, which was home to the calm waves of the Phyxtríalis Ocean. It was not until the early afternoon that she was able to find a suitable clearing to train. The woods thinned and were more open than in the midsection of the peninsula.

Neztríanis imagined a circle and walked to what she conceived to be the center. She took her bag off her shoulder and placed it in the imaginary center. Next, she found a small fallen tree, removed its branches, and picked up the trunk. When she returned to the spot where her shoulderpack was placed, she moved the satchel with her legs and drove the trunk into the ground. Moving the large piece of wood in a circular motion, the young woman bored a hole that signified the center of the apparitional circle. She scooped the loose dirt out with her hands and recited a story of her youth. After that, she picked the trunk up and stood on the north side of the cavity and walked ten paces from the center, dragging the log behind her. The trunk scoured a noticeable crease in the ground. Returning to the center, she did the same at each cardinal direction, giving the circle a diameter of about sixteen feet. Finally, she drove the log into the center hole and packed it with dirt so that it stood vertically. The trunk would allow her to measure the height of the hemisphere.

Drenched in sweat, Phesiana's daughter sat down and braced herself against the trunk. The trunk was heavy enough to require three or four able bodied persons to move it. Neztríanis did so alone with only temperate discomfort. She stuck her hand into her bag, retrieved a few dried and salted meat strips, and ate them greedily. Opening her water jug, she drank its entire contents. She felt too weak to train that day, so she decided that she would locate the nearest branch of the Xarkim River and find some of her favorite berries and nuts. She did not feel like hunting, and she still had a week's supply of dried meat.

After locating a small stream, about a quarter-length from her makeshift training ground, Neztríanis realized she had not taken a bath in well over a week. Although traveling unaccompanied, Neztríanis was vain and sure she smelled like someone who had been wandering for thirteen days and wrestled with a planet. Not too appealing. Neztríanis searched through her bag and laughed heartily when she discovered a large bar of soap her mother packed. The bar was so hefty; the daughter of Hopha broke into a fifth of its size just so she could wash herself without encumbrance.

Neztríanis wondered if her shoulderpack held magical powers because new things emerged from its belly every day.

Letting down her hair, the young woman combed and untangled the matted mess. After she straightened her hair, she undressed and walked into the stream. Using her powers of heat, she warmed the body of water, so that she might soothe her muscles. Soon the small area became like a hot spring. She reflected upon the phrase that conjured heat—"Mona fla renzgé ná"—and its possible meanings. She remembered that she not only said the words, she *sang* them.

"*Mona fla renzgé ná*," she sang, in a mezzo forte volume.

The water bubbled, and Neztríanis felt the local temperature of the stream rise moderately. This gave her an idea.

"*Fá'atoño má*," she sang at the same volume, but changed the key to a melancholy minor.

At once, her orange white aura emerged. The aura was noticeably thicker, but it did not spread out as far as she anticipated. It was as if her aura was protecting her from harm. She did not quite understand how intonation, syncopation, and volume affected her powers, but they were evidently linked.

Unfortunately, Neztríanis was very self-conscious about her voice. She could not imagine herself singing while dispatching her abilities. And it seemed bizarre that singing actually influenced her powers.

The daughter of Hopha cleaned herself and the soap's fragrance emitted a most wonderful scent. It reminded her of home. She submerged herself underwater and washed her hair. Once she resurfaced, Neztríanis exited the misty stream. She reached for a cloth to dry herself, but stopped suddenly. Instead, she petitioned her element of heat to dry her off, and it obliged. Steam rose from her naked body. She smiled to herself as the idea materialized. Steam was made of water vapor, and ice was made of water.

Concentrating, she gazed at a portion of steam in front of her hands and imagined a small cup that surrounded the steam.

"Zí mányx," she said with a quiet confidence. "Fá'atoño má."

Her white aura reached towards the steam and sputtered frost. Within seconds where there was once mist, an ice cylinder formed. Neztríanis laughed, rhythmically nodded her head, and performed a small dance of celebration. She soon realized she was dancing naked and felt embarrassed. Blushing, she put on her second set of clothes, a traditional leather dress, which was suitable for sleeping. Next, she laundered her other outfit in the stream then made her way back to the training ground. She hung her clothes up to dry on a nearby tree and lay down by the wooden post.

Neztríanis was drowsy. A pack of windhorses galloped to her north, heading northwest for the winter. The insects sung work hymns and gathered food for the oncoming freeze. Percussion and melody filled her ears. It did not take long for her to fall asleep.

***

What was she doing wrong? Three days passed, and she still was unable to make even a consistent sheet of ice. Every good intention was spurned into a chaotic or withering generation of her powers. At her best, she generated a small sheet of ice that started at her hands. But instantaneously, the sheet dropped due to gravity.

Resting against the pike, Neztríanis was completely spent. Her muscles ached, her head split, and her heart was nearing defeat. Only her qanín remained undeterred. Catching wind, she inspected her tiny proving ground and welcomed her new friends: the animals of the forest.

The first day she trained, small rodents and insects watched from afar. She barely noticed them. By dusk, a pack of windhorses also stopped their migration to gaze upon their sister. When she awoke the next morning, the animals were still there and were even closer. By the end of her second day of training, a traveling flock of birds found their way into the assembly. Once the wild animals realized the extent of her imaginary circle, they stayed a few feet outside of it. The spectators gave Neztríanis an incentive. She wanted to please the crowd.

Unfortunately, she was unable to even please herself. And by the end of the third day, she felt like giving up on the technique altogether. But the animals still appeared interested in her task. They possessed no fear of Neztríanis. It was as if they were able to grasp her Elemental and intentions.

She, however, was unable to grasp anything. How was she able to make the small "cup" of ice three nights ago, but now, she could not even make even a small hemisphere?

She recalled the memories repeatedly. But each maddening recollection made it more difficult to concentrate. She calmed herself by chanting, moving not so much into the memory, but its content. Neztríanis faced north, where the pack of windhorses was grazing, and focused on one of them. She examined beyond the exterior, and her eyes closed, yet she still was able to see, not just the *form*, but also the *content*. She gazed into the horse's body temperature, differentiating its various pockets of heat. The horse appeared to be aware of Neztríanis' examination and did not move, almost inviting her to continue. She graciously obliged her kin's request. After all, to many Nez Spiritans, the windhorse was their brother and sister. She experienced the heat of her brother, his entire spectrum of calescence. She *experienced* calescence. Conversely, she merely saw the steam. She *saw* the steam, projected her aura around it, and it froze. She *saw* the steam. But she did not *experience* the steam. The stallion bellowed and trotted off, in search for grass. Neztríanis experienced the creature's warm head tilt backwards, while it stood on its hind legs. The movement was clearly visible to her, not only through her sense of sight, but also through her qanín.

Her nod was solemn. She had to experience water vapor in order to make ice. No, it was not enough to experience all the molecular forms of water. She needed to embrace the various temperate dimensions of water.

She started small. Running to the stream with her water jug, Neztríanis filled it with water. She returned to the proving ground, poured the water on the ground, and made a puddle. Before the water seeped into the creases of earth, Neztríanis cooled the puddle rapidly and made ice. Soon, a mist developed and floated above the puddle.

Her orange-white aura emerged. Neztríanis concentrated and examined and felt the temperate dimensions of the ice, the liquid water that had not frozen, and the water vapor rising from the ice puddle. Each state of water occupied a different shape, a different way of storing and releasing heat, but they were connected. The water vapor molecule was the most erratic of the three, so the Sczyphamek let herself be immersed in its somewhat chaotic happening. It moved in and out of other gases in the air, forming, condensing, and cooling, yet rising and dispersing warmly throughout the atmosphere.

Her ignorance astonished her. Her element of *heat* allowed her to sense phenomena whose temperature was above freezing. Water vapor and liquid water were two of those phenomena. Mistakenly, she believed the technique required her cold Elemental *alone*.

Unable to maintain the necessary focus and energy for the exercise, Neztríanis hyperventilated. Stubbornly, she would not let herself give in to the instinct of stopping. Within seconds, nevertheless, she passed out.

The sun was about to set when she awoke. Dirt and leaves clung to her forehead, nose, and mouth. She was baffled. Somehow Neztríanis felt nearly as spent as she did when she battled the planet. Yet, her Elemental display was much more forceful then. How could something so mundane as water be so difficult to relate to?

Deciding it would be best to rest for the night instead of continuing to train, Neztríanis made a fire. The new moons were nowhere to be found which made the clear sky that much darker. However, Neztríanis sensed the diverse company all around. They had not given up on her, and neither would she give up on herself. All animal life on Qeauríyx was resourceful and smart. There was no wasted effort and no excess. The living were just eleven thousand cycles or so away from the Drift. It seemed that her kind was the only species out of sorts with the planet, and perhaps the témos as well.

The animal choir sounded rhythmic and melodic, driving the daughter of Hopha to remember the words she sang so many days prior.

"*Zí mányx que rai… Mona fla renzgé ná. Zí mányx que rai… Mona fla renzgé ná…*" she sang sweetly and softly, in an adagio tempo. "*Fá'atoño má. Fá'atoño má.*"

Amazingly, her Elemental was not burdened, even though she was exhausted. Her aura shone brightly, illuminating the campsite. The animals righted themselves, but they did not run away. Although she understood the necessity of chanting and praying, she had neither grasped the depth nor the height, the length nor the area of this necessity. Communion with her Elemental granted her the occasion to greatly increase her powers and mingle with phenomena unseen by the naked eye.

She concentrated and outstretched her right arm and chanted "Fá'atoño mona" and immediately a thick orange aura asserted itself between her right hand and elbow.

Holding out her left arm, she meditated and chanted "Zí mányx" and instantaneously a dense, white phenomenon graced her left hand. It was difficult to maintain, but she was able to localize her two, distinct powers in her hands.

But, why her hands? Why not her feet? Or her torso? She had not even considered such a feat, for her hands were the means by which she naturally "did" things. But her Elemental flowed through her entire body, and in order to make the ice hemisphere her full person needed to release her frigid Elemental. Even when she made the ice after leaving the stream, she concentrated on the area surrounding her hands. It was understandable that she did so, but if Neztríanis was on the offensive, most of her weaker yet quick attacks would instinctively emanate from her hands. If she faced a Sczyphamek or any seasoned fighter, they would discern that pattern in an instant. In order for her to truly walk the path of a potential Awakening, she would have to learn how to wield her Elemental in *any* situation and from *any* and *every* point of her body.

She grew discouraged at such a challenge. Because Neztríanis was quite gifted and because she picked up things faster than the overwhelming majority of her peers, her giftedness left her a bit lazy. But she had to put that character flaw aside now. For there was one thing she hated more than anything: *losing*. And once Neztríanis Phyxtríalis decided to win, she became a methodical beast whose only goal was to crush the competition. That habit earned her very few friends and teammates, but victory was always near her grasp. Her competitive nature made her people's subjugation by Tannódin and Damüda that much more unbearable.

Only two days remained until her journey's resumption towards Nextu. She would not let herself fail. She would win.

Studying her hands once more, she simultaneously shot a small bit of fire and cool air out of her respective palms and became extremely dizzy. Her heart fluttered rapidly and arrhythmically. Taking this as a serious sign, she lay down and went to sleep, obsessing over the ice hemisphere technique.

When Neztríanis awoke the next morning, she found herself a source of entertainment to the greatest crowd yet. The animals were also in it for themselves. Her residual aura gave them a place of warmth and protection during the night.

Instead of brazenly training without any preparation, the Sczyphamek chanted and meditated for two hours in order to concentrate and strengthen her Elemental. She concluded that one of the reasons she was unable to produce the hemisphere was due to a lack of "Elemental stamina," although there was probably a word in the Ancient Tongue that described the reality better. Regardless, the effect was the same. She spent too much energy clumsily (and accidentally) using her Elemental of heat to search for water vapor, instead of actually converting the water vapor into ice.

In addition, an Awakened Sczyphamek had to overcome the differences between Elemental and host. Arousing her Elemental had to be as ordinary as breathing. So far, Neztríanis counted four vital properties needed to successfully navigate and use her powers: belief, creativity, understanding, and stamina. But she was sure there were more.

After chanting for two hours, Neztríanis Phyxtríalis felt her aura growing more efficacious. In turn, the creatures surrounding her campsite backed away from their original locations, but still watched intently. Her orange-white aura was not only thick; it also dilated to a wider radius, fluctuating in a controlled, rhythmic fashion. Streaks of solid orange and white disambiguated from the initial orange-white amalgam.

With her Elemental of heat, she perceived the water vapor all around her. Instead of trying to make an ice hemisphere on her first try, Neztríanis attempted to construct a dense ice sheet, which would emanate from the front side of her body, with her hands as auxiliary support. Her element of calefaction gathered the water vapor, drawing the gas near her body. Meanwhile, her glacial Elemental increased in power and veracity. The area in close proximity to the Sczyphamek grew foggy.

"Zí mányx que rai," she spoke with belief and understanding.

In a matter of moments, a wall of ice appeared one foot in front of her. Its height was nearly seven feet and its width was four feet. It stood straight up, for sheet touched the ground which was also frozen. Neztríanis examined the mass' thickness. It appeared to be a foot thick at its base, three quarters of a foot thick near its midpoint, and a third of a foot near the apex. Even though her objective was to maintain a consistent sheet of ice, she was pleased that she accomplished the feat on her first try.

Standing in front of the ice sheet, she chanted in excitement, "Mona fla renzgé ná." An orange-blue flame enveloped the structure of ice, and within fifteen seconds, it melted completely. Her abilities were still primordial, but these first steps were building blocks to something larger. Her excitement turned to puzzlement one she smelled smoke, but saw no fire. Suddenly, she saw smoke rising from her backside. Looking down, Neztríanis noticed her left pants leg was charred. Frenetically, she patted the combustion out with her hands.

"Great," she muttered. "These are my favorite pants."

This happening led her to ponder an implication provided by her blackened leg garment: her clothes and maybe even her skin would burn if she was not careful.

She was about to resume her training when the *real* meaning of the observation assaulted her. Every time she used her powers, her Elemental protected her. When she used her powers of cold, her arm, hand, or fingers did not freeze. She reasoned that her fiery element guarded her. The same must have been true for the equation's corollary: when using her powers of heat, her frigid Elemental safeguarded her from cauterizing herself.

"Kíma," she cursed. "I must proceed with caution."

If she extended herself too far, without the necessary Elemental control, she would damage her surroundings and herself.

She held out her right hand and made a fireball by warming, superheating, and igniting her Elemental. Her Elemental acted as the "fuel" and heat for the fire. The gases of the atmosphere provided the occasion, which set off the chain reaction and produced the fire. She controlled the fire's shape by focusing both her frigid and warm Elemental around and in the flame. She was able to grasp and control this aspect of her power simply because of all the fires she had made in her life. However, blue and white flames required much nuance and control. And fire, in general, required restraint. Neztríanis possessed common sense and experience. One of her worst memories was of a forest fire that consumed a fourth of Hopha four cycles ago. What started as a social gathering and barbeque grew into a disaster that left many homeless and dispossessed.

When she extinguished the flame, her white aura retreated underneath her skin. Holding out her right hand again, she cooled the air around her and suddenly stopped the exercise. Quicker than a flash of light, her orange aura submerged into her skin. In order to wield enormous amounts of energy, she was going to have to (un)consciously create a barrier made of her aura between her skin and clothes and the surrounding environment.

A streak of defeatism crept into her heart. She wondered if she had set too lofty a goal. Would she actually be able to achieve the ice hemisphere by the end of the next day?

"Stay calm, Neztríanis," she said aloud. "You can do this." The woman meditated and breathed steady breaths. She would not be undone so easily. Neztríanis approached the pike and placed her back against it.

"Fá'atoño ma!" she belted with conviction.

In a burst of luminescence her orange-white aura returned, with great potency. Her eyes blinked, and when she opened them, her dark brown pupils were now an ashen auburn.

She thought about this moment the previous night, even in her dreams. Three layers of her Elemental were at work. The outermost layer of the hemisphere was the "hot" Elemental, that is, the Elemental that affected temperatures over freezing. Like tentacles, the outermost layer searched for the water vapor and gathered it for the second layer's use. The second layer was her "cold" Elemental. It converted the water vapor into ice, and as the outer layer extended and took in more water vapor, the second layer would "grow" the hemisphere. The third layer was her fiery Elemental, which would melt the backside of the hemisphere, superheat and recycle the ice into water and water vapor, and create food to transfer to her frigid Elemental to consume and transform back into ice; to the naked eye, it would seem like the ice was moving.

In short, the outer orange aura *made possible* the creation of the ice, while the inner orange aura *maintained* the structure and breathable space within the dome. How ironic that this technique required more work for the Elemental of heat than cold.

"Elements, please guide me," she graciously requested. All three happenings that constituted Sczyphamek Temperature had their assignments and, the elements knew that in order for them to grow they would have to test their limits. Neztríanis did not need to start fast. Her first task was simply to make a small, but sturdy ice hemisphere. Her goal was for the diameter to be six feet, the apex to be seven feet, and the thickness of the ice itself was to be at least five clips.

"Mona fla renzgé ná. Zí mányx que rai. Fá'atoño má."

A dark orange aura emanated from her body and collected the water vapor at a molecular level. Next, a white aura emerged about three feet away from the pike. In all directions, ice formed, as the orange and white auras formed an upside-down bowl-like structure. The orange aura extended further, and Neztríanis perceived various channels in the outer layer, like branches of a river or tree, sending the water vapor to specific spots on the white aura. The vapor condensed which made the ice continue to grow, and Neztríanis not only saw, she *felt* the structure's dimensions take form. The amount of information her Elemental sent to her consciousness was staggering. And they held back even more information for her sake.

The second orange aura shaped the inside of the dome, so that the thickness of the ice and the open space remained consistent. If there was a deficiency in thickness, the inner orange aura would move away from the space, and the middle, white aura, which controlled the creation of ice, would freeze water vapor to buttress that area. If the ice became asymmetrical or too dense, the inner aura would melt that area and send the water vapor to any surface that needed more ice.

The technique fatigued the Sczyphamek considerably. Neztríanis sat down, crossed her legs, and braced herself on the pike. She continued to chant and pray for forty minutes. For that half-hour, Neztríanis refused the temptation to open her eyes. She took the lesson the windhorse taught her seriously. She had to trust her Elementals and use their sight as her own eyes and let their movements happen like her own appendages and organs.

Although the temperature plunged, Neztríanis perspired as if she were in the middle of the Gemansu Desert. Her breaths were deep and frosty. Soon, her Elemental intimated to her that they were nearly done.

Opening her eyes slowly, she beheld fog and felt the humidity. Looking above, Neztríanis saw the obfuscated sky, made murky by the ice's refraction and reflection of light. Walking towards the wall of ice directly in front of her, Neztríanis knocked on the barrier, and the sound indicated the ice was about half a foot thick. Neztríanis levitated to the top of the dome and checked the thickness. After tapping her hand up against the top, she smiled to herself. It made the same sound as the lower wall. She could have used her Elemental to measure the hemisphere's dimensions, but she wanted the satisfaction of checking it herself.

The daughter of Hopha laughed and floated back down to the ground. Beaming with pride, she thanked the bipartite Elemental who had chosen her.

"What are your names?" she asked them.

They gave no response. Apparently, it was not time for them to reveal their titles yet.

"How am I supposed to get out of here?" she asked aloud.

If she heated the ice, it would rain down water on her head. She was so intent on seeing her task through that she gave no thought of escape. She should have designed and created an exit while fashioning the hemisphere. Her Elemental "shook their heads" at her in serious amusement, and the Sczyphamek understood why. She created an ice tomb.

Even with her lack of fighting experience, she understood that a battle was determined by action and counteraction. Therefore, the ice hemisphere's utility in battle was proportional to its *growth*. The expansion of the hemisphere would force distance between her and her opponent. As her adversary attempted to dodge or break the attack, it would allow her the opportunity to continue attacking before her opponent set up a counterattack.

Stop getting ahead of yourself, Nez, she thought. *We must make the hemisphere grow, first.*

Walking to the wall, she drew her left hand back, as it became engulfed in a blue flame, and took two quick steps to give her some momentum. Neztríanis punched the ice as hard as she could, and it melted, cracked, splintered, and altogether broke apart, making an opening in the glacial dome.

When she emerged, she grinned at all her newfound animal friends. Her left hand smarted slightly, but after her mediocre victory, she did not mind. The structure cracked and shifted. Suddenly, the hemisphere collapsed with a loud crash. The pike was broken into pieces by the heavy pieces of stone-like ice. The animals scattered at the sound.

Neztríanis shook her head. She was tired, but she did not want her campsite to be covered and eventually drenched by ice and water. Remembering her burnt pants, Neztríanis called forth her frigid Elemental, symbolized by a white aura. It covered her body, clothes and hair. Next, she chanted and brought forth a large amount of heat. The surrounding air became distorted and steam elevated above the ice. In order to best control the heat, Neztríanis used her hands to release the flames. Within five minutes or so of walking around the campsite, she melted all of the ice, but the ground remained a bit wet. Neztríanis was afraid to dry it completely, worrying that she might start a forest fire or scorch the que. Her Elemental was exhausted anyway, and so was she.

She gathered some rocks and wood, and made fire the traditional way, with kindling and a spark from a piece of flint. She ate a large portion of her rations and lay down. Her eyes closed, and she heard the animals returning to watch the awkward, but well-meaning, forest princess incant signs and wonders.

Two and a half hours of sunlight remained. Surprisingly, when she stood up after taking her nap, Neztríanis felt stronger than she did that morning.

It was time to try the full technique.

The ice hemisphere gave the illusion that it was moving and growing. It was growing, yes, but not *moving*. What was moving was her Elemental; the ice itself was forming, melting, growing and reforming, all the while maintaining the same level of thickness throughout. To the naked eye, it would appear moving. But for Neztríanis, it was more complex than this. She was unable to simply will the ice into reality. Her powers did not work that way. All three of the entities that comprised Sczyphamek Temperature were working at a molecular, physical, and spiritual level, which required immense concentration and practice.

She used the same approach she took with the first ice hemisphere: she did not concentrate on speed, but on her Elemental and the various factors that contributed to the successful completion of the task at hand. Though unlike the first, Neztríanis would make sure that the dome's dimensions were conducive for an offensive attack or a defensive stronghold.

Neztríanis sauntered to the hole that once anchored the pole to the ground and knelt. She chanted for an hour. Her Elemental had grown since morning. Apparently, they recovered faster than the person housing them.

Her Elemental of calefaction emanated eight clips in front of her and drew in the surrounding water vapor. Her glacial, white aura followed suit, and ice was quickly fashioned. Neztríanis completed the hemisphere in one minute. Next, the orange aura expanded and slowly moved towards the edge of the "circle" Neztríanis had dug into the ground. As it moved, the white aura followed closely behind, expanding as well, taking in more of the water vapor the outer orange layer gave to it. Inside the hemisphere the secondary orange aura melted and carved the ice, kept the thickness steady, and removed any ice that was excessive. Making good progress, Neztríanis decided to increase the power and range of her Elemental.

"Fá'atoño má. Zí mányx mona!" she exclaimed.

Before she could blink, the animals of the forest galloped, scampered, ran, and flew away in terrible, forecasting oncoming disaster. Neztríanis scanned her immediate surroundings. Her ice hemisphere appeared normal; the radius was now six feet and the apex was eight feet.

Yet through the ice, the Sczyphamek's outer orange-aura had swelled beyond manageable comprehension. Clouds appeared as the warm water vapor rose and condensed, and within seconds a large cumulonimbus emerged. Neztríanis stopped the hemisphere, but it was too late. The orange aura melted the ice and caused cooler air to form locally around the campsite, while warmer air rose ahead of the aura.

Without understanding, Neztríanis created a gigantic cloud, full of precipitation. Lightning struck; the wind accelerated, and the Sczyphamek smelled the odor of thunderstorm.

"Staxis" she said grimly.

The forces were chaotic. Neztríanis tried to use her Elemental to bring temperate equilibrium to the air. Within moments, the Sczyphamek realized that the feat was beyond her present expertise. Every attempt at cooling or warming made the disturbance grow larger. In the distance, Neztríanis beheld a clear sky with no clouds in all directions. The daughter of Hopha had created a strange thing on a strange planet in the Windhorse Peninsula.

Lightning flashed in quicker bursts, and thunder rolled so violently that the trees hummed and swayed. Neztríanis wondered how much energy she was actually dealing with, because the atmospheric reaction seemed exaggerated.

While frantically gathering her possessions, a bolt struck a Yarnínga close by and set it ablaze. Rain, sleet, and hail poured out of the local distortion, and drenched the surroundings. A large piece of ice hit Neztríanis on the head, which caused her to careen. Shaking the injury off, she tried to seek solace in a nearby collection of trees, and lay on the ground so as not to attract lightning.

For nearly an hour, the violent storm raged on, and the winds howled like the canine beasts of the forests. She was scared and guilty because this happening was *her* fault, and no one else's. She possessed so much power, compared to the rest of her species. But the exercise of power or empowerment did not bring understanding or right action. While fearing for her life amidst electrical discharge and sonic barrage, Neztríanis had no choice but to grasp this truth. Power was not necessarily proportional to knowledge.

"To master is to surrender..." Neztríanis recited. She was beginning to understand what the Great Mother had tried to teach her for cycles.

After awhile, the rain stopped. She was drenched and muddy. The storm had darkened the sky so much that Neztríanis did not realize the sun had set. Weary and aching, she returned to her campsite. Puddles of mud, chunks of ice, and snow-covered grass littered the area. She was tired of tidying up after herself, but the damage done to the area was egregious. Ignoring the mess—*her mess*—was tantamount to ecological malice.

How could she be so ignorant? Her creation and melting of ice in quick repetition undoubtedly disturbed the local atmosphere. Her focus on the ice hemisphere caused her to disregard her surroundings—in this case, the local, ambient state of water vapor. A Sczyphamek's powers were not easy to control nor were they without environmental consequence.

She decided to warm the area in a more subtle way. She recovered a blanket, which was soaked, and placed it on the ground. And lying down on it, near the place where the pike once stood, Neztríanis allowed a thin emanation of her orange aura to emerge and cover the entire campsite, providing a warm heat.

Gazing into the wilderness, Neztríanis spotted no sign of her animal audience. After that mishap, Phyxtríalis doubted they would return. She took sips of water from her water jug and meditated, and for five hours, she slowly dried the area, which exhausted her to the point of collapse.

She was dirty though, and Neztríanis *was* vain. She would not sleep in such a state. Staggering to the small stream, which had grown due to the rain, she undressed and washed herself and her garments. She put on her traditional dress and returned to camp.

She did not meditate, read, ponder, or eat. All she wanted was sleep.

"I lost."

Chapter Six: Complexity in Kamo

The sun shone brightly. The clouds were dispersing, and the day was growing quite beautiful.

He made it to the outskirts of the city in seven hours. But he had not stepped foot there since the days of his youth.

Kamo, his mother's hometown.

Nísephetsu,[1] Anámn's mother, was quite an elegant woman. Her smile dominated the coldest heart, but not the coldest mind. The mind corrupted all manners of qanín. Contradictory as that seemed, Anámn believed he grasped enough about this Cycle to know that existence was full of peculiarity and paradox. Although he was the only son of the most powerful man in Phmquedria, Anámn was the lowliest of all. The Tannódin'é liked to spout high knowledge and wisdom, but their methods betrayed their thinking. The more reason they claimed they possessed, the more wicked their intentions were.

Even as these musings swam unabated in Anámn's mind, the young slave felt a gentle current of emotion. No matter how harshly his father treated him, Nísyx Tekil[2] ju Xaníz loved her brother like no one else. Nísyx was a full-blooded Tannódin'é; in fact, the ju Xaníz line had ties to Sczyphamek Imperial. Alzhexph's father, four generations removed, was Imperial's spouse.

Nísyx was cared for by Nísephetsu when Alzhexph's wife, Nísyx's biological mother, passed away. Tekil, for her part, took care of Anámn after his mother's death. But as she grew older, her relationship with Alzhexph grew cold and strained. She left Euhilv ten cycles ago, returning every other cycle. However, those trips stopped three cycles ago. Nísyx and her father got into such a sharp disagreement that she left the Euhilv slave metropolis the next day, never to return. Shortly thereafter, Anámn began to lose all hope.

But in a matter of moments, Anámn forgot about his powers and hopelessness. The anticipation of seeing his half-sister dissolved all other thoughts. The slave had not experienced "home," but the presence of

---

[1] Nísephetsu (nee-seh-feht-su)

[2] Nísyx Tekil (nee-siks tuh-kil)

Nísyx was as close as he could imagine.

Anámn made his way to the town square, and memories of his childhood inundated his thoughts, which had been buried under the weight of ore and humiliation. He looked towards Lake Kamo, and remembered how he and his mother sat at its banks and watched the sunrise in the west. He had long forgotten his mother's words to him that day, at least twenty cycles ago. She told him that in the future he would return to Kamo free and with a warm heart. He let that prophecy fade a long time ago. His heart was far from warm, and he was damn far from free.

An intricate fountain stood before him in the middle of the square. The elyandir sculpture shined, sparkled, and drew water from the lake. The monument consisted of three statues: a fabled Nez Spiritan windhorse, a triumphant témo, and a representation of the sacred book, the Auría.

Why didn't the Tannódin'é destroy this fountain, the way they crushed all the other holy monuments in Phmquedria? Anámn wondered.

The slave located a sitting area near the fount and listened to the sweet sound of running water and children playing. Unlike Euhilv, Kamo was an indentured city, not a slave municipality. In fact, the locals enjoyed much more freedom there than anywhere else on the continent. For most Phmquedrians, Kamo was as close to self-determination as many would obtain.

His mother was taken from the city when she was just a young girl. Even though Kamo was indentured, it was a city in Phmquedria. And Phmquedria was ju Xaníz' jurisdiction. He could do and often did whatever he wanted.

Anámn did not know where or how he would find Nísyx. Though this was his maternal family's hometown, Kamo was more "city" than "town." And most of his mother's family lived in the southwestern section of the city. As far as Anámn remembered, Nísyx lived within its limits, yet that information was now three cycles old.

She's the daughter of the most powerful man on the continent. Someone knows who she is, he thought. *Maybe if I go to the town market, I can find someone who knows where she lives or at least knows how I could find her.*

Kamo was one of the earliest cities in Phmquedria. After the Drift's end, tens of thousands of Phmquedrians immigrated to the area. Since Kamo was near a great source of freshwater, advanced agricultural techniques were quickly developed. The city grew in stature and size, becoming an intellectual and creative haven for the continent. In the golden age of Kamo, the city gave rise to a period of great writers, mathematicians, scientists, and Mystics of the Auría. Educational institutions flourished, and the people built a city still known for its scientific genius. Because Kamo was located at the mouth of the river, floods were a chief concern. Therefore, 2500 cycles BGI, a group of engineers developed the first irrigation, drainage, and sewer system known to Qeauríyx.

The old town center was now located on the extreme northern portion of city. The area still maintained its traditional fare, though signs of modernization were everywhere. The buildings were made of stone, and the streets formed a grid pattern in and near the heart of Old Kamo. The town center was constructed with geometrical precision. There was equal distance between each building and walkway, and the height of each building decreased as one approached lakefront, which granted unbelievable shadows during sunrise and sunset.

Each street had a slender canal in the middle of it, so that running water was always heard in the town center. To his left, Anámn spotted two children hopping from one side of a small canal to another. They laughed as each tried to jump further than the other. One child slipped and fell in the water, causing the other to run towards the edge of the canal in concern. Anámn ran towards both of them, in order to save the submerged little one. And just as he neared them, the youth emerged and splashed water onto his friend, a girl. When she saw that he was unharmed, she laughed mischievously and held her arm out to pull him out. Reaching for her hand, the young boy hoisted himself out, but the girl let go and he fell back in the water.

Anámn laughed at the two, but then grew quite melancholy. He possessed few memories such as these.

Asking for directions to the market from a Phmquedrian vendor by the fountain, Anámn was told by his kinsman to listen for a moment.

"I don't hear anything but water," Anámn said.

"No," the man replied then chuckled. "You don't hear what's behind the water?"

Anámn concentrated and began to perceive faint voices in the distance. "I hear some folk talking."

"It's the sweet racket of trading," the man smiled. "The louder it gets, the closer you are."

"Thanks," Matriester said. "Uhm… Can I ask you one more question?"

"If you can buy one of these." The man held up a bottle of some sort of liquid.

"Do I look like I got any money?" the slave asked and brandished his threadbare garments.

"Well," the man said, "honestly… no…"

"So does that mean you won't answer my question?"

He sighed and shook his head, muttering something about "kímaz Phmmys."

"Follow the conversations, huh?" Anámn understood that his conversation with the vendor just reached its terminus. It took much restraint for him to hold his temper. His people were too liberal with the word "Phmmy."

Anámn neared the market and the clamor of buying, selling and trading filled the marketplace. He walked aimlessly amongst the crowd for half an hour.

Suddenly, Anámn detected someone's gaze directed at him. How was it possible? Providence? Purpose? Incalculable coincidence? Chance? He didn't care.

He glanced to his left and saw *her* speaking to a vegetable vendor. Her maroon eyes were as he remembered them.

Nísyx.

In disbelief, she stood still, gasped, hung then shook her head. Jogging towards her brother, Tekil's countenance grew congenial. Before he could brace himself, Anámn experienced an unknown (perhaps forgotten) emotion in his spirit. *Joy.*

Nísyx was a woman of medium height with irrepressible Tannódin'é features. Her skin was fair, with amber tones, and her cheeks were as rosy as a scarlet sunset. Her maroon eyes told the story of conflict and redemption. Her face had sharp edges, like most from Tannódin, and her light brown hair was long and a curly.

Although Nísyx possessed Tannódin'é traits and vocabulary, her accent was anything but. She had a distinct mid-eastern Phmquedrian enunciation, chock full of its slow, meaningful drawl and an excitable lightheartedness. It was a dialect that provided an escape to a shackled existence. She wore a brown traditional dress, cut just below the knees, and a white shirt, with medium sleeves. The woman was adorned with an elyandir necklace and a smile on par with his mother's. A brown bag full of vegetables hung across her left shoulder and torso.

"I cannot believe my eyes! Is it really you? Kíma! Anámn, it is so good to see you!" She embraced her brother with all her strength. "What are you doing here? Does father know you are here? Did you run away? Did you come to see me?"

"Well," he smiled, "it's a long story. But I did come to see you and I didn't run away. At least, not yet."

"Oh, thank goodness! Remember, we're supposed to run away together."

Anámn nodded and chuckled at the promise they made to one another twenty cycles ago.

Her face beamed with excitement and surprise. "Let's go to my home and then talk. I am sure you are tired from your journey. It must have taken over a week just to get down here."

"Actually, it took two and a half days."

His sister stared at him, baffled at this report.

"Two days?" she asked.

"I told you it's a long story," he said. "We'll talk when we get to your place. Right now, I'm just happy to see you."

They walked silently for a while, hand in hand, down one of the main thoroughfares of Kamo, simply content to be in each other's presence.

Experiencing the other's touch brought back buried remembrances long submerged by both of the siblings. Most of the recollections were intoxicating. That was why they had to be buried. The goodness was too painful.

When they were younger, Nísyx had no qualms hugging Anámn with all her love. She used to chase Anámn to a particular room in one of their father's mansions. The bedroom was ridiculously spacious with a gargantuan bed and mirror that defied reason. Anámn would hide under the bed, and Nísyx playfully dragged him out by the feet and tickled him to no end. Only when her enslaved brother grew close to wetting himself—then and only then—would she stop. After Anámn had composed himself and regained control of his bladder, the siblings would measure each other's height, standing back-to-back in front of the large mirror.

Tekil was never ashamed of him.

Héthyx found that out the hard way, when his face met her fist. She nearly broke his nose after she stumbled upon the overseer whipping Anámn. And walking down the street in Kamo, the brother felt the loving gaze of his sister once again. Neither time nor space had dulled her love.

She still was unashamed that she happened as his sister.

They were oblivious to the aghast stares they received from both Tannódin'é and Phmquedrian alike. Assumptions of unlawful miscegenation were rampant, but none of the onlookers considered that they were gazing upon a brother and his sister, although Phmquedria was filled with children who were the amalgam of the two lands.

Once the siblings realized their folly of familial love, they quickly untangled their hands and kept an acceptable distance between each other. Even after three cycles of absence and hurt, Anámn still found himself unable to celebrate and be joyful. Folk from Kamo, representing both continents, would not permit it.

The arbitrary line(s) were drawn long ago. Tannódin made them and the significant majority of Phmquedrians accepted them as law. Despising all logic and lessons learned from the Great Drift, both groups believed and acted as if they were different species of the same genus. In this sense, Anámn was an anomaly to be rejected by both, for his existence and others like him clouded the various "defined" structures of Global Initiative. A bit of the pain returned.

Trying to distract himself from the amaranthine ache, Anámn took in the surroundings and saw tall structures that drew no recollection from his childhood.

"When were these built? I don't remember these buildings."

"Over the past couple of cycles," she said. "Most of the material comes from the mines…" Tekil paused uneasily. She realized her next statement would lead to more resentment. "The House of Kaz calls it 'public works.' They say Global Initiative is for all of those on Qeauríyx. These buildings house many people who work for Tannódin and Damüda, but they are not indentured."

"*Public works*," Anámn's eyes glinted in disgust. "The metal and ore that they get doesn't come from the public. That work comes from labor... *slave labor*... and I thought this was an indentured town? Who in Phmquedria does 'public works' for Tannódin?"

"Some Tannódin'é and Damüdans, a few Brycians, but mostly Phmquedrians."

Nísyx Tekil spoke so matter-of-fact that Anámn almost ignored the implications of her answer.

"Wait. Did you just say *Phmquedrians*?" Anámn's face lost its slack grip on Happiness and reached for his old friends, Bewilderment, Disquietude, and Resentment. "What in Qalfocx is going on here? My own people work for the people who keep me a slave? Kíma!"

"I know Anámn." His sister broke social protocol and rubbed his back. "People in Kamo are just happy that they're not in the mines. They've forgotten that not so long ago, my people used them as indentured servants. That became too costly, so father instituted a new plan. He was going to let some Phmquedrians take part in Global Initiative."

"*What?* Why'd he do that?"

"It was not for charity..." Tekil muttered and clenched the strap strafing her torso. "This was one of the chief reasons I left... I just could not be a part of such deception."

The siblings walked past a light rail station, as one pulled into the area. Phmquedrians emerged from the steel monstrosity, heading in the direction of the buildings that Anámn and Nísyx just passed.

"What's this?" the brother asked, pointing towards the light rail system made of metallic alloys no doubt from Euhilv. "*Public works?*"

The sister nodded her head. "These were built in the past seven cycles. They connect the different portions of the city. Although the old town square is unchanged, the eastern and southwestern sides of the city have grown tremendously. Tannódin agreed to maintain the height restrictions on the old buildings in order to show those indigenous to Kamo that they were no longer interested in 'control.'

"This is one of the thirty-eight stations that traverse the city." Tekil turned towards her brother and displayed an inquisitive face. "Did you take the railcruiser to get here? There is a light rail station at the depot. You did not see it?"

Knowing that Nísyx's line of questioning would expose his true reason for visiting, which he himself was still unsure of, Anámn deflected. "I wasn't really paying attention. I was just trying to see you."

Nísyx smiled and motioned for him to follow her.

Anámn could only experience the next ten minutes. He could not understand what was happening. He witnessed Nísyx slide what appeared to be some kind of rectangle through an indented slot, which allowed both of them access to the light rail.

And then he sat next to Nísyx. *He sat next to Nísyx.* The light-rail was not segregated. There were parts of Phmquedria that were no longer segregated. Before he had a moment to take in that fact, the light rail sped underground and then above the ground, so that Anámn was able to see a greater swath of Kamo. Nísyx was right; the city *was* larger and more populated. East of the town center, a collection of skyrises sprawled for lengths.

After a few moments, Nísyx bade Anámn to leave the railcar. Apparently, they were at a transfer station.

The diversity of people overwhelmed him. Was that a Nez Spiritan or a Líachimian who sat opposite to him? He had almost forgotten that other continents besides Phmquedria, Tannódin, and Damüda existed. He grew claustrophobic in the sea of people and the techno-sociological gap between Kamo and Euhilv.

Yet in the midst of the madness, he felt her prescient touch. Nísyx clasped Anámn's hand without apology and with a sincere love. No one would have dared to say a word to her. Anámn clutched her hand, and his sister led him to another railcar, assuring him that they would be home soon. After three stops, they were at the end of the rail-line.

Nísyx and Anámn emerged from the light-rail station and found themselves in a less developed, suburban area. After walking five minutes on a paved road, a conspicuous dirt path opened up to their left. Instinctively, Anámn knew that was the pathway to his sister's house.

After traveling another length, the road became even more rural and serene. Anámn could not shake the starkly different worlds he traversed in less than two days and in less than one hour. There were two different worlds. Euhilv and Kamo were two different kinds of reality.

Such a contrast made Anámn insatiable. He needed an answer from his sister with regard to her prior comments about their father. "You said something about deception. What did you mean?"

Nísyx knew full well what Matriester referred to and recognized that she had opened a conversation not easily closed. "Brother, we have not seen each other in many cycles. We should be talking about something else."

"Nísyx, I am not a little boy anymore. You don't have to protect me. Besides, what else is there to talk about? Unless you've met somebody?" He grinned at her.

"No. You are such a joker." Her face became poignant and withdrawn. "Who would want to be with me?"

She was right. No Phmquedrian would ever approach the daughter of Alzhexph ju Xaníz, and Nísyx would not marry or associate with anyone from Tannódin unless that person was free of ethnocentrism. And from Anámn's experience, Nísyx was the only Tannódin'é he knew who appreciated other cultures and people besides her own.

The sister sighed and gave in. "It was deception because father has no intention of letting Phmquedrians participate in Global Initiative in any real sense. He figured that if he granted a few Phmquedrians access to the power of Tannódin, they would become enticed by its prestige and status. That way, he would not have to worry as much when it came to revolts, like his grandfather. He believed that if people in Kamo were granted access to even a small portion of power, it would create a buffer between Tannódin and those Phmquedrians most prone to revolt."

"Wait… What…?" Anámn was unable to ascertain the meaning of his sister's statements.

"If Phmquedrians saw other Phmquedrians doing well, they would stop conspiring against Tannódin, or at least Phmquedrians would become jealous of each other, which would deflect Tannódin's role in the entire situation." Nísyx said with sadness. "At least, that is what father said."

"And…?" Anámn asked.

"And *what*?" she replied.

"Did it work?"

"You just passed it on the way here. You saw it on the railcars and in the transfer station. It's not only worked, it has created more wealth for Tannódin and Phmquedria than originally expected. In all honesty, hard, physical slavery is not always profitable. There are other forms of slavery even more productive. If you can convince people that the 'unnatural' order of things is indeed the 'natural' order, even when they know better, then you've achieved true enslavement.

"People in Kamo settled for this reality, and other cities in Phmquedria are beginning to use the same techniques. By granting Phmquedrians access to Global Initiative's wealth and prosperity, the House of Kaz has effectively removed themselves from the ire of the locals.

"Disputes arise here and there, but they are normally between clans or groups fighting for the right to be included in this process. And as terrible as it sounds, many of the well-to-do Phmquedrians even participate in the sex trade. Some Phmquedrians speak out against this and other matters, but it doesn't matter."

"I know why," Anámn interjected. "Tannódin probably just kills them."

"No. Actually, they are silenced or ignored by their own kind." The woman sighed in discontent. "Those who propagate Global Initiative— they really do still see you and any other Phmquedrian as inferior, just not in the ways you were taught. But Phmquedrians now use inferiority and victimization to demand Tannódin'é rights."

Anámn became indignant. "So what? *We should get something back.*"

"Like being able to participate in the sex trade or *public works*?" Nísyx countered. "Tannódin'é rights are the foundation of Global Initiative. The only reason Euhilv has not changed is due to the harsh labor and unsafe environment. Some places are so fraught with desolation that you cannot cover it with lies. Only violent coercion can live there.

"No one can make Euhilv appear to be what it is truly not. It is not a place of mobility. Euhilv is the true face of Global Initiative. It remains the testimony of Global Initiative's genesis. Before the Solemn War, before the wars with Bryce and the Windward Isles… The first continent sought after, invaded, conquered, and exploited by Global Initiative was Phmquedria. The Tannódin'é and Damüdans can distance and justify themselves all they want, but Euhilv exposes their lies."

Suddenly, Nísyx stopped and faced her brother with eyes that could peer into the depths of the Infinite Deep. "Anámn, do not forget what I am about to tell you. Global Initiative—no matter what it claims and no matter how many advances it achieves—was, is, and will be built on exploitation and antagonism. The House of Kaz and the Damüdan Guild—and most Tannódin'é and an overwhelming majority of Damüdans—they believe that life on this planet is fundamentally antagonistic and violent. Their economics, politics, faith, and science are derived from this belief."

"I don't understand everything you just said, but as far as I can tell, the Tannódin'é are right about that. That is the one thing we do agree on. I think even other people in other lands believe that too.

"Who can argue against it? Qeauríyx is violent. Kíma, even before Global Initiative there was the Great Drift."

"*Brother whom I love so dearly,*" Nísyx quipped. Anámn waited for it patiently. The phrase was her favorite way of addressing him. He used to frown when she said it, but he had been anticipating the expression ever since he saw her in the market. "Brother, don't mistake your experience as the whole of reality. And do not think that antagonism and violence are the essential arbitrators of our planetary existence. That is the lie they want us to believe the most."

Anámn nodded his head. He had not thought on such a level before. It took so much concentration just to even understand what Nísyx was telling him. And because Anámn repeatedly turned down Nísyx's offers to teach him how to read, she felt no need to suffer his "pedestrian" vocabulary.

Even still, he *never* had a problem judging a situation. It was always easy to see who or what was right or wrong in every situation, even paradoxical ones. Kamo had brought a complexity that made Anámn uneasy. Tannódin was *always wrong* and Phmquedria was *always right. That was the order of things…*

But why would his people take courses of action like public works and the sex trade? Anámn had seen the sex trade firsthand. He could not imagine any slave or former slave voluntarily participating in sexual abuse after being economically, physically, psychologically, and sexually exploited.

Even though Anámn admitted contradiction, he attributed that to the inequities of ju Xaníz and Global Initiative. Life was simple; Tannódin had just disturbed the natural processes of life. Once they were gone, everything would return to the normal peaceful ways of the past, an idyllic time of natural splendor.

Yet, what was natural, and what was unnatural? And did he just admit that he and the Tannódin'é actually agreed on something? The conversation, the city of Kamo, and this newfound knowledge caused complication and shades of gray. Anámn scoffed at this revelation, seeing the complexity as compromise and compromise as paralyzing weakness. This was Kaimero and Hamin's blight as well. Why should he journey down the road of speculation when certainty was so readily apparent?

Silence beset him for ten minutes. Nísyx said nothing and let her brother meditate upon these new disclosures. Soon, Nísyx stopped, but Anámn continued to walk on, deep in thought.

"Anámn!" she laughed. "We are here, unless you were going somewhere else?"

Anámn about-faced and smiled. "I guess my mind was someplace else."

They were at the southwest outskirts of town. The nearest abode was a quarter-length away, and Nísyx's home was close to the outlying forest, giving Anámn the perfect opportunity to train in secrecy. After he took in the scenery, Nísyx beckoned her brother to enter into her dwelling. The house was relatively spacious. There appeared to be two rooms for lodging, a kitchen, bathroom, and gathering area. Anámn neared the kitchen, and the heat from the stove and oven touched his cheeks. Nísyx was in the process of making a slow-cooked stew.

"I went to the square for some fresh vegetables," she answered her brother's unasked question and walked into the kitchen. "Sit on the couch, while I put these vegetables in the soup. And I still cannot believe that we encountered each other at the market."

Anámn complied and also wondered how their meeting was possible. Nísyx sauntered out of the kitchen. Happy and confused was her countenance. She did not need to ask why he was there.

"Malchían gave me a ticket on the railcruiser line to come see you." Anámn told a half-truth. "You know that any slave in Euhilv can take a three week break from work."

"How did that old man get his hands on a ticket from Skylark to Kamo?"

Anámn shrugged his shoulders.

"Well, you're welcome here, if you want to stay. Honestly, I could use the company. Your uncle hasn't been by here in awhile."

"*Uncle?*" Anámn squinted his eyes and pursed his lips in confusion. "I have an uncle?"

"That's right..." His half-sister understood Anámn's perplexity. "You have not been here since you were a little one. You probably do not remember meeting your Uncle Huyé."[3]

"No." Anámn scratched his head and tried to conjure an absent memory. "I don't... I can't remember..."

---

[3] Huyé (hoo-y*ey*)

"Maybe I can arrange a meeting between the two of you, if that is all right with you."

"That's fine," Anámn said enthusiastically.

"How was the train ride? Was it cramped?"

"It wasn't so bad, 'cept for these two guys who wouldn't shut up. I almost thought about getting off the railcruiser because of them."

"I am glad you didn't." She eyed the meal cooking on the stove. "It's time to eat. I hope you are hungry."

Anámn had not eaten since his meal with Malchían almost three days ago. His only sustenance had been the water from the Kamo River. Even though he was no stranger to hunger, he was shocked that he traveled *so far* on one meal and with so little rest.

"Anámn?" Nísyx snapped her fingers to awaken Anámn from his pensiveness. "Are you all right? Are you hungry?"

Blinking and smiling, he responded, "Yeah. I guess I am."

He had forgotten how well his sister cooked. His mother had taught her many traditional Phmquedrian dishes. The siblings ate stew comprised of local red and green vegetables, seasoned with spices grown in Nísyx's garden, and marinated luku,[4] the best poultry that Anámn ever tasted. Nísyx also made some cold tea, sweetened covetously. Anámn ate two plates, while slurping down glass after glass of tea.

There was no conversation, and Nísyx giggled at her brother in surrogate embarrassment. She had forgotten how he ate. Anámn was a notorious eater in the slave camp. He rarely missed a meal when it was offered.

Anámn leaned back in his chair, burped, and sighed. "That. There. Was. Good."

The sister chuckled heartily. "I'm glad you liked it."

Anámn's eyes felt heavy, and noticing this, his sister pointed to the guest bedroom. "Go get some rest."

Anámn was too full and too tired to say no. Moments later, he was sound asleep.

Anámn awoke to the smell of bread prying into his nostrils. This was not Euhilv. However impossible it seemed, Anámn felt a sustained happiness in his heart.

Anámn stumbled out of the bedroom, cast his blurry vision settled on Nísyx's figure, and yawned. "How long was I...?"

"Twelve hours," she replied. "Anámn, I mean no offense, but you do not smell the best. Perhaps you should take a shower. I have some old work clothes here that your uncle used to wear when he helped around the house."

---

[3] Luku (loo koo)

Anámn did not respond. Neither was he embarrassed. His sister told him this out of love. Not to mention, he had not taken a shower with clean water in many weeks. Closing the door to the bathroom, Anámn turned the water on and undressed. As the warm water hit his dirty head, he noticed tears streaming down his face. One by one, tears collected around his pupils and fell to the rhythm of the water droplets in the shower. Soon, Anámn sobbed. He felt *content* in a *warm, clean shower*, at his *sister's home*.

Nísyx heard her brother crying. She wanted to comfort him, but Anámn was always distant when it came to his inner emotions. He kept them guarded, in a grip so tight, even water would be unable to find its way out.

Soon the shower stopped and Anámn emerged, clean and in his uncle's old clothes, which looked new compared to the rags he was wearing. His eyes were still red.

"Nísyx… Nísyx… I…"

He needed no more words. Nísyx pulled her brother close, embraced him, and let him cry.

Was this *"compassion"*? Anámn had no memory.

"Thanks for letting me stay," he said. "I missed you so much…"

Unable to staunch the flow, Nísyx was accosted by the punishing guilt that plagued her for the past three cycles.

"Anámn," she cried softly, rubbing his head. "It is all right."

She did not want to make any mistakes in grammar while comforting her distraught sibling. There was no chance she would say any word that spoke to a future happiness. Anámn would have closed up at those words. But, right now, yes, at that moment, in the meantime, it was *all right*. There was no ju Xaníz, no Héthyx, no smell of the mines, no whips, nothing but the love of his sister. Anámn let himself be held in her arms. He never let himself be cradled by any other person except his mother, but she died before he made twelve cycles. Nísyx was the last person who embraced him, when his mother passed sixteen cycles ago. After his mother's death, Anámn became hard and obstinate.

Tekil sensed the wrath he reserved for their father. It was unmistakable. She was relieved he had done nothing foolish enough to get himself killed. Her father had some malicious design for Anámn, one even she was unable to fathom.

"Thanks, Nísyx. You've always been there for me."

"Not like I should have, Anámn. Not like I should've. I'm so sorry. Only the Nameless One knows what you've gone through."

They sat in melancholy silence for a few minutes, and the young man drew away from his sister's embrace.

"Nísyx, I meant to ask you yesterday. What do you do down here? I mean, how do you make your living?"

"Hmmm… Actually, I make clothes and quilts to trade. And sometimes, I sell a few dishes here and there, when my credits run low. Things have been kind of slow lately. I haven't gotten the income I need to fix up this house, and I'm not asking father for anything. Many cycles have passed since I received financial support from him."

Anámn looked at the ceiling and the floor. "Yeah. Your roof needs some work."

"You noticed?" she asked, always amazed at Anámn's quick though erratic perceptiveness. "It hasn't rained here in three days, but we still have a duration left in the rainy season."

"I'll fix it, if you'll keep making those great meals," Anámn smiled.

"That is a deal, little brother," Nísyx Tekil said playfully. "There aren't too many people out here, so you can use the wood you find in the forest. I have some spare metal sheets out in the back. And, I must tell you. The entire roof needs replacing. That'll take more time than you have."

Anámn's smirk epitomized deception. "I think I can get it done faster than you think."

The next morning Anámn set out early with an axe in hand. Once he had gone a considerable distance in the forest, he found and cut down a large tree in four strokes. His physical might was incredible. His physical stamina and strength as a slave combined with his newfound powers melded quite well.

After he finished that quick workout, he sprinted near the lake's shoreline. But he stayed within the limits of the trees, in order to conceal his movements. His Elemental granted him more of an audience and although Anámn could not generate his aura, he noticed that he was able to sense different kinetic signatures of living creatures.

Returning to the fallen tree, Anámn tried to lift the entire trunk over his head without channeling or petitioning his Elemental. Gripping the felled tree's underside, the neoteric Sczyphamek hoisted it up. He could only raise the trunk to his midsection before the weight became more than he could bear. Grunting and blowing air out of his mouth, Anámn dropped the massive piece of wood, bent over, and coughed.

"Too heavy," he said. But he made a vow that before he left Kamo, he would be able to attain the goal.

With the trunk in front of him, Anámn smiled, made a fist, and punched the trunk with all his might. The trunk splintered and large pieces of wood broke at the point of impact, but Anámn was in too much pain to notice. Blood flowed from his knuckles. However, when he observed the broken pieces of wood, the slave felt a sense of accomplishment. He chopped one of the large pieces into five smaller logs.

Based on the sun's position in the sky, it appeared to be about midday. He walked back to Nísyx's carrying one log of wood with his hands and the axe tied to his belt. As he neared the path that led back to her abode, Anámn commenced rolling the log to his sibling's.

When he was not so far off, he yelled, "Nísyx, I'm back!"

Nísyx came out of the house and responded with amazement, "So soon?"

Stealthily investigating Anámn's body, she noticed his knuckles were bleeding in such a way that normal folk would cringe in pain, but Anámn did not even seemed worried. And the log Anámn rolled was so large that Tekil wondered how her brother was able to find it.

"You didn't steal that did you?" she asked half-jokingly.

"No," he feigned short breath. "I guess I just was lucky today. A tree had already fallen, so all I had to do was chop it with the axe."

Nísyx eyed her brother suspiciously. He was hiding something, but she was unsure what it was. She made a mental note to pay special attention to Anámn for the rest of his stay.

"Brother whom I love so dearly, have you learned how to read yet?"

"What?" he asked, although he heard exactly what she said.

"The Eastern barracks still have secret literacy meetings. Your mother and I helped start one, after all. I was teaching you before I left, and I was just wondering if you continued."

Anámn was quiet.

"We can start where we left off if you want. I mean, you don't have to… I just thought—"

"That's fine," he said begrudgingly. He still did not see the significance of reading. After all, he was a slave. But Nísyx and his mother had constantly preached to him about the necessity of literacy. However, he let Nísyx teach him out of respect and love, not because he valued the trade. "We can start after dinner," he added.

Meanwhile, he went into the backyard and started to hew the wood into manageable pieces to haul up to the roof. That evening, Anámn and Nísyx talked and entertained one another and ate dinner, after which, she taught her brother how to read. The siblings continued this trend for the first week, and were fortunate, for the seasonal rains appeared to be dormant, allowing Anámn to continue the roofing uninhibited.

***

"Uncle Huyé will be here any minute. Get out of there."

Anámn was not conceited, but this was the first time he met someone from his mother's family in his adult life. He wanted to make sure that he presented himself in the best possible light and did his mother proud.

"I'm coming!" He smiled and looked at himself in the mirror.

Nísyx's house was like a home he never had, and this was the first time he entertained company. The experience was alien to him. But after putting work into his sister's house and sleeping there night after night, Kamo did begin to feel like a place he could call home. Nísyx and Anámn purposefully avoided the *obvious* conversation and instead concentrated on their bond, without alluding to the first cause of their bond's existence. The two melancholy souls found rest in each other for those eight days.

Anámn emerged from the bathroom, dressed in traditional Phmquedrian attire, made just for him by his sister. Nísyx set the table: baked luku, an array of vegetables, and three kinds of bread. The knock on the door was right on time.

Nísyx opened the door and said jovially, "Uncle Huyé, I'm so glad you were able to make it tonight."

"Had to see Níse's son," Anámn heard an endearing gruff voice speak.

The man entered into the foyer. Anámn's eyes almost deceived him. Huyé looked almost exactly like his mother. He was tall and slender, just like she was. But, his face was round with dark brown eyes. He had a belly that protruded a bit from his gray shirt and over his belt buckle, which held up his black pants. As he took his cloak off, Anámn noticed his dark brown skin tone matched his mother's perfectly.

"You don't remember me do you?" he asked Anámn. "You were so little the last time I saw you, but I can tell by seeing you that you're her boy."

"And you've got to be her brother," Anámn smiled. "You look just like her."

"Well," he said, "not just *like* her. She was a woman, you know."

The three of them laughed.

"You look like Nísyx too though," he said, but immediately fell silent, for the remark signaled the siblings' common denominator.

The home entered into uncomfortable quietness.

"Dinner is ready," Nísyx interjected, rejecting the silence's hold on the atmosphere.

"Good," both men said.

They sat down at the table and held hands.

"May the Nameless One bless this food, and all those who partake in it. Let our Qaníns be filled with your presence."

"Fá'atoño má," Anámn and Huyé chimed.

Anámn's Elemental shifted during Nísyx's prayer, but he was unsure why.

No one talked during dinner. Nísyx impressed herself with the meal. It was probably one of the best she had ever cooked. After supper concluded, Anámn and Huyé sat on the couch. Nísyx purposefully let them be and washed the dishes.

"I'm sorry about your mother, Anámn," Huyé said.

"Yeah." Anámn's frown signaled his unwillingness to talk about it.

Perceiving his nephew's reticence, Huyé redirected, "Nísyx told me that you were fixing the roof. I was going to help, but I was delayed by other projects."

"What do you do?"

"I help build those new buildings you see in Kamo."

"*What?*" Anámn sneered.

"I am not over the project itself." Huyé did not catch his nephew's disdain. "I am just one of the workers. The pay is good though."

"I was telling Anámn about the public works program." Nísyx heard Anámn's displeasure and felt the need to become the conversational intermediary. She knew her brother.

"How can you work for them, Uncle Huyé, after what they've done, after what they did to your own sister?"

"I work for a Phmquedrian owned company," Huyé replied, becoming bit indignant, but understanding Anámn's frustration.

"Does that make it any better?" Anámn scoffed.

"Anámn," Nísyx interjected calmly. "Uncle Huyé has five children and six grand-children to care for. The land Tannódin left for public use is unsuitable for farming. How would he support his family?"

"There's got to be another way…"

"I was unsure about it at first, but now, I am happy to be a part of it," Huyé continued.

Nísyx hung her head, reminding Anámn of their conversation almost a week and half ago. Anámn did not know what to say. He did not feel he had the right to tell a man with children and grandchildren whom he was trying to provide for to not work. And his uncle favored his mother so much that Anámn's normal temper was pushed away out of sheer respect.

"I can tell the conversation is upsetting you," he said. "We don't have to talk about this." Changing the subject Huyé asked, "Anámn do you want to meet my children, your cousins?"

"My cousins…?" Matriester was still trying to grasp the idea of family, for it was such a foreign concept to him.

"Yes, they can be by a week from today, if you would like to see them. Two of them are around your age."

"I'd like that very much."

"Until then." Huyé rose from the couch. "Nísyx, thank you for the meal." He turned to Anámn. "If you get most of the work done, my family and I can put up the roof."

"No thanks," he said. "I told Nísyx I would do it, and I will."

"Don't hurt yourself." His uncle put his cloak on. "It was good to see you, Anámn. Nísyx, I will see you later."

Nísyx opened the door to let him out. Closing the door, she faced Anámn and began to speak.

"I don't want to talk about it," he said, unwilling to yield his ramparts.

"When? When will we ever talk about it?" she asked.

"Not tonight," he said, then went into the guest bedroom and closed the door.

***

Over the next two days, Nísyx saw her brother repair her roof at an almost unimaginable pace. Unable to sustain his rate of toil, Anámn's clothes became more ragged by the day. He had not cut his hair since he arrived and it grew into a short, kinky mess. Nísyx witnessed Anámn lifting pieces of wood that two or three able bodies could not harness. His stamina was also incredible; he was able to work for nine hours without a break for food or water. As a result, he had virtually finished the roof by the third day. Anámn seemed oblivious and carried about as if nothing was odd about his feats of strength. The mounting evidence enhanced her earlier premonitions about Anámn. Something was altogether different about him.

"Anámn, can you come inside for a few moments?" she called out.

"I just need to put these last two sheets on Nísyx. Give me five minutes."

It only took him two. He entered the house, drenched in sweat, but his breathing was steady. The knuckles he gashed almost two weeks prior were completely healed, without any lingering scar. Nísyx gazed at Anámn with pressing eyes and a scowl of apprehension.

"Something wrong?" he asked.

"Do not lie to me, Anámn. What in Qalfocx is going on with you? Never in my life have I witnessed such displays of strength and endurance. I wouldn't have believed it, if I hadn't seen it with my own eyes. You have been altered in some way."

Anámn was speechless. He sensed he was stronger, but he thought he had sufficiently concealed his powers. He should have known he could not have escaped the knowing eyes of Nísyx.

"Anámn," she said, "I happened as Nísyx Tekil, your sister. Please, tell me. What's going on? Or don't you trust me?"

"Nísyx," he replied warmly, "you are the only one I trust. It's just that... I didn't want to get you involved."

"Involved in what?" she asked warily. "Have you taken some mystical elixir? Did Malchían give you something?"

"No, Nísyx. It's not like that at all."

Knowing the conversation would be long, Anámn motioned his sister to the couch, and the young Phmquedrian told her the *full* story, about his powers and his encounter with Malchían, but *not* about the tree incident. Nísyx listened in amazement.

"And he did not tell you why you were supposed to come to see me?" she asked.

"No," Anámn answered. "Malchían... he just disappeared right before my eyes. That was all he said. I still don't know why, but I knew that he was right. I had to see you."

A kettle blew.

"Lunch is ready," she said.

Anámn's stomach growled. "Guess I am hungry… Can we finish this after lunch?"

Nísyx nodded yes. But after Anámn had lunch, his body felt the signs of overexertion, and he sat down on the couch and fell asleep.

Startled, he awoke to the sight of his sister. "How long…?" he asked.

"Fifteen hours," she said, smiling. "Anámn, you do not smell the best. Before we talk, you should take a bath. I drew some bathwater. And I went back into town and got you some new clothes and a razor. They are next to the tub."

"I don't smell that bad, do I?" he asked. Sniffing his armpit, his eyes almost rolled to the back of his skull. "Maybe I do…"

He took off his dingy shirt, and his back was completely exposed. Nísyx gasped.

"Anámn-" she stammered.

Anámn forgot because he had lived with them for so long. His back was scarred beyond description with whip burns and scars. Although his powers aided him in healing fresh wounds, his Elemental was unable to repair any of the ones he received beforehand.

"They've been busy," he told her, speaking of their father and Héthyx, the overseer. He entered the bathroom and closed the door.

The woman was greatly disturbed by her brother's scars, which only added to her anguish. Ever since she left Euhilv, and especially upon Anámn's visitation, Nísyx had been wracked with guilt. She left her brother alone with *him* for three cycles. He surely endured Qalfocx, gynix, and any other horrible geography the cosmos produced. He deserved better, and she owed him so much. He needed to be free from the glare of their father.

She knew what she had to do.

Anámn emerged from the bathroom, clean, refreshed, and in new clothes.

"Kíma!" Nísyx exclaimed. "Your sister has fashion sense."

She bought Anámn black boots and black-brown pants made of rain-resistant material. She also purchased a solid dark green long-sleeve shirt and a long black overcoat with a dark green inseam. The shoulders of the coat were also dark green, lined with white trimming, which made a semicircle on his upper back. Crowning his head was a charred green hat made of Phmquedrian wheatstraw, one of the most resilient plants on Qeauríyx.

The clothes were perfect for Anámn's tall, slender, yet muscular frame. He shaved his head, and his sideburns were groomed nicely. His light brown eyes radiated and seemed as neoteric as his clothes.

Nísyx was perceptive. When she heard that Anámn's aura was green, she wanted to make sure that she bought attire that would match and or complement its radiance.

91

"Thank you for the clothes, Nísyx. I haven't had anything new to wear in a long time. I know this must've cost a lot of money. I'll pay you back somehow."

Guiltiness consumed Tekil and prevented her from responding.

"Nísyx, what's wrong?"

"Anámn... I'm the one who must pay you back, and clothes are not enough." Ashamed and remorseful, Nísyx fell to her knees and begged for forgiveness. "I am so sorry for leaving you alone with him. What was I thinking? I let self-hate and guilt get in the way…

"Whether you happened as a Sczyphamek or not, you deserve so much better than this. And especially since you are coming into your powers, you do not need to be tied down to Phmquedria. You should leave this place."

Anámn was incredulous. "What? Leave here? Leave Phmquedria? Why would I want to leave here? That's crazy. This is my home."

"This may be your home," Nísyx Tekil replied, "but this place has not cared for you. I know you will come back, and you should come back. But not right now. Please trust me.

"There is much to do elsewhere. You will never be able to Awaken and become a true Sczyphamek here. The mines will take this gift from you. Phmquedria will take this gift from you. Alzhexph's hold is too great here. Sometimes, you have to leave and risk the worst in order achieve the best."

"Nísyx, if I leave, ju Xaníz will kill you. You know the rule. And even if he doesn't kill you, he'll find somebody to kill in your place. How can I leave with the runaway provision? I may be stubborn and mean, but I'm from Euhilv. I don't want others to suffer because of me."

The sister shook her head with determination. "I don't know. I will ask for your release. I will beg if it comes to that… I'll die in your stead if I have to."

"Nísyx, don't be…"

She cut him of before he could finish. "I will, Anámn. And he will have to listen to me… He has to… He *is our father*…"

"*Our Father?*" Anámn snapped full of wrath. "*…My father…* He doesn't even deal with me. *Father?* He's no kímaz father. He sends his middlemen like Héthyx to deal with me, Nísyx. His middlemen!

"He created me. I'm alive 'cause of his greed and his lust. But he don't want to deal with the thing he created—his own son. He won't even acknowledge me. He acts like he has no part in me happening, as if I just came out of the mines.

"He named me. And he doesn't even call me by my name. And my kímaz name…" Anámn trembled in anger and gritted his teeth. "My kímaz name doesn't even have a meaning! It means nothing in the Ancient Tongue, Phmquedrian or Tannódin'é… He gave me a meaningless name because that's how he sees me!

"But whose kímaz language do I talk? Staxis! Whose whip beats my back? His!"

Anámn sprang up and clenched his fist. The room became green as his aura emerged. Nísyx was frightened, but she could offer no rebuttal.

"When I act like the slave he wants me to be, Héthyx still beats me and humiliates me. And when I try to stand up for myself, he beats me harder and says I'm "breaking the peace"! *Breaking the peace?* Where's this kímaz 'peace?' Whose 'peace' is he talking about? Does peace happen in the mines? Is it on my back? Is it in those skyrises?

"*Peace, my ass...* There's no peace in Euhilv, or anywhere on this damn continent, and every time I scream and show what's already on my body— these scars and bruises—those Tannódin'é bastards act like they don't see it, while they keep on beating and whipping me...

"You wanna go to a man like *that* and ask for my release? You want to go to a man like that to suffer and be killed just so that I can go free? What kind of sick arrangement is that? What kind of terms are those? That's kímaz insane.

"That man doesn't even *see* the life I live. That man doesn't look at me in the eyes even though I am made from that damn piece of kíma! He made me!"

Anámn threw his hat down on the floor and his eyes overflowed in streams of misery and neglect. "He *raped* her, Nísyx! Raped my mother every day. I can still hear her crying... But, she just took it! Why didn't she resist...? Why couldn't I help her?" He stammered uneasily and staggered into a chair opposite of Nísyx.

"He drove you away... the last one who cared about me. His family, our family, is responsible for a 240-cycle slave trade. And now, you want to go to that man and beg for my freedom? I would never let you do that. *You should never have to do that...* Why do you have to beg to the one who has caused this Qalfocx?" Rubbing the tears from his eyes and calming down, he murmured, "Why do we have to ask him to stop, like we're the ones who're wrong?"

Nísyx drew close to her embattled brother and held him. "Anámn... I know you are hurting. I've spent my whole life trying to reconcile how I happened. Both sides of my family are directly responsible for Global Initiative. Alzhexph did rape your mother. And we both know that what happened to your mother was no accident. She gave up living. He broke her qanín completely.

"When Níse died, I had to leave. I couldn't live with him. I'm sorry Anámn." With tears falling from her maroon eyes, she muttered, "How can I love myself, when I know what I come from?"

The two siblings sat in silence. The sound of crying occasionally filled the room. Both held each other and fought against succumbing to the wretchedness of their existence. Vulnerability was in neither of their vocabularies, but after so many cycles and so many masks, Anámn and Tekil finally let their pain surface.

"Anámn," Nísyx reiterated, "do not go back to Euhilv. I do not care what happens to me. But, you need to leave this place."

Anámn was resolute. "I can't do that."

"Anámn, you have a gift from the Nameless One, an ability that can help so many people. What will going back to Euhilv accomplish?"

"When I go back, I *will confront* him." He hesitated, but summoned the gumption to speak the declaration. "Nísyx, he might be our father... but I'm going to kill him."

Nísyx was quiet.

"Sister, what're you thinking?"

She responded with careful measure. "Anámn, what will killing him do? What wrong will it right?"

"It'll right a lot of wrongs. Staxis! Don't you understand? The slave camp will be free..."

Nísyx shook her head. "Even if you kill him, they will just put another ju Xaníz or one like him in power. The House of Kaz is merciless and aggressive, and they'll come in a force much greater than that of our father. You know it is the truth."

"What if I don't care about the truth?" he asked, filled with uncertainty.

"You *do not* care about the truth, right, or wrong. You care about *revenge*."

"What does truth have to do with right and wrong?"

"It has much to do with them..."

"Maybe. But he deserves to die, and I can't forgive him for what he did to us, or to *my* mother."

"Why do you think Malchían told you to come to me? He knew that you would struggle with this." She placed her right hand in his. "Please listen to me."

He drew away with anger, stood up, and turned his back to her. "You of all people, I thought would understand. But you're blind to the real 'truth.' Power is all that matters on Qeauríyx. Those who don't have it are doomed to suffer."

"And those who have it cause more suffering. Which one are you?"

"Don't treat me like I'm dumb," he said with noticeable frustration. "I'm not stupid..."

"Anámn, you're not stupid. You've never been that. But you've been wronged and are filled with self-hate." Nísyx rose up and placed her hands on his shoulders. "I love you, Anámn. You know I love you. I would never do anything to harm you. You and I, we are all we have. Even though I moved here, close to your mother's family, they do not fully accept me. I am Tannódin'é, and worse, I am the daughter of Alzhexph ju Xaníz. They have taken me in, but I have not earned their trust, and I do not blame them."

Nísyx was ready to sob, but she steadied her breathing and would not let the tears flow. She straightened herself, cajoled her brother to turn around, and her eyes met Anámn's. Her eyes were filled with conviction, anxiety, and hope. "Brother whom I love so dearly, nothing awaits you in Euhilv. Not right now. Even though we can't run away together, you can still be free. If you are evolving into a Sczyphamek, continue down that path. Become like the Kylanín Sczyphameks of old, who fought for justice."[5]

"*Justice*… what is that? Justice…" Anámn mumbled. He did not want to, but again he turned away from the sister whom he loved. A great river of resentment crested in his qanín. "I know what justice is. I'll prove it."

"You are blind with anger; no, you are blind with rage. Anámn, do not go."

"You're acting like he's going to win, like he's going to beat me. I am a Sczyphamek, and I have the power to change this place."

"Into what? Your own image?"

With no understanding and unable to restrain his himself, Anámn violently backhanded Nísyx in the face. The belt lifted her off the floor and threw her onto the couch.

Stillness befell the room.

He could not look at her.

He failed her.

"Anámn…" Tekil's voice was engulfed in sadness, anger, and shock. Blood dripped from her nose and mouth. She spat out a tooth. Tears ran down her face. She could not push the pain and the betrayal away. Even her father had never laid his hands upon her. "Anámn… leave. Right now."

"Nísyx…" the ashamed brother said. "I'm sorry. I don't know what happened. Please, don't…"

"Leave," she repeated. "Leave… before you do a worse thing than this."

---

[5] Kylanín (kahy-luh-n*ee*n)

CHAPTER SEVEN: HEAVY BURDENS

19 Myaíz, 241 OGI

The elements awoke Neztríanis. Four distinct bodies of heat approached her. Frantically, she gathered up her things, ran towards a group of trees, and jumped high into the branches of a nearby Yarnínga. Perched far above the ground, she waited. Within five minutes, she heard voices.

"I think we are near the area where we saw that incredible thunderstorm last night," one voice said.

"Ah," agreed another. "Here are the remains of a fire. And what's this hole doing here by itself? The grass is well worn..."

With that discovery, the unknown foursome charged their energy weapons. Neztríanis was astounded. Somehow, she perceived energy cells of the AEARs without the aid of her eyes and ears. Her days of persistent training must have granted her the ability to detect heat signatures unconsciously.

Their accents were not indigenous to Nez Spirita. Because communication fostered survival, folk on Qeauríyx had evolved to be easily multilingual. But even though one understood the differing languages of their neighbors, dialect and vocabulary still made communication a most difficult task. The soldiers' delivery was extremely fast to Neztríanis' ears, and their inflections were quite haughty.

They had to be Global Initiative operatives.

She could not see them, but she was afraid to move the branches for a better view. The sound of rustling branches might alert the troops.

"Yeah. *Well.*" This time it was another. A female. She was restless. "Whoever lingered here probably decamped. Should we not get back to the unit, ah? We're at least four lengths removed by now."

Three of them continued to talk; however, one remained silent. Neztríanis' heart raced and her palms gushed sweat. Would she have to defend herself?

No, she thought. *I am not ready… This is too soon… But I cannot stay here…* She had never been in even the slightest of physical altercations, much less fought in combat. And she doubted her willingness to murder. Yet, *no one* could be allowed to hinder her mission. With a task as grandiose as the recovery of the Auría, Neztríanis never considered the mundane conflict she might encounter. And Vicious and Pre-Eminent were so legendarily despicable that she had little issue with their demise. But, what about ordinary people or nameless soldiers? How could she…?

"Sortie," the silent one ordered. "Someone is still around here. I know it."

Staxis, Neztríanis thought. *What am I going to do?*

She listened for ten minutes, but heard no sound from them. Focusing upon her Elemental, she sensed the operatives' whereabouts. Two were nearby, and the other two were quite distant.

If I fight them, they will certainly call for assistance. Even if I manage to subdue them, I do not think I can do so without the aid of my powers.

Confrontation was out of the question because secrecy was her greatest ally. Even though the soldiers saw the storm, they did not see who or what caused it. After all, Qeauríyx was a strange place full of weird happenings. And just because someone camped near the storm that did not mean that this person was responsible for it.

I must fly. She frowned in hesitation. The power was hard to control. *Elements, I need your help.*

Concentrating, she let out an emanation of lukewarm force from her body to make the trees rustle. This would aid in her evasion of would-be enemies. Continuing in her exercise of intense focus, she discerned the location of the search party's main unit. They were twenty lengths to her north, near Hero's Bay and the Xarkim River, heading east. She needed to fly west-southwest in order to avoid them.

The trees had been whistling for awhile, so Neztríanis levitated. And though the difficultly was extreme, she managed to fly for thirty lengths and forty minutes before her qanín faltered.

She settled in some trees near the southern beach of the Windhorse Peninsula. Climbing down, she sat on the ground, exhausted. Still in her sleepwear, the woman retrieved her shirt and pants from her shoulderpack. As she changed, the specter of death, confrontation, and the prospect of murder took hold of her qanín.

Why were Global Initiative soldiers in Hero's Valley? The valley was essentially uninhabited. Only the railcrusier line traversed the area, and that was on the northern shore of the peninsula. The non-aggression pact between the villages of the Windhorse Peninsula and Tannódin expressly prohibited Global Initiative military incursions. By custom and by law, Hero's Valley was a demilitarized buffer zone. Neztríanis pondered all of those facts, but could not think of an answer.

No matter the answer, her original route, following Xarkim River's main branch, was out of the question now. The soldiers were probably using the waterway. Neztríanis would have to follow the Phyxtríalis Ocean's shoreline then go through Nextu Village instead. That was the only way to circumvent the imperial forces to her north. Hopefully, the soldiers were not on their way to Hopha.

Her heart was troubled by the idea of her home's destruction. She longed for her mother, for her people. Spitefully, trepidation crept into her spirit and made her depressed and lonely. The heaviness—the old, long repressed heaviness of her youth, returned. The oldest scars never seemed to heal. New scars made the old ones fashionable or forgotten, but never remedied. Her old pain was back, steeped in solitude and abandonment. Though she had been in Phesiana's home for over two decades, Neztríanis still awakened at night periodically, drenched in sweat, believing that she would soon be abandoned again.

Traditionally, the Great Mother chose a female from a household as a successor when the girl was two cycles of age. Though the position was not hereditary, there were mores and norms to be followed. Phesiana, radical as she was, broke with tradition and decided upon Neztríanis, an orphan from a non-existent household.

Despite her social status as the Great Mother's daughter, Neztríanis was teased and resented by her peers. Because she was neither Phesiana's offspring nor from a prominent family, the hostility and jealousy displayed by some of the well-known families in the village was open and insidious. In fact, the acrimony was at its height during the earliest cycles of her stay with the Great Mother. Neztríanis was able to make some friends, but she never trusted them. She did not know if they were amicable for deceitful or egotistical purposes. Those early cycles had left their mark, and as a result, Neztríanis did not have a single close friend or confidant. All she had was her mother and a few acquaintances.

The Great Mother. Although aloof and suspicious, Nez never doubted Phesiana's love for her. Her mother was relentless yet loving, exacting yet fair. And the love and respect Neztríanis had for Phesiana was unparallel, even though she doubted her mother's sincerity from time to time.

But now Neztríanis was forced to look upon her mother with fresh eyes. Phesiana had foreseen that Neztríanis would happen as a Sczyphamek and purposefully raised an orphan and turned her back on tradition. To a certain extent, Phesiana was right. It did not matter who her parents were or even who the Great Mother was. Temperature's path was sure to be a heavy burden, and her mother's task was to instill in Neztríanis a kind of resolve that would not yield even under the most strenuous of adversity.

In discontent and acceptance, Neztríanis' heart fell. The pain was not just old; it was also new. Her path as a Nez Spiritan Sczyphamek was sure to be a lonely one.

She had to trust herself. She had to trust in the cycles that Phesiana poured into her. She had to trust in her Nez Spiritan heritage and the ancestors that preceded her. She worked hard to study and learn as much as she could in order to lead the village when her mother departed. Her greatest fear was disappointing her mother. Yet, in her heart, Neztríanis never wanted to be the next Great Mother of the Hopha.

Though scared, the daughter of Hopha was relieved when Phesiana gave her the present assignment. Searching, locating, and repositioning the Auría was an enormous task, but succeeding her mother seemed much harder. But she only possessed those feelings because she had firsthand experience of what the role of Great Mother required. Now that she tasted her first bite of this journey, leading Hopha did not seem like such a dreadful task. In either case, she returned to the same feeling.

She was alone. Just like when she was three and could not remember her parent's faces. Just like she was the day before she started on this journey.

Achieving her goals became a comforting solace. She learned at an early age to be competitive and strive towards excellence. It was an enjoyable game, a way to shelter herself from her incredible loneliness. As long as she focused on her next objective, then she would not have to face her fears. But becoming a Sczyphamek placed a newer and *wider* gulf between her and her kind, unlike anything prior. And if she Awakened…

The tears rushed to the front of her eyes, but she held them back. She kneeled and prayed to the ancestors and the One with No Name. While praying, she grew angry with Qeauríyx. Why did the planet test her when she was trying to help it? Why did Qeauríyx not attack Tannódin? It seemed that its time would be better spent on confronting those who were destroying its biosphere.

Still struggling with herself and her convictions, she walked out of the forest and towards the shore of the ocean. Although she believed, Nez still had questions about the One with No Name. Why did the Nameless One not help her people? Better yet, why did the Mystery allow the planet to fall under Global Initiative?

Why should I fight against the House of Kaz if Qeauríyx and the Nameless One do not?

While reflecting on these contradictions, her Elemental increased in stature. By seeking understanding, she remembered the teachings of the Great Mother: her questions were derived from her faith and practice. She questioned because she believed.

"Please increase my will," she petitioned. "Please, increase my faith… Fá'atoño má."

Neztríanis faced the Phyxtríalis Ocean and suddenly sensed twenty-five to thirty people heading down the coastline. Some of the heat signatures were faint. Erring on the side of caution, she ran back into the of the forest. Voices surfaced in the distance, and as they drew nearer, Neztríanis heard familiar accents. Nez Spiritans led the pack with energy weapons, and many slow-moving bodies followed them.

Feeling no fear of her own people, Neztríanis came forth from the edge of the forest and spoke with a loud voice. "Brothers and sisters, faring well, I pray." This was a standard Nez Spiritan greeting.

The leader of the pack halted, gave the order for those following to stop, and signaled two women from his party to run into the forest. He was tall, portly, and bandaged across his left arm, yet his size and apparel appeared deceptive to Neztríanis.

"Peace to you sister." Though the greeting was cordial, his countenance was apprehensive. "May I ask to see your hands?"

Neztríanis raised them. She understood their prudence. They had no idea if there were more of her kind behind the dark entrance to the forest. She walked slowly towards the company, palms open and hands away from her sides. "I was just wondering what you all were doing out here, brother? These lands are uninhabited by our people."

Seeing that she was no immediate threat, the man held his weapon down. "I could ask you the same thing."

Assiduously examining him and his party, Neztríanis concluded that they were survivors of a violent battle. There were wounded amongst their number, and the man himself was bandaged around his arms and legs. The women reemerged from the forest and shook their heads. The leader nodded.

"Are you all right? You appear to be injured," the daughter of Hopha said with concern.

"I am fine," he answered guardedly. "You still have not answered my question."

"And you did not answer mine," Neztríanis retorted with a smile.

Seeing that she was alone and unrelenting, he sighed. "We, my company and I, are all who are left from the battle of Lozé. We barely managed to escape and have been avoiding a unit of White Scythe for the past week and a half."

White Scythe! Neztríanis thought. *That is who they were!*

Her thought must have created a readable expression on her face because the man asked, "What? Have you seen them?"

"Yes," she said. "No more than thirty to forty lengths from here. I just—I escaped them the day before yesterday." Neztríanis corrected herself. It was no mere feat to travel such a distance in a half hour.

"Why were they after you?" he asked with suspicion.

Neztríanis said nothing and glanced in the direction of the wounded.

"You do not have to tell me," he relented. "There are plenty of things in this land that can get you killed. Saying too much is one of those things."

"Your company needs help. From what I saw of the Tannódin'é soldiers, you are in no immediate danger. You should rest here."

"Why should we trust you?"

"Why should you not trust me?" she countered and smiled to herself. The Great Mother rubbed off on her more than she cared to admit. Neztríanis was doing precisely what her mother would do if faced with the same situation.

Eyeing his troops, then gazing at the ocean, the man sighed deeper and wearier than the first time. His company was effete, and so was he. If they did not stop, they would have no strength to defend themselves if they faced White Scythe. He turned around and told those following him, "All right. We will rest here for the rest of the day and move out before dawn."

He threw the energy rifle over his shoulder. "I am sorry, sister. I have not introduced myself; my name is Rydín. I was the prefect of Lozé." Tears welled in his eyes, but he would not allow himself to cry. Though stopping almost allowed the rapids of sorrow to catch up with him. "For Lozé is no more," he whispered.

Neztríanis gasped; she knew the man's words were genuine. Indeed, Lozé was probably wiped off the face of Qeauríyx if Tannódin had anything to do with it.

Regaining his composure, Rydín asked, "What is your name, sister?"

Name? Neztríanis could not let anyone know her true identity, not even her own people. "My name is Mésa," she lied without flinching. In fact, "Mésa" was the name of her imaginary best friend when she was a child.

"Well, Mésa," Rydín said, "would you give us some help? I have eight wounded people here."

"Yes," she replied. "I know a Yarnínga mixture that helps with burns and reduces pain."

"Thank you, sister Mésa."

"You are welcome, brother Rydín."

***

Anzél, at one point a continent, plowed into southeast Líachim during the final millennia of the Great Drift. The collision caused the hallowed Mount Chabnev and Backbone Mountains to ascend. Most of Líachim survived the clash; however, large sections of Anzél fell into the Il'ectyx and Lancryptox Oceans.[1] The history of the continent turned peninsula had been unmerciful ever since.

The Backbone Mountains invariably split the continent-turnerd-peninsula in half—southeast and northwest—which added to the continental misfortune of the inhabitants. The mountains became not an obstacle to overcome in order to build community and solidarity, but a line in Qeauríyx. And those clans of the northwest built a great city called

---

[1] Lancryptox (lan-krip-toks)

Anmetria, from which their name is derived. The families southeast of the Backbones would not be outdone and fashioned a municipality of architectural genius, Focal.

No one remembered who started the battle; however, there was no point in arguing over the original sin. For reasons long forgotten, the Anmetrians and Focalites endured through millennia of war and anxious peace, which eventually left Anzél deprived and uncultivated.

They fought each other over land. They maimed each other because of illegal miscegenation. They beheaded one another for wealth and jealousy. They stormed and burned villages because of their apparent difference in phenotype: hair and eye color. Bodies were conflagrated and tortured for religious and philosophical purity. Justifying the wars became like a game of misdirection in order to conceal the real "reason" one side fought against the other.

Because after ten thousand cycles, there was no reason—none that anyone remembered—only the *feeling* of hate and wariness, the protocols of exclusion and domination, and a resilient mentality based upon chosen superiority. Anzél's springtime fogs, a weather event precipitated by the oceans and mountains covering the entire peninsula, personified the haze of combat and mistrust.

Much of the land was unfarmed with sprawling deciduous forests covering both sides of the isthmus; however, the yarla trees of Anmetria were of a green variety and the yarcés of Focal were blue-green, signifying even an arboreal conflict within the ground itself. Indeed, Qeauríyx's torturous history was on full display in Anzél.

Most of the inhabitants lived in large villages near the coast, and relied on seafood and bread for sustenance. There was only one neutral city on the peninsula, Laquína, located on the northeast side of Mount Chabnev. Aphaz, one of the largest cities on Qeauríyx, lay on the other side of the thirty-seven thousand foot mountain, in Líachim proper. The mountain once made land travel into either area impossible, but 200 cycles BGI the two cities made a ninety-five length tunnel through the mountain, using a rail system for travel. Sea travel was difficult; because of the mountain, a seafarer would have to deal with immense wind gusts, great waves, and erratic weather of considerable magnitude.

When the entire continent of Líachim (including Anzél) discovered that Global Initiative would be launched on their soil, the governor of Aphaz, Zotham, tried to coordinate a continental alliance. His father, six generations removed, brokered an uneasy peace treaty between the Focalites and the Anmetrians, which endured for 240 cycles. Zotham hoped that all of Anzél and all of Líachim would stand with him, resisting the Tannódin'é and Damüdan coalition. But local hate and fear were stronger motivation than geopolitics and cultural and historical annihilation.

In those 240 cycles of peace, both sides cultivated their own respective lands and only small skirmishes erupted from time to time. Yet distrust soon reared its seductive head. The Anmetria/Focal myanála agreed on one thing; both believed whichever side gained Tannódin'é support would crush the other. The fear needed no catalyst. The Anmetrians struck first, but in a conflict so immemorial, it hardly mattered. The Focalites response was violent, swift, and egregious. Both groups wanted the spoils of Global Initiative, and Anzél was not large enough for altruism.

Zotham pleaded with the antagonists, but his pleas proved futile. The head of Aphaz finally abated his attempt at reconciliation and focused his attention to his city and the rest of Líachim. When diplomacy with the House of Kaz failed two cycles ago, he and the other leaders of the continent, sans Anzél, prepared for the eventual battle while the Anzél peninsula lay embroiled in stalemated bloodshed.

Líachim was Qeauríyx's last line of defense against Global Initiative. Líachim was the third most populous continent on Qeauríyx; its economic and political structures rivaled Tannódin and Damüda, and its people possessed two hundred cycles of military preparation. If Líachim fell, Keotagosdi would be the last free continent, and although its denizens were irascible, its population was too low and too widespread to put up much of a fight. Yea, if Líachim fell, all of Qeauríyx would soon be under the banner of the House of Kaz.

The armed forces of Global Initiative arrived in spring, near the end of the second duration. Anzél, like all lands in Qeauríyx, maintained its climates antecedent The Great Drift. Since the continent was drifting in the temperate zones of the northern hemisphere before it crashed into Líachim, the continental peninsula was enjoying seasonably cool mornings and warm afternoons. The plants were beginning to bloom, and the days were growing longer.

On the 28th day of Myaíz, in the 241st cycle of Global Initiative, Kaz Késhal Supreme stepped upon the shores of Focal with 250,000 Blue Rapier soldiers, including their leader, Commandant A'reznu Feolenz. [2]

Breathing in the foggy, humid air, she noticed condensation collecting on her silver boots. Her footwear scampered to her knees, revealing her skintight, reinforced battle pants, made with a material so white that any reflection of light from them would cause momentary blindness. The pants ran seamlessly into her white top, which stretched to her shoulders and down her toned biceps, stopping just before the elbows. Both wrists were adorned with expanding elyandir bangles, covering her forearms. An exquisite glove, garnished with cometstone fragments, shielded Késhal's right hand. Her off-white cape, with a large Tannódin'é insignia, flapped in the wind. The cape was held by an elyandir pendant and chain that encircled the empress' neck. Underneath her mantle was a sheathed short

---

[2] A'reznu Feolenz (ah-res-noo fey-oh-lins)

sword that strafed her lower back horizontally.

Pulled back in preparation for the oncoming battle, her hair was dark brown, and Pre-Eminent's stunning maroon eyes were a symbol of planetary perfection. Her fair face shone brightly, accentuating her sharp features. Atop her head and down her cheeks—the platinum imperial headdress was of a skillful design, both artistically pleasing and protecting the ruler from trauma to the head, if such a feat was even possible. Her vestments seemed to correspond to another time and space, a time that even predated Global Initiative. It was the garb of the Sczyphamek Golden Age, which only added to Késhal's mystique.

Even the most hardened revolutionary knew the woman was gorgeous and deadly.

The once picturesque city of Focal lay in ruin. The Sczyphamek disembarked from her boat and mournfully shook her head at the desolation before her. Although she was certain the city would not compare to the technological genius of Tannódin, Pre-Eminent heard Focal's buildings and edifices of worship were visionary. But when Késhal walked the streets escorted by a splinter of her imperial guard, all she passed were abandoned homes, shops, and rubble. The city was leveled, stone over stone, and the once renowned buildings existed only as faint memory. Focal was virtually destroyed. Gravel crunched beneath her boots. Out of every crevice and broken brick, the fragrance of death reeked. The legacy of its past was drenched in the aroma of inane warfare.

She felt them, every last one of them.

Savages, she thought. *They have become savages.*

While still on a battlecruiser out at sea, A'reznu Feolenz contacted the empress via radio communication. "Pre-Eminent, we received word from scouts that a battle is ongoing, five lengths to the south and west of Focal. The rival factions are fighting each other. Our surveillance of this area appears correct. Anzél is in disarray."

Moved with pity, Pre-Eminent groaned in her qanín. "They will kill themselves off if I do not finish this. They have no direction. They are like a scattered herd with no leader, defeated and self-loathing. Let us end this quickly.

"Commandant, I will go there myself. Grant me a division for support. Divide the rest of the force as you see fit, and subdue the surrounding land. I want Focal and its vicinity secure by week's end."

"As you wish," A'reznu Feolenz replied.

Commandant Feolenz, or "Old Flint" as he was called by his troops, was over 100 cycles old, but he was more sharp and sturdy than any member of the imperial guard. Although his age was incredible, his strength and command were the real cause for awe. No one, not even Pre-Eminent, comprehended the man's vitality. He was not a Sczyphamek, but he wielded Blue Rapier longer than any before him.

Blue Rapier was found by a secret Tannódin'é archaeological expedition about three hundred cycles BGI within a crater in southern Bryce. The blade was made of an unknown metal, like White Scythe and the Violet Manacle, although all three were composed of different, pure minerals unlike anything on Qeauríyx. Many believed Blue Rapier to be from a heavenly body's fragments. And like White Scythe before it, by the time of Global Initiative, Blue Rapier had become a military chamber led by the Wielder of the blade.

The rapier was royal blue, extremely lightweight, and its hilt was exquisite. The grip was wrapped in leather, and Feolenz himself, who was also a master craftsman, welded the hand guard. It was composed of an alloy made of platinum, gold, elyandir, and silver. He ground ruby and diamond chips and added them to the alloy as well, making the hand guard one of the hardest substances on the planet. The guard completely shielded his fist and could smash through the toughest wood. The long, slender blade—though mainly used for defense, parrying, and thrusting attacks—could slice through rock if a swordsman or woman was adept enough. And Old Flint was more than capable. And if one believed an energy blast would damage the blade, he or she would be fatally mistaken. Blue Rapier discharged a defensive corona that deflected most attacks.

Feolenz had personally trained every General Maximum in swordplay for the past seventy cycles; indeed, he was heralded as the best swordmaster on Qeauríyx. His skill and speed were lethal, and his defense, impregnable. If not for White Scythe's superior power and constitution, Blue Rapier, in the hands of A'reznu, would have been the ultimate blade. At least, that was popular thinking. The blades, however, possessed qaníns of their own.

Feolenz's hair was so white that it diminished most of his other features. Long and perfectly kempt, the old man had not cut his hair in two decades. Half of it was pulled into a ponytail, which ran down to his lower back, and the other half covered his cheeks, ears, and forehead, casting a shadow over his blue eyes. His mustache sparkled white, and his beard fell halfway between his chin and clavicle.

Wrinkle upon wrinkle covered his face, and his skin was fairly pale, like most from the southern reaches of Bryce, his homeland. In fact, the southern isles of Bryce were only a few hundred lengths from the Qeauríyx's south pole. He carried no weapon, except the rapier, which was holstered on his hip by a leather belt with an intriguing metal buckle, a combination of the Tannódin'é and Blue Rapier insignias. His entire outfit was navy blue, with a thin white-yellow stripe that ran from the bottom of his pants to his underarms, and from his neck down the sleeves of his shirt. His jacket's collar was large and always folded up, covering his face. In fact, with his hair and beard covering most of his face as well, the ensemble of follicle and coat became like a mask that the old man wore into combat.

A'reznu spent his time rocking in a yardük[3] chair he carved himself, silently critiquing and creating war stratagems. On other occasions, he limped about, deceptively hunched over and dawdling around his troops, making sure they were ready for the unknown. His wife passed many cycles ago, and the majority of his family had been lost in the wars. Only his great-grandson and granddaughter were alive, and Feolenz made them promise that they would have nothing to do with Global Initiative, in terms of military service. He, however, would serve the House of Kaz to whatever end. Pre-Eminent's word was an authoritative canon that could be leaned on throughout the ages. He was the consummate soldier: she ordered; he followed.

Therefore, he informed his commanding officers of his plan, which would secure a thirty square length area by week's end. Unhesitatingly, the officers relayed the message to their subordinates, and so on, until Blue Rapier moved like one body, united in purpose. Like insects in the process of colonization, the first chamber of the war machine swept into the surrounding environs of Focal and into Anzél.

Meanwhile, Pre-Eminent dismissed her imperial guard to other matters and flew with determination towards the edge of the city. One length away, a great battle was underway between the Anmetrians and Focalites. The two sides had been fighting for days. Their energy weapons had long given out, and they were engaged in hand-to-hand combat. Even though Blue Rapier troops were present to the indigenous of Anzél, the fighting did not end. Emboldened, each side believed that whoever won the battle would win Tannódin's favor.

The Sczyphamek, repulsed by the carnage, met a division of Rapier soldiers, a number of about twenty-five thousand, and motioned for the field generals to come towards her.

She already knew what she was going to do.

"Generals," she greeted.

"Empress Pre-Eminent," they responded respectfully.

"Stay here," she ordered. "I will deal with them myself."

Without question, the generals commanded their subordinates to order the division to back away from the battlefield.

"Is a voice amplifier present?" she inquired.

With haste, the device was brought to the empress, and after grasping it, she continued her stride towards the fray. Solemnly turning back to her army, she commanded softly, "Make sure no one escapes."

She did not need to verify if her command was carried out. The division dispersed, so as to surround the combatants of Anzél. She was about a quarter-length away when both sides took notice of her. None of them had ever seen Pre-Eminent before, and the reports about her were mostly rumor. Most did not believe it to be her, shocked that she would venture

---

[3] Yardük (yar-*ewk*)

into battle without any imperial escort. When Késhal got within five hundred feet of them—a host of about fourteen thousand men, women, and some children—she stopped, stood, and assessed the battlefield and the combatants.

It happened within a matter of seconds. Those furthest away felt it first. They could not stand. It felt as if an enormous weight was placed over and in them; yea, even their lungs felt heavy. Dropping their makeshift weapons and collapsing to their knees, the multitude cringed in discomfort. Even the strongest soldier buckled.

Pre-Eminent stood motionless, surveying the underlying emotion of the crowd, for her Elemental was tripartite. Késhal was not only a gifted empath; she was also consecrated with the ability to manipulate the photons of over half the electromagnetic spectrum—from radio waves to ultraviolet—and gravity. And she had increased the gravity threefold in a two square-length area within seconds.

Gracefully placing the amplifier near her mouth, the empress declared, "Focalites and Anmetrians, choose this day whom you will serve, for judgment has reached your shores. Global Initiative will have no rival, and it is my wish that you all would be saved from your miserable and wretched lives."

She paused and looked at them knowingly and amicably. "I know you have heard otherwise, and I know this is hard for you to accept or believe, but I... no, not just I, but *all* those who fight for the ideals of Global Initiative are here to help you."

Suddenly, her countenance grew unflappable and aggressive. "But understand this now, today will either be your salvation or your damnation, for I know your hearts, and despite your greatest attempts, you cannot hide from me."

An indignant sensation swept across both sides of the battlefield. Although initially the Anmetrians and Focalites wanted to curry Tannódin's favor, many of the antagonists now grew offended at Pre-Eminent's disparaging tone. She knew nothing of them, their battle, or their culture.

Who was she to judge them? How could she offer them salvation? What gave her the right to impose her beliefs on them?

Her statements were out of place in Anzél, just like her garments; indeed, they belonged to another space and time. However, this realization came too late. Zotham warned them of the impending judgment, but they decided to win the demigoddess' favor instead of taking her down from her throne.

"Why do you always wish to fight us?" she inquired sorrowfully, sensing the fourteen thousand's dispositions, down to nearly every individual. "Why do you not understand that this is for your benefit?"

Saddened, Pre-Eminent's face crumpled and her maroon eyes watered, but she wiped the tears away. The first body flew in the air like a pebble from a catapult. The helpless scream died quickly, drowned in the collective cries of terror. Hundreds—no, thousands—soon ascended towards the heavens, through the clouds, at unimaginable rates, as Pre-Eminent selectively relieved the area of gravity.

Her tears dropped on the ground, which had been watered by the blood of so many throughout recorded memory.

Késhal wept.

She wept for the que of Anzél; it had suffered the horrors of civil war long enough. Its hurt was stronger than any cantankerous feeling that emerged from the combatants. Her resolve grew stronger. The dirt need clot no more. This would be easy. She would end this with bloodless crucifixion.

Judgment commenced, and she had to execute it impartially, with justice and mercy. For those who fully rejected her offer, she let their bodies float directly into space, where they were heard no more. Even as they inaudibly suffocated and froze to death in the vacuum of outer space, their emotions betrayed them. Fearful bewilderment gripped those damned to the emptiness of the galaxy, and yet, their vehemence still reached her qanín. The perverted unbelievers were cursing her. Soon, however, the pressure gradient of space would force the air out of their lungs, and their thoughts would be felt no more.

Next, those whom she judged confused, yet unrepentant, Késhal had mercy upon them and incinerated them, enveloping them in concentrated, powerful bursts of ultraviolet photon waves, so that they died instantaneously. However, she made sure that they would be purified through the heat on their way to gynix, so that all imperfections would be cleansed from their qaníns.

To those showing the promise of rehabilitation, she dropped their bodies back towards the ground but made sure the impact did not cause mortal injury. Their excruciating malady would give them the opportunity to rethink their perspective on Global Initiative. Only two thousand were found completely innocent and left untouched. After witnessing such an awesomely violent, *four minute long* spectacle, those two thousand were gripped with a fear and thanks so strong that their fidelity and service to Global Initiative would be irreversible.

She breathed heavily, and drops of fatigue sweated from her body. Many cycles had passed since Pre-Eminent displayed her power in that capacity. She did not even bother to chant or raise her aura. The exhibition was sheer willpower, and Késhal needed a few moments before she wielded her Elemental again. However, perception was often reality. She could not afford to appear weak. Pre-Eminent needed this story to circulate around not only Anzél, but into Líachim as well.

While reconstituting herself, the empress of Global Initiative fell disconsolate. Why did she continue to face so much opposition after all of these cycles? She had personally directed the talks with Líachim, hoping that they would sign a non-aggression pact. However, Zotham ("the

Ignorant," as she dubbed him) refused. He claimed that the elders of Phmquedria had signed a similar treaty cycles ago, yet in due time, the entire continent was enslaved. While that was true, Késhal, through her ambassadors, assured Líachim that Phmquedria was a different case. That continent required harsh measures, because of the Phmquedrians' well-documented inferiority and brashness. Pre-Eminent's grandmother, Sczyphamek Imperial, was responsible for Phmquedria's enslavement; so, the granddaughter would not stand for the legacy of Global Initiative to be tarnished by Líachim's noncompliance.

Imperial commenced Global Initiative's formal execution. Pre-Eminent, as a Sczyphamek and a granddaughter, was compelled to finish the task. Although Késhal did not want Tannódin, Damüda, Zorét, and Bryce to be involved in another large-scale military campaign, the daughter of Kaz broke off negotiations with Líachim and prepared for the eventual war that was to come.

Anzél, on the other hand, was another matter. Késhal tried to broker a non-aggression pact with the embattled peninsula as well. But the Anmetrians and Focalites were so consumed in civil war, they did not respond to the imperial invitation. From the clandestine intelligence gathered by the Eradicate, Pre-Eminent was briefed on the status of each faction. The Anmetrians were led by a woman named Cálo and the Focalites by a man named Lywa. Both of their hideouts were located somewhere in central Anzél.

Késhal's plan was methodical. The entire peninsula of Anzél had to submit to her rule before she entered Líachim. She could not fight a two-front war. That was her parents' mistake. They remained bogged down in a multifaceted conflict that stretched Tannódin and Damüda too thin. In fact, Késhal knew that the audacious attack on Phenplyacin would not have happened on her watch. Unlike her parents' failed strategy, she would make sure the march to Mount Chabnev was a march of absolute and irrevocable subjugation. Pre-Eminent would have to tame the wild frontier of Anzél, and Anmetria was the next locale on her journey.

Within moments, the elite Sczyphamek regained her wind. She promised her Elemental that she would soon convene with them, so that they could commune, chant, and pray together. She purposively kept her aura at bay. The peasant multitude had no right to see her in her full glory until they came into the knowledge of her sacred task.

Moans were heard lengths away. The majority who survived the Sczyphamek's judgment were now afflicted with a most terrible pain. Bones were broken, tendons snapped, and cartilage torn. The two thousand who were spared ran to their fallen comrades, approximately three thousand.

One Anmetrian saw a Focalite woman, whom he had fought, seized with agony. The Focalite woman was judged by Pre-Eminent and was suffering broken ribs, wrists, and metacarpals as the price for her rehabilitation. He wondered why Pre-Eminent let the woman live.

Yes, he thought to himself, *Pre-Eminent must've made a mistake.*

Picking up a sword, the Anmetrian decided to murder his incapacitated foe. With fearful eyes, his enemy gazed upon him. She was completely at his mercy and could not move—much less utter a plea. When the soldier thrust the blade down, he felt a grip on his wrist so terrible that it caused him to drop his sword and buckle. He winced and nearly cried, the pain was so horrid.

It was Késhal.

The man kneeled, shaking, aghast, unable to speak, and terrified. He was sure Pre-Eminent was almost a length away before he grabbed the sword.

"There is a saying..." she said poetically as the man plunged to his knees. "There is a saying that 'old habits die hard.'"

Kaz Késhal smiled sincerely at the broken woman who writhed on the ground then frowned at the vengeful man. "You must end your petty distinctions. Henceforth, you will no longer view yourselves as Anmetrians or Focalites. This woman is no longer your adversary. She is your sister. You are both a part of something larger now. Global Initiative is a new reign that forges new relationships." Letting his wrist go, she declared, "There will be no more of this."

The empress of Global Initiative picked the weapon up and tossed it to the heavens as if it was weightless.

"The mercy that was shown to you, show it now to your sister," she commanded softly.

Késhal moved on, walking slowly towards the sea. In the distance, the man saw troops in blue uniforms advancing their way from every angle, rounding up all who were judged innocent or capable of rehabilitation. An overwhelming feeling of dread entered into his heart. Although he accepted Tannódin, Líachim had not. Only Qalfocx knew what Sczyphamek Pre-Eminent had planned for them.

There would be no mercy.

***

By the time Neztríanis reemerged from the forest, the company of rebels had started a campfire. While gathering the herbs and leaves needed for the healing balm, Neztríanis constantly reminded herself that her name was "Mésa," a drifter from the outskirts of Pt. Sank, who had been traversing the Windhorse Peninsula for two cycles or so. While sleeping in the forest she saw some soldiers, and fled to the coast. That was when she met Rydín and his group. She repeated this story in her head over and over.

The smell of cooked seafood filled the beach, so did the sound of downhearted camaraderie. Stories of survival and death permeated the campsite. The escapees had been on the run for days with no chance to rest or reflect on the spectacle they witnessed at Lozé.

Neztríanis sauntered quietly towards the injured and applied the balm to their wounds. Many of them were asleep or unconscious, but an old man, missing his left arm and half of his right leg, lingered near death. His blood-soaked bandages had not been changed in days. Tenaciously holding onto life, he grimaced and scowled at death, denying its macabre advances.

Unconsciously and with saddened eyes, Neztríanis nearly drew away from the elder. Was this the fate of her kind: a debilitated wheeze that only delayed the inevitable? Before she could answer such a question, her empathy and solidarity overcame her desire to recoil and reflect. While humming a Nez Spiritan hymn, she redressed the man's wounds.

"So I encountered you before the end after all," he grunted in painful agitation.

"Shhh…" Nez lovingly rubbed his forehead. "Please, keep your strength."

"I saw… I saw you two weeks ago in a vision…" the old man sputtered. "My name is Wapla."

"You are tired, Old One," Neztríanis replied with great respect, yet in unbelief of the man's words.

He whispered, "I know why you lied, daughter of Hopha."

Neztríanis Phyxtríalis observed him closely and realized he must be a Mystic of the Auría, a guardian of history and the sacred teachings. There were only a few left on Qeauríyx. Most were dead or hunted down by Damüda's leader, Galís,[4] who seemed to have a vendetta against the Auría, its teachings, and its teachers.

"Mystic," she said. "I cannot…"

"You cannot endanger them with your mission," he interjected. "I understand. Be strong daughter. Be strong." His voice weakened, but he straightened what was left of his body and sat up. "I am happy to see the one who will rise against them. Do not despair. You will not face them alone. One person cannot save this world… It takes many… and higher powers still…" Unconsciousness and Death beset him, but he fought the siblings away one final time. "When you come to that moment of hesitancy, you must listen to your Elemental…"

His eyes closed; his breath grew fainter; and soon, he breathed his last.

Tears streamed down the Sczyphameks cheeks. "Sleep, Old Mystic. You have earned your rest."

Sensing Rydín's approach, she tried to stop crying, but the suffering of the land and her people was too great. Neztríanis had seen an elder's transition to death before, but it was never precipitated by violence. To Neztríanis' shock and dismay, her Elemental also grieved, which filled the Nez Spiritan with an indomitable depression.

---

[4] Galís (gah-lees)

"He was a good and fearless man. He told us to leave him in Lozé, but I could not." Judging from the defunct leader's tone, Rydín was plagued with remorse. "For as long as I can remember, I sat at his feet, soaking in all he instructed. Wapla served Lozé and the surrounding villages for many cycles. He taught us about Nez Spirita and the One with No Name. Now, he has returned to the land he loved."

"Yes," she responded tearfully. "Yes, he has…"

Neztríanis turned and saw Rydín was holding two makeshift plates filled with food. "What's that?"

Rydín looked at the plates and his demeanor changed. "Oh, yes. Mésa, we have prepared some seafood and wild berries from the forest. Please eat; you need nourishment."

Smelling the seafood was an olfactory delight, and Neztríanis was hungry. She had not eaten since she created the small storm. "Thank you, brother Rydín. I think I will have some. It smells delicious."

Rydín handed her the plate and motioned Neztríanis to a spot on the beach that put some distance between them and the rest of the camp. She followed him and placed her satchel on the beach. They both sat down, and as she ate, she grew more pleasant and less exhausted.

The leader of Lozé pointed to the northwest. "Sister, if you are heading that way, I must tell you something. That way is treacherous. Many pose as allies, but they are traitors. And the insincere can be the greatest of comrades. The Nez Spiritan mainland is a very different place than the peninsula."

Neztríanis nodded; she did not want to acknowledge his advice in a spoken capacity because she was afraid that it might give away her quest. However, she wondered why he was saying these things to her.

Rydín perceived her silence and went on. "In Nextu there is a middle-aged man on the northern side of the city. His name is Hafir; he is a good friend of mine and quite well-known. You should not have to tell him that you met me. He is a kind person, needing little reason to help strangers. He helped us get this far…" Rydín's voice drifted into painful memory.

Neztríanis rubbed the back of her Nez Spiritan relative with compassion. "Do you wish to speak about it?"

"No…Yes… I do not know," he answered bitterly and hurled inaudible curses at the waters. "There is nothing left to speak about. The General Maximum is as skilled as they say, maybe even more…" Rydín shook his head in disbelief, still bewildered and crushed by defeat. "You see Mésa, Sczyphamek Vicious did not even join in the attack. He simply observed it by hovering above the battle… He must be more powerful than anyone can imagine… So what does that say about Pre-Eminent… and *what does that say about us?*"

Neztríanis was confused. "How do you know that Vicious is more powerful? You did not see him fight. If he is that strong, why did he not participate in the battle?"

Turning to his inexperienced sister, Rydín educated her on basic rules of war and empire. "Those who are most powerful and intelligent only use an obvious display of their power when no other choice avails. Think of the statement that is made when even one's intermediaries can destroy you. It augments the perception of the powerful enormously.

"You must understand; Vicious is not lengths away in the comfort of his palace. Neither is Pre-Eminent. They ride into battle with their troops. They have an administration in Tannódin that sees to their governmental affairs. They are not cowards. Some leaders send their troops to fight and die in wars that they themselves would never fight. That is when the military becomes an impersonal tool of destruction and treachery. That is also why Phenplyacin remains such an indescribable moment…"

Neztríanis and Rydín both paused, recalling the stories of that horrendous event.

"*What does that say about us?*" The prefect repeated in self-examination and ethnic critique. "As soldiers, delusion is a crime against your brothers and sisters. There is a fine line between the upkeep of morale and delusion. Yet, Tannódin muddies that line like tilled soil after a spring rain. *We must fight*, but even so, the cause appears hopeless. Yet, life within Tannódin'é dominance is without hope… If a difference exists between gynix and Qalfocx, it must be in the hereafter. Here in Nez Spirita, they are one. Cycles such as these are doubly forsaken…"

Rydín put his hand in the ocean's waves and sighed. "Near the end of the battle, when I saw that it was hopeless, I and a few others escaped with some of the wounded through an ancient tunnel that cuts a path well beneath the city and into the caves of the eastern mountains. During the Solemn War, our forbearers built a small, self-propelled rail line through this path, allowing for relatively quick travel. For two days, we endured the dark and emerged 220 lengths later, into the western Nextu Forest. It took us longer than expected because of the injured. Despite this, we managed to cross the Middle Pass of the Nextu Range six days later. We lost many during that leg of the journey. On the tenth day of our journey, somehow we made it to the outskirts of Nextu…

"We thought we were safe there, but soon, we realized that White Scythe was hunting us. Somehow they heard that there were a few escapees of Lozé. And Tannódin does not leave a mission unfinished…"

Rydín shook his head in depression. "I should have stayed there; I should have died in Lozé…"

Neztríanis could offer no lies of consolation to her weary, newfound comrade.

"Mésa, I apologize for such talk. These past few days have been devastating. My followers look to me for strength, but…"

He paused, beheld his remaining comrades, and with his last bit of resolve, Rydín held back his defeated qanín.

"It is good to talk to an excellent listener," he said. He took a bite out of his seafood and searched for words that would quicken the tale's end. "Hafír could not meet with us personally; that would get him caught. But through some of his own contacts, we were resupplied and smuggled out of the city. We have been on the run since then, but I do not know how much longer we can keep this pace up."

Neztríanis nodded her head. Why was he trusting her with this information? She felt like saying more and divulging her own fears to the deposed leader. But she was afraid to burden Rydín with her issues, not to mention, she felt that if he and his party were captured, he could betray her through torture. Nevertheless, she needed information of her own, and she wanted to help her kindred.

"Brother Rydín, Hopha lies beyond the next range of hills. If you and your party can traverse them, you will find a village that will more than aid you. Of that, I am sure."

"I have heard of Hopha's kindness, but I do not want to bring trouble to the community," he replied.

"Hopha is a sprawling village throughout the forest, covering many lengths; you should be able to blend in with relative ease. The locals have no love for Global Initiative. Your fight is over; perhaps you can start a new life there."

"Perhaps…" his voice trailed, pondering her suggestion.

"May I ask," Nez continued probingly, "what news do you hear of Tannódin'é plans around Pike Metropolis?"

Rydín gave the impression that he anticipated such a question. He wished to know her motivations. Although he observed her exchange with Wapla, he did not know what their conversation entailed. However, he was no fool. The woman clearly was more than her appearance, and the Mystic purposefully used his last breaths to speak to her.

Wapla had been Rydín's religious and personal counsel since the latter was a small child. And now, the Mystic's combative and proud qanín burned in the daughter of Hopha. Neztríanis possessed an irrepressible inner strength. She reminded him of his fallen comrade, the valiant Syla, and the account of her bloody dismemberment at the hands of the General Maximum. Although he did not witness her demise, Rydín knew the description had little exaggeration. If there was any way he could spare Neztríanis Syla's fate, he would. Rydín had spent his entire life around Nez Spiritan resistance; Neztríanis' anti-imperialism wafted from her body with a strong fragrance.

"Mésa, listen…" He paused in order to choose his words carefully. "Tannódin does not reward mistakes."

"Huh…?"

"I do not know what you have planned, but I do not want you to suffer like I—like we, like all of us have."

"Rydín," the Sczyphamek replied hastily, unsure of what response she should give. "You misunderstand me."

"I do not think so," he countered with a smile. "I told you earlier, you do not need to tell me anything, but this course you plan to take is clearly worth lying about. I saw your exchange with Wapla. I do not know what you all talked about, and after all I have been through, believe me, I *do not* desire to know. And you seem like the type that would go to Pike even if I told you not to."

Neztríanis gave her fellow Nez Spiritan a sign of affirmation.

The prefect continued, "If you need any help while you are in Pike, there is an underground Miska Kea cell in the southeast section of town. They are located in a hostel named the 'Unseen Inn.' You must deliver a passphrase that they will recognize in order for them to help you. If you deliver it incorrectly, you will be killed. Tell them you received the sentence from me. If it is possible, I will alert them of the possibility of your arrival."

The sun was setting. The waves washed on shore. And the rising tide grew more noticeable. The man and woman let their feet become wet and sandy from the oncoming waters.

Rydín traced images on the wet sand. "There is a host of military activity north of Pike Metropolis in the Bitzroy Plains. No one knows why. Everyone knows that Líachim is next on Global Initiative's horizon. But rumor has it that the Blue Rapier troops training there are not preparing for Líachim. If you are heading that way, be careful. Other than that, all I've heard is gossip of a secret operation going on in the vicinity of Pike."

"Thank you, brother" she said. His last bit of intelligence referred to the Auría retrieval operation.

"No. Thank you. If Wapla believed you to be important, I know that it is you who deserves thanks."

Neztríanis' smile betrayed her sadness. Her heart was heavy, due to what she perceived as an enormous task. Even if she retrieved the Auría and made it to Sunrise Mountain, she would not be free of the burden. In fear, solitude, and amongst veterans who could fight no more, Neztríanis accepted the full brunt of the truth. She was one of the last "military" options for Nez Spiritan resistance.

The Sczyphamek was cut from an ever-shrinking cloth of Nez Spiritans. It was as if the survivors of Lozé passed the lonely and impossible torch to her—not only them, but all of her ancestors who had died while resisting Global Initiative. Neztríanis would not delude herself into believing that she was the second coming of Nez Spiritan resistance. However, the Sczyphamek saw herself in a long line of strong, peace-loving, and stubborn folk who fought only because they had no other recourse.

She would never yield to the House of Kaz. *Never.*

She had to become stronger before she made her next move, and that required her to leave Rydín and his company. The closer she was to Pike Metropolis, the weightier her quest became. Very soon, she would have little to no chance to outwardly train and enhance her Elemental.

Walking towards the two, a Lozé survivor signaled Rydín.

Rydín turned towards the daughter of Hopha. "We are about to pray, meditate, and speak to our ancestors. Would you like to join us?"

Neztríanis gazed at her brothers and sisters near the campfire. Then she looked towards the northwest.

"No." She replied with regret and grabbed her shoulderpack from the beach's care. "I must be on my way. Thank you for the information."

"Thank you for the help," he echoed.

Rydín wanted to give her some sign of comfort but he was motionless, sensing the weight of her journey. Neztríanis stood up and walked towards the forest. The prefect turned to his flock and approached the fire with confidence.

"May the Nameless One guide our steps," she heard the community recite, beginning the religious service.

Tears of loneliness streamed down the Sczyphamek's face, and the eldest Yarníngas tried to comfort her with tree light. However, they could not. Neztríanis felt a sadness and burden that moved beyond time and space.

Chapter Eight: The Slow Ache

İzdak?

His tears were like blades of grass in the fields of an uninhabited plain. Endless and long. Every time he thought he cried his last, tears from previous hurts surfaced in his consciousness. He sniffed, shivered, and curled himself up in the forest, where no one could hear his agony. He never dreamed that he could do such a thing.

It was his father's fault!

Ju Xaníz made him do it, made him wind his hand back, made him follow through, made him secretly *enjoy* it.

Anámn sobbed at the thought of hurting the only one who had treated him with love since the passing of his mother.

How could he?

Why did he?

No answers. Only tears. Only the misery of his existence. He did not care about becoming a Sczyphamek or whatever mission Malchían wanted him to accept. Nothing mattered except the pain. The more he tried to leave it, the more the depression pulled him in. Its girth was too broad and its density too immense. He grew tired of struggling against it, tired of making excuses, tired of his trivial life. There was only *one* thing to do now; only one event could give him satisfaction: murdering his father.

In the hellacious Qalfocx that was Qeauríyx, singular logic proved readily accessible and easily justifiable. One goal, one purpose, one essence. All things and actions must be made subservient to the immutable and necessary *one*. No higher calling or being existed.

Anámn finally ridded himself of all pretenses, all emotion, all action. All understanding was vacated, except for the rational, the only *one* true locus of knowledge. Based on his circumstances, it stood to reason that Anámn's existence was made for *retribution*. Vengeance and redemptive suffering.

He was a scapegoat after all.

But he would be damned if he would be the sole scapegoat in Euhilv. Others deserved damnation. In order to redeem, others must be damned. In order to transform, blood must be shed. Salvation was impossible without condemnation. In order for righteousness to reign, wickedness must be displayed. Someone must suffer. Salvation could only turn on the wheels of redemptive suffering and retribution.

As Anámn lay in the forest north of Kamo, the rains fell. The cold, springtime torrent had returned, hard and unforgiving. As the precipitation collected on Anámn's body, steam formed. The dark green aura returned. The Elemental could not separate itself from the pain of its host. It tried to reason with Anámn, but Anámn cared not to understand its intimations. And with wary regret, the Elemental was drawn into the Phmquedrian's rational anger. Violent emanations returned, without chanting or belief. Anámn willed the force into reality, without words or understanding.

Power. More Power.

Anámn craved it with no guilt. He sat up and spotted a tree directly ahead. Holding his right arm out and bracing it with his left, Kinesis opened his palm and let out a murderous discharge that ravaged the area. The blast was more controlled than before. His anger was more focused, more deadly, more reasonable, and more implacable than ever.

"Damn you…" He sneered and gritted his teeth. "Kill you… I am going to kill you…"

He would show Nísyx that he was right. He *would change* Phmquedria *his way*. The element pleaded with him to stop, but he ignored the petition. Ignorance was blissful anguish, and anguish was fuel to the flame of revenge. Anámn shook his fist towards the gray, ambivalent heavens and cursed the day he was born but blessed the oncoming day of his father's death. Unlike Anámn's birthday, his father's death-day would be a day of rejoicing, a day of celebration. For the world certainly mourned the birth of Anámn; surely, it would greet the death of his father with gladness and thanksgiving.

The aura crackled violently, yet it was noticeably shallow and emaciated. Anámn's face displayed a coy, maddening smile, unaware of his hollow aura.

"It'll be painful, you bastard…" he declared, as his Elemental retreated, "…I'll make sure of that. You'll bleed like I've bled. You'll join me in this Qalfocx… We will go together… Father and son… We'll go into the Deep together…"

He promised Qeauríyx, the wind and rain, the remaining trees, and the River Kamo itself. He would either obtain recompense or depart while striving for it. This gift from the absent Nameless One was given as a divine pronouncement against the sins of his father, to be exacted by the son, who in being in similar constitution, would reap where he did not sow and cut down that which planted him.

Malchían was a fool and had misinterpreted the signs of the times. This was not a time for reconciliation; this was a time of judgment. The jury had spoken, and his father was deemed guilty. Guilty of not considering others, guilty of acting without justification, guilty of raping his mother, guilty of driving his sister away, guilty of creating systems of violence and exploitation. If violence ushered Anámn into this world, then it should take his father out. Woe unto Alzhexph ju Xaníz and all of his ancestors. Their line was going to end by the hands of their bastard son.

Lightning flashed, and his eyes became like the thunderbolts. Anámn beat his chest thrice, and three times the clouds thundered and rolled. Atonement would soon be at hand. He wiped his hands of the verdict; he was only the executioner.

The drifting Sczyphamek had six days before he had to return to the village. He needed to practice and develop his powers. He wanted to be at his best… when the time came.

***

Damüda was his homeland. Zorschwin, his favorite game.

It would take the General Maximum some time to compile a final report for the battle of Lozé. The search for the Hidden Tabernacle was going slowly. And Vincallous' Elemental seemed invigorated and anxious. It was a perfect time to train. Therefore, Vicious informed his subordinates he would be leaving for three weeks.

Vincallous journeyed from the Bitzroy Plains to the Fire Fields of Nez Spirita—a rocky, volcanic area that jutted out into Hero's Bay east of Nextu Forest. Desolate and charred, the Fire Fields were subject to constant plate tectonics. The place reeked of the Great Drift.

Most continents in Qeauríyx had large mountain ranges and dormant volcanoes, but the Fire Fields were still quite active. The Fields reminded Vicious of the Volcanic Line that surrounded the Cape of Comphyx on the western shores of Damüda.[1] Cycles ago, he spent countless hours there, covertly heightening his Elemental. Indeed, that was the sacred space of his Awakening, at the Barrier Island Pass, nearly thirty cycles ago.

Had time passed so quickly? As a Sczyphamek, he aged slower than the rest of his species. Vincallous was fifty-seven cycles old, yet his appearance was that of a young man. And he had over three lifetimes of experience, which was not due to age.

Scratching his goatee, the Damüdan pondered the irony of his life and the love he never thought existed in him. He walked along an ashen path, thinking of his youth, meeting Késhal, and his time as a soldier in Blue Rapier and White Scythe. The co-leader of Global Initiative lifted his head towards the gray, smoke filled sky. It was times like these that he truly

---

[1] Comphyx (kom-fiks)

missed Késhal. If present, she would probably smile at him and comment upon his strange sentimentality.

He was ready.

To his left, a volcano erupted and birthed a massive earthquake. Feeling at home, the Damüdan smiled. The shock would have frightened the most unflappable of folk, but Vicious happened as a Sczyphamek, whose bipartite Elemental was connected to sonic vibration and the que, yes, even Qeauríyx itself. And even though the quake caused the ground to crumble and shift, the Sczyphamek neither moved nor swayed.

Volcanoes were a metaphorical comparison for Fierce. He was the earthen, magma-filled dome, a quiescent, reflective warrior, with only the occasional smoke or small earthquake to warn one of danger. But all should beware when this thing exploded, for no one was safe. Indeed, the Sczyphamek known as Vicious was personally responsible for one of the most reprehensible acts of destruction in the history of the planet.

A caustic cloud of debris rushed to his position, but Vincallous held firm.

"Fá'atoño má. Dé'wa." he chanted. "This should be interesting."

How many times had this scenario happened in Damüda, while he was secretly preparing himself for revenge? It took him six cycles to smolder the lava filled rock that was his own body, spirit, heart, and mind, so that he could coldly carry out his plan of unfailing vengeance. Despite laborious obstacles, he had to conceal, yea, even bury his pain for countless cycles in order to draw near the House of Kaz.

Van Fénüra[2] perished, and Vincallous Fierce, a saturnine, wretched, and calculating individual, was incarnated. He left his home at nineteen and entered the ranks of Blue Rapier as an unknown volunteer. He departed from his old name, as well as his old life, except for that quiet, excruciating *ache* and the memory of playing Zorschwin with his parents and friends.

The cycle happened as 184 OGI. Van Fénüra was born in the eastern Damüdan highlands, in the city of Nosgüth,[3] the northeasternmost town on the continent, located on the shores of Glacier Bay. Back then, the highlanders were notorious for two things: their love of Zorschwin and their acts of rebellion against any imperial advance.

Zorschwin was a game of Damüdan origin made of two opposing sides. The game was played on a hill or incline, with an offensive team of twenty climbing uphill and a defensive team of fifteen holding various defensive positions. In order to score, the offense had to seize a flag and a témo's canine, which were both held by the defense.

The defensive team protected these two items by throwing a finite number of small leather balls at their adversaries. If an offensive player

---

[2] Van Fénüra (van *feh*-new*r*-uh)
[3] Nosgüth (nos-*gew*th)

were hit on any part of the body, that player would be removed from the field of play. An offensive player's only assistance was a small shield. Each team had eight chances to score.

Zorschwin was a game of strategy, quickness, and luck. The offensive team was always at a disadvantage, because climbing uphill was its own battle. The games, therefore, were low scoring, but highly competitive and entertaining. Zorschwin's purpose was not limited to play. The game also doubled as military and critical thinking exams given in the form of sports. The goal of the game was to force the players into finding ways to win despite impossible odds. Van was an exceptional offensive player. He was so good at Zorschwin that he dreamt about playing in his sleep throughout his childhood.

Nosgüth was a rebellious place, so Zorschwin was an apropos game for its inhabitants. The terrain surrounding the city allowed for excellent protection from both ground and water invasions. Mountain ranges covered its western and southern flank. And Glacier Bay was frozen the majority of a cycle. Not to mention, rough seas shielded its eastern shores. By the time any travel-weary invader reached the town, the people of Nosgüth had an overwhelming tactical advantage.

As a result, the city was free from disruption during the first millennia of the Tannódin/Damüda alliance. Nosgüth grew to be quite large and self-sufficient, and by the time Van was born, the city possessed a population of about 200,000. Since they represented a small section of Damüda, the House of Kaz and the Damüdan Guild tolerated the highlanders. But over time, Nosgüth grew increasingly critical of the Tannódin/Damüdan alliance, and 190 OGI, the city leaders publically sympathized with the cause of Miska Kea. Relations between the highlanders and the imperialists remained quiet and cool for a few cycles. Then Global Initiative airlifts dropped paratroopers into the highlands in 197 OGI.

The destructive plume neared him.

Vincallous shook off his historical reverie and turned his full attention to the present. Vicious chanted and incited four immense chunks of terra to rise up nearly two lengths in the air, which created an enormous crater in the que. Simultaneously, he choked the volcano's blast from the depths of Qeauríyx by closing off the magma vents beneath the crust.

Each chunk of excavated land was massive, nearly half a length in height and width. While humming an incantation in a minor key, Vicious and his Elemental began their display of supremacy. Invisible to the most proficient observer, the Sczyphamek drew the molecules in the earthen slabs closer and tighter together and fashioned a resilient shield. The shield was behind a harmonic buffer that would repel and weaken the oncoming soot and rock.

Some two lengths beneath the surface, where no mere person could see,

Vincallous displaced sediment and bored a twenty-length long hollow tube for the magma to rush through and out into the Hero's Bay. The topsoil expanded, and small mounds rose from the surface.

The fiery debris crashed into the dense earthen barrier, absorbing the debris' force and matter. Vincallous, with his left arm outstretched, made the earthen wall tip over. And slowly but resolutely, Vicious forced the debris into the Sczyphamek-made crater.

A few of the molten shards managed to sneak through at a titanic speed. The shards were made of Qeauríyx, and Vicious felt each one. Obeying his command, the volcanic detritus halted and caused a backlash that ripped through the area. Soon the dust settled and the volcano grumbled against the fatigued Sczyphamek, angry at the Damüdan's unwanted interference and insolence.

Exhausted, Vicious kneeled on one knee and gasped for air. His thoughts filtered back to Tannódin's punitive invasion of Northeast Damüda 197 OGI.

When Blue Rapier parachuted into Nosgüth's vicinity, the villagers acted with the same revolutionary fervor as their ancestors, except this time, the conditions were different. The environmental edge was lost due to technology and long-range ordinance. Within two days, Blue Rapier subdued the majority of the highlands. In response, the citizens of Nosgüth utilized guerilla tactics to fight their enemy. Vincallous' mother and father participated in the fight and were the leaders of their neighborhood division.

The imperial coalition was swift and thorough, and before long, there was no doubt that the resistance would end in defeat. Nosgüth lay under siege for one cycle, and Blue Rapier was ominously patient. They did not bomb and level the city.

One by one, Nosgüth's neighborhoods were eventually depleted and defeated. Hunger reared its ravenous head. Rations were thin, and the troops of Global Initiative moved systematically from ward to ward, crushing their opposition. In those days, the imperial war machine only offered armistice once. If peace on the imperialists' terms were rejected, the enemy would be subject to horrific repercussions.

They came in the daytime. Young Van Fénüra was eating a meal with his parents, a rare occurrence due to the fighting and low rations of food. A battalion of Tannódin'é forces stormed his family's house. The sentries of the neighborhood were killed covertly, and with no one to alert each household, Blue Rapier easily moved from house to house, seizing the insurrectionists.

When the troops surged into his home, Van was grabbed and placed in a chair. His mother and father pleaded with the men and women in blue uniform to leave their child unharmed. But injury was more than physical violence. And after what Van Fénüra experienced, he wished Blue Rapier had killed him that day.

Instead, they held him in the chair and made him watch as the male soldiers tortured and raped his mother in front of his eyes. Not a single Blue Rapier female uttered a word during his mother's degrading abuse and murder.

Van was ashamed of his father; his father who begged the soldiers to stop the violence; his father who was unable to save his own wife.

After the male soldiers slit his mother's throat, a sobbing Fénüra was forced to watch the female soldiers fondle, rape, castrate, then bloody his father for thirty minutes, making sure they did not damage any of his vital organs. Finally, his father collapsed from the pain and died at his son's feet.

Every soldier's blue uniform, hands, and boots were drenched in blood.

And suddenly, the troops left. The house was quiet. Fénüra sat in the chair frozen and in shock. All he thought about was Zorschwin. Traumatized, the young boy could not grasp such brutality, neither could he understand why they left him alive. Apparently, Blue Rapier had done the same to every neighborhood leader and spared the children out of "mercy."

"Mercy" never again entered Fénüra's moral vocabulary. Tannódin taught him the value of "mercy," and as a categorical imperative, it drew little respect. The ache had commenced, and it would not be satisfied without extreme recompense. Zorschwin obtained a new meaning for Vincallous.

Only the death of the emperor and empress, the "flag and tooth" of the House of Kaz, the "parents" of Global Initiative, would atone for the sins of Tannódin and Damüda. Only then would the game be won. He would become a retributive god of vengeance, and all gods required submission, blood, punishment, and sacrifice. Mercy was only a fleeting illusion before the specter of true justice. At the age of thirteen, Van Fénüra made a vow of blood atonement and swore to himself that he would never relent.

To carry out his plan of retribution, Van would have to become the happening he hated most. He was certain other children, from other lands, who suffered similar fates, had probably tried to execute such a predictable, adolescent, and stock plan of revenge. He recognized and admitted the plan's stupidity, its pedestrian simplicity, and that recognition and admission gave him an edge the other children did not possess. They deceived themselves concerning their vow and did not calculate the time and space—the patience, hard work, and self-hate—it would require.

But he was a master of winning uphill battles, no matter how much the odds were against him. When he was nineteen, Van entered Blue Rapier, the same force that killed his parents. Every day, he wore the uniform whose fabric was mingled with the blood offering of his parents. He enshrouded the anger and the pain with determination and loyalty to Global Initiative. Only a stellar career would grant him access to the House of Kaz.

Then the unexpected happened.

It was 209 OGI. Vincallous was twenty-five cycles old, still dreaming and recalling his days of playing Zorschwin with his community. He had been under the authority of Old Flint for six cycles and given his first command in the northern country of Phmquedria. Miska Kea was disrupting the lumber plants, and Fierce was ordered to reinforce four plants.

The assignment was not that noteworthy per se, but neither was the moment he was drawn into Qeauríyx's spin. While sitting in his tent that fateful night, Vincallous became dizzy, unaware that he had tapped into the planet's spin and orbit around the sun. An extreme sense of vertigo beset him, and he could neither stand nor speak. Falling to the ground, he closed his eyes and focused. That was when Dénque,[4] his earthen Elemental, spoke to him. His element of vibration, Wanesé,[5] emerged within him two weeks later. At first, Vicious believed that no mediator instigated his encounter with his Elemental, until he realized Qeauríyx itself took the initiative.

Brazenly revealing his powers would only grant him death, for the House of Kaz would have no competitor. As an unawakened Sczyphamek, Vincallous was easy prey for the General Maximum or Commandant Feolenz. White Scythe had already dispatched Sczyphameks in previous cycles. And Feolenz's skills as a swordsman were indescribable. Even to the present day, Vincallous believed that he had not seen the true measure of Blue Rapier's power. So as a neophyte Sczyphamek, he needed time to train and Awaken his powers. But he was an enlisted man and could not terminate his tour of duty. Leaving the military would make his plans for revenge almost impossible.

Vincallous did not wish to kill the leaders of Global Initiative lengths away by simply causing their palace to crumble with them inside. No, he required a personal relationship with their demise. He wanted them to know who the avenger was and from whence he emerged.

He trained covertly for five cycles, even though it normally took a Sczyphamek one to two cycles to Awaken. Yet because he could not train while on duty, Vincallous endured slow progression. Using every moment he was away from service, he would travel to uninhabited locales to pray, chant, and train. His mental resolve grew, and both Elementals understood his secrecy and complied. All parties comprising Sczyphamek Vicious related to each other quite well. The elements knew his plan of retribution and gave their blessing. They were just as aggressive, coldly ration, and complex as Fénüra, which made for a cataclysmic combination.

He was thirty when he Awakened and was four durations shy of transferring into the ranks of White Scythe, in order to serve as a

---

[4] Dénque (de*h*n-k[w]eh)
[5] Wanesé (wah-nis-*ey*)

Secondary in the imperial chamber. Vincallous was close to achieving his goal. As a master tactician, he recognized that his faith and practice were not at the level required for his plans of revenge. Although he was versed in the history of Sczyphameks, Vicious gave little thought to the three Sczyphamek factions. In truth, he did not care for any of them.

He only cared about the ache and the game.

And he was so deliberate now that patience was not an obstacle to be overcome, but his greatest ally. Yet, nine durations after Vincallous' Awakening, he perceived the Awakening of another Sczyphamek, much to his stupefaction. Vincallous wondered if the new Sczyphamek happened as a Benevolent, Apathetic, or Malevolent?

If the Sczyphamek decided to fight for justice or was neutral, then Vincallous would consider it a blessing. And even if the Sczyphamek was Malevolent, that did not mean this person was aligned with Global Initiative. However, there was a worst-case scenario. And Vincallous had to think of the worst-case scenario. The newly Awakened Sczyphamek might be a loyal agent of Global Initiative. Therefore, for four more cycles, he continued to train covertly and develop his powers until they became potent and awesome. Refusing to rest on any achievement, Vicious strived to new Elemental heights. During that span of time, he never gave himself the opportunity to believe that he was strong enough to take on the General Maximum, Commandant Feolenz, Isürus Tekil, the imperial guard, and perhaps a Sczyphamek.

Vincallous became a decorated soldier in White Scythe. He amassed medals of honor and much recognition. His skills as a Secondary were undeniable. He personally led the attack on the Windward Isles in the spring of 218 OGI, which all but eradicated the insurrection without a single death on White Scythe's side. As a result of such an astounding feat, Vincallous was informed that he would be given the prestigious Medal of Kaz.

The son of Nosgüth had kept his past secret for twenty-one cycles. He had gained many friends and comrades while serving in Global Initiative and even found himself somewhat enamored at the aims of Tannódin. He made a life for himself and was respected and feared among his peers. Nonetheless, his chance had come and he would not be deterred.

The ache exerted its rightful place in his life again.

It was time to play Zorschwin.

Vincallous Fierce was summoned to Megaphyx Bonicin,[6] on Civix Setrin, Tannódin, during the summer of 218 OGI. It was the first time he set foot on the continent. The imperial palace was located in the heart of the hallowed city. Since Vincallous was receiving the highest honor of military service, every leader from the military branches would be there, so

---

[6] Megaphyx Bonicin (meg-uh-fiks boh-nahy-sin)

would the most elite members of the House of Kaz's imperial guard. Vicious and his Elemental, "Dé'wa," as they liked to be called, had waited long enough. He believed that he was capable of killing all who stood in his way to achieve his goal. The flag and the tooth were at his fingertips.

The brilliance of the moons jostled Vincallous out of his remembrance. Although night reigned, the stars and moons gave the atmosphere a transparency that revealed the Firmament. The Sczyphamek surveyed the Fire Fields. The smoke from the volcanoes had subsided and nearly dissipated. Lying on his back, he gazed towards the sky and hummed a tune that was quite moving. His sonic element also granted him remarkable pitch control.

With a morose demeanor, he laughed. "Qeauríyx, you are a strange place, bending the rules of fate and chance to suit your own ends."

He knew that truism more than anyone. Qeauríyx taught him that lesson the day he was awarded the Medal of Kaz, the day he was *supposed* to obtain his revenge.

While walking in the imperial procession, moments before obtaining his medal and his reprisal, Vicious sensed something foreseen yet theoretically improbable: the other Sczyphamek. He could tell by the residual aura that the Sczyphamek had Awakened. His Elemental became agitated. He tried to discern the Sczyphamek's identity, but the crowd was so great that he was unable to locate the other Sczyphamek's position with any precision.

One thing was certain. The other Sczyphamek knew he was also an Elemental warrior.

This unknown person had to be closely allied to the House of Kaz. It was no mere coincidence his or her presence was felt in the imperial palace. Vicious had been on every other continent in Qeauríyx, with every military branch, and never sensed the other Sczyphamek.

Vincallous Fierce was an excellent strategist. He could not ascertain the Sczyphamek's identity or the extent of their power. After all, he or she might have been stronger than him. It was foolhardy to attack without knowledge of his potential foe.

He choked his ego, the game, and the ache down, and let the emperor and empress of the House of Kaz pin the medal on his chest (while he imagined impaling theirs). Somehow, he managed a smile of thanks and respect.

It was only a matter of time before his Elemental kindred confronted him. The moment came sooner than he wished. That very night, while staying in the imperial palace as an "honored" guest, he felt a concealed aura approaching his bedchamber from the outside. The Sczyphamek's speed was phenomenal.

Vincallous readied Dé'wa for the oncoming meeting. He sat up in the bed, knowing that it was only a matter of seconds before he was to meet his potential adversary.

"You know I am out here," a voice said outside his window. It was a woman. "I am coming in. I hope you are dressed."

The lady entered charmingly through his open window. The lights were dimmed. He just made out her silhouette, but he sensed her Elemental. She was powerful and completely veiled with a hood over her head and a black cloak that covered her entire body.

"I imagine your surprise was as great as mine, Vincallous." The beleaguered man was struck by her calm and sweet enunciation. "*Vincallous Fierce*. Heheheh… That cannot be your real name."

"You have me at a disadvantage," the Damüdan said while plotting various attacks in his mind. *Ignore her voice, Van.* "You know my identity, but I do not even know your name."

The woman removed the hood from her head and stepped into the light. She looked familiar and was lovelier than anything Vincallous could imagine. He did not know how or why, but he was instantly attracted to her. This feeling intrigued and scared him. Vincallous was a virgin, primarily because he cared little for anyone who might complicate his plans. Though he had many acquaintances, he only let himself get close to two of them. But something about this woman made his guard drop slightly. Was it because they were both Sczyphameks? No, it was more than that. Behind Fierce's iron grimace were sweaty palms and nervousness.

Her maroon eyes reflected elegance and care, and she looked upon the man with an amicable gaze. "What is your title?"

"My title?"

"Yes. I happened as Pre-Eminent."

Vincallous paused. One's title signified much. It was given to a Sczyphamek; the host did not create the name. She was so direct. What was her game?

"You do not wish to answer?"

"It's not that, ah. You asked for my title. Again, I do not even know your birth name."

"You do not know my birth name? I find that hard to believe, Vincallous." She had not looked away from his eyes yet. "Tell me, what is your title?"

"I happened as Vicious."

"*Vicious?* That is a foreboding name."

"And 'Pre-Eminent' is supposed to be a sign of meekness? I think not." *I must seize control of this situation.* "And besides, those names are only half of our happening."

Pre-Eminent stepped forward and ran her fingers through her dark brown hair. "What faction do you belong to?" Her smile was sincere, but her eyes were ready for battle. She was asking if he was a Benevolent, Apathetic, or Malevolent Sczyphamek.

Vincallous shook his head. "Faction, ah? That's a trick question. I don't belong to any faction. I happened as a Sczyphamek. I do not believe in the factions of the past. Not to mention, there are not enough Sczyphameks to speak of factions."

"I cannot feel your emotions." Her face was a mixture of puzzlement, intrigue, frustration, and admiration. "Amazing. I have no way of determining the truth of your answers."

"Your Elemental…"

"Is tripartite, unlike yours," she finished his sentence. "I sense two elements within you."

How did the woman discern the composition of his Elemental? He did not have that ability, but the fact that she was unable to use her empathic abilities was advantageous to Vicious, for that put them on a potentially equal footing.

"Once again," he replied respectfully, "you have me at a disadvantage. I am sure I have seen you before, ah. Are you going to reveal your identity or not?"

"You *really* do not know who I am?" She stuck her head out in playful irritation. "Are you serious?"

"I would not have asked you if I did not," he responded with a smirk. "*Really.*"

"You received the Medal of Kaz from my parents and do not recognize me?"

"No…" Vicious muttered. His heart forebodingly wrenched. Qeauríyx could not be that unkind.

"My name is Késhal. I am the daughter of Emperor and Empress Kaz."

The Damüdan did not flinch. "So will you tell your parents and the Daknín about my true identity? I've worked hard to keep the secret because I happened as a soldier more than a Sczyphamek. This ceremony is proof enough of that." He had to press her; they were past the point of no return and the element of surprise was no longer on his side.

Késhal sat down in a chair only two clips from Vincallous. "Do not worry. I will not say a word." She leaned over and was face to face with the Damüdan. Her eyes were not seductive or predatory; they were confident and *lonely*. A sliver of her aura emanated and her maroon eyes became teal. "Plus, I am stronger than you anyway. *Much* stronger."

Her Elemental was suffocating and crushing.

For the first time in cycles, Vincallous felt true fear. But he had no desire to fight or fly. Though more powerful than he, she was a sheltered novice. Her admission of her stature said as much. Those who had direct experience of battle never showed their full hand until absolutely necessary.

"Ah. Stronger…" Vicious snickered. "Strength is relative."

Késhal was surprised by his answer. She pulled back her aura and away from Fierce. Her eyes softened. "Strength is relative? What about attraction? I do not need my empathic abilities to sense how you feel. You like what you see."

I hate what I see, Vincallous thought. *And I love what I see. Kímaz Qeauríyx.* The Damüdan smiled and his gray eyes sparkled in the night. "I'm not the only one staring, Késhal. And I do not need empathic abilities to see that you are lonely." *You know nothing of true loneliness.* "As a fellow Sczyphamek, I understand. But based on your lineage, I can only assume that you have had even less friends than I."

Késhal blushed and leaned back in the chair. She bit her lip and folded her arms. "I suppose misery loves company."

You know nothing of misery, wench. "I suppose so." *This is the most beautiful woman I have encountered in all my cycles. Staxis...* Vincallous smiled. "But company can provide other, more pleasurable alternatives to misery." *Have I lost my kímaz mind?*

Késhal laughed. "Kíma! You are bold."

"No bolder than a woman breaking into a half-naked man's room in the middle of the night to confront him about his identity on the most important day of his professional career. Ah?"

Pre-Eminent blushed redder than before and stood up. "I must go. We will speak again. Farewell." And just as suddenly as she entered, she left. But a deposit remained.

Before Vincallous righted himself, he had already forgotten some of the rules of Zorschwin. And for some reason, the ache for revenge seemed more distant than usual. That night, he dreamed of making love to Késhal on a steep hill. They were wrapped in a large flag while they had sex. The next morning he woke up, erect and with a dry mouth and sweaty palms.

***

There was nothing worse on Qeauríyx than a wandering Sczyphamek. They were living incarnations of the Great Drift.

Every insect and small animal hid from his aura. The planet gave them warning. The elder evergreens denied him their luster. Their radiant leaves turned mysteriously gray and casted an eerie shadow over him. The atmosphere was veiled around him. At night, he beheld no stars in the heavens. Even the blades of grass attempted to move out of his path. Anámn drank water from a river branch, but the taste became bitterer with each swallow. Finally, the river branch retreated from his presence, becoming little more than a trickle.

Anámn paid no attention to these happenings. Training as if possessed, sweat poured from his face. He pushed himself harder, running alongside the river Kamo at speeds far beyond a windhorse in full stride. He was consumed and believed his power had grown astronomically due to his physical displays of aggression.

He deceived himself. He and his Elemental were at unbelievable odds, and Anámn fought with it daily. Although his physical abilities continued to improve, his kinetic powers grew increasingly harder to conjure, yet Matriester neither meditated nor prayed. He only promised himself his father's demise.

He grew quite hungry. All of the large game, which was normally prevalent in the jungle, disappeared, forcing Anámn to hunt further and further away from his campsite.

At night, Anámn's dreams were nightmarish images of planetary struggle. He felt the planet speaking to him, hearing no fewer than six distinct voices at a time. The experience was maddening. His Elemental seemed to be drawn to a particular voice of a particular kinetic signature.

It was only during the nightmares that Anámn felt connected to his Elemental, but he did not understand the voices of the planet, nor their kinetic frequencies. The planet was too erratic. Anámn believed Qeauríyx to be as misbegotten as he was. However, this comparison did not evoke sympathy, only disdain from the son of ju Xaníz. The world was just as much to blame for this gynix as his father.

At least I am going to do something about my problems, Anámn thought.

Two days before his vengeful return to Euhilv, Anámn's spirit was heavy. He found himself accosted by his exchange with Nísyx. Trying to calm his qanín, he chanted and prayed. He did not know why—perhaps because every other method of distraction proved futile. However, his guilt and some unknown weight wore relentlessly on his qanín. He sat down near the river and meditated, hoping to erode the ineffaceable haunting, so he could resume preparation.

Intently, he stared at the river. He perceived the molecules of the water bouncing off each other. His tears became one with the stream. Anámn continued to meditate, and during his fifth consecutive hour of prayer, his Elemental awoke, which allowed his aura to return. The aura was emaciated.

The Sczyphamek became disgusted at his lack of command and power. But angst would lead him nowhere. So he continued to chant and petitioned his Elemental to speak to him. But with an aggression of enigmatic and epic distortion, Qeauríyx ambushed him.

Anámn felt the core of the planet emotionally and kinetically at odds with itself. He was thrust into the Great Drift. Past became irreversibly linked to future and present—in a medium that wrenched life out of Anámn. He felt the energy, the momentums of the great earthquakes of the past. *They were inside him.*

Every tectonic cataclysm reverberated in his consciousness and drew him nearer to the planet. His Elemental, now heavy and dense, crackled and hissed, and the trickling creek grew into rapids. Kinesis was torn asunder by Qeauríyx's internal conflict. He tried pleading with the planet, but suddenly realized that he was speaking in an unknown language: the Ancient Tongue.

"É müz keh... É müz keh fíp Téza má..."[7]

He knew not what he spoke, but the depths of his qanín experienced the historical weight and consequences of his words. So much so, that his estranged Elemental grew even larger. Anámn's clothes rustled; the yarkés careened; various wood chips and rocks lifted off the ground and swirled about his aura.

In the midst of the torturous experience, Anámn glanced at his hands and beheld the power he possessed. A prideful smile etched itself across his face. The planet felt his pride, and for recompense, rewarded Anámn with scorching agony. However, it was not just Qeauríyx; his Elemental was also responsible for his affliction.

The evidence was irrefutable. Anámn was forced to concede that a Sczyphamek's powers were connected to the planet. Elementals were almost pieces of Qeauríyx's personality. Anámn had only incited his Elemental; its blossoming was the planet's doing. His pain increased at this newfound revelation. And at that moment, Anámn realized that he was battling the planet for his Elemental.

While chanting, Anámn focused his will on the pain of his past, believing that he could defeat Qeauríyx with his personal history. Relentless, Qeauríyx shunned his foolish self-centeredness and brandished upon Anámn its own cataclysmic background. Its wretchedness was unsearchable, but its hope was incomparable. Anámn tasted them both. Even though the planet suffered such a tumultuous yesterday, Qeauríyx had not lost hope. Indeed, the planet was neither good nor evil. It happened.

This non-binary truth shattered Anámn's perceptions. He was hurled through time and space and saw images of places, things, and people unseen. Somehow Anámn sensed a connection to them. The onslaught receded, but Anámn did not notice. Something dawdled in the haphazard milieu of time and space, an image he was unable to ascertain. A vision of his mother; she appeared younger and tearful. The time and place of this image escaped him.

As soon as the vision faded into the planet, Anámn Matriester felt a warm darkness approaching. He thought it was his Elemental; however, the anomaly presented itself with only a sliver of its emanation. His aura receding, Anámn scanned the forest. He tried to sense movement, physical or otherwise, but was unable to perceive anything. Yet, something was out there, an undisclosed production of qa,[8] and its own negation. It moved, but remained motionless.

"What in Qalfocx...?" he asked himself, fearfully.

---

[7] É müz keh fíp Téza má (*eh myoos* k[ih] fíp *tey*-zuh mah)

[8] Qa (kah)

Hurriedly, Anámn tried to escape this thing, running at great speeds through the jungle, faster than ever, nearly two lengths per minute. Nevertheless, his haste was matched by antithesis, and the ambience, though it moved even slower, somehow bested his speed and passed him.

Escape was pointless and impossible; so Anámn sat down near the base of a yarké. With clenched fists, he was ready to confront the unknown presence. But the moment he thought it would reach him, it moved away.

Anámn was frightened, but he was ready to battle whatever was there. He could not die until he killed his father. And in his mind, the fact that his Elemental stayed with him and not the planet was confirmation that his course of action was correct.

Exhausted, Anámn rested his head on the trunk of the tree and fell asleep, murmuring to himself about the need for more strength.

Chapter Nine: Nextu

27 Myaíz, 241 OGI

She arrived in Nextu exhausted.

The daughter of Hopha traveled by day, trained by night, and slept only when her body gave out. She felt no portent of doom from the elements after leaving Rydín's company. Therefore, she decided to follow the schedule she set earlier and took a week to augment her abilities and learn new incantations, while traveling towards Nextu. In those eight days, her speed and strength increased threefold. Although flying remained difficult, it was not as excruciating as before. Her Elemental also increased in stature. She was now able to wield her aura in small displays of power without the need to chant. Her fiery Elemental was harder to control than her frigid, and although she still had not completely perfected the ice hemisphere technique, she felt fairly confident about her powers.

Displaying her powers now, however, was forbidden. Nextu was the third largest municipality in Nez Spirita and the roads to Pike Metropolis were sure to be well traveled. Neztríanis planned to meditate and pray every day, in order to increase her faith, practice, and Elemental. Yet, overt training was no longer possible. She hoped her preparation was enough. The first snow was about four to five weeks away, and she would have to move towards Mount Xarkim with haste and precision.

Her face was swathed in dirt. Her clothes needed washing, and her boots were so worn, her feet had no support. Nez's black hair was a tangled web of strands and wood chips, and that was just her physical appearance. Under the surface, every muscle she possessed ached. She felt soreness in places she never knew existed.

The wearied Sczyphamek required a place to recuperate for a few days. Rydín had given so much advice; it was hard to manage it all…

Hafir…

Rydín said he could help her. She needed to find him, without drawing attention to herself. Since Nextu was a large, extensive village—much larger than Hopha—it was routine to see travelers. Neztríanis believed this fact would grant her some much-needed anonymity, as long as she stayed away from the community's center where the elders of the village lived. Though remote, there was a possibility the elders would remember her, and she did not want to involve them.

Since she possessed no firsthand information regarding the path of least detection into Pike Metropolis and to Mt. Xarkim, Neztríanis required some help. The megalopolis was at least 400 lengths from Nextu. According to the stories she gleaned from Nez Spiritan travelers in Hopha, the four roads that connected Nextu and Pike Metropolis were full of military checkpoints and they were well-traveled through much of the day and night. She was not advanced enough in her powers to sustain long periods of flight, and she could not risk being spotted while flying. That would put Nez Spirita on notice that another Sczyphamek had emerged. She had no other recourse except to travel by foot or windhorse. But, she did not know the trails and roads or the best time to travel. If someone could help her avoid Tannódin altogether, that would be advantageous.

However, the fledgling Sczyphamek was vexed. Neztríanis, though cautious, loved her fellow brothers and sisters of Nez Spirita, and she genuinely trusted in them, believing none would ever follow the rule of Tannódin willfully. If Rydín said Hafir could assist her, the young woman from Hopha would not inherently doubt the information. And yet, Rydín advised her that some Nez Spiritans were not her allies. That was hard advice. She had seen her brothers and sisters dispute, even fight one another, but she had not encountered any Nez Spiritan who had love for Tannódin.

Staying near the outskirts of the city, Neztríanis made her way to the northern section of town. Inconspicuously, she asked around for Hafir, and before too long, she learned who he was, where he lived, and even what his favorite meal was at a local restaurant. He was quite popular in Nextu, and most spoke well of him.

She was astounded by the number of Tannódin'é in Nextu. They walked freely and lived peaceably among the Nez Spiritans, and from what Phyxtríalis gathered, there was an imperial armory every two lengths or so within the village. The integrated reality of Nextu required Neztríanis to immediately adjust. Hopha was completely Nez Spiritan. The only Tannódin'é she had seen were those passing by on the railcruiser line. They hardly set foot in Hopha; it was just a stop on the way to Point Sank or Nextu.

With each step and at every turn, Nextu overwhelmed and discombobulated Neztríanis. One could walk through an area comprised of a collection of traditional huts and outhouses, but within a few hundred feet, stone and concrete structures were planted firmly in their midst.

Electricity was wired and running water was granted to the newer buildings, while the huts remained without power and plumbing.

Beyond a shadow of doubt, Nextu was in a period of great transition. Even though clusters of time-honored, Nez Spiritan abodes were still scattered about the village, Neztríanis remembered Nextu had fewer "modern" structures the first time she visited.

The place was unmistakably a hybrid area; however, the signs of change were impossible to miss. Nextu was no longer a village or a part of the Nine Houses of Peace. It had become a great city indebted to Tannódin'é persuasion and technology. Motorized vehicles and paved streets crisscrossed the area, along with those Nez Spiritans who still rode windhorses. Twelve cycles had passed since she last set foot in the city, and to Neztríanis' knowledge, no violent conflict had arisen in Nextu.

Yet, Nextu had fallen. The Nine Houses of Peace were reduced by one. Only Hopha and Hero remained. Who or what was responsible for such a drastic change? If the Great Mother knew of the Auría expedition, she certainly knew that this fate had befallen Nextu. Due to the distance and railcruiser proscription, only the elders of the village and the Great Mother traveled to Nextu, and their travel was once every four years. Somehow, Phesiana and the village elders kept Nextu's fall top-secret. As best she could, the daughter of the Peninsula did her best to hold her tears of sorrow, defeat, and anger back.

While occupied with those thoughts and others, Neztríanis was assaulted by the mundane. She was going to need new clothes. Many Nez Spiritans wore the garb and fashion of Tannódin. She surmised this phenomenon would only increase when she arrived in Pike Metropolis. Unfortunately, Neztríanis was short on money; Phesiana had only given her a few hundred credits.

The sun set and the moons rose. She would not be able to reach the northern section of town that day. She had no choice. Throughout the entire night, the daughter of Hopha kept trudging north. She tried not to think about the obvious implication. Pike Metropolis was at least seven to eight times the size of Nextu. How would she, who possessed little money, traverse the capital city without stopping for food or for rest?

By noon the next day, Neztríanis finally neared the neighborhood where Hafir reportedly lived. She was unsure if she was in the proper location, for it was a neighborhood filled with mansions, recently paved streets, and other structures unknown to the daughter of Hopha.

She could not turn around. She had come too far and was enervated to the point of collapse. Neztríanis staggered towards a large, brown, three-story house, which was made of earthen brick. She felt nervous. Nearing the front door, she became seized with doubt.

Who was she to knock on the door of a stranger? What was she doing? Maybe it would be better if she went about her business and moved on; after all, she knew the general path to Pike. The Nextu Range was plainly visible to her west.

If I follow the base of the mountains, they will lead me to the Infinite Circle. I should just leave, she thought. *But I am so tired.*

"May I help you?" a friendly, sonnet-like voice spoke, as the front door opened.

Neztríanis was so gripped with indecision and exhaustion that she did not feel the heat signature nearing her. She had not knocked on the door and was unready for conversation. But she had to say *something.* "I-uhmm… My name is Mésa, and I am looking for Hafir."

Timid, the young woman did not look at her interlocutor. She knew from the voice that it was a woman.

"Hafir is not here at the moment," she replied.

Neztríanis froze. She did not expect Hafir to be absent.

"Mésa," the voice said. "Are you all right, daughter?"

Hearing the affirmation and inflection in the word "daughter" snapped the *daughter* of Hopha back into normalcy.

"Yes," Neztríanis glanced up at the woman. The Sczyphamek's eyes were heavy with bags underneath. "I am fine…"

"Would you like to come in and wait for him?" the woman asked. She was elderly, about ten cycles older than the Great Mother. Her attire was traditional Nez Spiritan. A tan, one-piece dress ran from her neck to her lower legs, and her grayish black hair was cut medium length so that it fell just by her shoulder blades. Her tawny, russet face was wrinkly, but she was still a lovely woman. In Nez Spirita, elders grew more beautiful through the passage of time.

"Elder, I do not wish to impose," Neztríanis graciously answered.

"Nonsense," the woman countered. "I could use the company, and he should not be too long."

The young Sczyphamek was lethargic and possessed no strength to argue. It was probably best if she took the woman up on her offer. Her thighs and calves were near implosion. Nodding her head, Neztríanis followed the elder inside the home.

She was amazed at the size of the house, its architecture, and furniture. The entryway opened into a large room with a high ceiling. The walls were adorned with various paintings; they appeared to be artistic renditions of many Nez Spiritan cites and holy places.

One, in particular, caught her attention. It was a picture of a mountain—*the mountain*—Sunrise Mountain, the second tallest peak on Qeauríyx, standing over 47,000 feet. It was rendered quite large and snowy. The picture appeared to be drawn from a distance, which was still remarkable. Few even dared to venture towards the rock; most stopped at the Crag Mountains, the "gateway" into the northern, icy wasteland. Supposedly, the temperature was so cold that most would freeze to death in a matter of minutes. Even Tannódin left the area alone. Only a rare person could survive there. That was why her mother told her to take the

Auría to the frozen badlands. Vicious and Pre-Eminent would be unable to endure the cold, but Neztríanis' abilities gave her an edge.

"Hafir painted those," the woman said. "That is his favorite one. The one you are looking at now."

"Hafir journeyed to Sunrise?"

"Just 100 lengths beyond the Crag Mountains," she replied. "He painted that picture during the middle of summer, in the tundra, before the ground turns completely into snow and ice, about four hundred and fifty lengths from the base of the mountain. The day was unusually clear and warm, and the mountain is so immense, you can make out its dimensions, even if you are that far away for it stands alone. Oh, and when I say 'warm,' I meant it was ten degrees below freezing."

Phesiana's daughter was floored by the painting's exquisite detail. She almost tasted the snow. "He is very talented," Nez commented.

The elderly woman smiled. "I try not to boast, but he is my son."

At that point Neztríanis realized she had not asked for the elder's title. "I am sorry. I did not ask your name."

"Namí," she replied.[1]

"Faring well, I pray."

"Yes, I suppose I am, although you must not be from around here. Most young ones from Nextu do not speak like that anymore." The woman sighed with a hint of nostalgia. "Would you like to sit? I was about to make something to eat. Are you hungry?"

The Sczyphamek was about to say "no," when her stomach objected and voiced its case rather loudly. The elder snickered and motioned to Phyxtríalis, inviting her to sit on a large couch, while she went to the kitchen to prepare some food.

Neztríanis was too tired to complain. Upon sitting down on the sofa, she nearly fell asleep. She had not felt anything so cushiony since the morning she woke up in her bed and left Hopha. Sleeping on the ground became so common that she forgot the seduction of tactile softness. She tried to stay awake, but the more she fought sleep, the more it reeled her in. Her head felt heavy. She hoped Namí would be back soon.

Hafir's mother was on cue. "All right. The meal is ready."

The elder prepared smoked luku sandwiches with melted cheese, fresh vegetables, and sauce and a tall glass of cold citrus juice. Neztríanis' drowsiness turned into salivation when she smelled the sandwich. The meat was hot and steaming. Nine *long* days had passed since the young woman consumed hot food.

Namí set the platter down on a table in front of the couch. She handed Neztríanis a washcloth, and the daughter of Hopha cleaned her hands. After which, Namí held out her left hand, and Neztríanis clasped it.

---

[1] Namí (nah-m*ee*)

Namí prayed, "Thank you, O Nameless One, for this food. Let us use the energy we gain to do justice to those living and dead who made this meal possible."

"Fá'atoño má." Neztríanis chanted.

"I hope you are hungry."

"I am."

Neztríanis picked up the sandwich and took a bite. Her eyes closed. She moaned in satisfaction and shook her head in ecstasy. The Sczyphamek savored every morsel. And the juice! Its sweet and sour taste was magnificently balanced. She did not know if it was because she had not eaten a meal like that in days, but Neztríanis did not believe she had partaken in a sandwich or juice that delicious in all her cycles. This was not berries, nuts, dried meat and water.

"Mother Namí," she groaned in satiation. "That was so good. Thank you so much."

The Nez Spiritan elder laughed and nodded. "You are welcome, Mésa."

Neztríanis' yawn came before she could stop it. Her mouth stretched wide again. Embarrassed, she pursed her lips together.

Namí's laugh reemerged. "Are you tired?"

"I suppose I am." Her eyelids felt heavier than ever. The call of sleep was much louder than before. "Perhaps it would be best if I returned some other time. Do you know where I can find some suitable lodging in the area, Mother Namí?"

"Nonsense Mésa," the woman replied. "I told you, Hafir will be here, and if you need to rest a bit, I can show you to one of our guestrooms."

Neztríanis was enamored by the woman's traditional approach to receiving guests. She was obliged to accept such a courteous offer.

"Yes, Elder."

Namí rose from the couch. Neztríanis followed her with every step growing harder to take. The two Nez Spiritan women ascended the stairs, and Namí motioned Neztríanis to a room down the main hallway.

Namí opened the third door on the right. "This is one of our guestrooms. It has a bathroom inside so that you may wash up."

"Thank you. I am very appreciative." Neztríanis bowed her head and entered into the room.

"It is but a small thing to help one's brother or sister, especially when one has the means," Namí replied and rubbed her hand on Nez's dusty back. "I will not disturb you. When you awake, come downstairs, I am sure Hafir will be here by then." At that, the elderly woman shut the door.

The room was large as her entire hut back in Hopha. It seemed ridiculously extravagant to her, but she was impressed by the décor and use of space. Hafir's gift for artistry and design was undeniable.

Unable to sleep in such a soiled condition, Neztríanis made her way to the bathroom. The daughter of Hopha was taken aback by the enormity of the shower. The showers in her village were shared and much more humble in appearance. Running water was a new phenomenon in Hopha, made possible by a group of ingenious villagers. But, Hafir's shower warmed itself, and as she turned the knob to open the water valve, steam immediately formed.

How was such a technological leap possible? Just twelve cycles prior, Phesiana and she visited this same village, staying with prominent families, and not a single household boasted such technology.

She was too tired to think anymore, so she undressed and stepped into the shower. The temperature would have scalded anyone else, but she was immune to its effects, due to a certain white aura. She thoroughly cleaned herself, scrubbing and rinsing away the muck from her body. There was hair cleanser inside the shower, so she washed her hair as well. By the time she was done, her washcloth and the shower's floor were brown from all of the dirt she removed. Neztríanis, vain as she was, felt embarrassed at her slovenly appearance.

Searching through her shoulderpack, Neztríanis dug towards the bottom and found the sleeping attire she wore ten days and seven hundred and fifty lengths prior. When she emerged from the bathroom, she was ready for the bed. She pulled the quilt back and snuggled under the cover. Within seconds, she was somnolent.

***

There were two heat signatures in the house. Neztríanis had no idea how long she was asleep, but the sun was up. When she went to bed, dusk was four hours away, so she clearly slept through the night. Exiting the covers, Neztríanis checked her bag to make sure no one rummaged through it while she slumbered. Apparently Namí or Hafir reentered the room while she was asleep for there was complimentary mouth rinse and a Yarnínga brush for her teeth. Neztríanis brushed her teeth and gargled with the rinse. After she was done, she straightened her hair, pulled it back in a tail, and followed Namí's advice by making her way down to the first floor of the house.

Sound emerged from the kitchen. A man and a woman were talking softly.

"Hello," Neztríanis spoke from the sitting room with reservation.

"Mésa," she heard Namí say, "Come on in here."

Neztríanis moved into the kitchen. There, she saw a tall, slender, yet solid man. He was absolutely striking. His copper skin was of a dark variety, and his black hair was cut short, but its density was thick. He wore a traditional blue shirt with a Yarnínga tree appearing on the front. His brown slacks were like a Tannódin'é, however. His feet were uncovered.

"Hello Mésa," the man said. "My name is Hafir. Faring well, I pray."

Neztríanis, still struck by his good looks, stammered, "H- hello, Hafir, my name is Mésa... which you just said... uhm..."

Hafir and Namí laughed at Nez's awkwardness.

Namí's laugh tapered into a giggle. "Mésa you have been hibernating for eighteen hours. You were very tired. I placed some things in the bathroom last night, and you hardly moved."

"I saw that," she replied. "Thank you, Mother Namí."

"*Mother* Namí?" Hafir asked with surprise. "Mamisí, I know you told me she spoke in such a manner, but I did not believe it." The man smiled and chuckled in appreciation. "Mésa, no one your age uses such pleasantries anymore in Nextu. Where are you from?"

"Point Sank," she lied. "But I have been traveling in the peninsula for many cycles. It has been a long time since I was home."

"What brings you to Nextu?"

Neztríanis looked directly at Hafir and suddenly grew serious. "I was on my way to Pike Metropolis, and I was told that I could arrange travel with you."

Namí and Hafir looked at each other, grunted and nodded.

"A road less traveled, I assume?" Hafir asked.

"That would be my wish," Neztríanis affirmed. "Hafir, I must tell you now. I do not have that many credits, so I will not be able to pay you—"

"Who told you about me?" Hafir interjected with a pleasant trepidation.

Neztríanis paused. She was caught off guard by Hafir's interjection. "I was told by various people in Nextu that you were kind to strangers."

"I do not know what you are talking about, then." He folded his arms, apparently unwilling to help the daughter of Hopha.

Namí nodded. "Mésa, you must trust us if you want us to trust you. I offered you our house, food, and hospitality."

"I know, Mother Namí."

However, Neztríanis was unsure if she should even give them a foot into her quest. But she certainly needed help. They were forcing her hand.

But what if Rydín was captured and tortured? He could have told Tannódin that he met a young Nez Spiritan woman and gave her information about Hafir. In fact, the man before her might not even be Hafir. What if he was captured and replaced by an agent of Tannódin? Informants were one thing, but were there actually Nez Spiritans who actually *worked* for Tannódin?

Namí and Hafir's countenances were unrelenting; they were not going to speak until she spoke. But Rydín had given her instructions; he said that she would not have to tell Hafir anything.

"I cannot say..." She was quiet but resolute. "If that means that I must leave, then I will do so, and compensate you for whatever I have used."

"What?" Namí and Hafir both inquired.

"I will not say..." she repeated, this time louder and firmer.

Namí slammed her hand on the counter in irritation. "That is your answer after we have extended our home to you?"

"Yes."

"Rydín's description of her was very accurate. He told us that she appeared to be quite resolute and serious, Mamisí," Hafir stated nonchalantly. "Do not be too angry with her."

Neztríanis tried not to seem astonished, but her eyes gave her away.

"You did meet Rydín," Hafir continued, "did you not?"

Neztríanis said nothing. Her mind raced for an answer and an escape.

"'How do I know these are not Tannódin'é agents posing as Hafir and his mother?'" the artist stated with a friendly smile. "That is what you are asking yourself."

Hafir took a sip of some hot tea and added some sweetener. "Mésa, let Namí and me tell you a secret: When Tannódin comes, they come as a force that gives one no possibility of escape. Meeting Rydín and the escapees of Lozé should have taught you this lesson.

"The conversation we are having means that I know about your encounter with Rydín. But that would also mean that I know you are a potential threat to Tannódin. This line of questioning has put us past the point of no return. I am not prodding you for information; I am calling you out. And again, when Tannódin calls for you, you *will* know. Of course, you may be a Global Initiative agent, yourself, trying to get me to talk…" Hafir took another sip from his cup and laughed. "Mésa, you should see the look on your face…"

Namí burst into laughter. Neztríanis' mouth was wide open and her face was blank, yet nervous.

Acknowledging her blown cover, Neztríanis relinquished, but resolved that if either of them made any suspect movements, she would have to incapacitate them. "I met Rydín nine days ago in Hero's Valley, with a company of about twenty. He was fleeing White Scythe. I helped tend their wounded. After telling him that I was on my way to Pike Metropolis, Rydín told me to see you, but that I should not mention to you that I met him."

"And normally, I would not ask, but things have changed just in this past week. We had to be sure that you were trustworthy; so, I am glad you maintained the lie. Rydín has made it to Hopha and sent word through recondite means that he met you. But I just learned that I have been placed under surveillance by Tannódin, and I cannot afford to take any more chances for awhile."

"How do you know this?" Neztríanis inquired.

"We have 'friends' in many locations," Namí explained, took her hand out of her blouse, and revealed a large knife, no doubt meant for Neztríanis if she had not lied to them. "I did not suspect your sincerity from the moment I met you, but Tannódin is extremely cunning. They have used our own to spy on us on a few occasions."

That was the same thing that Rydín said to Neztríanis, and one of the reasons the Sczyphamek was reluctant to trust Namí and Hafir.

"Mésa," Hafir's face, tone, and body emanated a grave seriousness. "For your safety and for ours, you must stay here for quite some time. If you leave this house after a few days, Tannódin will become suspicious and probably follow you to Pike Metropolis and place us under greater watch."

Neztríanis scowled. This was exactly what she was afraid of. The more she involved other people, the greater the attention she would draw to herself.

Hafir let the woman grunt her displeasure, but remained steadfast in his countenance. "I know a trader named Jennó.[2] He is a traveling merchant from Northern Bitzroy who does a few 'favors' for me. He is due here in three weeks. It will be his last run before the winter snows commence, when the roads become completely impassable. I am sure he will be able to guide you into the city with the least amount of imperial interference."

"Three weeks!" Neztríanis exclaimed. "Kíma... Are you sure? Is there no other way? What will I do for three weeks?"

"You will get to know Nextu," he answered with a charming smile. "The ever-evolving Nextu. Namí and I will be your chaperones. You are our distant cousin from Point Sank, and your name is Mésa. We would not want you to lie twice about your name," he laughed.

"Staxis," she cursed. "How did you..."

"We are masters of living double lives," Namí said, moving towards the stove. "Cousin, would you like some breakfast?"

∗∗∗

And so for the next twenty-three days Neztríanis lived with Namí and Hafir. Though Hafir was only in his mid-forties, he was a prominent man in Nextu. Actually, he was one of the most important persons in the town. He was responsible for the architecture and the building of new structures in the village-that-was-also-a-city. This task was assigned to him by the elders of Nextu and by a Tannódin'é diplomatic group.

The sight was unimaginable to Neztríanis: Tannódin'é and Nez Spiritans working together. But what was once cringe-inducing fantasy was now reality. In fact, Hafir was a Nez Spiritan who sought Tannódin'é help and technology in order to rebuild and "modernize" the city.

His status and activities perturbed Neztríanis. Some days she felt that he was a traitor who sold the inheritance of the Nine Houses of Peace to the House of Kaz, a house of war and destruction. On other days, she remembered her own doubts concerning Nez Spiritan resistance and how isolated she felt Hopha had become due to the non-aggression pact. Each morning, she tried to give Hafir the benefit of the doubt.

However, one day, during her second week in Nextu, while visiting a construction site, Neztríanis lost her wits. She observed her fellow brothers

---

[2] Jennó (jin-*oh*)

and sisters creating structures that were *Tannódin'é* in origin, *Tannódin'é* in design, and for *Tannódin'é* and Nez Spiritan use. Then, to make matters worse, she walked into Hafir's construction site office, and he was talking to a *Tannódin'é* foreman.

"Cousin," she said with great agitation, "I must speak with you… *Now.*"

The foreman glared at Neztríanis and then looked at Hafir in confusion.

"Can you excuse us for a moment?" he asked the Tannódin'é.

The foreman took his leave and closed the door behind him. The architect sighed and glanced at his guest in frustration. Hammers and saws banged and buzzed in the background. The concrete mixing tanks whirred and boomed. Neztríanis perceived a blacksmith's blowtorch welding two slabs of metal together. Indeed, sparks were flying, but they were not in the genus of passionate affection.

Hafir put down a sheet of paper, which revealed the structure's finished design. Judging from the sketches, it would be a four-story building, with a sculpture of a Yarnínga tree in the front. Looking down at the paper, and then back at Hafir, Neztríanis scowled. Nextu was so baffling.

"Mésa, I do not have to tell you that you are *my guest.*"

Neztríanis was calm yet firm. "Cousin, I apologize. However, I cannot remain silent much longer."

Hafir realized that she was deeply troubled and signaled her to take a seat. From the moment he met her, he knew this day was inevitable. "We will not have this conversation here if you cannot control yourself."

Neztríanis remained standing with her arms crossed, but when she saw that Hafir was unwilling to talk unless she completely calmed herself, she sat down.

The Sczyphamek tried to hold her peace, but the dam of patience and merciful understanding cracked and split under the pressure of history and exploitation. As a descendant of Hopha, the Third House of Peace, Neztríanis considered herself to be a Nez Spiritan Kylanín, a Sczyphamek of justice and peace. She could not accept Nextu's path for Nez Spirita or Qeauríyx.

"How can you work with *them* after what they did to us?" she murmured.

"I ask myself that question every day. I never stop asking that question."

"Then why?"

Hafir stood up and looked out of a window in the front of his makeshift office. "Mésa, come over here, and let me show you something."

Neztríanis complied and examined the construction site and workers outside the window.

"Six cycles ago, this plot of land was a large shantytown full of poverty and misery. In fact, even prior to that, the entire village was in a state of distress. The elders of our village were unable to maintain our way of life with any kind of efficiency." He glanced at her with knowing eyes. "It is not just I who has said this, even the elders would agree.

"Lozé had begun to give the House of Kaz more problems than they would admit. And because of the sanctions, embargoes, and constant military clashes in and around Lozé, a refugee crisis emerged.

"Most people from Lozé fled to Pike Metropolis, but about twenty thousand made their way to Nextu. At the time of their arrival, Nextu was already in decline. People were leaving here to go to Pike as well, because there was no work or barter. And our crops were completely ruined. Surely, you remember the summer and winter nine cycles ago."

"How could any Nez Spiritan forget?" Neztríanis replied. "It was said that a cycle had not happened like that in many spans... A severe drought in the spring, summer, and fall, a paralyzing cold in the winter, followed by no rain the next spring and summer."

"Yes." Hafir agreed. "And because it came without warning, we lost over half of our crops before winter arrived. In a word, the situation was desperate." Through the window, he gazed upon the sun and then at Neztríanis. His face was quite melancholy. "Because of those conditions, combined with Nextu's population, a terrible woe dispersed amongst our people. Over eighty percent of our population became malnourished and lived in extreme poverty. The elders of the village were ill-equipped to handle such a catastrophe, and to be fair, most leaders would have crumbled just as they did."

Neztríanis recalled the extreme duress Hopha befell during that same period. Many starved, but the situation was not as dire because their population was not the size of Nextu, nor did many folk immigrate to their village. But there were too many days where Neztríanis did not eat. She remembered that particular hunger, sickness, and death all too well.

"The next cycle, in the middle of summer, a Tannódin'é envoy arrived here with little fanfare and with little weaponry. As you can imagine, we were distrustful at first. But we soon learned that Pre-Eminent had allocated resources to rehabilitate areas of Nez Spirita that were destroyed during the Solemn War and the drought."

"*You must be kidding.*" Neztríanis was taken aback. The Great Mother must have withheld that information from Neztríanis—not because Phesiana took the foreign aid in secret but because Hopha would have never considered such a bribe. Resisting Global Initiative was a right bestowed upon all indigenous Nez Spiritans. The Sczyphamek scowled and voiced her musings. "Nez Spiritans I know would rather die than accept assistance from Tannódin."

"*Die?* We had died. We were already dying. We are dying today. And what will be left of us if this continues?" Hafir pressed Neztríanis to bear the weight of his questions. "What will Nextu be if there are no more Nez Spiritans here? If the Great Drift taught us anything, it was survival. Is this any different? What are we to do when great change will not occur in our lifetime? What are we to do in the meantime? Do you have an answer?"

Neztríanis did not know how to respond to the man who clearly wrestled and continued to wrestle with those questions.

"The elders *were* against any assistance at first, but as the cycle drew on, the famine reached extreme proportions. We asked for aid from the surrounding villages, from the mainland to the peninsula, and they gave what they could, but in the end, their aid was insufficient. Of course the aid was insufficient; times were hard for those populations too.

"Our children and elderly died, while the adults watched on. My mother grew very ill, and I lost my father. He was quite a man..." His voice trailed off in wistful remembrance. "Yes, those times were more than hard.

"I, along with a few others, petitioned our remaining elders to change their hearts regarding Tannódin'é aid.

"They did. Within weeks, we drew up a proposal with Tannódin, which ensured our rights and status, as well as our land and governmental structure. Surprisingly, they agreed, with one condition: they wanted to place a contingent of Blue Rapier soldiers in the area, for they anticipated reprisals from Miska Kea. We agreed; that is why you see the small military installations every two lengths or so throughout the city."

Neztríanis nodded. Somehow she was able to understand Tannódin's concern, although she believed they had ulterior motives. "That is all?" she asked. "That is all they wanted? Surely they were concealing something."

"They were and are even to this day," he said. "Many of us know that. But at the same time, we have accomplished so much. Within two cycles of their assistance we were blessed with a surplus crop cycle. Through the use of refrigeration technology, we have been able to store our food for longer periods of time. We are building housing units that will give our homeless a roof over their heads. The elders still make the decisions, along with various civic committees—"

"Then why are you helping me and others like me," she pressed, referring to Rydín's company. "And why are you under surveillance?"

"Because I do not trust them," he stated matter-of-factly. "My father was a brilliant artist, although formally, he was an arbitrator for village disputes. He taught me a most valuable lesson in life. And it is this: those who are keen and powerful only play their full hand when absolutely necessary. Anyone in league with such people must always remember this. It is the desperate or ignorant who normally become extremists."

Neztríanis shook her head. "You are playing a deadly game. I pray nothing will happen to you."

"Something will happen to me." His eyebrows furrowed and his eyes hardened. His fate was certain, but he would resist. "I just have to have the foresight to anticipate it."

He turned and faced Neztríanis with a radiant smile, and she blushed. He was remarkably handsome. "You see this room?" he asked. "This room had a recording device placed in it just last week by Tannódin."

"Then why are we—"

"I confronted them about it. I went to the regional head of Tannódin'é affairs, threw the device at him, and verbally berated him."

Neztríanis was shocked.

"Of course, the regional director knew about the device. He probably gave the order to have it placed here." He smirked. "But he denied it that day, and I knew he was lying. Just like he knew he had ample reason to place me under surveillance. But, I put them on notice that day, that I was no fool, and that I was a valuable asset worth keeping around." Fidgeting in his pocket, he pulled out a small device.

"What is that?" Neztríanis asked.

"Have you seen a microphone before?" he asked.

"Uhmm… no."

"It is a voice amplifier that allows a person's voice to be heard and recorded from far away distances, and it picks up the smallest of sound."

"I see," she said. "It is a smaller version of a megaphone?"

"Something like that. Very simply, this device can detect a microphone or any other surveillance device."

"How did you obtain that?" she asked.

"I have some friends in this world who love liberation," he said, clearly playing on the word "Miskanyx," which in the Ancient Tongue meant "to release," "liberate," or "save." He was speaking about Miska Kea.

"Staxis," Neztríanis cursed with admiration and in fear for her interlocutor. "Hafir… Why are you telling me this?"

His response was without hesitation. "Because Mésa, *they will kill you too.* After all, who helps escapees from Lozé? I do not know your intentions, but from the moment Namí and I met you and received word from Rydín, we knew that you were a danger to Tannódin, and if they knew who you were and where you were, they would question, torture, and then kill you."

Neztríanis was jarred by his words. They were harsh and discomforting, yet true.

"Now cousin," he stated amicably, "I have to get back to work. Some of my brothers and sisters need some housing right now, and I need Tannódin'é help to make that housing a reality."

***

"Fá'atoño má. Fá'atoño má. Zí mányx que rai. Mona fla renzgé ná. Fá'atoño má," the Sczyphamek chanted and sang in her room quietly. Although she participated in home and communal worship services with Namí and Hafir, she did not utter her Elemental incantations around her new friends. Though difficult to tell, she felt like her relationship with her Elemental had grown. However, she had not conjured a visible expression of her powers in nearly three weeks.

"Mésa!" Namí called out from downstairs. "It is time for dinner."

"I am going to miss these meals," Neztríanis whispered to her elements. It was the last day of her stay with the mother and son. Jennó, the traveling merchant, would be by Hafir's residence around midnight, in order to lead Neztríanis safely to Pike Metropolis.

"I am coming," Neztríanis called back. The woman galloped down the steps and smelled the most heavenly aroma Qeauríyx ever produced.

"Mother Namí, I will miss your cooking. You are, by far, the best cook I know." She lovingly hugged the woman who had become a second mother to her. She and Namí wove quilts together, visited the sick, prayed together, and Namí even let Neztríanis handle some of the household's business matters. Namí was a dying breed of Nez Spiritan within the city of Nextu.

In turn, Namí kissed the daughter of Hopha on the cheek. "You are always welcome here, daughter."

"Did you hear what *our* mother said, Hafir?" Neztríanis said playfully to the artist who was drawing a portrait of a Yarnínga tree. "I am always welcome here."

Hafir put his pencil down and chuckled. "I heard what she said, but that does not mean I like it or you."

Laughter erupted within their midst.

"I am going to miss you both very much," Neztríanis said. "Thank you for everything. I hope I did not cause too much trouble."

"You? Cause trouble...?" Hafir asked in a lighthearted, accusatory tone. "Not yet..."

Namí moved to the table. "Let us say a prayer before my daughter takes her leave."

Neztríanis became choked with emotion and almost cried. All three sat down, around a most delicious spread of culinary genius. Though they entertained guests during her stay, the Sczyphamek was awestruck that Namí prepared so much food for so few people.

"O Nameless One," the elder prayed. "Protect our friend on her journey ahead. Guide her and keep her in your presence. Help us, we pray. We pray for those at the battle of Focal who were slain and for those who survived. Be with the peninsula of Anzél; strengthen those in Líachim; and inspire Nez Spirita. Empower us all to do your work. Fá'atoño má."

"Fá'atoño má," Hafir and Nez responded.

It was quiet for a few minutes, as food was passed around the table. Neztríanis bit into a roll that had the taste of rapture baked into its most inward parts. The taste nearly made her forget the news.

"I still cannot believe the reports," the daughter muttered. "The numbers seem inflated."

"My sources tell me that there were originally forty-five thousand who participated in the battle. Twenty thousand Anmetrians and twenty-five thousand Focalites. By the time Pre-Eminent arrived most had either fled or perished in the conflict. But about fifteen thousand were still present."

"Pre-Eminent could not have been so ruthless as to kill ten thousand." Neztríanis spoke.

"She is a Sczyphamek, Mésa," Namí answered nonchalantly. "Killing is easy for them, whether it is one person or thousands. Do not forget about Phenplyacin."

Neztríanis was taken aback, feeling insulted, but she remained quiet. They did not know her true identity.

"She is a *Zananín*,[3] Mamí," Hafir corrected. "Kylanín Sczyphameks would never do such a thing."

"Whatever you say," the sagacious old woman muttered.

"The newsprints reported that she was making her way to the city of Aphaz to seek a peaceful resolution with its leader." Neztríanis tried to steer the conversation in another direction.

Hafir looked at his plate blankly. "She has already made her intentions clear. Most of that story was propaganda. Pre-Eminent used that battle as a warning to Aphaz..." Hafir put his fork down and sighed. "If Líachim falls, it is all over. All of Qeauríyx will fall under the House of Kaz's control." Distraught and angered, the man beat his hand on the table, which caused the plates to shake and the glassware to career. "What am I doing? How can I work with them?"

"You made an imperfect decision in an imperfect world," his mother stated plainly. "What more can any of us do?"

Once again the dinner table became mum. Neztríanis ate her food slowly and thought of many things.

"Will the One with No Name not send us any help? Will Qeauríyx abandon its own people?" Hafir asked in exasperation.

"Do not worry," Namí said before Neztríanis could respond. "This too will fall and pass, just as the Drift. The First Sczyphamek taught us that."

"You are correct, Mother Namí," Neztríanis joined in. "The First gave us a chance to live differently."

"Maybe." Namí stopped in mid-thought in order to pace her response. "But I sometimes wonder about her motivations..."

Hafir grew suddenly and conspicuously annoyed. "*Mamí*, please, not again. Not tonight."

"I just think that we should not assume that our interpretation of her intentions is completely correct."

Neztríanis injected herself within the discussion with interest and veiled disdain. "Are you saying that she was selfish in doing what she did? That is blasphemous, Mother Namí. She sacrificed herself so that we could live."

"Sacrifice does not necessarily lead to obedience. We have a tendency to valorize sacrifice at the expense of understanding," she barbed. "Nor is sacrifice always central in any story. It may be a piece, but it is not everything. One can sacrifice for a cause that is wrong."

---

[3] Zananín (tzahn-nuh-n*ee*n)

Namí paused, as the man and woman frowned at her. "And both of you were not listening to me, anyway. I said we should not assume our *interpretations* of the Great Extinguishing are completely right. Not that the First did not try to accomplish something for our good. But, it remains to be seen if her death proved anything except revealing her own power and the power it was derived from.

"I am only wondering what the effect has been on us. And that is still a lingering question that has not been answered. After all, by stopping the Drift, Global Initiative became a possibility. Is this worse than the Drift? I do not know…" Namí stared at the ceiling and then at her half-finished plate. "May the Nameless One forgive me if I have misspoken, but that is how it appears to me."

Neztríanis was perturbed by Namí's comments, but she did not want to appear ungrateful for all that she and Hafir had done for her. Namí was an elder of great faith, but her reflections departed from the teachings Neztríanis believed to be true. It was another addition to the list of mystification and paradox found in Nextu.

"Mésa," Namí said, in a different, less rigid tone. "I have something for you." The elder got up from her chair and went into the kitchen.

"And I have something as well," Hafir smiled, leaving to go to his study.

Neztríanis was silent; she did not expect any more hospitality. And their friendliness was not out of fear or obligation. It was out of love. Neztríanis resolved in her heart to show her loving appreciation by completing the task given to her by the Nameless One. Both of them returned to the dining room, with their hands behind their backs.

Namí was first. "Neztríanis, you will be traveling for some time, and I thought that you may need something larger than your water jug so I purchased this windhorse hide water container."

Namí handed her guest the present. The hide was dark brown, and it was smooth to the touch. It was larger than her original jug, capable of filling twice the amount of water. It also had a long, padded strap that was meant to strafe her torso.

Namí continued, "I have seen your shoulderpack. If you can carry what is already in there, you certainly will be able to manage the weight of this canteen even if it is filled to the brim."

Before Neztríanis could thank Namí, Hafir spoke up. "Mésa, you are heading to Pike Metropolis, and you cannot be seen wearing such attire. Most in the city do not dress as you or my mother do. So, I purchased you a new outfit to wear."

"What?" Neztríanis was incredulous. "You… you did?"

He brought his hands forward, revealing new clothes. The clothes were semi-traditional, yet also displayed a more modern, Tannódin'é fashion sense. At first glance, she noticed the dark brown boots and matching socks. She was in desperate need of new footwear.

Hafir was also holding brown slacks that were thick and heavy. They would protect her from the oncoming winter. The medium-length jacket matched the pants perfectly. Hafir then handed Neztríanis a gray, long-sleeved, shirt with a picture of a Yarnínga tree on the back. The tree was a representation of Hafir's design. There was also a white undershirt, which appeared rather small for Neztríanis liking.

"I do not know what to say…"

"How about, 'I want to try this on, right now'?" Hafir laughed.

"I want to try this on, right now," Neztríanis said playfully.

"I guessed your measurements, but I think I was correct."

Neztríanis entered the downstairs bathroom, in order to change clothes. Hafir and Namí smiled at one another, waiting for her to come out.

With her old clothes tucked under her arm, Neztríanis emerged from the bathroom radiant and beautiful. Her new boots were a dream to wear. The soles were so soft and gave great support. The pants were a bit tight, in most places, which was a new feel for Neztríanis. It accentuated her legs and derriere, but did not exploit them, still allowing for a full range of motion. The shirt was a bit loose, but the undershirt was small, keeping her breasts close to her body. Although she did not give much thought to it at first, on second examination, she realized the advantage of the undershirt, for it would aid her in nimble movements. The jacket was lighter than she expected, but the material had the potential for storing and maintaining a body's warmth. These were not parting gifts for a quick trip; these were clothes and a water container for someone on a long, arduous odyssey in the middle of a Nez Spiritan winter.

How did they know?

Perhaps they did not know everything about her journey, or even who she was. But true to themselves, Hafir and Namí realized Neztríanis had a need for something and they supplied it.

Her tears fell with little reservation. "Mother Namí, Hafir… Thank you. You have been so wonderful to me, and I extend my heart and gratitude to both of you."

"Remember what I told you, the day we first met, three weeks ago?"

"Yes, Mother Namí. You said, 'It is but a small thing to help one's brother or sister, especially when one has the means,'" Neztríanis replied, touched by their kind gestures. "Hafir, Namí, please let me tell you my real name."

"Tell us when you come back." Hafir walked over to Neztríanis and assessed her new clothes. "Those look very nice on you, Mésa. You are certainly a daughter of Nez Spirita, beautiful beyond any painting I have drawn."

Neztríanis blushed. "Thank you, Hafir."

Before they could say anymore, there was a knock on the door.

Looking at a clock hung in the foyer, Hafir commented, "He is early. He is always early." Walking to the front door, the artist asked. "Who is it?"

A deep, sing-song voice answered, "Who do you think, Hafir? It's me, Jennó. Early, as usual."

Opening the door, Hafir let the merchant in. His cloak was dark and ruddy, and his shoes were well worn; clearly the man was seasoned. His pants were as dark as his cloak, and for the life of her, Neztríanis could not tell what their original color was.

He was Nez Spiritan, but his copper face had a scar on the right side. His black hair was neat, but his goatee was scraggly. His slender nose accentuated his black eyes.

He was a walking oxymoron.

Even though he appeared unkempt in some ways, there were also signs of conceit and luxury. He wore an elyandir ring on his right ring finger, which was freshly polished. And on his back was a backpack, which looked ridiculously expensive, but worth every credit, for it probably housed just as much, if not more than Nez's shoulderpack.

"Have I missed any of Namí's good cooking?" he asked, smiling. "That's why I'm early tonight. I was afraid I'd miss a meal that I won't have the privilege of eating 'til next spring."

"You know I would have saved you a plate," Namí said. "The food is still on the table. Help yourself."

"I will. Thanks. But first, let me catch a gander at this 'Mésa.'" Looking in Neztríanis' direction, he smiled and grunted. "*Kíma*. You all didn't tell me Mésa was so *fine*. If I knew that, I would've gotten here even earlier."

Jennó started to laugh, and Neztríanis felt embarrassed and unnerved. She was going to have to travel with this man for seven days?

"Uhmmm... yes..." Hafir was flustered himself. "Let's discuss some things at the table."

"All right," he said, following Hafir. As he passed by Namí, the elder kissed him on the cheek and then swatted him on the back of the head. "Ow. What was that for?"

"You know I do not tolerate cursing in this house."

"Yes, Mother Namí," he said respectfully. "I'm sorry."

"That is better. But yes, Mésa is rather lovely."

The two men sat down at the table and started to discuss news and details of the trip. Namí motioned Neztríanis upstairs.

"We should go upstairs, daughter. Jennó, if anything, likes to be early. So, if he can leave here before he was originally scheduled, he will. We need to pack up things and put them in your bag."

Neztríanis followed the elder up the stairs and into the room that had been hers for three weeks. While Neztríanis placed random items into her shoulderpack, the elder went into the room's bath area and gave Neztríanis a supply of mouth rinse and another Yarnínga toothbrush.

"Where did you get this wonderful shoulderpack?" Namí asked. "It seems to possess endless space."

Neztríanis laughed. "Yes, I often wonder about that myself." Unsure of the journey ahead, she stopped packing. "Mother Namí, is Jennó trustworthy?"

"He may seem and sound a bit brash, but he is a good person. He has helped us with a few favors over the cycles, and we do not ask him to do anything that would put all of us in real jeopardy."

Neztríanis hung her head as a sudden onset of sorrow rushed over her. Namí drew close to the daughter of Hopha, placing her hand on the Sczyphamek's face, and then stroked her long rich, black hair.

"Daughter, what is the matter?"

"I know I have to go." Her tone betrayed a doubt that originated from her qanín. "But… I do not want to. I do not know where this road will take me."

"It will take you where it will take you," Namí countered. "The question is whether you will let that stop you." The elder pulled Neztríanis close and hugged her warmly. "Mésa, you are a woman of strength. You must not turn away now."

The Sczyphamek wanted to embrace her forever. The daughter of Hopha thought about the day she left her home and Phesiana. If Neztríanis had known the true weight and loneliness of her task, she would not have released the Great Mother from her grasp that day.

Gathering herself, Neztríanis stammered, "I love you. I will not forget you or Hafir, or what I have learned these days in Nextu."

After all of the solitude Neztríanis had experienced from her first memories up until her present journey, Nextu, perplexing as it was, gave her the opportunity to encounter a connection she had longed for. Namí and Hafir did not know who she was or what family she belonged or did not belong to; yet, they accepted her with open arms. Prior to her stay with them, Neztríanis believed the Great Mother was the only person capable of appreciating and loving her for who she was. However, the mother and son did not fully *know* her, for she was more than what she appeared. But, so were they, and despite the layers of lies, facades, and distance, they created a palpable and genuine friendship.

"You better not forget us," Namí cried. "Or I will come after you with my knife."

They tearfully laughed and finished stuffing the shoulderpack. The women returned downstairs, finding Jennó stuffing his face with Namí's good food. Neztríanis laughed. She was the same way when she ate Namí's luku sandwiches.

Hafir rose from the table, and walked towards Neztríanis. "I have arranged everything, Mésa. Stay close to Jennó. Although you will pass through Pike Metropolis, Jennó can help you avoid every kind of entanglement. He has made his last run of the season, and is traveling back home, unaccompanied."

Neztríanis frowned at Jennó, who waved at her playfully.

"Do not be deceived by his appearance, Mésa," Hafir continued. "He has moved contraband throughout all of Nez Spirita, from Point Sank to Nextu to Pike to the Crag Mountains and has never been caught. He is good at what he does."

"That's right." Jennó gulped down an animal-sized portion of Namí's berry punch. "I'm *gooooood* at what I do." He rose from the chair and entered the bathroom.

Hafir's eyes became red. "Be careful."

"I just cried upstairs with Namí," she said. "Do not make me cry again."

The toilet flushed and the sound of water was heard. Namí and Hafir neared Neztríanis and gave her a warm embrace. Namí went into the kitchen and returned with some wrapped food as well as some dried meat strips. She also filled Neztríanis' jug and new canteen with water. Neztríanis strapped the new canteen over her shoulder, and put the water jug and food in the shoulderpack, and closed it. The three of them exchanged loving glances.

Jennó's cough signaled it was time to depart. Hafir opened the front door, and the light from the inside of the house and a small flickering street light revealed two elegant Nez Spiritan windhorses.

"Do you know how to ride one of these?" Jennó asked.

"Yes, I have ridden a windhorse once or twice," she lied. In fact, Neztríanis had been riding windhorses her entire life.

"They are good horses," the merchant said. "Since we'll be traveling off-road most of the time, an auto was out of the question. We will take these to the outskirts of the southwestern side of the Infinite Circle. From there, we'll travel on foot. The southwestern pass is the least used, mainly because it's treacherous and narrow. Not to mention, every other pass has a Tannódin'é checkpoint."

"I am ready." Confidently, Neztríanis walked toward the windhorses. Turning back, she looked at the door of the house she was so afraid to enter, so afraid to knock on, but now extremely thankful she did. "Goodbye, my friends."

"Goodbye," they said.

Jennó mounted his horse, and Neztríanis did the same with hers. Heading north and following behind her new guide as they left Hafir's neighborhood in the middle of the night, Neztríanis vowed she would return to Nextu.

CHAPTER TEN: FIRST CAUSE(S)?

10 Ízdak, 241 OGI

While on his way back to the Bitzroy Plains and after his three-week training stint in the Fire Fields, Vincallous, airborne and gazing at the Nez Spiritan nighttime sky, was radioed by Haptian Spiax, the lead biologist for Tannódin and current mastermind of the témo extermination program. Spiax was an elderly man from Keotagosdi, the northernmost continent in the western hemisphere of Qeauríyx. He had been in the employ of the House of Kaz for several cycles as their lead scientific innovator and researcher, and many of Tannódin and Damüda's recent technological leaps were under his watch. Pre-Eminent understood enough history to grasp that war led to some of the greatest advancements in Qeauríyx. So when Késhal rose to power in 221 OGI, she added a permanent department of scientific discovery to the government. There was no doubt that Spiax would control that wing of the bureaucracy.

"We've found two of them." Spiax's voice crackled through Vicious' radio transceiver, located on the Sczyphamek's hip.

"Staxis. I utterly despise radio wave communication," Vincallous replied and placed the device to his mouth. "Our correspondence can be overheard by the rebels with the most minimal of technology. When will be able to establish high frequency communication systems, Haptian?"

"We are six to ten durations away from our goal of modernizing all of central Nez Spirita, from the Crag Mountains to Nextu. It all depends on how harsh a winter we will have, and from all indications, it will be harsh."

"One cycle and not a moment later," Fierce commanded. "Where are you now?"

"Pike Metropolis," the scientist answered.

"Where are they?"

"On one of the northwest isles of the Crossroad Islands, of all places. Our Eradicate trackers are having some difficulty with these two. We lost contact with them five days ago. We've sent two Blue Rapier naval search

154

parties to locate them or the témos, but neither party has returned or checked in."

"They are dead." Vincallous was matter-of-fact. "Of all the banes in and of this world, témos rank near the summit. Allow no more parties to enter the island; just keep them contained. Send word to the Blue Rapier naval contingent that I am coming there myself."

"Is that necessary?" Spiax asked. A dash of alarm flavored his inflection. "Aren't you supposed to be meeting the General Maximum for a debriefing? It's been weeks since you've overseen the Auría…"

"They can wait," the Sczyphamek interrupted. "Things have been quiet since the battle of Lozé. This research is vital to our long-term goals.

"I have received no urgent word from the Auría expedition parties and quite frankly, I am in no rush to retrieve the Auría. It may well be a fool's errand, not to mention the first snow is less than a duration away."

Vincallous stared at his hands in the nighttime sky and frowned. "The truth is, too many cycles have passed since I've seen any real combat. Tell Lo'Marc I will return soon, and that he is charge of all of my affairs until then."

"Yes, Potentate."

"The male I will kill, and the female will soon be ours."

"I am appreciative," the scientist said graciously. "I am a few more specimens away from unlocking the science of their power."

"Only a few more 'specimens' remain on Qeauríyx," the emperor of Global Initiative chided with disdain. "Those animals believe they hold the keys to justice and have judged our cause malevolent. Although they feign impartiality, they are far from it; however, they are powerful enough to overthrow this entire undertaking, with the right amount of help."

"Yes sir."

"They dishonor the First Sczyphamek's sacrifice." Vincallous' aura flashed in anger and he changed his direction in midair. "I am on my way there now and should return in about two weeks or so."

"Understood," the imperial biochemist responded and broke radio communication.

"Témos," Vincallous muttered to himself. "Returned home, ah?"

The Crossroad Islands were a collection of small to moderate isles about eight hundred lengths from the extreme eastern shore of the Windhorse Peninsula. At his maximum velocity, the Sczyphamek could rendezvous with the tracking vessels near the westernmost isles in four to five hours. He did not want to delay. Once he arrived, he planned to completely suppress his Elemental; for every témo possessed the innate ability to sense mystical warriors and weapons, including Sczyphameks, whether they were Awakened or not.

Only a trained mind could accomplish such an ensconcing. And suppression was especially difficult for elite Sczyphameks, since the host and his/her Elemental existed as a complete entity. If the témos sensed him before he even began his hunt, they would flee, which would make the task of catching them drag on longer than Vincallous cared. More likely, the témos would be killed in an escape attempt, but they needed the female alive.

That being said, the lives of his subordinates would be risked no longer. Témos were a problem primarily for Késhal and him. The enlisted of Blue Rapier should not have to suffer any more casualties because of a five thousand-cycle-old feud. Plus, the Eradicate was tasked to handle the témos anyway.

Theoretically, he needed about four days to mask Dé'wa's presence. Most would consider the measure foolish. Témos were dangerous and extremely intelligent. Any advantage over them was considered a boon, particularly since no one dared to hunt one, let alone *two* témos by oneself. However, Vincallous was a formidable opponent before he happened as a Sczyphamek, and although he embraced his Elemental, he routinely trained as if he did not possess them. In fact, he endured the last week of his Fire Field excursion without the aid of his Elemental.

This was not a test of ego alone. If allowed to reproduce, témos would threaten Késhal and Vincallous' plans, especially if a Sczyphamek judged benevolent were allied with them. Témos were uncanny. They were the only other animal species on Qeauríyx capable of audible, spoken language. They were also consecrated with the extraordinary ability to act as conduits for a Sczyphamek's Elemental, which could multiply an Elemental warrior's power exponentially. However, such amplification had not been achieved since the Bitter War.

Haptian Spiax wanted to harness the felines' power through science and metaphysics, but the House of Kaz wanted no chance of their continued propagation. All males were to be killed, and females were to be held, surgically sterilized, and probed for research, in the hopes that Spiax might bioengineer a new breed of animals loyal to Pre-Eminent and Vicious. His research provided some breakthroughs, such as the development of nightshades that allowed soldiers to gain nocturnal sight. But the bioalchemist was still unable to harness the full potential of the témos. If he was able to accomplish anything other than extermination, the House of Kaz considered it a bonus.

Within four and a half hours, the emperor touched down on a medium sized boat, anchored in the southwest Lancryptox Ocean. He was greatly fatigued, since he had already been pushing himself to the limit in the Fire Fields, in hope of learning new incantations and techniques.

The témo tracking squad was notified of his forthcoming arrival, and once Vincallous was over the ocean and free from possible radio interception, he requested that a ship be brought to a location two hundred lengths south of the isle where the témos were hiding. The ship was not a large battlecruiser, but a smaller, faster model, called a "seawinder." Seawinders were used for quick sea transport and held a crew of thirty or forty.

As soon as the Sczyphamek landed on the windy deck, the captain and his underlings stood at attention. The captain and crew, from the Blue Rapier naval division, were all wearing standard nautical uniforms: long beige slacks, black boots, gray shirts, and beige coats, with Blue Rapier's symbol on front and a Damüdan crest on the back.

"Do not worry about protocol." Vincallous was out of breath. He could not remember the last time he flew that long or fast. "Lead me to my quarters. I require food and water twice a day. Do not disturb me, unless you receive a direct word for me or if the position of the témos changes. In those cases alone should I be notified."

"Yes Potentate," the captain replied in hesitation.

"Is there an issue, captain?" Vincallous prodded.

The captain's fear was palpable. "I am sure you are aware of this, Potentate… but the témos are inhabiting an island two hundred lengths to our north. Is there a reason why you asked us to meet you this far away? Would you like us to return quickly or at a slow to moderate speed?"

"Ah. Feolenz's training does not disappoint," he said, commenting on the insight of the commanding officer. "I require the latter. I must prepare myself before our arrival or they will be sure to perceive my Elemental. This will require at least four days."

"Then, we will stay afloat here for four days and await the Potentate's command," the captain replied with diligence.

"Very well captain," he said wryly. "What is your name?"

"Captain Säkno."[1]

"'Säkno,' ah? You are from Damüda?"

"Yes sir, Southeastern Damüda. From the Anplo coastal region, as is my entire crew."

"Well, Captain Säkno, you must be a good Zorschwin player," Vincallous smiled. "White Scythe may be in need of an officer like you. Show me to my quarters and await my command."

"Thank you, Potentate."

The captain beamed, and his Damüdan crew looked on with pride.

***

For three days, Vincallous and Dé'wa worked tirelessly, attempting to conceal their power. Vincallous diligently meditated, ate and slept, never leaving his room. Screams of agony emerged from his quarters, as he tried to place the symbiosis in temporary hibernation. The ensconcing was excruciating. But as Vincallous struggled, he became convinced that his course of action would help him and his Elemental become stronger. If

---

[1] Säkno (s*ahh*k-noh)

anything, he would relearn how to control his Elemental to the point that he could not be detected by either a témo or a Sczyphamek. A useful technique indeed.

The crew was concerned for their leader's safety, but none dared to check on his condition. Vincallous had given his instructions.

The first night, the boat was tossed about in the sea due to his Elemental's power. Dé'wa was one with his qanín and hiding them was like ripping out a piece of himself. Sweat poured from his body as he placed Dé'wa in what could only be termed an alternate dimension of reality. He wrapped the Elemental in a self-sustained, infinite layer of spiritual, physical, and mental energy. If Dé'wa had been unwilling to cooperate, the task would have been impossible. The bipartite force fell to an almost death-like, paralyzed, state. Meanwhile, the Sczyphamek—nay, no longer a Sczyphamek—Van Fénüra exerted himself with all the strength he could personally muster, pushing his Elemental to pseudo-oblivion.

The days passed. Vincallous' appearance changed. He looked about fifteen cycles older. His hair became a grayish-brown, a dominant follicle trait of the middle-aged from Damüda. Some of his muscle mass was lost, and his voice lost some of its deepness, but none of its reflective mystery. He would not admit it to anyone except Késhal, but he had not been this horrified since his parents were murdered before his eyes. Although his Awakening inspired awe and fear, this induced slumber of his Elemental, his friend, bordered upon existential terror.

On the fourth day, he emerged from his quarters. The crewmen and crew-women gasped at the body, countenance, and figure they once apprehended as Sczyphamek Vicious. This person was unknown to them. He was almost unrecognizable, even though his physical features were still relatively intact. However, his imperial garb, sword, and overwhelming stature were gone. Vincallous even wore the same outfit the crew was wearing.

"Crewwoman," he said to the sentry guarding his quarters, "take me to the captain."

"Yes, Potentate," she stuttered.

Fierce followed her lead, up the metal stairs to the main deck. After three and a half days of being locked away in his dark quarters, the sun's rays caused his eyes to strain and readjust. Vincallous slowly regained ocular focus and watched the sea. He only heard what his natural ears perceived. He no longer felt sound, the vibration of air molecules. He no longer felt the spin and elliptical orbit of Qeauríyx around its sun, Zénan.[2] His Elemental was totally submerged, but still very much alive.

"Potentate Vicious," the captain stammered.

"Do not call me by that name right now," the sedated Sczyphamek commanded. "I am simply Commander Fierce."

---

[2] Zénan (tz*ey*-nahn)

"Yes, sir," Captain Säkno replied. "You've accomplished your goal, ah?"

"For the most part, yes."

"Shall I give the order to move towards the island?"

"Give it."

Säkno motioned to his first officer. The signal was relayed to the helm, and soon, the boat was en route to the north.

Vincallous walked towards the front of the boat and requested that the captain join him. Säkno saw it on the emperor's face: Fierce was exhilarated. Phenplyacin was probably the most recent occasion; yet that was twenty cycles ago.

But the exhilaration he felt now was incomparable to the terror he would experience on the island. He embraced it. Fear was to be embraced, accepted, and overcome. Fools denied the existence of fear, and only cowards let it hinder and control them. The strong, on the other hand, they were of a different constitution.

Breathing in the salty smell of the sea, Vincallous smiled eerily, and Säkno was taken aback. The captain beheld the emperor in person only one time prior their present meeting. They were at a commemoration service for Commandant Feolenz two cycles ago. Vincallous' mien was so stern and awe-inspiring back then that Säkno believed the Sczyphamek was incapable of happiness.

"I require an energy rifle and pistol, a machete, long knife, tranquilizers, and a week's supply of rations," Fierce stated. "And of course, camouflaged attire."

"Yes, Commander," Säkno responded. "We also have a small motorized boat pre-"

"No." His voice was firm but not menacing. "No motorized sea vessel. That was their first mistake."

The captain blinked and employed his excellent skills of analysis. "Their hearing is that sophisticated?"

"Ah, especially higher frequencies. They must be unaware of my coming." That type of knowledge was not deemed classified. And although the Eradicate normally captured and killed the témos, the Blue Rapier retrieval squads needed to know such information. Spiax oversaw the affairs of the entire témo program. However, Vincallous sometimes wondered if the scientist enjoyed *too* much authority over the program. "Spiax did not inform you of this?"

"*No. We were not informed.*"

"I will speak with Haptian myself," Vincallous said while looking at the ocean once more. The Damüdan did not tolerate unwarranted suicide missions. Returning his gaze to the captain, he resumed his orders. "Keep the boat at least five lengths away from the coast." He closed his eyes, ground his teeth together, and prepared his strategy. "How many tracking ships do we have in all?"

"Two battlecruisers and four seawinders, including this boat."

"Those battlecruisers are excessive; they should be heading towards Anzél... Have one of them anchor fifteen to twenty lengths offshore to the east of the isle and the other on the north side maintaining the same distance. Have two seawinders anchor five and two lengths off the western shore. We will meet the remaining boat five lengths from the southern coast and move within two lengths of the isle. Once the boats have anchored, keep all power consumption, radio and voice communication at an erratic pace until I reach the island. Send a few volleys of ordinance into the island, but aim for the outer edges, with occasional shots inland. Once I arrive, cease all firing and communication."

"Yes, Commander." Säkno processed the implications of Fierce's instructions. He walked over to his first officer and relayed the commands. The first officer went to the helm and carried them out personally.

Säkno returned to the emperor and stated, "We should arrive in the next two hours. And your strategy is very clever sir, their natural escape route will be to the northeast, but that is where the heaviest ordinance will be, and they will be unable to hear your infiltration of the island. And since she is pregnant they would not dare—"

"*The female is with child?*" Vicious interjected and stared at the captain. His body language betrayed his uneasiness.

"Yes. I thought Spiax informed you."

"No. *He did not,*" Vincallous sneered. Once again, he fixed his attention to the sea. What kind of game was the old scientist playing? *You knowingly withheld declassified intelligence and seemed nervous that I was heading here myself. Ah. You want the female to deliver the cub. That's the only explanation.* "How far along is she?"

"We haven't seen her in awhile, but she is probably a duration away from delivering."

Fierce sighed in relief. "Good, there is still time."

Säkno fidgeted, adjusted his coat, and breathed in the salty air. The question had plagued him too long. And though Vincallous terrified the man, the captain reasoned that some knowledge was worth the potential retribution. "Sir, pardon me, but are the témos that dangerous? No one has ever posed you, Empress Pre-Eminent, or your forces any major problems."

Still surveying the stirring sea and the northern horizon, the Damüdan emperor measured his reply. "Every star, even the greatest, no matter how bright it burns or how enormous its gravitational pull, has the same potential and inherent weakness. It can become blinded by its power, its brightness, leaving it ignorant concerning its place in the universe."

"Ignorant sir?" Though wise, Säkno did not grasp Vincallous' enigmatic metaphor.

"This Cycle continues to prove this one truth: Some happenings—when combined with the right energy and constitutive parts—can produce a force much greater than the aforementioned star. This new star could collapse the old star, or it could cause a gravitational event that allows for the colliding of the two stars, destroying star systems."

"I see…" The captain silently pondered the meaning of Vincallous' words.

"Of course, it may not be a star. It is misconception that allows the idea of a mutual nemesis, one who must mirror the protagonist in all ways except for belief…" Vincallous Fierce laughed to himself. This type of verbiage was exactly why Késhal heckled him so relentlessly. "Témos, combined with the right Sczyphamek, could undo everything we have strived and bled for."

"Everything?"

"You are from southeast Damüda, captain. So you know how Zorschwin came about."

Säkno grew mum and cautious. "We are not allowed to talk about the origin of Zorschwin. It is against the law."

"I won't tell anyone." Vincallous smiled. "Ah?"

Säkno laughed in fear. "Ah, Zorschwin was created by témos and Damüdans. It celebrated their strong relationship, particularly the Damüdans from the east." He could not believe he was having an illegal conversation with the most powerful man on the planet, a man whose word was *law*.

Fierce nodded. "Correct. The flag and the canine were symbols of camaraderie and respect."

"Ah. In the original game, one témo would join the Damüdans on offense as they tried to capture the flag and tooth."

"And although the odds were against those fighting an uphill battle…"

Säkno understood perfectly. "Even though the odds were against them, if a team was formidable enough. They could undo the best defense."

"*They could undo everything we have strived and bled for*," Vincallous repeated.

"Yes sir." Säkno was unsure, but there seemed to be remorse underneath the emperor's steadfastness. "Do you require accompaniment?"

"No."

"But, sir, you are our leader. If something should happen—"

"A leader should never ask his followers to do something he himself is unwilling to do," Vincallous interjected. The captain was drawn into Fierce's emphatic and impassioned delivery. "Make sure no one in this company follows me."

"But the lengths…"

Fierce scowled. He stepped towards his countryman and forced Säkno to return his stare. "Is it normal protocol for a captain to question the orders of his superior officer?"

"No sir, it is not normal." The Damüdan captain nearly cowered, but his desire to know continued to override self-preservation. "But if I may venture another question, Commander Fierce?"

The sleeping Sczyphamek chuckled in stern amusement and prodded the captain to continue.

"Is it normal for a Sczyphamek to do what you have done?"

"Hmmph," he grunted. "It is not. However, our cause is noble, and honestly, I trust this task to no one else."

"Yes sir." Säkno agreed, but he was unconvinced. The captain knew that the co-leaders of Global Initiative did not participate directly in the témo extermination program. So why was this task, this cause, so important now? What necessitated Fierce's willingness to hunt the témos and ensconce his Elemental?

"Where is the equipment?" the emperor asked.

Säkno led Vincallous to the small armory on the boat, and once inside, the commander took an energy rifle off the wall. He fastened a black belt around his waist, which held ten covered tranquilizer darts and a pistol for firing them. Examining a wall of knives, he chose one of medium length and twirled it with his right hand fingers, displaying his proficiency with the weapon. There was a holster for the knife on the wall, and Vincallous placed the knife inside its covering, and snapped the holster onto his belt. Finally, he moved towards the energy pistol rack, and removed one. Pulling his jacket up above his waist, he placed the gun, uncharged, in between his back and his pants. Letting his jacket fall back down, he strapped an energy rifle across his chest and a machete across his back.

Vincallous Fierce turned around and faced the captain. There was no smile, no frown, or any sign of emotion on the face of the current patriarch of Global Initiative.

"These are not too heavy," he commented to himself, judging the weight of the armaments. "I should be able to move and react quickly…"

"Your battle fatigues are in your quarters, sir. Won't you need a secondary energy pack, in case you discharge your entire weapon?" Säkno asked.

"If I discharge my entire AEAR and they are still alive, I will not have time to change cartridges. I will be dead."

"What about this?" Säkno handed Fierce a pressurized bottle that contained the scent of a témo.

"Did the other squads use this?"

"Yes," Säkno responded.

The commander shook his head. "That was folly. If this is applied, even though it would match the general scent of the témos, how would you then be able to distinguish this from the actual smell of the témos? This spray is only advantageous if you are aware of the exact location of a témo, otherwise, a témo could hunt you and you would not even know it."

Säkno said nothing, crushed under the expertise of the leader. What appeared to be technologically advantageous was actually a death note.

"Now, about your third question, Säkno… the real one…"

"Third question, ah? Commander, I only asked you two."

"You asked two questions, ah. But you have another." Vincallous smiled at the captain. "'Are the témos that dangerous?' 'Why have I gone to such lengths?' There is a natural third question: 'Why do they just not kill the témos?' That is your question, correct? If they are a threat, why do we capture the females and study them? Why not flatten the island with our incineration bombs and kill them? Why are our men and women of Global Initiative dying for such an animal? Why did I choose to hunt the témos now?"

The captain was speechless.

"You have an excellent military mind, Säkno," Vincallous said, "but, you lack the understanding of historical perspective.

"Témo's deserve better than such an end. They deserve an ironic end. If we augment ourselves with their power, how much more powerful would we become? And how much more would that diminish them? After all, témos are just another piece of kíma in this Cycle. And this place will raise another 'nothing' in their place to fight against us. We must use their strength and make it our own.

"They deserve to die at the hands of a sleeping Sczyphamek, who has descended from his natural state, so they may come to realize how weak they have become and that their use on this planet has reached its fitting conclusion.

"As a commanding officer, you must not downplay symbolic victories. Symbols hold much power. Gaining control of symbols is half the struggle of all combat. It is the difference between dying as a failure or as a martyr."

Säkno absorbed the wisdom of Vincallous and vowed he would appropriate and master it, in order to serve and guide his own officers to the best of his ability. "Thank you, sir."

Fierce displayed another wry smile, for only a moment. At once, his expression changed as the first officer approached both men.

"Captain, Commander," the first officer greeted, "we will arrive at the southern shore within the hour."

"Exceptional," the emperor stated. "Prepare a small boat for me and place the rations there. I will go to my quarters to change clothes and we will go over any remaining logistical matters."

"Yes sir," the first officer replied and left.

Turning to the captain, Vincallous' face became the only memory Säkno had previously possessed of the man: *stern*. "You are in charge of this operation Säkno. I demand nothing but perfection, and if you fail me, the consequences will not only be dire for you, but your entire command."

"Yes, commander."

Vincallous walked out of the room, but Säkno called after him. "How will we know you have succeeded? How many days should we give you?"

"Three days at the most. And do not worry. You *will know* when I have succeeded. And if you do not hear from me in four days, incinerate the island. That is an order."

***

The air was filled with smoke, sand, and chunks of earth. Vincallous kept his gaze straight ahead and rowed towards the isle's southern coast. Though deafening and a length away from the shoreline, his mind was in a quiet, still reflection.

How did Qeauríyx and the One with No Name produce such a self-righteous creature?

Témos were late bloomers in the evolution of Qeauríyx. Thenceforth, they were the last of the animals that emerged from the ground. There was no record of them before the Great Extinguishing of the First Sczyphamek. Many believed their genesis commenced with the dispersal and fracturing of the Sundry Elemental. Whatever the case, témos were first noticed a half a millennium or so after the Great Extinguishing.

Legend held that seafaring inhabitants of the continent Meve were journeying to Nez Spirita, and while stopping in the Crossroad Islands, they happened upon them. The Mevites were astonished. Their ancestors had navigated through the Crossroads for many cycles (since the end of the Drift made sea travel far less dangerous) but they never encountered animals such as these. Large felines were commonplace in Qeauríyx, especially in Phmquedria and Keotagosdi, but felines with wings?

The Mevites shock soon turned to mystification when they spoke in front of the témos and discovered that the animals could not only understand speech patterns, but were able to converse with their own form of sonic communication as well.

Continental and regional languages developed after the Ancient Tongue. But the inhabitants of Qeauríyx—those who were capable of linguistic, grammatical, and aural communication—were blessed with an evolutionary knack for picking up new tongues. Due to the transient and cataclysmic nature of the Drift, learning how to communicate became an indispensible attribute for survival. Témos did not pronounce, but instead used a mixture of growl, tone, rasp, which had a grammar and syntax of its own.

Although the témo's communication was alien to the ears and language patterns of the Mevites, both groups were able to understand each other quite well after a short period of time. The Mevites and témos realized that both species had as much in common as they had in difference. But they were the only animals on the planet who audibly conveyed memory, ideas, and reality to one another. Thus, the Mevites and témos decided upon a word to call their collective ancestry: Chénínqua,[3] a word from the Ancients, whose closest approximation was "the Blessed Gathering" or

---

[3] Chénínqua (shey-neen-kwah)

"Multitude" in any common tongue.

However, "Chénínqua" was now deemed a word of insurrection by the House of Kaz. Mentioning the Chénínqua was a criminal offence. In the eyes of the House of Kaz, témos were lesser forms of life, with no right of assembly, whether it was with their fellow felines, or with the other half of the Gathering. The fact that Tannódin instituted its own lexicon as the de facto vocabulary and grammar of the planet was like a caustic salt in the already deep wounds of Qeauríyx, for témos were anatomically incapable of speaking like Tannódin'é.

The first language the témos learned outside of their own tongue was that of the Mevites. However, that language was now a dead language, like the continent of Meve itself. The natives of Meve fled their homeland 1300 BGI, due to the looming threat of the Infinite Deep and the melting of a large glacier. Prior to these cataclysms, the people of Meve were known as exceptional seafarers, and some témos journeyed with them as they explored the planet. As a result, circa 6000 BGI, témos had established "Dens" on every continent within Qeauríyx. They lived in peace with most of their new neighbors, settling in the wild and feeding on the surrounding plants and animals. Témos were able to maintain equilibrium with their surroundings with exceptional precision.

By 5500 BGI their population numbered about nine hundred thousand. The majority of them lived in their homeland, the Crossroad Islands, but a significant number lived on various continents, particularly in Phmquedria, Damüda, and Nez Spirita. Their first encounter with Sczyphameks occurred nearly five hundred cycles later, when the first large wave of Elemental warriors appeared after the First's Extinguishing. No one knew how or why, but evolution and grace struck a mystical connection between the témos and Sczyphameks.

It was called "The Synthesis."

Like most marvels and inventions, the Synthesis hinged upon a series of accidents that lead to discovery. The Sczyphamek's name was unknown, but the témo's name was Lanp, a feline from the Phmquedrian Den. Somehow, the témo transformed according to the powers of the Element, which was recorded as magnetism. This allowed the power of the Sczyphamek to double, as the témo amplified the warrior's ability. The témo deployed the Elemental warrior's powers without significant taxation and drew metal from the surrounding area and made a skin of alloyed metals for himself. The Sczyphamek and témo were known as the Myanín,[4] which meant the "group of two" in the Ancient Tongue. The designation was ironclad. Every Sczyphamek and témo who had partnered and synthesized since, carried the name.

Concurrent with this astounding development, the témos organized themselves according to their own standards. After living with the

---

[4] Myanín (mahy-uh-n*ee*n)

inhabitants of the continents for millennia, the winged felines became familiar with the Auría, the beliefs in the Nameless One, and the Great Drift. While they accepted some of the creeds of the variegated beliefs of the men and women of Qeauríyx, the témos found their faith to be too species-centric. In response, the témos mapped out a system of beliefs, law, and society that married the principles of justice, mercy, and a respect for the life of the entire planet as core tenets. After much discussion and debate, they developed a complex, democratic governmental structure whereby absolute power was nil and the unity of the témoic species with the planet was held in deep respect.

There was no one "head" of the témos, just The Keep. The first branch of The Keep was the "Principle," an executive board of five témos. This board was comprised of two members elected from the "Enclave," a group of témos that represented the homeland of the Crossroad Islands, and two members elected by the "Den," the group that represented the témo establishments on the other continents. The final member of the Principle was the eldest témo alive, whether from the Den or the Enclave. The Den and the Enclave were also the names of the legislative branch of the government. They consisted of ten members per group. The Den and Enclave could decide on no law that the Principle would not approve.

Once those three chambers approved a measure, it proceeded before the Adjudicate, a group of seven judges, who maintained legal order. No law could be passed by the Principle, Den, and Enclave without their final approval. The judges, appointed by democratic election, were legendary for ruling on the side of justice, mercy, and equity. Corruption and extreme partisanship were not tolerated, and a judge would be excommunicated from the Adjudicate if this tendency was displayed. In time, due to its incorruptibility, the Adjudicate was petitioned to hear cases and disputes from people and interests throughout all the continents of Qeauríyx. Most codes or laws used on Qeauríyx thenceforth, and even during the present age of Global Initiative, were based on témoic principles.

The final group was the Orators, the only group in the témoic democracy that was determined by ancestry. During the Golden Age of the témos, there were at least sixteen Orators at any given time, who were supported by an entire household of record keepers. Témos did not write; their entire history was recorded orally. The Orators were responsible for keeping this knowledge fresh and mediated all governmental process. No official business took place if three Orators were not present. This seemingly complex system worked with efficiency and with little bureaucracy.

In addition to their governmental chambers, the témos were supported by their own volunteer army, the Austere, who were only engaged for defensive purposes. The témos would not strike unless provoked and tried to stay clear of most skirmishes of the "upright," their name for the men and women of Qeauríyx. It was an age of prosperity for the témos, but it was not meant to last. On Qeauríyx, the call to justice is often the call to a tragic path.

When the Synthesis was discovered, circa 5000 BGI, the Myanín presented themselves to The Keep whose home was located in the Crossroad Islands. It was the témos who named the first Sczyphamek of Justice, "Kyla." And thenceforth, all Benevolent or Justice Sczyphameks were called Kylanín. The Keep decreed unanimously that témos and Kylanín were allowed to synthesize without the approval of the Principle, Den, Enclave, or Adjudicate. This statute held for almost 2400 cycles, until the questionable acts of the Kylanín in the Black Staff incident. For over two millennia Kylanín and témos traversed Qeauríyx, and the Orators recorded their great exploits.

As the cycles grew, the Malevolent Sczyphameks arose, and the témos once again assembled and judged their aggression as detrimental to the planet, and they were summarily labeled "Zananín" ("zana" was an ancient word approximate to ruthless, unmerciful order). Témos were not allowed to associate or synthesize with them under the penalty of death, the first and last occasion the Keep sanctioned capital punishment. The penalty was a signal to the Zananín, not so much the témos, for no témo would join the ranks of an adversary of the Kylanín. And from that moment on, Zananín and témos became immortal enemies.

In 2594 BGI, the Black Staff Incident—precipitated by the rise of White Scythe—forever changed the dynamics of Qeauríyx and put the témos on course to a slow, baneful extinction. The controversial event caused the Kylanín and Zananín to irrevocably splinter, and a third party, the Zephanín,[5] was born. The Zephanín (rooted in the word "zeph," which means "aimless" or "unconvinced") were labeled by The Keep to be unlawful and apathetic. Furthermore, the governing body refused to allow any témo to synthesize with them. However, many témos were already partners with some of the former Kylanín-turned-Zephanín and would not leave their comrades.

This internal conflict came at an inopportune time, because one cycle later, White Scythe surmounted the entire continent of Damüda. The témos from the Damüdan den requested help, and both Zephanín and Kylanín participated in the decimation of White Scythe. This did not heal the wounds of the split. In fact, it exacerbated the problem.

The Zephanín, who interpreted the First Sczyphamek's Extinguishing quite differently than the Zananín or Kylanín, did not believe that Sczyphameks should interfere with or actively shape the course of Qeauríyx. They saw the rise of the Zananín as confirmation that if Sczyphameks continued down that path, Qeauríyx would be crushed under the weight of their power.

---

[5] Zephanín (tzeh-phuh-neen)

The témo establishment saw the Zephanín view as cowardice. Their core principles left them no choice but to fight, placing them at odds with a growing minority of their species who had seen their numbers decline because of the constant battles with Sczyphameks and mystical weapons. The minority of témos did not believe in isolationism, but they felt that if their kind continued to police the planet, all témos would suffer recurrent casualties. Those témos sympathetic to the Zephanín left the Den and Enclave, which accelerated an ever-growing fissure between the felines. The infighting between Sczyphameks and témos spread throughout the planet, which soon fractured the Chénínqua.

As a result, the Zephanín withdrew from the historical milieu and marshaled their movement. The Zananín laid in secret, plotting their next move. The Kylanín maintained order whenever they were so harkened. All was quiet for over a millennia, and Qeauríyx saw one of its most beautiful periods, except for the témos. The rift between the felines grew, intensified, and exacerbated violent confrontations.

In 1502 BGI, the Zananín struck with a series of assassinations upon the Kylanín, which eventually drug the Zephanín into what became known as the Bitter War. The battle spilled into the ranks of the témos and plunged them into civil war, which had been brewing for centuries. After the Bitter War eradicated the entire Sczyphamek population, the témos were alone, but still embroiled in their own dispute.

They put an end to their fighting in order to quell the resurgence of White Scythe. White Scythe was under the leadership of a new General Maximum, and the mercenaries struck soon after the deaths of the Elemental warriors. The people of Qeauríyx had grown accustomed to Kylaníns aid whenever trouble reared its head. With no Elemental mediation, Tannódin was caught unaware and easily conquered by White Scythe. The menace of White Scythe was so severe that the témos were forced to reunite. However, their numbers had decreased to less than ten thousand. Instead of going to war, the témos worked with the leaders of the remaining continents and taught them how to defend themselves against the eventual onslaught of White Scythe. They also engaged in diplomacy by helping each land restructure their government and armed forces, only if requested.

The témos were hailed as wise teachers, masters of knowledge from a time long forgotten. Many communities responded to them favorably, especially the Phmquedrians and Damüdans. Témos possessed instinctive clarity and foresight. The Keep understood that the témoic journey would come to a conclusion at some point, just like every species on Qeauríyx. They wished to leave a positive legacy to all on Qeauríyx.

It was just a matter of time before the blade of destruction and the General Maximum would strike again from their new homeland, Tannódin. The winged felines grew in numbers once again, but only reached a fifth of their previous golden age population. The témos consolidated their political system and issued a decree for the Orators to codify their accounts, by way of a Nez Spiritan tribe known for keeping historic annals. This task took nearly three hundred cycles, but the Témoic Annals were completed in 657 BGI in northwest Nez Spirita.

For a millennium, Tannódin bided its time, advancing in technology and weaponry, and in 509 BGI, the Tannódin'é launched a preemptive strike against Damüda. The Damüdans and témos fought against White Scythe on various battlefields throughout the continent for twelve cycles. In the tenth cycle of the conflict, the Violet Manacle was discovered deep in the mountains of northern Tannódin by a Tannódin'é oligarch and archaeologist named Wézko Tekil.

The mystical weapon's emergence marked the turning point in the war and ultimately led to the destruction of the Damüdan Den. All of Damüda fell, except for the province and city of Nosgüth. Due to the war's length, the témo population was decimated down to the tens of thousands. The winged felines retreated to Phmquedria and advised the elders of the continent to draw up a non-aggression treaty with Tannódin and the elders agreed. However, the témos were betrayed and murdered by many of the elders' descendants five hundred cycles later, at the dawn of Global Initiative, when the first Sczyphamek in over fifteen hundred cycles ascended to power, the Zananín, Sczyphamek Imperial.

With their population hovering around five thousand, the témos withdrew from all of the remaining Dens and returned home to the Crossroad Islands. Their wish was to remove themselves from all conflict. But they knew not Sczyphamek Imperial. Her anger burned against the témos, a hate soaked in the cycles of absent Zananín Sczyphameks and amplified by the insatiable imperialism of White Scythe. Imperial was an astute student of history and would not allow témoic "corruption" to infiltrate the ideology of Global Initiative. Most folk on Qeauríyx forgot about the Synthesis, Sczyphameks, and the old wars of the past, but Imperial had not. She understood that if a Kylanín came forth, her aims would be greatly jeopardized.

Tannódin and Damüda invaded Nez Spirita in 2 OGI. A few cycles later, Imperial dispatched a Blue Rapier division[6] and her imperial guard[7] to the Crossroad Islands in order to massacre the remaining témo population as well as to seize the témoic oracles of the past. The témos scattered, but not without heavy losses.

Imperial ordered that all Témoic Annals be burned and issued an absolute mandate to hunt down and kill all témos. Any person or community in collusion with or hiding the felines was put to death. The imperial guard enforced this mandate. When Pre-Eminent came to power,

---

[6] Blue Rapier was discovered 280 cycles before Global Initiative.

[7] The imperial guard was commanded by the wielder of the Violet Manacle, a member of the Tekil household.

she tweaked the mandate, allowing for the capture, experimentation, and euthanasia of the females, and the immediate destruction of the males to be carried out by the Eradicate, under the jurisdiction of Haptian Spiax.

Because of Imperial, témos kept out of the active history of Qeauríyx—with the exception of Phenplyacin, which reduced their numbers to the hundreds. Since that defeat, the témos had almost become myth, hiding themselves and staying clear of the House of Kaz. They were hunted constantly and no one was certain how many remained.

***

Under the cover of sand and smoke, Vincallous made it ashore, and within thirty seconds, all bombardment ceased. The slumbering Sczyphamek readied himself and breathed in the charred air.

Dé'wa was so far from him, Fénüra could not perceive their voice.

He took a sip of water from his canteen, got out of the boat, and armed himself. Looking back towards Säkno's seawinder with his binoculars, Vincallous observed two flashes of light: the signal that the témos did not flee from the island. Next, Vincallous overturned the vessel, walked towards some trees near the beach and gathered some fallen branches. The trees were relatives of the Nez Spiritan Yarnínga, but the leaves were broader and thicker. He covered the boat with the branches and sand and moved towards the trees once more.

Fierce saw no further than a few feet. The cluster of trunks, branches, leaves, and shadow was stifling. He felt the ground; it was muddy and wet. He rubbed mud over his face and his hands in order to mask his scent. Next, he took some of the leaves of the forest, wetted them and placed them in his satchel and pockets and chewed on them. The taste was bitter and rancid, but it was edible. Vincallous, as educated as he was indomitable, studied the Crossroad Islands extensively while he was in the ranks of White Scythe. He knew which plants were harmful or otherwise.

It was an hour before sundown, after which he would be at a supreme ocular disadvantage. His best chance of survival was to erect an inconspicuous shelter and camouflage himself there. For a brief moment, he almost second-guessed his decision to ensconce his Elemental, but negative thinking precipitated negative outcomes.

Still, as Zénan set to the East, Van Fénüra understood that if he was not careful, he would die on the island. There was no hyperbole in his admonition to Säkno. Chased and pushed to the brink of extermination, témos had become much more violent and aggressive. A far cry from their more "civilized" days.

There would be no discussion, no banter between him and them. Any murderous reservation they possessed was unshackled weeks ago. They would kill him on sight if they could. The male would do his best to protect the pregnant female at all costs. If Van could kill the male somehow, his chances of victory would increase tenfold because the female would instinctively hold back due to her need to preserve their line.

Without his Elemental, Fierce was forced to rely on his wits and five senses. The latter had dulled since he became a Sczyphamek. Again, a hint of nervousness struck the Damüdan. But his lot was now cast. He was the co-leader of Global Initiative. He could not go back to his subordinates in fear or defeat. He had instructed Lo'Marc and Reníz[8] on the necessity of focused determination in difficult situations.

Fénüra took a quiet, heavy breath.

If he perished, Késhal would understand. She knew the stakes and history. Empire building tended toward absolutes. Victory or death: those were their only options.

"I will not fail," he said in a low tone. "I will not."

Shaking all dread aside, Vincallous stepped into the caliginous, dense forest. His energy weapons remained uncharged. Témos were able to sense high pitch dissonance from lengths away. It took three seconds for a standard issue to charge and fire a normal burst. Témos could run at speeds of over one hundred lengths per hour, and their maximum aerial velocity surpassed three hundred lengths per hour. However, because the jungle was thick, the chances of them flying towards him at full speed were slim. It was their ground speed that concerned Fierce. He needed to spot them first, so that he could maintain a safe distance that would grant him ample time to charge, aim, and fire his weapon.

Taking the long knife out of its holster and the machete out of its sheath, Vincallous trudged ahead, able to see very little. Säkno briefed him on the isle's topography before he left the seawinder. It was mostly forest from the beach to the inland area, but there were two moderate hills in the middle of the isle, and surrounding them was a grassy field.

He could not go into the grassy field; that would leave him out in the open and visible to his game. The couple would then use their flying ability to tear him apart. If pushed to his limit, he did not know if he could simply and hastily call his Elemental forth in any meaningful way after such a radical submergence. His appreciation for Dé'wa hastened with every step, but he was determined to see his task through. Becoming angry at his constant relapse into fear and regret, he reminded himself of harder challenges.

And suddenly, Vincallous smiled and almost laughed. Although presently unaware, these témos would soon know what kind of happening had drifted ashore. It was their doom, their decline, their capture, and their death: another memorial for a bygone species. Whether one with his Elemental or not, he was still a Zananín, and témos were his enemy.

After carefully advancing inland for a few minutes, he righted himself against an immense tree. Both moons were present in the sky. It was nearly

---

[8] Reníz (rhin-*ee*ss)

winter. Most of the foliage lay on the ground, which made the canopy penetrable to light. He felt around the trunk, which was an ever-bloom and twelve feet in diameter, and found an opening. The opening was just large enough for him to squeeze into. It was a perfect hiding place.

He sat down in his makeshift lodging, opened his bag, and procured some rations. He ate a double portion of them quickly, so not to allow the scent of food to permeate his surroundings. Next, he drank some water and placed the wrapping for the food back in his bag. He scrubbed more leaves over his bag and chewed on them again so that his breath would not smell like his rations. Feeling no apprehension, Vincallous piled nearby rocks and fallen branches around the opening and fell asleep. He would need all of his strength in the morning.

"Van, look! Témos used to live in this cave…"

After Phenplyacin, he could not remember his dreams, but Fénüra awoke with the same melancholy feeling he had been subject to for thirty-five cycles. Judging from the shadows and the position of the sun, it was early in the morning. Although feeling a bit claustrophobic, Vincallous did not move and breathed quiet breaths. He was alive and intended to stay that way.

For thirty minutes, he let his ears adjust to the sounds of the forest. He heard the leaves, the insects, running water, and migrating fowl. Concentrating fervently, he sensed the nuances of the woodland. He had to trust his ears and nose more than anything else. Peering out of the opening, Vincallous checked for any signs of the témos.

As his left leg emerged from the hiding place, a flock of fowl dispersed at a phenomenal rate. The insects stopped buzzing and burrowing about, which made him take serious pause. Vincallous drew his leg back into the tree trunk. He barely perceived them: the steps were light, but there was heaviness behind them.

The Damüdan's eyes widened and his heart's pace quickened as a blurry, large, fifteen-foot long mass of gray, black, and white appeared sixty feet ahead. As soon as he saw it, it disappeared into the upper tree area.

A témo. It was enormous.

Although he only caught a glimpse of it, the long, muscular, yet sleek trunk was unmistakable. Besides the color, that was the only physical feature Fénüra determined. He stayed perfectly still for another twenty minutes, making absolutely sure the creature had passed. He listened for other animal activity and used their eventual lack of anxiety as a gauge for his safety.

He surfaced from the tree, stretched, and drank some water. It was colder than the night before. By all indications, the late autumn trend would continue. He could not make a fire. That idiocy would give away his position. He had to capture the female in a few days or he would grow sick and weak. And even if had not ensconced his Elemental, Dé'wa could not fully insulate him from the cold.

By his reasoning, the témos were located on the other side of the island. Based upon Tannódin'é reconnaissance and zoological research, it was known that the felines hunted away from their dens. Since the female was close to term, they had probably picked an inconspicuous place that was hard to enter.

What are they hoping for, ah? The témos must understand their chances of survival are slim, and yet they continue to linger on this isle. Why?

While in deep self reflection, a cold wind blew over Vincallous Fierce's face and he shivered in response.

Of course, he thought. *The winter.*

The inclement weather spawned by winter would discourage any search parties. Although foreign to Blue Rapier, the Crossroad Islands were the témo's natural environment. A patient war of attrition. This was their Zorschwin gambit. With each passing day, the felines gained more of the upper hand. Though the plan was dangerous, the témos could escape once the female delivered. And once winter commenced, the days would be shorter, cloudier, and more precipitous. The seas would be rough and inhospitable, complicating their capture.

If they wanted to play the game that way, Fierce preempted an equal response. He already ordered Säkno to smolder the island if he did not return in four days. The témos were hoping in vain. No matter the means, the outcome was the same. They would be killed.

He advanced northeast slowly, cautiously, and low to the ground. He headed towards the northern side of the isle and stayed clear of the island's center. Every five minutes, he marked his path on the bark of a tree, near its base, so that he would not get lost. After about three hours of walking and sensate absorption, the Emperor of Global Initiative neared the center of the island. Glancing to his left through the trees and towards the open field he stopped. Even though he was half a length away from the grassy field, the smell was pungent.

Every soldier knew that stench. It was a dead body. And from Vincallous' urge to vomit, there were more than five. It was both expedition squads.

How could they have been so arrogant as to assault these creatures in the open field, He thought to himself. *You underestimated them. That is unlike you.*

Blue Rapier soldiers were bred on the powers of observation. Something went terribly wrong with their plan if they to ended up there—unless their plan was to draw them out in the open and kill them through the power of numbers. The soldiers obviously misjudged the témo's flying speed. An understandable folly, but Vincallous was capable of flying at similar speeds. He would not make the same mistake.

Although curiosity made him reach for his binoculars, he swatted the instinct away. Light would reflect from the binoculars' lenses and give away his position. He resumed his walk to the northeast, and to his surprise the revolting aroma became more local and stronger. Directly ahead, he saw dried blood on the base of a medium-sized tree. The trunk was bent and suffered a large gash due to some large projectile. Looking down and under fallen branches and leaves, Vincallous almost stepped on the body of a fallen insect-ridden corpse of a Blue Rapier soldier.

Using environmental and forensic analysis and judging from her wounds, Van Fénüra reasoned that she was mauled by one of the témos. A deep bite mark spanned the entirety of her neck, a killing technique employed by the felines. He searched for her firearm but could not find it. Looking back towards the open field, Vincallous saw a path of snapped branches.

"Amazing."

The woman had been killed in the open field, and the témo had flung her limp body at an unbelievable speed towards the forest, a distance of nearly half a length. Her body created the path of bent branches and had nearly broken the tree in half. Once she hit the tree, branches and leaves dislodged and fell on top of her.

The Blue Rapier expedition parties had treated them like other animals. But, témos were as intelligent as they were, perhaps more. The felines had their own terrain at their disposal, and their physical strength was greater than twenty soldiers combined. The Rapier's species-centric tactics contributed to their slaughter and mutilation. If that were any other animal, the plan would have worked with standard Blue Rapier efficiency.

But témos were not any other animal. They were creatures *who* taught *people* how to govern themselves and fight. They were creatures *who* fought against mystical weapons and Sczyphameks. They taught Damüdans how to play Zorschwin.

Vincallous' arrogance subsided. His hate and circular logic had clouded his judgment. He remembered the implications of all he told Säkno and the evidence he just encountered. Arrogance would kill him just like it killed those soldiers. The témos rejection and slaughter of the previous messengers signaled their blasphemous noncompliance *and* their strength. Even if they were just a remnant of an olden species…

Stop, Van. Let go of the hate. You must remember.

They would not convert and deserved desolation, but even so, they were still to be respected in their own right. He needed a healthy dose of fear to quell his arrogance and hate. In his haste and malcontent, he forgot.

Remember…

Témos had already killed Awakened Sczyphameks in previous cycles.

"Staxis," the *man* cursed.

He knew he could be killed. But he could not acknowledge *how* it might happen. Cycles of empire building and constant victories had blinded him to his own shortcomings. A younger Vincallous Fierce was not so arrogant. He was a person who embraced patience and humble calculation. Did he listen to the metaphorical lecture he gave Säkno? This recent incarnation of Vincallous Fierce needed a dose of humility. He had become soft in his hardness. This assignment was his choosing, but its outcome would not proceed by his design alone. There was risk involved. This was still a two-sided game.

I'm still playing Zorschwin.

A broad grin grew on the Damüdan's face amidst the trees, death, and fear. He actually thought he had reached a plateau with regards to his potential. Happily, he was wrong. He still had room to improve. Other than Késhal, Lo'Marc, and Reníz, few happenings excited him anymore. But he forgot about the unpredictability of the planet. This self-imposed mission forced him to rethink his motivations and goals. The descent into the dark forest was a rite of passage, abounding with temptations of pride, terror, grandeur, and false security. Even if his and Késhal's aspirations were just, those aspirations needed to be perfected and proven in the untamable wild. Global Initiative's success required his entire qanín.

"May the Nameless One grant me strength," he prayed in earnest. Suddenly, another thought—no, remembrance—entered his qanín. "No…" Van shivered in discontent. "No. I will not…"

Using the dead body as an opportunity, Vincallous relieved himself so that the stink of the corpse would mask the smell of his urine and excrement. Next, he ate and drank a small amount of water. He did not want any distractions. The male témo needed to be dead by the end of the night.

I must remember it all.

Wiping the tears away from his face, Van resumed his brisk pace. Fénüra watched, smelled, and listened for any indication that he was near the témo's den. Vincallous reached his northern destination by mid-afternoon.

Without hesitation, Fierce added fresh mud to his face and hands. He was in enemy territory now and made preparations for conflict. He took the energy rifle off his shoulder and gripped it with his right hand, so that he could charge the firearm at a moment's notice. Sheathing the long knife, he grasped the machete in his left hand. He placed his back against a tree, and breathed deep breaths through his nose. A faint scent, which contrasted with the previous smell of the forest, entered his nostrils. Sniffing again, he confirmed it. It was a témo's scent.

Staying low to the ground, Vincallous gathered some nearby moss and needles and placed them on his head, while sticking branches in his boots and jacket pockets. His camouflage was excellent for the terrain. The trees were thick. He just needed to make sure that he moved low and slowly. He crawled a few feet every ten minutes, drawing nearer to the smell of témo. Serene, his heart's pace was nearly unnoticeable, even to himself.

After two hours of dedicated movement, the Damüdan made his way to a small, underground cave opening with three small boulders nearby. This was their enclave. Most of the animal life tapered off about a length from the area. There were a few birds, high in the trees, but the small, ground animals were nowhere to be found. The sun had begun its nocturnal journey and would soon be overtaken by the moons.

Vincallous was about two hundred feet from the opening, in a small trench by a large tree. Understandably, he grew nervous. He could not retreat under these conditions, because even in darkness, the témos would see him. He could not use night vision goggles anymore than he could charge the energy rifles. A témo's hearing was extremely sensitive to high frequency. Even the smallest electrical device made a sound. In such close proximity, any such mistake would grant him a hastened death, which was why he left the goggles on the boat in the first place.

The setting sun casted a discriminating shadow on Van's position. He discreetly laid his energy rifle next to his right hand and kept his finger on the "charge" switch. With his left hand, he placed the machete down and quietly covered it with leaves. No sooner had he done this, the activity of the forest halted and the hair on the back of his neck stood on end.

Deep, snarly inhalations and paws thumped the que.

Vincallous cautiously turned his head to the right.

It was the male témo.

The animal weighed at least six times his own weight. Its long, lustrous frame was so solidly muscular that every move from the témo appeared as if his muscles would tear through his black coat, which was strafed with gray stripes. When his large, white paws hit the ground, the sound was like a bass drum reverberating through the soil. His whiskers were long, pointy, and regal. His calculating eyes were green and black. The gray wings of the animal were drawn and folded in on its back, parallel to his torso; they were at least six feet in length, unexpanded. The canines of the beast were protruding, lengthy, and cuspidate. His tail appeared as muscular as the rest of his body. Vincallous reasoned that if he were struck by the appendage, he would suffer possible incapacitation.

This is neither an animal nor beast, Vincallous repeated to himself. *This is my enemy. Remember, Van, the témo is a* "he," *not an* "it."

The feline walked toward the cave, but suddenly, in mid-stride, the témo precariously paused, sniffed, and then resumed his course. However, after a few steps, the winged creature turned and raced in Van Fénüra's direction. The témo possessed a ferocious, feral presence in his eyes and was ready to pounce on his newfound prey.

The Damüdan had been spotted, or perhaps sniffed out was more accurate. Vincallous was so preoccupied with the creature's aural capacity that he underestimated their extraordinary sense of smell. He charged his AEAR, but the animal was too close. It appeared he underestimated the distance between them as well.

In an instant, Fénüra threw his concealed machete at the témo. The feline eluded the attack, but his elusion gave Fierce the three seconds needed to arm the gun. The commander rolled to his right and aimed at his opponent's frame, but his adversary was as agile as he was muscular. Since témos were not that bulky, the male jumped and easily dodged the discharge in mid-stride.

Glaring at Vincallous with canines flexing, the animal roared a terrible warning. This encounter would end in one of their deaths.

Expanding his wings to half their wingspan, the témo flapped and caused branches, leaves, and random debris to be thrown in the air, which obscured the vision of Vincallous and upset his aim. Immediately, the témo ascended into the branches above and made no sound.

A growl emerged from the cave: it was the pregnant female. In a move swift as the wind, Fierce fired a tranquilizer dart her way, but it missed its mark. The female had already retreated back into the cave. No sooner had the tranquilizer fired did the male témo descend from the trees and fly over Van. The force was so great, due to the témo's speed and mass, that it caused the Damüdan to fall to the ground.

Vincallous tried to right himself, but he saw claws in his peripheral vision. The female reemerged and swiped her claws at his face. He pulled back and put his gun between he and the barbs. The gun was easily sliced into four pieces. The feline's nails also grazed his forehead and right cheek. Although the wound was superficial, he bled as if he was severely lacerated.

He had little time to recover as he heard the sound of the male témo land thunderously on the ground. Van Fénüra's eyes stung from his blood. He would be lifeless in seconds if he did not do something extreme.

Fashioning his smaller energy gun, Vincallous fired at the male. The discharges smacked the male témo on the wings. He buckled somewhat, and both wings smoked and blood poured from the damaged areas. Though flight was no longer an option, the témo shrugged the blasts off and batted his tail in violent anticipation.

Probability continued to mount. The Zananín scowled. He was about to be executed by the line of self-righteous, false-hearted judges.

The male rushed towards Vincallous and brutally slapped his left shoulder, with claws retracted. The Damüdan flew twenty feet to his right and landed in a patch of mud, near the opening of the cave. The impact caused him to drop his gun, his shoulder to dislocate, and his humerus and clavicle to break. Lying in the soil, Fierce screamed in acute displeasure.

"Get back in the cave," the male intimated calmly to the female and scanned the area adjacent to the den. "We do not know if there are more."

The belt delivered to Vicious was intentionally non-fatal; it was an attempt to draw out more of his comrades. Most fatal blows left one open to attack, and the témos would not take such a wild chance. Little did the témos know that it was Vincallous who had taken the road of negligence. He was completely alone.

The female retreated back to the enclave. Vincallous, battered and bloodied, glanced her way, and with his remaining strength and mental concentration, threw his long knife at her abdomen where her baby nested. The male ran to the blade's target, in order to preserve the life of his mate and child, but his acceleration could not gain enough ground to overtake the trajectory of the weapon. The female crouched and leaned backward but could not avoid the blow directly. Her right shoulder was pierced by the blade.

"It is not bad," she purred.

The male dislodged the blade with his teeth by its grip, whipped his head and released the blade in the Damüdan's direction. Vincallous dodged, but he had to contort his body in a manner that made his dislocated left shoulder and broken clavicle overwhelm his nervous system. He groaned in intense suffering.

The male témo shook his head and growled in bitter disbelief. "Your attack was meant for the cub. You are truly malevolent. Prepare yourself, upright."

"You know all about 'malevolent,' don't you?" Van Fénüra coughed and muttered, cursing and rejecting his oncoming execution.

In the distance, Vincallous saw the machete. Too far away. Both his energy pistol and his tranquilizer gun were fifteen feet away; there was no chance he could make a break for the weapons in his condition. His legs would collapse if he took another step, and his urge to cower would not be rebuffed. Despite his attempts to quiet the instinct, Vincallous drew back from the témos. He needed a miracle; he needed to be born again in his true form.

Although in considerable pain, he clenched his fists together, righted himself, and yelled at the felines with reddened eyes. "You sicken me. You deserve extinction. You are partly responsible for all of this! And I will not be put to death for the sake of your sanctimonious, archaic laws!"

Glowering at the animals in disdain, his chant was angry. "Fá'atoño má. Fá'atoño má. Dé'wa. Dé'wa."

The témos halted in astonishment. The ramifications of Vincallous' chant resonated in their historical subconscious. The Damüdan's eyes turned from gray to charred yellow. A deeply instinctive identification crept in the témos' qaníns.

"A Zananín!" the male témo yelled. "It's Vicious!"

With little reticence, the témos lunged towards Vincallous with violent intentions. The injured female seemed completely unconcerned about her unborn child and unhurt from the bloody wound in her shoulder. Although dodging the knife to protect the cub a few moments prior, she was now willing to sacrifice the cub and herself in order to see Sczyphamek Vicious dead.

"Fá'atoño má." Van's chants were desperate and quick. He pleaded for Dé'wa to break through the wall he had placed between them. "Níyama haito![9] Níyama haito!"

The témos were only a few feet away from placing their canines and claws in him, when Fierce felt a red trickle seep through the astral wall and out of oblivion. His Elemental was returning, but he would have to absorb the oncoming strikes and hope he would persevere.

The female mercilessly slashed his legs. Vincallous' skin ripped and his tibia was punctured and splintered. Unconsciously, the Damüdan hunched over in pain. That move, however, was the first step in a two-part design. With all his might, the male murderously head-butted Van Fénüra, hurtling the Sczyphamek backwards. Vicious somersaulted through the trees, until he finally crashed into pile of rocks, nearly a quarter of a length away.

The blows should have left him without both legs and killed him. *Would have*, if his powers were not somewhat restored two seconds prior. His forehead bled ostensibly, and the pain, localized in his cranium and legs, was enough to paralyze his attempts to stand. Indeed, without his powers, that strike would have collapsed and shattered his skull, but Dé'wa gave him just enough Elemental protection to absorb the head-butt and enough extra energy to stand amidst the rocks.

His camouflaged outfit was ripped and torn, with holes and crimson marks spattered throughout. Vincallous' left hand twitched uncontrollably. Blood streamed down his face, over his eyebrows, down his nose, and onto his beard and goatee. His pants were soaked in his own constitution, but he would not yield to this enemy.

The animals looked at him in contemptible terror, shocked that he had somehow survived the assault and fearful of the implications of such a fact.

Enraged and in horrendous agony, Van's scream was primal and crazed. The flag and canine were his.

It was their turn to suffer.

Forthwith, a high pitch ring emanated out of Sczyphamek Vicious, which caused the témos to shudder and fall. Other animals capable of hearing the pitch squealed and squawked along with the témos, and the rocks behind Vicious began to crack under sonic duress. The forced use of his drowsy Elemental caused Vincallous' to drop on all fours and gasp, but his Elemental continued to assert itself. Standing up once more, Vicious scowled at his adversaries with wild eyes and a malice that bespoke robbery and indignation.

"What gave you the right to judge us malevolent? Who appointed you judge of our cause?" Vicious bellowed, demanding a response. "Why were we denied The Synthesis? Tell me!"

The témos writhed in torment. Dé'wa oozed out of Vicious, leaking out of his left shoulder and dripping down his arms. His aura crept up his shoulders to the top of his head. Slowly, his features regained their younger

---

[9] Níyama haito (*nee*-yah-muh hahy-ih-toh)

expressions, and his lost muscle mass returned. He was a long way from his Awakened power level, but it was just enough to pauperize the témos.

He began to walk, but quickly tumbled. Gathering what little of himself and Dé'wa he could, Vincallous crawled wearily towards his energy pistol. After picking up the firearm, he staggered towards the male témo. The male sensed the coldness of Fierce's qanín and shuddered.

Vincallous wiped his nose, mouth, and chin clean of blood, only for more to pour out of his wounds. He spat a tooth out of his mouth and declared, "Your species cannot naturally achieve the abilities of a Sczyphamek, and yet you think you understand the First's intentions. I am a Zananín by name only, and when we kill the rest of your kind, all memory of this title will die with you."

The male témo lunged towards Vincallous, but missed due to the extreme disorientation caused by the sonic disruption. Vincallous, having recovered some of his Sczyphamek strength, barbarously kicked the male témo in the stomach, fracturing the témo's ribs and the Sczyphamek's metatarsals. The male whimpered, and Vicious nearly buckled from the effort, as more blood poured out of his right leg.

Staring at the female témo in angry languor, a groggy Vincallous huffed, "I want you to see what will happen to your mate and what will happen to you and that unborn kíma of a cub inside of your misbegotten body."

Retrieving a tranquilizer, he tossed it into the rib cage of the female. She lost motor control, but not consciousness. Vicious increased the gun's charge and aimed the pistol at the male and shot his four legs. The male yelped in affliction. Immediately, Vincallous stopped the high pitch ringing. Now that his adversaries were downed, he did not wish to cause he nor Dé'wa any more unnecessary stress.

The female témo looked on, unable to move, but able to think and emote.

Picking up his machete, Vincallous trudged towards the male ominously. He clutched the struggling feline by the head with his left arm and ignored the distress of his shoulder. Instead, as he drew his broken right arm back, Vicious channeled his pain into his right hand, in order to return a double portion of what the témo had given him. In violent, successive blows to the animal's neck, the Sczyphamek beheaded the male témo while tears streamed down the face of his pregnant mate.

The Damüdan's expression was savage. He wheezed and hacked and his blood-soaked hand dropped the machete on the ground.

"You all are trophies… relics of a bygone era," Vicious panted. He stumbled towards the female and tossed the severed head in front of her. "This next tranquilizer will completely render you unconscious, although when you awake, you will wish you died here with your mate."

The Sczyphamek laid his own bloody head on her belly and rubbed it, while stabbing another tranquilizer in her right hind leg. "Do not grow angry at me, témo." He relaxed his head on her rich fur. "It was your kind who began this. If you had not seen us as enemies so long ago, then I would not be here today. If you had not attacked, I would not have become your destroyer, would I?"

He wiped his eyes with his soiled hands, but tears continued to fall down the Sczyphamek's face, and his aura flickered then bloomed. The texture of the témo's fur felt like his mother's favorite blanket. The tactile remembrance precipitated his bitter weeping.

He still possessed vivid memories of that day. On his twelfth birthday, his family hiked in the hills of Nosgüth and happened upon the cave.

"Van, look!" his mother exclaimed. "Témos used to live in this cave. Long ago, they taught our village how to fend for ourselves and fight against Tannódin and White Scythe. Although we play Zorschwin for fun these days, the témos taught us that game as a way to defend and fight for ourselves against impossible odds."

"The highlanders of Nosgüth, our ancestors, helped them escape after most of Damüda fell, seven hundred cycles ago," his father added. "But this cave used to be a great meeting place for them. They were very kind and gracious to our ancestors. Remember Van; their strength now lies in you."

To use the tools of resistance to build the master's house...

Kaz Vincallous Fierce gazed upon the anesthetized, pregnant témo with hatred, sympathy, conviction, and self-loathing... and sliced open her abdomen.

CHAPTER ELEVEN: JENNÓ

"What're you thinking about back there, Mésa? Staxis, you haven't said a thing since we left Nextu. I mean, can I get some conversation here? We're six days away from Pike Metropolis, and we're going off the main road within the hour..." Jennó glared, scowled, and sighed disapprovingly at the blank-faced woman. Patting his windhorse and murmuring inaudibly, the man looked at the well-worn trail ahead and then glanced back at his Nez Spiritan sister. "I mean, Nez Spiritans love traveling together, right? That's one of our marks as a people, y'know? It's what makes us happen as us, y'know? You are from Nez Spirita, right? Hey... hey... Damn it, are you even listening to me? Staxis..."

Neztríanis, although perturbed by Jennó's voice, had fallen back into her traveling self. She did not talk much while journeying alone from Hopha to Nextu. So it was strange to try to enter into Jennó's banter. She recalled Namí and Hafir's reassurances. Although he was abrasive, she could tell just by traveling with him for one day that he was a man who knew his way around Nez Spirita.

"I apologize, Jennó. I guess I am used to traveling by myself."

"Where are you from again?" he asked. "Point Sank, right?"

"Yes," she lied. "More like the outskirts..."

"Oh. Villages are few and far between out that way... No wonder you're used to traveling quietly. But you see, I just got this itch to talk, and I've gotta scratch it. *Scratch, scratch, scratch...*" His sing-song voice was as entertaining as it was annoying.

Neztríanis, unable to maintain a solemn face, smiled. His expression was quite comical.

"Is that a smile? By the Nameless One! It took sixteen hours! And here I was, thinking I'd lost my charm. You were close to the record."

"Record? Who holds it?" she asked with interest.

He grinned. "My Mamisí."

"Why am I not surprised?"

"Ahhh," he said in his sonnet voice and scratched his goatee. "She can make a joke too?"

The two were mum for a few minutes as the horses trotted up the path. The daughter of Hopha and the trader from the North passed few people or checkpoints, which made the Sczyphamek wonder why she was so afraid of traveling by herself or felt the need of a guide in the first place. Perhaps she overestimated Tannódin's presence on the road to Pike Metropolis. The first snow was now a few weeks away; they had probably pulled back their forces in preparation for winter. Neztríanis doubted herself. Stopping in Nextu added three unnecessary weeks to her journey. Although grateful for meeting Namí and Hafír, the daughter of Hopha reconsidered her actions, especially since the winter season was sure to plunge most of Nez Spirita into a frozen wasteland. Again, she was forced to trust another stranger. And no matter what her friends in Nextu said, she would *never* trust this brigand of a merchant. Jennó seemed like the kind of person who would sell out his own mother if the price was right. Avarice, ever the opportunist, was by its qanín, insatiable. It respected no ethnicity or culture.

These musings were brought to a halt when Jennó suddenly stopped his windhorse. Without hesitation, Neztríanis followed suit and sensed her surroundings. At first she felt nothing. However, after about a minute she detected them coming towards their location. She had no idea who they were, but they were about fifty in number and all of them were armed. There was a mechanized vehicle as well, and soon Neztríanis began to hear the signs of what she sensed.

"This way," Jennó whispered, moving off the trail and into the forest at a steady clip.

Neztríanis hastened. The windhorses galloped at half their top speed; twenty minutes or so later, Jennó stopped, dismounted, and motioned for Neztríanis to do the same.

"We are going to stay here for the night. That was a standard Blue Rapier patrol; they cover a ten-length radius in each direction from the road. But they backtrack their steps every two hours. I'd hoped we could use that path for a little while longer." He ran his fingers through his hair and scratched his goatee. After which, he guided his horse by the reins and led it west, prompting Neztríanis to follow. "We need to find a small stream from the Xarkim so the horses can have something to drink."

Neztríanis used her Elemental to sense for the nearest running water, which was furthest away from the soldiers. She located a small brook, two lengths to the northwest of their position.

"We should head this way." Neztríanis pointed in the direction of the brook. "I have a knack for finding water."

"Alright." Jennó's face betrayed his confusion. "That's where I was going to take us."

They made it to the brook in about a half an hour, but Neztríanis wondered why they did not use the horses to travel.

He answered her unspoken question. "The horses are gonna work hard starting tomorrow and for the next three days. And my butt hurts."

Neztríanis shook her head in amusement. "How did you know about the troops? You perceived them before I heard a sound."

"Cycles of smuggling and moving contraband, I guess," he said. "When you've been in this business as long me, kíma, some things start coming naturally. I know these roads well... well, Qalfocx... Heh heh heh... I pretty much know all of Nez Spirita, from the Crags to Nextu, down this kímaz peninsula, and back up to Point Sank."

The man spoke in such an arrogant, low brow, self-congratulatory manner; it was comically agitating to the Sczyphamek. "I see." Neztríanis smirked, but her pressing stare at him revealed her dissatisfaction with his answer.

"I heard the sound of their machinery and movement towards us. It was faint at first, but when you're so used to hearing something, even the slightest noise 'll warn you." Jennó patted his horse on the side and reached into a satchel on the horse's back, pulling out some food for the stallion. He placed his hands in front of its mouth, and the horse ate the food. The sun was setting to the east, and they would have to make preparations for a fire.

Neztríanis walked to the stream and was about to put her face in the water when Jennó yelled, "Mésa, stop! What're you doing? Get away from the water!"

Neztríanis immediately backed away.

"This water is from the Xarkim River, but it is north of the Nextu water treatment facility. It might be contaminated with poisonous runoff from Pike Metropolis. We've got to test the water before we drink it."

He reached into his pants pocket and pulled out a capsule. Next, he took a small cup from his backpack. He passed Neztríanis, scooped some of the water out of the stream, and placed the capsule in the cup. It dissolved and a green pigment appeared.

Neztríanis inquired, "What does that mean?"

"It means, you'd've been lucky," he sighed. "Green means that the water is safe to drink. Orange means that the water is undrinkable. If it's neither, it's the drinker's call." Jennó poured the water out of the cup. "Just as well, I think we should boil this water, to be safe. It should be good for the horses to drink though."

The smuggler walked back to his horse and led it to the stream. Neztríanis did the same.

"How long since you've been to Point Sank?"

Neztríanis was uncertain how to answer. "A while, I guess. Why?"

"They built a water treatment facility there too, about five cycles ago, with Tannódin's aid. No one drinks water outside the city anymore, unless it is far upstream on the Kyan River, before the industrial factories."

"Well, I left there before they made those changes."

"I see. Well Mésa, how about this: How about you don't drink from any water source until we test it?"

"That is acceptable," the woman affirmed affably and tried to appear normal. She realized that Jennó was so talkative that she would be in a state of fabrication for the foreseeable future. She needed to cut down on the conversation and remember every story she made up.

Jennó left to search for firewood while Neztríanis cleared an area suitable for sleeping. This was her first night out in the open in some time, and she felt a bit cold, even with her powers. Before long, Jennó returned with ample kindling and made a fire. Then he took a covered pot, went to the stream, and filled the pot with water. He returned and placed it on the fire. Neztríanis turned to the river and sat down in a reverential posture, her back to the merchant. She chanted some of the Fragments to herself while gazing at the running water.

Jennó studied his traveling partner silently.

After about thirty minutes, the daughter of Hopha turned around, faced the campfire, and laid her eyes upon a spread of food prepared by Jennó. Neztríanis was astonished and wondered how he was able to do so much in such a small amount of time. Some of the meal was the leftovers from Namí's feast the night prior, but he had also made a pot of some sort of stew. It smelled delicious.

Before Neztríanis opened her mouth, the talker spoke first. "How often do you chant and pray?"

"Whenever I can afford the time," she responded. "How did you fix that meal so fast?"

Jennó scratched his goatee and ran his fingers through his black hair—clearly an unbreakable habit—and smiled, "I fix food about as good as I talk."

"Oh." Neztríanis peered into the pot with an inquisitive frown and asked, "What kind of stew is that?"

"The kind you eat..." he grinned. "I ain't telling you, Mésa... Staxis, you probably won't try it if I told you."

"*That* comment is supposed to make me want to try it?" Neztríanis smiled at her guide, who grunted to himself.

"Look, Mésa..." Jennó's tone became apprehensive. "I don't want or need to know what you are doing out here—Hafir's credits were enough for me—but I do need to know where your final stop is so that I can plan the rest of this trip. If you want to pick a point that's close to the destination, that's fine, but, trust me, things'll get harder from here on out... I made all of this food, because we won't be eating a hot meal again for about three days."

"Why?"

"Troops from Blue Rapier and White Scythe are everywhere right now. They're searching for escapees from the battle of Lozé, and they're performing their annual pre-winter sweep of the area so that no major contraband can be smuggled in or out of the city. Even I cease with the hustling this time of cycle.

"Once the snows begin, you can't leave or enter Pike Metropolis unless you're on a stratojet, railcruiser, or you're crazy. All of the mountain passes are completely impassable; even the trains don't run as often. Because there isn't a great deal of normal traffic in or out of the city for nearly two durations, Tannódin makes sure that no one or nothing important is trying to sneak in or out before it snows.

"That means Blue Rapier will be all over these parts. Anyone who is caught and unable to provide identification will probably be put in prison or at least questioned. You picked one of the worst times to travel like this. Kíma, judging from the weather, we're about two weeks out from the snows…" He eyed her carefully and continued with a congenial tone, "But, lucky for you, I am a master in getting around these parts."

"I see."

"*Do you see?*" he pressed. "We'll be off the major roads from now until we reach Pike Metropolis. When we get there, stay close to me. We'll be taking public transportation at a few places. Make eye contact with no one, and say even less. If the snows start and we're not out of Pike Metropolis, then we'll be stuck there. No, let me rephrase that. *You will be stuck.*"

"Why are you telling me this now?"

"I am going to tell you this every night so that it will stick. Every night I will repeat this, because I am not going down for your sake. If at any point you look like you will get caught, I won't be coming to your rescue."

"I guess your payment didn't include that," she said with noticeable disgust.

"Damn right," he replied and poured some of the stew into a small bowl. "Like I said, I don't want to know what you are doing. You may very well be a harmless insect who just doesn't want to get involved with Tannódin. But that probably ain't true. Times are changing; even random Nez Spiritans don't get stopped for no reason too much anymore, except for this time of the cycle…

"Come to think of it, I bet Hafir himself probably doesn't know who you really are or what you're really doing. That guy would help anybody he feels is in need. He's a true Nez Spiritan." Jennó's last comment displayed a genuine admiration for the man who had given Neztríanis a house and a home for three weeks.

"Yes," the woman said sadly in fond reminiscence. "He and Namí are wonderful people."

She placed some of the stew in the bowl Jennó provided for her, and put some of Namí's food in the dish as well. The young woman scanned for any possible traces of Tannódin'é or Damüdan forces. She felt none.

"Why did you choose here to stop?" Neztríanis asked. "I was thinking as I meditated that a likely place to stop would be the—"

"Wait, Mésa," Jennó interrupted. "You didn't answer my original question."

"What was it? I cannot remember because you talked so much…"

He laughed at that barb. "Funny. My question was, 'where do you want me to take you?'"

Neztríanis thought for a moment and decided it would be best if he took her to the Bitzroy Plains, even though it was further than Mount Xarkim. That was fine, however, because he would not know that she would be doubling back. "If you can get me to Bitzroy, about a hundred lengths northwest of the Infinite Circle, near the Eastern Gemansu Range…"

"Bitzroy," Jennó echoed. "Staxis… it's hot in Bitzroy right now." The man slurped down some of his food and continued his instructions. "Don't talk to anyone Mésa. No one travels this time of the cycle except for merchants, Global Initiative envoys, sex traders, criminals, or fools. You are one of the last two… maybe you are both…"

Learning from her experience with Namí and Hafir, Neztríanis' face was impossible to read and she spoke nothing.

"We gotta go through Pike Metropolis," he continued. "It'll be quicker than going around the western side of the Infinite Circle. We'll cross the mountains at the southwest pass; no one uses it anymore, not even Tannódin. It is too treacherous and steep. Plus a wealthy Tannódin'é farmer owns the land on the Nextu side of the pass. I happen to know this farmer, and he doesn't mind if I use the road as long as I do him some favors come springtime.

"We'll use the horses to cross over the Nextu Mountains. That pass is about three thousand feet. Once we cross there, we'll be near my 'friend's' farm. We'll leave the horses there and go into Pike on foot. The southwest pass… it's well over six thousand feet, and the climb is downright ugly. Mechanized vehicles and horses can't make it up those inclines. But we will enter into an underdeveloped part of the city. There's no official Tannódin'é checkpoint there, just some contracted help that doesn't mind looking the other way. Especially when the other way leads to credits…

"Well, all that will come later. We need to make it first. You seem like you are in shape, and your legs…" Jennó smiled, gazed at the daughter of Hopha's lower body and chest, then lasciviously grunted and nodded in approval. "*Yeah*, I think you'll be *just fine*."

The Sczyphamek was both angered and embarrassed by Jennó's unambiguous flirtatiousness.

"I will be *fine*." Her tone was severe, matched by the indignation emanating from her eyes and body. "Do *not* look at me like that again."

"I'm sorry," he smirked. "I won't do it again… or at least, you won't see me do it again…"

"Why do we not travel around Pike?" Neztríanis was wary of Jennó's reasoning and plan. She did not see the merit of venturing into Tannódin's imperial headquarters in Nez Spirita.

"Good, I like questions…" Jennó laughed. "You don't trust me. I get it. We can go around the circle if you want. But we will die. So then, I guess you can go that way and die.

"The Gemansu Range—which is really two mountain ranges—is the western way. By the time we cross them, the first snows will already be falling. No one survives out there in the winter. If this was summer, we wouldn't be going through Pike. *I* don't want to go there, but it's the only way now.

"You're nervous and scared. I get that. But as long as you do what I say, no harm will come to you." He said this as sincerely as Neztríanis had heard him speak thus far.

"The way around to the east, the Limestone Mountains…?" Neztríanis inquired with less suspicion and hostility.

"It's the same. Even though it's just one mountain range, we'd have to go through rocky terrain before we even made it to the range itself. And if we even made it there before the First Snow, most of the area in the Bitzroy Plains north of the Limestones is filled with troops. You got any more questions?"

She shook her head and sighed.

Phyxtríalis ate her meal slowly; surprisingly, it was not that bad. Perhaps Jennó was not *that* bad either. Their conversation benefitted Neztríanis more than he knew. First, she could have been sickened or worse if that water was actually toxic. In addition, the Sczyphamek possessed no knowledge of the patrols around this area, nor the fact that Pike Metropolis was placed on a virtual internment for the winter. That information, combined with the knowledge that the survivors of Lozé were still being searched for, was eye opening. White Scythe, clearly a relentless adversary, was sparing no expense to find Rydín and the remaining survivors of Lozé.

Neztríanis had not perfected the skill of detecting heat signatures, so it was to her advantage that she was traveling with someone who could avoid discovery. And most importantly, Temperature realized she had grossly underestimated the weather. She had experienced winters in Hopha, yes. But the elevation of her hometown was much lower than Pike Metropolis and more obviously, Mount Xarkim. She could not afford to be on that mountain when the snows started. She doubted that she could stay alive there, even with her Elemental. Since Jennó lived in Northern Bitzroy, he would not linger any more than he had to in any place. His destination was further than hers, and there was very little time left. The daughter of Hopha considered all of this and understood that Jennó must have made a trek like this before, probably countless times.

It seemed the Nameless One and the planet was once again generous to her. She was quite fortunate to have met Rydín that day, which seemed so long ago. He was just like the Nez Spiritans of Hopha: dedicated, congenial, and most of all, he had no love for Tannódin. Although Hafir worked with the Tannódin'é, it was clear that he was still cut from the same cloth as Rydín and her clansmen and women. And despite Jennó's bravado, greediness, and lowbrow behavior, he too embodied these characteristics. They were her extended family; they were all connected, yet distinct. They were like her brothers, and Namí was like another mother. Somehow the verses she read in the Fragments and the memory of the ancestors found a space within her journey.

Nez Spiritans… We really are all kin, she thought in wonder.

Neztríanis was filled with an inner peace, a strange inner peace, which was the cognate of her name in the Ancient Tongue. "Nez," translated, meant "peace," and the approximate meaning of "tríanyx" was "to be filled (with)."

She was becoming more confident in her abilities, journey, and faith. Who knew this feeling would emerge in the company of such a scoundrel? The random unfolding of time and space made for weird pairings.

Jennó stood up and took a swig from a flask, filled with a fermented beverage. He downed it in gulps, wiped his mouth, and cleared his throat. He smiled at Neztríanis awkwardly and put the food and the pot away. Then he lay on his back and wrapped himself in a thick blanket. The merchant yawned and stretched. "Tomorrow is going to be long, Mésa. You should get some rest. We shouldn't run into anymore agents until we reach Pike Metropolis."

"I am about to lie down." She hesitated, but spoke in earnest, "Thank you, Jennó. I know you were paid, but you did not have to do this."

"Yeah," he smirked and scratched his rear. "You're right about that. But then, I wouldn't have had the pleasure of traveling home with an attractive woman like you or making a few extra credits. Luckily, my consort won't know about this."

"*Right,*" Neztríanis frowned humorously.

"Mésa?" Jennó called out in an unfamiliar tone. "Do you think we can chant together, just once? I don't do it as often as I should… Actually, I haven't done it in a long time… I was just wondering…"

"That is fine," she smiled.

"Thank you," he said and turned over.

Neztríanis spread her own blanket out. Although she was not cold, she had to play the part. She ate her last bit of food and stretched out on her back. The horses grazed near the river then huddled next to one another. Judging by the wood and burn rate, the fire would last for at least three more hours.

***

The windhorses huffed and panted as the terrain became thicker and steeper.

Jennó did not exaggerate. The days were grueling.

They did not sleep or rest for any substantial period, and the moments of rest were due more to the horses' fatigue than their own. Every day grew noticeably cooler. The snows would commence in no more than two weeks. Customary for the wintertime, the sky became grayer as clouds rolled in from the North Country. The entire continent would soon be covered in the dreary haze of Sunrise Mountain. In the winter, the mountain shared a small but overwhelming portion of its saturnine coldness and precipitation with the rest of the continent.

On the few occasions Jennó and Neztríanis rested, she invited the merchant to chant and pray with her, followed by the sharing of a sacred meal. She recalled leaving Rydín and his group abruptly when they were about to begin a similar ritual. She still felt guilty, but grew comforted by the fact she could atone for her departure by celebrating and eating with the talkative trekker. It was unsurprisingly natural for an uneasy rapport to develop between the two, for Nez Spiritans rarely, if ever, traveled by themselves on long journeys. Although Neztríanis valued her Elemental, she was quite lonely during the first leg of her quest.

By the end of their second day of traveling, the Elemental warrior was feeling rather spent, which made her wonder how Jennó possessed a wind that allowed him to move with such vigor. Competitive as the Nez Spiritan woman was, she would not let on that she was tired. Her species *happened* indomitably, a necessary adaptation due to the Drift's influence on Qeauríyx. But, spending time in Nextu for three weeks had dulled the Sczyphamek's burgeoning physical skills.

On the fourth day of travel, they crossed over the Nextu Range at a natural open plateau, and moved down into a small valley. Nestled away near the base of a large hill, a mansion fit snugly into a groove in the small mountain. Neztríanis was worn, and even Jennó finally appeared to be exhausted. They planned to shower and spend the night at his acquaintance's house once they arrived.

Throughout the past three days Jennó also proved to be a man of his word. He recounted his plan to her every night, and added more information with each repetition. As they neared the mansion, the daughter of Hopha titled her head upwards and saw a mountain peak almost directly behind the large hill.

"Is the pass near that mountain ahead?" she asked Jennó.

"The mountain *is* the pass," he commented.

"Who built the path?"

"Our ancestors, probably; but it hasn't seen much use in many cycles. I and a few others like me are the few who use it now. The mountain is over twelve thousand feet."

"And the house we are going to?"

"No one you need to know about," he said flatly. He was unwilling to grant her any information that might compromise him or his partners-in-trade. "As a matter of fact, you are not even going to meet this person. It would be better for everybody if you remain in the dark as possible.

"There's a guesthouse for us, so you won't need to go anywhere else. We get running water and a warm bed to sleep on. Sleep hard tonight, Mésa. The climb tomorrow will be like nothing we've done so far."

Neztríanis did not reply but focused her attention on the mountain ahead. It was still daytime, but it was unusually clear for the season, so the summit was visible. There was not much of a snowpack, but the winds were threatening. Thin clouds swirled in a manner that signified strong air currents. Her horse bellowed wearily and she patted its head and rubbed its mane.

"Your journey is almost done, my friend," she whispered.

Hers was still just beginning.

She slept well that night. In fact, Jennó woke her for the first time during their travels. Their meal was heavy. The merchant did not want to stop until they made it to the pass, which was five thousand feet, one and a quarter lengths above their present location.

They departed at two hours before dawn. The days were growing shorter. In the throes of Nez Spiritan wintertime, Zénan provided a mere five dedicated hours of sunlight. In order to traverse the pass in one day, traveling in the dark was a necessity

Jennó left her in the mansion's guesthouse, while the merchant exchanged pleasantries with his mystery contact. Based on Hafir's testimony and Jennó's own admission, the man's operation was not entirely legitimate. Jennó's entire livelihood was caught up in his continental mercantilism. He could not afford for Tannódin's meddling hand to disrupt his economic affairs. And though Nez had no love for criminals, the Sczyphamek realized that she was a "criminal" in the eyes of Global Initiative. Temperature was comforted by the fact that she was not the only one who broke or would break Tannódin's rule of law. Still, she trusted Jennó as much as she did when she first met him: very little.

The trail on the first leg of the incline was manageable, but steep. Jennó assured her that the path would be more treacherous every thousand feet or so. She was instructed to stop at any moment she felt more than drained. The air was thinner, the temperature was colder (even she grew a bit chilled), and the wind was filled with enmity. Her calves strained and flexed, as she carried the weight of her shoulderpack and canteen. She was not used to the altitude's air and neither was Jennó it appeared, for their pace had slowed in order to compensate for necessity.

While hiking, Neztríanis focused on her Elemental and chanted silently, trying to enhance their power and attempting to forge a better connection with them. She had become an expert in locating water vapor, water, and ice through the use of her elements during the trip with Jennó. Heat signatures were another matter altogether. Each animal, from the tiniest insect to a windhorse, had unique heat dispensations. Neztríanis was truly inspired by that observation. Windhorses possessed similar signatures, but beneath the similarity was a distinction. Locating and locking onto a heat signature required the active knowledge of this duality. Jennó's heat signature, however, was now almost a part of her consciousness. If he were in her vicinity, she would know.

The growth of this ability was advantageous. The daughter of Hopha realized that every Sczyphamek used their Elemental in a similar way. Pre-Eminent and Vicious doubtlessly utilized their distinct abilities to locate and lock onto specific signatures. Tales of Phenplyacin abounded, but no one could describe the powers of Vincallous with much accuracy, although they probably had something to do with ground manipulation. But Neztríanis knew that ground manipulation could only be a half or even a third of his Elemental.

Based on the reports from the battle of Focal, Neztríanis surmised that one of Pre-Eminent's powers was in the form of gravity and some other ridiculous force. Though various reports corroborated the general outline of Pre-Eminent's attack, Neztríanis was still unable to process how Késhal wielded her Elemental in such a stupendous yet precise manner.

Neztríanis shuddered. She did not even want to think about what her next move might be if she was able to retrieve the Auría and take it to the North Country. What terrible fate would beset her then?

Just climb, she told herself. *Just keep climbing…*

It was dusk.

Pulling his hood back, Jennó proclaimed with a sense of accomplishment and finality, "There it is."

They stood atop the frigid southwest pass, at an elevation of 8750 feet, and marveled at the breathtaking panorama of technology and rocky splendor. Neztríanis, dusty and thirsty, took a drink from her water jug, closed the cap, and wiped her mouth. Moving her windblown hair from her face, Neztríanis' brown eyes fastened upon one of the most magnificent venues on Qeauríyx, the Infinite Circle.

Mt. Xarkim was unequivocal, unspoiled, and unopposed. Its cloud-covered, snowcapped peak dwarfed the other adjacent mountains, while its river cut across Pike Metropolis with determination. Mt. Xarkim's summit, well over twenty thousand feet, was shrouded in misty solitude, and the other mountains complimented its splendor. Neztríanis looked clockwise around the majestic range of mountains and embraced a closeness to her elements previously unknown. The view provided a glimpse of the inspiring potential of Qeauríyx. The Infinite Circle, with nine peaks near 14,000 feet and three around 8000 feet, circumscribed Xarkim Valley with heavenly protection. The daughter of Hopha caught her breath and felt the breeze on her face, the beauty of the Nameless One, and exhaled.

"Wonderful…" she said in joy and admiration.

Then she saw *them*. They were unmistakable, three towers looming portentously over the entire valley. The tallest one was in the center, and its rooftop brandished a revolving bright light that drew attention to its haughty ancestry. Neztríanis visibly scoffed at the building. Although impressive, the structure was a testimony to the arrogance of Tannódin. Only the Tannódin'é would rob the magnificence of the mountains, by placing their own version of ascension in the middle of Xarkim Valley. The very fact that she could see such a structure from such a distance sickened her.

"How large is the valley?" Neztríanis asked.

"For all intents and purposes, the valley is almost a perfect circle, with about a 127 length diameter from any part of the circumference."

"Are the Triple Skyrises at the exact center of the circle?" Neztríanis inquired, with noticeable agitation.

"How'd you guess?" Jennó smiled. "That light is so bright that if you were under it, it would appear as if it was daytime. Of course, we're not going anywhere near that place."

The population of the capital was massive. A tremendous amount of heat flowed from the city, not only from its inhabitants but also from the many lights and machineries flickering about the Circle. Pike Metropolis was one of the largest cities in all Qeauríyx, and its sheer scope baffled the daughter of Hopha. Although Hopha was a collection of villages, with a population of about 150,000, her home was much more rural and spacious.

"How many people?" Nez asked, dumbfounded.

"Thirty-nine million," Jennó replied. "Thirty-three million live within the Circle. Another six million live on the other side of the mountains; the greatest concentration of those is on the northern side, heading towards the Bitzroy Plains."

As his custom when explaining things, Jennó ran his left hand through his black hair. "The city is about half Nez Spiritan, a third Tannódin'é, and the remainder are from the other continents. Most Nez Spiritans are employed in various buildings and businesses throughout the city, working for Tannódin'é or Damüdan companies."

As he spoke, a stratojet flew overhead, revealing its underbelly, wings, and fiery thrusters. The plane was noticeably quiet, considering the size of the mechanical monstrosity. Neztríanis was both startled by its proximity and the self-evident, technological gap between Tannódin and the majority of Nez Spirita. The ship was probably flying from Tannódin or another distant continent, and yet the journey from Nextu to Pike on foot was longer than on a transcontinental stratojet flight. Time and space were constricting for some, but for others, an entire way of life was being torn asunder, replaced by a shrinking distance that measured genocide. Neztríanis started to understand Hafir's position a bit more after seeing

Pike Metropolis.

Before she descended, Neztríanis breathed the crisp air. The pass she and her guide traversed was also a rite of passage. With each step toward Pike, the gravity of her mission pressed upon her. Turning around and heading back to Hopha became less and less an option. Jennó was a couple of paces ahead of her; his cloak was drawn tight and his hood flapped in the wind. She took one more gaze at the picturesque scenery, promising herself that she would visit the vista again, and then she started down the mountainside.

***

They made it down the mountain by the end of the day and stayed at a small place for lodging on the southwest outskirts of Pike. It was almost deserted, giving credence to Jennó's plan thus far. They had not encountered a single Global Initiative operative since back on the main road five days ago. The trek had been difficult, but she was almost near Mt. Xarkim.

Jennó suggested they stop and rest. The next day, they planned to cross the entire city by way of the massive light-rail and subway system. The transit system connected the metropolis through a network of stations and tracks, and certain stations contained large security detachments. After explaining the transit's layout, along with the geography and demography of the city, the merchant gave the most detailed instructions henceforth concerning their course of action.

First, they would take the light rail and subway system through the districts with the least amount of law enforcement and military presence. However, there would be three occasions where they would have to walk on the city's streets to bypass transit security forces. Once they made it to the northern side of the city, which swarmed with Blue Rapier, White Scythe, and local law enforcement, they would come to their most dangerous part of the trip: secure passage on the Pike Metropolis-Plains of Bitzroy railcruiser line, which burrowed underneath the northern Infinite Circle. A security checkpoint was unavoidable.

Jennó's instructions to her were simple. Say nothing to anyone unless someone of importance said something first. Her identification would be scrutinized. But Hafir had provided her a legitimate identification card, which he obtained illegitimately. Her bags would probably be searched, but she could not flinch or appear upset. As a precautionary measure and for practice, Jennó rummaged through her bags in an acerbic manner. Seeing her things tossed aside so uncaringly *did* cause her to lunge towards the merchant.

"*No.*" Jennó was as serious as he had ever been towards her. "*Never, ever* move towards or look like you will move towards a Global Initiative agent. That will be the end of it. I will not come to your rescue, because that will be the end of me."

"They would kill me?" Neztríanis was incredulous. "I know the Tannódin'é can be savages but I did not—"

"*Savages?* 'Savages...' Mésa..." Jennó's laugh was speckled with irritation. "Who on Qeauríyx talks like that? The Tannódin'é do what they have to do. They do what they must do, in their own eyes. Whether we agree or disagree is another thing. We have to do what we need to do in order to get out of here."

The woman shook her head, and after some hesitation, nodded.

"Isn't your goal worth this inconvenience?"

"Whatever."

"Yeah, whatever. But, if it is *that* important then you should have no problem with this."

"Jennó, I think we need a secondary plan just in case things go awry or if we get separated."

"If we get separated or if things turn into kíma, then there will be no seconds to spare. We will be caught. This is Tannódin and Damüda. This is Global Initiative's Blue Rapier and White Scythe. This is local, imperial law enforcement. Mésa, *this is it.* Now, you can walk away tonight if you want, and I'll go on without you. I can't afford being with someone who'll get me caught because they are unsure and will hesitate.

"Then again, if you do get caught then you probably will be questioned... meaning you're probably going to crack and give up me and Hafir and whoever else is counting on you." Reaching into his cloak, he brandished an energy pistol, armed it, and aimed it at the woman before she could react. "*Staxis.* I ain't going down for nobody. This gun—it's either going to leave you dead here, tonight. Or, it's going to make you continue through fear. Trust me, if Tannódin catches you, you'll wish that you were dead. They make no secret that they torture prisoners."

She hardly recognized Jennó. "You can put that away," she said quietly. "I will do it."

Jennó hid the weapon back in his cloak. His threatening countenance changed, as he scratched his goatee and ran his fingers through his hair. "Good. Get some rest. And don't worry. By tomorrow night, you'll never see this face of mine again."

The next morning, they took a transit rail halfway through the southwest portion of the city. The train was located underground, and Neztríanis was forced to contain her awe at the novelties she experienced in the great city. Jennó did not threaten her again. It appeared that his dramatic delivery was a last ditch effort to motivate her. She did not know if he would have tried to kill her, which unfortunately for him, would have ended in his death. Once again, the Sczyphamek was chilled by Namí's words concerning how easy it was for a Sczyphamek to kill. She was still deathly afraid of taking a life, but her exchange with Jennó, the night prior, was possibly providential. The merchant placed her in a situation where she was forced to realize how quick death occurred. She had to keep her wits about her no matter the situation. That was what Jennó was trying to teach her. Neztríanis vowed to herself that she would learn this technique.

They did not speak nor did they make eye contact with each other while riding the train, just like Jennó ordered. After about a half an hour, Jennó gave the signal to disembark. Once they left the station, which was located on the northern fringes of southwest Pike Metropolis, they headed north towards the midwestern section of town.

The merchant informed the Sczyphamek that the midwestern borough was the most diverse section of town. Inhabitants from every continent lived there. Secretly, Neztríanis anticipated this part of the journey. Other than Nez Spiritans, she had only encountered Tannódin'é and Damüdans in her lifetime. Therefore, the daughter of Hopha only had imaginary pictures of the other men and women of the planet

A length into their walk, the sidewalks became more and more crowded. Jennó's face signaled surprise. Before too long, the horde grew so dense that the travelers could no longer advance without great difficulty.

With such a close proximity to others, Neztríanis heard random and broken conversations between folks in the multitude.

"I heard it's on its way down this street."

"That's the fifth one they've caught this cycle."

"They should leave them alone."

"I heard that Vicious captured this one."

Neztríanis did not know who "they" or "it" were, but something about the exchanges and proclamations made her wary. In the midst of nondescript locutions, she heard the sound of a large engine. The crowd turned towards the hum, and Jennó and Neztríanis followed the herd's gaze.

Within moments, a procession of autos followed by a large truck passed their way. Behind thick bars and being pulled by the large truck, the Sczyphamek's incredulous eyes looked sorrowfully upon a témo. It appeared injured and depressed.

"Oh no," the daughter of Hopha gasped. "No... no..."

Jennó turned and looked at Neztríanis with eyes of empathy, then motioned that they move on to a parallel street.

But the Sczyphamek *could not* respond. Her Elemental almost engulfed her; her aura nearly burst forth. The connection between the témo and her elements was beyond Neztríanis' understanding. Temperature's Elemental was distressed and *furious*. Never had either of her elements been so frenzied. Perhaps her Elemental was once part of a Myanín. The heat signature of the témo seared Neztríanis' qanín. She would remember it always.

Gritting her teeth in silent fury, the Sczyphamek closed her eyes and took a breath.

"That's right!" a Tannódin'é bystander shouted. The belt woke Neztríanis out of her astral meander. "*Kill it*. Kill those kímaz animals. Their time has passed! Global Initiative is now and the future!"

Some in the crowd chanted "House of Kaz." A Damüdan and Nez Spiritan behind Neztríanis stood with clenched fists and bitten lips. Others were holding back tears; others yelled slurs and threw trash at the témo. Still others cheered for the troops of Tannódin and Damüda who risked their lives to capture the winged feline.

Neztríanis was visibly overwhelmed. There was a tug on her shoulder. It was Jennó. Taking his thumb, he wiped away her tears, grabbed her hand, and led the woman out of the crowd and down an alleyway that connected to a parallel street.

The Sczyphamek fell into somber and angry reflection as they continued to walk north. She still detected the témo's heat signature even though it grew farther and farther away.

Neztríanis was so sullen; it took her a few moments to realize that her Elemental was a different kind of restless. At first she thought that the elements' agitation was caused by the imperial processional and the caged témo, but something else grabbed their attention now. After ten minutes of deducing what the elements discerned, Neztríanis concluded that two heat signatures had been following the duo since she and Jennó exited the transit rail. Soon, Neztríanis noticed other, particular heat signatures tailing them. With so many pedestrians on the sidewalks, she waited until she and Jennó traversed ten intersections before she grew seriously apprehensive.

Turning to Jennó, she stated, "I am thirsty and a bit out of sorts. Can we stop and get something to drink?"

Jennó smiled. "Guess that was kind of rough. We're making good progress, and we've got time. Sure. I know a place that's very close."

The uneasy woman did not respond, but followed her guide into a food establishment some ten minutes later. There were Tannódin'é, Nez Spiritans, and Phmquedrians in the eatery. However, the Tannódin'é appeared to enjoy their own dining section. Although Neztríanis had not seen a Phmquedrian before, she knew they possessed darker skin tones than most on Qeauríyx.

"I did not think a Tannódin'é would eat in the same place as a Nez Spiritan and Phmquedrian," Nez commented.

"Things are different than many Nez Spiritans believe," Jennó said with concealed agitation. Neztríanis barely discerned his irritation, but her emotions were so raw that she was able to sense any emotive variation.

"There are many integrated establishments," the merchant continued. "Although Tannódin keeps some things segregated."

Glancing over her shoulder, the young Sczyphamek sensed five distinct people enter into the restaurant. They were the same heat signatures of those who were following them on the street, in the crowd, and on the light-rail.

That was beyond the laws of probability.

There was only one answer. She admitted to herself that somehow she was compromised. How? She talked to no one, and Namí and Hafir were certainly on her side...

It was him. It had to be *him.*

Thief. Hustler. Merchant. Backstabber. Avarice personified...

"What a kímaz day this has turned out to be," she muttered darkly. "Staxis."

"Something wrong?" asked Jennó. "Something's got your attention."

Neztríanis was scared but maintained a congenial countenance. She did not want to believe it. But it had to be him. Of course it was him. Jennó was an informant for Global Initiative. Of course he was. He must have sold her out the night before they arrived in Pike Metropolis, the evening they lodged at the ranch behind the southwest pass.

"I am fine," she reassured him. She did not want the man to know she knew he had betrayed her. Nervously, she ran her fingers through her hair and began to formulate a plan of escape

Overt use of her powers was prohibited. Jennó had already pilfered enough intelligence from her.

A waiter came to their table and asked for their order. Jennó asked for a Brycian beer, while Nez ordered a glass of mixed berry juice.

Why did Jennó choose her? Was Rydín captured? Were Hafir and Namí compromised? It did not make any sense. There was nothing about her that suggested insurrectionist or person of interest. Or was there?

The waiter returned with their orders and Jennó picked up his glass, eyeing Neztríanis.

Jennó's face became wary and he sipped his beer cautiously. "Damn, you're better than I thought. This trip's over. It appears that I won't get to meet your friends. But I see you've already noticed mine."

"What are you talking about?" Nez matched his tone.

"You've been trying to control your gaze towards my agents since we entered this place, only confirming what I already suspected: your mission is so important that you cannot help but assume that you have adversaries."

"This is not the time to joke." Neztríanis spoke confidently.

"They've been following us for the past two lengths," he said.

The Sczyphamek realized he was serious, but she could not tell if they were actually with him.

Jennó nodded in affirmation. "You glanced over your shoulder at them three times while we were walking, and twice just now. So, no, I am not joking, *Neztríanis.*"

Did he just speak her name, her real name?

The shock in her eyes gave her away, but she feigned innocence anyway. "What… what did you call me?"

"That is your real name, is it not?" His voice was calm, but his dialect, grammar, and cadence grew more erudite with each sentence.

"I told you; my name is Mésa," she stumbled.

"You lied. I have made a life of lying about my names. 'Mésa' is not your name."

Jennó was clever. He picked the perfect place to hand her over. There were probably agents already seated, not to mention those who had followed them inside the building. Surprisingly, she felt no energy weapons on Jennó, or any of his cohorts. So they were either unarmed, or they had not charged their firearms yet. That meant they knew she was unarmed. *He searched her bag the night before…*

But how did he realize she was a person of interest? She had not revealed anything pertaining to her mission, and it was not uncommon for Nez Spiritans to hire travel guides, since Nez Spiritans rarely journeyed alone. Suddenly, she remembered Hafír's chilling warning to her concerning Tannódin: "*When Tannódin comes, they come in a force that gives one no possibility of escape.*"

"Did you not think we would notice if the daughter of Phesiana Phyxtríalis, the Great Mother of Hopha, went missing?"

Again, Neztríanis' eyes widened before she could stop them, but this time her anxious face was accompanied with an audible gasp. She had to relax. Her mother warned her of this possibility, so there was still a chance that Jennó only believed that she had run away or was preparing herself to lead the village. His talk of her "mission" might have been a ploy to get her to yield more information. He was unaware of her true purpose, and there was no way he would risk her harm, due to the peace treaty between Hopha and Tannódin. That treaty was one of the few things that Tannódin actually respected since the rise of Pre-Eminent.

Jennó adjusted himself and took another gulp from his beer. "You were not from outskirts of Point Sank. Even a child there knows that you should not drink water outside the city unless it is checked for contaminants. Not only that, but your accent and mannerisms placed you somewhere between Nextu and Hopha itself. But, that only added to what I already knew."

Neztríanis looked at the man she never trusted, whom she frequently lied to, and a steady anger entered into her qanín.

"Once you stayed with Hafír, we started collecting our data. I did some checking myself and realized who you were before I met you, although Hafír and Namí did not ascertain your true identity."

There was no reason to deny his accusation. They were past the point of no return.

"I do not want to go back." Neztríanis played along. "Why should Tannódin care if I ran away? I don't want to lead the village. Should you not be happy that I am gone?"

"Believe me, nothing would make me happier… *if that was the truth.*"

"The truth—"

"*Shut up.*" His voice became like a knife's edge. "No more lies. You don't understand what I am saying to you, Neztríanis Phyxtríalis. You are a novice playing an expert's game. I am not some Nez Spiritan merchant selling you out for credits. I told you, those are *my* agents. I am Eradicate. Seeing through kíma is what I do. And I have grown quite adept at it, *sister.*"

The Eradicate? Who were they? *His agents…?* It was one thing for Jennó to be an informant, but that was not the implication of his words. He was a Nez Spiritan in the employ of the House of Kaz.

"By the Nameless One," the woman stammered with palpable resentment. "That… that is kíma. A Nez Spiritan who works for our oppressors… Kíma."

Jennó was unaffected by her anger and shook his head. "When I first met you. I believed that you were running away. Everything about your actions said so, and that was probably what Hafir thought as well. I was content to be your guide and size up the daughter of the Third House of Peace. Just by traveling with you, I would be able to tell how the village views us, and that information would be invaluable. Kíma, maybe if I was lucky, I could've even had sex with you.

"You have good instincts, but you are too careless and inexperienced. You became more apprehensive and secretive with each passing day. That could only mean one thing. You are not running away nor are you entering into some ridiculous rite-of-passage. You are on a mission of secrecy.

"I do not know what this mission is, but once we drug, torture, and rape you—*repeatedly*—I am sure we will find out. Hopha… Kíma…" Jennó snarled in deprecation. "The remaining Houses have been a bane to this continent for too long. If you have broken our non-aggression treaty, we reserve the right to attack."

The apparent master of espionage lacerated her story with precision. Neztríanis did not offer a rebuttal. She was angry and frightened: angry that she was disrespected in such a manner and scared because she could tell how staid the man was. Judging by his recent statements, Jennó appeared to be a Nez Spiritan who genuinely disdained the ways of the Ancestors. But then again, it was possible that he intentionally misled her with those comments. If there was one thing Neztríanis was certain about in the midst of her uncertainty, it was that Jennó's countenances and words were sweet and shifty anathema mixed with foreboding and gentle fondness. He was impossible to read with an untrained eye.

"I wanted to find out who your contacts are or what mission you are on… but then again, these missions never go according to plan, do they?" His smile grew into a menacing glare. "Neztríanis, you have two options. You can tell me what your mission is and who your contacts are right now. Or you and I can take a ride to the Triple Skyrises with my friends, and we can discuss the matter there. The choice is yours."

"That is not a choice. And I do not know what you are talking about. I am not on a mission; I am running away."

"Cléth," [1] the spy cursed. "I will not repeat myself again. *Do not lie to me.*"

"Jennó, I will not repeat myself. *Do not call me out of my name.*" Vitriol oozed from her mouth. She was livid that he used such a derogatory name to refer to her.

Jennó laughed heartily, clearly unmoved by her threat. "What's wrong? Has the daughter of Hopha never been called a 'cléth' before? That's what you are to us. A kímaz cléth."

Neztríanis searched for an escape path. Maybe if she acted as if Jennó threatened her, the customers would confront him. After all, she was surrounded by Nez Spiritans.

Jennó followed her eyes and her reasoning and anticipated her conclusion. "Don't even think of making a scene," the spy warned. "This isn't the peninsula. These people will not come to your aid. Observe."

Before Neztríanis had a chance to defend herself, Jennó violently struck her in the face. Even with Neztríanis' newfangled strength and greater threshold for pain, she experienced a considerable amount of soreness on her left cheek. Jennó was *strong*.

The establishment grew quiet, and everyone stared at the adversarial table. Jennó scanned the room venomously, with contempt for his fellow Nez Spiritans.

"Say something," he barked at the patrons, and his agents, seven in total, stood up around the eatery, with visages of tyranny.

No response. No protest. Folk went about their business as if nothing happened. The imperial operative turned his attention back towards his captive, who was bleeding from her mouth, and threw Neztríanis a napkin.

"Clean yourself up, cléth," he smirked and motioned to his agents to sit back down. "You cannot escape. And since you don't want to talk here, I guess I'll have to take you to the Skyrises for a more *formal* debriefing."

She wiped a small amount of blood from her mouth and trembled in rage. *Too much.* It was too much. She *hated* Global Initiative. Tannódin and Damüda had created a world that celebrated the genocide of témos. The House of Kaz employed Nez Spiritan collaborators, those who would betray, torture, sexually assault, and kill their own brothers and sisters for imperial gain. And to make matters worse, her own people would not stand up for her after she was accosted without provocation.

Was she one of the last Nez Spiritans with a qanín of resistance and pride? Was the majority of her kind on the slow, inextricable march of assimilation?

---

[1] Cléth (cléyth)

It took Neztríanis' entire qanín to not freeze then burn Jennó alive. It was going to take more than one reason for her not to kill him that moment. Before Jennó, she had never been struck by anyone; she had never been called out of her name by anyone; she had never seen a Nez Spiritan balk at the ancestors so strongly; she had never known a Nez Spiritan to collaborate with and completely submit to Tannódin and Damüda; and she had never seen her continental brothers and sisters appear so *weak*.

Her desire to kill arrested the rest of her thinking and feeling. She craved his death. Where was the Neztríanis who was afraid to harm? She was afraid of (though not deterred by) her resentment, cold-heartedness, and rational decision to kill Jennó.

Lucky for him, two realities prevented her from striking him down that instant. First, she could not reveal her powers in a Pike Metropolis eatery. Eyewitnesses, word of mouth and newsprints would ensure that the entire planet would learn of another Sczyphamek within a week. And her fear of Vicious and Pre-Eminent guaranteed her reticence to kill. Her exposure meant that their gaze would be turned to her, and they would find and destroy her. Second, any action she took now would place Hopha, Namí, and Hafir in grave danger. Her actions would be interpreted as a sign of aggression against Tannódin and the armistice between her village and Global Initiative would be void. Her hands and her Elemental were tied. Without a doubt, Jennó had the upper hand, even though she had more brute power than he. Escape without violent confrontation was her best and only option.

When Jennó saw that Neztríanis had given up on the conversation, he signaled his agents to arrest her. After Jennó's violent demonstration, Neztríanis expected no help inside the restaurant. The Tannódin'é welcomed another captured insurrectionist, and no Nez Spiritan or Phmquedrian aimed to share her fate.

Dour, imperial agents encircled Neztríanis and Jennó's table. One of them, a fair-skinned man with wide shoulders, a chiseled face, and a hardened grip, placed his hands on her shoulders tightly. The eyes of all the patrons were fastened upon her, and the restaurant became a sonic vacuum. Neztríanis was almost drawn into the weight of the silence, until she heard some meat sizzling on a stove.

A stove!

Focusing, in a manner as to avoid detection, the Sczyphamek got up from her chair and incited the heat in the stoves and ovens, until they became virtual incinerators, suddenly smoldering the food in an incandescent yet smoky blaze. The appliances themselves began to melt. Some exploded. Commotion ensued. The cooks ran out of the kitchen, unable to control the growing conflagration. As the fire raged, smoke filled the eatery. The customers became frenzied, clamoring towards the exit.

The agents tried to react but the tide of people was uncontrollable. The threat of immediate conflagration superseded imperial domination. Jennó and his company were almost stampeded. The hardened agent, caught in the growing eddy, lost his grip on Neztríanis, allowing her to break free. Jennó screamed to his other operatives, but to no avail. The force of the crowd was too great; it took almost all of Jennó's strength to prevent him from being trampled.

Exiting the eatery, Neztríanis masked herself in the oceanic crowd. Once outside, she ran towards the Triple Skyrises, attempting deceptive misdirection. She tried to sense Jennó's heat trace; however, the crowd was so dense, she was unable to retrieve it. She plunged into an alley, jumped skyward onto a rooftop, and lay on her back for countless moments.

She replayed the exchange and past few days in her mind over and over again, for she sensed something else while Jennó was speaking. Gasping in disconcertion, she understood. Rummaging through her bag, she took hold of the Fragments. Shaking the book wildly, so much so that she nearly broke the spine, she noticed a small device fall out its pages. After her time with Hafir, she knew it was a tracking device. Every electronic gadget, no matter how small, emitted heat from an electrical signal, so Neztríanis concentrated and memorized the device's heat signature. Then, she crushed the device with her hand. In disbelief and alarm, Neztríanis shook her head. There were two more. One was planted in her traditional clothes and the other was in the inseam of her jacket, in a small hole where her left sleeve began. She destroyed one of them and threw the other one to the west with all her Sczyphamek might.

He played her. And even more telling, he played Namí and Hafir. Jennó was formidable. *She was a novice,* playing a game with no rules and merciless objectives.

She did not lie when she told Jennó that she was scared of Pike Metropolis. She was a woman from the country trapped in one of the largest cities on Qeauríyx, and she knew no one. If she had a hard time adjusting to Nextu, Pike Metropolis was sure to crush her.

The Sczyphamek slowed her breathing and concentrated. After a few moments, Neztríanis was able to locate Jennó's heat signature. The crowd had dispersed, and Jennó was two lengths from her current position, heading west-southwest. Emerging from the alleyway, Neztríanis walked north at a quick pace. Until she figured out her next move, she saw no other choice. Her destination was the Triple Towers. Unsurprisingly, her Elemental did not object.

Neztríanis already knew why.

CHAPTER TWELVE: THE CAUSTIC COMMANDER

How could a living creature sound so tortured and resilient? Neztríanis, hooded, hid in a dimly lit alleyway near the Triple Skyrises when she heard the témo's squeal. Her Elemental was distraught. The cries of vicissitude were unspeakable. She did not want to see. The young woman had just escaped Jennó and was gripped with anxiety, afraid that her inexperience would place her in another compromising situation. But her Elemental demanded that she look. It had been trying to convince her of something since she saw the feline, but Neztríanis feigned ignorance.

She could resist neither the temptation nor the persuasion of her Elemental. Even those walking on the city streets stopped their stride because of the clamor. Cautiously, Neztríanis peered around the corner to add her gaze to the crowd. That was when she saw its eyes. The témo growled, hissed, and screamed as imperial operatives poked and prodded the feline with electrical staffs.

The motorcade had come to an end at the base of the Triple Skyrises. A small crowd had gathered. The pack was mostly comprised of Damüdans and Tannódin'é; however, a few Nez Spiritans were mixed in the group.

Suddenly, a Nez Spiritan man sprinted towards the motorcade and threw a bottle at the imperial agents. "We stand with you!" he shouted to the témo. "We are Chénínqua!"

Before Neztríanis mustered the courage to stand with her brother, soldiers and imperial law enforcement swarmed the man. With the butt of their rifles and electric staffs, they beat the dissenter to near death, bound his comatose body, and dragged him into a police vehicle.

"Get that damn animal in the building!" yelled an old man. He was not Nez Spiritan or Tannódin'é. His inflection and accent was extremely aggressive.

A large door opened upward and revealed a garage. The agents moved the cage inside of the structure, Skyrise One. Yet, as the témo was almost

204

submerged in the skyrise, the eyes of the creature and Neztríanis' met. The témo's eyes were stricken with pain and loss, ensconced in black and contoured with red-green ferocity. For the first time, Neztríanis felt a connection with the creature that was not due to her Elemental. But just as soon as the feeling arose, the garage closed in front of the building. The crowds dispersed; the parade was over.

Uncertainty clutched the daughter of Hopha. However, she was certain that she could not stand in front of the Triple Skyrises. She might draw attention to herself, and she did not feel like outrunning imperial agents again.

An integrated cantina stood two blocks away, so Neztríanis pulled her hood down even further and went inside to think about her next move. Using some credits obtained from Hafir, she bought a cup of hot tea and a sweet and sat alone in a corner. Erring on the side of caution, she scanned for Jennó's heat signature every five minutes or so.

She had no relationship with the témo, but her qanín and Elemental acted as if they were friends of old, filling the emerging Sczyphamek with sympathy and guilt.

This type of feeling will bring me trouble, she thought. *What in Qalfocx am I thinking?*

She barely escaped Jennó without overtly revealing her powers. The chance of rescuing the creature without the use of her Elemental was slim to nil. She felt over two thousand distinct heat signatures from ground floor to the center of the building alone. The top floors of the skyrise were quite insulated and reinforced; who knew how many agents awaited her there? The size of the main tower was indecipherable. Its apex was near forty-five hundred feet, and its width was large. Not to mention, Skyrise One was connected to both Skyrise Two, a military installation towering at thirty-eight hundred feet, and Skyrise Three, the residential wing scaling thirty-six hundred feet. Each tower had its own population...

Suicide.

Due to the buildings' extraordinary height, each was anchored to the other by connecting bridges and reinforced by beams that jutted upwards from the roofs of Skyrises Two and Three to the top of Skyrise One. Neztríanis wondered how deep the Tannódin'é engineers dug in order to lay a strong enough foundation, but she was certain that Qeauríyx provided the ingredients needed for such a formidable structure. Yet, how could she enter into such a building? Genius and effort were clearly involved in making it. How much more then would Tannódin guard it?

Still afraid of outright confrontation and life-taking—not to mention the specter of encountering Jennó and his kind again—Neztríanis decided to leave Pike Metropolis and go to Mt. Xarkim in search of the Tabernacle of the Quickening. However, the creature's stare continued to fill her qanín.

The elements shifted inside of her.

"This is not my problem," she told the elements. "My mission is to retrieve the Auría."

Témos had been steadfast allies to the Kylanín and Zephanín Sczyphameks of old. Her Elemental chided Neztríanis to remember this.

"They are nearly extinct," two melded voices responded inwardly. "Will you leave her to die?"

Neztríanis gasped. The elements spoke to her; she was amazed that she heard them so clearly.

"By the One!" she whispered. "You can speak?"

The elements did not respond. They intimated what they needed to say. Elementals had qaníns of their own, and it was up to the Sczyphamek's faith and practice to harness them.

"Why should I? How can I?" she questioned herself.

What strange turn of events placed her in such a circumstance? Her plan had gone to kíma. Why did she walk down *that* street at *that exact* time? Is that why she experienced the three-week delay in Nextu? However, it seemed illogical that she should somehow break from her task because of such a randomly powerful event. Sipping some tea, she remembered the old mystic's words to her over a duration ago: "When you come to that moment of hesitancy, listen to your Elemental."

The old man must have foreseen this moment, she thought.

Or maybe he did not, but recognized that her journey would require her to make difficult choices, choices that would cause any rational person to hesitate. Then again, maybe the mystic's words were aimed at this exact place and time. Her elements chided her to trust that this was the moment of which he spoke. Why this one, she did not know; but, she could not turn away from her Elemental.

Some saw these moments as fate; others saw them as coincidence. Neztríanis did not care about the definitions as much as she hated the implication: inescapability. The Ancient Tongue had a word for the phenomenon that Neztríanis was now experiencing: *chénala.*

"Infinite points," she translated to herself. "Kíma. Why now of all times?"

Finishing her tea, she rose out of her seat, and a Tannódin'é man approached her. Neztríanis was suspicious and eyed the man with distrust.

"Excuse me," he said. "I was just wondering if I could interest you in another drink."

Neztríanis was embarrassed and irritated. Smiling, she replied, "No thank you. I must go."

Persistent, he grabbed her hand and attempted to pull her hood back. "You are a beautiful Nez Spiritan." His tone was unambiguous. He wanted to have sex with her. "What is your name?"

She did not have time for the advances of some arrogant Tannódin'é man. Who did he think she was; some wench that he could have anytime?

"Let *go*." Her whisper was severe. "It would be best if you unhand me."

Grabbing her wrist even tighter, he said, "It'd be best if you took this like a good Nez Spiritan whore." At this, he swiped his hand against her backside.

Neztríanis was infuriated, by a level of disrespect previously unknown. She had to keep calm, although her instinct was to burn her ignorant solicitor alive.

She noticed the stares of many within the cantina so she played along and feigned congeniality. "Can we discuss this outside?"

He placed his arm around her shoulder. "That is more like it."

Neztríanis was repulsed, but held her temper in check. When they exited the establishment, the man pulled her to a dark, deserted alley. Removing her hood, Neztríanis smiled, and the man smiled back.

He had no clue.

"I am glad that you had some sense, girl. You should feel honored that a Tannódin'é from Civix Setrin would want to have a Nez Spiritan."

Neztríanis was unrepentant for what she was about to do. Due to her Elemental perception, she was able to anticipate his every move. Heat and muscle movement had become synonymous for Temperature. When her assailant tried to fondle her breasts, she effortlessly sidestepped out of the way and grabbed his left arm. She twisted then broke his arm in two places, covered his mouth to drown out his wail, and tossed him to the ground.

The sexual predator cried out in humiliation, "You cléth!"

Reaching for a knife hidden in his boot, the would-be rapist stood up with a ruthless glint in his eye.

"Oh, yes. Please..." The incensed Sczyphamek smiled. "*Please* keep giving me a reason, Tannódin'é."

He lunged for her, clumsily swung the knife, and missed. Neztríanis gave her right hand a little heat, and punched the man in the jaw. He flew about ten feet backwards and crashed on the concrete, falling unconscious.

Perhaps now he will think twice before he approaches one of my sisters, she thought.

Amazed how easily violence escalated once commenced, not to mention her increased reaction time, she was both alarmed and pleased with the progression of her powers. Neztríanis looked around and saw that the event went unnoticed. She was furious, but she did not kill the man. Only the Nameless One knew how many women he had raped.

Wait, she thought. *How many has he raped? No one even sees us here...Staxis, how many of my sisters has he raped? Who does this Tannódin'é think he is? No one even knows we are in this alley... How many?*

Suddenly, a deep anger and hate roiled Temperature's qanín. Her right hand erupted in a condensed white flame. Neztríanis looked down at the man, and before she knew it, her trembling, open palm was directly above her comatose assailant. The air between them became unsettled by the ever increasing heat emanating from her unmerciful hand. She breathed hard and did not blink. Finally, she bit her lip.

"No," she said to herself. "Killing only breeds more death."

She powered down, walked out of the alley, and refocused her attention upon the rescue of the témo. Time was not on her side. Who knew what that old man with the aggressive voice was planning? However, she had no chance of breaking into Skyrise One without some help.

Rydín and Hafir had told her of a covert Miska Kea resistance cell within Pike Metropolis. Remembering their words, she recalled that they were located in the southeast section of town, which was made up of predominantly Nez Spiritan poor men and women. Neztríanis realized she should have listened to Rydín in regards to Jennó. Not all Nez Spiritans were her natural allies. Some had actually assimilated within Global Initiative and were working for the House of Pre-Eminent. Scarier than that fact was the knowledge that Jennó fooled even Hafir and Namí, and those two were experts at sifting through lies. He was clearly a frightening enemy and a master of information and misinformation, which meant some within the city would possibly betray her, seeking reward from Tannódin.

If the resistance was located in the southeast section of the city, Jennó likely sent lookouts to the borough. He suspected her of being an "insurrectionist" and no doubt knew that rebel activity was present in that part of Pike Metropolis.

Yet, the southeast section of Pike was too large. He could not have eyes *everywhere*. She needed to move quickly. Since it was nighttime, she had a better chance of remaining inconspicuous. Taking a gamble, Neztríanis levitated to the top of a building some three lengths southeast of the Triple Skyrises and changed her clothes. Jennó knew what she was wearing now, but he had not seen her in her traditional dress. She also took her hair out of a tail and combed it out. The southeast section of town was many square lengths in area and contained millions of Nez Spiritans. Hopefully, her outfit would not stand out that much. Under the cover of darkness, she focused her Elemental and jumped carefully from rooftop to rooftop, above the buildings, while scanning for the heat signatures of Jennó and his five agents.

***

When she arrived in southeast Pike Metropolis, it was nearly dawn and she was exhausted. The colossal size of the city almost overwhelmed the Sczyphamek since she was unable to take public transportation. Her awe turned to dismay once she entered the southeast portion of the megalopolis. The overt, abject poverty was shocking. Housing was a desperate, unimaginable comparison to the luxury she left in central Pike. Homes were poorly constructed, made of various semi-diaphanous materials. In some ways, it reminded her of the rural life in the peninsula.

She had to stop using rooftops for transportation. It was no exaggeration; she would have collapsed the tops of the shacks if she stepped on them.

A smell of forgotten personhood fragranced the air, reeking of selfishness, feces, and neglect.

Temporarily effacing her ire, she focused on her mission. Rydín said that the leader of a Miska Kea cell was located in an old hostel called the Unseen Inn. She remembered the name of the place because it was so unique and conspicuous. Why would a resistance group pick a location with such a name?

Seeing an elderly man sitting in front of his shack, she cautiously approached him and said, "Elder, faring well, I pray."

The old man smiled. "You are not from around here are you?"

"I am traveling from Bitzroy and I wanted to know where I might lay my head for the night," she explained. "Have you heard of the Unseen Inn?"

The old man's face changed from joviality to trepidation. "Why do you want to go *there?*"

"My business is my own. But I was told that it is a place where poor travelers can find rest."

"Indeed," the elderly man said. "In that case, wonderful daughter of Nez Spirita, the inn is located down the way about one and a half lengths. Make a right, when you see a house with an old woman out on the porch cooking. Keep walking until you get to a vegetable field—"

"*A vegetable field?* "In the middle of a city?"

The old man smiled. "You'd be surprised at what folks can make when life is as hard as the concrete you live on. Anyway, when you pass the field, on your left will be a broken sign that says, 'Inn.' That's it."

Neztríanis' face showed the signs of bewilderment.

"What's wrong, young one?" he asked.

"Why do you not use the street signs for directions?" she asked.

"It's not like the streets are for us," he replied. "Sure, we can live on this or that street, but in reality, we are not really living on 'our' street. We own nothing… So, we make our own space down here. I gave you directions that matter, and they still tell you how to get where you need to go."

Neztríanis smiled at the man's righteous indignation, "Yes elder, they do."

"Be careful."

"I will."

Neztríanis did as the man instructed. When she passed old female cook, the meal smelled so delicious that she asked the woman if she could buy a plate. Obliging, the woman sold her a plate of spicy green vegetables and barbequed luku, marinated over two days. Neztríanis licked her fingers, finished her meal, and passed the vegetable field—between concrete and shanty. It undoubtedly belonged to the entire community. There was no fence or sign to ward off trespassers. While marveling at this garden of hope, she saw a dingy sign that read "Inn." Neztríanis would have been upset at the lowly establishment, if she had not noticed a group of six Nez Spiritans at the entrance eyeing her with suspicion.

Rydín had given her the password; so, she headed to the entrance, unassumingly, with her hands in visible sight. Two of them were packing concealed energy weapons, and one had a power cell fully cycled. They were clearly up to something. They went inside the building and prompted Neztríanis to follow. Reluctantly, she walked into the foyer and stopped. The Sczyphamek could go no further; a wall of hard-edged persons with unpleasant demeanors blocked her path.

Directness was probably the best move.

"Rydín of Lozé wanted me to tell you that 'the day is not for everyone, only for those who awake to its luster,'" she said, though mentally scoffing at such a banal passphrase.

A shadowy, saffron-yellow woman emerged from the group. She was shorter than Neztríanis, dressed in all black, and armed with the fully charged weapon. She was not Nez Spiritan.

Pointing the rifle at Neztríanis in the middle of the lobby, she said, "I have quite the ability to see through kíma. So do not lie to me, and if you hesitate on any answer, I'll kill you where you stand."

Neztríanis remained calm, although the woman's statement was strangely familiar.

"How do you know Rydín?" she prodded in a bellicose tone.

Neztríanis was resolute. "I met him on the way here on the southern coast of the Windhorse Peninsula. He was fleeing White Scythe. He and about twenty-five others were all that was left of the city. He told me that if I needed help, a small contingent of Miska Kea in Pike Metropolis could help me."

Reading her intently, the woman asked, "What is your name?"

The Sczyphamek did not hesitate. "My name is Neztríanis Phyxtríalis. I am from Hopha."

"You are a long way from home, *little* sister," she said, her finger still on the trigger.

Neztríanis grew upset and impatient. She needed to save the témo with haste and she was having a horrible day. "If you do not want to help me, then let me go on my way. I will deal with them myself. At the very least, please remove the firearm from my face. I have neither traveled this far nor been chased through this city by imperial agents nor assaulted by a Tannódin'é to receive such treatment."

The woman smirked. "She's all right. It's the one Rydín sent word about. Mésa…"

The aggressor dropped her weapon, reduced its power, and held it to her side. Her company appeared less hawkish and went about their business. Neztríanis realized Rydín was a saving grace, incredibly wise and prudent in foresight. How did he know? Perhaps he did not know, which meant the stakes in Nez Spirita had been raised considerably since the fall of Lozé.

"That was you yesterday, wasn't it—the one who almost got caught in west-central Pike?" the woman asked.

Neztríanis nodded skeptically, shocked that the woman possessed such recent intel. She escaped Jennó less than a day ago. How did the Miska Kea cell obtain such information? Were they that advanced in their espionage?

Motioning those in the lobby outside, the woman ordered, "Make sure she was not followed here. I want a two length perimeter."

Immediately, the group dispersed, following the command of their superior.

"If you were followed and they find out that you've been here, you'll have destroyed cycles of work," the woman warned sternly. "You've been found out already, and you aren't even a part of us... If you have brought *your* trouble to us..."

They waited silently for half an hour while the woman's subordinates checked the area for enemies. Soon, all reported back with nothing to tell. The woman sighed in forthright relief then told them to go back out into the streets for a few more hours, as a matter of precaution. And at that moment, the daughter of Hopha realized she had just stepped into a world she truly did not know.

While reentering the inn's foyer, the woman said, "My name is Kéma'fém,[1] but everyone calls me Kéma,"

"Kéma..." Neztríanis said rhetorically. "'To be at one with the planet...'"

Kéma stopped and turned around. "What?"

"That is what your name means in the Ancient Tongue: 'to be at one with the planet.'"

"*Oh,*" she said with a bemused smile. "You *aren't* from around here, are you?"

"No," Neztríanis laughed guardedly. "No, I am not."

"You can still laugh. Kíma..." Kéma was impressed. "That's good. Maybe you can make him laugh..."

***

Those Tannódin'é bastards. The whole pack of them... They won't stop until this planet is turned to Qalfocx." The grizzled man scratched a scar on his left cheek. "They're all the same: violent and arrogant. And the only way to beat them is to become more arrogant and viler than they are."

Stopping in mid-thought, the veteran ran his fingers through his short, dark gray hair, and lit a daggerweed cigarette. Inhaling, he continued in a

---

[1] Kéma'fém (*key*-mah-f*ey*m)

harsh, poetic tone, "There's only one way to stop them. You hear me? Only one way... Kill them. You gotta kill every last one of those cléths."

He blew smoke from his nostrils. The opaque mist created a haze over his yellow-brown face. His gnashed knuckles and fingertips looked as if they had never scratched the itch of happiness. "Kíma... Damn every single one of them to Qalfocx..."

Neztríanis sat wide-eyed. Never had she encountered such baneful speech. The man's voice brimmed with hatred and disdain, revealing cycles of violence and bitter disappointment.

Kéma had led Neztríanis to a room in the little, three-story hotel. Apparently, it was a place where a traveler could lay one's head. Many rooms were occupied. Nez Spiritan janitors cleaned the hallways and bedrooms. When Kéma took Neztríanis to the second floor and opened the door to an unnumbered room, she was told to sit down and wait for him. She did not know she waited for this...

"And who do you think you are anyway?" He gave Neztríanis a piercing glance. "Trying to just traipse into the Triple Skyrises? If you got a death wish, I can think of plenty of ways for you to satisfy that. Bastards..."

He stood up from his chair and sighed. The man was shorter than Neztríanis expected, but his malcontent was so commanding, it heightened his appearance. His shirt was white, but his pants were the color of midnight. A violet-blue jacket hung on the back of his chair. His hip was adorned with a radiant firearm of antiquity: a combustible 11-shot revolver, with shells of ammunition across his belt. However, nothing caught Neztríanis' attention more than the black headband on his forehead. The band seemed to be a part of the skin on his face. An insignia of a sword was its only marking.

The commander noticed her staring at the headband. He pointed to his forehead. "This thing... This thing I got when I was in Keotagosdi. That's where I am from. Keotagosdi. I was born in Veta. My parents were Líachimian and Phmquedrian, a desert nomad and a runaway slave... What a mix... I went to a rogue military school there, where I learned the stupidity of battle..."

Flicking his cigarette down to a position on the carpet that revealed floor burn and ash, he picked up a cup and gulped down a large portion of some drink. The swallow was accompanied by five seconds of coughing and wheezing. "I took that stupidity and this kímaz headband and have been fighting these malignant bastards ever since."

Confused, Neztríanis glanced at Kéma, who was behind her. Kéma returned Neztríanis' stare by shaking her head.

"Why do you want to rescue that témo? Like it matters a damn."

"Commander—" Neztríanis started.

"Call me, Bíoske.[2] Kíma. There's no glory in these titles... I'm only a commander because everyone else deserted or died. Can't blame the bastards either..."

"Bíoske," she continued, "témos are nearly extinct. They have aided us in the fight against Tannódin for a long time. They have no right to hold her."

Unable to argue at that fact, Bíoske sat down. Témos *had* fought against injustice since long before the Bitter War. And for that, their number was dwindling. The soldier respected the fact that témos were the ultimate fighters for a cause. No. He could not argue about the témos, but he *could* argue about...

"Aided *'us'*...? Who in Qalfocx is *'us'*? I don't know you, and I don't give a damn what Rydín said, or the fact that you may or may not have met Hafir. I don't know you from the kíma out of my ass.

"All I know is that you were almost caught by the Eradicate and you got a death wish—daydreaming about rescuing that témo. Staxis..." Bíoske softened after he saw Neztríanis' stupefied face. An alluring smile emerged from the gruff. "*I'll tell you what.* We will help you, if you agree to help us destroy the Triple Skyrises and everyone in it."

Neztríanis stared at the commander with disbelief.

"What?" he asked. "You got some problem with that, Nez Spiritan?"

"Did you not just imply that I am a novice? What makes you think I can aid you in such a task?"

"Whatever..." Bíoske said. "You aren't so much of a novice. You escaped them somehow. Unless they let you escape..."

Neztríanis looked down, battling her own personal struggles. "That building appears impregnable; how and why would you even think of trying to do something like that? What will killing everyone do except bring more of Tannódin? Not only will there be more of them, they will come with greater destruction."

"*Destruction?* 'Destruction' is already here. From what I hear and from your own mouth we know Lozé is gone. Tannódin has not only destroyed this land, they've almost exterminated its people and their spirit. What more destruction can there be?"

"That is not what I meant..."

"Who cares what you mean?" he barked. "Tannódin doesn't. They don't give a damn about you or me. So why show those cléths compassion when we don't receive theirs? They don't show any remorse when they violate the men and women of this land..."

Neztríanis remembered her stock, random, and terrifying encounter with the Tannódin'é man just hours before. He did not value her as an equal. Neither did Jennó, and he was Nez Spiritan. Her exchange with both of them was devoid of respect and consideration. She was just an object to

---

[2] Bíoske (*bee*-ahs-k[eh])

the rapist and the spy. Had she not gained control of her Elemental, she would have left the eatery with Jennó as his prisoner. Indeed, if she were not a Sczyphamek, she would have been raped in a dimly lit alleyway, amidst the trash and silence. And, if she had put up a fight, either the rapist or spy would have killed or beat her where she stood, with impunity—just like the Nez Spiritan man who had been violated when he had protested the témo's incarceration.

Perhaps that was why she *wanted to* kill both of them...

But she did not. The teachings of the Auría were clear: murder begets murder. No doubt, the rapist had probably taken the will and life from so many Nez Spiritan women. Even though she stopped him, he would probably return to his sexual predation. He was just a representation of Tannódin. Neztríanis was not blind; she knew that Tannódin would not give up without a fight. However, the moment she lost her compassion would be the moment she lost herself. She could not bring herself to kill anyone.

"And what if you have to?" His gaze and his questions were unrelenting. "I've seen that face. You haven't had to make that decision yet. You still live in the world of ideas. Reality is all that matters. You will *have to* kill before this is over."

"You do not know that," she snapped. "What good is reality without hope?"

"Hope gets you killed... softens you. It drugs you to sleep." He took out his revolver and plucked the ammunition from his belt. "*This...*" He injected the rounds into the chamber in ecstatic malaise. "*This is all that matters.*"

"So you live to kill?"

Slamming the weapon on the table, his caustic aura nearly eroded the room. "I live to hurt those bastards as they have hurt me and my kind. And I will continue to hurt them until I stop hurting... or die."

"Vengeance does not ease hurt; it only causes hurt."

He grew beleaguered, then numb at those words. "Kíma... what do you know? You're just a girl in this."

"Bíoske," she pressed, "will you help me? I need your assistance, but I will not participate in murder."

"Heh. 'I will not participate in murder'... " He laughed an empty, heartfelt laugh. "Damn, you are like an ignorant child... You participate in murder when you do nothing. You participate in murder when you don't stand up to Tannódin, when you feel sympathy for an enemy that feels no sympathy for you. You participate in murder when you care for the murderers over your own people." He took a sip of his elixir of wrath, choked the bitterness down, and resumed his diatribe. "You participate in murder when you believe in that Nameless One, who does nothing for those who suffer, while apparently aiding every whim of a malicious enemy. When you believe in something that escapes this Qalfocx instead of dealing with it!"

Neztríanis' eyes flashed. The daughter of Hopha was infuriated, yet scared of Bíoske's brutal logic. This caustic, brazen soldier of misfortune was attacking her beliefs and her calling. However, the Sczyphamek could not deny the fact that she was struggling with the same questions. But, his tone, his qanín, appeared to be so vacant.

The daughter of Hopha shook her head. "I do not know what made you so callous. You would be no better than Tannódin if this war were won. You would switch places with them."

"You don't know me!" he yelled at her, grabbing his pistol off the table.

"And you do not know me." Temperature looked in the commander's eyes with strength, although she was very afraid. "It would be best if you holstered your firearm."

He gazed at her with discerning eyes. She was not bluffing. Somehow, she had the upper hand. The caustic commander holstered his weapon, meditated on this fact, sat back down, and calculated the conclusion.

"Kíma... I hate you guys..." he mumbled, then said loudly, "Go kill yourself. Leave me and my people out of it."

The room fell uncomfortably silent.

Kéma positioned herself within the conversation. "With all due respect, Bíoske, you do not speak for all of us. Once the group hears about this and Rydín's approval of her, they'll want to help. It is the perfect opportunity. We've been preparing to infiltrate the Triple Skyrises in order to steal Tannódin's tactical shipping and deployment plan for Líachim. Although we wanted to wait two or three days before the first snow, extracting the témo will provide an even greater sleight of hand. She'd be a perfect distraction."

"The First Snow?" Neztríanis inquired. "I don't understand."

"The less you know about us the better," Kéma snapped. "I've said too much already. And I told you; things were in the works long before you asked for our help."

"I did not mean to offend you," Neztríanis apologized. "The First Snow is the beginning of hibernation for all living creatures on Nez Spirita. Without adequate shelter and food, one would perish in a Nez Spiritan winter."

"And that means that even Blue Rapier and White Scythe must desist in their activity," Kéma smiled. "Bíoske, I'm right, and you know it."

Neztríanis understood completely. Unlike her, Miska Kea wanted the First Snow to arrive. It would assure the rebels an entire season to put distance between them and their adversaries. But whoever decided to trek in Nez Spirita during the winter was either crazy or formidable.

"As if it matters a damn," the commander said with some acquiescence. He closed his eyes, lit another cigarette, and mentally materialized military stratagem. "You would still have to worry about the troops beneath you... Skyrise One is heavily fortified, damn it." He gave

Neztríanis an awkward though somewhat filial smile. The man was a soldier, and like Neztríanis, he loved a challenge. "Kíma. And just how do you expect to rescue that témo?"

Neztríanis smirked. "With your help."

"Staxis…" he grumbled. "This is asinine… Heh. So stupid that it just might work… Kéma, are we still good in Skyrise Three, the residential one?"

"Yes. We have obtained all the access codes to the main tower."

Dumbfounded, Neztríanis asked, "How did you manage that?"

The acidic commander smiled with an ever-noticeable change in countenance with every syllable spoken. "We got a couple of insiders in the Residential Tower. Namely, us."

"What?" Neztríanis asked. "Are you telling me that you work at the Triple Skyrises?"

"Janitor for Skyrise Two," Bíoske said nonchalantly. "My team has been there for the past six cycles. As a matter of fact, my shift starts in six hours."

Before Neztríanis responded, Kéma added, "I'm a custodian for Skyrise Three. I've been employed for six durations and have already received high marks for my work in the commissary."

The revolutionaries *worked* for Tannódin. No wonder Kéma was so perturbed by Neztríanis. The amount of time and effort needed to infiltrate the Skyrises was beyond what the daughter of Hopha cared to know.

Bíoske explained, "Tannódin uses outside labor for janitorial duty. They're too lazy to clean up after themselves. Over the past six cycles, our entire group of thirty has slowly gained insignificant employment there and just recently has managed to steal some codes to the two connector bridges from the Residential Tower to the main skyrise."

"How did you get a job without them placing you under surveillance?"

"Help. The same kind of help that let us know about you almost getting caught," he said guardedly and cryptically.

Neztríanis was not going to receive any more of an explanation than that. At least she knew how they had found out about her and Jennó. She was impressed that Miska Kea's intelligence gathering ran that deep.

"I see. So does that mean you will help me?"

"Kíma! You're one persistent Nez Spiritan! We'll help, but this isn't for your benefit, and it damn sure isn't because I believe in this cause of yours."

Neztríanis was floored by his erosive response.

Bíoske slapped his fist into the palm of his hand. "We have to do *something* now that Lozé has fallen. I've analyzed Pre-Eminent's war strategy, and she has a habitual hate for two-front wars. I can't blame the cléth either; those things are worse than Qalfocx."

Neztríanis barely noticed, but she had an inner disdain for Bíoske's use of the word "cléth" to describe Pre-Eminent. Neztríanis searched Kéma's face for some sort of confirmation, but Kéma revealed no emotion either way.

"The war here is over. Lozé's decimation put an end to it. Kéma is right; Tannódin will strike Líachim soon, now that Nez Spirita has been quieted."

"Líachim *is not ready* to defend itself against Tannódin yet," Kéma said. "We are at least eight durations away from—"

"I know, Kéma." Bíoske's empathy surprised Neztríanis. "We have to give them a fighting chance to turn those bastards back because it isn't like the Nameless One is going to help us."

The daughter of Hopha held her ire and fashioned a face of determination.

Bíoske took a swig from his cup and muttered, "Yeah, just as you should be." Concentrating and staring at the wall, the soldier snarled, "We have to send a loud message to Tannódin—loud enough to make them take pause over their assessment of the Nez Spiritan conflict. So far, Global Initiative—Pre-Eminent and Vicious' version, that is—has strived to crush their opposition, rebuild on the ruins, and maintain their position. They have achieved the last two goals here. Lozé was their attempt to achieve the first and last objectives. They meant to crush the city before winter.

We've got to deprive them of this final objective as long as we can. Attacking them right before winter—it's an audacious plan, but it would buy us two and a half durations." He glared at Neztríanis, smiled, moved close to her, and whispered in her ear, "And once they find out about you, they will pause, won't they?"

Stunned, the woman finally saw past Bíoske's chiseled cloak of gruffness and foulness. His statements had become sharper and more acerbically rational with every sentence. He was a military mastermind hiding under some unknown canopy, obscuring the casual observer's vision. His vocabulary cloaked his understanding. Undoubtedly, he surmised she was a Sczyphamek after less than an hour of conversation. The last jab at the One with No Name was used precisely for confirmation and to voice his disagreement with her. He also knew a Zananín's hatred of témos would keep one from even proposing a plan of rescue, which meant he was well-versed in the cycles of Qeauríyx.

"Neztríanis," Kéma said pensively, waking the Nez Spiritan out of her thought. "Neztríanis, this is the real thing. While you may not agree with Bíoske, your negligence will kill us all. Even if you do not kill, you must subdue every enemy you encounter. Is that understood, sister?"

"Yes, Kéma. I understand."

"Good," she replied then turned towards her commanding officer. "Bíoske, what's your plan?"

The soldier remained quiet. His mind hunted for the right pieces of the puzzle, going through multiple scenarios in his head at a speed unknown.

For six cycles, Bíoske had coveted and prepared for this attack. He knew the entire schematics, patrols, and contingency plans of all three buildings by memory. Spies had risked their lives and some were killed for obtaining the information. The least Bíoske could do was to use their sacrifice to develop the best gambit. But Neztríanis was a new, unknown variable; all of his stratagems needed to be recalculated, critiqued, and tweaked. After opening a cabinet with multiple locks and passcodes, Bíoske retrieved detailed maps of the three skyrises and laid them on the table. He stared at them without blinking.

"That won't work," he muttered. "What if we... Kíma... Bastards are too good for that... Need to move fast... but not too hasty, or this won't work... Two days preparation... Misdirection... I don't know..." he continued to talk to himself, lost in thought.

While Bíoske mused, Neztríanis turned to Kéma and whispered, "I wanted to ask you something..."

"What is it?" the woman replied.

"Are you not worried about this location? It seems rather obvious that a building called the 'Unseen Inn' would be a place of revolutionary activity."

Kéma laughed. "I wondered that myself when I first heard of the name but—"

"Can you two talk about this outside?" the commander asked brusquely. "Staxis. You think it's easy coming up with an asinine *and* effective plan?"

Kéma rolled her eyes and motioned the Sczyphamek out of the room.

"Like I was saying, I thought the name was ludicrous, honestly. But then I learned about the history of this place. It was actually a music club created a few cycles after the Solemn War. The place was quite popular and the owner, who was Tannódin'é, built an inn right beside it.

"But as Pike Metropolis grew, this community became older and economically depressed. Nez Spiritans and Phmquedrians moved here and eventually took over the area, while the Tannódin'é and Damüdan population 'escaped' to the northern area of the city. In its better cycles, the Unseen Inn was known for being a place where a traveler heard a good song, had easy sex, and laid in a cheap bed. In fact, the third floor is still a favorite love nest for the locals."

Neztríanis' used her Elemental and searched the floor above. She felt the bodies of men and women extremely close to one another, generating a heat previously unknown to her. The lasciviousness of the story and the corroboration by her Elemental made the woman blush. The old man who gave her directions to the inn probably reasoned she came to the hovel for sexual satisfaction.

Kéma laughed at the Sczyphamek's flushed countenance. "So after I learned this, I realized the genius of Bíoske. No one would suspect a place like this to be a home for rebels. And the southeast section of Pike is home to more than six million people. The Unseen Inn is just one place out of many. The real owner of this place is as subversive as they come. You don't need to know who it is. Let's just say she is an interesting Tannódin'é."

"Tannódin'é?" Neztríanis asked with unbelieving ears. Then again, if Jennó betrayed her, it was possible that there were Tannódin'é dissidents.

"That's right, 'sister,'" Kéma said playfully. "This place may be run down, but this hotel boasts some surveillance technology that rivals Tannódin's. And you'd be surprised who comes here for intercourse. We've gotten some pretty good information because of the third floor."

"If you all are through talking about sex," Bíoske yelled out to them, "we can discuss more important, yet less pleasurable matters."

The women went back into the room, and beheld an enigmatic glow about the commander.

"Misdirection. It's risky, but life is risk..." Bíoske flicked the half-smoked cigarette to the floor burn. "This strategy is predicated upon damage and diversion. The main objective is the retrieval of the tactical information, but Tannódin needs to be completely oblivious to that. So we gotta make it appear like structural damage and the rescue of the témo are our primary objectives. This plan hinges on solo missions for the both of you. Kéma, I know you can get the job done. And, Neztríanis, there is more than meets the eye with you. It takes an extraordinary person to risk their life for a témo.

"How much battle experience do you have?"

Neztríanis could not even stammer a lie.

Kéma grimaced in disappointment. "Staxis... are you telling me you don't have any?"

"Kéma..." Neztríanis' had no choice. She had to reveal she was a Sczyphamek.

"Let's see how she does in training." The man was no fool.

Kéma shook her head. "Bíoske, I will admit I made a mistake. I thought she was skilled, even though she was nearly apprehended. But, clearly that was a fluke. We cannot risk our lives and our only opportunity on an untested, unseasoned girl from the peninsula's countryside just because Rydín gave her his blessing."

Though Neztríanis just met Kéma'fém a few hours prior, she felt like she had been besmirched and marginalized by an old friend.

The caustic commander laughed inexorably. "Kéma, relax. I already knew she hadn't seen any action. I wanted to see if she was honest. She's gritty, but she doesn't have the look."

Kéma gazed at the daughter of Hopha as if for the first time. "Yeah. You're right."

The Sczyphamek did not know what they were talking about. She could not waste time deciphering "the look;" she needed to convince them—rather, Kéma—she was indeed capable.

"I factored her lack of experience when I made the plan," Bíoske explained. "But I think she can compensate for that."

Kéma's face voiced her disapproval and displayed her unwillingness to accept the sell.

"Just listen to the plan first," Bíoske pleaded. "If you still got a problem with it, then let me know. How about it, Kéma'fém?"

"Yeah, whatever."

Bíoske smiled sarcastically, stood up, put on his jacket, and prepared to rehearse. "We are going to pull this off at night, two nights from now, during the late hours. Fewer on guard, you know?" He snarled at Neztríanis. "And that should make *someone* happy... We'll infiltrate Skyrise Two by posing as janitors, and we'll have three points of entry."

Kéma, in a state of persistent skepticism, frowned again. "Three points of entry? That does not make sense. There are only two connecting bridges between Skyrises One and Two. We cannot enter through the ground floor entrance of Skyrise One; we would never make it."

The man grinned mischievously. "Staxis, Kéma. I said voice your displeasure after I'm done. But you're right about the main entrance." Bíoske placed his finger on the schematics of the buildings and pointed to Skyrise One. "The vent shaft on the 242nd floor... that is Neztríanis' point of entry."

"*What?*" asked Kéma in disbelief. "You cannot be serious! How can she even reach that? The height of that shaft is almost thirty-six hundred feet. Impossible. She cannot climb that. What do you expect her to do, cross over there from the roof of Skyrise Two?"

"Yes. That's exactly what I expect. She seems quick and agile. She can use the mooring stilts that connect to Skyrise Two's rooftop or *other* means."

Kéma stared at Bíoske then gazed at Neztríanis. The young woman from Hopha seemed unaffected by Bíoske's words, almost as if she expected nothing less of herself. Kéma would not let herself believe what that might mean. *She could not.*

"Qalfocx... No. No way..." The operative was unwilling to hope. "How can she do that? She already has very little battle experience, much less..."

The commander cut her off. "Leave that up to us, Kéma. That shouldn't be a problem; should it, Neztríanis?"

"No. No problem," the Sczyphamek replied. "I can do that."

"Good," he said, as Kéma fell silent in mystification. "Now let's continue. The height of the shaft is around 3600 feet, and the gulf between Skyrise Two and One is 500 feet. So Nez, you've gotta make sure your execution is flawless. Once inside, you'll have access to the main vent shaft, which has its own ladder system. Ascend eight floors, to the 250th floor. The main power conduit is adjacent to the vent shaft at this point. The lab/research area is on the 252nd floor. It is the only place large enough to hold a témo. When you get to the 250th floor, create a diversion by destroying the main power, wait a few moments, and then set off a radio scrambler in an inconspicuous place.

"The scrambler will cut off all radio communication within all three buildings. That'll add to the confusion, while simultaneously leading everyone to your position. By knocking out the main power, the building will be reduced to auxiliary power, so most of the lighting will be dimmer, aiding those who do not wish to be seen. *Like us.*

"You are the first hinge. We cannot enter until you make your move. Once you do that, head to the main stairs at your own discretion and rescue the témo. The 252nd floor is comprised of three rooms. One is a great chamber, which will probably remain lit, an extensive laboratory, and a large conference room.

"I must tell you, there will be at least fifty guards between your point of entry and the main chamber. Do whatever you need to do to achieve your goal. If you want to sneak around and avoid them, fine. Even if it gets you killed, you will at least draw attention away from Kéma."

Neztríanis took a deep breath and let the nervousness cover her body like a shroud. This would truly be her first testing of her abilities. She had to trust the elements and herself. She had to have faith in the Nameless One. She could not let her newfound compatriots down. Her hands shook in fear and anticipation. She tried to calm down by taking larger breaths, but the excitement, danger, and unknown ravaged her thoughts. She felt a hand on her shoulder.

It was Kéma. Her facial expression had tempered. "Don't worry. Everyone goes through this. If you can get into that vent, something tells me you will be done with the hard part."

"Nez." Bíoske lit another daggerweed. "Can I call you Nez?" She signaled "yes." He responded by inhaling almost half the daggerweed in one breath. "Nez, let me reiterate; you've gotta go in first and draw attention to yourself. The plan rides on it. Your commotion will draw the troops away from Kéma. Once or if you even reach the témo, you must find your own exit out of the building. Understand?"

"Yes."

"You cannot withdraw under any circumstances. If you do, you will jeopardize the whole mission, and I don't need to tell you what that means."

"I understand."

She did understand. Her mission would end in death or success. If she failed, the Auría would be lost. If she failed, Pre-Eminent and Vicious would have no potential rival. Her Elemental knew this too, but *still* desired to rescue the témo. She had to trust them.

"All right then," he said. "Kéma, your point of insertion will be the main connector of the Residential/Main tower on the 210th floor, commanding two teams of five. Once inside, you will leave your teams at the side stairway near the military connector, and covertly make your way into the Imperial Access Room on the 215th floor. Meanwhile your primary team will blow the minor connecting bridge to the military tower. The secondary team will give them cover fire and support after demolishing the main staircase. That should keep a large force off your back."

"How can I be covert when I have to climb five flights of stairs?" she asked. "I will run into someone."

"Not necessarily," the commander replied. "If Neztríanis can get their attention, and then set off the scrambler, everyone will go to her location, leaving only a minimal contingent for you to face. Be quick though. Hack into the main computer and steal the tactical plans and whatever else you can get your hands on.

"Kéma, I know you already know this (this is more for Neztríanis' hearing)—but you cannot announce any trace of your presence. If alerted, the sentries on that floor will delete those files directly. The Access Center is Global Initiative's computing, military, communication, and intelligence hub in all of Nez Spirita. So the files will not be deleted unless the floor itself is at risk. But once the deletion sequence begins, it can't be undone, and all files will be deleted within five minutes. If that happens there may be a chance to synchronize some information with your minicomputer, but the information would be piecemeal at best. You've always bragged about being one of the best hackers and covert operators in Miska Kea…"

Kéma brimmed with confidence. "Don't worry about me. What is my point of extraction?"

"You have to make it back to the Residential Tower the best way you can. If possible, put your janitorial garb back on and leave the building."

"What about you?" Neztríanis asked. She was amazed that the man had come up with such a multifaceted plan so quickly, although it certainly appeared that Bíoske had spent many hours studying the schematics and personnel movements of the Triple Skyrises. His six cycles in Tannódin'é employ was not for naught.

"I'll be on the 114th floor with a team of nineteen. Our objective is to take out the elevator system and main stairway, and to destroy the main connecting bridge to Skyrise One, the military wing."

Kéma'fém's expression was the definition of reticence. "Bíoske, that floor contains a force of at least one hundred security personnel at all times. How will nineteen take on one hundred?"

"We haven't shirked at the odds before, and we won't now. Once our job is done, we will be out. Besides, Tannódin's forces in the buildings are reduced, due to the battle of Lozé and the annual pre-winter Nez Spirita sweep, so we should meet an enemy at fifty to sixty percent."

Seeing that Kéma'fém was assuaged by his answer, Bíoske concluded, "Remember, this plan hinges on diversion. Does everyone understand their assignments?"

Neztríanis nodded, but she had her doubts. "Bíoske, I am asking many questions—but I have to know—how will we smuggle so much contraband into that building without capture? And my image is surely in circulation throughout Pike Metropolis. I am sure Tannódin has taken precautions against such a plan, and I cannot imagine that I won't be recognized once I step foot into the Triple Skyrises."

The commander smiled. "Actually, I don't mind this one. We have two Tannódin'é connections, namely two Blue Rapier soldiers, who will grant us access. That is how we are going to get you in, even though you do not work there.

"As for your blown cover, we're gonna get you some new clothes, change your hair up some... But, I'm sure our contacts will help sneak you in somehow. It may be difficult for you to believe Nez, but there are many Tannódin'é and Damüdans who are against Pre-Eminent and Vicious—"

"And there are many Nez Spiritans and others who are for them," Neztríanis completed his statement. "I learned that yesterday. It is difficult to accept, but the evidence is irrefutable. I will not ask the names of these Tannódin'é, but you all should know the name of the operative, for I truly believe his presence will be felt again. His name is Jennó. At least, that is *one* of his names..."

"Damn, Neztríanis," the commander cackled, "you speak so... Anyway, 'Jennó' huh? We'll see if we got any information on him."

"You won't. He is the type that finds you, not you, him."

"At any rate," Bíoske continued, "we can't worry about that now. I will ask our contacts if they've heard anything or if the Skyrises have been placed on high alert. We also need to see when or if the témo is scheduled for euthanasia. If the témo is dead or the security has increased then this mission is scrapped. I don't do suicide missions anymore. Are we clear?"

The two females nodded.

"All right. Kéma and I will brief our teams. And we will run through this drill four times today, and four times tomorrow. The day after next, we will strike. There hasn't been any major action in this city in ten cycles. That may be to our advantage."

Kéma exited the room in order to tell her comrades the news. The commander was about to leave when he stopped. His back faced Neztríanis.

"I can't stand chénalas," Bíoske quipped. "A bunch of coincidences coming together that exert a powerful gravity that pulls most people in, although some can escape."

How can Bíoske be so reflective and astute in the Ancient Tongue? Neztríanis thought to herself. She wished she could see his face, but her qanín knew that if she made him face her, he would not have the conversation.

"Chénalas are not always about coincidence," Neztríanis corrected him.

"Damn them and damn whatever you think," he spat. "Coincidences or no, they're kímaz meaningless."

"Bíoske, you can't believe that."

"Don't tell me what I believe. When you've seen what we saw, you would understand it too."

Neztríanis shook her head in disagreement.

"You think there are factors beyond us that shape the course of events in the world? Kíma. That's kíma, Neztríanis. Randomness creates gravity too. Just as much as fate. And who gives a damn anyway?

"Seems to me that you left Hopha on some mission that wasn't even about this témo. But then you met Rydín, and then Hafir, and then you happened upon a témo at a moment you least expected, and soon after you were betrayed by Jennó. All of these things placed you on a path that led you here. And somehow, we were days away from striking the Triple Skyrise, which let you just slide right into our plan. And what's more, you made all those decisions without the presence of an absolute power whose method is control. But it isn't just about you, is it?

"Rydín escaped from Lozé then met you. But, he suffered through a horrible loss just to meet you. Lozé had to resist Tannódin for over two hundred cycles just so he could meet you. Hafir, as confused as he is, distrusts Tannódin and helped you because he knows in his qanín that Global Initiative is one of the most violent campaigns Qeauríyx has ever produced. Vincallous captured that témo and had it transported here. All these random events—born of suffering and death—all of your decisions and my decisions began to twist and pull together and became what some consider as fate. Infinite strands and cycles that coalesce and create a kind of pull on space and time. The chénala is one of the main reasons people believe in a Nameless One."

Neztríanis started to grasp the implications of all that he spoke, and she grew unsettled. "What are you saying?"

"I am saying that chénalas are meaningless. Just like the Nameless One. No matter how complex they make it, people bicker over the myanála. They argue over whether a chénala is fate and providence or coincidence and randomness.

"That's not what I'm saying. I'm saying that whether fate or coincidence or some combination, this is all senseless. I'm saying that chénalas and the Nameless One don't exist. We use them to justify our causes and suffering." His tone was calm, yet somehow impassioned.

"I won't deny that a strange sequence of events placed you in our company, and I won't deny that things seemed to work out this way, but that means that the témo and Nez Spirita *had* to suffer in order for this moment to occur. That's kíma. And even if the témo did not need to suffer for this moment to happen, it still doesn't matter because the témo did suffer."

Ignoring his cosmological and theological point, Neztríanis asked a question more local and fundamental than those. "Then why are you fighting?"

"You won't understand, because you didn't live through it." Bíoske was guarded and cryptic. "You remind me of Syla so much."

"What are you talking about? Who is Syla?"

Turning towards the Sczyphamek, Bíoske looked at the woman in the eyes. She could tell by his body language that the prior conversation was over.

"Neztríanis, it's clear that we got differences of opinion, but I know that there is something remarkable about you. Even with word from Rydín, we were skeptical. But, Kéma and I trusted you from the moment you told us about your objective. There was no way you were a spy. As bluntly as I can say it: this mission is too kímaz ridiculous to be an Eradicate ploy. Like I said, not too many people—well, nobody actually—would risk their lives for a témo.

"You've got a misguided, yet great cause and inner-strength, even if you are *one of them*. Don't lose that in this stupidity. Never lose that." His reassuring face changed to one that was more worrisome. "But, this will be your first battle, and the lives of all of us will be tied to what you can accomplish. You do not strike me as some bastard who makes a promise they cannot deliver. You aren't one of those damn pieces of kíma are you?"

"No," Neztríanis chuckled. "I do not believe so."

"I didn't think so. Have you ever fired an AEAR?"

"What is that?"

"That means 'no.'" He sighed and almost reconsidered the plan altogether. "It is an Automatic Energy Assault Rifle."

"No, I have not," Neztríanis admitted, but quickly added, "However, I learn new things easily."

"Learning how to fire the gun is easy. Learning how to aim the gun takes a bit of practice. Learning how to pull the trigger on a live target comes without warning. Lucky for you, your enemies are strong, and there is a 'non-lethal' setting on the damn thing.

"You trained enough for this? Your stamina won't fail will it?" he asked with knowing eyes. "Kéma doesn't appear to know the history that both of us know. And even if she did, I can tell she wouldn't let herself believe that you are—Staxis, *even* I don't want to believe it. That may be the last, but best thing we need... Your kind habitually complicates this world..."

Neztríanis was tired of keeping the secret and did not act shocked by the insinuation. "I have trained for this. I'll be fine." But, she honestly knew that was a lie, because she was about to wield her Elemental in full bloom for the first time, and she had not conjured her aura in over a duration. But she had prayed and chanted every day. "I happened as a—"

"Don't say it. *Staxis*," he cursed. "Don't let anyone know about that here. I don't want them getting their kímaz hopes up. Especially if you get killed or something. This gynix is hard enough as it is. I'll just tell them that you are a highly-skilled operative."

"Bíoske, what happened?" Neztríanis pressed the man for a response.

"We never wanted to talk about it. And now she's dead, and who in Qalfocx knows where Brenko is... There are some things in life, no one should have to go through, even those Tannódin'é bastards."

Bíoske heard his sentimentality and searched for a daggerweed and lit it. The commander took a deep inhale and blew the smoke out of his nose and mouth. "I don't give a damn what you think you can do, you are obviously the weakest link here, and I am going to make sure you are not a liability for this mission. Do you understand?"

"Yes, I do. Thank you Bíoske. I cannot do this—"

"And don't get nervous or scared now," he said loudly, but reassuringly. "That'll come later. If you need to relax, there are some men upstairs I know who can help you."

Neztríanis' face became red in embarrassment. "I do not believe that will be necessary." Although tempted, she did not need sex. She needed to chant and pray. And she was a virgin anyway. She did not want her first experience to be at the Unseen Inn.

Leaving the room, she saw Kéma, who exploded in laughter at Neztríanis' red face and Bíoske's comment. After calming herself, she gave the daughter of Hopha a serious smile, "Get some rest. We will train in three hours. The first thing I want to see from you is your physical conditioning, because this mission will fail if you are not in shape. And if you are not, I will be most disappointed in you, sister Neztríanis."

"I will not disappoint you."

Chapter Thirteen: All According to Plan...

3 Gamíz, 241 OGI

There was an explosion.

Something is not right, Neztríanis thought. *I am the first hinge.*

Alarmed, she stood on the rooftop of Triple Skyrise Three. Everything had gone smoothly until then. Neztríanis left Kéma only ten minutes ago. All of them entered into the residential tower posing as cleaners in full janitorial vestments.

What went wrong?

Neztríanis spotted the airshaft some one hundred feet away and then looked down. Concrete, mobiles, and death lay beneath her. It did not matter if the plan had gone awry. She knew the mettle of her comrades; she had spent the past three days training and bonding with them. Without question, they would see this mission through to the end.

There was no time to waste. She tore off her janitorial costume, revealing new apparel given to her by Bíoske. He informed her that the clothes she received from Hafir would hamper her movements and were not suitable for combat. Her new pants were a dark, deep blue, tight at the waist, hips, and thighs, while loosening beneath the knees. A solid, thin white stripe ran down the sides. Her top was also dark blue and skin tight, with a short jacket that carried the same color. It too had a white stripe flowing from the shoulders to the wrist. Her head was crowned with a snug blue beret hat, and her black hair was tied in a long, tight ponytail (courtesy of Kéma). Her shoulderpack and animal-hide canteen, which she hid in a trash container while making her way through the building, straddled her torso. She gripped a modified AEAR in her right hand—the firearm was larger than the normal issue and possessed three times the destructive power—and placed her bag and canteen on the rooftop. She would be back to retrieve them.

She was supposed to cross the chasm by using one of the steel anchors that girded the top of Skyrise One and diagonally descended to the rooftop of Skyrise Three. That would take too long now; she had to be more direct.

"Zí má," bowing her reddish-brown face, she sang. *"Zí mányx que rai…"*

Her breath grew cold and misty, while her left hand sputtered frost. Deftly holding her hand out, Neztríanis let loose a beam of coldness that traveled across the municipal ravine, found its mark on the vent, and froze it instantaneously into brittle. The adolescent Sczyphamek backstepped, ran across the top of the building, and jumped from the ledge and over the abyss. She flipped and straightened her body feet-first in mid-air, drew her energy rifle, and blasted the vent into pieces while still gliding. Her aim was nearly perfect; she slid directly into the shaft.

The experience was exhilarating, but Neztríanis remained focused. She crawled to the large, main air duct and jumped as high as she could. Reaching her apex, she hovered and searched for heat signatures. The témo was two stories above; therefore, she surmised that she was on the 250th floor. She also felt an intense amount of heat in two places. The battle was underway, and time was of the essence. Kéma's distinct heat signature was already moving up the side staircase. There was no time to delay. A group of soldiers from the uppermost floors were already heading Kéma's way.

Cycling her power cells to sixty-five percent, she chanted, "Mona fla renzgé ná."

Holding the rifle in her left hand and powering her right full of heat, she extended her arms horizontally.

"We must," she said to herself and the elements.

Her Elemental was ready.

With her left index finger, she pulled the trigger, and with her right hand, she released a fiery combustion, obliterating and melting the walls to her left and right with a great commotion. The top fourth of the building shook, and the main power block was destroyed. Her protective aura retreating, she waited a few moments and felt the troops in Kéma's direction reversing course. Next, Neztríanis turned the radio scrambler on, dropped back down to the floor of the shaft, and left it there. Then, she ascended once again and into the next portion of her mission: rescuing the témo.

Exiting the sizzling vent shaft hole to her right, the young Sczyphamek sped down the dark, smoky hallways to the main stairway. Enemies approached from her left. She brandished a flash grenade and rolled it down the hall. Emitting a bright light, the explosive blinded her adversaries. Neztríanis gave them no time to recover. She raced into action, crudely punching and kicking her way to the main stairway.

Swiftly running up two flights of stairs, she sensed a large contingent of heat signatures in the main chamber of the 252nd floor. Stopping short of the chamber, Neztríanis perceived their positions. Bíoske was right; there were twenty-five armed soldiers. Her weapon's energy cells were down to thirty-three percent. Setting her AEAR to stun, Neztríanis decided to wait until the last possible moment to reveal her powers.

Although the majority of the building was reduced to emergency power, the white chamber was somehow well lit. Neztríanis created a dense fog by cooling the air in the hall, and amidst the bright lights, the visibility decreased. The Blue Rapier cadre became confused. However, their disorientation turned into pain, for the daughter of Phesiana Phyxtríalis was upon them and assaulted them with restrained brutality.

Although foggy, her movements were still traceable for the trained Blue Rapier fighters. At once, the imperials opened fire, and the room became consumed by yellow energy bursts. Temperature felt nearly every firearm's discharge: its speed, direction, and point of release. Dodging the shots with agility and speed, Neztríanis launched herself upward, twisting and turning, and returned fire while still in mid-air.

The experience was invigorating. Her reflexes had become more heightened than she realized. She had not displayed her abilities in nearly five weeks, since before she entered Nextu. However, she prayed and meditated daily. Clearly, prayer and meditation yielded great results, but she began to feel the onset of minor fatigue.

She had subdued about half of the force when her weapon gave out. Breaking her spent AEAR on the face of an adversary, Neztríanis sensed the soldiers who were pursuing Kéma's party had arrived. Her distraction was successful. They were a force of fifteen, and the twelve remaining soldiers from the chamber made twenty-seven assailants. The chamber was silent, and the few lights that were still operational flickered discordantly. The Global Initiative forces regrouped and surrounded Neztríanis. Their rifles stared at her with cruel intentions.

Her breathing slowed. Time was of the essence. She still had not reached the témo.

"Staxis…" a soldier remarked. "What is she?"

"Fá'atoño má," she replied quietly. "Fá'atoño má. Fá'atoño má." Her orange-white aura emerged with power, blossoming in radiance. Her dark brown eyes became an ashen auburn, and her body gave off cold heat.

"She is a Sczyphamek!" a soldier yelled. "Kill her!"

It was time to try.

"Zí rai, mona flanyx," she sang softly.

The response from both elements within her was not so soft. A hemisphere of ice instantaneously materialized from her body, growing in speed and magnitude, and rushed towards the walls of the room. The soldiers tried to breach the small glacier with shots from their weapons, but to no avail. Slamming into her enemies, the dense ice shattered against their bodies and the walls, leaving their bones broken and their bodies indisposed and gripped with frigidity. The walls of the room were also gashed and frozen. She had incapacitated almost forty in a matter of moments. Although she did not have time to rejoice, Neztríanis was ecstatic that she was able to master the ice technique.

Bíoske, she said to herself. *You were right; I needed my powers.* She shuddered at his other prediction: she would have to kill someone before this ordeal was over.

Sensing the témo just ahead, Neztríanis resumed her mission. She opened a large, bolted door directly ahead of her. As soon as she stepped through the threshold, a massive, singular heat source descended upon her. She had little time to react as the témo pounced on her with unrestrained savagery and attempted to bite her right arm off. Neztríanis barely dodged the attack and placed her arms around the animal's mouth.

"I am here to help you!" she fearfully appealed.

The animal hissed and violently threw her off, causing the Sczyphamek to crash into a wall. Gathering herself, Neztríanis discerned the témo's eyes and realized it knew neither friend nor foe. The daughter of Hopha was filled with dread.

The témo's whiskers appeared sharper, like needles of death, ready to inject their poisonous experience into her. Its black fur had lost its regal tone, and the blue stripes that disparately ran across its stout and muscular trunk seemed jagged, while the stripes that crossed its head appeared as scars.

With instant brutality, the animal went on the offensive and attempted to gore Neztríanis, but she evaded the attack. However, her arm was grazed by the animal's claw, which caused the young woman from Hopha to cringe. Neztríanis instinctively punched the témo in the jaw, sending it flying backwards. She conjured heat in her left hand and made a fiery barrier between herself and the venomous animal.

The canines of the beast protruded with malice, and its adjacent teeth accentuated its loss and hurt. The wings of the témo appeared to be injured, but their luster was undeniable. They were a beautiful black, with royal blue artistically spattered across the wings. Its yellowish eyes, with a hint of red, burned against the Sczyphamek. The creature stepped back into the shadows, staring at Neztríanis through the flames, preparing for another attack.

"I saw you outside..." Neztríanis pleaded and held her injured arm. "Do you not remember? I am a Sczyphamek... A Kylanín... Please. Listen to my Elemental..."

The animal hesitated, and its eyes somewhat relented.

"I... saw you," it intimated, with a hardened, yet saddened vocal display. It was a female, by the sound of its inflection, although her vocalization was laden with heaviness. "It *was* you. You *are* a Sczyphamek."

"Yes," the daughter of Hopha replied, quenching the barrier of fire. "My name is Neztríanis Phyxtríalis, but my Sczyphamek title is Temperature. As soon as I saw you, my Elemental persuaded me to help you. I trust them and came to free you."

"Why? What is the point anymore...? Tannódin is too ruthless... I sense that you have not yet Awakened. It is impressive that you made it this far, but I…" Her countenance became unnerved and grave. "I have sensed Vicious… and you stand no chance."

Her directness cut the heart and hope of Neztríanis, but the young woman had no time to critically reflect. She dropped the sizzling fence altogether and moved towards the creature, inwardly chanting and petitioning her Elementals for strength and healing.

"We will cross that bridge when we get to it. Right now, you are my primary concern," she said with compassion. "What is your name?"

The animal hesitated, but Neztríanis held her arm out to the winged feline, and the témo drew closer to her.

"Timura,"[1] she sorrowfully purred. "One of the last témo's."

"Last? I know your number is near extinction but…"

"They have killed most of us off," Timura interjected. "Those females remaining were dealt with… just like me…" Tears clouded her eyes.

"I do not understand…" Neztríanis said.

"Vincallous… he robbed me. He sliced open my abdomen and put a knife through my cub. I was only one duration away from delivering. He killed my cub, but made sure I would survive. Since I have been here, they destroyed my reproductive system… but my… my cub."

Tears of devastation rained from her furry face. "We hid from Tannódin once we caught wind of their plot against us. Yet, somehow, we were located. No, *he* found us. I was one of the last témo's capable of reproducing… They performed some experiments on me as well; I think…"

Suddenly, the building was rattled by a fearsome explosion. Within a few moments, Neztríanis sensed the minor connecting bridge was destroyed.

"What is happening?" Timura asked.

"The minor connecting bridge of the military wing is down. Circumstances are going according to plan," she replied. After chanting silently for a few seconds in an attempt to heal her wounds, she turned to Timura. "We must leave. I do not think that we can linger here much longer."

She scanned the building for the remainder of her comrades.

Kéma's team had either made it out of the building or they were dead.

Kéma was alone on the 215th floor. She wondered what happened. Did Kéma actually kill all of them? She would not be alone for long. Twenty soldiers were heading her way.

And Bíoske—what was he doing? Something had gone terribly wrong.

She wanted to go to both of them, but only one of them could receive her aid.

She had no choice. Líachim was too important. Kéma was by herself and forty soldiers still remained, ten floors above her position. Half

---

[1] Timura (ti-moor-uh)

appeared to be on the move towards Kéma's position; the other half were heading Nez's way.

"Can you fly?" Sczyphamek Temperature asked Timura.

"I am unsure," the témo replied. "My underbelly and wings are quite sore. Probably not for long."

"You will be fine," Neztríanis reassured the témo and received newfound energy from her elements. "Timura, please, you must trust me. My Elemental is telling me our lives are intertwined."

Timura begrudgingly nodded her head, agreeing to the Elemental pronouncement.

Neztríanis returned her attention to Kéma, who would soon face a large contingent. Kéma could not escape. She was in trouble. Neztríanis ran to the other side of the lab and threw open another oversized door, revealing a room with a large window. The Sczyphamek needed to move.

***

They had just changed out of their janitorial garb and were in front of the connecting bridge to Skyrise One when an explosion beneath them occurred. Something was wrong. She signaled her two teams to open the access door.

"Team 3," Kéma said. "You must go to the minor connecting bridge and take it out, no matter the cost." There was no need to reiterate the seriousness of the command. "Team 4," she continued, "give them cover fire until you reach the main stairway. Set your explosives two flights beneath this floor and detonate them as quick as you can." After giving these short instructions, she motioned her soldiers to follow her.

Extreme confusion beset the 210th floor, and the two teams made it to the main stairway with little resistance, dispatching the disoriented guards effortlessly.

Kéma looked at her brothers and sisters-in-arms with confidence. "Be careful. Perform your tasks and leave."

Finishing these words, the stealthy Líachimian ran up the stairs to the intelligence room, while Team Four went down the steps and began to set charges. The members of Team Three made it to the minor bridge, but a moderate contingent of Blue Rapier was already crossing from the military wing.

"Grenade!" the team leader yelled as he threw the explosive onto the bridge.

It went off, killing some and wounding other Tannódin'é who were traversing the minor connecting bridge; however, the structure itself was undamaged.

Motioning to his group, the leader ordered his team forward for demolition. While they were setting the charges on the bridge, shots rang out and two team members were hit. The team leader turned and saw a large reinforcement of Blue Rapier on the other side of the bridge. Just as he was about to give the signal to fire, a percussive detonation made the bridge lurch and creek, putting the floor on emergency power. Recalling the strategic briefings, the leader reasoned the blast to be the handiwork of Neztríanis.

The Blue Rapier troops lost their balance and tumbled over each other because they were so stacked together. Seizing the opportunity, the captain set the final charges and threw a flash grenade towards his adversaries, blinding them for a few seconds. He set his remaining grenades on the bridge, and ran back into the main tower and positioned himself behind a wall, detonator in hand. The surviving two members of his team gave him cover fire. He ordered them to make their way back to the Residential Tower. However, his comrades would not leave him behind. Blue Rapier was closing in on their position and the bomb, laying down heavy fire.

"Get down!" he yelled and pressed the detonator.

After an explosion followed by a loss of main power, Kéma gathered herself and poked her head in the entryway of the 215th floor. Unable to use their radios due to Neztríanis' wave scrambler, the Blue Rapier soldiers yelled messages to one another. They switched from their normal patrol to a more sophisticated protocol.

Although Kéma was unaware of their precise tactical deployment pattern, ten incredibly skilled Blue Rapier soldiers safeguarded the floor. Their primary task was to protect the information war room. The information war room not only housed the supercomputer that contained the Líachim war plans. The room was also home to the only communications device in Nez Spirita capable of reaching all of the continents. In other words, it was the most important piece of imperial real estate in Nez Spirita. The soldiers would only destroy the room and computer if there were no other alternatives.

When Kéma asked Bíoske why the floor possessed so few troops, the commander from Keotagosdi laughed and told her that she of all people should know the answer to that question.

"One exceptional fighter is better than ten average fighters," he said. "When you're guarding sensitive material, you don't want those who panic easily guarding it. The more people, the greater the chance that the 'herd mentality' will kick in, even for soldiers. The unquestioned importance of the information and the threat of death over against the possibility of the information falling into the wrong hands—only the best should be placed in those scenarios. And Kéma, you will be going against the best. Ten of them. I hope your fighting skills are as good as they told me."

Kéma breathed deeply and silently. The next few moments required her to subdue ten exceptional fighters without causing the slightest commotion. During her preparation in Líachim, she was deemed the most nimble, swiftest, and strongest of all her contemporaries. Her speed and agility in this exercise would be tested to no end. However, six durations of cleaning bathrooms and mess halls had diminished some of her skill. This part of her mission could not be simulated. As long as she engaged each adversary individually, under the element of surprise, she stood a chance.

The floor was on emergency power and dimly lit. Kéma'fém reasoned visibility was no more than five feet. She was dressed in black; that alone would aid in her in avoiding detection. A black strap, fastened around the Líachimian's waist, held an armored pouch, tranquilizer darts, and her sheathed weapon of choice, a long argent knife she called "Feather."

Across her mid-back was a sword, mystically sealed in a dark hazel casing. The sword's base was elyandir, and the aciculate, dreary blade, minutely serrated near the edges, was made from the metals found in Mt. Chabnev. Her mentor bequeathed the sword, "Affliction," to Kéma after she completed her training at the Sacred Keep in Líachim. Affliction could only be unjacketed by her hands.

The fingers on her left hand were adorned with platinum rings, which expanded on notice to become platinum knuckles. Her right hand gripped an AEAR and four grenades strafed her torso.

Two enemy soldiers patrolled the entrance to the floor. From Kéma's calculations, their patrol kept them no less than ten feet from the opening. There was no way to pass them unseen or without tipping off their comrades. She hoped the two guards would have taken Nez's bait and followed the rest of the soldiers up the floor, but they were excellently trained. They would not abandon their posts unless under extreme duress. Kéma had to precipitate such duress.

Quietly hopping up two flights of stairs, Kéma charged her AEAR to two percent with a twenty-second countdown. She sat the firearm on the steps and stealthily made her way down one flight below the Imperial Access Center. The discharge from the firearm would only be loud enough for the closest guards to hear it. Hopefully, they would only be curious and check out the noise and not alert the other guards.

The plan was dangerous. Her breaths were spastic. She needed to calm herself.

She thought of her hometown of Aphaz on Líachim and the august Mount Chabnev. Her eyes closed, and fear was replaced with righteous determination. Her shadowy xanthic face became the countenance of acceptance. She accepted the next few minutes of what might become the last moments of her life. Bíoske would not retreat, and Neztríanis had done her job. And she—she was a Cílal,[2] a covertly trained mystical engine of death, one of the last heralded warriors of Líachim from time immemorial. It was in her hands now.

---

[2] Cílal (see-lahl)

The AEAR discharged. The two guards closest to the stairway ran out to assess the situation. The first soldier scanned the steps, while the second covered his position. The Cílal, hiding in the shadows, clenched Feather tightly and threw it at the second guard. The long knife made a bloody incision in the guard's neck. In writhe and gurgle, the second soldier collapsed. The first solider turned around; however, his reaction time, though outstanding, was still too slow.

Kéma sprang from the steps; her platinum knuckles expanded; her arm drew back, ready to deliver the blow. The Tannódin'é soldier attempted to aim his gun but for naught. Kéma'fém's punch was a violent eruption, nearly beheading the man as she struck his forehead. Kéma dislodged Feather from the other guard's neck, and ran into the large room.

The room became narrower and led to a small door which opened into the floor's main hallway. Cautiously, she knelt at the door and stuck her head around the corner. Near the middle of the main hallway, an intersecting hallway led to smaller rooms. The computer room was at the end of the main hallway to the right.

The entire floor was nearly pitch-black, apparently without power. Kéma recalled Bíoske mentioning that the Rapiers on guard did not possess dark-vision instruments. The goggles were a new invention and had not been mass-produced, _yet_. This was advantageous, for fighting well without the sense of sight, smell, or sound was a staple for all Cílals. Stealth was indispensable, and stealth was her expertise.

Making her way down the corridor, she realized the only way to make sure her mission would be completely untraceable was if she destroyed the entire floor and those adjacent, which would make the demolition appear to be part of the plan. It was not what Bíoske advised, but then the plan was already unraveling, was it not?

Besides, Tannódin would not consider such an audacious attack to be anything but an attempt of disruption and sabotage. With at least three different engagements going on, the destruction of the Imperial Access Center would be a logical step to an attack built upon damage. Once she convinced herself of this strategy, her thoughts turned deadly. The most time efficient method involved eight more bodies, charred in a way to conceal the cause of death. Her heart grew surprisingly troubled at her cold rationale, but she could not examine moral law now.

Taking out her tranquilizing darts, the Líachimian rebel continued towards the intersecting hallways. She was about to move into action when a colossal explosion jolted the building. Kéma nearly stumbled into the intersection, but she intuited a small, preliminary tremor, milliseconds before the large jolt. She braced herself; however, two sentinels to her left and right fell into hallway's intersection. Kéma's reflexes were impressively mercurial. She tossed the darts with precision into their legs, and instantaneously, they collapsed.

That explosion was very close, she thought. *The minor bridge must have been destroyed.*

According to her count, six Blue Rapiers remained. They were undoubtedly aware of that last explosion, which would only heighten their vigilance. Kéma, being ambidextrous, unsheathed Feather with her left hand and drew her last three darts out with her right. Like a predator avoiding detection by its prey, she ran down the hallway.

Observing a soldier with his back turned to her, she clandestinely dispatched him with her long knife in mid-stride then covered his mouth in order to silence any noise. While her hand muffled the sound of writhe and gurgle, the Cílal spotted a silhouette down the corridor. She tossed a dart near the apex of the obscuration and her enemy buckled. At once, Kéma'fém heard the sound of a weapon arming around the corner where the incapacitated soldier had fallen.

Unhesitatingly, she threw Feather towards that direction, quickly running behind the blade and briefly matching the knife's speed. A weapon went off at the glint of Feather, and as the blade lodged itself in a wall, Kéma slid on the floor headfirst, throwing her last two darts at the soldier who discharged the weapon, hitting her in the thigh and hand. That shot was sure to alert the last three soldiers on the floor and in all likelihood the file shutdown sequence had begun, so the Líachimian priestess of suffering took Feather out of the wall, sheathed it, picked up the soldier's AEAR, made two quick lefts, and scampered up the hallway.

If her calculations were correct, only three patrollers remained, and the main computer room would be the second door on her left. As she passed the first door, she listened for a sound but heard nothing, even with her vivid senses.

Moving on, she saw something in the shadows moving. It was a Blue Rapier soldier. Suddenly the door she had just passed flew open, and a second combatant emerged behind her. Just as Kéma surmised, the discharge alerted her remaining adversaries, and they moved into another defensive protocol.

Well trained, the Rapiers did not fire their AEARs due to their proximity with each other.

They needed Kéma alive. She needed them dead.

The guard behind her knocked the rifle out of her hand, while her other foe punched her in the jaw. Kéma stumbled backwards into the guard, and somehow escaped his waiting grasp while her platinum knuckles expanded. The soldier to her rear grabbed her right hand, but she knelt and punched him in the kneecaps with her knuckles. He blurted out a shriek of pain, soon to be hushed as Kéma unsheathed Feather and effortlessly sliced the Blue Rapier soldier in the throat, all in a matter of what seemed to be a millisecond. She turned and faced the other guard, only to step into a murderous backhand to the face, jarring Feather from her clutches. Kéma bled from her mouth and nose, and her vision blurred.

She had to end this.

Her skilled assailant lunged for her and drew his leg back for a kick to the abdomen. Kéma blocked the kick, sizing the man's face for a platinum engagement; however, the masterful soldier was quick to counter her punch by knocking her left arm down with his right, while trying to deliver a head butt. Kéma dodged the attack, narrowly, and kicked her adversary in the shin, causing him to career backwards. The Líachimian warrior ran at her enemy and clotheslined him, unleashing a vehement barrage of force that caused him to flip in mid-air. As he landed violently on his head, Kéma'fém picked up her long knife, winced in pain, and ran towards the computer room.

Mentally and physically distracted due to the scuffle, the Cílal forgot about the last remaining guard, much to her chagrin. No sooner had Kéma opened the door to the computer room, did the final soldier rammed the butt of her rifle into Kéma's upper back and dislocated her shoulder. The Cílal grunted in audible torment. As a secondary blow came in tempo, Kéma'fém had just enough strength to block the punch with her knuckles and break the fingers of her nemesis. Kéma wasted no time and crescent kicked the woman in the face while simultaneously unjacketing Affliction. The female soldier fell to her knees, and Kéma ran her through, back first, with the sword, and swiftly returned Affliction to its jacket. She moved towards the computer, muttering, angry with herself for forgetting about the last guard.

The deletion process had commenced, and only had three and a half minutes remained to retrieve any information. Hurriedly, Kéma took out her minicomputer from the protective pouch around her waist and linked it with the computer. She bypassed the security blocks with ease and managed to sync and download the information before it was completely deleted.

While the minicomputer retrieved the data, Kéma clamped her teeth together and popped her shoulder and arm back into place. She whined, breathed heavily, and sat down at the base of the computer. Livid, the Miska Kea operative knew that the information she obtained would only be partial files and images. She hoped that whatever data she obtained would be useful, but in general, her mission was a failure.

Giving herself only a minute to rest, Kéma'fém put the second phase of her plan into action. She rounded the entire floor and set each soldier's AEAR on a 100% charge, laying her grenades in strategic places. When she had finished dispersing the weapons in such a way as to cause the most structural damage, she went back into the computer room. The minicomputer had obtained whatever information it could. Kéma covered her tracks, erasing all clues pertaining to her espionage.

Her mediocre satisfaction was replaced by apprehension when she noticed a silent alarm flashing. The alarm was undoubtedly connected to the floor's secondary power source. She was in trouble.

The Cílal placed the minicomputer in her armored pouch, and returned to the room antecedent, where the guard had emerged behind her. An armory was located inside the room, filled with grenades and energy weapons. Kéma took two bombs from the cache and set as many energy rifles to maximum discharge as she could.

While arming the explosives, she heard the steps of her adversaries approaching. They were a heavily armed detachment, and on each gun was a light projector. Kéma refused capture; she knew too much and Tannódin routinely broke even the most recalcitrant minds. It seemed fate was not kind to her this day; neither would it be kind to her enemies. As she peered down the long hallway, she saw nearly twenty soldiers coming her way. Behind her was an extended window that led to death by concrete. There was no way out, except the way of death. The method of death appeared to be her choice.

"Put down your weapon, *or else*," one of the soldiers threatened and flashed the light in her eyes.

Eyeing the weapons room, Kéma replied with misty breath, "Else."

A shivering Cílal observed the guards seemed to be looking beyond her and at the window behind her. Kéma heard the sound of cracking glass, and she grew even colder. The temperature had dropped precipitously in a matter of seconds. Amidst the splintering glass, Kéma detected the sound of a growl that became louder and closer. Instinctively, the woman dove into the computer room, and the entire window shattered behind her. Before she could stand upright, Kéma harkened screams of agony and energy bursts. When the Cílal reentered the hallway, her eyes almost deceived her: A témo was afoot, mauling and maiming the guards, and Neztríanis was beside it, punching and kicking the remaining soldiers with incredible speed and power.

"Timura," Temperature ordered, "get behind me!"

The témo retreated behind Neztríanis as she created a blockade of ice between the guards and their position. Kéma did not want to believe when it came to her mind three days ago, but Bíoske staked everything on it. Neztríanis was a Sczyphamek, and a Kylanín at that.

Kéma gathered herself and yelled, "Nez! We have to get out of here now!"

Neztríanis sensed the cycled firearms from the weapon room and frowned. "*Kéma...*"

"No time," Kéma perceptively countered and threw an armed grenade into the cache room. At that quick rebuff, Kéma strapped an AEAR around her torso, ran towards the shattered window, and jumped out.

Neztríanis and Timura followed with urgent haste. Just as they exited and started their descent, the entire floor exploded with a jarring shockwave. Flames and concussive blasts spewed from the windows and roiled Kéma in midair. Plummeting towards the hardened gravel below, the Cílal was grabbed by a soaring Neztríanis, who simultaneously created an ice shield to protect them from the cascading debris.

They made their way to the top of Skyrise Three, with the témo close behind. There were a few soldiers on the roof of Skyrise Three, gazing upon the damage and fires raging in Skyrise One. Before they could react, Kéma fired seven shots, which struck and killed all of them. When the two women touched down on the roof, Neztríanis nearly collapsed. Kéma assessed their immediate situation, barricaded the rooftop door, and perceived no sudden danger. She spied Neztríanis' shoulderpack and windhorse canteen sitting near the edge of the rooftop. She retrieved them, and upon hearing the sound of water within the pack, she found the water jug and handed it to the Sczyphamek. Neztríanis took the jug and consumed its entire contents and breathed heavily, almost losing consciousness.

"This is her first great employment of her Elemental," the témo explained. "Temperature is naturally winded."

"Temperature?" Kéma asked.

"Tha-..." Neztríanis gasped for air. "That is my given title. Brace yourselves."

Drawing her wings in, Timura crouched down on all fours, and Kéma was puzzled until she perceived a small tremor. Suddenly, a catastrophic explosion rocked the entire area and boomed throughout the vicinity. Although Skyrise One partially hid the happenings, Kéma, stumbling backwards, knew the major connecting bridge was destroyed. After regaining her balance, the Cílal ran towards the edge of the building. Ablaze, the main building had taken considerable damage, but showed no signs of structural collapse—a somewhat ominous sign of the times.

"Bíoske..." Kéma'fém muttered.

***

In the residential tower, Skyrise Three, the grizzled veteran—his team in tow and wearing their janitorial vestments—observed the connecting bridge to the main tower. His speculation had to be accurate. Neztríanis was probably a Sczyphamek and would at least be able to carry out the first leg of her mission. That was the only thing that explained her frenzied search for help and her unremitted motivation. His team needed only to wait for the signal before they began their phase of the plan. They rehearsed this plan eight times in two and a half days. This *plan*...

"Ah, what are you doing over there?" a voice in the distance asked. The Damüdan accent was thick. "This floor should have been cleaned three hours ago."

Misfortune had found them. Too many comrades underestimated the cunning of their enemy. Twenty janitors would never congregate in such an area. Blue Rapier was not a second rate military branch of the imperial war machine. Feolenz instructed and held his pupils to the strict code of observation. Old Flint believed that commanders and soldiers who did not grasp the nuances and cues of battle and situation were destined to make major military blunders. As a result, each Blue Rapier soldier's training consisted of adroitly perceiving circumstances, forever expecting the unexpected. It only took Bíoske's team's presence to alert them.

As the guard quickly grabbed his radio in one hand, he stealthily clicked a button four times and drew a weapon with his other hand. Bíoske smiled at his enemy and laughed, then lit a daggerweed cigarette.

"You bastards are damn perceptive," he said after inhaling. "Damn perceptive..."

The move was like lightning. It was as if the sound of the combustible firearm's discharge arrived before he unholstered his weapon. The first bullet disabled the radio; the second lodged itself in the heart of the soldier, causing him to stumble back into a wall.

"Staxis," Bíoske cursed. "This is no good. We're gonna have to go in first."

As a conditioned field officer, Bíoske knew most plans never went according to plan. But there was a gnawing feeling in him this time. This would be the night he would redeem all those lives lost at Phenplyacin. This would be the night he would ransom his unknown first cousins and aunt who were murdered in recompense for his mother's escape.

She never talked about it much, but his mother had been haunted by her actions. She was born in the forests of northeast Phmquedria in a slave town built upon the lumber industry. His father was a member of a resistance group that planned to destroy a lumber factory in order to upset the economic wing of Global Initiative. Upon arriving, however, he met a young slave woman and they soon fell in love. This story of old did not enjoy a blessed epilogue.

"Bíoske," he heard one of his soldiers say. "What do you want us to do?"

Clearing his mind of distractions, he declared, "I'm sure Blue Rapier troops will be greeting us on the connecting bridge when we cross." Gruffly nodding towards the fallen solider, he grunted. "The bastard damn well probably alerted them to our presence. We can't wait for Neztríanis."

Peering through the window of the security doors over the other side of the connecting bridge in Tower I, the commander saw a team of Blue Rapier soldiers gathering their strength, ready to seize the rebels. Undoubtedly, more troops were already heading their way from inside the residential building, the present location of Bíoske and his team.

"Kíma," he cursed in admiration of his foes. In a caustic whisper, he commanded, "Give me two charges."

One of his subordinates objected. "But sir, do you think we will have enough to take out the military bridge."

"Wenal." The commander replied with compassionate reassurance to his personal aide. "Don't worry. We'll think of something. Now bring me those damn charges."

Peering through the window again, Bíoske spied a group of about twenty agents crossing the bridge. His team set the charges at the door, and once they had finished, Bíoske motioned them to stand back and seek cover. Bracing himself against a wall, Bíoske pressed the detonation button.

The numbness took hold. Explosions were second nature to him. It would take exactly four tenths of a second for the charges to blow, and in that short instant, he returned to remembrance. Memories flashed like lightning in his mind, leaving indelible imprints upon his subconscious.

He had to repay the crimson oblation of his comrades and enemies, who died at Phenplyacin, and his unknown family, who were executed under the ju Xaníz runaway provision as a ransom for his mother's freedom. He owed it to them. They could not run from their deaths, neither would he run from his.

Payment, debt, enmity, and guilt. Bíoske believed that the faithful of Qeauríyx chained themselves to these metaphysics of relationship. This was precisely why his parents let their guilt consume them. They never stopped praying to the One with No Name for forgiveness. His parent's attitude repulsed Bíoske now, and he sought to remove himself from the bondage of such religious and philosophical terror.

The payment was impossible to redeem, for the interest upon the principal act was indefatigably egregious. Verily, the enmity would never be gone, only appeased. This enmity was not of the absentee deity. Rather, his species would not allow the erasure of divine wrath. Mendaciously, they were trying to escape into an omnipotent, omnipresent, omniscient cultural production. And as long as they continued to act as if they were bound to this dramatic farce, they would infinitely rehearse their own fateful tragedy of damnation, guilt, and the spilling of each other's blood. Such was their chénala.

Not Bíoske.

His duty was clear: Bíoske would make his life a living sacrifice. Not to the Nameless One or to some inane comedy, *but to the plotline and cult of reality.* His theory, hypothesis, and observations had been tested and proven, with only one *minor* exception: even within this new frame of reference, he still found himself actualized and victimized as a spiller of blood.

The charges exploded. The door blew open. The floor rattled. Shrapnel flew. A large ball of fire shot into the connecting bridge.

"Let's go!" Bíoske ordered.

Immediately, he and his group moved into action blasting their way across the smoke-filled bridge although most of the soldiers were dead. Those that were not were dispatched by the insurrectionists. Daggerweed still in mouth, Bíoske ran towards the main hallway's the elevator shafts. Without words, he signaled his explosive team to prepare for demolition, while he and others laid down cover fire, as more guards advanced to their position. The demolition team obliterated the elevator doors and placed adhesive charges on the inner walls of the shaft. Within moments, the job was done, and the nod of affirmation was given to Bíoske.

"Move!" he commanded.

But they were unable to execute the next phase of their design, for a second wave of Blue Rapier soldiers arrived. One group was from the military wing, the other from the residential. Bíoske and his team were surrounded.

"Nez, you better had—" Bíoske grunted. "Damn…"

At that moment, the building lightly swayed; the lights went out; and moderate tremors shook the floor. The Rapier soldiers were startled but Bíoske was not. Two flash grenades were already in the air, and gestures were given to his compatriots signifying the next course of action. As the grenades emitted their signature glow, the fighters of Miska Kea moved into a room adjacent to the elevators. There was not a second to delay, for the grizzled commander had also motioned to blow the charges in five seconds.

Bíoske understood that many on his team would not survive the forthcoming explosion, but neither would his foes. And those Miska Kea operatives that lived through the blast possessed little to no chance of surviving the entire mission. Did Syla perceive this as well? He pleaded with his longtime comrade not to go to Lozé but she was persistent. Maybe Brenko was right after all, having gone underground for the past fourteen cycles.

The three of them were in the same platoon on the shores of Phenplyacin. And they were the only ones from their group to make it out alive. Although he had no proof, from what he gathered from Neztríanis, only Rydín and a few others had survived the battle at Lozé. Syla would not have let herself be taken by the enemy. She was probably dead. And judging from his current circumstance, Bíoske would soon be joining her. Their godforsaken luck was coming to an end. The battle was almost over.

War was anything but a lovely enterprise, and death came without pomp and circumstance. There was no grandeur, no orator to present the tale of a valiant warrior. The dead were celebrated when they were dead. But in the few milliseconds it took to breathe one's last—and Bíoske had seen it too many times—only a macabre transition took place. There was no escaping this lot.

Brenko was a fool. It was their fate to die on the battlefield.

Indeed, Bíoske was completely tangled in the metaphysical web he so loathed. Even if the means were different, they were only different roads to the same chthonic destination.

"Kíma." He spat out his cigarette and curled himself up.

The discharge ripped through the main hallway. The walls, which protected the Miska Kea agents, were soon obliterated as shrapnel, dust, fire, and concrete rained.

He still felt pain. He was still alive. His left arm was unresponsive. He was alive.

Ears ringing, he coughed and laughed insufferably. "Not yet, you bastards; *not yet...*

"Who's still here? Kíma."

A few moans and groans answered his question; however, nearly three-fourths of his company were killed by the concussion, including his entire demolition team. Only five remained.

"Damn kímaz probability," he muttered. Even as he drew up the plan, the man from Keotagosdi knew that probability dictated this outcome. There were too many unknowns. The mission was suicidal for one of the groups. It might as well be his. Silently, he apologized to his fallen comrades and almost shed a tear.

Almost.

They knew the risk as well as he did.

"Get up!" he barked at his remaining squad-members and removed any salvageable munitions from the corpses. He ripped a shirt off a fallen comrade and tied it around his blood-soaked arm. Using his good arm and his teeth, he made a tourniquet for himself. If he was right, that last explosion bought them at least ten minutes before any reinforcements reached their position.

"Take your real clothes off and put those janitor suits back on." Bíoske pointed to their dead allies. "And take their janitor clothes off and bring them with you." The remainder of his team appeared hesitant, which made Bíoske's scowl grow into an abyss of aggression. "Do it now!" he commanded maliciously.

The remaining Miska Kea operatives, inspired by Bíoske's relentless tenacity, did as their commander ordered. They removed the janitorial garb, which revealed their battle uniforms. Next, they took those off and then put their cleaning outfits back on. The commander assigned a man and a woman to remove the cleaning attire from their fallen friends and pick up all of the remaining clothes. They complied, and the living followed Bíoske out of the room.

The hallway was destroyed. Craters and holes littered the floor. Moving cautiously, the caustic commander stepped over bodies and gingerly made his way to the major connecting bridge, while ordering three of his troops to take any operating energy rifle they found. They only found twelve usable weapons.

While on their way, they passed a Blue Rapier soldier with a mortal wound and in considerable pain. Bíoske stopped, looked at the man, and punched him in the face, which knocked him unconscious. His squad puzzled over what seemed to be an unusually cruel act.

"He won't suffer as much that way," Bíoske explained. "Come on."

Suddenly an awesome blast rocked the building. The minor connecting bridge to the military wing had been destroyed. When they reached the major connecting bridge—it was nearly eight hundred feet across—Bíoske and crew looked above through the reinforced glass windows. The bridge was wide and jutted out of the 114th floor of Skyrise One and was met halfway by an escalator system that descended to the military wing.

Debris and shrapnel rained down on the entire walkway, but caused very little structural damage; most of the pieces fell onto the concrete below. No*thing* was on their side that night. There was a seventy-eight percent chance that if the minor bridge was destroyed, it would cause significant structural damage to the major bridge.

Instead, the bridge stood there with minor scrapes and laughed maniacally at the remainder of the foolish Miska Kea agents. The steel, shipped in from Euhilv, and mortar, made in the Bitzroy Plains, continued to cackle neurotically: what Cycle did Bíoske think he was in? He had picked the wrong chénala to meander.

Gazing across and down the way, Bíoske observed there to be no sign of any immediate resistance.

Like it mattered. There was no end to the random folly and diabolical tease of existence. Evil and good were both infinitely cursed and frustrated in their cyclic designs.

"Won't even give us that, huh? Where are you when we need you O Nameless One? Qeauríyx? Probability? Staxis… Chénala, my ass… All of you are kímaz useless…" he muttered sarcastically. Turning to his companions, he ordered, "Set the charges and clothes in the middle of the bridge."

Bíoske ran towards the other end of the walkway and opened a large door that led to the military wing. On the other side, he pressed the "close" button on the control panel and set a charged AEAR nearby. Bíoske strafed through the closing door and moved back to the middle of the bridge. The energy rifle discharged and destroyed the control panel. Blue Rapier could not approach them from that way. Neztríanis had crippled their communication system, and the only way the door could be opened was if a soldier radioed the request to a control room. But the control room was probably on minimal power or destroyed too.

Bíoske returned to his company and noticed Wenal's long face.

"What's the problem?"

Suffering a head injury and wincing, his subordinate answered, "Six charges left, sir. You told us it would take nine to destroy this bridge."

Bíoske cut his eyes at his assistant. "I did, didn't I? Wenal, perhaps you can convert your enormous gift for the obvious into something useful, like helping us come up with a solution."

Bíoske's sigh betrayed his weariness. "Give me all your energy rifles, and get out of here as if Qalfocx itself were chasing you. You're still dressed like janitors. They'll probably hold you for questioning, but when they find our dead comrades in a different dress, they'll believe they were the only ones involved in the conflict. Since you all took off your real clothes, even if they strip search you, you won't appear to be anything but Nez Spiritan janitorial help. After all, you do work here. And with our 'help,' you should be able to get out alive."

"Bíoske, we are not going to leave you here." Wenal's face was firm.

"Then you'll die here."

"Why can't you use the detonator?" a soldier asked.

"This detonator?" Bíoske held up a broken electronic device. "Now cycle those cells to maximum discharge and place them at the ends of this bridge, damn it, and get out of here." Bíoske unholstered his firearm of antiquity and smiled; it too was damaged beyond repair. He could not shoot the charges with his gun, and he needed the remainder of the AEARs to explode in order to complete the destruction. He searched for his lighter, but it was also smashed.

"Staxis. Why are you all here? Leave," he growled while emptying the combustible rounds from the chamber.

"Why even try to detonate the bridge?" the aide asked his commanding officer of ten cycles. "Let's just get out of here while we can. There's nothing to be gained anymore; one of the bridges was destroyed—"

"I will not let them have died for nothing…we've got to give Líachim a chance. That was our mission…"

"And it failed," Wenal countered, "that does not mean that you failed…"

"The enemy must—"

"The enemy is not here! Look around, Bíoske!" Wenal yelled. "Where in Qalfocx is the enemy? I only see a bridge."

"This is my last response, Wenal. My enemy was always more than Tannódin, or Blue Rapier, or whatever bastard that crawled out from under the ground. My enemy is this—*all this*… what this bridge is… *this whole damn thing*… You know me, and I'm not about to explain it now. We are four minutes away from being killed…"

"Bíoske," Wenal said softly, "this is not the time to prove Brenko or Syla wrong."

Bíoske smiled at his comrade and friend. Wenal returned the sign of affection. He did not see the blow coming, as Bíoske moderately rammed the butt of an AEAR into Wenal's head, knocking him unconscious.

"Get him out of here," he told the rest of the soldiers quietly and solemnly. "Get out of here and live… Carrying him like that should give your story more credibility. Our 'friends' will help you escape once you're detained." Bíoske turned to the pile of explosives and set them for detonation.

Begrudgingly, his last few underlings followed his command and made their way back to the residential connecting bridge. Crossing over the bridge into Skyrise One, they made their way down a staircase, and as they continued towards the exit, they were stopped by Blue Rapier soldiers.

"Hold them for questioning," the commanding officer stated. "The rest of you, follow me."

The Blue Rapier troops headed for Bíoske. The rebels hoped he finished the job in time and were astonished by how quickly Bíoske created stratagem. Even though their plan was botched from the beginning, somehow, the commander was ingenious enough to devise an alternate plan. If they were right, Bíoske changed out of his janitor's clothes to look like their dead friends. He only had five or six minutes before he would be greeted by Commandant Feolenz's troops.

Back on the connecting bridge, Bíoske had indeed changed out of his worker's garments. With great speed, he had removed the gunpowder from his combustible shells over the past three minutes, placing the powder on the main charges. There was enough powder to create a large spark, which would ignite the main charge. He just needed to create a small spark. Taking the metal butt of his antiquated firearm, Bíoske smashed the end onto the broken cigarette lighter.

Over and over, he bashed the firearm onto the lighter. A small hint of orange-blue appeared before his eyes, and he closed them, smiling to himself. It was over. He did not know if there was an afterlife, but he was certain he would not find his way to whatever place his aunt, cousins, Syla, and Phenplyacin now resided. He heard the steps of Blue Rapier in the background, but they were too late.

"Bastards," he grunted, and the spark grew into a flame. "It's about damn time."

Chapter Fourteen: A Dim Reflection

30 Ízdak, 241 OGI

In order to return home before the murder provision went into effect, the slave stowed away on a railcruiser three hundred lengths north of Kamo.

Hard were the rains of Euhilv.

Anámn took apprehensive steps in the muddy ground that late afternoon.

Upon entering his district's outskirts, he saw not one person. Inconspicuously, the Sczyphamek headed towards his shack in the shantytown located on the eastern side of the city. The dirty streets brimmed over with waste and litter. Like always, Euhilv's remedial drainage system could not handle the rainy season. The pus of slavery oozed onto the streets, a sign of the chronic infection that lay beneath. The smell of raw sewage wafted into Anámn's nose. Somehow he had forgotten that demonic smell.

No matter. Vengeance was at hand. The noose around his father's neck was tightening.

Dilapidated streetlights peppered the squalid shacks and streets. But they only revealed the gray monotony of Euhilv, not so much giving off light as revealing the miserable obvious. The few folks Anámn encountered greeted him, relieved that he was back from his sojourn. None knew if his father would have Héthyx kill random slaves if Anámn did not return, since he had no next of kin nearby. A few asked Anámn if he had seen Malchían, because the elder had not appeared in the village since both left twenty-four days prior. Anámn lied and answered "no."

According to the slaves, his father and all the overseers were pleased by Malchían's departure, having longed for such a day for quite some time. Evidently, the old man was the only bondsman free of the murder provision.

By the time he arrived at his shack, Anámn's ire was in a slow, inextinguishable burn. Upon stepping through the entryway, he noticed immediately that he had been robbed, probably by one of his fellow slaves.

His food was gone, along with a few dingy possessions.

He grew dismayed... angry at their deceit, their *weakness*. The conditions of slavery caused Anámn to hate his own kind, the wretched of Qeauríyx. He knew the hate was misplaced but that could not stop the hatred from entering his thoughts, feelings, and actions.

His father would atone for his misdirected malice.

Touching his bed, which was more like a mat of straw and linen, Anámn knelt down by its lower end. He moved the mat over, revealing the woodchip and earthen floor, and dug with his bare hands. Eventually, after about ten minutes of digging, he clasped his hands upon it, the only keepsake of his mother that he managed to save: a small bronze bracelet. Scraping the dirt off the trinket while bracing himself against a wall, Anámn clutched the only heirloom he possessed.

His hands were dirty. His fingernails held chips and mud. His heart was like the eye of a typhoon. Destructive thoughts and memories swirled around him like storm clouds; yet at that moment, Matriester was enraptured by the scent of his mother, her love, and her hope in him. A tear rolled down his cheek.

But the teardrop was not the condensation of melancholy remembrance. The calm eye of the storm had passed, and the torrent was about to resume. Placing the bracelet in his pants pocket, Anámn stood up and stepped out of his shack.

Héthyx's garrison was his first stop.

Euhilv was comprised of eight districts, with eight overseers. Each overseer had his or her own garrison, where their family and major subordinates lived. Each overseer also employed a litany of support from his or her own personal cadre, in order to enforce bondage. The overseer's subordinates were in charge of maintaining control of a specific area of the expansive slum that was Euhilv. The overseer's responsibility was to make sure that the eight mines within the nameless mountain continuously produced the ore necessary for Tannódin'é and Damüdan consumption. In some respects, the slave system developed in Euhilv mirrored the military chain of command. Intermediaries carried out commands that were given from a distance. And the system ran mercilessly and with extreme efficiency.

When Anámn was seven cycles old, Héthyx became the overseer of the eastern district. There was immediate tension. Out of all the overseers, Héthyx was the most parsimonious and scurrilous. He demanded the most from his slaves, with little incentive. He was Tannódin'é, from the northwest coast of Civix Setrin. Anámn's father personally recruited him. Raised and nurtured in Tannódin'é aristocracy, Héthyx's disdain for Phmquedrians was mythical.

To the aristocrat, "Phmmys" were but useless play things trapped in bodies of labor. Inferior in design and in utility, only their quantitative numbers brought them salvation, and as a deacon of prosperity and progress, he would baptize them in the name of industry, commerce, and war. Global Initiative left no other standard. Allegiance to or belief in anything "other" than the cause of the House of Kaz, no matter its apparent "goodness," was anathema to Héthyx's qanín.

Closing in on Héthyx's garrison, Anámn passed the overseer's personal slaves. Their knees knocked and their mouths quivered at the sight of the Sczyphamek's countenance.

"Don't go starting trouble, Anámn," they warned. "It's been quiet since you been gone, and we getting along just fine this way."

Anámn let his sneer do the talking. *"Quiet?" "Getting along?"* This Qalfocx had destroyed his people, taking their heart and sanity. This kíma of a life was troublesome in itself. And here they were, admonishing Anámn for starting trouble. He suffered no pity for them. They were traitors, comfortably living with Héthyx, while those who worked in the mines suffered tremendously. However, Anámn had little sympathy for the mineworkers, for they mocked and stole from him at a moment's notice.

They were all Phmmys.

Anámn shrugged off the complications, the complexities of systems, the collusion of institutions, and the webs of power. They just got in the way. Narratives of vengeance demanded nothing less than the acceptance of—

Though it seemed impossible for the rains to fall any harder, the sky thundered and brought forth a deluge so absurd, visibility decreased to gray obscurity. Anámn saw nothing in the murky distance that would grant him his bearings. Phmquedrian bodies and faces became ashen, charcoal shadows moving behind a film of muddy, lifeless refuse. Anámn's hands were almost invisible to his eyes. Never in his life were the rains so indomitable.

Yet even as the clouds wept uncontrollably, the son of Alzhexph was not lost. He needed no marker in the distance or close by to help him find his way. He had walked toward the garrison on so many occasions; he had been dragged to the garrison on so many occasions; he had been humiliated and beaten at the garrison on so many occasions—all Anámn had to do was follow the scent of his memories, which would never be dulled by the rain. The rain washed away all of the other smells, sights, and possibilities of the slave's story.

Anámn neared the gate of the overseer and was stopped by Tannódin'é guards, who searched him for contraband and weapons.

"Look who's back, eh?" one guard said. "It's the bastard."

"Bastard!" the other exclaimed (for that is what the Tannódin'é called him). "Hey bastard. *Bastard?* You damn piece of kíma. I am talking to you!"

Not yet, he thought.

"Where did you get those clothes from, bastard?" the first guard asked and pulled on his jacket.

"He probably stole them from someone," the other one replied.

"Can I go now?" Anámn asked, fermenting in insolence.

The hard slap on the back came without warning. The second guard struck the son of Alzhexph so hard that it almost knocked his hat off. Anámn turned and scowled with such hateful nerve that the sentry took two steps back.

"Let him go," the other guard ordered. A pensive fear and respect filled his voice. "Héthyx will deal with him anyway."

Anámn passed through the gate and sauntered toward the large, stony, three-story garrison, attempting to sense the movements of those inside and on guard. His Elemental was giving him some difficulty, but Anámn was able to make out twenty kinetic signatures throughout the complex. It was mid-evening, and Héthyx's subordinates were completing their daily census tallies around the district, which left the amount of support at the garrison at its lowest. He knew where Héthyx was, in the main chamber, at his study, near the fireplace Anámn built with his own hands and the lash as motivation. Nearing the door to the room, the angst-ridden slave passed two more guards.

When he entered the enclosure, Héthyx was alone, sitting in a shiny, black leather chair, in comfort and luxury, and smoking a daggerweed pipe. The study-chamber was idyllic, removed, pristine, and noble. There was no medium to compare it to the shitty reality of Euhilv, and it was only one room, in one garrison. Oppression wrought a staggering gap. The quakes, which tore Qeauríyx apart in the past, had found a home in Euhilv.

The room was large and circular and littered with full bookcases, maps, and antiques. Héthyx prided himself on being a cultured man. He spent many an hour reading classic Tannódin'é and Damüdan literature and writing poetry when he was not focused on the mines.

A large, silver chandelier dangled in the middle of the room, which held sixty-seven light bulbs. At times, the room became so hot that the fireplace seemed excessive. And excess was all Anámn saw in Héthyx. Excess waste, a leftover from Qeauríyx's dark days. More electrical wattage flowed in Héthyx's chamber than in an entire subarea of the eastern district. A témo's stuffed head hung above the fireplace, and beneath it, on the mantle, rested the electric "Whip of Eons," timeless and never ceasing in scarring a slave.

The fireplace itself was made of granite and cometstone. Anámn built it in one cycle, and although his craftsmanship was unparalleled, the slave felt no accomplishment in his work. He owned nothing his hands produced. He was estranged from his own artistry, labor, and creativity. It was time to collect his stolen wages.

Héthyx swung the chair around and faced Anámn. His face was the picture of nonchalance. "Welcome back."

Anámn did not return the greeting. He was too busy plotting his revenge and escape route. He had given no thought about its execution; so confident he was in his strength.

"Are you here to report in, bastard?" the aristocrat asked. His Tannódin'é inflection sickened Anámn, and his dress was just as ghastly.

The overseer was in full casual Tannódin'é garb: brown slacks, a gray shirt with the Tannódin insignia. His arrogant fair freckled face, with nicely combed brown hair and cocky mustache displayed centuries of self-righteous superiority. "You have been gone for twenty-four days. That was pretty close. Since you do not know how to count, I was worried that you might confuse your absence."

"You think you're so much better than me…" Anámn muttered, tilted his wheatstraw hat up, indignantly shook the rain off his coat, and wetted the floor.

"Anámn." Héthyx shocked the slave. The overseer rarely called him by name. "Anámn, let us not do this tonight. Do not tempt me, swine."

"Tempt *you?*" Anámn scoffed. His almond skin reddened with madness. "You serious? You got no idea…"

Héthyx ignored his statement. "Where is Malchían?"

"I don't know. Why?"

"Just as long as he is gone… That is all that matters. And I asked you a question, bastard. 'I don't know' is insufficient." Héthyx's tone matched the son of ju Xaníz.

"*Bastard…* You're the bastard, Héthyx. I'm telling you; you don't know temptation. Call me 'bastard' again and I'll show you."

"Are you actually threatening me? The last time I saw you, I pulled your worthless body out of the pit. Would you like to return?" Héthyx asked with clenched teeth and started towards his whip.

Anámn's speed was swift, and before the overseer reached the whip, the bondsman was in front of him, grabbing his hand, squeezing it venomously, and causing Héthyx to stumble back into a bookcase and fall to his knees.

"Where is my father?" Anámn inquired with intimidation. "*Where?*"

In fear, the overseer lost control of his bladder. And in pain, Héthyx's whimper was nearly inaudible. "I don't know!"

"'I don't know' is an insufficient answer," the Sczyphamek smiled darkly.

Dispassionately, Anámn broke the overseer's right arm and shoulder. This time, Héthyx screamed in agony. The sound alerted the two guards, and Anámn sensed their movements. They were already at the chamber's door.

The Sczyphamek ran to the door, locked it, and moved an enormous caisson in front of it with ease. Héthyx was petrified by Anámn's strength. It took five able-bodied slaves to move the dresser into the room.

The guards did not have energy weapons. They would have to go to the armory to retrieve them, which would give Anámn at least five minutes of uninterrupted pain for pleasure.

"What are you?" Héthyx yelled.

"I asked you before; do you think you are that much better than me?" Anámn queried, turned around, and stared at his prey. "Don't lie to me."

The son of Nísephetsu walked ominously towards the man who was his father's intermediary. The man whose whip was responsible for the scars on his back. The man who placed on Anámn heavy burdens he could hardly carry. The man who starved him, mocked him, and spat on him. Anámn's boots were timpani of retribution, sounding the percussionist's intentions.

"Do you think that you are that much better than me?" he asked once more.

"Yes." Though his hurried breaths revealed his suffering, Héthyx had managed to calm himself. "Of course. I am a Tannódin'é, and you are just a Phmquedrian. That is the order of things."

"What gives you the right to tell others that you are better?" Anámn asked and smashed Héthyx's lower left leg with his fist.

The yelp was pure suffering. Tears welled in Héthyx's eyes.

"Yeah," Anámn answered the overseer's unspoken question. "I'm gonna kill you."

Outraged by the Phmquedrian's audacity, Héthyx spit in Anámn's face.

"If you are so much better than me," Anámn Matriester smiled eerily and wiped the saliva from his cheek, "then why am I a Sczyphamek and you aren't?"

"Kíma!" the overseer cursed. "You are lying."

"Where is my father?" Anámn reached for the whip that had cratered his back on so many occasions. "I don't have time to search for him after I kill you. Which house is he staying in tonight?" He asked this because his father had nine mansions in the city, and he stayed in a different one every night, in case of a rebellion.

Héthyx was quiet. *Anámn plans to kill my master and the bastard's own father.*

"How many times have you beaten me with this, Héthyx?" Anámn snickered while gazing into the whip's creases. "Too many to count."

He snapped the whip back and created a force so great that it decimated almost a fourth of the room, causing the bookcases to tumble, the antiques to break, and the fire to blaze.

"No…" Héthyx stammered aloud in disbelieving bigotry. "How could the Nameless One be so insane as to allow a bastard Phmmy to become a Sczyphamek?"

"Which house? Or I'll go into your wife, mistress, and kid's room next…" Anámn threatened. There was no mercy in his eyes. He was resolute. He would kill anyone that stood in is way.

Héthyx gulped and acquiesced. "He is in the mansion in the northern district. Please, leave my family alone…"

Sensing the guards had returned with energy weapons, Anámn smiled. "You're lucky the first person I want to kill is my father. But if you lied to me, I will come back."

At that, the drifting Sczyphamek struck Héthyx with the whip so hard, that it tore into and cauterized the overseer's thighs, severing his lower legs from the rest of his body. In shock, Héthyx fell unconscious.

Anámn opened a large window in the chamber, jumped out, and ran like a galloping windhorse towards the northern mansion.

His smirk betrayed him; he delighted in that act of vengeance.

***

It did not take Anámn long to reach his father's mansion. The guards had surely found Héthyx by now. Whether the overseer was conscious or not, Anámn's father had been alerted to his presence via radio communication. The neoteric Sczyphamek would have to fight his way to his father because Alzhexph always kept an armed contingent nearby.

As usual, Anámn's Elemental was not cooperating. He would have to achieve his goal with only a minimal use of his kinetic powers. That suited him just fine. Anámn wanted the satisfaction of knowing that his Elemental did not help him in any overt way. As long as he was able to detect the movements of his adversaries, he would have the advantage. Even without his Elemental powers, Anámn reasoned his speed and strength would be more than enough.

He neared the mansion's front gate and sensed two signatures to his left. Anámn gave the sentries no warning and knocked them unconscious with two punches. Sprinting towards the front door, which was quite large with great ironwork canvassing the wood, Anámn deciphered the positions of everyone in the house. Fifteen guards stood on alert. His father appeared to be in his main bedroom with someone. Anámn was surprised. He was sure his father would have gone to a safe room or fled. Five guards with energy weapons neared the front door. Anámn perceived their power cells cycling. Indeed, they were warned.

There was no time to sneak around.

The Sczyphamek kicked the door off the hinges and splintered it in two. The two large bits rammed into three of his father's bodyguards, nearly goring all three of them. The other two door guards were so taken aback, they became motionless. Before they had a moment to recover, Anámn was already in the air and landed a boorish kick to the face of one and gave the other no chance of rescue, as he threw her into a priceless painting of ju Xaníz's ancestral line.

Anámn felt the shots go off before he heard them, and he nimbly dodged the blasts from two guards upstairs. The avenger ran towards the banister of the steps and launched himself upwards, ready to deliver a punishing blow to one of the guards when a voice rang out.

"Stop this now!"

It was Alzhexph.

At the sound of his command, the remaining guards lowered their weapons. Anámn stared at his father with anger so severe, he could hardly contain himself. His father's expression, however, was indecipherable.

Ju Xaníz was middle-aged and tall, with short gray hair and a finely groomed mustache, a towering disposition, and veiled blue-gray eyes. His face was fair, yet tanned, and he wore immaculate rings on both of his index fingers. His frame was solidly muscular and the blue-collared shirt, which was unbuttoned, stretched, showing off his physique. His countenance appeared deceptively congenial, although Anámn noticed his pants were loosened.

"Cléth, get out of my room. My son is here."

Anámn almost gasped. For the first time in Anámn's life, Alzhexph addressed him as "son." While the young man stood in half-shock, a Phmquedrian slave woman emerged from ju Xaníz' quarters, half-naked and crying, which snapped Matriester back into reality.

The patriarchy, the domination, the exclusion, the imperialism, the sexual exploitation, the ethnocentrism, the chauvinism, the power... *it was too much to take...* The amount of power and oppression that flowed from this one man—who had become more than a man—was incalculable. Redemption and reconciliation were never viable options. Only annihilation. The knot was pulled close to his father's neck and Anámn was ready to hurl him off the gibbet.

His father pointed to his intermediaries. "Go outside and wait for my command. Tell everyone in the house to evacuate. I do not want us to be disturbed. I do not care what happens or what you hear, you are ordered to stay outside. Do you understand?"

The guards nodded in affirmation and took their leave, helping their injured comrades out of the mansion while the slave woman ran down the steps.

"Don't worry," Anámn called to her. "He'll be in Qalfocx by the end of the night."

His father cut his eyes at Anámn. "Indeed? We shall see, shan't we?" Motioning to his son, the father's grin was pure condescension. "Come to my room, Anámn, so that we can talk. I am sure there is a lot you want to ask me before you kill me."

His father entered the room and sat down comfortably, in a large, shiny burgundy chair. Anámn followed, eyeing him suspiciously. How did his father know that he wished to confront him before he killed him?

A cold sense of familiarity entered Anámn as he trailed Alzhexph into the master bedroom. The room was unforgivably spacious, with a bed so large that four adults could sleep in it without touching one another. There was also an oversized chest-of-drawers opposite the bed and an enormous mirror by a window, which was to the right of the bed. The floor was covered in luxurious fur. And although the room was dimly lit, its dimensions were not lost.

This is the room me and Nísyx used to play in when we were little, he thought.

"Finally, you are strong. At last, you are worthy to be called my son."

Anámn was flabbergasted. "*What?* Don't try to talk your way out of this."

"I am not, nor will I need to." His father was confident. "You may be strong, but you do not fully grasp the dynamics of power, my boy. You will not even touch me tonight."

Angrily, Anámn ambled towards his father in order to strike him down that instant.

His father shook his head and sighed, placing his right hand on his right cheek and his left arm across his abdomen. "How foolish. I incited you to kill me. You only approached me this moment because I told you that you would not touch me. Before this, you desired to talk to me, and then kill me.

"Predictable. You are still only responding to my authority. *Such a victim!* Are you *certain* you are strong? Maybe I was mistaken…"

Lightning struck and the rains beat against the windows of the master's bedroom. An awkward silence filled the room. The only audible sound was the rain falling in a quick meter.

"Do you know what I am?" Anámn asked. "I—"

"You are a Sczyphamek," his father interrupted wryly. "What of it? Do you think that matters?"

"Héthyx thinks it does." Anámn beamed. "You won't be using his services anymore."

The father chuckled, quite entertained by the son's statement. "Héthyx is a fool, like you. He is a replaceable pawn with little understanding. He hates Phmquedrians because I and others like me trained him to do so. He responds to manipulation and shallow emotion quite easily, like most people on Qeauríyx. Though he feigns enlightened aristocracy, Héthyx has learned nothing. He does not think about his actions or why he believes what he believes. True investigation in his mind is a waste of time. Reactionary ideals are easier to handle."

"If I gave him a gun and told him to shoot you in the name of peace, he would. If I withheld the firearm and told him to be nonviolent in the name of peace, he would. All I need to do is make him believe that he believes in the gun or nonviolence and that he came to this belief based on his own choice even though he really believes in my manipulation. He, like most, will not ask what I meant by 'peace' or if there were other means to achieve it. The argument, the fun, the desire, the manipulation happens as myanála. Violence or nonviolence.

"In time, Héthyx will create his own self-made justifications as to why he desires a gun or why he desires nonviolence. He will latch on to them. He will stake his identity on these justifications. Before long, he will believe in the justifications more than his own qanín.

"Inevitably, he will forget my power of suggestion. Discerning how peace actually happens is too uncomfortable for his kind. Asking if firearms or nonviolence can actually lead to peace takes too long. And because he worships brute power, he forgets that other powers exist besides violent or nonviolent brutality."

Shaking his head, the father frowned and his face was unequivocal. His eyes, mouth, and hair follicles emanated stoic conviction. "All of you are delusional. Feckless, banal, and hopeless. All of you remain capricious. That is why none of you are fit to govern yourselves. This is precisely why Global Initiative is needed so badly."

Anámn did not fully understand his father's diatribe, but a bedeviling feeling seized upon him. The Sczyphamek did not have the upper hand.

"So you are motivated by hate and revenge, and some blind sense of justice and retribution," ju Xaníz continued. "That is just a response as well. You are still under the authority of that which has scarred you, and even if you kill me, you will still do it because of *my actions*. Even your revenge is precipitated by what I have already done. I am responsible for your *satisfaction* if you kill me, because if it were not for me, you would not even feel justified in your vengeance." The father's laugh was short. "You actually believe that freedom is synonymous with vengeance. All that means is that your understanding of power is based upon a flawed desire to happen like me."

"You are trying to confuse me." Anámn felt somewhat shaken by his father's logic. "I am in control of my own actions right now."

"*Really?*" his father mused with much interest. "Senseless boy, you may have partial agency in this. But you also are here because of me. You were born a slave. You have settled into your victimhood. Your reaction towards me is based on that relationship, a relationship *I created*."

Anámn was quiet, remembering what Nísyx had told him about the Phmquedrians of Kamo.

"I could have killed you the moment you returned to town. Informants alerted me to your presence the second you reached your shack." Alzhexph gazed perceptively at his son. "That is correct, Anámn. I *let* you enter into Héthyx's garrison, knowing full well of your violent intentions. My first reaction was to have you slain, but things would not be as interesting as they are now. You are a bastard, yes, but you are still my blood. And mercy is as entertaining as vengeance."

Suddenly, his impassible countenance became furious. No. Not fury. Wrath. "However, it took a great deal for me to forgive you for striking Nísyx."

Anámn was stunned.

"Oh yes. She was here four days ago, pleading for her 'dear brother's' release. Are you that surprised, Anámn?"

Guilt-stricken, Anámn recalled his violent exchange with his sister once more. He could not believe that after he was so cruel to her, she still sacrificed her dignity and pleaded for his release. That only made his actions that night even more reprehensible than they already were. Anámn realized what he always knew, but forgot in the heat of the argument: Nísyx loved Anámn more than any person on Qeauríyx.

"She was quite persuasive, and I almost let you go." He stopped and pounded his right fist in his left palm. "*Almost*. But when I realized that she was injured both physically and emotionally, I knew you were responsible, despite her attempts to convince me otherwise. So, I waited for your return. You left quite a bruise on the left side of her face..."

Ju Xaníz stared at Anámn, clearly angered at his son's misdeed. However, the patriarch was in full control of his emotions. "Her countenance suggested that you would seek me out. She told me that my 'cruelty' towards you had driven you mad with reckless vengeance."

"I didn't mean to hit her..." Anámn's regret breached his makeshift dam. "It was your fault..."

"Perhaps," his father replied, clanging the rings on his index fingers together. "But at least I am strong enough to acknowledge my wrongdoings."

"Where is she?" Anámn asked.

"Why should I tell you?" his father retorted. "Do you wish to blemish her face once more?"

This was not the court of judgment Anámn had imagined.

"I hate you..." he muttered spitefully. Even now, Alzhexph was toying with him. Only his death could terminate this game of one-upmanship.

"Did you enjoy striking her?" he asked insidiously. "Did you enjoy your first taste of power?"

The paternal adjudicator had rendered his son—a slave—mute and empty.

His father stood up, walked towards him, and placed his hand on his son's shoulder. "Do not be hard on yourself, Anámn. How could you understand all of these things or acted otherwise? You are just as ignorant as most Phmquedrians—even the Tannódin'é are like you—and I did not teach you these things." He looked around the room in cold nostalgia. "But tonight, I saw it in you. I saw your face, and I realized that you were ready."

"What are you talking about?"

"I witnessed firsthand the pleasure you took in hurting my guards, and I am sure you reveled in pleasure as you bloodied Héthyx. Just like when you struck your own sister. Though immature, you began to understand the true dynamics of power. And believe me, son, power is the great equalizer.

"There is no difference between anyone in Qeauríyx except for their understanding and wielding of power, whether Tannódin'é or Phmquedrian. You wield it as brutes do, but you do not understand nor can you control it. And like most, you secretly worship it and desire to be entertained by it. So believe me when I say, I can help you, Anámn..."

Anámn drew back, although a portion of him was greatly intrigued by his father's offer.

"I don't want to have anything to do with you!" he yelled.

"This is the room where it happened, you know," Alzhexph said impersonally. "This is where I raped your mother for the first time. This is where she conceived you in order that you might become a Sczyphamek. Right here. On that bed. In front of that mirror. I beat and had your mother all night; and she cried Anámn. She pleaded for me to stop, but I could not. A chénala, perhaps?

"She should have been happy of the honor, and you should be thanking me for impregnating that cléth whore, for I am responsible for the power you enjoy right now."

Anámn's eyes flashed, his sickly green aura emerged, and he grabbed his father by the throat and held him against the large mirror.

"*Yes*," his father choked and gasped. "*That is the face...*"

Anámn was ready to exact his revenge, but somehow he was thrown back and remembered the vision he had while wrestling with Qeauríyx, the image of his mother crying. Pulled out of time and space, he was engulfed in the moment, and the scene drew back, depicting a wider angle. His father was raping his mother, pulling her hair, and cursing her condescendingly. The bed was violently moving due to the force of his sadistic penetration, and his mother clasped the sheets, with clenched teeth and tears streaming down her bruised face. He could see the other slaves in the house weeping for her.

And then Anámn saw it. Anámn saw his father's face, and while glancing in the mirror at his own reflection, he realized that they *were* one in the same. The twisted, gruff smirk and power-drunk expression: Anámn *was* Alzhexph's son. The slave desired to be the slave master.

"I..." Anámn sobbed, unsure of how he tapped into Qeauríyx's historical memory and consciousness. Releasing his father from his grip, he stammered, "It can't be. I... Mamí... I'm so sorry..."

Marred with grief, the Sczyphamek found himself unable to shake the scene. His Elemental was so moved by his pain that it emerged and covered him, blossoming and causing his father to draw back.

"Leave, Anámn," it whispered. "This is not the path for you, for either of us."

Weeping bitterly and incapable of facing his father, Anámn opened the window and jumped out, running with all his might southwest, stricken and ashamed.

"You cannot run away from me forever!" his father yelled through coughs. "I will await your eventual return. And if you do not come back on your own, I have the means and connections to find you!"

***

The jungle became denser and the rains subsided. But a stream of tears marked his path. Anámn had never been so far southwest, but he journeyed on, praying his steps would undo the past. He had been running nonstop for five straight days. He should have been amazed at the feat, but displays of power only caused regretful memory.

"Where are you going, Anámn?"

Anámn saw nothing, but someone was out there. Concentrating, he used his Elemental to locate the source of the speech.

"Malchían." The young man's eyes were still red from crying. "I should have listened to you. I should've..."

Although he thought he had no more tears to shed, the remembrance of Malchían's proclamation of his "obstacle" and his advice to visit Nísyx caused the defeated Anámn to brace himself against a tree and hang his head. He had no one to blame... except...

Malchían emerged from the trees wearing his yellow cloak. The robe was completely dry, although the bottom was blemished by dirt. Anámn was not sure, but he believed that this was the first occasion he ever witnessed Malchían's cloak soiled. The medicine man's countenance was somberly sober. The glisten in his eyes had darkened, and his steps were heavier. He was wounded somehow.

"I greatly wished that you would have chosen a different path," he stated. "Now the road is more arduous than you can imagine."

Anámn had no words.

"You learned a lesson that could have been learned in other ways, but it does not matter. It cannot..." His low tone was fraught with uncertainty. "What matters is that you find your own path."

"How'd you know I was gonna try to kill my father, and why didn't you stop me?" Anámn pressed the man for an answer. "You had the power to tell me, but you didn't. You're connected to the Nameless One, right? Why did Global Initiative happen in the first place?"

"You know this is wrong. I may be wrong too, but I'm beginning to understand that this isn't just about me. So why don't you help? Why don't you show people like my father and me what real 'power' is?"

Malchían's eyes were caring. "You are starting to question. Good..."

"You didn't answer me," Anámn pressed.

"If there was no answer, could you live with that?" Malchían retorted.

Sczyphamek Kinesis paused and pondered the matter. He could not answer the old one's interrogative.

"A journey lies ahead for you," the white-haired Phmquedrian said. "And I do not know where it will take you, but I can tell you this: you must meditate and chant Kinesis. You must understand Qeauríyx and your Elemental. The ancients are calling you. Their resistance lies in you. Their hope lies in you. You are not alone. But this journey will answer some questions, only for new ones to arise."

"I don't think I can do this." The slave sat on the ground in weariness and doubt... "I don't even know where to begin. Everything I think and everything I know—it's all been given to me by people who want to control me. Why should I even trust you?"

"Heh..." the old man smiled in his own kind of fatigue. "Why should you indeed! You are free to do as you please just as It. While you have been victimized, that isn't the only way you've happened. So, you do not have to trust me, but you should eat something. It looks like you haven't eaten in five days."

"I do need *something*. It's not just food. I need something, *one thing*, to hold on to..." the slave responded. "How will I know that I'm doing what I should do? How'll I know that I won't be like my father if I don't have a real, *real* sign that I'm on the 'right' path?"

Malchían smiled solemnly at Anámn, with a sympathy and love so unambiguous, that Anámn was shaken to his very qanín. Malchían walked to the young man and lifted him up by the arm. The elder placed his old, soft left hand on Anámn's trembling head, then his quavering heart, and finally on his taught shoulder. "Why do we search for '*the reason*' instead of '*reasons*'? Can we truly not handle these *happenings*? Are they really too much to bear?" His words were more like laments than questions. "Can the many weaken the one and the one weaken the many, even though they still exist together, and we have yet to perish...?"

"You..." the Sczyphamek replied with some understanding. "You're talking about the myanála..."

"*The* myanála?" Malchían corrected in a deep, reflective voice. "*Myanálas*, Anámn. *They are infinite, no matter how false the overwhelming majority of them are.*"

His reply was staggering. Anámn stood in shock and tears. The man with the soiled yellow cloak turned around and walked out of Anámn's view and back into the woods.

"Malchían..." Anámn droned. "Wait..."

Chapter Fifteen: The Dying Birth

Anámn made his way to Minusía quickly; time was fleeting and his Elemental seemed on edge. However, he was not about to turn away, for the element had been trying to guide him since the beginning of his quest. Gaining its trust now would prove difficult. Though possessing no thought of his final destination, Anámn still recognized how far he strayed, and out of deep contrition, he repented. Matriester was left with no choice. Trusting his Elemental was his only option.

Malchían told him to meditate and reflect on his actions of the past three weeks. Repentant, Anámn followed his instructions and more. He realized the recklessness of his decisions. Above all things, he had brought unwarranted attention to himself, in addition to alienating Nísyx. Concerning the former, his father was sure to alert Tannódin that a waking, vengeful Sczyphamek was roaming the Phmquedrian countryside.

He was exposed and unprepared. Easy pickings for imperial agents. Someone would surely come searching for him, perhaps Vicious or Pre-Eminent themselves. The thought of the Zananín in dogged pursuit almost loosened Anámn's bowels and bladder. His only advantage was the fact that Sczyphameks' could not sense those who had not Awakened. This was little assurance, for Anámn was certain his likeness was circulated to imperial agents around the continent.

He could not return to Kamo to attempt reconciliation with Nísyx, now. She was probably under constant Tannódin'é surveillance.

His father's last words continued to chill his thoughts. He was *expecting* Anámn's return; did this mean Alzhexph did not consider Anámn an escapee? Would he not invoke the runaway provision? It appeared the manner of Anámn's return did not concern his father. Although the son was cycles away from desiring another homecoming, he realized, just as his father, that at some point, he would have to return to Euhilv. For now, his father had won the first battle.

Convincingly.

Matriester doubted Euhilv would go under the murder law, however. It was not to his father's benefit to institute the law. Alzhexph ju Xaníz held the advantage, and the slave master was too smart to make a rash decision that would alter his position. More than this, Anámn had placed a mark on his own head. It was only a matter of time before he encountered a Sczyphamek or agents of Global Initiative. The truth was that he was no longer a runaway; he was an imperial fugitive.

After his encounter with Malchían, the runaway traveled west-southwest for four more days, entering into a strange valley. Once inside its rocky walls, Anámn spent the next two weeks traveling northwest in the barren place, understanding that his Elemental had led him to the Valley of the Ancestors, which lay between the Sternpain and Noble Mountains. When he was not traveling or sleeping, he prayed and meditated, twice a day.

He desperately desired to rid himself of his obsession with strength, viscerally reacting to the vision of ju Xaníz raping his mother. He was scandalized by the resemblance of his face with his father's during the violation. To that end, he did not try to evoke physical displays of his power while he chanted. He only wished for direction from his Elemental. After a few days his Elemental began to respond to his qanín. While repeating "Fá'atoño má," Anámn earnestly tried to grasp the meaning of the words, and his Elemental granted him an audience, revealing to him his next course of action. He was given an intimation to travel to Minusía in northern Phmquedria, a journey of about thirty-seven hundred lengths, with no accompanying explanation. His Elemental was testing him and rightfully so.

The Valley of the Ancestors had only two trails, on the eastern and western shores, and they were vitriolic and cumbersome. The middle of the valley was eroded and littered with sharp, wet rocks, lashed constantly by the Spine River, a rancorous, wide rapid of a waterway that flowed southward from the northwesternmost peaks of the Sternpain and Noble Mountains. There were four peaks over fifteen thousand feet, and streams collected on various slopes of the mountains to form the source of the waterway. It raged down the Valley of the Ancestors swiftly, creating a giant gorge at the city of Corsound, on the southern shore of Phmquedria. At over twenty-five hundred lengths, the Spine River was the second longest river in all of Qeauríyx, and the amount of water it released was incomparable, except for the glacier source of the Silent/Tur River system in Keotagosdi.

Downstream, the river boasted a most virulent current, along with natural widths as great as eighty lengths and depths as much as four thousand feet. If it were not for the meeting of the mountain ranges near Portal, the southwestern portion of Phmquedria would have been a large island. No boats dared travel the river, and few people traversed the path. Even Tannódin left this craggy and watery artery to the wildlife and greenery that was able to survive in such a hostile environment. Rain constantly fell due to the large volume of water and the prison-like mountain ranges, which prevented the rainclouds from moving. When it was not raining, the climate became unbearably hot in the daytime and cold at night.

During his time in the Valley, Anámn meditated and was drawn into the qanín of the planet once more. This time, however, he chose not to battle the planet; instead he followed his Elemental, which drew him into the history of the Valley of the Ancestors. Astonished at such a clear vision, Anámn realized his abilities were not only physical. Indeed, he was able to grasp and understand phenomena in ways previously unimaginable.

The valley was created during the Great Extinguishing of the First Sczyphamek. When the Sczyphamek used her powers to terminate the Great Drift, the planet's tectonic plates fought against her with all their might. The engagement was undeniably destructive, causing massive earthquakes and a chaos never before witnessed on Qeauríyx.

Anámn never thought about it, but the loss of life on the planet during the Extinguishing must have been enormous. The First must have possessed the foresight to perceive this, but chose to continue anyway. At the time of the Extinguishing, the Valley of the Ancestors was not actually a valley, but a fertile plain, one of the first and few places on Qeauríyx suitable for sustained living. The First's actions created the Sternpain and Noble Mountains, as tectonic plates pushed and pulled against one another.

Anámn was used to the torrential downpours of the Kamo region. But the rain he now experienced was stubbornly asinine. He made good time despite this, and although the trail was burdensome, it had not presented him with a difficult challenge. The road was ancient, made in a time long forgotten. Whoever conceived its course, however, was a genius. The passage was nearly a length above the river, at an altitude of about seven thousand feet, on the edge of the mountains. In fact, the area Anámn now trod was an expanse canyon, aptly called the Deep Chasm. There, the Spine River showed its strength most forcefully, carving an elaborate gorge with peaks as high as twelve thousand feet.

The ravine was desolate, and if Anámn had not hunted and gathered food before he entered, he would have surely starved to death. Looking above, he spied the snowcapped tops of two mountains to his north, which had been losing their white color during his journey. Looking below, he gazed into the river and was drawn into its hypnotizing current.

But as the days passed, he grew more alarmed; the once small streams flowing from the peaks were becoming more vigorous. The caps were melting at an alarming pace. Summer was only a few weeks away. At his next chance, the Sczyphamek would have to leave the area. If he stayed, he would be placing his life in jeopardy. His powers were still too unrefined to endure such inclement conditions. In the far distance, there was an opening near the two mountains.

On the canyon's slick slopes, Anámn made his way along the winding, muddy path. A nearby tributary swelled, and its current grew more aggressive. Water splashed onto his boots, and he grew anxious, afraid the entire trail would be swept away. He jumped towards a large rock some twenty feet above; however, the boulder was loose and dislodged from its position. Anámn tried to regroup by hanging onto a ledge, but what was once solid dirt turned into mud. The slave's grip was rendered ineffective, and slid down the side of the canyon. In panic, Sczyphamek Kinesis attempted to levitate and find his way back to the path, but his concentration failed. He managed to locate a moderate indentation in the rock, which acted as a small cave.

His breathing was volatile, so panicked he was. His Elemental, on the other hand, was in a complete calm. Anámn tried to allow it to permeate and bind him, but the sight and sound of the water was too distracting. He heard the element speaking softly to him, cajoling him to be at ease. He listened intently, receiving guidance. Without words, the element of kinetic energy intimated to him, admonishing him for spurning the ambient energy around him.

"Rejecting it is rejecting me," it expressed.

"But it's water, not energy," Anámn replied, translating the Elemental's nonverbal communication. "Isn't my power related to energy?"

"Is it?"

Was it? No. Yes. Anámn both outwardly and inwardly searched for the reason of his element's stillness. While gazing into his qanín, he encountered the Elemental, wrapped in a dark green covering; it was his aura. The color was luminous and thick. Pulsating in a steady tempo, his Elemental appeared amorphous, changing into different shapes with every pulse. With his entire qanín, Anámn outstretched himself to the element. It was so flexible, yet formidable. Within his body, mind, heart, and spirit— no, these descriptions of entities in relation were inadequate—within his qanín, he felt energy all around him. He was unafraid. His aura emerged, within the small alcove, shining brightly and giving the rain a green tint. His eyes turned from their original light brown to a golden crimson.

"Do you see it? Do you feel it?" he and the Elemental asked together, in one voice.

"I feel it," Anámn responded.

"I am in the water," the element expressed.

"*We are the water*," they spoke together. "*We are yet. We are not yet. We are energy.*"

The experience was intense, and Matriester lost his focus. His aura grew even larger, causing the mountain to crack and the rain to turn into steam. There was so much energy, active and potential, around him, within the clouds, water, rocks, air, and himself...

It was everywhere.

He felt so insignificant and ashamed. There happened a reality so much greater than he, and yet he had been consumed by what now seemed to be miniscule in relation. His personal torment was not to be pushed aside; however, he felt the groaning of Qeauríyx, and he realized his pain was added to its infinite wail. But its hope was so incredible. It was like being wrapped in a blanket of warmth; it had great potential, like Anámn, yet something lingered. He felt energy from the raindrops, the latent energy in the rainclouds, the potential energy from a loose boulder three hundred feet above; all this caused his aura to blossom into a beautiful dark green color. Between his fingertips, Anámn perceived what was invisible to the naked eye, waves of energy collecting in his qanín and into his body.

He apprehended the presence of the *something*. He was sure of it, but he did not deify this feeling. He would not allow it. However, he could no longer speak, only murmur and shake. Anámn had been hiding behind his anger for so long. His true pain surfaced; it was of a robbed childhood, a great indignation against the Nameless One, one he had felt since his youth. He projected much of his anger onto his father, but truthfully, he was angry with It.

It might not even exist, but *It* created all of this. *Its* cause was first, and *It* was responsible for his lot. But his mother prayed to *It* constantly, sang songs in *Its* honor, recited broken fragments alluding to *Its* love. Anámn saw no love, no faithfulness to his people. Should he be thankful that Phmquedrians were still alive and not killed by slavery? Should he be elated that his life seemed infinitely meaningless in the cycles of this Cycle? The One with No Name was a powerful, *aloof* deity, purposefully toying with those created in capricious frivolity.

And yet…

And yet, some *Happening* was drawing near Anámn, filling him with power of a different kind.

His weariness emboldened him to yell to the Firmament. "I don't want this! I didn't ask for this! What? Why do you always do this to me? To us…? Did you create me for fun?"

Uttering curses and muttering spitefully, the runaway shook his head. "How long are you gonna sit around and do nothing? How long? Damn it! Tell me!" Anámn bent over and shoved his tears of agnostic anguish away from his pupils. Something was happening inside, around, and through his body. His abdominal cavity felt pricked by sensations language could not describe. "Don't touch me… Please…Don't touch me… Don't embrace me… It's not enough…"

His breaths grew short once more. He tried to calm himself by chanting, but he did not know why he was repeating the phrase.

"Fá'atoño má. Fá'atoño má. Fá'atoño má. Fá'atoño má. Fá'atoño má. Fá'atoño má. Fá'atoño má. Fá'atoño má. Fá'atoño má." Every chant brought him closer to crying, but also closer to understanding himself and his element.

"I don't know if I'm ready," he told his Elemental. He cried till his body shook, and his aura retreated. "I know this is why you brought me here. I won't... I can't leave this place if I don't get this right. But, I've gotten so many things wrong... I'm sorry..."

"Why are you making it rain so terribly, Kinesis?" his Elemental asked.

The aforementioned question surprised Anámn more than the fact that the Elemental spoke to him.

"What do you mean? I'm making it rain..."

Silence. The element had spoken. There was no point in trying to make it converse with him once more.

I'm causing the rain, he thought.

His thoughts turned back to his time in Euhilv. The rain was so hard. It was bizarre. However, the precipitation in the valley was even stranger. Although he did not understand the scientific dynamics of meteorology, Anámn was certain that kinetic energy had something to do with it. After he left his shack, before he arrived at Héthyx's garrison, when his anger was foulest, the rains were falling the heaviest. Somehow, he unconsciously connected himself to the weather. Even while he was in his father's bedroom, the lightning and thunder crashed almost too perfectly. It was as if a (meta)physical script was placed in the exchange.

However, Anámn now realized that during the pauses of their conversation, when he was the most unstable—secretly desiring speech and repentance from his father—it was then the lightning and thunder struck, somehow voicing his own displeasure. Reckless indeed, Anámn had placed considerable people at risk.

His Elemental did not retreat out of displeasure with Anámn alone; it was also trying to protect the planet, animals, and Anámn from himself. The potential of the kinetic Elemental was amaranthine; however, it was fraught with complications. Out of all the many Elementals given to Sczyphameks, Kinesis realized that his was one of the most challenging. Energy was everywhere and in large supply. If he could not control himself, he would never Awaken, or worse, kill himself, through his inability to control or contain energy. His power did not have a switch to regulate or even turn off its effects. There was a long road ahead before he would be able to ascend to the next horizon.

"I've gotta learn how to read and study," he stated quietly.

The exercise of literacy would teach him patience and would open up new ways of thinking he did not yet comprehend. Perhaps this is what Nísyx Tekil tried to induce within Anámn. He was still unsure about his faith and about the One with No Name, but he would not deny that he just experienced the presence of something greater than himself and Qeauríyx. Even he could no longer debate that truism; however, Anámn would not equate the experience as an encounter with the Holy.

Anámn thought of the rain again. Clouds were made of water. Malchían used to tell him that once the clouds were filled with too much water, the water would fall back to the ground.

"It didn't rain when I was with Nísyx," he said, recalling his sojourn in Kamo. "I was calmer, happier."

Since the time he realized he was a sleeping Sczyphamek, he had been unconsciously interrupting the normal weather pattern of Phmquedria. He simply did not grasp the science behind it. However, since the weather was such a large energy well, especially during the springtime durations, it was only natural Anámn displayed his powers in such a hackneyed, unintentional way. In some respects, it was a testimony to how fragile he truly was, for weather was a quite visible and common phenomenon. Even without understanding the dynamics of meteorology, one could understand at a basic level that incredible power and energy is at work during a thunderstorm. And when Anámn was content and taking in every moment with Nísyx, he was draining the local atmosphere of its potential energy, storing it within himself. He must have released the energy in a controlled, seething way. *No*, he did not release it. His Elemental did. And it did so in a way to draw attention away from Anámn. If Anámn went around Phmquedria obliterating trees and homes due to flashes of energy, he would have been quite noticeable. The Elemental released the potential energy back to its original place, but there was so much contained within Kinesis that any haphazard discharge would still be catastrophic.

A lingering question entered into the runaway slave: what would happen if he took too much potential energy from any given phenomena?

"I... I am weak," he stated, matter-of-factly. "*I am weak.*"

His father was correct in at least one thing; power was not measured in brute strength alone. This adage was now reality for Anámn Klyphaju'an Matriester. Restraint was a sign of strength, a true sign of strength. Those who were weak had nothing to restrain. By disregarding forbearance as strength, the brash Sczyphamek had truly shown his glaring folly. What was potential energy at all, but restraint, action that was not yet? Every decision he made heretofore alienated him from his true power, whether he was a Sczyphamek or not.

The rains had subsided since his inward journey began. He viewed the starry sky through the clouds. The two moons of Qeauríyx, Mashé[1] and Parce,[2] illuminated the Firmament. They were beautiful. And as Anámn gazed upon them, he took a breath and embraced his Elemental with his entire qanín.

"What's your name?" he asked the kinetic element.

"You know my name," it intimated. "You spoke it in the jungles of Kamo."

"*Téza*," he said with complete confidence. "Thank you for your patience."

---

[1] Mashé (muh-sh*ey*)
[2] Parce (pahrss)

He expected no response.

"Fá'atoño má," he chanted softly, with a melancholy smile. "É müz keh fïp Téza má."

For the first time, due to his own conscious volition, his aura displayed itself.

"I'll embrace you with everything I got; please, do the same."

He stepped towards the ledge of the cave, walked out on the air, and levitated. He had not yet mastered flying but he somewhat discerned the belief and practice necessary to use the ability. Ascending to the path above, Anámn settled down with little fanfare. He raced towards the two peaks in the distance. Their summits were made visible by the ample moonlight. His speed was incredible, and he dodged most of the treacherous spots on the path by focusing on the trail's potential to collapse and give way. Within five hours he cleared the Valley of the Ancestors and made his way due north, towards the Lumber District of Phmquedria.

He had no idea of his route or means to Mínusía; however, he was certain he would make it there. He needed to keep a low profile on his journey, but he needed to move expeditiously. Téza seemed on edge, and, for the first time, afraid of the future.

***

He could not speak. Lo'Marc was too nervous.

The scythe rested in his quarters, but his countenance was not so docile. P'tan's blue-green eyes betrayed incertitude. Pacing outside Vincallous' encampment made it no better. But, he could not enter just yet. His mentor had just returned two days prior and not spoken to anyone. Lo'Marc only obtained one piece of credible information concerning Vincallous' sojourn into the Crossroads: Vicious encountered two témos and suffered injury. Nonetheless, the emperor did not wish to take any more time for recuperation. The excellent and meticulous war commander he was, Vincallous wanted to review the now two-duration-old battle report from Lozé with Lo'Marc.

Running his right hand through his short, dark blonde hair, Lo'Marc sighed. Although he had virtually destroyed Lozé, a few insurgents managed to escape. His arm had healed nicely, aided by White Scythe's mystical powers, but he was disturbed that a Nez Spiritan was able to harm him in combat. Then again, it was *her*…

Lo'Marc did not know how Vincallous would react when he received the final report. In fact, he had been pacing near the tent for the past twenty minutes, so much so that dust had collected on the bottom of his gray war fatigues and boots. Vicious stressed absolute perfection in military command. Yea, many generals and officers had cracked underneath the pressure. Only Violent Fist, Feolenz, and he, the General Maximum, were able to handle it. Reproach by Vicious was hard on any commander, for he was quite an intimidating man. His very appearance caused even the most hardened veteran to become tense. Fierce's gray Damüdan eyes seared and disheveled a nel'asmív's spirit, burning and disintegrating a woman's metaphysical innards until her outward appearance was reduced to mere groveling.

Lo'Marc gathered his composure. He remembered his matriculation through the ranks of Blue Rapier and White Scythe and the five cycles he spent preparing himself to become General Maximum. Those cycles crippled and destroyed even the best and the brightest of Tannódin and Damüda, yet somehow he was chosen by the blade. For five cycles, he trained in the highest levels of Tannódin'é Néwan. However, even before then, Vicious had groomed his prized pupil for the position. When Marc entered into the Skill of the Scythe military school, Vincallous prophesied his protégé would become the General Maximum. Vicious' confidence in him was one of the few things that remained fresh during the torturous preparation—that and Kazen'lo.

Kazen'lo was Lo'Marc's ardent rival. Verily, their names were given the title "lo," which meant "last" or "ultimate" in the Ancient Tongue, symbolizing their achievement as the final two candidates for the leadership of White Scythe. Neither Kazen nor Marc was expected to be finalists when the competition began, but after the third cycle, it was clear that they were unsurpassed in intelligence, strategy, strength and technique.

Every candidate entering into the running for General Maximum knew the rule: if one were not chosen, the blade would smite that individual to add to its power. Each cycle the trials evolved, becoming ever more brutal and rigorous. The candidates were tested in six assessments: survival skills, mental puzzles, war simulation/strategy, hand to hand combat, weapon to weapon combat, and torture. Torture was a necessary component to the examination process, for it was the only way to ensure that a soldier would be able to handle the blade's bloodlust. There would not be another General Maximum Fifty-Six, who, after gripping the blade, killed her entire family, cabinet, and surrounding village, before finally taking her own life. Indeed, the blade required mental acumen and emotional strength, not just the will to fight.

The competition took place on Zorét Major and Minor, the inhospitable ice and desert islands, and home of Skill of the Scythe. Although the islands were proximate to one another, their climates were anything but. Between them lay the auspicious Edaw Peak, at 55,249 feet, the highest mountain on the planet. At the pinnacle of Edaw's precipice, the First Sczyphamek extinguished herself and stopped the Great Drift, although this was not altogether true.

Even though most of Qeauríyx stopped drifting cataclysmically, Zorét Major and Minor did not; instead, they circled counterclockwise around Edaw Peak. The Extinguishing was so powerful that it caused the continent of Zorét to break apart into two major islands with smaller isles lying between them. Tannódin suffered the same fate as well, and a mountainous volcanic line emerged from the deep producing the Memory Ridge, which ran from the North Pole through Edaw and down to the South Pole.

On Zorét, the two main islands became subject to extreme weather patterns, due to the enormous energies released into the atmosphere by the First. The smaller island, Minor, was covered in a blizzard that lasted eight cycles, and the larger one saw no rain for ten. The islands continued to circle around Edaw, and in time settled into their own climates, both intemperate and hostile. It was a perfect retreat for White Scythe after their defeat in Damüda by the Kylanín, for no mortal dared step foot on those islands. The shattered continent also made an ideal location for the selection process. Only the small isles near the main islands provided noticeable relief from Zorét's harsh conditions.

Cometstone Island—named after the rare mineral found only on Zorét and the isle closest to the desert island—was home to the Great Hall. Within the Great Hall lay the Haven, White Scythe's resting place between wielders. Cometstone was sixty-eight square lengths in area, and Edaw Peak was always visible, even from great distances. Depending on the season, Lo'Marc would gaze in a different direction towards the immovable snow-capped dome to gain strength. The islands made two revolutions per cycle; therefore, small earthquakes were common on Zorét. Yet because the path of orbit occurred for such an extended period of time, the continental movement was almost unnoticeable by feel, only in change of perspective.

Indeed, perspectives would change as one endured the hurdles to become General Maximum. The actual selection only happened twice or thrice an average lifetime, and since the selection process commenced after the death of a General Maximum, the blade remained unused for five cycles. In the absence of a General Maximum, the highest ranking Secondary assumed temporary command of White Scythe. The Skill of the Scythe Military Academy never closed its doors, due to Global Initiative mandate.

Every eldest child from Damüda, Tannódin, and most recently Bryce was subject to universal conscription for at least five cycles of duty, not including basic training. All draftees were sent to Blue Rapier's proving grounds, which were held on Tannódin at the ruins of Phenplyacin or in Corsound, Phmquedria. If a family had more than three children, another child was able to enter into the military. The Tannódin'é and Damüdan alliance was strict in its views about family. A family would not become extinct through the battlefield. The spoils of war should be enjoyed by and given to all who *deserved* them.

Lo'Marc, the youngest of five children, volunteered his service for Tannódin, despite great protest from his clan. Despite his family's social standing as farmers, his parents kept themselves informed about the happenings in Qeauríyx. Lo'Marc's father vehemently opposed GI, though he said nothing to anyone outside his family for fear of repercussions. After losing a daughter to the draft and to shrapnel, Marc's father tried to persuade his son to reconsider. The youngest P'tan would not heed his father's pleas.

On the eve of summer, in his seventeenth cycle, Marc left his home near the southeast coast of Loama Setrin. He found himself under Blue Rapier command within a week. Although simple and agrarian in appearance, internally, Marc's timid tenacity was undeniable. So was his lust for command. On the ruins of Phenplyacin, during a training exercise overseen by Vincallous Fierce himself, the potentate noticed P'tan. Although there was nothing outwardly observable, Fierce realized his potential through Marc's interaction with his comrades, and petitioned that he be sent to the Zorét as a member of White Scythe.

No one entered the ranks of White Scythe without the petition of a commanding officer. The military structure of Tannódin was quite sophisticated, yet streamlined. There were three branches of the military, Blue Rapier, White Scythe, and the Eradicate. Each wing was headed by the greatest warriors Global Initiative could offer: Commandant A'reznu Feolenz, the General Maximum, and Violent Fist. They were hailed as the Daknín.[3]

Each of the Daknín held a mystical weapon: a rapier, scythe, and chain; however, the title "Daknín" did not start with the current wielders of the weapons. The name was derived from the Ancient Tongue, signifying a group of three, and the term had been in circulation since the genesis of Global Initiative. Although the members of the Daknín were seen as equals, it was generally agreed that White Scythe was the most powerful weapon on the planet (though ancient rumors loomed of a mystery brand that could hold its own against the deathblade).

Despite its power, the actual military branch of White Scythe was not the highest in stature. The Eradicate, Pre-Eminent's recalibrated imperial guard, reserved that honor. Only three hundred and fifty enjoyed the privilege of serving under Violent Fist, the wielder of the Violet Manacle. The Eradicate was comprised of veterans who were the paragon of both Blue Rapier and White Scythe. Some of these soldiers were simply great fighters and others were extremely intelligent, but a spectacular few were both. There were also a small number who were personally added by Violent Fist and the Zananín. Besides protecting the House of Kaz, the Eradicate's other objective involved covert operations around Qeauríyx. However, every soldier's roots were in Blue Rapier, which made it no less significant in the promulgation of Global Initiative.

After a cycle of basic training and four additional cycles in Blue Rapier,

---

[3] Daknín (dahk-neen)

the soldiers who were nominated to enter White Scythe and the Eradicate would leave the watchful eye of Feolenz. At this point, preparation under each Daknín took its unique turn. Blue Rapier soldiers had their special training, while those at the Skill of the Scythe learned their own. Only a member of White Scythe who had completed the two-cycle basic training was eligible for General Maximum.

When Marc received word the eighty-third General Maximum had finally been taken by the blade, he was in outskirts of southern Bryce on assignment. Marc P'tan was no coward, but he did not know if he was capable of harnessing the power of the mystical weapon. However, those under his command and Vincallous persuaded him to enter into the competition.

When Marc arrived on Cometstone Island, he was amazed by the number of entrants. In fact, it was the highest number of competitors in centuries. There were one hundred and twenty-seven candidates, and all were seasoned White Scythe veterans. All were aware of the consequences. There was less than a one percent chance that any of them would become General Maximum, and there was a greater than ninety-nine percent chance that they would be killed by the blade sooner than later. However, this fact did not hinder the men and women of White Scythe. They believed in its cause, its historical weight in the happenings of Tannódin and Damüda, and its role in Global Initiative.

Each cycle, the class grew smaller and more competitive, until the final cycle, whereby the "lo" candidates were chosen. And for that one cycle, the final two endured some of the most extreme challenges, while creating a bond of suffering that would draw them fornent. Indeed, as cycles went by Kazen and Marc became best of friends and bitter adversaries, yet never losing respect for one another's prowess. However, in the recesses of both their minds, the Ascension meant one of their deaths.

The Ascension was *the* rite of passage for the General Maximum; it was his or her last step in wielding the blade and required the death of the final candidate rejected by White Scythe at the hands of the newly chosen General Maximum. This was the "lo" test, for even the most heated competitors came to value each other due to the intensity of the selection process. The blade had no predetermined favorites; only one person was worthy of its power.

Kazen'lo was from Civix Setrin and a poet at heart. He spoke in meter and metaphor, with the proud inflection of a true Tannódin'é, but there were times when his words were as melancholy and gentle as a springtime breeze. Lo'Marc, on the other hand, was not so eloquent; many attributed this to his geographical lineage, for Loama Setrin was viewed as the simple and country half of Tannódin. Yet, in reality Lo'Marc simply had no use for verbiage. That did not mean he did not appreciate a good recital.

During the final cycle of their murderous training, Kazen'lo frequently recited various poems or epic tales after a grueling session, although he would always return to his favorite:

"Night, yea the night has darkened their eyes
And the morning's light is pale luminescence,
The twilight yields the moment of clarity
Opaque in the time of tribulation
Unspeakable agony, wretched delight
Fraught with anticipation of a new arrival
This blade of power shall usher a new horizon…"

The poem was part of the epic speech of the Thirty-Fourth General Maximum, the great warrior who conquered Tannódin after the Bitter War. Kazen'lo, during his waking moments of sleep deprivation, would recite that verse and others with weakened vigor. Lo'Marc utilized his own weapons of sedation and renewal to bear the pain. However, Kazen'lo's poetic utterance was remarkable, and even in the midst of hardship, his meter was impeccable. Lo'Marc never admitted it, but Kazen's speech kept him from quitting some days, just as his own actions kept the native of Civix Setrin from losing his sanity as well. Indeed, the training fostered this heartfelt appreciation purposively, making the last selection even more wrenching.

By the time the Rite of Ascension arrived, Lo'Marc and Kazen'lo had not seen one another in a fortnight. After those sixteen days, the finalists were led into the Great Chamber of the White Hall, escorted by the Curators of the Scythe. Lo'Marc could still see the sight as clear as Vincallous' tent in front of him. The Secondaries of White Scythe, Blue Rapier, the Eradicate, and Sczyphameks Pre-Eminent and Vicious—they were all there that night, encircling him and Kazen. They chanted the hallowed song of Damüdan and Tannódin'é origin, "Comet's Blossoming," which chronicled the story of White Scythe's mythical origins.

Seven cycles had not dulled Lo'Marc's memory, and the General Maximum's heart raced and swelled with emotion.

After the song's completion, Lo'Marc and Kazen'lo were guided into The Haven of the White Hall, where the Curators could no longer follow. The inner sanctum was meant only for the Lo candidates. However, the melody of the hymn saturated the enclave. The entryway was made of two stone pillars that gleamed from the opaqueness of the deathblade. On each side of the pillars was an altar that housed helmets worn by the General Maximums from time immemorial. The walls were artistically crafted with a mural history of White Scythe. As the congregants chanted in the main hall, their reverberations echoed into The Haven, and the blade's power drew nigh, hearing the call.

Lo'Marc and Kazen'lo looked at each other, nodded, and stepped through the entryway. The scythe's luster of oblivion was horribly magnificent. Neither candidate realized that he was crying until he gazed at the other. There was no turning back, no words to pronounce. Kazen'lo was Lo'Marc's best friend and strongest ally, and vice versa. Stretching out their trembling hands, both men gripped the blade. At first there was no sensation to be felt. However, in an instant, Kazen'lo was thrown back, and Lo'Marc's grip became much stronger.

The blade had adjudicated; its decision was without appeal.

Anointed by White Scythe, Lo'Marc turned around with power and faced his fallen comrade as tears streamed down his eyes.

"Do not mourn for me, brother," Kazen'lo said with poetic genuflection. "I have only one supplication."

"What is it?" Lo'Marc P'tan asked with a sympathetic bloodlust.

Removing a finely detailed metal gauntlet on his right hand, which portrayed the Battle of Bonicin, the same battle in which General Maximum Thirty-Four delivered his immortal speech, Kazen'lo said, "This glove was passed down throughout the ages in my family. I wish for it to live on in your hands. I see nothing more apropos than for this gauntlet to aid you in your reign as General Maximum."

Lo'Marc took the gauntlet of antiquity from his dearest friend and secured it upon his right hand. Its weight was tremendous. He was scarcely able to raise his hand or even make a fist, much less hold the scythe in a battle position. But if Lo'Marc could wield the glove as if it were his own hand, he would be able to use White Scythe in a manner none had seen.

"Thank you Kazen'lo," the General Maximum said graciously.

"No. Thank you. For I am the first to see the Eighty-Fourth General Maximum, the first to be smitten by his blade."

With a bowed head, Kazen'lo knelt in front of his superior, and Lo'Marc drew the blade back for a death stroke. There was no sound of flesh ripping; the blade completely consumed Kazen'lo and absorbed his body, his life force, his entire qanín. His power was added to the blade, filling Lo'Marc with a sense of gladness. Even if he was estranged from his family, the General Maximum's best friend would always be close by.

In deep memory, Lo'Marc rubbed the hallowed gauntlet as he stood outside Vincallous' tent. He began to feel no shame in his command.

"I sense you have stopped pacing," Vicious called out. "Does that mean that you are ready to go over these battle statistics?"

"Yes, Potentate." P'tan responded with confidence.

Upon entering his mentor's tent, Lo'Marc almost gasped. A noticeable scar ran across the Sczyphamek's left cheek and a large bruise rested on his forehead, both wounds no doubt from the témos. Vincallous also required a cane in order to stand and walk. Although Sczyphameks recovered quickly after a battle, wounds from a témo were nothing to shirk. The scar would never completely heal; the bruise would take a few weeks. Vincallous' broken legs had just been mended to the point where he could finally walk, but he would suffer a limp for a few durations.

The General Maximum was astonished. Vicious, physically injured, was an unknown sight to P'tan.

Fénüra glanced at Lo'Marc with keen eyes, "Only a fool believes that war is a perfect enterprise. Execution may be flawless, but this planet is full of unforeseen scenarios and devices that render even the most trained mind and body useless in regards to seeing all ends."

This was a rare side of Vincallous. However, the elite Sczyphamek had been engaged in quiet reflection since his time at the Fire Fields. And his encounter with the two témos plunged him into an even deeper introspection. When he returned to the Bitzroy Plains after his battle on the Crossroad Islands, Van was unable to shake the dull sense of depression he thought was long buried.

"Understand me." Vicious' countenance grew firm. "This battle must be won at all costs, and with a brutality so relentless, it will cause a historical fear in all who dare to oppose us. We must be diligent, but do not feel disconcerted because that woman was able to harm you. Syla was one of our most formidable opponents. Pride can lose a battle and a war."

"Yes, Potentate," Lo'Marc responded respectfully.

The Sczyphamek sighed. "Lo'Marc, you do not always need to call me that."

The General Maximum grew awkwardly silent.

Vincallous laughed heartily. The leader of White Scythe wondered if he was in the midst of an impostor.

"You should see your face Lo'Marc." Fierce smiled. "Do not be so foolish to believe that even the 'Great Sczyphamek called Vicious' is incapable of laughing."

Lo'Marc gathered himself from his uncomfortable disposition and replied, "Yes, sir."

"Staxis," Vicious said with a melancholy air.

"It is just that…" Lo'Marc trailed off. In many ways, Vincallous was the closet person he had to a father, since he left home so many cycles ago. "What should I call you?"

"You decide," the Sczyphamek replied. "I did not train you to be so timid." Looking down at the map of Nez Spirita in front of him, along with other sheets of random information, his tone changed. "Give me a summary, General."

"Lozé is virtually destroyed. The rebels suffered ninety-nine percent casualties, with eighty percent of them resulting in death."

"Excellent," the potentate coldly interjected.

"The remainder are imprisoned and are being interrogated for any information at our barracks here in Bitzroy," P'tan continued. "Regarding the one percent who escaped, I dispatched a force of White Scythe to find them. We believe they are heading southeast towards Nextu and down into the forests of the Windhorse Peninsula. I am sure they will be found and executed."

"If they make it to Hopha, leave them be."

"Sir?"

"If they escaped our pursuit and somehow made it to Hopha, leave them be."

"But what about…"

"No. We signed a treaty with Hopha, and we will not break any treaty so long as I am co-leader of Global Initiative. Lozé was destroyed. The Nez Spiritan Rebellion is crushed. Crumbs always remain. But this continent has lost its will to fight."

"Yes sir."

"Any reports from the Eradicate in the Windhorse Peninsula?"

"Nothing too substantial. An agent reported a possible Miska Kea suspect near Pike Metropolis, but there has been no major terrorist activity in the city for cycles." Marc paused. "I almost forgot; Spiax is already experimenting on the témo you captured. He believes that there can only be about five females left on the planet capable of reproducing."

"Those témos have been quite vexing throughout the ages," Vicious mused and rubbed his scar. "They will not be missed."

"I also received word from Anzél. I thought you would like to know that as soon as possible."

"Saving the best for last, ah?" Vincallous smiled. "And you acted as if you never met me."

The General Maximum returned the smile. "The shores of Focal have been taken. We should establish radio communication within the week."

"Quit enticing me. How is she?"

"Empress Pre-Eminent is well," Lo'Marc answered. "She and Commandant Feolenz are on the move to Anmetria next. She sends her well-wishes, and wants you on Líachim after the Auría is recovered."

"The *Auría*," Vicious echoed. "The search is proving harder than our archaeologists thought, and the First Snow is imminent. I may go out to those mountains personally now that our business with Lozé and those témos is concluded…"

Lo'Marc barely perceived it, but Vincallous sounded as if he possessed mixed emotions concerning the Auría's retrieval.

The sound of erratic footsteps neared the potentate's enclave. A White Scythe soldier entered the tent without asking, already signifying the seriousness of the message; no one dared to enter Vicious' quarters unannounced.

"Potentate, General Maximum," he saluted. "I apologize for my entrance, but the Triple Skyrises were just attacked and have sustained heavy damage. The military connecting bridges are destroyed as well as the Imperial Access Center."

"*What?*" Disbelief struck the General Maximum. "Who would be so foolish…?"

"We do not know; however, we believe Miska Kea is involved."

The soldier stopped, displaying some trepidation.

"What is it?" Vincallous inquired. "Speak."

"Sir," he replied. "We have reason to believe that a Sczyphamek led the attack."

"Do you have any proof?" Lo'Marc inquired.

"The imprisoned témo was freed, and several Blue Rapier eyewitnesses have confirmed a woman with extraordinary powers attacked them."

The room fell still. Lo'Marc looked at his soldier, and then at his mentor, and grimaced in anticipation. He had seen *that* look before. Vicious' smile was dark and disquieting.

"*At last,*" he said. "I knew Qeauríyx would not make it this easy. Send the report to Pre-Eminent, and ready my airlift. I am going to Pike Metropolis myself. Lo'Marc, arrange a meeting with the Eradicate agent who reported on that possible terrorist. I am sure there is a connection. Put all of our forces in Nez Spirita on high alert. I want this woman found—*alive*. Kill the témo on sight."

Chapter Sixteen: The Ascent of Mount Xarkim

After Neztríanis regained some of her strength atop of Skyrise Three, she and the Cílal were transported by the témo to the northwestern fringes of Pike Metropolis. Despite Timura's wounds, she persevered and was able to support both of the women's weight. After searching for heat signatures, Neztríanis picked a location near a small creek where they would be many lengths from any person. The two women made an encampment and started a fire while Timura searched for game in the darkness of night.

"Where will you go now?" Neztríanis asked Kéma.

The two women stood near the end of the tree line on the southeast slope of Mount Xarkim. Sighing, Kéma'fém looked towards the lights of the city in the distance and then back at Neztríanis. The signature light of Triple Skyrise One had been rendered powerless. In its stead was a smoky haze made partially visible by the surrounding lights.

The Cílal knew that Tannódin's retribution would be unmerciful. She tried to quiet the dismay, but her anticipation of the blowback could not be mitigated. Kéma's face and voice dwelled in angst. "I'll make my way back to Líachim, through underground channels. Hopefully the fragmented data I retrieved will be good for something."

"Do not worry." Neztríanis rummaged through her bag, searching for the attire she received in Nextu and her water jug. "I am sure the information will be more than adequate."

Timura returned with a mountain fawn and set it down in front of the two women, prodding them to take their share of the food.

"Bíoske would be proud of you, Nez," the Líachimian said warmly.

Neztríanis stopped her activity. "Bíoske…"

"Don't say it. I can tell by your face that he's dead."

"Kéma, I am so sorry." Though Neztríanis spoke words of consolation, she wanted to be consoled herself.

Gazing at the wounded Timura then glancing at Feather, the Cílal kicked the snowy ground. "This war... this life... happening like this... it seems so pointless sometimes..."

Nez placed her hand on Kéma's shoulder. "That is why we must continue. Future generations deserve better than the repetition of hollow battles and the futility of life."

"You are *not* from around here, Neztríanis." Kéma laughed wearily at the Sczyphamek's strange speech. "Hopha must be an interesting place..."

Kéma approached the slain fawn, unsheathed Feather, cut off some choice meat, and brought it to the fire for roasting. Timura, after seeing the portions removed, ravenously swept down on the dead animal, tearing into her first real meal in weeks. Neztríanis and Kéma stared and blinked, which caused the témo to stop and sheepishly laugh at the women.

"Why do you not travel with us?" Neztríanis asked the warrior of Líachim.

"And just where are you and the témo headed?"

The winged feline stopped feasting and turned her attention to Neztríanis in curiosity. Timura did not know their next move either.

Resolutely, Neztríanis angled her head to the heights of Mount Xarkim. "Up that way. The House of Kaz desires the Auría's recovery. I must retrieve it from the Hidden Tabernacle before they can."

The Cílal shook her head. "What do you mean, '*the Auría*'?"

Timura's ears perked up; her wings flapped; her tail beat against the frosty ground, and her hair stood on end. The Auría in the hands of the House of Kaz portended catastrophe for the entire planet. In the breath and palms of an elite Zananín, its verses would usher in the onslaught of doom and despair. Even the words of the Nameless One could become the vehicle for destruction. Divine inspiration did not preclude righteous misinterpretation.

"Are you certain?" Timura asked Temperature.

Phyxtríalis was quiet for a few moments. "This was revealed to me by the One with No Name."

"Through what intermediary?" the knowledgeable feline asked.

"My mother, the Great Mother of Hopha, Phesiana..."

Kéma, still shaken by the pronouncement that the Zananín were searching for the holiest, most variegated of books in Qeauríyx, interjected with an uneasy laugh. "Kíma. You are full of surprises. This keeps getting easier and better."

"We could really use your help," Nez replied.

"Maybe..." Kéma'fém took a few moments and pondered her options. "No... I can't. I must see to Líachim, my homeland. There's more happening on Qeauríyx than perhaps both of us know.

"Pre-Eminent is marching with a large contingent of Blue Rapier across the Anzél peninsula, making a straight line for Aphaz, in order to subdue the entire continent. And you say the House of Kaz is here trying to retrieve the Auría. That means Vicious is somewhere close by. And Miska Kea also received information that Galís, the Damüdan vassal lord, has been rounding up the Mystics of the Auría. Many thought that this was due to his desire to destroy them, but maybe he is trying to gather information for the expedition here. I've heard there are many incarcerated Mystics at The Gate."

"The Gate?" the uninformed Sczyphamek asked. "What is that?"

"The Gate," Timura explained with historical perspective, "was one of the sites where the Kylanín and Zephanín Sczyphameks of old and my ancestors defeated White Scythe, where it was believed at the time that the deathblade had been destroyed."

"Now," Kéma continued, "the city doubles as a penitentiary for elite war criminals and the capital of Damüda itself. The Interror, Galís' personal army, operates the jail. Those jails are worse than the dungeons of old. I feel sorry for anybody who finds their way to that Qalfocx.

"But if the Mystics have succumbed to their torture, it is possible that they handed over vital information concerning the Auría and the original Fragment's locations. Even so, it appears that the House of Kaz has not yet found it. I am sure we would know if they did…"

Timura chimed with her raspy intimations. "We *would* know. They are still searching. The Auría is in any one of the twenty-seven sacred temples on Qeauríyx. But, these Zananín never do anything piecemeal. They must be sure of their choice. Even if the Auría's whereabouts were narrowed to the Tabernacle, no one knows its precise location; only that it is near one of the mountains in the Infinite Circle. And all of the mountains have mythology or legends that claim the temple's ruins are in their rocky belly. Are you certain Mount Xarkim is the place we should search, Temperature?"

Neztríanis felt the doubt rush to her qanín. How could she find a temple that even the Mystics could not find? But, her mother told her to go to Mount Xarkim. So, the Tabernacle had to be there. There were likely to be some hostiles in the area doing preliminary reconnaissance. She would have to plan her search carefully; they could risk no detection.

She needed to assume the worst: after her actions at the Triple Skyrises, Jennó would deduce she was somehow involved, and that she was the Sczyphamek involved in the assault. He would undoubtedly relay this message to Vicious, who, in turn, would probably scour all Nez Spirita for her and Timura. It was not to Kéma's advantage to travel with Neztríanis. If anything, the daughter of Hopha, as a distraction, would make her trip back to Líachim a little easier. Bíoske was right after all; a new Sczyphamek would cause the leaders of Global Initiative to take pause.

"Staxis," the young Sczyphamek cursed with resignation. "There is too much heat in this group."

"Yes," the Cílal replied. "You are quite right, sister."

"When will you leave?" Neztríanis asked.

"In the morning. Neztríanis, if you and the témo succeed and make it out of this (which I pray you do) and find yourself in Líachim, I'll be in Aphaz. Look for me there. You can ask for me openly; it's a 'friendly' city."

The women sat around the fire and ate. Timura licked her mouth in satiated enjoyment and purred. Soon, the témo's black fur and deep blue stripes heaved heavy breaths, and the animal fell into deep slumber, her first undisturbed sleep in durations. While Timura purred and hummed, Kéma sharpened Feather with a stone. Neztríanis searched her bag for the Fragments of the Auría. She hoped its verses would give her some insight regarding the entrance to the Hidden Tabernacle.

While studying the sacred writings, she noticed Kéma unstrapping the jacketed sword across her back. Neztríanis was unsure, but she believed Kéma was a Cílal, one of the great warriors of Qeauríyx. Most reports of the Cílals were scattered rumor and myth. Legend held that they were exceptional warriors trained in an undisclosed location in Líachim. Their order was shrouded in mystery; few who saw their skill lived to tell about it.

"Are you a Cílal?" Neztríanis asked bluntly.

Kéma laughed to herself. "Why do you ask?"

"I was just wondering. Since my youth, stories were told to me about the Cílals of Qeauríyx, the wielders of special swords, fighters for justice… and sometimes for money…"

Kéma grunted and smiled. "I see our reputation still precedes us…" Kéma's voice suddenly became somber. "'Fighters for justice…' Staxis… Those titles belong to an age when there were enough of us to form a reputation. But yes, Neztríanis, I am a Cílal, what some on Qeauríyx call a 'silent slayer.'"

Conversation stopped once more. The Cílal continued whetting her short blade.

"Someone told me that the sword of a Cílal never dulls," Nez prodded. "Is that true?"

"I've heard Sczyphameks are invincible and never tire," Kéma responded playfully. "My primary sword does not dull, as long as I continue to believe in my cause; however, my secondary blade, Feather, can become naturally weary." Holding the blade in front of her, and twirling it gracefully in her left hand, the Líachimian continued, "I've wielded Feather long before I became a Cílal."

Kéma's playful banter embarrassed Neztríanis. "I have not Awakened yet; that is why I tired so easily after battle. Once I fully Awaken my Elemental, I should greatly—"

"I was joking Nez," Kéma'fém chided in irritation. "It was not meant to stir you." The young Sczyphamek's quick defensiveness made the Cílal uneasy.

"Oh."

"After all, whether Cílal or Sczyphamek, or anyone else, we happened as nel'asmív," Kéma said with tempered conviction.

"Nel'asmív..." Neztríanis echoed. "Yes. That is how we happened."

On Qeauríyx, the species of men and women were called "nel'asmív," a shortened version of the Ancient Tongue's "Nelon Ásmivü."[1] "Nelon" carried many meanings, but its most approximate was the word, "paradox." Ásmivü was also difficult to interpret; however, its closest definition was "corporeal breath" or the generic "entity." The title was a bit redundant; however, no less striking. The name went unchanged throughout the history of Qeauríyx. No one knew its origin, and out of their many redefinitions, the Tannódin'é did not attempt to alter the word designated for the men and women of Qeauríyx. They happened as entities of paradox in body, heart, mind, and spirit—in qanín. Neither was pure, neither did evil. Like Qeauríyx, they were what they did and vice versa. They happened.

"I cannot remember the last time I heard that word," Neztríanis spoke in solemn reflection. "Kéma, I do not wish to disturb you. I need to decipher these fragments and prepare myself for the journey ahead as well."

The Cílal shivered. "Neztríanis, I'm still cold. Can you increase the fire's intensity for a while?"

The daughter of Hopha did not realize the temperature was below freezing, even though snow covered the trees and ground. Quite some time had elapsed since she had "felt" hot or cold.

Walking towards a large Yarnínga, Kéma unjacketed Affliction and in a move so fast—Neztríanis almost missed it—the Cílal felled a large branch. The one incision made the branch break into eight parts. Neztríanis moved towards the dismembered branch and picked up four pieces. After placing them in the fire, Temperature extended her arm and expulsed a controlled, small fireball onto the conflagration. Kéma returned with the last four pieces and set them down by the larger, warmer embers. She was amazed at Neztríanis' powers and allowed herself a moment of hope.

The rebels' cause seemed hopeless without the aid of a Sczyphamek, and here was one, right before the eyes of the Líachimian. Zotham would be elated to hear the news. Kéma hoped Neztríanis would survive long enough to aid them, but there were no guarantees. Their actions had all but secured the elementary Sczyphamek a hard road.

Phesiana's daughter read the Fragments, while the silent slayer yawned wearily. Lying close to the fire, Kéma'fém fell asleep. Neztríanis studied the Cílal with great interest. How many cycles had Kéma seen? She appeared about five to ten cycles older than the Sczyphamek. Her weary face showed

---

[1] Nelon Ásmivü (neyl-on ahs-meh-vyoo)

the signs of death and battle, but underneath the scars, Kéma was beautiful. Timura and she were her first comrades-in-arms.

An unfamiliar sentiment crept into Neztríanis' heart.

She was not alone in the fight against Global Initiative. She had allies. That brought Neztríanis comfort. She could not take on such a task alone. Even though Rydín, Hafír, and Namí assisted her, she had not been in combat with any of them. Indeed, they risked their lives, and Nez appreciated their help.

But these new comrades were of a different stock and different kind, to be respected in a different way. Her thoughts shifted to Bíoske. He had only known her for three days, yet he trusted her with his life. He gave his life for her goals. Even though he disagreed with her faith and ideals, he respected them unto death. With such an example, she could do no less.

Like Bíoske, she too would have to be unafraid of death. He was neither a Sczyphamek nor a Cílal, but like them, he happened as nel'asmív.

***

The next morning Neztríanis awoke, and as expected, Kéma was already gone. Timura was up, pensively circling around the campsite.

"Good morning, Temperature," the témo rasped. A deep misery lingered in her voice. "Kéma wishes us well. She departed two hours ago."

"Good morning, Timura," Neztríanis replied. "How are you feeling?"

The winged feline trotted to her companion and sat. This was the first time Nez beheld Timura in full view and sunlight. Her black fur was beautiful, and the light blue stripes that found their way around her body were quite elegant. The témo yawned and stretched; her wings emerged from the top of her trunk to a considerable degree. Her wings were more immense than Neztríanis realized, appearing like a malleable metal lightly covered in thin fur. Although the wings were altogether natural for the témo's body and constitution, they were completely distinct and nearly indescribable. They were neither similar to a bird nor an insect's wing, nor any other flying creature. They resembled shields that protected the body of the témo. But, they were clearly damaged by the scientists' experimentation.

This was also the first time Neztríanis saw the stitches on the closely shaven belly of the témo.

"I dreamed I was still pregnant last night… that my cub was still within me. I gave birth to him, amongst my kind, and we all rejoiced at a new generation. I heard him purring and sleeping in my coat," Timura lamented. "When I woke up, I realized it was only fantasy."

Though reticent, Neztríanis moved closer and put her arm around Timura's neck and lovingly embraced her. She did not know how the témo would react; they had not even known each other for one day. The Sczyphamek wondered if she was overreaching, but her qanín sincerely ached for the feline.

"I am so sorry," she whispered and ran her right hand through the témo's fur between the ears. "Maybe you should—"

"Leave?" Timura interjected. "What would I do? Where would I go? Témos mate for life, and mine fell at the hands of Vincallous. My unborn child was taken from me. I have no other reason to go on."

Timura's loss was unimaginable to Neztríanis. She felt emotionally paralyzed by the feline's pain. But she forced herself to say something.

"We will go on together." Neztríanis suddenly thought of her exchange with Bíoske and paused. Her voice evinced a wary confidence. "I will not speak of predestination, for only a sick providence would unite us under these conditions. However, I will not leave your side, until I am taken."

Timura attempted to shake her sorrow. "A Kylanín and a témo have not roamed Qeauríyx for more than one millennium. They were called Myanín many cycles ago. I believe the House of Kaz has always feared this moment."

"The Synthesis?"

"That is correct," Timura replied, in her raspy, yet beautiful vocal intimations. "Most nel'asmív are unaware of it or its potential. I am sure there were scarce verses in the Fragments that prophesied about it."

"Most were vague and cryptic, leaving more questions than answers." Neztríanis picked up the sacred book she had been studying all night. "My Elemental has related the gravity of the Synthesis to me, but I am still not altogether sure what it means."

"In time, you will. But only an Awakened Sczyphamek is capable of wielding that kind of power. We must focus on greater matters anyway." The témo drew away from Neztríanis, righted herself, flapped her injured wings and caused a breeze to blow over the Sczyphamek's face. "Temperature, until I am taken, I will not leave your side."

"Fá'atoño má," Neztríanis chanted.

At once, her orange-white aura emerged and enveloped Timura as a sign of Elemental acceptance. Just as the emanation shone forth, it soon drew back, and the woman and the feline were among the Yarníngas. Neztríanis looked at the sky then at the trees. A few flakes had already fallen while she was nearing Pike Metropolis with Jennó. From all indications, the first major snow event was only days away. She needed to find the entrance to the temple before then. Once the snowpack formed, it would be nearly impossible to find an opening or get her bearings.

"Where should we begin?" Timura asked.

"The Fragments revealed very little to me, except that an entrance would be in the higher elevations." Neztríanis sighed heavy thoughts and possessed too few answers. "I am not sure what we should do. There must be some semblance of a path above the tree line. Once we reached it, I planned to chant and focus my Elemental. Perhaps, I may be able to sense something and—"

Simultaneously, the Myanín turned southeast. Timura smelled and Neztríanis sensed them.

"How many?" Timura asked.

"Seven," she replied. "They are about one length away."

Timura lifted her front right paw, and extended her claws and retracted them. "I will deal with them."

"No, Timura." Neztríanis voiced her dissent as friendly as possible. "I am not your master, nor are you my chattel. But killing them will only hasten the arrival of more sentries. I know Tannódin hurt you, and there will be a time to fight. But right now, we must find the entrance to the Tabernacle."

Drawing in her temper, the témo gazed towards the southeast once more. "You are right. But, we must do something about this campsite. They will ascertain that someone happened by here."

Neztríanis nodded and gathered her things, while the témo placed the carcass of the fawn on the smoldered fire. Motioning Timura to step away from the campsite, the Sczyphamek extended both of her arms and called forth her element of frigidity and covered the campsite in a thick layer of snow and ice. Even to the proficient eye, it would be hard to discern the camouflaged area.

Throwing her shoulderpack over her back, Neztríanis walked uphill, smiling and feeling confident that she was able to create the conditions for snow without much concentration. Her powers were growing to such an extent that she no longer needed to consciously search for water vapor.

"Temperature," Timura called out. "They will notice and then track our footprints. We must either fly or move through the trees."

"I should have known that." The embarrassed Sczyphamek shook her head. "I am sure you could tell that I have not mastered flying, and your wings and underbelly are still injured. You were pushed to your limit transporting Kéma and me here. I think it would be best if we used the trees for as long as we can."

"I agree, but the tree line will end in another 5000 feet around the 16000 foot mark. Last night, as we flew to this spot, I surveyed the area while still in flight. Xarkim is over 26000 feet. And at some point, both of us will struggle. If the altitude does not slow us, the snows will."

Risking their lives was never in question. They both leapt into a tree, and Neztríanis covered their tracks by making fresh snow. They hopped from tree to tree, up the mountain. From their higher elevation, Neztríanis made out the figures of those nearing their site. The crew was not carrying standard Tannódin'é issue. Their energy guns went almost unnoticed by Neztríanis.

"They must be a search party for the Auría," she told Timura. "But, for them to be this far out, so close to the first snows, makes little sense."

"Vicious has learned of you. He has sensed your quest for the Auría."

"How do you know this?" Neztríanis was alarmed. She believed the core of her mission, although pressed, was still uncompromised.

"He may be violent and arrogant, but Vincallous is no fool. He has enough insight into Qeauríyx to calculate this probable outcome. Undoubtedly, he learned of my rescue by your hands. Although témos and Sczyphameks fought together in the past, this reason alone is insufficient for you to be in Nez Spirita, especially as an unawakened Sczyphamek. No, there must be a greater purpose. The Auría is the most likely reason for your arrival.

"But Vincallous does not know the location of the temple, so he must be quickening all of the reconnaissance teams and placing more in the field, in order to retrieve it before you. Even though he is a great Sczyphamek, he cannot search all twelve major mountains that surround this area. It would take him weeks to do so, and just like us, the First Snow would paralyze any effort. Not to mention, the injuries Vincallous just sustained are not easily overcome..."

"Even if what I just said is not true, we should act as if it is, so that we can focus on our task. Our greatest advantage now is that we know which mountain to search. We will not enjoy that advantage for long."

Neztríanis sensed over seven different search parties within a ten length radius in all directions, validating Timura's claim. Though appearing youthful, the feline's fighting and tactical experience belied her true age. Her mother once told her that most témos reached over two hundred cycles.

"Kíma. We are surrounded by Tannódin'é forces. They seem to be combing the upper tree line area."

"We cannot delay," Timura said. "We need to get above them. They cannot cover as much ground as we can. Once we get to a safe altitude, you must find the entrance to the temple as soon as possible, or else—"

Neztríanis and Timura froze.

"*Wha- what is this I am feeling?*" Neztríanis stammered. Her hands and body shook. Her blood ceased its flow.

"It is Vincallous. He is near," the témo replied calmly although her hair stood on end.

"Unbelievable," she gasped. "How can he...? How is his Elemental...?"

"Crumbs, Temperature. Remember, he is injured... Those are but crumbs."

Neztríanis was silent and quieted her Elemental. Vincallous would be unable to sense her unless he was extremely close.

"You must not move or speak until I signal it safe," Timura said solemnly. "Even though he will not be able to perceive your Elemental and is thousands of feet in the air, his powers allow him to sense sonic vibration, to the smallest degree. We cannot take any chances."

Neztríanis did as her companion ordered. Vincallous was twenty lengths away to their north, at high altitude, in an airlift. Somehow,

Temperature sensed the heat generated by its engines. Keeping completely still, she tried to think of the most serene moments of her life, like cooling her feet in Hero's Bay during the summer or the smell of Elder Namí's luku sandwiches. She was so enveloped in those memories; she barely heard the machine pass by.

After only a few moments, Timura purred and they resumed their ascension. Neztríanis would not let herself become discouraged at what she felt when the plane was closest to their position. His Elemental was unimaginably intense, even in a state of rest and injury. She would be killed or worse if she met Vicious in her present condition. His power bordered upon absurdity.

Within the hour they had moved to the outskirts of the tree line, searching for an upward path. During their climb, Timura and Neztríanis stayed clear of all resistance, zigzagging their way up the southern slope of Mount Xarkim, quietly exchanging conversation. Timura was impressed by her partner's abilities, since Neztríanis had only been happening as a Sczyphamek for a little over two durations.

The témo revealed that she was ninety-two cycles old and was the last of her family. Apparently, only twenty témos remained on the entire planet, eight females and twelve males. Six of the females were pregnant, and all were in hiding throughout Qeauríyx. They made a vow to distance themselves from all fighting and nel'asmív until their number reached at least fifty. And although témos were known for only having two to three cubs per den, all mated felines accepted the mandate of prolific reproduction.

"I doubt any more of my kind will be able to aid us," Timura added.

They rested near the fourteen thousand foot mark, on a southern cliff of the mountain, overlooking the Infinite Circle.

Both were short of breath, due to the altitude's thin air. Neztríanis sensed her surroundings. She was confounded. Somehow her abilities appeared to be increasing in veracity every moment. With little concentration, she felt the air cooling and the water vapor turning to ice. It would not be long until their position would be covered in clouds, maybe even heavy snow.

"We have to stop here," the Sczyphamek gasped for air. "One spot is as good as any now."

"Your powers have sharpened since yesterday," the témo observed with interest. "I wonder if the Auría is causing this increase in your Elemental."

"That would be good," Neztríanis replied. "Are you cold Timura?"

"Not yet." Suddenly, the témo's instincts gnawed at her from the inside, indicating danger in their vicinity, but there was no one around. "Is anyone nearby? The winds are affecting my sense of smell."

Neztríanis scanned the entire south side of the mountain within seconds. "No. The closest party is at least four thousand feet downhill from our position." Temperature gazed at Timura; the feline seemed distressed. "Is something wrong?"

"I feel a great threat close by," the témo responded darkly. "We must be careful."

The daughter of Hopha nodded, sat down, and crossed her legs. She chanted quietly, searching for anything that would guide them to the temple. Timura crouched on all fours and insulated herself from the oncoming cold. The clouds continued to form and roll in with wintry vigor. The situation would be dire within a few days. Nez Spiritan winters were harsh and grueling, especially in the mountain ranges. Besides Pike Metropolis, the eastern Bitzroy Plains and the Gemansu Desert were the only locales on the continent that occasionally reached above freezing in the daytime.

"I will soon join you in chanting," Timura rasped. "But, I have one more question. Where will we take the Book if we find it?"

Neztríanis stopped chanting. She dared not look at her complement directly. "Sunrise Mountain," she whispered.

Timura responded by chanting and praying. *May the Nameless One protect us.*

The Sczyphamek undoubtedly meant the *Place with No Name*, whether she knew it or not. The Nameless One had indeed used her mother as an intermediary. Nez Spirita's northern country was notorious throughout all of Qeauríyx. Although it was thousands of lengths from the South Pole, Sunrise's temperature rivaled each anti-pole of the planet. Timura doubted that even Neztríanis could survive there unless she Awakened, which meant that Timura would freeze to death. At its coldest, the temperature only warmed to one hundred and fifty to one hundred degrees below freezing.

Neztríanis' shoulderpack contained three weeks' worth of rations. Water would not be an issue, due to the snow, and if they made it to the entrance of the temple, Timura was sure there would be underground water sources. The dyad chanted together, matching pitch and tempo. With Timura's friendly growl added to the petition, her Elemental grew larger. However, Neztríanis withheld a visible display of her aura.

***

"Ah. Jennó, I have received remarkable reports regarding your work."

"Thank you Potentate," the spy replied graciously. "Your time is valuable, so if you do not mind, I will tell you what I know."

Vincallous arranged for the meeting at the Triple Skyrises in order to survey the damage and for a thorough debriefing from all remaining commanding officers and eyewitnesses. Jennó was the first person he wanted to meet. Reníz continuously extolled the man's work and acumen. The emperor and spy met in the large room adjacent to the témo's previous holding area. The massive window still lay in ruins, courtesy of

Neztríanis and Timura. Only one and a half days had passed since the attack, but Vicious detected no residual Elemental signature. The inference was clear: this newfangled warrior was unawakened. As for Jennó, he quickly deduced that Neztríanis had something to do with the freeing of the témo as well as the destruction of the building's major and minor bridges.

"Tell me what you know, and then tell me what you think," Vincallous stated.

"Her name is Neztríanis Phyxtríalis, although she called herself Mésa. Her speech and knowledge of the Auría placed her near Hopha or its surrounding villages. Some of my agents did some reconnaissance and confirmed that the daughter of the 'Great Mother' of Hopha was missing. We had little intelligence on her since we are not allowed to permanently spy on that area. However, after I met her, I could tell she was from there. Hopha is one of the few places that still clings to old tradition."

"You say that with venom, Jennó," Vicious observed.

"No, sir," the imperial agent lied. "It is a statement of fact. Anyway, she lived with Hafir (an architect and community leader in Nextu) for three weeks, under the pretense of being his cousin. Based on the intelligence I have gathered, I am positive Hafir had and still has absolutely no knowledge of who he was truly dealing with.

"As far as the attack goes—you may have heard this from your commanders here—"

"No," Fierce interrupted and tapped his cane on the floor. "I do not care about that, as I am sure you understand. Include what you have learned here in this briefing, but only as it pertains directly or indirectly to this woman."

"Yes, sir. Although there is some disagreement, it seems that she broke into the airshaft on the 242nd floor, although I am still unsure how she did it. Evidence shows that she was a part of a three-pronged attack, coordinated by a local Miska Kea group here. Quite frankly sir, the plan was ingenious. The level of sophistication points to one of the three…"

"It was Bíoske," Vincallous replied. "Syla was killed personally at the hands of the General Maximum at Lozé, two durations ago. Our intelligence and the blade confirmed this.

"Who would have thought that another one of those three was right beside us? Even in such a decrepit state, Miska Kea is still resourceful."

"If it was Bíoske then his body was not recovered," the Nez Spiritan continued. "Two of them dying so close to one another… perhaps we should try to locate Brenko. These deaths might pull him out of hiding. His death would put an end to the hopes of many who oppose Global Initiative. Even though a new Sczyphamek has emerged, I doubt she will be blessed with the tactical skill of those three.

"I am not agreeing with them, and I think you will understand when I say that they were formidable opponents, the likes of which we probably will not see for a while. If we captured or killed Brenko, that would be a great blow to their cause. Maybe we should alert all Eradicate agents about this development..."

"Excellent point," Vicious smiled coldly. "I will give the order when this meeting is done. You may continue with your report."

"The Sczyphamek engaged Blue Rapier twice, once while freeing the témo on this floor and again in the Access Center. She killed no one in the process. The témo, however, was quite another story. Some of the few surviving soldiers were maimed beyond recognition..."

Vincallous nodded. "That was to be expected, in terms of the témo. But this Neztríanis—she killed *no one*? She is showing restraint... or..."

"Or she doesn't feel comfortable taking a life. And judging from what we know about the powers of an Awakened Sczyphamek, coupled with her unwillingness to kill, I think she is still immature in her powers. From what the witnesses have said, her power is connected to ice.

"Maybe you would understand this better than I, but when I arranged for her capture, she was able to escape because a stove caught fire *a bit too conveniently*. I know you told me to hold off on my speculation, but I strongly feel that her power was connected to this event and that her abilities are beyond ice creation.

"As far as the Access Center, we do not know if any information was stolen from the main computer. If someone tried to steal something, they are as skilled as our own elite programmers. The system's failsafe was armed, but because the floor was all but obliterated, we have no way of confirming or ruling out espionage. Only three soldiers survived that battle.

"Lastly, we have no prisoners, which means that—"

"They received help from within our ranks. It is the only explanation," Vicious said bluntly. "No matter how adept Bíoske was, it is extremely unlikely he executed this plan without inside assistance. The challenges are mounting, from within and without..."

"Yes, sir; I agree. Four Blue Rapier guards on duty that night are unaccounted for. And we now know that some of the rebels actually worked in the Skyrises. We do not know how they bypassed our security checks, but in order to do so, they must have allies who are commanding officers. These are all the facts I possess."

"Implications?"

"I do not think that the témo was Neztríanis' original mission. The animal arrived here while I was still with her. When we encountered the témo in a parade, I witnessed her shock and depression personally. She was shaken by the experience. She must have decided to rescue the témo after she escaped me.

"In addition, she asked me to take her to Bitzroy. She clearly did not want to be entangled in anything that would place her close to our forces. But even the average Nez Spiritan knows that Blue Rapier and White Scythe have made southern Bitzroy their home. I do not think she intended to go there, or else she would have asked me to lead her beyond the plains.

"Whatever her goal was, she was to do it alone, and with minimal interference. Therefore, I think she is after the Auría, and judging from the point she asked me to guide her, I can say with confidence that she believes the Temple's entrance is on the northern half of the Infinite Circle."

Vincallous looked out the northern window towards Mt. Xarkim and the mountains that strafed it to the west and east. Clouds subsumed the top of the mountain, while the lower elevations displayed the signs of emergent snowfall. Cold wind, emanating from the mountainsides, rushed through the broken window and on the face of Van Fénüra. He winced as the chill groped his scars.

There were five mountains on the northern rim, and any of those five could house the temple. But they sought not the temple. They were searching for the *entrance* to the temple. The Tabernacle was underground and possibly in an adjacent mountain. In other words, even if the temple was in Mt. Xarkim that did not mean the entrance was. A journey to the Auría was a journey through time and space.

"She has not Awakened. Even I cannot survive in those conditions. I just called the expedition parties back due to the weather. Whether her Elemental is tied to temperature is beside the point. Only an Awakened and *trained* Sczyphamek can survive out there. She will be fighting against Qeauríyx the entire time…What is she thinking?" Vincallous muttered half-caringly and half-spitefully. "The témo joined her, which means that ill-conceived animal believes her to be a Kylanín at best or a Zephanín at worst. Staxis… We worked so hard here in Nez Spirita… I cannot allow the possibility of the Synthesis…"

Jennó barely caught any the emperor's words, and growing uncomfortable, he placed himself back into the conversation. "She had no access to our information, from what I can gather. I do not know how she found out about the Auría."

It told her, Vincallous thought. *Probably through some mediating source… Could they be…? No… the Nameless One is a trickster at times…*

"Potentate?" Jennó's interjection was bathed in hesitation. "Are you all right? Would you like to finish this briefing at some other time?"

Vincallous did not turn to face the man, but replied, "Proceed."

"I was going to deploy some of my contacts to the Hopha area—"

"No," the Sczyphamek sighed. "We must honor the treaty we signed with Hopha. The House of Kaz does not break its armistices… anymore. If this is how they are playing this, then there is no point of trying to stop it now."

"'They,' sir?"

"I would tell you, but you are not ready. And we cannot go rounding up Nez Spiritans. We just put Lozé down permanently. It was the only municipality that openly opposed us. Any violent imperial action now could start another uprising, and Global Initiative is futile if everyone dies in the process.

"We have made much progress here. Your own presence is testimony enough. But, this Hafir concerns me. The Eradicate briefed me on him before."

"I do not think he is a problem, or that much of a problem," Jennó countered.

Surprised by the agent's parry, Vicious turned around and his eyes met those of the Nez Spiritan. "Are you defending him?"

"No," Jennó lied though his heart skipped not a beat. "I just think he is more valuable to us alive, and Nextu would most certainly revolt if you killed him. Nextu, though changing, is still a proud House. This is Nez Spirita, not Phmquedria."

Fierce perceived that Jennó's pulse had remained unchanged during their entire conversation. He was the first person other than Pre-Eminent who had shown no fear of him in their first encounter, or at least, could pretend that he was not afraid.

"Do as you see fit, but leave the Sczyphamek to me," Vincallous stated. "Jennó, you are a valuable member of the Eradicate, and you do not disappoint. Violent Fist told me that your investigative skills rank near top of the imperial guard."

"I am pleased I have the confidence of Mistress Bläno. I hope I have or will earn yours."

"There's no need to bait me, Jennó. Pre-Eminent and I were the ones who gave our final approval. After all, our agents answer only to Bläno or us.

"What are your plans now? I doubt you will go back posing as that merchant."

"No. I will not. I spent six cycles living that life. Mistress Bläno just informed me of another task. But first, I must find the person who broke into the Access Center. All Eradicate agents in Nez Spirita are mandated to find her. It is possible, yet unlikely, that she was a Cílal."

"A *Cílal*?"

"Yes. Only one of the guards survived her attack—he's dead now—but, she was the only one sent to this floor. Again, we are uncertain of her objective—whether she meant to destroy the floor and cripple our tactical efforts here, or if she was to steal valuable information, or both. That is a penchant for Brenko's group: attack in all directions so that your enemy will pursue in all directions, only to be spread thin and weakened."

Vincallous stood silently. That was troubling news. The stolen data had direct consequences for Old Flint's plan to destroy Aphaz and move into Líachim. The elderly commander had worked on that strategy for two cycles.

Pre-Eminent and I cannot take Líachim by ourselves, Vicious thought. *If Feolenz's plans are compromised...* "We must assume she retrieved the information. Find and eliminate her. But before you do, make sure she did not give that information to anyone. Her capture and elimination is more important than anything, even more important than that Sczyphamek."

"I am scheduled for surgery after this meeting," the agent replied. "My recovery time is two days, but my team will start as soon as we conclude."

"Your third face?"

"Yes, sir," Jennó replied.

"Well, we cannot delay. Tell your team and all agents to move quickly and judiciously. We may need to pull our Wind…"

The Sczyphamek felt the pace of fast steps and the racing heart of Haptian Spiax before the bio-alchemist entered the room. Spiax was elderly, but unlike his contemporary, Commandant Feolenz, the scientist seemed like he would die any moment. He was bald, wrinkly, and wheezed even while resting.

"Vicious." Spiax whispered through raspy breaths. "Ur… urgent news from Phmquedria."

"What is it?" Vincallous' eyes sparkled nervous anticipation.

"A message from Alzhexph," he gasped. "I was able to set up high frequency communication with Phmquedria for only a short while, but I was told that it was extremely important." He paused so that he could catch his breath. "Another Sczyphamek. Alzhexph confirms another Sczyphamek in Phmquedria. It is his son. He escaped from Euhilv, but is believed to still be on the continent."

"*Another.*" Vincallous' smile was calm and maniacal. "*A chénala.* Good… two Sczyphameks, a Cílal, a témo… this may be the battle we need… or not…" The emperor's smile morphed into a stoic countenance. "Jennó, before you find that Cílal, alert all Eradicate agents in Phmquedria to be on the lookout for…"

"Anámn," the bio-alchemist responded. "His name is Anámn Matriester."

"Scour Phmquedria for him," Vincallous ordered. "Do whatever it takes. He must be found alive. Pre-Eminent will want to meet him personally. Has she been informed?"

"I have not spoken a word, since the information is so sensitive. I believe an Eradicate courier should deliver the news personally," Spiax said. "We cannot allow anyone to intercept this information."

"Agreed," Vincallous and Jennó said together and then looked at one another.

"I will see to it," Jennó said. "I'll contact one of our most clandestine operatives in the field. And my comrades in Phmquedria will be sure to find Anámn.

"As for the possible Cílal—if she is smart she wouldn't dream of telling anyone on this continent that she has seen a Sczyphamek. That would start a rumor trail that would lead us right to her."

Vicious eyed Spiax while discreetly nodding to Jennó. "Spiax, what can you tell me about the témo? I take it you disposed of the cub I killed?"

The old man nearly hesitated. "Yes, I did. Genetic analysis revealed that she is from the line of Orators. She possesses the knowledge of the Synthesis, without a doubt."

"Staxis," the Emperor cursed. "How many did you say were left?"

"Around ten altogether, but we believe that this témo was one of only five who could be pregnant."

"Make sure those on your staff and under your jurisdiction remain uninformed about these Sczyphameks, Spiax. And the témo project is becoming too dangerous for us. Kill all remaining témos you come across."

"Yes, Potentate."

"You may leave us now. I need to finish my debriefing with Jennó," Vincallous said to Spiax. "And Haptian, double-check to make sure all of the Auría expedition parties are out of the mountains. The weather will only get worse."

"It will be done."

"Exceptional."

The imperial scientist left from their presence. No sooner had he done so, Jennó spoke quietly, "He is lying about the témos, Potentate. I am a master at lying. I am unsure of his plans, but he is not being truthful."

"I needed to be certain," Fierce stated. "Place a Wind agent on him, one of our best. Haptian is no lackey."

"Yes, sir," the spy replied. "If I might ask, Potentate Vicious, what is the 'Synthesis'?"

"You will find out on your own I am sure, but if you pass the information along, I will behead you, *personally*," Vincallous placed his hand on the spy's shoulder and squeezed it gently. "That is no threat. It is a promise."

Jennó's heart skipped.

"You are dismissed. Ah."

The master of espionage bowed before the emperor cautiously and slowly treaded out of his midst. Vincallous set his sights upon the mountains in the north once again. He could feel the que growing cold. If he searched for Neztríanis, he would be caught in a snowstorm or worse. Though on the mend, Vicious' injuries were deep, and the inclement weather made sonic detection nearly impossible.

At no time can a Sczyphamek's powers exceed Qeauríyx's qaníns or the intersection between Lo'Ché and Kímaios'lo, Vincallous thought. *The Nameless One will not actively intervene on her behalf. Does she know about these things? She has not Awakened. Death would await even Pre-Eminent in the higher elevations. Sczyphameks are mortal. We are not gods.*

"Do not die. We need you alive. You *must* live."

***

10 Gamíz 241 OGI
Myalé

Days passed. The climate grew colder and harsher. Timura and Neztríanis devoted nearly all their time during the day to chanting and exploration. Before dawn, they would scramble to find adequate shelter. If weather permitted, Timura searched for wood and hunted in the lower elevations, in order to maintain their rations and fire supply, while Neztríanis continued to comb the surrounding terrain for any opening she could find. During this time, they had found five locations around the 18000-foot mark of the mountain that were suitable for survey and shelter. Neztríanis did not allow herself to become disenchanted. She reminded herself of the gravity of the situation and that the Tabernacle had been lost for over ten thousand cycles.

On the sixth day of exploration, the daytime was filled with snowfall and night was bitterly cold. Even Neztríanis felt chilly, which meant Timura was hours away from hypothermia. Their predicament would only worsen as the hours loitered. Only a blazing fire gave them some heat.

Neztríanis asked Timura, "How are you faring?"

The témo shivered. "I am fine. But, I will not survive under these conditions much longer. Soon, even your Elemental will be taxed."

Suddenly, a misty gust of wind descended upon their position and quenched the fire. Neztríanis tried to make another, but every effort was surmounted by a stronger gust.

"Do not exhaust yourself," Timura roared, for the wind was howling. "If you do not find the entrance in a few hours, we *will* descend."

"We cannot leave!" Neztríanis' yell was one of anger and desperation.

"We will return during the daytime," Timura reminded the Sczyphamek. "I can use my night vision to guide us down."

"The weather will only get worse." The daughter of Hopha tried to relax her growing anxiety. "But, you are right. We cannot stay here much longer. That fire was our last source of sustainable heat. I did not want to use my Elemental to keep us warm. I do not believe I have grown enough to sustain such an ability while searching for—"

Neztríanis stopped. And even without her night vision, Timura saw her eyes brighten.

"That is it!" she exclaimed. "The fire was a distraction. Timura, please, chant with me."

It was freezing throughout the vicinity. But if there was an opening, any opening—even if just a small fissure—the air behind the rock face would have a higher temperature than the outside. Neztríanis truly believed that the opening would be revealed by the One with No Name. But a new plan of discernment now entered into her thoughts. She could measure the temperature of the rocky surface, and where there was a temperate gradation of even a decimal of a degree behind the surface, she would focus upon that position. Warmer air had to linger within the cavern that led to the Tabernacle. The largest and deepest temperature discrepancy between the air outside and the air inside would be the signal of a cave or a tunnel.

While considering her course of action, a vengeful gale of a high velocity fell upon them and slammed Neztríanis against the mountain. The Sczyphamek winced in macabre clarity. If it snowed now, they would face horrendous blizzard conditions.

No.

They would face death.

The Myanín meditated. Neztríanis readjusted her focus. Immediately, she felt over fifty fissures around the mountain within a four thousand foot radius. Within forty minutes, the Sczyphamek had become completely engrossed in her Elemental. She had not felt this way since her training in the forests of the peninsula. The cracks in Mt. Xarkim became visible while all other surroundings turned into complete darkness. Mentally and perceptively, her Elemental demarcated the fissures as grayish white flames. One by one, Neztríanis searched. And using her Elemental like a thermometric shovel, she excavated the rock face in order to find any air that was warmer than the outside temperature. Once Neztríanis confirmed the temperature discrepancy, she checked to see if the space of air reached deep into the belly of Mt. Xarkim.

Systematically, from the lowest elevation to the highest, around the entire rocky palisade, she surveyed and measured the temperature gradation of each crack and reached into the space to see how far the warm air traveled with minimal obstruction, and within ten hours, she had narrowed the entrance to two possibilities.

The sun was rising, but it was colder in the daytime than it was at night. Timura would not be able to last another day in the same spot, and Neztríanis was also spent.

"Timura." Neztríanis nearly hummed her name.

"Yes," the témo coughed. The creature had curled up and her wings were covering the majority of her body. "Did you find what you were looking for?"

"I found two possible entrances. But both are too far up the mountain to discern adequately."

"Where?" her partner inquired.

"Fifteen hundred and five thousand feet above." Neztríanis response was drenched in cold and sweaty anger. "I wish I was an Awakened Sczyphamek. We would have been inside the mountain by now."

"Do not burden yourself with such thoughts," Timura said.

"Vicious will be sure to find the opening if he decides to begin his search here," Neztríanis complained. "What will we—"

"Stop," Timura growled. "Vicious is not here. And even if he was, it would not be as simple as you grumble. The Auría is partly responsible for your finding the opening in the first place. Remember, this mission was given to you by the Nameless One."

"Then why does *It* not help..." Neztríanis, exasperated and fatigued, stopped herself from completing the sentence. Apparently, Bíoske made an impression upon her.

But she keeping on was her only option. Regardless of the mission's origin, the melancholy ascent was mandatory. Not just by divine commission, but because of the consequences if she did not carry out the task. However, she continued to ponder the apparent lack of care or power the deity displayed. The témo offered no words and let Neztríanis struggle with her faith.

The daughter of Hopha surveyed the path before them. At times, the climb would be vertical. Ice and snow now covered the upper limits of the mountain, and the winds were sure to pick up. Jumping and the use of flying would be at a minimum. So far, the climb had only been taxing. But now Neztríanis wondered how the témo could possibly make the upward journey with her.

"Can you climb that?" Neztríanis asked.

The témo extended her front right paw and revealed her claws. She swiped at the face of the rocks and they crumbled. "These claws can cut through rock," she said. "They can anchor me to stone as well."

Neztríanis opened her shoulderpack and retrieved her water jug. Then she opened the large, animal-skinned water container given to her by Namí, so that Timura could drink. Next, she handed Timura seven choice pieces of meat, while she consumed one large piece and some nuts and berries.

The implication of the meal was clear. Timura and Neztríanis would not eat or drink again until they arrived at the entrance—if not, this was their last meal. The upper elevations of Mount Xarkim awarded no safe havens. No one who attempted to climb the tallest peaks on Qeauríyx ever returned, in any season, much less a Nez Spiritan winter.

Hurriedly, they ate and drank, after which, Neztríanis heated some nearby icicles and refilled both containers with water. After putting on another layer of clothes, she extended her hands over Timura and warmed her completely, drying her wings and coat. Anxiety gripped the fledgling Sczyphamek. Even that small feat made her dizzy.

Closing the shoulderpack and slinging it over her back, she started to scale, with the témo behind her.

Neztríanis searched for heat signatures in the lower elevations, but she felt not a single nel'asmív nor any other animal. The Tannódin'é search party was apparently on winter hiatus, and the last of the animals had left the area.

With the First Snow so imminent, Timura was right about one thing; the situation was about to grow so dire that even Vicious would not be able to survive on the slopes of any mountain of the Infinite Circle.

Neztríanis did not know if that was a good or a bad thing. She simply did not know…

They made it to the first fissure in two hours. It was nearly fifteen hundred feet above their prior location. However, after careful though fraught examination, Neztríanis accepted that the fissure was not the entrance. Though the air was warmer and there was a small cavern behind the rocks, the cave was not a pathway. After a half-length, the air met a wall of dense rocks.

The Sczyphamek almost hung her head, but this was not the time to give up hope. As flakes of snow fell, Neztríanis signaled to Timura that they must continue the ascent. Timura nodded.

Although they were on the south side of the mountain, the second fissure was on the western side, at a height of about 23,000 feet. Not only would they have to scale the crag, they also had to strafe the ominous cliffs in order to achieve success.

Soon, Timura and Neztríanis were engulfed in a large snow cloud. Visibility was reduced to two to three feet. Ice formed on the woman's face, and for the first time in a long while, Neztríanis *was* cold. And since her body had become unaccustomed to experiencing the temperature, the Sczyphamek's every movement was accompanied by some muscle burning in discomfort. Her sweat froze. Frostbite was at hand. And so was temptation. It took every ounce of will not to call upon her Elemental. She needed to conserve her energy.

The cloud did not move and became so thick that Neztríanis could no longer see Timura behind her.

"Timura," she gasped. "Are you… are you there?"

There was no response, but after a few seconds, Neztríanis heard a purring sound.

"I am here," the feline wheezed.

The ascent was punishment to the already injured témo. Neztríanis decided that every five minutes she would extend her aura around herself and her companion for half a minute. She hoped the act would keep both of them from freezing to death and that she could maintain such an Elemental display throughout the climb.

The cloud passed, and the weary Sczyphamek took in the scenic view to her south. Pike Metropolis seemed so small; she could not even see the Triple Skyrises anymore.

Only five hours of sunlight remained, and there was no place for them to stop and rest. If they did not enter the cave by nightfall, neither would survive the night. The two moons were rising, and without regret, Neztríanis cursed the sky and the seasons.

Gazing down at Timura, she witnessed the unhindered fatigue of her partner. Timura's exhaustion was not due to any flaw in the témo's physical conditioning, but rather to the limitations of life. Timura was massive and required more air than the daughter of Hopha. However, breathable air grew thinner and thinner the higher they climbed. That Timura had climbed to their present location was beyond amazing.

The feline would not be deterred. She had seen her mate and cub killed at the hands of Vicious. Her kind was nearly cadaverous. After such losses, she would never fear her own death. Qeauríyx had stripped that natural inclination away from her. The témo growled and reached even deeper into her qanín and ascended upward and upward to a realm of cynical consciousness and chthonic elevation, a realm of heavenly dissatisfaction.

Six hours later, only a sliver of sunlight remained. As they neared the fissure, the duo began the ebbing flow towards death. The rocks were slippery, and the air was chimerical. Every breath became a sadistic tease, like being given a bead of water when one was utterly dehydrated.

Whether through her Elemental or numbness, Neztríanis became somewhat accustomed to the temperature. The Sczyphamek continued to extend her aura around Timura so that the témo would not freeze to death. After the fourth hour of that exercise, the effort became more exhausting each time she conjured it.

Flying was out of the question. The winds were so erratic and powerful, one would be swept away only to be hurled back toward the jagged rocks.

Neztríanis' fingernails dug into the icy stone, and she pulled herself aloft. More clouds returned, and snow now fell at a heavy clip. A wrong move would hurry their journey to death. Timura was behind her, panting irregularly. The témo had to be cumbered beyond belief because even the daughter of Hopha was worn, and she was less than half the témo's weight.

Finally, her Elemental displayed the signs of impuissance.

"Ti-… Timura," Nez gasped. "We are very close."

Covered in wet snow, Timura nodded in affirmation. Her canines chattered, and her whiskers were iced over.

The next ten minutes were excruciating. The climb was vertical. Gravity was real. The winds were insatiable. Irritable snowflakes blew into the témo's eyes and stung them. Sensing Timura's core temperature drop rapidly, Neztríanis allowed her aura to fully blossom around her partner. The témo was a warrior. Timura was unwilling to let Neztríanis worry about her until the last possible moment, if at all.

Climbing and extending her aura while in desolate air demanded considerable effort, and Neztríanis' Elemental strained beside her. Her qanín felt as if it was ripping under the strenuous conditions. She nearly lost consciousness, but summoned enough energy to continue the ascent of despair.

"Arrrrghh!" She grimaced, stretched her arm out, and lifted herself to a small indentation on the mountain's side.

Timura scampered up behind her, but suddenly lost her footing. Frantically moving her front legs and trying to latch onto anything that could support her weight, the témo slid down the mountainside.

Instinctively and without regard to her own body, Neztríanis grabbed Timura's front paws although her claws were still protracted. Ignoring the pain as the crooks tore into and through her palms, Neztríanis hoisted the témo up to her position, using most of her remaining strength. The young woman's hands were bleeding, but they were so numb, she could barely feel any pain from the wounds themselves. Wickedly and obligingly, the cold air pricked them.

Her fingernails were black from grit, and her face was covered in snow and dust. The Sczyphamek was thirsty. She reached for her water bottle, but the water inside was frozen. Timura hyperventilated and wheezed. Her large trunk shivered uncontrollably, and she was too weak to say anything.

"Fá... Fá... atoño..." Neztríanis tried to chant in order to beckon her Elemental, but she was too fatigued and grew colder by the second. Her skin blanched, and she nearly fainted. They needed real shelter or they would freeze to death in minutes. She leaned back in the indentation and sat down. There was hardly enough room for both of them to fit.

Examining the face of the rock, the Sczyphamek saw a crack. She put her hand over the fissure and felt air blowing out of it. The air caused an even greater stabbing sensation on her palms. Balling up her hand, a tight yellow-orange flame emanated around it. She drew her fist back. And with what remaining energy she had, the daughter of Hopha bashed her hand into the glacial stone.

Whimpering in pain, the Sczyphamek's right hand broke along with the sizzling rock, which revealed a passageway into a cave. With nothing left to give, Neztríanis passed out. In great affliction herself, Timura slithered to the opening, grabbed Neztríanis by her collar with her teeth, and dragged her into the cave.

It was only slightly warmer than outside. They needed to move further into the mountain's belly in order to have any respite. Even if it cost Timura her life, she would give Neztríanis a chance to survive. For five excruciating minutes, the témo tugged the Sczyphamek and pulled her limp body away from the outside until she could go no further, falling unconscious.

Neztríanis' head lay next to the mouth of the témo. The Myanín breathed dangerously short breaths.

CHAPTER SEVENTEEN: A TRAGIC CONTAGION

17 Namíz, 241 OGI
Kazlé

She sat alone in the room. Blue Rapier had overtaken two-fifths of Anzél in a little over three durations. They were ahead of schedule.

Schedule... Plans... Ideas...

They were nothing more than illusions. When height, width, length, time, and qanín interrelated, one could only pray and forge ahead anyhow.

The house Feolenz commandeered for her did not disappoint. Even in the midst of ruins and dilapidation, the Commandant found the best accommodations. Old Flint was tireless and micromanaged every battle, surrender, and victory. His war plan was ingenious. With allies such as him, the cause had the possibility of fulfillment. She just had to lower or destroy other competing possibilities.

Sad and alone in thought, she tapped her finger on the table rapidly. The woman glanced at the imperial headdress, battle outfit, and sword, all used by her grandmother so many cycles ago. Covered in an elegant dark purple robe, Késhal pulled her hair back into a double tail.

Two Sczyphameks. *Two...*

She was as unsurprised as Vincallous, whom she missed more with each passing day. But if their own stories taught them anything, it was that nothing was impossible.

The report she just received from ju Xaníz was more detailed than the message sent by the Eradicate some time ago. Késhal was most intrigued by the slave, Anámn. Though distant and lowly, he was still family. He was a descendant of her grandmother, Sczyphamek Imperial.

How was that possible? It threw out every orthodox assumption and convention.

Sczyphameks were not known to bequeath their powers to their offspring or genetically. They were chosen by the elements. Pre-Eminent was the first recorded Sczyphamek who was a direct descendant from

301

another. Outwardly, Késhal professed this to be a sign from the Nameless One. Inwardly, she believed her Sczyphamek lineage was a random phenomenon. At some point, the aberration was *bound* to happen. But Alzhexph's son was now an Elemental warrior. And like it or not, he *too* was Imperial's grandson, four generations down. Something strange was happening. She needed Anámn found and brought to her so that she might speak to him and his Elemental.

Knowing her consort, Vincallous was probably combing Nez Spirita relentlessly for the other Sczyphamek, Neztríanis. His premonition was correct. All of the cycles they had invested in training would yield them an insurmountable advantage.

It was no mere coincidence that Anámn and Neztríanis emerged around the same time. If she captured Anámn she might be able to convince him to join Vincallous and her. However, the fact that a Phmquedrian slave was a Sczyphamek was alarming. His hate for her and Tannódin might be too strong, and understandably so. If that were the case she would have to kill him. That the Nez Spiritan and témo would be her enemies was a foregone conclusion. She needed no intelligence to confirm her intuition.

She hesitated. Maybe she was wrong… after all, was not Van once an enemy of Tannódin? Nothing was impossible, if only improbable…

***

Her parents were torn. On the one hand, Vincallous was one of the most honored Secondaries in White Scythe. There was even talk of him becoming the next General Maximum. On the other, it became increasingly clear that he and Késhal were growing enamored with one another. Her extended family and Tannódin'é nobility were also suspicious of the Damüdan and believed he courted Késhal for his own personal ambitions. Her parents had commanded their imperial spies to check on Fierce's background; however, they got no further than his appearance into Blue Rapier when he was nineteen.

The tension only worsened because of Fierce's standoffishness. The Damüdan did not acknowledge her parents unless they spoke to him first, which they found extremely disrespectful. And when Vincallous did speak, it was with the tiniest shred of grace and respect. In addition and when time permitted, he and Késhal would disappear for weeks without leaving any clue to their whereabouts. The pair easily escaped the agents assigned to them. Her parents did not know that the couple trained together on the uninhabited continent of Meve, and when they were not training, they constantly expressed their love romantically, sexually, and passionately.

"Why do you not tell my parents that you are a Sczyphamek?" Késhal asked him one day while being held in his arms.

They were on the eastern shore of the fractured continent of Meve. In the distance, the sea churned heartlessly. The five giant whirlpools that happened as the Infinite Deep whirred and caused a strong wind to blow onshore. Késhal and Vincallous were dressed in White Scythe black battle fatigues, made in Phmquedria. Their uniforms were soiled, tattered, and charred. They sparred against one another for four consecutive hours at least twice a day. The Sczyphameks had grown quite proficient in combining their abilities to wield even greater displays of Elemental power.

"Why do you always ask that, Késhal?" Vincallous replied irritatingly. "I told you; I will tell them when I am ready. They think I am a threat and not 'worthy' of courting you. They would order my death if they knew how involved we really are."

"My parents are a bit haughty, but that was uncalled for." She was dismayed and personally insulted. "You are exaggerating. The House of Kaz does not participate in unmerited murder."

Vincallous loosened his hold on her and moved away. His black hair flapped and he fixed his gaze towards the sand on the beach, in a doomed attempt to dam his cresting anger and sadness.

Even though they had known each other over a cycle, Késhal still wished she could read his emotions. She could not feel what he was thinking, even when she knew he was distressed.

"What is wrong, Vincallous?" she asked. "Did I say something to upset you?"

"No," he lied. Trying to change the subject, he redirected, "I will be gone for quite some time on this next assignment…"

"Why do you do this?" She grimaced, stared at the sand, and pulled him towards her. "You know I love you. You know I care for you deeply. I would never do anything to harm you."

Vincallous was unable to keep two tears from trickling down his face. It was true. She would not hurt him. But she was *stronger*. She did love him. Yet she happened as the beautiful spawn of a violent contagion that destroyed his life.

Why could he not escape?

He wanted to keep his distance after they met for the first time.

He tried.

But somehow he found himself desiring to see her again. And every time he convinced himself to end the relationship, she appeared and looked at him with her incomparable maroon eyes.

Why did he allow himself to be caught in such a mundane, yet gripping cycle? This was the stuff of dreams and childish fantasy. Was there a chance for a "happy" ending? He knew better than that. His life was a testimony to the lie he continued to live. Qeauríyx permitted neither endings nor happiness.

He wiped his eyes, turned to Késhal, and looked at her with melancholy care.

She blushed in attraction. Even sad, Vincallous was still striking. "When are we going to talk about what has harmed you?"

"Not today," he quipped.

The waves washed on the beach.

Vincallous stepped back. "Are you ready?"

"Yes."

"Fá'atoño má!" they chanted together.

Their auras emerged, red and purple. The ground cracked and careened, and the ocean receded. The rush of calling forth one's Elemental never grew old.

"What are we doing this time?" he asked, wrapped in a red haze.

"We have used our Elemental abilities all week. Let's concentrate on flight and speed."

"Good idea," he said. "Let's race to the other side of the continent, through the volcanic lines, with no help from our Elementals."

"That is fine." Her purple aura pulsated calmly. As they levitated, ready to begin the competition, Késhal nudged closer to Fierce and put her hand on his shoulder. "Tell me the truth, do you embrace that I love you?"

"I do," he answered. Then, Vincallous took a purposeful chance that would bind him for cycles to come. "Késhal, I know I do not... I love you too," he said clumsily. "Please believe and trust me."

Pre-Eminent was speechless. She knew that he loved her, but he never said the words because he was so guarded. She nodded in affirmation, drew close to her partner, and they kissed lovingly. After which, she moved back into position.

"You give the word," he said.

"Now."

Their auras caused a local disturbance, and within a flash, they were off.

***

It was very early in the 221st cycle of Global Initiative. Késhal's father had died four durations prior. Her mother, Phenicia,[1] although still a strong leader, would soon be buried with her husband and her parents in the Imperial Catacombs. Power would be handed to Késhal in half a cycle. Her mother pressed her to cut ties with Fierce, claiming that they knew too little about him. Phenicia was right.

Vincallous had been deployed since her father's passing, and Késhal could stand it no longer. She needed to discover his true identity. He kept her at bay for three cycles and still had not told her parents that he was a Sczyphamek. She felt torn between her obligations as the future leader of Global Initiative and her love for Fierce. She wanted to pledge herself to him. But she was unsure about his motivations, though she was certain he loved her.

---

[1] Phenicia (fin-ih-see-uh)

Yet, her suspicion was not only directed at Vincallous. Over the cycles, Késhal became increasingly critical of some of her mother and father's foreign and domestic policies. She inspected the reports—reports that revealed malicious practices by every sector of Global Initiative. She also realized that Fierce was being sent on remoter and more dangerous missions, which if the trend continued, would eventually lead to his death if he did not use his powers. When she confronted her parents about both of these issues, she was told that her thinking was "juvenile" and "petty." Was that the reaction Vincallous feared? Her parents had concealed many of their decisions, and it was obvious they did not place their full confidence in her. She was an excellent fighter, but they doubted her ability to lead.

She performed her own investigation and learned that questionable operations had taken place in Damüda when she was just a child. It was no secret that many Damüdans felt discontentment toward Tannódin'é. Although they fought and died with the Tannódin'é, Damüdans were still treated as second-class soldiers and citizens. Moreover, there were rampant grumblings of Tannódin'é entitlement and unwarranted meddling in Damüdan affairs.

Késhal wondered if Vicious was using her to lead a Damüdan rebellion against Tannódin. But she had no proof and felt she was being too pessimistic. Késhal was ever the optimist. Negativity never found a permanent home in her qanín. Damüdans were her allies and should be treated as such. Global Initiative was for every person on the planet. It was unfortunate that many did not see this and required violent conversion. However, Damüdans were not just another people. They were centuries-long of the Tannódin'é. When she ascended to the throne, she wanted to make sure that she reestablished good ties with the continent and its leaders.

Traveling to Fierce's homeland presented her with a good opportunity to investigate Vincallous' past and Tannódin's role in Damüda. If she was lucky, the two would coincide and she would be able to reconcile both.

She effortlessly snuck away from Megaphyx Bonicin, made her way to Damüda, yet maintained an unbreakable empathic link with her mother in case she fell gravely ill. Phenicia was accustomed to her daughter's excursions and had to attend to more urgent matters. There were rumors of a massive attack against Global Initiative by Miska Kea. In response, Phenicia deployed a loose network of spies throughout the planet to find out any information pertaining to the plan. So far, the spies had gathered no useful information, and those that did never returned to Tannódin.

For three cycles, Miska Kea designed, planned, and implemented an attack on Tannódin's own soil. The plan was patient and ingenious. Durations before the attack, the rebels amassed a fleet located in the southernmost islands of the Memory Ridge Archipelago, which ran from Zorét through Tannódin and down towards the South Pole. Once the fleet had assembled, they moved up the islands, surreptitiously and carefully. At the time, the resistance group flooded Qeauríyx with disinformation. Every once in a while, they would act upon the spurious intelligence to keep Tannódin and Damüda guessing.

In 221 OGI, the House of Kaz was engaged in a two front battle: Miska Kea and Bryce. Bryce had long been a pest to Tannódin; it was the only continent in the eastern hemisphere Tannódin had not completely subdued. Bryce was sparsely populated in many places, which granted ample occasions for guerilla tactics. It was also the oldest continent on the planet, full of the most stubborn, reclusive, ill-tempered wretches Qeauríyx ever created—so said Phenicia.

Fighting both Miska Kea and Bryce spread Global Initiative forces terribly thin. Enlistment was down, outside of the mandated conscription. There were even signs that Tannódin was losing its foothold and dominance in Nez Spirita.

The soon-to-be Empress was going to inherit a host of problems, and Késhal wanted to make sure she would not lose the support of Tannódin's closest ally, Damüda. Her mother was foolish to believe Tannódin could govern Qeauríyx by and for themselves—so thought Késhal. And yet, the daughter respected and loved her mother dearly.

Phenicia had instructed Késhal concerning the latter's training, and it was the former's efforts that granted Pre-Eminent's Awakening. But their bond ran even deeper than instruction. Phenicia was Sczyphamek Imperial's only daughter, and Késhal was Phenicia's only child. Imperial birthed children well beyond the childbearing cycles of a normal nel'asmív, since she was a Sczyphamek. In fact, she had six sons by three consorts. Phenicia was the daughter of her fourth and last partner. Though Imperial cherished her sons, the creator of Global Initiative always wanted a daughter. Késhal hailed from a line of strong matriarchs and would never tarnish their legacy.

Pre-Eminent flew to Damüda unaccompanied and donned a more casual set of clothes worn by "common" folk. She set out with a pack of supplies, credits, and food in tow. Vincallous said that he was from northern Damüda, but that was undoubtedly fabrication. The easternmost portion of the continent had a history of raucous behavior, so she made her way there. Spies visited those lands as well, but turned up nothing. She was unsurprised. The spies were Tannódin'é. How could a Tannódin'é gather information from people they refused to mingle with in friendship and respect?

She planned to speak to and live among some of the locals for two and a half durations, all the while using her empathic abilities to understand how the everyday Damüdan (from the continent's most disruptive district) responded to questions about Tannódin. Their experience would be a great barometer for the rest of the continent.

Believing her to be a spy (her features were definitively of Tannódin), the Damüdans were distrustful of her. They were generally and genuinely afraid of the House of Kaz. Why would Damüdans possess *brazen* fear and distrust towards their allies? Within two durations of travel, she realized why.

Reportedly, Blue Rapier performed an operation in the town of Nosgüth nearly twenty-five cycles prior, and in the aftermath, many "instigators"—those Damüdans against Tannódin in rhetoric only—disappeared and were not seen again. Neither Nosgüth nor these other incidents were known to Késhal. She did not recall her parents or the Daknín talking about it. She almost dismissed the Damüdans' claims. But every person who talked to her (or avoided talking to her about it) *believed* something had happened. Their emotions did not lie. As an empath, the Sczyphamek learned that dismissing a person's emotions led to unimaginable folly, for feelings were a major component of all motivation, understanding, and existence.

Kaz Késhal Supreme made her way to Nosgüth slowly and deliberately, to such an extent that she got to know folk from the Damüdan countryside and grew enamored with them. They possessed many of Vincallous' sensibilities. Her empathic abilities allowed her to assess and understand people quicker than the average nel'asmív, although, like Fierce, some folk were impervious to her abilities.

Her element of empathy screamed and moaned the moment she neared Nosgüth's outskirts. The city was deserted. An undeniable sorrow and anger tarried. A terrible blood had been spilled. The southeastern Damüdans had spoken the truth.

The streets were silent, and the houses deserted. Késhal searched for at least one nel'asmív, but she sensed none. Even the wildlife remained in the hills. She passed a clearing that should have contained houses and an intersection. Instead, there was a flattened piece of land and a large mound.

Késhal would not reject what was so obviously true; it was a mass grave.

Her Elemental tugged her, and she followed. A tragic contagion lured her empathic element to a particular house. While walking, she noticed distinct burst patterns, and although they were old, they could only be attributed to Blue Rapier's custom AEARs.

Suddenly, she stopped. Késhal detected Vicious' qanín, even though he was in Phmquedria on assignment.

How?

She knew the answer, but she did not want to concede the truth. With each step, she placed more and more distance between herself, her mother, and her grandmother. With each step, the angelic Global Initiative she idolized transmogrified into a demon of the Drift.

She wanted to turn back. She wanted to close off her feelings. Her sheltered existence demanded retreat.

The refrain of her progenitors bade her to remain silent and turn around.

Bury it deep. Close it down. Shut it out. Forget it forever. Leave it alone.
Her legacy was at stake. Global Initiative would not be the same if she continued. Walking this path required her to rethink the history she knew was a myth and might be a lie.
Bury it deep. Close it down. Shut it out. Forget it forever. Leave it alone.
But the wound in Nosgüth was still open. Qeauríyx would not keep quiet.
Bury it deep. Close it down. Shut it out. Forget it forever. Leave it alone.
"No," she whispered. "I love Vincallous, and I want to know the truth. I cannot bury this. I must know what happened."

Tears poured from her maroon eyes as she took slow steps towards Van Fénüra's house. The aroma of the contagion was an intoxicating desolation. She no longer felt his misery alone. There were at least a hundred other miseries, and the misery was not of adults. No, they were childlike and adolescent. These were the wails of little ones.

Something dreadful and appalling happened in Nosgüth, and Vincallous was there when it happened. She could *feel* him.

Was it because he left it there—he left his feelings in the ruins of Nosgüth? Did he leave his feelings for the contagion to devour? The capacity for sadness was related to the capacity for happiness. In other words, Késhal had learned that successfully reading emotions was only possible when all ranges of emotions were present. Vincallous had left all of his grief and happiness in the house and in the city.

She felt apprehensive about entering into the dwelling, but she had come too far to turn back. She stepped through the front door and inspected the dilapidated structure. Dust reigned, and the hardwood floor squeaked and crunched under her feet. She pulled her hood back. Her eyes glimpsed upon a small chair, overturned and wrapped in cobwebs.

His ache was there. He returned there very recently. She felt a small trace of his Elemental signature.

What happened?

Why did he even involve himself with her?

More pressing than those questions, she realized—with no attempt to hide the truth—he hated her parents. They were ultimately responsible, were they not? The event happened under their watch and they gave approval for its execution.

Yet Vincallous joined Blue Rapier; yet he participated in Global Initiative...

To what end?

***

A knock on the door jarred her from remembrance.
"Empress."
Old Flint.
Pre-Eminent wiped the teardrops from her face. "One moment."

The co-leader of Global Initiative sauntered towards the door of the house and opened it. The commandant's beard was so long and white, it made the woman smirk every time she saw it. A'reznu entered the abode, wearing the same uniform he always wore. It was a longstanding joke that the leader of Blue Rapier probably slept in his uniform. When Késhal closed the door, the old man turned and bowed reverently to the Empress.

Késhal blushed in embarrassment. "Feolenz, I told you that you under no obligation to bow."

"I want to," his elderly, yet strong voice replied. "May I sit for a few moments, Empress?"

"I am in one of those moods," the woman said. "Call me Késhal, please."

The old man made some face, which was probably a smile, but because of his sideburns, beard, and wrinkled forehead, it was hard to interpret any of his facial expressions. "I suppose being called your title grows as weary as I am."

"You are not weary. You rode into battle with your soldiers during the last fight. I heard what you and the rapier did."

Feolenz glanced at his hip, which holstered the rapier, and tapped it caringly. He took the jacketed sword off his waist and sat down in a rocking chair. Supreme turned her chair towards his and smiled. Few nel'asmív were as endearing as A'reznu. She could always sense his emotions. Appropriately nicknamed, Old Flint happened as a rock. His faith in Global Initiative was unshakable, yet measured. The wise man had seen more than his fair share of battles and circumstances. He was the sagest of nel'asmív in the eyes of Késhal.

"I can tell you want to be alone right now," he said. "So I will make this quick as I can. We've found the hideouts of both Lywa and Cálo, leaders of the Focalites and Anmetrians respectively. The Eradicate confirmed this information and sent it to me within the last hour."

"Good. We may have an opportunity to end the conflict in Anzél. Capture them and bring them to me."

Feolenz's bushy eyebrows raised in interest. "You do not want them killed? They have joined forces since our arrival…"

"No. They are more valuable to us alive, and we should never kill anyone unless it is absolutely necessary. If I can convince them to join us, then they can add to our numbers when we finally fight against Líachim, and Aphaz in particular."

"Most wise. That is most wise," the commandant agreed. "I will see to it."

"How many have we lost so far, Old Flint?"

"Nearly three thousand have died and four thousand have been wounded from our ranks."

Késhal shook her head. "This battle with Líachim must be decisive. We cannot lose and we must send a message. We have been at war for over two hundred cycles. It must end. Too many have lost their lives. Too, too many…"

The old man looked at the Empress the way a proud parent gazes upon a successful child. "Késhal, you are a wonderful leader, greater than your mother and grandmother.

"Yes, we have been at war, but both Nez Spirita and Bryce have significantly drawn down their hostility towards us. Phmquedria continues to evolve out of its backwardness, which is at least half our fault. And our relationship with Damüda could not be stronger.

"War and death can take their toll on anyone. But do not undervalue what you have accomplished. Imperial and Phenicia would be proud of you."

"Thank you, Old Flint," the Sczyphamek said. "Alert me when you have captured those two. I want to speak to them myself."

The elder rose from his chair. The Empress stood up, waiting for him to bow, but he did not.

Instead, he walked past her and said, "Vincallous will soon be here. I know that will make things a bit better for you. You always seem happier when you are in his company. If there is any decision that you should feel confident in, it was your decision to pledge yourself to him." The chief of Blue Rapier opened the door and said, "When they are captured, you will be notified." At that, he closed the door.

Késhal stood and stared blankly at the walls. Feolenz did not know how hard of a decision it was…

***

When Késhal returned to Tannódin after her trip to Damüda, she arrived with the news that her mother had taken ill. Pre-Eminent took on more responsibilities, and prepared herself for the throne of leadership.

Though she had been back for nearly a duration, she still would not let herself think about Nosgüth. She was certain that she had to undo the damage her parents' administration had done to Damüdan/Tannódin'é relations. However, she did not share these sentiments or any of her other revelations with her mother or with any of her advisers.

In mid-autumn 221 OGI, Vincallous finished a grueling tour of duty and traveled to Civix Setrin to see Késhal. The moment Vicious arrived, he knew something was wrong. There were no guards on duty by her quarters, she did not meet him at the skyport, and he had received no word from her in over three durations.

When Vincallous closed the door to her room, Késhal would not make eye contact with him and kept her distance. She did not know where the conversation would lead. Though Vicious was unarmed, Pre-Eminent's sword strafed her back in plain sight, and her right hand stayed close to its hilt.

Vincallous drew close to her, and she instinctively recoiled. Even she did not understand her revulsion.

"What is it? Why are you armed?" he asked. His wariness was palpable. "I know I have not been—"

"I do not know who or what you are Vincallous!" Késhal screamed, unable to contain herself. She had been holding in the angst of betrayal, fear, and imperial pressure for too long. "I doubt that is even your real name."

"My name..." Vincallous' distress turned into defensiveness. "What has my 'real name' to do with this?"

"I went to Damüda," she confessed. "I went to the eastern lands. I was told about Nosgüth."

He did not feign ignorance and whispered, "Did you go there?"

She nodded.

"*You went there?*" He raised his voice. "Who told you to go there? What gives you the right to go there? What gives you the right to question me about Nosgüth?"

Késhal was silent. She remembered the pain of the boy, who was now the man standing before her.

"I felt your misery," she cried. "I felt—I can feel your hurt... It was there in your old house..."

"You hypocritical cléth." Vincallous' long-repressed venom emerged, and he moved towards Késhal, intending to strike her—repeatedly. "How dare you go into the place where they killed them! And you come here and question me about who I am? And now you draw away from me as if I have participated in 'unmerited murder.'"

Vincallous raised his hand to slap then punch her, but his arm grew heavy. Pre-Eminent had created a local gravitational pull on his arm. She had reopened an unfathomable wound on Fierce. He would have never allowed his guard to drop or his Elemental to wane in such a manner unless he was completely distracted.

"Why did you go there?" The Damüdan trembled in anger. "I convinced myself that I'd let them die. Your father passed away and I lay not a hand on his damned body. I hope that he is in Qalfocx and gynix, that irredeemable piece of kíma."

Késhal gasped. "What... what did you say?"

"It is obvious that your mother finally convinced you. Then you are just like her now; are you not? Cold, calculating, with some self-righteous attitude of omniscience... *They were right...*" His gray Damüdan eyes burned against her, and his aura emanated. His grimace was callous and unafraid. "Késhal leave now, before I kill you too. I see now that I should have not allowed my emotions—this foolish love—to get in the way."

"I cannot let you kill my mother." Késhal's purple aura asserted itself.

"Then I suppose we are at an impasse."

His eyes conveyed the gravity of his conviction. He was willing to kill her if it meant getting to her mother.

"We do not have to do this."

"Yes, we do."

"What about Reníz?"

Van's face, for a moment, softened, and his eyes wavered. But he brought Zorschwin, Nosgüth, the témos, and his parents to mind. Within a blink of an eye, his countenance returned to insatiable resentment and measured vengeance. *"Do not bring her into this...* One of us will be left to care for her, and that's all she needs."

"Please, Vincallous," Pre-Eminent reiterated caringly while dropping her aura. "Please tell me what happened."

"Raise your aura, Késhal. Because after I tell you, you will know that I will try everything in my power to kill her then you, and I will not hold back."

He was not lying. His emotions, for the first time, were completely open.

"In 197 OGI, your parents approved Nosgüth to be wiped out. Blue Rapier paratroopers landed, and everyone in the city engaged them for quite some time. But they were patient and held the town under siege for durations. Soon they moved borough to borough, killing any person that stood in their way."

His gray eyes became charred yellow. "They killed everyone except the children. They brutalized and raped my mother in front of my eyes for fifteen minutes, while my father and I were forced to watch. Finally, she collapsed and died. Every time my father tried to step in, they would hit him on the head with the butt of their energy rifles, and would say, 'you are going to get yours soon enough.'"

His red aura thickened. "They laughed as they tortured my father. They shot his feet, bound him by the hands, struck him, raped, and castrated him. All the while he told me he loved me and not to worry. After twenty minutes, he stopped moving. The soldiers continued to kick him in the head and in the chest."

Tears gushed down his face, but Késhal wept more than he. Yet, Van Fénüra was unmoved by her sympathy. His Elemental had been aroused to heights of violent anticipation.

"I did not recognize him after they were done. I did not recognize myself. I was only a child, damn it! But I was not the only one. Ninety other children befell the same fate. Blue Rapier was ordered to target the leaders of the community and make them suffer for their rebellion. If children were there, they were supposed to watch and be spared out of 'mercy.' But there is no mercy for those who are weak. Even the little we had was taken from us.

"There were other children in the village but they were killed. Tannódin needed survivors to tell the story so that Damüdans would not try to arise against them again. But who would fully believe the tales of children? So the story became more myth than truth, and once the myth drew ample circulation and fear, Tannódin killed anyone who told the truth or corroborated our story. Of the children that survived, I am the only one alive. Most took their own lives after their parents were killed, a small few found more productive suicides and killed a few soldiers who had defaced and murdered our parents.

"My goal was clear. I would kill the parents of those who killed my parents. *Your parents*. I let your father die a natural death, but your mother deserves what my mother had to endure. I'm going to bloody that imperial whore. There's no point in holding back anymore."

Késhal dropped to her knees. Her aura flickered and soon dissipated. She wept. She loved her mother and Vincallous, yet it was undeniable that her parents were ultimately responsible for Vicious' suffering. As a leader, difficult decisions came with the position, but her mother and father had crossed the line by approving that sort of homicidal measure.

Was this the legacy they would bequeath to her? Was this how Global Initiative happened? *Allies should not be enemies*. On the same token, she would not allow herself to be killed; she was from the House of Kaz and destined to promulgate Global Initiative.

Vincallous walked past Késhal, heading towards Phenicia's quarters. His aura was oppressive. It was just about as strong as hers. When and how did that happen?

"What is your real name?"

"Van Fénüra."

Késhal rose and wiped the tears from her eyes. "Van, I will help you. I will help you kill my mother."

"I am not ignorant. You do not expect me—"

Her eyes were resolute. She was not bluffing. "I told you. I love you and I will never harm you. But you must promise me that you will never harm Global Initiative."

"Global Initiative?" he asked in bewilderment. "What has that to do with this?"

"Everything," she said. "The policies of Global Initiative must change if it is to be successful, and when I become Empress, you and I will make sure to institute those changes. But Global Initiative is more important than either of us. I cannot allow you to destroy it for the sake of vengeance. Even you cannot deny that it has improved the lives of millions. I will not deny that it has caused grievous injuries in the process, but we can change that together. Certainly, you have seen its positive potential."

"I have." He made the confession regrettably. "But, Késhal, I cannot ask you to—"

"You do not have to. This is what must be done."

"Are you doing this for me or for Global Initiative?" he asked, demanding an answer.

"I am doing this for both and hating myself in the process."

"You do not have to do this."

"*Oh, yes*. Yes I do. *No one* is above Global Initiative. *No one.* This task was given to us by the Nameless One and Qeauríyx." She turned and faced him directly. "Van, no person will ever come before you when it comes to my love, but Global Initiative must be continued, no matter the cost."

She clasped his hands and drew close to him. "Am I not to suffer the loss that you have? Am I supposed to ask my people, our people, to do something I myself am unwilling to do? A leader should never ask a subordinate to do something she is unwilling to do."

"You have not taken a life before," Fénüra objected. "Do not—"

"No more," she commanded. "No more. When we are pledged to each other you can do what you feel like, but at this moment, I outrank you, Vincallous Fierce."

When they arrived at her mother's chambers, some strangeness pressed upon Vincallous' heart: an inevitable weight that still felt escapable.

Késhal opened the doors to the immaculate room, which was filled with art, antiques, and books that dated back to the Ancient Orality. Phenicia's chamber was the finest expression of what Tannódin had to offer to the world. The empress lay on her back, coughing and wheezing. Késhal took slow steps towards the woman who gave her life, the woman who taught her how to use her powers even though she herself was not a Sczyphamek. Her mother helped her learn how to govern. Phenicia and her father protected her and loved her. Phenicia was the daughter of one of the most awesome Sczyphameks to have ever walked Qeauríyx. Késhal trembled intractably as she took small paces towards her chénala and genesis.

"Késhal," Phenicia called out lovingly, "are you there?"

"Yes, mother," she replied. "Vincallous is with me."

Her mother gasped in disbelief. "He *is*?"

Vincallous kept quiet but eyed Késhal intently. He had made up in his mind that he would kill both of them if Késhal did not act.

"How could you approve the destruction of Nosgüth?" Pre-Eminent spoke without pretense. "Why did you let Blue Rapier commence with that attack?"

"Nosgüth..." Phenicia's voice matched her daughter's openness. "Hmmmm... That was Imperial Order 531, I believe. All records of that operation were destroyed. How did you find out about that?" Turning on a lamp next to her bed, she sat up wearily. "Vincallous, was it you? Did you tell her?"

Again, Fénüra remained quiet.

"I went there, Mamisí," the Sczyphamek answered. "How could you and father approve such a measure?"

"*Approve*? I did not approve it. It was my idea, and I gave the order personally, over the objections of Feolenz." She smiled sarcastically. "That was the first of three times that lowly man has ever disobeyed or objected to my orders. The Eighty-Second General Maximum had to coordinate the attack."

"What?" Vincallous grunted. His aura emerged, and it was ferocious, albeit controlled. "*You gave the order to have my mother and father killed?*"

"So that is where you are from!" the old woman said with interest. "That is why we could not find out who you were. *And you are a Sczyphamek?* We would have killed you sooner if we knew that. We hoped that you would have died as a martyr on those suicide missions we kept sending you on. Your death was clearly merited. But now I see why you survived."

Késhal's cosmovision continued to crumble by the hand of Phenicia's dispassionate logic. "How can you say that to him?"

"You will not let him kill me, daughter. He is a threat to everything we have worked for. I have felt this for quite some time, but his work was excellent. And earlier in his career, he was more useful to us alive. I may not be a Sczyphamek, but I do not fear him."

The daughter frowned at her mother. "Why did you give such an immoral order?"

"Immoral?" Phenicia chuckled in irritation. "Morality has nothing to do with this. Morality is used to control the peons and to give their life purpose, but the rulers cannot be and have never been bound by such constraints.

"Global Initiative is more important that morality, and it was more important than some children or Damüdan families. It is more important than some obstinate villagers in Damüda. Their kind deserved to die. The children should have been happy we did not kill them, but they were of such weak character that they killed themselves. Well, all but one it appears…

"We thought we had accounted for all of the children, but you slipped through the cracks."

My mother cannot be this cruel, thought Késhal. *She cannot be this evil… There had to be a reason… This cannot be how Global Initiative has happened… This changes everything… I've been sheltered from reality… I am weak…*

Vincallous looked at Késhal and powered down. A strange feeling beset him. He was no empath, but he saw the emotional torment on her face. He did not know what made him angrier, the fact that her mother had killed his parents or that she was harming her daughter's innocence, both done unrepentantly.

Little by little, Pre-Eminent's aura began to emanate and grow. "Damüda is our ally. If they were rebelling, then they should have been brought to trial as citizens of Global—"

"*Tannódin is Global Initiative!* We are Tannódin'é!" her mother yelled with her remaining strength. "Staxis, you have always been weak-minded and insufferably compassionate. I should not be surprised. You displayed your ineptitude the moment you brought that promiscuous commoner into our house. Staxis. You soiled the House of Kaz for the sake of some pedestrian, slack prostitute from the Windward Islands."

Pre-Eminent gasped. Her purple aura flashed then retreated. "You will not refer to Reníz in that manner again, *Phenicia*," Késhal warned. "She is our legacy."

"Legacy? Whose legacy? This is about preserving our legacy, maintaining our way of life, and making sure that Qeauríyx follows the same. I have always worried that you would not be up to the challenge of being the Empress of such an empire. Difficult decisions are required if you happen as a leader and your resolve must never falter, even if the masses paint you as evil.

"Imperial would be ashamed of your spinelessness. I tried to raise you like my mother raised me. However, your strength is not in leadership, but in being led. And since you are unfit to lead, listen to me. Kill Vincallous, *now.*"

Késhal beheld Vincallous, then her mother, and drew her sword. Vicious gazed at Pre-Eminent intently. She was truly about to kill the one who had given her life.

"Goodbye, mother." Tears pricked her maroon eyes. Her mouth quivered, and her hand shook.

"*What are you doing?*" her mother asked in a state of shock. "You would raise your hand against me?"

"My hand and this knife," she retorted. "This is neither the Global Initiative I believe in nor the one I will lead. I am only upset that it took this long for you to be judged by your own standards and that Vincallous is killing a woman far past her prime when his mother was taken from him when she was probably more than half your age."

The Tannódin'é Sczyphamek straightened her body and resolve radiated from her purple aura. Késhal nodded her head and pointed towards the Damüdan Sczyphamek. "Empress Phenicia, I love Vincallous—I love Van Fénüra with everything I possess. I am pledging myself to him and him alone. What is mine will soon be his. And the pain that is his will now become yours."

Vicious rushed to her side and gripped her hand that held the sword, in order to try to take it from her. But her grip was firm, and she shrugged him off.

"No," Phenicia pleaded. "Do not do this. This is wrong. Children should not take the lives of their parents."

Késhal ignored her mother's supplication. "How did they kill your mother, Van? Please, do not lie to me."

Vincallous hesitated in his response and although he did not understand, he choked up. But the emotion was not tied to his pain alone. Finally, Van answered in a low voice, "They slapped her awhile, punched her for three minutes, and kicked her until she died…"

Before Fénüra said another word, Késhal slapped her mother across the face with restraint, so that she would not kill her. Fierce was jarred, but before he could react otherwise, his hand was already delivering the next blow. Phenicia, ill and elderly, screamed in pain. The empathic backlash Pre-Eminent felt was massive, and it caused her to drop the weapon.

"I am your mother," she pleaded, as blood poured out of her mouth and nose.

"You are the killer of his mother," she responded. "Am I strong now? Do you see? I *can* be committed to action."

Késhal grabbed her mother's ankle, squeezed, and crushed it dust, but before her mother could wail, her daughter backhanded her him the jaw. Phenicia nearly passed out from the violence done to her body.

This was not the vengeance Vincallous desired. The remembrance of his mother's death filled his qanín. "Késhal," he whispered. "Stop."

"No. We must make her suffer like your mother did."

"This is enough. Nothing will ever compare to that. She deserves death, not torture. I don't want to happen like her."

He recovered the sword Késhal dropped and looked into the eyes of the woman responsible for the ache—the ache he now realized would never heal. Even as he drew his hand back, Vincallous knew that her death would not grant him the satisfaction he so desired. But, *she had to die*. He felt Késhal's hand grip his, and they stabbed her mother in the chest three times. Phenicia squirmed and yelped with each thrust, but soon, she lay limp and soaked in blood.

Késhal stepped away from the bed. Her eyes were unfettered and mania beset her. The Tannódin'é's body shook so violently that no comfort could be given her. Vincallous did not know what to say or what to do. He saw that his hands were covered in blood, so he retrieved a towel from Phenicia's extravagant bathroom, wet it in a water basin, and wiped his hands. He walked over to Késhal and washed her hands, as she murmured and droned inaudible words.

Suddenly, Késhal yelled at the top of her lungs, fell to her knees, and sobbed bitterly. Vincallous used his Elemental to mute her shriek so as not to alert the imperial guards.

"You know I love you?" She had lost her wits, and grasped and clawed at his body frantically. "Please tell me you love me; please tell me! What did I just do? I killed my mother! Mamisí... Please tell me you know that I would never hurt you... How can I lead? I love you. Please say it. Please tell me you love me, Van..."

Vincallous knelt beside the woman whom he loved more than his own life. He held her closely, ran his fingers through her hair, and gently rubbed her back. "I love you, Késhal. You won't have to do anything like that again. I—"

Before he finished his promise an explosion boomed near the periphery of the city. Vicious used his Elemental to sense the surroundings. "That came from the outskirts of Phenplyacin."

Seconds later sirens sounded and footsteps neared Phenicia's quarters. Késhal and Vincallous stood to their feet and met the contingent outside the murdered matriarch's room before the agents arrived.

"We just gave the Empress a sedative for the night," Pre-Eminent lied. "What is happening?"

The imperial agent was shaken and stuttered, "Reports confirm that Phenplyacin is under attack, Lord Pre-Eminent. We do not know how many troops there are. But, this must be the attack Miska Kea was planning."

"Do not be afraid," she said to him. "Order all our troops in the area to attack, and make sure that our entire coastline is secure. Let no one draw near my mother's estate."

The agent bowed and ran to relay the message. When he had gone a distance, Késhal turned to Vicious, and tears fell down her face again.

"Who do they think they are?" she asked spitefully. "I did not happen as my mother or my grandmother. Why are they forcing my hand? Do they think we will respond lightly?"

"Késhal, are you all right?"

"Remember your promise," she said and looked at Vincallous with great clarity and perception. "Global Initiative must not be harmed."

"Yes," he said.

"I will deal with my mother," she reasoned aloud. "You go to Phenplyacin." She held his hand and her confidence appeared to return. The threat to Global Initiative superseded her own personal hurts. "They underestimated us. They do not know who we are. They do not know we are united. Do not go to battle as General Fierce, but as the Sczyphamek who happened as Vicious."

The Damüdan beheld his love and knew that she was torn, hurt, and confused. But her resolve made him love her all the more.

"Make them pay." Her countenance was stern and dark. "*Make them all pay.*"

"All?" he asked.

"*Everyone.* Our ascension will not be born in weakness. Miska Kea attacked us on our own soil. But Phenicia and Imperial's policies made this day possible. And our forces allowed them to breach Tannódin'é shores.

"Make them pay.

"We Tannódin'é have punished others unjustly. We are self-righteous and have lived with a false sense of security long enough. We have killed people anonymously and without acknowledging their lives as real. Should your wrath and the wrath of Nosgüth's children escape us?

"We deserve retribution.

"And Damüda was not the exception. Surely similar events and murders have taken place in Nez Spirita, Phmquedria, and the Windward Isles... Surely Global Initiative has perpetrated injustice in those lands too...

"For Reníz's sake, make them pay.

"Do whatever it takes to stop this. Do whatever it takes to right the wrongs. Do whatever it takes to let go of the pain. Do whatever it takes to turn Global Initiative in a new direction. Global Initiative is yours as much as it is mine. You can redeem us. You will not need my help. I trust you."

Vincallous' aura emerged, and as it did, Késhal leapt toward him and kissed him. Her kiss was sweet, bitter, and savory.

Van Fénüra said and thought nothing as he flew towards the battle. His heart was broken. Késhal would never be the same in the wake of that murder. Despite her words of strength and conviction—and indeed, they were convincing—some light and hope had faded out of Pre-Eminent's maroon eyes. Reality had claimed another victim. Optimism lost some of its luster.

Fénüra hated Qeauríyx.

Van hated his life.

Vincallous hated that he felt just as tortured as he did twenty-four cycles ago.

Fierce hatred.

Dé'wa was altogether insatiable now. Vicious had never openly used his powers, and the Elemental was more than willing and ready to show all spectators its abilities.

Phenplyacin was unaware of the historical and personal angst-ridden wrath soon to be unleashed upon it. A wrath born of a contagion that infected the city of Nosgüth and other lands. An ache that would never heal. The rupturing tragedy that caused the most beautiful woman in the world to become emotionally maimed. The children of Nosgüth who committed suicide when their parents died.

Contagion: Unearned wounds caused by intentional transgressions and cosmic reproach.

Could redemption... *should* redemption ever flow from such injustice?

The son of Nosgüth cursed it all.

It was the changing of his name, his identity, all for the sake of mediocre retribution. It was the emptiness of all the cycles he wore that damn Blue Rapier suit. It was the venomous irony of vengeance, the brittle apotheosis of revenge. The recompense of murder did not bring the dead back to life, and left another mortal wound in the infested victim.

Contagion: retributive "justice" and a redemption based on the currency of death, damage, and absurdity.

The contagion had spread without mitigation and finally metastasized into a cold, critical, palpable, fiery, Fierce mass.

Phenplyacin would come to experience its toxins personally. Qeauríyx would never forget it.

Contagions were meant to be spread.

CHAPTER EIGHTEEN: STORIES OF QEAURÍYX

? OGI

Coughing, Neztríanis felt the hard, cold, but not freezing gravel underneath her body.

She opened her eyes.

There was nothing to see.

Clinging desperately to her precarious composure, the woman groped around for any sign of Timura. Her right hand throbbed in pain so she used her left.

"Timura?" she whispered. "Timura?"

Her hand brushed against the témo's fur. Neztríanis placed her head on the animal's trunk to check for breathing and a heartbeat. Timura was alive. The feline's heartbeat had slowed, and her breathing matched the pace of her heart.

In the darkness, a sliver of light languidly ambled its way to the Myanín's position. They were in a cave. Her elements had guided her well.

Neztríanis unfastened her shoulderpack and retrieved her water jug, which was only partly frozen now. Somehow, the temperature was above freezing. The daughter of Hopha drank what water she could and swallowed four meat strips and some nuts.

Her weary composure had been dangled over the abyss of despair on too many occasions, and the gravity of her situation was ineluctable. She shuddered and fell into the chasm.

The Sczyphamek's hands shook.

Her Elemental felt distant. The ancestors no longer reached her qanín. Her mother's scent had given way to the odor of sediment underneath her nose. And the Nameless One...

She shook her head.

She did not want to let the despair in.

She shook her head.

She did not want to let the loneliness sink in.

320

She shook her head.

She did not want the coldness to sink in.

She nodded her head, rocked back and forth, and held herself tightly.

She groaned.

The insanity of her quest finally broke her qanín. Her hometown of Hopha, the Great Mother, Hafir and Namí, Kéma—they were all gone. She and Timura were the only ones left, and they nearly died. Their only companions were an ever-dwindling pack of supplies.

What little light there was cast its luminescence on a teary-eyed, tired, and helpless face. Her mission was suicidal, and she had yet to retrieve the Auría. If she did retrieve it, perils worse than these were sure to await her. She almost died while ascending Mount Xarkim; so what chance did she have in the North Country?

"*Nameless One*," she cried aloud. "Why was I given this task? Why?"

For five inconsolable minutes, Neztríanis, infuriated and scared, sobbed in abandonment.

Her tear ducts utterly spent, Phyxtríalis tried to rise to her feet, but her right hand erupted in an intense, piercing pain. The agony was so excruciating, she fell back to her knees.

Her teeth chattered and her body shivered. With her last bit of resolve, she crawled towards the opening. She told herself that Vicious could find their location at any moment.

Wincing, she stood up and hobbled toward the light, and within two minutes, she made it to the opening on the western side of Mount Xarkim.

It was almost daybreak, and the sky was unusually clear. The western horizon beamed due to the rising sun. The sunlight warmed her qanín. Gazing at the lower elevations, the daughter of Hopha witnessed the ascent Timura and she had engaged. When she surveyed the path of their ascent, the Sczyphamek was left in a state of shock. Their previous position in the lower elevation seemed cycles away. Her present height was above all mountains in the Infinite Circle, and to her northwest lay the East and West Gemansu Mountain ranges. The Bitzroy Gap was clearly visible from her position as well, but she had no time to view the lovely scenery.

She did not know how many days she was unconscious, but it was only a matter of time until someone saw the opening to the cave. The cave's entrance had grown since she initially broke into the bedrock, and it was clearly visible from the air. Glimpsing above, the Sczyphamek observed some loose rocks held by a large amount of snow.

She had to do it. How could she turn back now?

She stretched her left arm up and chanted, "Fá'atoño mona."

A small wave of fire shot towards the snow, and Neztríanis backed away from the entrance and gazed at Zénan. She was certain she would not see its rays again for quite some time or perhaps never again. The avalanche descended, and Neztríanis withdrew into the cave. The sound was deafening; the rocks and snow crashed onto her position and down the side of the mountain. She heard the echoes booming from the inside of the cavern. Because she felt the air blowing out of the crack before she shattered the original fissure, the daughter of Hopha reasoned another exit had to exist, or at least another air source.

Picking up a few slabs of rock with her left hand, Neztríanis felt the wall of the dark passageway with her right shoulder, and soon made her way back to the témo's position.

Setting the stones on the ground, Neztríanis covered them in blue flame for three minutes. The act nearly made her faint, but she fought to stay conscious. The slabs were superheated to an almost white color, giving off a heat that warmed the immediate area and shed some light on the Myanín's location.

Neztríanis turned to Timura and said, "This should help."

She pushed the unconscious Timura's body towards the hot rocks. Then she sat back against the rocky wall.

The next time she awoke, she noticed her breathing neared its normal pace. Her lungs were adjusting somewhat to the thin air. It was pitch black and the once white-hot rocks had lost their color, light, and heat.

Neztríanis listened for the témo's sighs and used her powers to locate her companion. The core temperature of Timura's body had regained its standard heat dispensation and the témo's breathing was steady. Nez moved closer to the témo and lay her head on the abdomen of the winged feline.

"Tem- Temperature," she groaned in her hoarse, mid-tone voice. "Where are…"

"Shhh," the woman hushed her partner. "Do not spend your energy."

"Water," the creature rasped. "I am thirsty…"

Neztríanis fumbled in the darkness, searching for her animal-hide water container. Upon finding it, she placed it in front of Timura, and the feline sucked the water from the canteen.

"I do not know where we are." Neztríanis despaired. "I just don't know…" She would not allow herself to cry, but stinging tears still found their omnipotent way to her pupils and down her soiled face. "I have not moved since I collapsed the entrance to this place. I cannot see and needed to regain my strength."

"It was a wise decision," Timura said in an encouraging, yet weak voice. "You must not leave an opening."

Neztríanis grunted in affirmation and wiped her dirty face of tears. "Timura, I need your eyes. As soon as you feel capable, we must move. I sense warmer air ahead. We might be able to find a water source."

"How much food do is left?" Timura purred.

"After the rations I am about to give you, one week's worth." Neztríanis placed three large pieces of meat in front of Timura, who ate them slowly. "I have lost track of the days," she continued. "But I can feel that the First Snow has commenced."

"I am sorry about your hands," Timura intimated while munching on the food.

"Oh. *My hands*... That is interesting. Hmmm..."

"What?" the témo rasped with curiosity.

"I cannot explain this, but I do not possess scars on either of my hands, and my right hand is no longer broken."

"Are you certain?" Timura turned her head to Neztríanis. "Wounds from a témo leave scars that remain visible for a lifetime. I am sure Vicious still carries the scar I gave him. It does not matter how many days have passed, you should show signs of damage."

Neztríanis was just as mystified as her partner. She remembered the pain of her broken hand quite vividly. But because she and Timura had no way of ascertaining how much time elapsed, it was impossible to tell the rate at which she healed. However, the extent of her recuperation was phenomenal. "Maybe my powers are responsible."

"Even if that is true, I have never heard tales of a Sczyphamek recovering at such a rate or being scarless after such a wound."

The Myanín exchanged silence and sat in complete darkness. Again, Neztríanis lost track of time and fell asleep. At some unknown moment, Timura arose and stretched.

"I am ready," she called out to the daughter of Hopha.

Neztríanis responded by elevating her aura to a candescent state. The candescence almost blinded her and caused her eyes to twitch and strain. She would have to create some light ever so often in order to keep her vision. While the aura shone, Neztríanis gathered up her things and placed them in the shoulderpack. Looking upward, the Sczyphamek noticed the ceiling was about two arm-lengths above. Stalactites hung down, with some unknown mineral embedded within them, and they sparkled, casting an uneven luminescence. Her aura continued to reflect off the diamond-like deposits and projected scattered, visible light ahead of the Myanín.

Neztríanis could not see the end of the passageway and saw no evidence of nel'asmív markings, much less any edifice of Nez Spiritan design. The path was at least ten thousand cycles old, yet the ground felt incredibly sturdy and smooth.

Her aura retreated, and the cavern soon became impenetrable to Neztríanis' eyes. Staying close to Timura's left, the Sczyphamek followed her partner. After what she perceived to be an hour or so, she would light up the cavern.

They could not keep a precise track of time. Neztríanis could only guess at the intervals to brighten the cavern. She did not feel the sun due to the density of the rocks, although some unspeakable happening also upset her Elemental. When she tried to use it to gaze into the temperate constitution of the cave, she was unable to distinguish any warmness or coldness.

The terrain was just as ambiguous. Some moments, the path descended, at other times the path maintained a level plane, and yet in others, they stumbled up a considerable incline.

Soon, the Myanín lost all track of space and time. The spatiotemporal disorientation of the darkness was enough to drive one mad, but they passed the time by talking about their pasts and exchanging light and thought-provoking conversation.

Luckily, they encountered water sources. Some water dripped from the ceiling; some poured down the side of the cavern's walls. The only way Neztríanis was sure a week had not passed was due to their food supply.

"Timura," Nez said, "it is time to eat."

"Must we?" the témo asked.

Neztríanis understood her concern. She was already rationing the food into smaller portions to stretch it out as long as possible, but Neztríanis was starving and exhausted. Timura had to be hungry and fatigued too.

"Yes," the Sczyphamek affirmed. "We must."

"Temperature," the témo said with interest, "there is a wall marking ahead."

"Really?" the woman asked pensively. "You are not kidding me are you?"

"Témos do not 'kid,' Temperature, although we do possess the appreciation of humor."

Neztríanis smiled. "Where is it? Should I use my Elemental?"

"Not yet," the feline responded. She was about to begin another sentence, but she suddenly stopped. "I... I hear something."

Neztríanis strained her ears and quieted her thoughts. "I hear it now."

"It sounds like musical notes, almost concerted," the feline observed. "This song is unknown to me."

"*I know it*," the Sczyphamek said. Her Elemental shifted and demanded attention. "*Zí mányx que rai. Mona fla renzgé ná*," she sang the notes which had been revealed to her over two durations ago. They were the notes that allowed her to build an ice sphere of massive proportions when Qeauríyx attacked her.

The phrase... that contained the names of her Elemental: Rai and Renzgé. Yes, those *were their names*. Neztríanis embraced it to be true. The cavern walls were emitting this same sonic configuration, the same melody in the same key. It was calling her and *them*.

"How is this possible?"

The témo needed no explanation to understand Neztríanis' question. "Your Elemental must have triggered something within the cave."

Triggered? They passed no physical apparatus of detection. But, perhaps "physicality" was just as unnecessary in Mt. Xarkim as time and space.

As they resumed their walk towards the music, another melody emerged within the composition. It was piano, and nearly undetectable. The nearly inaudible melody possessed a subtle percussive quality. The tempo was slow and meaningful, and the harmony of the main movements followed the meter of the submerged melody. The time signature appeared to possess three beats per measure, and recycled every two measures.

"*Fá'atoño má*," Neztríanis sang, believing the melody on the underside of the composition was the chant of ages. Neztríanis was perturbed. She was sure something would happen if she sang the words according to the meter and music.

"Your pitch is too low," Timura explained. She purred the melody to her partner. The notes were fine-tuned, but the sound was bizarre to the nel'asmív's ears. It sounded like the notes were muffled and echoed, yet they resonated with melancholy purity.

Neztríanis was nearly moved to tears. Wondering if she could match such musical prowess, she admitted with nonchalance, "I never liked to sing."

Timura stopped singing and replied with noticeable gravity, "If you do not sing, you will not Awaken. All Sczyphameks, whether they had the ability or not, developed a portion of their Elemental through singing."

"I still do not understand how or why singing should affect one's power..." Neztríanis complained.

"Elementals have been greatly strengthened after singing. Singing is not only about pitch and tempo," the témo explained eloquently. "It is also about confidence and emotion, a radical connection between the song, performer, and audience."

Neztríanis smiled in admiration and surprise. "Timura, I had no clue that you had such a deep grasp of music or a Sczyphamek's powers."

"You know my line is from the témoic Orators of the past. Much history and understanding has been passed down throughout the cycles."

"Clearly," the daughter of Hopha affirmed. Sighing and fidgeting about in the darkness, Neztríanis sang, "*Fá'atoño ma. Fá'atoño ma.*"

Timura joined in with her in harmonic accompaniment.

It happened.

The Bombardment

Breathe me...
Breathe me, Sczyphamek
Hear me, Orator of the Témos
Glimpses of the Past, your past, our past...
Through your eyes.
Extend O Elemental, Extend...
Rai, Renzgé
We are one
We are one
We are many
See the myth
See the history
Of Our Creation

Neztríanis hardly breathed. The air grew dense and thickened as visions and emanations sprung forth from the wall—no; the wall, the cave had all but disappeared behind the veil of the image. The light continued to pulsate in front of her, causing her aura to extend to the heights of the cavern. But what was once a cramped, stalactite infested, low ceiling had now opened into a limitless heaven. "Timura," Neztríanis stammered. "Can you see... do you see this?" "Yes," the animal intimated, no less flabbergasted than Neztríanis.

Breathe me... Hear me...
And Witness, be the witness of an Ancient Time...
Still forgotten, whose memory lives to this day

Immediately, Neztríanis felt a gravitational sensation towards the light as if it were drawing her closer. Her feet instinctively dug into the ground, and she hung onto the side of the cavern walls with all of her might, but instead of wall, she felt nothing. Timura's claws dug deep into an ever more disintegrating floor. Looking at the Sczyphamek and then at the light, she purred calmly, "It wants us Temperature; there is no point resisting now." Retracting her claws, the témo was sucked into the light. Neztríanis surrendered herself, her qanín, to the current.

Darkness. Do you see the darkness?
Do not fear it.
The Darkness was our home.
The darkness is our home.
See us in the abyss of space, in the beginning of distance
At the emerging of time…

The voice was a quiet boom to the Sczyphamek's ears, although she wondered if she was actually using her auditory senses. Her senses were confused. She could no longer differentiate them in the medium of this bodily revelation. What she should have heard, she tasted and touched. Sight never heard and felt so overwhelming. Timura was intimately present to her; yet, the distance between them—incalculable. Darkness surrounded her. She encompassed darkness. It was cold, but not freezing. In the distance she perceived a light. It was murky, barely visible to the naked ear. Barely heard or noticed by the eye. Her nose almost touched it. Her fingers almost smelled it, if not for the infinite distance that separated her from it.

The Darkness! Not the Light!
Gaze there, only then will you know…
We chase for what is
But seek for what is not
This happens as unsearchable truth
Pursue what does…

Who was speaking? The poetic words and verses were cryptic and elusive; but Neztríanis tried to comply. Comply. Comply? Comply! Shifting herself, shifting her qanín, the light lost its primacy in perception. With the light now behind her—or was it above or beneath her?—the darkness was fully before her. The darkness, the Deep, she witnessed it. She felt not what she saw, but she tasted *it*. It was large, and she was hurling towards it at an incredible speed. Or was it hurling towards her? So large, round and jagged. The darkness became peaceful to Neztríanis. What does? What does darkness do? It illuminates. How could darkness illuminate? Neztríanis realized illumination was only possible because of darkness, because of its contrast. The large, round object grew even larger, and its gravity was so intense, Neztríanis felt as if she would pass out. She wanted to call on her Elemental, but in her heart, she knew she should not. Reaching her hand(?) out, she tried to sense the darkness, and as her fingertip(?) grazed its surface, the Dark erupted in a blaze of magma, ash, and fiery rock. The explosion drew no sound.

No sound.

"Space," Timura growled. Her silhouette alone emerged from the darkness. "We are in the Firmament." "The heavens...?" Neztríanis whispered. She saw it. It was impossible for her mind to understand the shape, the contours, although she had learned about the shape of Qeauríyx and its moons when she was younger. She was not conscious of it; she required the rest of her qanín to understand... It appeared to be a planet or some heavenly body. It was—she was—covered in lava and volcano, ash and fire. But Neztríanis did not lose sight of the darkness. It was still there, as impenetrable and enlightening as ever.

Can you "hear" us Sczyphamek?
Can you understand the futility of such a word?
Qanín draw near...
Draw near Creatures...
Nigh
Hear them coming
Hear! they come
They have come
They are here...
Witness through your own gaze
Witness the happening
For it has happened and continues

Sound. She heard. Timura heard. Sounds launched at them. No understanding could be drawn. No sense was made. *But she sensed.* Space was the terminus of sound. The roar was deafening. Neztríanis' perspective changed. It was not *a* roar, but *roars.* There were four of them, hurtling slowly towards the dark mass of ash and lava. They were not "of" the darkness. She consumed their qanín, inhaled their particulates in the vacuum of space. Rage, compassion, aggression, pain, hope, domination, apathy, woe, indefatigableness, mercy. She tasted them all, in relation to the Dark, in relation to the place of lava, ash, and fire. Four. Four roars. Four heralds. Four manifestations of indeterminate purpose announcing to the dark their visible intentions. The Dark pulled them in. They sought the dark. They were illuminated. "Timura," she thought. "What are they?" Somehow she and Timura's thoughts were merged, though she knew neither when nor how. "I do not know," was the response. There was a fearful edge to the Témo.

Violet Illumination,
White Incandescence,
Viridian Radiance,
Blue Glimmer,
They have come, they came from nebulous spaces

There were four of them. Somehow Neztríanis beheld their approach, although such perspective was normally impossible. But the Dark saw them. So did she and Timura. Four of them—they were blue, viridian, white, and violet. Neztríanis perceived them as space rocks. More. *They were more.* The starry hosts became obscured by the glory of the four bodies. Streaking across Temperature's arms and legs, streaking towards her core, her—their—qaníns, the bodies of rock and purpose rippled through the heavens. The impact would be devastating, yet Timura could not curl up and Neztríanis could not defend. Such things were impossible, were they not? They were coming. The impact would be devastating, yet they drew them in anyhow.

Prepare, Sczyphamek
Prepare, Orator
More shall be One
More shall be Us
Soon you shall all happen…

They were ready. There was no atmosphere to slow them down. No friction to destroy their mass. The impact was devastating. The Firmament saw it all.

The Nameless, Ineffable, Thing(s)

The purposeful rocks struck deep.

The Dark was not as large as it once happened. Darkness, Blackness would have covered them, if not for the gathering of the Four. Viridian. Blue. White. Violet.

The Craters were vast and deep, pulsating, vibrating, seeking the Dark. Tempting the Dark.

But the Dark was all (so?) alluring.

Intentions were unclear.

Misunderstanding drew nigh.

Chaos and calamity erupted on the Dark-with-the-Craters.

"Qe.[1] Call us Qe."

Chaos and calamity erupted on Qe.

Blue against White. Viridian and Black against Violet.

Intentions were unclear.

Misunderstanding continued.

Earthquakes and eruptions transpired on Qe.

White, Blue, and Violet against Viridian.

Black...

Overtake. Conquer.

Destroy.

Defend.

Squirm.

Qe grimaced. In the void of space, Qe grimaced. Yelling to the heavenly realms of space, Qe grimaced.

Darkness gave way. darkness gave way to fire, ash, lava, volcano, and the Four.

A scream in the vacuum of space. A scream for life on a lifeless Qe.

And yet there was life.

Darkness still dwelled.

And yet there was light.

A tortured laugh. A rejoicing wail.

The utterance reached Its ears. That which has no Ears.

---

[1] Qe (key)

The scent of chaotic hope reached Their nose. That which has no Nose.
This Nameless and Ineffable Thing.
Gathered Itself across the heavenly firmament.
Gather, gather, commune, communicate.
Reveal.
Marshalling Its currents, It streamed.
This Nameless, In/effable… Happenings.
What shape could shapelessness afford?
What sign can be assigned to that which is Nothing?
What words will fail to describe that which is Something.
It advanced.
It encounters.
So shall It continue.
A comet?
One symbol is as want as another
For this In/effable Mystery.
The request was a desperate, conflicted cry.
Dark-with-the-Craters—Qe wrestled with itself.
Yelling before it could stop itself.
Yelling before it knew, before it understood its own name.
The Nameless Comet approached.
Its aura was silent majesty.
Its train leapt off Its back into the Firmament only to touch Its face.
It met Itself at Qe.
They found Itself at Qe.
It discovered Themselves at Qe.
They were with It. It was with them.
And many were in the train of It.
The Comet, Its train, and the Darkness-with-Craters—Qe.
They met in the infinite space and chance.
Although overwhelmingly incandescent, the Happening(s) burst in a light
that caused Darkness to erupt, and the Craters to rise.
Yet. They were there.
A Mist from the train, the particulates in the train, the It in the enveloped
Qe.
Ascended and Descended into Qe
Traversed and Intersected Qe
The cry was solicited. The response was unsolicited.
They danced. In dissonant arrhythmia they danced.
They danced.
In harmony and rhythm they danced.
They sang. They cried.
The mist became they and they performed the mist and the mist
capacitated the In/effable and the In/effable indwelled the mist, but was
also the train that met Itself at Qe.

It Breathed.
It Graciously Breathed.
The Mystery Breathes…
All words are wanting.
The Nameless, In/effable Doing lingered.
And the Cycles, which had already commenced, neared the Infinite they already encountered.
You are in my pages, Sczyphamek.
What will you do?
The ----- stayed.
Can you hear It?
Can you hear what emerged?
The hum was there, Sczyphamek.
The hum was there, Témo; you who therefrom emerged last.
The Chant began there.
Fá'atoño má.
The phrase that means --- and Nothing.

The Rain and the Waters

The drowning overtook her. Neztríanis knew how to swim, but this water, this pool was inescapable. Her qanín could not interpret the words that imprinted on her mind just cycles(?) ago. *Fá'atoño má.*
No time.
She had no time to chant.
Swim.
Swim.
Swim.
She did not want to drown. Yet how could one drown in the water that brought forth life?
She emerged from the pool at this revelation.
She was not in a pool. For reaches and reaches, all she encountered was water. It was warm. It had no taste.
"I am here," Timura purred before the Sczyphamek said a word. The témo was soaked, which on any other occasion would have caused Neztríanis to laugh, but the seriousness of their situation did not allow for such a response.
"What is happening?" the Daughter of the Dark-with-Craters asked.
"I do not believe any answer I offer will suffice," the témo responded. "I am—we are at a loss."
Beneath her, through the aqueous haze, the témo saw the indications of lava and volcanic eruptions. In the sky were limitless clouds, pouring rain on the waters.
They were moving. She felt them—Qe—moving.
A wave of great heights emerged from the waters and crashed down on them, plunging them into the Deep. Viridian, Violet, Blue, White... their color was obfuscated by the murkiness of the water, but their presence was undeniable. Diving towards Timura, Temperature inhaled the breathable water. She reached the témo and wondered how she had the strength to even swim. Moments(?) ago, she was so hungry and tired that she was scarcely able to walk.
Timura's widened eyes spoke compositions. Turning around in the depths, the Myanín observed a wave of water, in the ocean of water, barreling towards Neztríanis. This wave was violet, and the pain it wrought pierced the very fabric of their qanín. The Sczyphamek/Nelon Ásmivü and

Témo felt four distinct pains, but the infliction claimed the same origin. Neztríanis' Elemental jostled in suffering and yelled in displeasure, causing a violent ripple in the waters.

Before the Myanín had a chance to right themselves and recover from the stinging agony of the violet water, blue precipitation cascaded upon the duo in the Deep of the waters. She grew wetter than they already were, and the blue made the témo feel confident, arrogant, yet quietly withdrawn and defensive. As Neztríanis lingered in the reflective deluge, the Myanín gathered themselves, only to be sliced by the blue drops of rain, as if the duo was one entity.

They *were* one.

They were not bleeding.

Preparing herself for the next onslaught, which she reasoned would be either viridian or white, the témo was surprised to find themselves approached by what could only be described as a black solution. Covering them, the black mass swirled and rushed in out of the foreground. The power was unlike anything they had ever felt, but there was little control or purpose in the darkness. Yet, Neztríanis perceived the black holding back its entire qanín. A portion, a large portion, ensconced itself in mystery. Its energy appeared untranslatable.

A viridian whirlpool developed within the blink of an eye, sucking the Myanín into its currents. The warmth and the aesthetic hope it produced amazed the body. Timura wished to linger there for the rest of their experience(?). The whirlpool felt immature and distinct from the previous waters. More than anything, Neztríanis realized it was the gentlest and humblest of all the colors, yet its strength was just as disproportionate. Two… there were two of them.

The Sczyphamek felt their anticipation as the témo looked ahead. A white mass headed toward the viridian whirlpool, and the whirlpool would have it no other way, even though it wanted no part of the encounter.

The white liquid crashed into the whirlpool. It gulped the viridian and tried to swallow the Myanín. Timura felt as if the very life of her was being drained by the enormous pressure exerted on them. Neztríanis screamed in the water but before the impossible sound was uttered, the white siphoned off the pain from the scream and made it its own. It appeared insatiable, without purpose or design. Neztríanis did not understand its intentions, if there were any.

Soon all forms of liquid joined in the fury of the viridian and white waters, churning, rising, and beating the Myanín with a terrible, yet unintentional backlash.

This did not feel like a vision. Neztríanis felt as if she and Timura would die if this continued.

Chant?

Chant.

Chant!

"Fá'atoño má!" she chanted(?), in the water.

"Fá'atoño má!" the témo roared(?) in the water.

The waters stopped churning and kept their distance from the Myanín in the ocean.

Neztríanis' aura extended over Timura, whose qanín gave off its own brownish orange glow. Timura's mass grew and the hair on the feline's back became much more rigid and pointy. The Sczyphamek's orange-white aura let out a blast of force that shook the waters for reaches.

"We happened as Rai and Renzgé," her Elemental spoke in one voice to the colorful waters. "We are Temperature; we were Sundry; we are Qeauríyx; we happen with *It. We are with the témo.*"

Neztríanis was shocked. Her Elementals had now verbally revealed their names. Why now?

"Temperature," Timura intimated softly.

The daughter of Qeauríyx faced her partner and gasped. Timura's form was obfuscated, but Neztríanis knew that she was witnessing the beginning of the Synthesis. Steam rose off the back of the témo and her front paws gave off a cold heat. Her wings emerged, crystallizing in fiery ice, and a black heat emitted a strange warmth.

"Not for one who has yet to Awaken," the waters and some other voice(s) reverberated and rushed the Myanín. Their velocity was unimaginable.

The impact between the Myanín's aura and the waters launched the Chénínqua into the atmosphere and out of the waters. The experience would have been terrifying if a song of hope had not filled the air...

The Emergence of the Ground

We emerge from the heart of the Deep
I emerge from the heart of the One
You emerge from the atrium of hope
They emerge with heated blade

The Ground-land
Que

Emerge! Kísanque…[1]
The Land emerges underneath the waters.

Rumbling out of the Deep
Ten ground-lands Emerged from water
And the waters were so, so still
And *It* said we must live
Epicenter is ready
Epicenter Swirls
Epicenter is open
Epicenter Gives

And *It* said we must live
So Live!

Kínand…[2]

The four, even the five, cannot pin us down…
The Firmament calls us forth
My, my! What is this?
Let's call it grass
"Ménan"[3] is its forgotten name.

Emerge! Kísanque!
Kísanyx Níse tzo Qe![4]

---

[1] Kísanque (kee-ahn-k[w]eh)
[2] Kínand (k*ee*-nahnd)
[3] Ménan (m*ey*-nahn)

To Emerge from the Firmament and Dark-with-the-Craters!
What cursed joy is this?

Yarké, Yarcé, Yardük, Yarnínga, Yaré, Zéyar, Yartan, Yarla
Help me breathe
Help me grow…

Their wings emerge from me
Their fingers emerged, clawing and gasping for air
The insects emerge, singing and carrying about
The rocks emerge, granting us a strong foundation…

An element burns within me
We know not its purpose
We know not its origins
We know it warms…
It feels like *It* and Qe
It feels like *Them* and Qe
Wrapped together
Huddled together
Struggling together

Y'skax![5]
You are Sundry!
Tríana Y'skax chíos[6]
The Elemental filled to the full
Kísan! Kísan!

You lands are nameless…
Emerge Nelon Ásmivü
Emerge from the soil and from the grass and from the trees…

Just as us emerged from you…

Yet, the shaking has not ceased.
It is Infinite.

---

[4] Kísanyx Níse tzo Qe (kee-sahn-iks nee-sey tsoh keh)
[5] Y'skax (ih-skaks)
[6] Tríana chíos (tree-ahn-uh chee-ohs)

The Cycles of the Drift: The Temple(s) and Auría(s)

The Land shakes day by day
Cycle by Cycle
The misery of the day crushes the feet of our children
Yet, their smile endures infinitely
Just as their tears fall ceaselessly

Surely, we appear like the pebbles,
Cast down and forgotten.

Where lies our comforter?
The power of It nears exhaustion
in Its unfailing love and wonder.

The pebbles stack, they gather, stone upon stone
Rock upon rock.
They topple only to rise again.

What is such a thing as a "temple"?
What is this "tabernacle"?
How did these words enter our thoughts?
How did this sacred space emerge?
How does possibility happen?
How is *It* possible?
How are we possible?

This world is our home and it has loved us enough to give us life.
This world is our home and it has hated us enough to give us life.
This world is our home and it cares not—whether we live or die...
This world cares for us and sustains us.

The Rainbow, its colors are at war.
Blue over Violet, Violet over White, White over Black, Black over Viridian
Yet, tomorrow, the arrangement is different.

The rains are the same.
The Great Sky pours...
The Land Shakes...

338

Yet, how do you stand O Temples?
How do you, Tabernacles, reach into the heights, without crumbling?

Yes, it is a sign.
Yes, it is a sign from It.
How could we ever doubt, that which is undoubtable?

It here.
So we here.

We enter into this strange edifice that provides us shelter.
It looks different to everyone
But we know we behold the same things

Some sit

Some stand

Some kneel

Some lay

We hum it softly.
Its meter not lost
Its rhythm. Untarnished.

It means Nothing; yet we hum it anyway.
It means ------; yet it brings us little peace.
It means Everything: We must carry on.

Fá'atoño má.

How do we know these words?
How can we read these words?
Words we have spoken but have never seen
Words we have heard but never have written
It has written, although written is not the word to call It.
It speaks, but speech does not describe.

The Land shakes.

Here the words lay.
Our words

Its words

A planet with an incomplete name gives voice in its pages.

The Four are here as well.
They are in Me.
They are in My pages.
My pages that falsify and speak the truth
My pages that prophesy and create
My pages that codify

My pages are written, heard and witnessed anew, day by day
Cycle by Cycle

My words are as swift as the lands
For I am they.
The windhorses, the insects, the animals, the rocks
All who struggle for life on this emerging planet
I am Nelon Ásmivü
Nín, Nín
Togetherness.
Qa.

Trían wu qanín Ché
Trían mu qanín Kímaios

Qe
I am part of your consummation
Auría
This is the name the words choose.
Auríyx.
I do this.

Qeauríyx…
This is your name.
This is our name.
Forever linked, forever separate, forever one, forever many, forever bound,
forever scattered…

The Cycles of the Drift: The Emergence of Anplo

My mother is giving me that look again. It's always the same. "Anplo," she says. "Anplo, quit looking at the water. It's going to shake soon."

"It's always shaking, Mamí," I say back to her.

"*Anplo...*"

"I'm coming."

I just like looking at the water. I always have, ever since I can remember. Some say I am little, but Kanoso tells me I'm the oldest child he knows. So I step away from the water's edge and hurry back into the cave where we have lived for over two hundred cycles.

Why am I the only one who sees what glows in the water?
Why am I the only one who hears the whistling of the ground?
Why do they still call my friends, Rai and Renzé, imaginary?
Can they not feel them?

Today/Cycle was bad. The ground shook so hard even the cave grew unsafe and we were forced outside. Zénan and Mashé are quiet concerning our destiny. My friends tell me that their parents say that we won't last. Yet somehow, we last.

I don't want to die. I don't want to lose everything that I know. One of those "don'ts" will come true though. If we stay here, even a "little" child like me can see that something bad will happen. But leaving here is another kind of death, isn't it? Kanoso keeps telling me that I am only ------ and should not be thinking about such things. I asked him when ------- was considered young on this planet. One is considered old if they make it to forty -------.

The steps are so cold. They are so silent. They are so worn. I feel like I have done this before. I feel like these steps are not my own. My hands

341

fashion ----- but I do not recognize my ------. How many have been taken? I cannot remember home anymore. We never gave it a name out of fear. O nameless home, what did you look like? A Cycle has passed, and I can't remember you. But I still remember the water.

Why was I the only one who saw what glowed in the water?
Couldn't they see that we would never get away?
Why was I the one who heard the whistling and singing of the ground?
Didn't they understand that it was trying to tell us its name?
Why are they still saying that my friends, Rai and Renzgé, are imaginary?
Can't they feel the warmth and coolness they give off?
Can't they feel their relationship with the water?

I don't know who you are, but I know you see them. Don't you? You have traveled with us for this past Cycle, but you have said nothing to me. That creature that travels with you, what is it? Why does your Elemental speak to me, but you remain silent?

The First Sczyphamek

She said nothing as she sauntered up the mountain.
"What is your name?" Neztríanis' question was desperate.
She said nothing as she advanced. The planet shook so violently and insanely that it no longer shook. Neztríanis was almost swallowed in her aura.

O her lustrous aura!

The Sczyphamek hummed thousands of melodies and various colors emerged and disappeared within her aura.

The Sczyphamek's face was a plethora; many were her face. Shades of nameless peoples from continents unnamed. With determined steps and misty breath, she climbed.

"Do you see me?" Neztríanis yelled, but amidst the crashing of the planet, her cry was hardly a faint whisper. She was in the aura. Rai and Renzgé were there. Temperature was there.

The Sczyphamek uttered a thousand chants simultaneously, as Sundry as the Elemental she inhabited, which also made its home within her, around her, through her.

O warm embrace!

The Sczyphamek stood atop the snowy peak, at the edge of the magma filled dome.

"Fá'atoño má."

Sundry as she chanted the elemental phrase which means ---- and ---- emerged from the ----

"I do not understand," Neztríanis spoke, as tears of revelation streamed down her face.

"Keh mányx --- phen --- pet --- ...." A singular chant sprouted forth, but Neztríanis could not witness, nor did she fully comprehend the phrase spoken.

The Sczyphamek outstretched her arms and beheld the sea. An unknown kind of lightning struck and the heavens swirled in accompaniment. Erstwhile, the waves roared and Qeauríyx careened.

"We must leave," Neztríanis heard Timura say. "We are not meant to see this. We will be destroyed."

"Then why were we brought here?" Neztríanis thought aloud. "Someone should witness this. The factions started because of this. Everything happened because of this!"

As soon as Temperature spoke those words, the First Sczyphamek looked in her direction and nearly blinded Neztríanis. The Sundry's aura was incredibly intense.

The Sczyphamek's face was impossible to read. Her words were impossible to translate. Her emotions were as distant as the gulf between... The energy the First conjured was terrifying. And the atmosphere soon became consumed by the Sundry. Ahead of her, something emerged from the waters.... It was the Fragmented Colors...

Before they came to realization, the Myanín was hurled through time and space...

Témos emerge...........................Temples
endure........................
....Continents are named
......Sczyphameks.........Black
Staff.........Synthesis............War.............White Scythe.....
Betrayal... ExtinctionBlueRapierViolentManacle... Damüda...
Tannódin... PhmquedriaNezSpirita... Imperial...
Neztríaniscouldnotbreathe. Shecouldnotthink. Itwashappeningtoofast.
Timewasmovingsofast. Spaceshiftedtooquickly. Aterribledangerahead.
Shescreamed. Timuraroared. Inpain.

It was dark. Soaked in sweat and fatigued to the point of disintegration, Neztríanis dropped to her knees, while a faint Timura staggered a few paces ahead of her, crouched on all fours, and soon lay on her side.

"What was that?" Neztríanis wondered aloud and felt an oncoming rush of nausea. "Was that… were we really there…?"

A solid wall of rock lay directly behind them. The path that they were once on was no longer discernible.

"And where are we?"

Neztríanis vomited.

Wiping her mouth, she searched her surroundings, and to her amazement, she detected a residue of her aura lengths away to the northwest. If what she was sensing was correct, she and the témo had traveled through time *and* space, not only in the visions, but also from their original location. Her Elemental's potency had increased tremendously since the revelation began. Never had she been able to discern heat sources from such distances.

"Temperature," the témo intimated wondrously. "Look."

Ahead of them was a large chamber that somehow was incandescent, even in the midst of the darkness.

"Are you hungry?" Timura curiously asked the daughter of Hopha.

"Actually," she responded in bewilderment, "I am not. I am tired, but I do not believe I have ever been so satiated in my life."

"I believe it was from the waters," Timura replied.

Neztríanis was quiet. She and her clothes were soaked, but her shoulderpack and its contents were completely dry.

"So did we actually—was that real? Did we see *her*?" Neztríanis asked, nearly brought to tears by such a powerful religious and personal experience.

"You are asking a question that cannot be answered, except through living," the témo answered solemnly. "Only our forthcoming actions can validate the revelation."

"…*Right*," Neztríanis responded, unsure of what Timura's words implied. However, Timura *was* a témo… "I guess…"

For the next few minutes, the duo attempted to retrieve their bearings. Somehow and amazingly, the area was not pitch black. It was difficult to see, like the last sliver of the sun setting during the new moons, but the nel'asmív's eyes were not deceived. Something illuminated. Her ears heard it. Her qanín felt it.

It hummed.

"I hear it too," Timura said quietly.

Though debatable, she believed she heard the hum from the moment the wall came alive, throughout all the experiences, even during the First Sczyphamek's ascent. As they walked closer to the sound of the hum, which was almost like a rhythmic pulse, the cavern grew brighter and warmer.

"Temperature, I wanted to be sure, but I believe your hair has grown." The témo was correct. Neztríanis ran her fingers through her loosened hair and found it three or four clips longer than before. It would have taken her nearly half to three quarters of a cycle to grow her hair that much. Were they older? How much time had passed?

The sound grew louder; or rather, the Myanín became more conscious of it. And the space continued to grow in luminosity. Neztríanis was able to discern colors and shades.

Stopping for a moment, she turned around and stated, "Timura, let me see your abdomen."

Timura understood the Sczyphamek's hypothesis. Sure enough, the témo's wounds were healed. That meant her wings had mended as well. So, the experience was not *purely* cognitive, spiritual, and emotional; it was immensely corporeal. Their entire qaníns were subject to the experience.

"What was that happening we experienced? How long were we truly gone?" Timura purred solemnly with reverence and mystification, allowing herself a moment to grapple with the... No words could describe it, and all subsequent attempts would forever prove to be wholly inadequate.

The Myanín continued to walk. Soon they entered into an area where the pathway split in two.

Neztríanis did not hesitate and chanted, "*Fá'atoño má.*" In response, the pathway to the left erupted in orange-white luminosity, mirroring her aura.

"Temp... Temperature..." Timura was flabbergasted. Her partner's Elemental had grown to unbelievable heights, although she still had not Awakened. *But she was close.*

Neztríanis' hair lifted and pulsed, and her clothes rustled. She was as amazed as Timura. With clarity unmatched, she heard her Elemental, Rai and Renzgé. She nearly grew afraid of herself and settled down.

They continued to walk to the left for a short distance, when the subterranean trail opened up into another large area. Their eyes fastened upon an unknown structure. They knew it nonetheless. It was the Hidden Tabernacle.

Its height was lowly, a true testimony to the life of nel'asmívs during the Drift. It was no more than eleven to twelve feet high and no more than one hundred feet in width. In front of the structure, parallel and parabolically placed rectangular pillars jutted out of the ground, their height increasing the closer they were to the structure, which had only a small staircase leading into the edifice.

Cautiously, the Myanín sauntered nearer and nearer to the entrance of the temple. Neztríanis' heart leapt in anticipation. The first part of her quest was at hand. She thought about Rydín, Hafir, Namí, the Great Mother, Bíoske, Kéma, and even Jennó... they seemed so far away, so far removed, but they were all so integral to this moment's possibility. Her hands trembled in expectation. With great passion, she wept.

Timura looked on with empathy, for her thoughts turned to her cub and her mate, and their destruction at the hands of Vincallous. She thought about the remaining remnant of her species, wondering what hope they actually had. And yet, one of the most hallowed treasures of the planet was only a few steps away: A book whose existence was known through the Fragments and oral tradition.

For a moment neither Neztríanis nor Timura felt helpless and hopeless.

Ascending the small steps, Neztríanis and Timura walked into an open chamber. Somehow, the chamber was filled with a low, yet revealing light. Scattered across the floor lay the remains of people long forgotten. With reverence, Neztríanis said a prayer on their behalf. Just as she surmised, an altar was present at the front of the temple. She expected the book to be lying there. But it was not. However, the hum was so present now; the book had to be close by. Silently, the Myanín methodically searched the tabernacle's floor for the Auría.

"Fá'atoño má," they both chanted together. It appeared that their mental connection remained partially intact since the end of the visions(?).

In a corner, under dust, ash, and pebbles, something grew bright and then the color of absolute darkness. Walking slowly to that part of the temple, Neztríanis stepped over what was left of the skeletal remains of her ancestors. Removing the debris from the area, Timura and Neztríanis laid their eyes upon a book. Its dimensions were average, but as the hum continued, they heard voices, speaking words they could not understand. Some sang, some spoke, yet all were present, and some had yet to speak… stories yet to be chronicled.

Overwhelmed with emotion and fearful of new paradigms, a quailing Neztríanis reached down and picked up the aural book. She opened the first page. Nothing was written. She opened the second page, an unrecognizable scribbling was uttered. She skipped to the fifth page. Words abounded.

As soon as she took a breath to read to Timura, the book spoke in the Ancient Tongue, Nez Spiritan, and témoic iterations, "The end continues to happen."

Neztríanis and Timura shared a bewildered look. Flipping to the end pages of the document, Neztríanis noticed an inordinate number of pages were blank. Trying to find the final written page, Neztríanis gasped in disbelief.

Written in her own handwriting, the page proclaimed, "Herein chronicles the account of the Sczyphamek called Temperature and her steadfast ally, the témo named Timura."

Why was their story to be included in the book? And what did a sacred book with no ending mean? Neztríanis was somewhat irritated for she thought that finding the Auría would grant her answers not more questions.

Grumbling to herself, she tried not to focus on the aural pronouncement, "Timura, how are we supposed to get out of here?"

"I think we should follow the other path. Who knows where it will lead us, but I observed no exits here or in the antecedent chamber."

Placing the book she was dying to read in her shoulderpack, Temperature nodded. "Agreed. We have no way of discerning how many days have passed, so we must continue as if everything depends on this… because it does."

Timura growled in agreement.

Neztríanis' power seemed to have doubled since she held the Auría. And if that was the case, there was no telling what would happen if Vincallous held it. One thing was certain. The Auría *wanted* to be found by the Myanín.

Chapter Nineteen: The Coward in Minusía

After three weeks of traveling through the lumber district of Phmquedria, Anámn neared the outskirts of Minusía. In order to sustain himself, he took odd jobs as a migrant worker, a commonplace occurrence in the lumber district. Workers were paid a meager daily wage from Tannódin'é mills. There were two Phmquedrian-owned lumber plants, and though their pay was higher than the Tannódin'é mills, they were unable to hire at the same rate. Most of the Tannódin'é lumber companies did not ask for legal documentation. They did not care if the workers were runaways, free, or indentured.

This was Phmquedria. Exploitative labor was as endemic as the breathable, smoke-filled air. The land was to be exploited. The people were to be exploited. The seller was to be exploited. The buyer was to be exploited. The continent was a land of unregulated business and bottom-line profit. A merchant's paradise. A place where liberal business practices and free exchange veiled power relations, ethnocentrism, death, and depression.

Workers outbid one another for labor and wages each day. Over the cycles, owners of each lumber mill constantly sought to monopolize, in order to shut down their fellow Tannódin'é competitors out of the market. As a result of this practice, only three Tannódin'é lumber companies remained. The two Phmquedrian companies were upstarts, partially aligned with the Global Initiative Public Works program, and partially entrepreneurial ventures. In the lumber district, one rule remained cross-cultural and universal: those who cut down a tree and processed it the fastest—power and credits were theirs.

Wood was in great demand throughout Tannódin and Damüda, and Phmquedria was the closest continent that could provide the necessary supply. Because Loama Setrin was a farming island, and Civix Setrin was almost completely covered in a sprawling metropolis and mountainous ranges, Tannódin was especially strapped for wood that could be used for continuous urban expansion.

The yarkés of Phmquedria were furious. Anámn only needed to work in the lumber plants for one week before the pain of the yarkés became too much for him to bear. Large sections of forest had been flattened into savannah. Ecosystems withered, and plant and animal species fell extinct. Sustainability was ignored and forest revitalization was spurned. Instead, Tannódin'é, Damüdans, and Phmquedrians continued to raze the que, once known for some of the most diverse habitats on Qeauríyx.

Matriester felt the anguish of the trees, but his need for money outpaced ecological concern. Although he knew not the route he would take to get out of Phmquedria, he was certain that it would involve the exchange of credits. Anámn never worked more than two concurrent days at any one company. He did not want to be noticed, only paid for his work and forgotten. Likewise, he engaged in very little dialogue with any of his coworkers. From time to time, he would ask about the news of the day, but most of the workers only knew what was happening locally. The time they spent away from the lumber mills was for recreation, sleep, and delusion. Working was a hard enough reality; the laborers had no desire to be compensated in the currency of complex interconnection. Even Anámn, with his powers, became fatigued after the first week. Each shift was fourteen hours, and the mills operated seven days a week and granted only one day of rest.

Though the slave trade had ceased in the lumber district, the sex trade was alive and well. And unlike Euhilv, even Phmquedrians took part in the practice. Many of the laborers—men, women, and children—without solicitation, told Anámn story upon tale about the district's large supply of sex slaves.

The district's conditions were brutal and harsh for everyone, even the bosses of the mills. Many escaped into their own world of domination at the expense of the body and dignity of other nel'asmívs. However, according to the lumber-hands, the "sexploitation" (as they called it) was on the decrease. For some unknown reason, the global side of the business had been hampered. Therefore, many of the new workers at the plants were former smugglers of bodies, who were now out of work because the trade was no longer profitable.

Nísyx Tekil was right. For some reason, Phmquedrians were assuming Tannódin'é patterns of behavior. And Anámn soon realized that this was not only Phmquedrian or Tannódin'é behavior; it was nel'asmív behavior.

The lumber district contained an irrepressible desperation. This was Kaimero and Hamin's home. No wonder they questioned their own history. Even though the labor was for pay, in some respects, it was crueler than overt slavery. At least Anámn knew he was a slave. Credit payment was a facade: paltry compensation for the most ridiculous labor. Indeed, Phmquedria bore the brunt of Global Initiative's underside. Faced with this truth, Kinesis knew he ought to do something. But after his exchange with his father and sojourn in the lumber district, the runaway was clueless as to what direction he should take. The mess was too complex to tackle haphazardly.

The days were growing longer and warmer. Anámn had long lost track of and care for time. It felt like midsummer, which meant that he had been on the run for nearly two durations. The forest became thicker as he migrated north. Anámn surmised that he was leaving the Lumber District and moving into the northernmost reaches of Phmquedria, the Minusía peninsula's Shipping District.

He used every bit of means to get to Minusía as fast as he was able. He stowed away on railcruisers, walked, ran, and even flew (for a few moments). The journey he undertook since his escape from Euhilv was not the most direct; however, in the end, he had traveled over 5100 lengths. He could not have covered half that distance in two durations if he had not stolen his way onto the rail lines at every opportunity.

Three weeks had passed since he last worked in a lumber plant. During these twenty-four days, Anámn dialogued with Téza constantly. He chanted at least once a day, for three hours. As a result, he increased in knowledge of his powers. Of all the things he learned, he confirmed he *was not* a telekinetic. He could not "move" objects with his mind. His powers were much more nuanced and enigmatic.

Thinking over Malchían's explanation, Anámn gathered that his ability converted potential energy into kinetic energy and vice versa. The ability was context sensitive. The more potential energy surrounded him, the more he could "siphon" off this energy and convert it into actual energy. He could release this energy in a myriad of ways. The opposite was true as well.

Once, during a thunderstorm, Anámn tried to sense the kinetic signature of each raindrop. The exercise almost caused him to pass out, so he focused on the local, aggregate rainfall instead. Concentrating, he "robbed" the raindrops the motion due to them, because of gravity. His experiment created a shockwave that threw Anámn backwards. It was an easy lesson to learn: Anámn could not control gravity, just the energy that gravity caused. Instead of robbing the rain of all its energy, Anámn reasoned that it would be safer and easier to borrow *some* of the energy. In the case of the raindrops, the outwardly visible display of this ability caused them to fall slower.

Anámn was unable to control his power on a large scale, however. He found it difficult to differentiate the stages of energy. He did not understand or intuit the basics of energy flow, and Téza would not be the one to teach him. The Elemental still held a grudge against Matriester. Anámn had forfeited instruction from the Elemental due to his prior actions.

Before Anámn entered the city, he washed himself and his clothes at a small hostel about a half day's journey from Minusía. He was surprised how well his clothes held up considering the amount of work he had performed and how far he traveled. There were a few holes and spots of discoloration, but all in all, his sister's judgment in apparel was genius. Even still, he decided to change into a cheap but efficient secondary set of clothes he had purchased on his way north: brown pants, sandals, a gray shirt with a thin scarf, and a light brown jacket. He stuffed his coat and other garments in a recently obtained midsize traveling bag and set out for the city around midnight.

Minusía was a port town, located on the western face of the northern Phmquedrian shoreline. It was the main commercial junction between Damüda, Tannódin, Keotagosdi, and Phmquedria. Beyond its shores lay the Anplo Sea, the waterway to northern Tannódin, Zorét, and Damüda. Persons of every sort moved about and through the city. At every turn, the runaway encountered unknown dialects, faces, and skin tones. Minusía had been an important shipping city for over a millennium.

He arrived at the city's outskirts before dawn. Although he had never seen one up close, Anámn had heard the sound of a stratojet enough to know he was close to a skyport. But the aircrafts' roars soon dissolved under the screech of a railcruiser. The skyport and railcruiser line were only a few lengths from one another, probably to make shipping and commerce flow easily.

The layout of the city confused the Sczyphamek. He discerned no systematic design, no commercial center, nor a central location of lodging. It was as if the city was erected with minimal civil planning and engineering. When Anámn made it to the coastline, he was astounded. For lengths in either direction were piers, filled to the brim with all kinds of boats, seawinders, and battlecruisers. The port stretched over twenty lengths at least. Looking inland, Anámn finally gained perspective of the city. The ports were the center of commerce; everything was built in relation to them.

Anámn walked towards the tallest building near the shoreline. There lay no reason behind his course of action. And asking Téza for directions was pointless. The Elemental had already spoken. And Téza was just as surly as Anámn.

Matriester pulled his hat low and kept his head down. He eyed no one and did his best to appear anonymous amongst the sea of people. Anámn passed many Global Initiative troops, no doubt from the ranks of Blue Rapier or White Scythe. He decided against talking to anyone in a straightforward manner. His father had surely sent word to all the coastal towns. And because Minusía was a city of massive transportation and trade, it was a likely place of escape.

Matriester was still in Phmquedria. Minusía was still the domain of Alzhexph ju Xaníz.

Anámn approached the tall building with reservation. The structure was round, tall, and slender, and its top contained a large revolving light. Its height was greater than any other building in the city. He wondered what its purpose was. It seemed to be too out of the ordinary. He almost had the mind to ask someone, but something stopped him.

His stomach growled in discontent. Matriester had not eaten decent food for quite some time, other than insects in the forest. His stomach growled again and louder than before. Anámn searched for an eatery, one that was frequented by Phmquedrians more than any other ethnic group, so that he would blend in.

Anámn inhaled and smelled a wonderful aroma of cooked seafood. His watering mouth and nose led him to a square filled with many different eateries. Anámn spied a Phmquedrian seafood café and entered it. A host invited him to sit anywhere as it was still early in the day. Anámn complied and sat near the back so that he could see who went in and out of the restaurant. He ordered seafood stew with bread and water. As was his custom, when the food arrived, Anámn slurped, chewed, and pulverized his meal with an appetite so intense that the cook served the runaway another bowl on the restaurant's tab. Upon finishing his meal, Anámn drank the water. The water was *cold*, but there was no ice.

Cold water. How was that possible? Thanking the cook, Anámn paid for the meal and left the eatery questioning his own senses.

He exited towards Minusia's inland and walked down a stony street. A multitude of people was standing around and reading some sort of paper. The front cover sported a picture of a large building that appeared to have suffered major damage. At the bottom of the picture lay a caption with large letters.

He was illiterate; therefore, the slave had difficulty understanding the meaning of the pictures. Frowning his face and concentrating, he tried to make out the words, but he did not recognize them. The little literacy he possessed was due to memorization, not phonics. Nísyx had told him that memorization was not actually reading, but he always ignored her. Another thing to add to the ever-growing list of things he regretted.

"D' ya need some help?" he heard a female voice inquire.

Turning in the direction of the inquisition, Anámn saw a young woman, who seemed about four to five cycles his junior, staring at him. Although apprehensive, Matriester felt no warning from his Elemental or his own senses.

"Well, yeah... I guess so..." Anámn said. He gazed at the ground in embarrassment. "I uhm... I can't... I can't..."

"It's fine." She smiled cheerfully. "I'll tell you what this says if you wanna know."

Like words on a page, her genetic composition was indecipherable to Anámn. To his eyes, she appeared to possess Phmquedrian features, but she also displayed phenotypes unknown to him. The woman did not possess Tannódin'é or Damüdan blood. She had a brownish-yellow complexion and was shorter than him, and she was wrapped in a thin brown cloak and hood that obscured her face and eyes. But that was not the give-away; the irrefutable evidence lay in her dialect. Anámn was familiar with Damüdan, Tannódin'é, and Phmquedrian speech patterns, but her pronunciation baffled him. Her meter was steady and rhythmic, but there was a deliberate poetic quality to the somewhat broken delivery.

Anámn pointed to the collection of bound paper she was holding. "I saw the cover of this thing."

"It's a newsprint." Her tone continued to grow more amicable. "This is a Tannódin'é newsprint dat covers news throughout the entire planet."

"Huh? The *entire* planet? Kíma…" Never in his life did he think about the other continents as real, as being "newsworthy," as truly existing or impacting his life on Phmquedria. They seemed just as far removed as the One with No Name.

The young woman studied Anámn's face. "Yeah. Da cover's a picture taken from Nez Spirita. Pike Metropolis to be exact. They're the Triple Skyrises. You ever 'eard of dem?"

"No," Anámn said nonchalantly. "Are they important or something?"

Shaking her head, his interlocutor was emphatic. "*Yes*. They're quite 'portant."

"Oh." Anámn blinked. "So what happened to them? They looked kinda damaged…"

"Well, I guess if you haven't heard of dem, den you haven't heard th' news. These towers are da base for Global Initiative in Nez Spirita. Two durations ago, a group broke into da building and did a great deal uh damage."

"Two durations ago?" Talk of durations made Anámn realize that he had completely lost track of the days. "What day is it now?"

"You serious?" she asked. "Where you from? Why don't you know what day it is?"

Anámn was uncertain how to answer her question, so he paused and responded, "I've been traveling for a while, working here and there. I don't keep up with the days and durations, just as long as I get paid for the number of days I worked."

"Hmmph… Well, it's Namíz… the thirteenth day, Fürnlé…"

"It's *Namíz?* Namíz… Staxis… how long I been traveling?" he muttered to himself. Returning to their conversation, Anámn continued, "So if that building was attacked two durations ago, why's the newsprint reporting old news?"

The woman laughed at Anámn's erratic perceptiveness. "*Dat* is a good question. Tannódin still hasn't found nay one perpetrator." She chose her words carefully. She did not trust him. "Dis issue is about th' 'vestigation. Da Eradicate has blamed Miska Kea—"

"The Eradicate…" Anámn trailed. "Who in Qalfocx are they?"

"Spies and agents for Global Initiative and Pre-Eminent's personal soldiers."

"What a kímaz crazy name for a group…"

"And just what's *your* name?" the woman asked, surprising the runaway. "We been talking here for five minutes, and this conversation don't seem like it's gonna end soon with them kind of questions."

"Huyé," Anámn answered without hesitation. "My name is Huyé. What is your name?"

"Lénü," she replied and looked Anámn directly in the eyes. "Lénü'íque."[1]

"I won't waste any more of your time, Lénü." Anámn nodded appreciatively. "I'm sorry that I asked so many questions. I should've learned how to read a long time ago." His apology was sincere and carried with it a repentance born of willful ignorance.

"*There's something about this report that they are leaving out*, Huyé," she said, bypassing his apology. "There been some rumors going around dat this was not the work of Miska Kea by themselves..."

"Huh?" Anámn was lured into the gossip. "Another group...?"

"No, not another group." She drew very close to him and whispered, "A Sczyphamek..."

Anámn stood still.

"Huyé?"

Anámn could not believe that.

"Huyé, are you all right?"

"Are you *sure*?" His face was serious and stern. "Is that even possible?"

"That's what they say," she replied. "You know, *they*..."

"By the One!" Anámn quietly exclaimed.

The woman drew away and scanned her surroundings. "Well den, Huyé, I must be going."

"Thank you for the news, Lénü."

Anámn was filled with gratitude and a newfound hope. However, a feeling of apprehension came before the hope acquired a permanent dwelling. The power cells of four AEARs had just cycled.

He glared at Lénü, believing her to be his betrayer, but she was not carrying the weapon. She glowered back at Anámn until she noticed four Blue Rapier soldiers eyeing them in the distance. Anámn looked beyond her and saw three soldiers coming from the other direction. They were trying to corner one of them in some sort of trap.

"Staxis," they both cursed.

"That was a good story, you piece o' kíma. You Eradicate bastards're getting pretty good if you fooled me so easily."

"What? You're the one who set me up, damn it."

"What?" she balked. His face did not lie. He was just as nervous as she. They were both targets. "Who're you? And what'd you do?"

"You don't wanna know," he answered. His delivery was humorous but his countenance was solemn. "Just like I probably don't want to know who

---

[1] Lénü'íque (*ley*-nyoo-*ee*-k[weh])

you are… Staxis… I really need to learn how to read…"

"Maybe they just want you," she said warily. "I think I'll go now…"

"They're behind you too," he replied. "I think they want us both."

The approaching contingent did not know he was a Sczyphamek. If they had been notified, there would have been more of them. His father had probably only relayed Anámn's full identity to the highest levels of Global Initiative. It made sense that the average soldier was kept in the dark. There was no need to alarm them with the possibility—however small—of defeat. And it was not to Anámn's advantage to use his powers in public.

Grabbing Lénü's arm instinctively, the Euhilv runaway said, "I think it'd be best if you came with me."

"Let go o' me," she whispered and attempted to free herself from his grasp.

"No," he stated matter-of-factly, but he knew neither where they were going nor why he was taking her with him. "Come on…"

Anámn spotted an alley and ran towards it with Lénü in tow. The soldiers broke their nonchalant saunter and burst into full pursuit. Reaching in her cloak while running down the alley, Lénü pulled out an uncharged energy pistol and powered it up.

"Don't do that," Anámn sighed.

Lénü disregarded the runaway's warning and fired the weapon at the soldiers, who halted and took cover in the alley.

"Stop," Anámn ordered, this time more sternly.

"Don't tell me what t' do," she snapped.

"You just told soldiers who weren't looking for us, where we are," he said. "Put that away, please."

Reluctantly complying, Lénü'íque holstered her pistol. "Well, what're we going to do?"

Anámn nodded towards a three-story building ahead of them and pointed. "In there."

Lénü'íque's retort was primed but shots rang out before she could extend her displeasure. "Staxis…"

They darted into the structure as energy bursts grazed their path. The kinetic signatures increased; Anámn now sensed ten pursuers. The building was a hotel of some sort, and the duo was not welcomed when they entered. Evidently, the lodge was a segregated establishment—Tannódin'é and Damüdans only. Before the dismayed concierge uttered a word, Anámn spotted a staircase, yanked his unwilling compatriot by the arm and compelled her to follow. Anámn threw open the door to the stairway, and they bolted up the steps as quickly as they could. The troops were only a few paces behind.

"And you thought d' Eradicate was a crazy name," she sneered through huffs. "Their agents were the ones who probably located us and relayed the message to Blue Rapier."

"It's still a dumb name."

"You don't know what 'eradication' means, *do you*?"

"No. Why?"

"I t'ought so…" she smirked and rolled her eyes. "If you can find a way out of here, I can take us to a place where we can hide."

"That sounds like a plan."

Though afraid, Anámn had spent the past two or more durations by himself. His constant travel had left him quite lonely and antisocial. Just being in a dialogue—no matter how contested and forced—gave Anámn a sense of connection and identity.

They scrambled to the third floor and stumbled into a hallway. A guestroom's open door availed itself, and Anámn signaled Lénü to follow and quietly closed the door behind them. There was a bed and a chest-of-drawers in the chamber. Though no one appeared to be in the suite at that moment, the room was occupied. The bed was unmade and clothes filled the open drawers. On the far side of the room was a balcony.

Lénü heard the steps of their adversaries. The soldiers knocked on the doors to every room, prodding the inhabitants to open. If no one responded, the Rapiers kicked in the doors. The sounds of the knocks and kicks became louder and angrier. Time was not on their side.

Anámn locked the door. "Move back to the window, Lénü."

She complied. He effortlessly picked up the chest-of-drawers and pushed it against the doorway. Lénü had no time to be shocked at his feat of strength, for just as quickly, she heard the banging of Blue Rapier troops on the door.

"Dat won't hold 'em."

"I just needed to give us some time. Remember the deal, right? You know a place where we can hide?"

"Yeah. But I still wanna know how we're gonna get out of here, Huyé…"

"Anámn. My name is Anámn. Hop on my back."

"Aná—wait… your *back*?"

"Yeah, my back."

"Are you kiddin'?"

"Do you wanna get caught?"

Anámn opened the balcony door, stepped out, and moved towards the guardrail.

"Come on; we don't have time!"

The woman acquiesced and jumped onto Anámn's back.

"Hold on." He gripped his hand on the balcony's guardrail.

"Wait… what're you…? What the… No… No, no, *no, no, no*…. Anámn!"

The Sczyphamek jumped over the rail with Lénü'íque screaming and gripping his body tightly. She did not feel the impact. There was no impact. Opening her eyes, she realized they were floating high above the hotel.

"Where is this place, Lénü?" he asked and turned his head back to her. "What direction?"

"How? Oh, kíma!" she gasped in disbelief.

"Lénü," Anámn said with a calmness that even surprised him. "Lénü, don't worry. I'm a Sczyphamek."

"A… Sczyphamek…" she whispered and noticed a small green layer surrounding them both.

"Which way, before they see us," he repeated.

Coming to her senses, she murmured, "Go north, up the coast."

"Hold on tight, and take a deep breath."

She pressed her body against his, clenched his jacket with a violent grip, and closed her eyes. The sensation was indescribable. Her stomach shifted and the air almost completely rushed out of her lungs. When she opened her eyes, they were already a length from their original position.

Anámn's velocity was swift. He quickly grew fatigued, but pressed on. No one detected their presence, and their altitude removed any chance of a noticeable shadow. After about a minute, Lénü could no longer hold her breath and exhaled. Aware of Lénü's discomfort, Anámn slowed his pace so that she could inhale without gasping.

"Down there." The woman nodded towards a collection of old and underutilized warehouses.

Sensing for nel'asmív, Anámn chose a spot to land where they would not be seen.

"We are going to have to get down there pretty quick," he warned. "Please, don't scream."

She gave a sign of affirmation, and within a millisecond, the descent started in all its haste. After five or so seconds, they were on the ground, in another alleyway between two warehouses.

"Lénü," Anámn said. "Lénü, you can let go… Hey, Lénü…" Turning his head back, Anámn looked into her feverish eyes, which correlated with her short breaths and racing heartbeat. "Lénü, you alright?"

"Yea," she gasped and let go of Anámn's jacket. "A Sczy… phamek…"

"Yeah." Anámn hunched over with his hands on his knees, breathing heavy and perspiring. He had not flown that fast since the tree incident. But he exhibited an incomparable amount of control versus then. Yet regardless of whether he exhibited control or not, the exercise of flying was still terribly taxing.

After catching his wind, Anámn scanned once more for any possible enemies who might have tailed them to the location. He made a hand gesture in Lénü's direction, which signaled that no one was around, and prompted her to take the lead.

Lénü fidgeted about. Her guilt consumed her, so she interjected softly, "Anámn, I'm sorry."

"For what?"

She reached into her pocket and pulled out a small sack that was strangely familiar to Anámn. "I took this from you back d'ere. We needed the money so dat we could get out of here…"

He brusquely searched his pockets and satchel, and without a doubt, his wallet was missing. "That is mine! When did you…?" The Sczyphamek retraced their entire twenty-minute relationship. "When you drew close to tell me about another Sczyphamek—that's when you stole my credits!"

"I didn't know who you were," she said remorsefully.

Somehow Anámn maintained his composure despite himself. That money represented the first time he was paid for his labor in his entire life, no matter how unfair the wage was.

"The story you told me—was that a lie too? Is there a Sczyphamek in Nez Spirita, or did you just tell me that so I wouldn't notice that you robbed me?"

"That was not a fabrication. I would not lie about something like that. Such a thing would be evil." Lénü'íque responded with sincere repentance and her grammar and vocabulary suddenly became pristine.

Kinesis paused. *Evil.* Yes, it would be. As rare as anyone or anything was called that word, such a statement would have embodied evil. A potential Kylanín had not happened in over 1700 cycles. Not too many folk would have lied about *such a happening.*

The pickpocket extended her arm and handed the pilfered wallet to Matriester in contrition. "If I'd known, I wouldn't have taken it from you." Her voice wavered as he took his wallet back. "A-are you," she stuttered. "Really… Did you honestly happen as a…"

"Yeah." Anámn chuckled. "I'm an illiterate Sczyphamek. My title is Kinesis."

"Kinesis… I don't wanna believe it. He won't believe it…"

"*He?*" Anámn asked. "Who's 'he'? You said something about 'we' earlier, too."

"My father… well, he's like my father." The woman's countenance changed. "C'mon."

Lénü walked out of the alleyway and towards a large shipping warehouse. The Sczyphamek followed her lead, just as she followed his earlier. A deal was a deal. The closest person Anámn sensed was half a length away, but a faint kinetic signature emanated close by.

"I can sense somebody very close to us," Anámn whispered.

"It's just one person?"

"Yeah."

"It's him."

Opening the door to the warehouse, the two walked inside. It was completely dark. Only the light from the outside, which found its way in through the cracks in the ceiling and under the doors, gave the space any illumination.

Anámn wondered why the door was unlocked. If it was such a secure place, why were there no security precautions?

"Hold mah hand, and step only where I step," Lénü warned with an intentional edge. "If we make one mistake, he'll start shootin', and I'll prolly end up dead."

"Then let me use my aura to light the way."

"*No.* No lights. If he sees lights he would think it was someone other than me, and he would destroy this place."

"How do you switch talk like that? And why don't you just say that you're back?"

"*No.*" Lénü responded with exasperation. "No yelling or he'll start firing. Anámn—just do what I say, please?"

Anámn discerned potential energy everywhere and in extreme amounts. It only took a few moments for him to realize what that meant: traps and alarms were littered throughout the warehouse. The potential energy represented the many snares that had yet to be activated. They zigzagged their way around the shadowy, dank edifice, and soon, Anámn lost track of their direction. He held onto Lénü's hand and remained quiet. After ten minutes of what appeared to Anámn as random movements, they stopped.

"Alright, we are done," she declared. "We're here."

Lénü tapped an arrhythmic beat on the ground, which was countered by two knocks underneath their position. Anámn rolled his eyes and wondered what kind of person required such an obsessively intricate system of identification and entrapments.

Lénü stepped back and pulled a concrete floorboard up. She was stronger than she appeared. Light emerged from the hole in the floor, and the Sczyphamek used what little light there was to glimpse around the room. However, the light was unable to cast any revelation on the warehouse's innards. Whoever designed the setup was a genius, which meant Lénü was extremely gifted in her own right because she navigated through the maze by memory alone. Down the hole was a ladder, and Lénü went down first, Anámn behind her. When they made it to the bottom, they ambled through a hallway that led to a greater source of brightness.

"Who'd you bring back here?" a slurred, masculine voice demanded. The light obfuscated his body.

"I tol' ya not to start drinkin' again," Lénü barked.

"Who'd you bring back here, damn it," he repeated even harsher than the last time.

Anámn didn't say a word.

"Brenko," she said. "I don't think you'll mind once you—"

"*Brenko?*" Anámn blurted out. "No way…"

"Kíma," the man's retort was as rancid as the rotten carcass of a diseased canine. Even the scavengers stayed clear. "Why do some legends die and others live on?"

What emerged from the shadows was hardly legendary. His fair face was round and covered by a scraggly beard. The countenance that surrounded his blue-green eyes and rested upon his face was so forlorn and mysteriously confident—an anxious coolness perhaps—Anámn had to question his eyes. The man was too overweight be a legend, too unkempt to be a legend. His clothes were a ragtag of black pants and a blue shirt that did not match. Based on his demeanor, the slob cared not if he matched or if he clashed. In his trembling right hand shook a cup, and three open bottles were on a table behind him. The smell of liquor was paralyzing.

No. He could not be *that* Brenko. *That* Brenko was a legend, a hero—the one who led and survived the attack on Phenplyacin. Everyone had heard of *that* Brenko. *That* Brenko was purportedly the best military mind in this span of cycles.

This Brenko... *This* short, pudgy, slurring, balding, non-matching, stumbling, droopy, slack, smelly, and truculent fraction of a man *could not* be the Brenko of legend. Anámn shook his head at this. The story—turned legend, turned myth, turned truth—of Phenplyacin was circulated throughout all of Qeauríyx. And every good story had clear-cut representations of good and evil and a setting where these forces would do battle. Phenplyacin was the site, Brenko was the tragic hero, and Vicious was the reprehensible malefactor. Anámn had heard the story countless times in all its various permutations, but he also remembered Malchían's apparent disdain for them.

Yet something else also filled the Sczyphamek's qanín. This particular meeting was also the doing of Téza. Somehow his Elemental knew that Brenko was in Minusía, although the runaway was oblivious as to how such a feat was possible. But, it was a highly unlikely coincidence that Anámn met the daughter of one of Qeauríyx's most notorious characters by mere happenstance.

Téza wanted this to happen... Searching his Elemental, Anámn felt it to be true. *But it can't be true... Téza can't predict the future and ain't no way this guy is...*

"Lénü," Anámn stammered, "is this *the* Brenko?"

The woman shook her head. "Unfortunately, yes."

"That's a good word." Brenko dropped his cup on the floor, which spilled the remaining liquor he had not consumed. "*Unfortunate.* That about sums it all up; doesn't it?" The man got down on his knees and sucked and slurped the spirits from the floor.

"He is much nicer when he does not drink." Lénü apologized in a dialect and grammar that tried to make up for the drunkenness and lowliness of Brenko.

"*When I don't drink?*" The brigand righted himself. "I am always drinking, even when I don't drink... I drink. I've drank. And I've drunk... this liquor ain't the worst of what I drunk, Lénü. Those bastards..."

Before he could finish his rant, Brenko slumped over and fell against the wall, and Lénü rushed to his side. Anámn was dumbfounded. Even during the worst periods of his life, Anámn had not been so resigned. He was defiant, but not resigned. He had tasted despair, but his anger made despair a vacation, never a home. This sort of resignation frightened the Sczyphamek to the innermost parts of his qanín. What made a paladin like Brenko become such a perforating, cracking, and withering shell of his former self?

"Kanoso,"[2] Lénü muttered.

The runaway grew more uncomfortable. He could not remember the last time he heard the word "kanoso," and he was obviously in the middle of a private matter.

"Anámn, I know he doesn't look like it, but he is a good man. At least, he was…" She shook away the reflex to cry. "He can still be…"

Brenko lay comatose, breathing laboriously.

"And you don't need to ask. He never tol' me what happened either. Can you help me pick him up and put him on his cot?"

The runaway walked towards the man and his daughter and hoisted the drunk up, carrying him to the cot, which was located by the table with the open bottles. He placed the drunkard on the bed, and Lénü knelt beside him and covered him with a blanket. The woman stood up and motioned the Sczyphamek to another room. Once he entered, Lénü closed the door and switched on a light. Somehow they were able to receive electricity to the building without anyone knowing about it. The man and the woman were resourceful and clever. The room itself contained an old couch, some sort of machine, and a barebones bed.

Anámn did not know what to say, but he thought it would be best if he changed the subject. "You said that you all were trying to get out of here. Does that mean you have a way?"

Shaking off her sadness, the woman answered, "Yes… well, maybe. D'ere's a man Brenko knows who pilots a stratojet. If we pay him enough, we can get out of here. As you've noticed, Phmquedria has gotten a little too hot for us."

"For me too." Looking at Lénü again, he could not stop wondering where she was from and how her dialect and grammar came to be so indescribable. "Uhm… Lénü, I don't know how to ask this right; so I'm not even going to try… But *what* are you? I mean, where are you from? I've never seen a nel'asmív that looks or talks like you."

"Really?" she asked in amusement. "Where you from, Anámn?"

Anámn smirked. The woman had a penchant for answering a question with a question. "Euhilv."

"*Euhilv?*" she gasped. "You are a runaway *and* a Sczyphamek?"

"Well… that and…"

"And *what?*"

"Alzhexph ju Xaníz is my father."

Lénü'íque winced. She was in the company of a runaway Sczyphamek who *happened* as the son of the most powerful man on the continent. The

---

[2] Kanoso (kuh-noh-soh)

female sat down in angst. Out of all the possible combinations of a fugitive on Qeauríyx, Anámn was the worst one, at the worst time, on the worst continent.

"I am from Bryce," Lénü said. "My mother was half-Brycian and half-Phmquedrian. My father was from Dynasty, Líachim, a major shipping city. But he was half Líachimian and half Nez Spiritan." She unwrapped herself out of her cloak and pulled her hood back, and what emerged was beyond Anámn's reckoning. It was as if the cloak provided an obscure veil over the woman's beauty—with one terrible blemish. A scar ran from her left temple, down her neck, and into her shirt. Her hair was short, black-brown, and quite lovely, and her brown eyes were mysteriously free-spirited.

Anámn tried his best not to gawk at the wound. Repeatedly, he told himself not to stare, but his eyes would not listen to the sincere direction of his mind. He must have appeared quite awkward, because Lénü somberly pulled the hood back over her head.

"I forgot about the scar. Don't know how, since 's so obvious."

"No. That's not…" Anámn felt guilty for embarrassing her. "I'm sorry. I didn't mean to make you feel like…"

The Sczyphamek was at a loss for words. Pulling his jacket off and his shirt up, Anámn turned around, his back facing the woman. He heard the gasp. She saw them. Scar upon scar. To the woman's eyes, his back appeared burned many times over. Long black-brown streaks crisscrossed and made indistinct patterns that carried no meaning other than the torture and pain they were meant to provide. The top of each scar revealed the pathways of tears and blood that had streamed from the body of the slave. Lénü's right hand touched her face while her left reached toward his back. When Anámn felt her caring palm against his superficially healed wounds, he nearly wept. Her hand was warm, and this was the first time in many cycles that something other than his shirt or a whip had touched his back. Her fingers delicately traced the scars—nearly one by one—across and over his entire back.

"Who- who did this to you?"

"Most of them were from a Tannódin'é named Héthyx," Matriester whispered. What was he doing—opening himself to a stranger?

"*Did ya kill 'im?*"

Jarred by her question, Anámn pulled his shirt down and put his jacket back on. "Why do you want to know?"

"Any man who did 'at to the son of the most powerful man on this continent has surely done worse to those who got no rights he has to respect. A person like that deserves to die," she stated coldly.

Kinesis was agitated by the woman's quickness to judge. It reminded him of himself. "I didn't kill him. It wouldn't have done any good. Did you kill the person who did that?" Anámn pulled her hood back down and touched her face.

She recoiled, but could not completely withdraw from the caring feel of his hand. "Damn right, I did. I killed the cléth, and it did a lot of good."

"Maybe we should talk about something else."

"Why? Brenko will be sleep for at least half a day," she responded. "He's gonna try to keep you from comin' with us when he wakes up. I know the man... But I won't let him... and when he hears what you are..."

"I don't understand. I thought he was one of the best—"

"He is the best!" Lénü's scream evinced fatigue, defensiveness, and hopelessness. "I'm sorry. We been on the run now for so long..."

"How long have they been chasing you all?"

"Which 'they' do you mean?"

"Blue Rapier and the rest..."

Lénü looked away.

"What? Are you telling me they aren't the only ones looking for you?" Anámn's stare pressed her for a response.

"You better sit down, son of ju Xaníz. This story's gonna be long. I got a knack for being indirect and loquacious."

"*Lo*-what?"

"You talking better than me, and you cain't read, but you don't know the words I do 'cause I can read. Staxis... I think it would be better if I talked more like a Tannódin'é for this part."

Anámn nodded and smiled. Her dialect and vocabulary confused him from time to time, though he was amazed how effortlessly she switched back and forth. The woman was more adept at the skill than Kaimero and Hamin.

"'Loquacious' means I can talk too damn much. Now about who was chasing us..."

"I like stories," Anámn interjected and sat down next to Lénü. "But I hope this story tells me how in Qalfocx you all managed to create a makeshift base underneath an abandoned warehouse."

"*This* place? This is our home. This is where we've plotted against the sex trade the entire time."

"*The sex trade?* You all fought against the leaders of the sex trade?"

"Leaders?" Lénü asked. "What makes you think we were only against the leaders? Leaders are only one part of anything. Brenko taught me that... No, Anámn; we plotted against the *entire* sex trade."

Anámn thought back to his time in Prosephyr where he worked as a hired hand. Some of his co-workers did say something about the sex trade not being as profitable as it once was.

"But why the sex trade?" Anámn inquired. "I thought Brenko was a soldier. It doesn't make sense that he would fight against—"

"When has Qeauríyx ever made sense? Brenko never told me why he chose to do this. I think it was out of guilt for leaving..."

If any part of the Brenko story was *completely* true, it was the fact that the tactical mastermind deserted Miska Kea a few cycles after Phenplyacin.

Miska Kea was shattered into factions after Brenko's departure, but many had hoped he would return.

"I honestly don't know for sure why he left… I met him after his fourth sex trade assassination," Lénü continued.

"His fourth assassination?"

"Oh, I'm sorry. See, there I go 'gain meandering."

Shifting her weight on the couch, the woman thought about how she should tell the story, while Anámn vowed to cease his inquiries. Every time he asked a question, it made her stray even more. Lénü seemed scattered, deceptively scattered.

"Let me try this again; and don't say a word to me unless you have to."

The Sczyphamek nodded.

"Brenko told it to me like this: a few cycles after he left Miska Kea, he was traveling around the planet and noticed that sex trading was happening everywhere. In some ways, its reach was greater than Global Initiative."

Anámn inwardly agreed. Even in Euhilv, he had seen the trade firsthand—men and women being forced into sex and disappearing from the slave camps with no warning. Tannódin'é men and women were both involved in the enterprise. If a bondsman or woman withheld sex from a Tannódin'é, the penalty was clear: "family dissolution." It was one phrase that Anámn understood too well. Families were broken up and shipped to other areas on Phmquedria, or their young children were made to work deep in the mines. Most of the little ones who worked there did not survive.

But as terrible as the Tannódin'é were with such threats, they were not alone in their exploitative activity. Anámn observed the wealthy Phmquedrians in the lumber district also participated in the trade. Even Nísyx said something about it when he visited her in Kamo. The problem was not endemic to Phmquedria alone. Yes, it was more *global* than "Global" Initiative.

"So you've seen it here too? I'm sure. Well, it's everywhere Anámn. I asked Brenko why nel'asmív did this to each other, and all he said was, 'Why not? Meaningless people do meaningless things…'

"He relocated here in Minusía. At the time, he looked much different than he does now. I think he gained the weight on purpose and by accident. He grew his hair and his beard out and mastered four distinct languages and dialects from different places on Qeauríyx. And he changed his name to 'Plenz' and began drinking himself to death when he wasn't plotting something.

"Brenko… he's such a damn fool… a fool of a genius. He figured out a way to cripple the entire sex trade."

"How?" Anámn asked. "I thought you said that the trade is global. How can one person do that?"

"One person cannot. Success requires the death of a lot of people and the sabotaging of important equipment in strategic places. For two cycles

Brenko traveled the planet gathering information on the trade, from the top to the bottom. He came back here, in this room no less, and schemed. He figured that it would take him twelve cycles to complete the task, if his calculations were correct."

Anámn was scared and curious as to how someone possessed that kind of mastery of the art of patience, sabotage, and premeditated murder.

"His first assassination was somebody that most folk would hardly mention. Even the elites of the sex trade didn't notice. They replaced her quickly. But Brenko had done his research. The person he killed had connections to every major interest in the trade. Her replacement could not completely duplicate her role. For six durations, Brenko waited and watched to see if he was right. And he was. The slave trade was subtly made inefficient and less profitable.

"To shorten this up, like I said, we met on his fourth cycle of doing this. I was fifteen cycles old. My mother was already gone and my father died the previous cycle in Dynasty. Wasn't much for me there. I tried to find work, but no one would hire me. 'Fore I knew it, I was homeless and kidnapped by sex traders. For half a cycle I was raped and beaten and sold."

She paused. Although hardened, the woman could not altogether stifle those repeated violations.

Anámn was stupefied. He felt a simultaneous compassion and shame for Lénü. Was it because she reminded him of his mother?

"Brenko bought me, under the lie of being in need of a new whore slave. But as soon as the deal was done, he set me free, with enough credits for me to live on for one cycle." She paused again, and this time, a few tears fell down her face. "But where was I gonna go, and what was I gonna do? I didn't know what to do, and Brenko saw it on my face. He must've... I wasn't the first person he'd set free, and I wasn't the last, but unlike the rest... I couldn't...

"He took me in, educated, and trained me. That's why I am able to talk both ways like I do. Brenko taught me how to interact in any environment and with any person. 'Language, grammar, and dialect is the first give away,' he used to say to me..."

Lénü's eyes grew firm. "He was—he became like a father to me. When he thought I was ready to handle it, he told me about his plan to deal with the sex trade. He didn't need to ask me if I wanted to help. I volunteered.

"My first action was during the sixth assassination. 'Twas in Keotagosdi... We've been working together ever since then. Brenko taught me how to be passionate about my work but dispassionate in its execution."

"Lénü, I don't mean to stop you, but—"

"The eighth assassination," she continued, ignoring him, "was a mass killing. We killed over twenty-five men that day. A captain and his entire crew. They were responsible for shipping men, women, and children throughout the planet. After that, the major players figured something was wrong. Brenko had been silently crippling their operation for seven cycles and the crew we killed—just like the first woman—was irreplaceable. Now, what did you want to say, Anámn?"

Her narration left her unaware of Anámn's growing disaffection, which he had to vocalize. "You make this seem so easy. I mean, you're killing people!"

"Yeah. So?"

"Don't you think something is wrong with murdering people?"

"Don't you think the slave and sex trade is wrong? *This is like for like*, Anámn."

"That doesn't make it right," he stated.

"You haven't seen the results. And we are not killing everybody who has something to do with this..."

"Something about this still seems wrong..."

"Oh?" Lénü asked spitefully. Her countenance and delivery changed with amazing speed. "D' ya think you're gonna persuade Pre-Eminent to stop killin'? D' ya think somebody like Vicious'll respond t' anything but murderous force? Ya haven't even heard what Pre-Eminent did singlehandedly in Anzél. Staxis, you don't even know where Anzél is, do you? Before you start judging us, maybe you should read a little bit. Oh that's *right*... Ya *can't* read, *can you?*"

Amazingly, Anámn held his temper. "For you to react like that, only means that you're as clueless to the answer as I am."

Lénü'íque was about to respond, but held her head down. "Now you sound like Brenko... I'm sorry I insulted you. 'At wasn't called for."

"That's alright. Just finish the story. If you all were so successful, then what happened? Why are you on the run now?"

"It's called probability. Damn probability. Every execution made the likelihood of us getting caught more and more a possibility. By the time we pulled off the eleventh plan, we figured that we were close to being found out. We hadn't been in this location for over a cycle though, so we knew this base was probably a safe place for hiding. But I am getting ahead of myself.

"Our last target, the twelfth one, was a woman in Dynasty. Actually, she was one of the head suppliers and beneficiaries on the planet. She was so powerful that the Eradicate frequently visited her for information."

"Wait. Tannódin is working *with* the sex trade?"

"No. They are not, but the Eradicate can't infiltrate every community. So they use intermediaries to act as listening posts. But then again, I guess they are workin' with them, since the sex trade became planet-wide through the expansion of Tannódin'é technology."

"Oh... I get it. So was this woman the same person who was over the trade when you were kidnapped?"

"Yeah. One and the same," she muttered.

"What happened?"

"What happened is that we tried to kill her five days after the Triple Skyrises were damaged."

"What does that have to do with this?" Anámn asked. "Didn't you say a Sczyphamek caused most of the damage?"

"I also said that Miska Kea was involved. And the leader of that group took part in the attack. He knew Brenko."

"He did?"

"Actually, he and Brenko, and another woman—they survived Phenplyacin together. They were the only three from their division to make it out alive."

"I can't even imagine what that was like."

"Sometimes, Brenko still screams at night about it, but I can't tell what he's saying…" Her eyes tarried towards the room where the drunkard slept. "Although Brenko was the most famous, he used to tell me that those two were just as intelligent and strong as him. Anyway, Tannódin had also learned that the woman who survived with Brenko had also died in a battle earlier this cycle. Because of this, the Eradicate believed that Brenko would soon make his move against them. They combed for his location, and they used all their resources to do so."

"How do you know that?"

"Brenko always found ways to check in on those two, and I know he doesn't look like it, but, he is the smartest person I have ever met. He figured all of this out using his experience, his connections, and his mind."

"I see."

"Stop, Anámn," Lénü chuckled playfully. "You're making this story take too long."

Anámn smiled.

"Now, this woman in Dynasty—based on the information the Eradicate gave her, and due to her own connections with the sex trade— she reasoned who Brenko was and that he had help. Brenko was the one who was going to kill her, through poisoning, and if he got in trouble, I was his backup. We knew where her favorite eating establishment was. Brenko had connections at the eatery, so that he could place the poison in her food. It wouldn't kill her quick, but she would die in a few days."

"I'm sorry, but I have to ask, Lénü. Why didn't you just get somebody else to do this?"

"Brenko doesn't trust any job to anyone unless it is him or me. That's just how he does things. Maybe we should have though, because things were botched from the beginning. There was a very good chance that we were being set-up. But we had come so far, so we had to see the job through… although sometimes I think that Brenko wanted to end up killed, and that's why he went ahead with the plan.

"As soon as the woman—Gisé, that was the cléth's name—she had informants everywhere she went. And as soon as she saw Brenko in the eatery, she had her people try to capture him. It's too bad that those cléths underestimated the fool of fools. That man can fight like the wind, and he's an excellent shot with an energy rifle. The first three who tried to touch him were down before they knew it. The place erupted with shots firing everywhere. Once I heard the gunfire, I armed and hid my AEAR and went in. Brenko had given me clear orders: no matter what, Gisé had to die. While she was rushing outta there and I was running in, we crossed paths at the entrance…"

Lénü stopped in midsentence.

"What?" Anámn asked, deeply involved in the story. "What happened?"

"She had an Eradicate agent with her. He was the one who gave me this…" She pointed to the scar on her face. "I didn't even see the sword, but I did see the blood… my blood."

She stopped for a moment and recollected herself.

"He didn't see my energy gun though," she smirked. "I killed that bastard, and then I shot Gisé five times, before I lost consciousness. When I awoke, I was in a great deal of pain, and we were on a seacruiser, already on our way back here. Brenko told me that I had been unconscious for a week. He managed to get us out of Dynasty. Only the Nameless One knows how…"

"And you've been here ever since?"

"Yeah. We've been keeping low for the past three durations or so. We figured that our other hideouts were compromised. But that was where most of our credits were. We don't have too much money here—"

"Where is Anzél and what did Pre-Eminent do there?" Anámn interrupted.

"Anzél is a large piece o' land that's part of Líachim. Pre-Eminent been there since nearly the beginning of this cycle. The day she arrived she killed twenty-five thousand people."

"Twenty-five thousand! Twenty… no way… that is…"

"…Insane is what it is. Evil."

"How can one person do that?"

"She's a Sczyphamek. It's easy."

Anámn was silent and pondered his own powers. There was no way he could defeat Pre-Eminent or Vicious. Even if he Awakened, he wondered if he actually stood a chance. But where did that thought come from? Why was he thinking about battling Pre-Eminent and Vicious? He never possessed the thought before or the slightest motivation to enter into such a conflict. But then again, the conflict was inevitable; was it not? His father was sure to have alerted his cousin, Késhal, and judging from Lénü's explanation of Tannódin and the Eradicate, the empress would never stop searching for him. And if he resisted her, she would order his death. But did she actually kill twenty-five thousand?

"That number is wrong." Anámn searched his connection to the planet for confirmation. "Something tells me that it wasn't that many."

"Maybe. But if it was half of that, would it matter?"

Neither of them said a word for a few minutes, until Anámn mustered up some courage and spoke. "Lénü, I don't have anywhere to go. I think my Elemental led me here to the both of you. I don't know how that's even possible, but I know it's true. And, I don't want to be a burden to you, but..."

"Don't worry about it, Anámn. I told you; you're comin' with us, no matter what Kanoso says."

"How long do you think he's going to be asleep?"

"Awhile, why?"

Anámn had nothing to lose. "Can you help me learn how to read? I kind of know a little bit..."

Lénü'íque looked at the runaway Sczyphamek with sympathetic eyes, which caused Anámn to blush.

"Yes," she said. "Course I will. Just promise me that you'll give Brenko a chance."

First impressions were hard to shake, but Anámn would try. Hearing Lénü talk for an hour was interesting enough; she switched in and out of two different voices the entire conversation, showing a mastery and disdain for grammar and vocabulary. One could not judge her by first impressions...

"All right."

***

The moment Brenko awoke, disorientation beset him. The first attempt to lift his head brought a heaviness he knew too well. His knowledge of this thing never made it any lighter. He would have to negotiate with it. Yes, once again, it was time to reenact the banal ritual demanded by the gods of inebriation.

"Lénü?" Brenko groggily called out. His mouth was dry, and his breath was so rancid, his nose objected every time he opened his mouth. Rolling off his cot, with no memory of how he had gotten there in the first place, Brenko hit the hard, cold floor, knees and palms first. His head felt as if a large stone was tied around it.

"Staxis," he muttered. "Either I need to go ahead and die from this, or I need to quit drinking."

He took measured breaths while kneeling on the cold ground. Soon, he distilled the sound of faint voices. The urge to vomit was not as present as he thought it would be. But, he had not been awake that long, had he? Stumbling and bracing himself against the hallway, Brenko made his way to the voices. Lénü heard him, but she was not going to come to his aid this time. She was serious when she said she would not support him in his addiction any longer. It appeared that also meant she would no longer help him when he was severely hung-over.

"Kíma," he burped, trying to win over his esophagus and stomach. Opening the door, Brenko gazed at the figure of a young man who nervously and sadly looked the other way.

"Why in Qalfocx is he still here?" Brenko asked with vitriol.

"I see you're up and stumblin'," Lénü said. "You should sit down."

Brenko made an inhospitable face at his guest. "Who are you? And how'd you get Lénü to trust you?"

"My name is Anámn."

"Anámn…that's a weird name. *Anámn…* What in Qalfocx does 'Anámn' mean? I don't remember encountering a name like that before…" the drunkard trailed. "And why does my daughter, who trusts no one, trust you?"

Lénü smiled. "Because he saved my life. And you should sit down."

Complying as gruffly as possible, Brenko plopped himself between Anámn and Lénü. Anámn nearly moved away. The man smelled terrible, and as a slave from Euhilv, Anámn had smelled the worst of the worst. However, Brenko was one of the rankest things he ever encountered.

"What? I stink or something, Anámn?"

"Yeah. You smell like kíma."

"Ha!" the man exclaimed. "I do stink don't I? I got this bad habit, Anámn. I drink too damn much, but one day—"

"'I'm gonna stop,'" Lénü finished the statement. "This time you are though. You won't be drinking anything when you find out who Anámn is."

"Hmmm… We'll see about that. I'll tell you what Anámn. If you can shock me like Lénü claims, then I'll stop drinking. Kíma, I won't even kill you."

Anámn smiled. "I am Anámn Matriester, but my family name is from my mother. My father is Alzhexph ju Xaníz."

Brenko suddenly found himself sober.

"I am also a Sczyphamek."

Shaking his head and nearly wetting himself, Brenko jumped up from the couch. He paced back and forth and scratched his head. "No… no, you can't be one of them… I don't believe it."

"Fá'atoño má," Anámn chanted. His dark green aura shone forth; the emanation was powerful enough to scare even him, for Anámn was sitting down and at rest. When did he get so strong, yes, *really* strong? Within seconds, Téza and Anámn—Sczyphamek Kinesis—retreated from observation.

Brenko stood in disbelief and Lénü stared at Anámn in wonderment. She desired to see his powers again, but had refrained from asking. They had spent the past six hours asleep, and before that, she was teaching him how to read. Yet, her mind constantly drifted to the memory of their flight together.

Brenko, on the other hand, appeared as if he saw a frightful image.

"Da Eradicate found us, Kanoso," the daughter said.

"Damn it," Brenko snarled. "Now I gotta stop drinking…"

"Brenko…"

"I heard you, Lénü." The tactician gazed at Anámn. "Sczyphamek… *kíma*. What is your title?"

"Kinesis."

"Kinesis, huh… Kinetic energy—that your power?"

"I guess. It's got something to do with kinetic and potential energy, but I don't understand all of it. And somehow, my Elemental led me to you."

Brenko, still in shock—first, because he would have to sober up and second, because the likeness of his waking and living nightmare was now in his company—paced back and forth while rubbing his protruding belly. He was deep in thought and impervious to emotional or psychological analysis.

Their meeting could not be coincidence, but it could not be entirely providential either. A chénala, perhaps? No matter what it was, Brenko had to try. If anything could keep another Phenplyacin from happening…

He would not let himself think about the possibility of victory, for he believed that to be as asinine as the thought of defeat. He had tasted defeat. Defeat was bitter, biting, acidic, and tepidly sour. He did not want to taste it again. If that meant he was a coward, then so be it. The foolish underestimated sheer defeat and hopelessness. *Yet*, Anámn presented him an opportunity. The runaway might not be the opportunity of victory, but maybe he happened as the opportunity for the possibility of an elusive outcome.

Anámn said his Elemental had something to do with this, Brenko thought to himself. *Potential and kinetic, huh? I wonder…* Suddenly, the tactician stopped pacing, faced Anámn, and asked, "*Are* you a Sczyphamek?"

"I am." Anámn said.

"Are you?" Brenko questioned mysteriously.

"Am I *what*?"

"A Sczyphamek?"

"*I am*."

"But you aren't too," Brenko added. "You happen differently."

"What is that supposed to mean?"

"'*Is*?' You keep using these words—'is, am, are, be, was'—like they mean something. They can only indicate something partial."

"What…? What in Qalfocx are you talking about?" The runaway sunk deeper into bewilderment.

"Don't do this Kanoso," Lénü cautioned.

"Do what?" the tactician answered innocently. "No, Lénü. He's got to know that he is and he ain't what he claims to be, and if he doesn't realize that, he'll be just like *them*, and he won't understand a damn thing about his powers."

"Who?" Lénü and Anámn asked.

"Pre-Eminent and Vicious," Brenko stated in a quasi-religious tone and threw his hands up in faux adoration. "Anámn, are you who you were two minutes ago? Are you who you were before you found out you were a Sczyphamek?"

"No. I've changed."

"You're right; and you'd be lying if you said something different. But tell me, are you still the same? I mean there are things about you that cannot be changed, even if it's just your story up until this point."

"Yeah. I guess that's true," the young man responded, still unsure of Brenko's point. "So?"

"So you aren't just a Sczyphamek. You are and aren't who you say you are. You ain't even a Phmquedrian."

Anámn's face contorted in a humorously aghast manner. Was Brenko still inebriated? "What kind of kíma are you talking?"

"They want your mind too, Anámn." The genius' last statement was clothed in ominous enunciation. "Your body is equally important, but they've enslaved that already."

The room grew tense. Anámn and Lénü silently pressed the deserter to continue.

"They want you to think that things can't change when they can, and they want you to think that things can change when they won't."

"I don't get—"

"Do you think the first people on this land, on this continent, called themselves Phmquedrians?" he interrupted. "We don't know what they called themselves, but it probably wasn't that. Scholars from Kamo believe the name for the continent arose one hundred and fifty cycles after the Extinguishing.

"There were no names for the continents, because no one understood the concept of 'continent' until continental travel was possible. All of the continents received their names after the Drift, even Tannódin. It wasn't until people met others who were different that the names of land began to have meaning.

"But your ancestors, both Tannódin'é and Phmquedrian, did not call themselves those names."

"So?" Anámn asked, understanding what the tactician was saying, but missing the implications.

"All I'm saying is that you are Phmquedrian and you are something else. You are both. Don't let them convince you that what they say you are is what you truly are. What happens, what has happened, and what you do is more important. Understanding this should help you understand potential and kinetic energy as well."

Thinking back to the exchange with his father, Anámn tried to apply this newfound knowledge. He did... *he did see*. He went to his father as a slave who happened to *be* Sczyphamek. But he went as a slave first. He let the identity of a slave dominate his actions, even though the identity was first created by his father and those like him. He, like many others, maintained the identity after that, believing that they *were* slaves, even when they knew better. *That was power, was it not?* In that, his father was not lying. Anámn and Héthyx were the same on that account. They had both acted within the bounds of Tannódin'é identification, and because of that, their power was indeed limited. The potential of Anámn's power was subject to the relationships he perceived, the identity he constructed. The more he was able to broaden his scope and context, the more aware he would be of potential and kinetic energy and himself. His existence was irreducible to being or doing...

He, like all of his surroundings, was in a constant moment of *happened, happening, and will happen*. He like all of his surroundings was located in particular and generic spaces.

Brenko smiled. "I can see on your face that you do understand what I am getting at."

"I happened as a nel'asmív, right?" Anámn felt as if he was nearing a new plateau of understanding. "I happened as a nel'asmív on an unnamed continent now called Phmquedria on a world we call Qeauríyx... Right?"

"More or less. Yes and no. You're happening as a nel'asmív right now. But later, you might happen as a nel'asmív and Sczyphamek. Right now we happen to be in Phmquedria but who knows where we might happen later on. But where we go from here is in some ways contingent upon where we happen to be now—at least, as nel'asmív."

Nel'asmív. That was the name that signified their species, a species that was as variegated as the continents, Aurías, and elements. Difference was not different. Diversity was as ordinary as life itself. Spontaneously, routinely, and unapologetically, difference happened. The Tannódin'é made difference appear hierarchical or unnatural. They made difference being or doing different. They had taken a self-evident factor of reality and made a system of oppression and domination.

Anámn scowled.

"Stop with that hateful face," Brenko warned. "That other way of thinking was in the works long before Tannódin, although they did help popularize it. Truth of the matter is that this has been going on since the end of the Drift."

Anámn did not respond. He was too busy recounting his conversations with Kaimero and Hamin and his sister.

CHAPTER TWENTY: THE DEATH OF A MYANÁLA

3 Opíz, 241 OGI

The stratojet, which *appeared* rickety and *sounded* terminally ill, lay before them.

Appearances and sounds deceived.

Brenko gazed at a rising Zénan. Behind him, the mumblings of Lénü and Anámn reached his ears. Again, they had remained awake into the late hours of the night. Teaching the runaway how to read provided his daughter a newfound demeanor. Perhaps if it were another time and space, Lénü'íque would have happened as a great teacher. But they lived on Qeauríyx, where destiny happened as the amalgamation of foolish mishaps, chaotic determinacy, mingled with cycles of disaffected, conflicted choices.

And he—he was Brenko; he happened as nel'asmív. What else could a paradoxical creature do on an enigmatic planet but go on?

For the past three weeks, Anámn's skill with his Elemental had grown as much as his literacy. Not only was Matriester displaying more control, the power behind his abilities was maturing. Brenko could only assume that the son of ju Xaníz was finally grasping the complexities and nuances of potential and kinetic energy. Or maybe two weeks without intoxicants had dulled his perceptions.

One thing that had certainly dulled was Tannódin's efforts to catch them in Minusía. The three of them had remained in the safe area for three weeks. After those three weeks were finished, Brenko scouted the city and found that a large contingent of Blue Rapier and White Scythe had left the city. The tactician's gamble was correct.

"Stop dragging," he yelled at the Sczyphamek and his adopted daughter.

Anámn and Lénü appeared as somnolent corpses; with half-open eyes, they stumbled along behind him.

He could not go home to Bryce. Neither could he return to Líachim. Tannódin was a location that cried idiocy. Keotagosdi was too obvious. Nez Spirita… *Vicious was there*, and he never wanted to see that cléth of a man *ever again*. Meve was sinking, freezing, erupting. Who would go to Zorét? Not them. Damüda was their only option. Although a vast number of nel'asmív loyal to Global Initiative lived there, Damüda had only a few densely populated areas. And its southeastern regions were traditionally hostile to Global Initiative but had tentatively drawn back their angst since Vicious became co-leader of the House of Kaz. Even still, Brenko was sure that he could live out the remainder of his days there.

The challenge was getting there. He arranged transport to Barrier Island, which neighbored the western coast of the continent. Their passage to Barrier Island was secured through Brenko's old acquaintance who went by the name of Yerna.[1]

Yerna was a Damüdan pilot of the airlift, "Dark Nimbus." He took pride in his stratojet. The craft was made from disparate parts, but the old man painted, shined, and retooled the exterior, while adding his own modifications to the inner-workings of the flying mechanism. The lift was a moderate size. Brenko had experienced bigger and smaller crafts, but he was partial to Dark Nimbus.

Although the wings were retracted, there were a total of six, two tail and four lateral. When the airlift was grounded, a novice's eye would only see four wings. However, once airborne, the fifth and sixth wing would emerge from the belly of the craft, aiding in maneuvers that only Yerna could pull off. The craft's agility was matched by its speed. The lift possessed three aft thrusters, with each individual engine capable of propelling the craft three hundred lengths per hour at maximum output. When all three were engaged, Yerna's airship reached speeds in excess of eight hundred lengths per hour.

Yerna's face was wrinkled, nicked, and scarred. Each wrinkle had seen too many cycles, and each scar, too many fights. Brenko discerned long ago that no one wished for or sought out the first scar. Subsequent scars were, on many occasions, by choice, although that did not preclude the fact that they might be just as random as the first.

"This everyone?" Yerna asked with a voracious Damüdan accent: nasal, reflective, and melodic.

"Yeah," the tactician replied.

The sun barely showed itself in the horizon. It was still an hour or so from daybreak. A sliver of purplish-orange candescence peered into the nighttime sky. The airman signaled Brenko to follow him and come aboard. They made their way up the steps into the cargo hold, which was capable of transporting freight of a decent size or up to ten passengers. There were no seats in the traditional sense, just two benches and backrests on each side of the fuselage's interior. The benches were uncomfortable, but during dangerous times, one was forced to strap themselves in and sit on them while Yerna took evasive maneuvers. Brenko hoped the flight would not include such a necessity, for he greatly enjoyed sitting on the floor in the middle of the hold.

"Yerna…"

"I've told you for the past two durations; staxis, I've told you for the past cycle, Plenz. I cannot land there, ah. Nimbus will be either be searched or shot down on the spot. Barrier Island is as close as I can get. You're going to have to make it the rest of the way by yourself."

"*Staxis*," the critical thinker cursed.

"I didn't make it this way. Only military or approved commercial flights

---

[1] Yerna (yurn-uh)

can land in southeast Damüda unsearched. I don't make the rules."

Didn't make the rules… Who did? Bíoske would say no one. Only Eternity knew what Syla would say. But even Brenko was unable to answer the question… the question no one could answer: How did this existence happen? How did it come to pass? If not the Nameless One, then who? If not pre-existent matter, then what?

His existence and experience revealed that everything emerged from something else, something prior. What did Qeauríyx emerge from? And what predated that pre-emergence? And the one before it… and so the question cycled and spiraled into infinity. No matter the method, knowledge, or intent, only arrogance allowed nel'asmív to believe they had answered that question with any legitimacy. Neither faith, nor experience, nor language, nor empiricism, nor theory—nothing would grant anyone access to that information.

Smiling to himself in a melancholy manner, the tactical philosopher knew there was at least *one* rule that applied to the cosmos. Some kíma in this Cycle was *wrong*. Phenplyacin was wrong. Those who died there were a part of a terrible tragedy.

"Plenz, are you all right?"

"No," Brenko answered. "But when have things ever been 'all right?' Kíma." Looking back at Anámn and Lénü, he responded to his question with another question. "And when have things been *all wrong* either?"

The old man smirked. "You're a strange nel'asmív, Plenz."

"Quit calling me 'Plenz,' Yerna. No point anymore."

The aviator's grin was slight. "Who's the young man with Lénü'íque?"

"You don't want to know, old man," Brenko replied. "Trust me."

"Does he got sympathy for Tannódin or The Guild?"

"None whatsoever. He probably hasn't even heard of The Guild."

"Well then, Brenko, I don't need to know anything else, ah."

"His name is Anámn. You can ask him *what* he is later."

No sooner than the Brycian finished his statement did the young man and woman enter into the cabin.

Lénü'íque greeted the Damüdan with a smile. "Yerna."

"Hi, darling," the pilot said, which caused Lénü to giggle. Yerna had called her that ever since she met him five cycles ago.

Anámn gazed at the pilot, unsure of who he was and how he should be addressed. "Hello."

"Anámn," the man responded nonchalantly.

"Anámn, this is Yerna," Brenko said. "He and I have known each other for a long time. He doesn't tolerate stupidity. He's even worse than me. But, he is the best pilot I know."

"This lift looks like it's got four wings, plus the two tail wings," Anámn observed. "I was wondering if that was normal. This is my first time near an airlift, but from the sky they always seemed like they had two wings coming out of the sides."

Yerna smiled appreciatively; the Phmquedrian must have been a builder in his lifetime. "Ah. There are six wings, and yes, most lifts or stratojets have two lateral wings. Dark Nimbus is one of a kind. The retracted wings are very thin, but they grant me aid when I have to maneuver in ways that one should never maneuver. I also modified the tail wings. There's not an airlift created that's as nimble as this one."

Yerna said the last statement with pride. Indeed, he worked hard to modify and augment Dark Nimbus. Experience had taught him that agility was more valuable than speed or strength. The ability to squeeze out of tight situations was a covetous boon on Qeauríyx.

Anámn smiled and sat down on the bench located on the right side of the fuselage, next to Lénü. He saw her harnessing herself to a safety strap, so he did the same. Brenko sat down on the left and strapped himself in. Yerna studied Brenko's body language. The coward-tactician only traveled with Lénü.

The Damüdan made his way to the cockpit and closed the cargo bay doors. He fired up the engines of Dark Nimbus, and the craft rumbled to the runway.

An interesting trip lay ahead.

***

Hours passed. The monotonous, meticulous hum of the engines grew maddening to the runaway. It reminded him of the small rail car on his way to Kamo. Although the Dark Nimbus afforded more room, he still became claustrophobic.

"What's wrong Anámn?" Lénü asked.

"Nothing," he sighed, fidgeting and twirling his wheatstraw hat on his left index finger.

"He's bored," the tactician said. "He's been twitching the past hour or so."

"I'm *fine*." Anámn's agitation was tactile.

The mastermind ignored the runaway's attitude and rubbed his belly. "You still don't get it Anámn."

Matriester had grown weary of Brenko's unapologetic smugness. Just because he was smarter than everyone did not mean that he needed to be so arrogant.

He exhaled in exasperation and put his hat down on the floor of the cargo hold. "What don't I get now?"

"Your restlessness is due to your Elemental, more than likely." Brenko remained calm and ignored the runaway's aggressive tone. "You think because you're not moving physically—or should I say bodily—that means that you are not moving."

Anámn tried not to be curious, but Brenko's explanations were always so alluring.

"That is not true," the Brycian continued. "You are moving. Right now. We are all moving. The plane is moving. The planet is moving. The moons are moving."

"I *know* that," Kinesis barked. "Why didn't Téza choose you, since you know so damn much? Kíma!"

Lénü had to put out the flames before they truly started. "Anámn, Kanoso is just trying to help."

Anámn looked out the window of the craft and stared at the clouds. He did not understand why he was so frustrated.

"I won't say anything after this, Sczyphamek Kinesis, unless you ask me to." Brenko's tone, plus the fact that he addressed Anámn by his full title—the first time anyone had done so—caused the son of ju Xaníz to turn and face him. "It is a hard thing to come face to face with ignorance, especially our own. Facing ignorance is facing our limitations. We all have limitations one way or another. But ignorance exposes our limitations to a considerable degree.

"It hurts. Being and acting ignorant hurts yourself and others. But it isn't just personal. I think that's why your frustration and anger is so intolerable at times. You waver, Anámn. You waver between feeling that your ignorance is entirely your fault or all somebody else's fault.

"But you are wrong... *It's both and neither.* No more, no less. Once you accept that, your anger should be more controlled, and—."

"And, I 'should be able to understand my powers better.' How many times have you said that? You talk like you know me," Kinesis said softly and returned his gaze to the floor of the airlift. Catching himself, he faced Brenko and became stoic. "You don't know anything about me, only what I've told you."

"And what I observe," the Brycian added.

"Yeah. Well, if you are so smart and observing, then why didn't you use that power to help your friends? What gives you the right to lecture me?"

Brenko unconsciously reached for the inside pocket of his coat to pull out a flask, but it was not there. He sighed at Lénü in irritation. She returned his sigh with a smile and confirmed his suspicion. She had taken it. Why did he promise to stop drinking?

"Staxis," he cursed.

"You aren't answering my question," Anámn pressed. "Lénü doesn't know either and probably is smart enough not to ask. But, kíma, you know I'm not. Why are we heading to Damüda?"

"To escape from the Eradicate."

"I may not be as smart as you are, but I've been on the run for almost four durations. Sometimes I knew where I was going, but most times, I didn't. But you already planned this, whether you were on the run or not. Lénü told me that another continent is about to go up against Tannódin. Why aren't we going there?"

"It's Líachim. That's where we just escaped from, remember? Why would we go back there?" the Brycian countered without hesitation. "You don't know what you are talking about."

Anámn would not give in. "But you weren't in Líachim because of Global Initiative. You were there because of the sex trade. You don't think you could find people in Líachim that would protect you in exchange for your help?"

Brenko was quiet. Anámn did not yet realize how smart and discerning he truly was.

"Why're we going to Damüda? Why'd you plot against the sex trade? Why did you leave your friends when they needed you most?"

"You weren't there," Brenko murmured.

"Does that matter?" Anámn asked. "You don't have my powers or know my story, but you like to tell me all about them."

Groaning in annoyance, Yerna emerged from the cockpit and curled his lip at Anámn. "'*Does that matter*'? *Sczyphamek*, you of all people should know better than to ask such a stupid question. Then again, you're ignorant, ah? You've heard stories. You've heard tales. *You've heard kíma.*"

Anámn was about to give the pilot a tongue-lashing of his own when Brenko interjected, "He was there too, that day."

"You?" Anámn and Lénü asked.

"Ah," the old man said somberly. "I was a soldier in Blue Rapier."

Anámn and Lénü's eyes widened.

"That's right," Brenko chimed. "We were supposed to be enemies that day."

"But Vincallous had other plans," Yerna finished.

"Damn right." Brenko nodded at his Damüdan comrade. "*Damn right, he did.*"

The aviator returned to the cockpit and reemerged with a bottle of spirits.

Yerna tossed the bottle to Brenko, who caught it, looked at it, swished it, and muttered, "Is this supposed to be a test?"

Brenko laughed inexorably at his predicament. Should he even repeat such a story? Could he do so after he committed himself to give up drinking, even though he was about to speak about the event that caused him to become a drunkard in the first place?

"Kímaz irony," he spat out. Now he was starting to sound and think like Bíoske.

Silence exerted itself for a few moments until Anámn blurted out, "Who in Qalfocx is piloting this lift?"

"Don't worry," Yerna replied calmly. "Dark Nimbus has autopilot, radar, and radio wave communication."

"Yerna is right, Anámn." The cowardly philosopher disregarded the previous statements. "You talk as if this was only fiction. You still don't understand the amount of power you wield."

Suddenly, he threw the bottle at the Sczyphamek and instinctively,

Matriester robbed the bottle of its energy. The observable sign of the event was that the velocity of the object rapidly decreased. The Sczyphamek raised his hand slowly and caught the bottle.

"You're getting better," Lénü commented. "You didn't chant at all."

Yerna was speechless, yet unsurprised. Anámn's power seemed so local, so harmless. But he understood Brenko all too well. If the Sczyphamek ever Awakened...

Anámn, for his part, was bewildered.

"Kinesis, what did you do with that kinetic energy from the bottle?"

"Huh?"

"What did you do with the energy? I told you, energy doesn't disappear. It has to be stored or transferred."

"Oh... I remember you telling me that now. Hmm... I don't know where it went."

"What do you mean, you 'don't know?'"

"I guess I stored it somehow." Searching his Elemental, he confirmed it. "Téza stored it."

Brenko was thankful to the runaway's Elemental. Clearly, Téza understood Brenko's pedagogical style and the Elemental had protected many people from Anámn's inadvertent lack of understanding. At times, Matriester was pure, unbridled kinetic energy. Uncontrollable and chaotic. And Téza was forced to play the role of the calming storehouse, filled with potential. As long as Anámn allowed that myanála to continue, he would never Awaken, Brenko surmised. It made the thinker wonder why the Elemental *did* choose Anámn...

"Why'd you do that Brenko?" the Phmquedrian asked, holding the bottle, which Lénü promptly grabbed.

"Because she'll keep it from me, and I wanted to demonstrate something. You did that unconsciously just now and you have not Awakened. Can you imagine what might happen if you were?"

The son of ju Xaníz was mum. He had not thought about the full extent of his power since his confrontation with his father.

"No; actually, I can't." A spirit of doubt, frustration, and inadequacy crept back into the Sczyphamek's qanín.

Brenko and Lénü looked at Anámn with their own respective concerns. The Euhilv runaway had struggled his whole life to give his hard existence some meaning. And when he finally had a reason to believe in some sort of purpose, he was linked to one of the most complex relationships the cosmos had to offer.

"Don't feel sorry for me," the slave said indignantly. "I don't want your kímaz pity. And I don't want you acting like a high and mighty teacher. I need your help, but don't act like those Tannódin'é missionaries who used to try to convert us 'unbelieving' and 'confused' slaves. No matter how low I've been, I still happened as a nel'asmív. Treat me like one."

Brenko bit his lip and nodded in shame. Unlike Brenko, Anámn had known oppression and degradation from the moment of his birth. Despite these circumstances, Anámn and others in his community still struggled for personhood and purpose. If the Phmquedrian could go on, the Brycian had to try.

Coaxing himself into conversation, the coward muttered, "The plan was flawless."

Anámn and Lénü looked at Yerna who nodded in steadfastness.

"That was our best chance. I mean... We really... we really had a..." Brenko hung his head.

"Nobody knew about Pre-Eminent or Vicious," Yerna explained, giving the Brycian time to gather himself.

"But I heard..."

"Forget what you heard, Sczyphamek. I'd been in Blue Rapier for over ten cycles by that point. Nobody except Pre-Eminent knew that Fierce was one—*nobody*, except for maybe Reníz Bläno. And only Supreme's parents and the Daknín knew that she was one."

Brenko nodded in agreement. "None of Miska Kea's intelligence suggested anything along those lines either, and we had infiltrated deep into the ranks of Scythe and Rapier. Our infiltration was a major reason why the House of Kaz was clueless about our plan.

"The Brycians, my people, for once, decided to do something that benefitted something or someone other than themselves."

Anámn's blank stare was almost enough to make Brenko reconsider telling the story. He knew the obvious questions Anámn had. Even though Lénü had taught the runaway the continents and their geographical positions, she did not have a chance to fully educate him about the planet's recent history.

"Yerna, how long until we land in Pod to refuel?"

"It's over three thousand lengths... so about five hours."

Nodding, the tactician smiled and his hands trembled. Deep in his heart the coward wanted nothing to do with Phenplyacin or its story. Explaining history to Anámn might bore and distract the runaway.

Lénü knew her father would back out on the smallest of pretense and summarized, "Brycians are traditionally isolationists. The only reason they fought Tannódin to begin with was 'cause Tannódin invaded d'eir homeland. Kanoso ain't ya typical Brycian. He left d'ere when he was young an' joined Miska Kea."

"Thanks for the lesson," Brenko said obnoxiously. "That was such an incisive review..."

"Yeah, Anámn, something like that. We got a lot of my people to agree to use Bryce to fight a proxy war. Basically, we used the battlefields in Bryce to move weapons, people, and equipment past Tannódin without them realizing it.

"We gathered a large fleet of ships, even some battlecruisers that had braved close proximity to the Infinite Deep in order to sail to the southernmost sections of the Memory Ridge."

"Whose idea was this?" Anámn asked. "The plan seems so… Wait… You didn't… It wasn't you was it? You'd've only been about…"

"I was twenty-six cycles. I wasn't the leader of Miska Kea, but the leaders accepted the strategy. It took me, Syla, and Bíoske two cycles to come up with the plan. Then we had to pitch and execute it."

"Syla and Bíoske?" Anámn inquired. He could not believe that Brenko was so resourceful at that age. "Are those the two people you were talking about, Lénü?"

"Yeah. 'Ats dem."

"So the three people who came up with the plan survived? That…" Anámn stopped himself. He finally felt the enormous weight and responsibility Brenko carried.

"Give me the bottle, Lénü," the Brycian said in a cumbersome attempt to hide his surging grief and guilt.

"It won't help," Lénü'íque said.

"It never has," he responded. "I didn't start drinking to help myself. I drank to numb myself. Now give me the damn bottle."

"You need to let this burden go," Lénü said. "You have placed something on yourself that is not yours alone."

"Be quiet, darling," Yerna said with cool sweetness. "You haven't experienced war, ah. The longer it drags on, the more things like guilt, morality, and responsibility die. They become meaningless."

Offended, Lénü sneered at the old man. "I done my share o' killing and have gone through things too."

"Darling, you're taking this close to the qanín, ah? The Sczyphamek has been through things too, but you don't hear him talking crazy anymore. *He knows.* He knows he *doesn't understand.* After traveling with Brenko this long, you should've realized the same.

"You and Brenko planned those sex trade killings. But in war, battle is unplanned. It is 'kill my enemy before my enemy kills me.' In the end, that's what it comes down to when the energy bursts begin. The overall 'goal' becomes lost. The aims of Global Initiative: gone. The aims of Miska Kea: pointless. None of these things matter if you are dead or if everyone dies.

"So *you* kill. And *you* maim, and *you* injure, because *they* will kill, maim, and injure *you.* It's like for like… But, Phenplyacin… it changed all that." Yerna's forehead wrinkled and his facial scars flexed. "War is madness. Phenplyacin… Phenplyacin was worse. *It happened as Qalfocx.*"

The way the Damüdan said "Qalfocx" was chilling. So chilling, Anámn would think twice about using the word liberally.

"By the end of it," Brenko continued, "Blue Rapier, White Scythe, Miska Kea… those distinctions meant nothing. We were all helping each other, just trying to make it, just trying to survive…

"A terrible beauty and compassion happened there. We were ready to kill each other, but in a matter of minutes we became comrades…" Brenko paused. He wanted his question to be as conditional and meticulous as possible. "Is it only in competition and catastrophe that strangers can come together? But it could have gone the other way just as easy… It could have been every nel'asmív for themselves. So what did everybody die for?" The tactician stared at the blurry bottle in Lénü's hand. The tears stung. How long, how many durations, how many cycles had it been since he cried *sober?*

"Yerna is right about battle," he continued. "I never understood how or why killing ourselves or others solved our problems. But even a thinker like me, who figured war was asinine… I couldn't keep myself from killing. I tried to tell myself that I was different, that I didn't kill out of a love for violence and death. And believe me, there were some in Miska Kea who fought for that reason alone."

"Same on our side," Yerna added. "I saw many a nel'asmív kill just for the pleasure, 'cause when dying means losing, and living means killing, killing can be a source of satisfaction. We were trained to respect our enemy but not to have compassion for them.

"I joined Blue Rapier because I believed in Global Initiative. And after every battle I used that belief to help me move past the violence I had seen or done. A soldier with no vision or mission isn't a soldier. That's a wild untamed beast of ages past. A killer with no purpose.

"But it's inevitable, isn't it? The longer it goes on… the moment comes when it all becomes meaningless."

"But there was meaning too," Brenko sighed solemnly. "Meaning I wish I never knew."

"But don't you have to fight?" Anámn was growing uncomfortable at what seemed to him mere abstract reflection and idle talk. "Global Initiative is wrong."

The Phmquedrian's dismissal of he and Brenko's pain infuriated Yerna. *"Of course you have to fight;* but that doesn't make it any less pointless."

Brenko nodded. "Fighting an enemy that's trying to kill you does call for resistance. But resistance can easily turn into mimicry. Global Initiative is one of the most violent programs ever undertaken in the history of Qeauríyx. As a result, those who have fought and continue to fight against it have matched and in some brief moments, exceeded its violence."

Anámn was silent and withdrew into a moment of introspection. *He's right. I ended up hitting Nísyx. And my reflection in the mirror…*

"But we can't let them take land, enslave people, kill people, and say that they are in line with the planet and the First Sczyphamek," Lénü continued a quieted Anámn's argument.

"That's how you see it," the pilot said. "But me, when I was young, I saw my first airlift, which was invented because of Global Initiative. I saw advances in technology, weaponry; I saw my hometown grow, and my people unite because of it."

"But they are responsible for—" Lénü blurted out, hardly able to contain her anger.

"Both," Yerna replied. "They are responsible for both. Yes, the growth and expansion is at the expense of Nez Spirita, Phmquedria, Bryce, and even Damüda."

"Even Tannódin," Brenko added.

Yerna gazed wearily at Anámn. "It's like Sczyphameks can't help themselves."

"Or those three blades," Brenko responded.

"Or nel'asmív and témos," the Damüdan finished.

"But it doesn't matter. Because no matter how noble the cause, it dies in pain along with everybody else on the battlefield. Never will you see some of the most atrocious and loving acts than in the heat of war."

"Just like Phenplyacin. Self-preservation kept us as enemies, and self-preservation made us allies."

"No," the Brycian said. "Vincallous Fierce *made us friends… that kímaz day.*"

Kaz Vincallous Fierce. A name Anámn encountered on so many occasions. Kaz Késhal Supreme. The very utterance of the title evoked fear and trembling. They were evil forces, responsible for numerous acts of violence and brutality. They were to be feared. They were incarnate entities of Qalfocx and gynix, capable of a kind of destruction that was indescribable, reminiscent of the Great Drift.

But I'm one of them now, he thought. *I happened as a Sczyphamek. If I Awaken, it's gonna happen. Won't it? I'm gonna cross them sooner or later. I'm gonna have to face them because I'm never joining them.*

Kinesis took a deep breath. He did not want legend or myth, varnished with sheens of sensationalized anecdotes. He wanted to know what happened, what actually took place. He no longer wanted to hear a story; he wanted to take hold of the event. He wanted to embrace that particular intersection of space and time, with all its concomitance and ambivalence. He needed to understand what he was up against. He needed to comprehend what an Awakened Sczyphamek was capable of *twenty* cycles ago. He could no longer stay the same.

"Brenko. Yerna. Tell me what happened. I've gotta know. You know why. Y'all may not want to fight anymore, but I doubt I got much of a choice."

"No," Brenko muttered. "Not much of a choice. I am sure they're sparing no expense to find you and your contemporary."

"You can be sure of that, ah," Yerna added. "You should know what you are up against. They'll not rest until you've either joined them, or are killed at their hands."

Brenko looked out the window and at the clouds to settle himself.

"Destabilization was our plan. Our mission was to decimate Tannódin's home force and assassinate the entire house of Kaz. We figured that if we accomplished those two goals, at least one of the following would happen: (1) Damüda would cut its ties to Tannódin'é or try to wrest power from them, which would plunge them into war; (2) one of the Daknín would try to capture power, leading their own forces into war; or (3) at the very least, those lands that had been conquered by Tannódin would revolt now that they saw a tangible opening.

"All we sought was massive deterioration, not complete victory. That would, at least, keep them at bay and, at the most, lead them down the path of internal destruction. Tannódin is an imperial entity. And all empires have the seeds of unrest and hate sown in their very core. We were just trying to make those seeds sprout.

"Since radar had not been invented yet—"

"It was invented within two durations after the attack," Yerna added.

"Yeah," Brenko stopped in mid-thought. "There's no denying that radar technology and other military advancements were pursued because of the attack."

"It's amazing to think that we created energy rifles before detection devices," Lénü commented.

"Not necessarily," Yerna cackled gruffly. "It's easier to create something to help us kill or for greed than something that can help us live and be peaceful. Most progressions in technology have been made in large part because of death. Even the very airlift we are in now."

"*Staxis*," Anámn cursed. "Do you and Brenko always think and talk like *this*? This… this… whatever kind of talk this is, is crazy. I mean, damn. *Who talks and thinks like this?*"

Brenko and Yerna looked at one another. Anámn needed to recognize what kind of event caused Nelon Ásmivü to question their very existence.

Paradox

The three friends/comrades/warriors/sages were located five lengths outside Phenplyacin to the east-northeast in the hills.

Lighting a daggerweed cigarette, Bíoske looked at Syla and Brenko, inhaled, blew smoke out of his nostrils, and grinned. "These bastards don't even see this coming. They're so arrogant."

"Like you're not." Syla snatched the cigarette out his mouth, flicked it on the ground, and stomped it with her feet. "You do realize you're breathing smoke don't you? Those things are going to kill you one day. And what are you trying to do… give away our position?"

"They can't see us from here."

Brenko shook his head. "You guys should hurry up and pledge yourselves to each other for the rest of your lives. Only the two of you would carry on when we're in the heart of Tannódin two hours before a battle that might change history."

"*Will* change history," Bíoske corrected. "The Nameless One is with us, Brenko. And our plan has made room for every contingency."

"*Every contingency?*" Syla smacked Bíoske on the back. "Damn. You brag too much."

"What?" His smirk was wary, but confident. "We worked hard on this kímaz plan."

"Is everything in place?" Brenko asked.

"Yes," they responded.

Syla beheld the Firmament. Mashé was full and Parce was a quarter. Still, the moonlight could not penetrate the amalgam of lights in Phenplyacin. "What time is it?"

"Fifteen minutes until the first bomb goes off in the hills." Bíoske gazed at his time-keeper and handed it to Syla. "I don't need it anymore. You keep it. And I'm telling you, nobody in Phenplyacin will see this coming.

"Even you have to admit their security was lax. You can tell that they don't think anyone has the guts to do what we're about to attempt. And there are over seventy thousand troops here."

Syla nodded, strapped the watch on her hand, and made sure her hair braid was in no danger of loosening. Then she checked the sheath and the sword that laterally straddled her lower back. "You are right about that. All that disinformation was worth it. Tannódin and Damüda are strategically confused. But we've lost a lot of good people to make this possible."

Brenko tapped his right foot nervously. "That's why we can't fail."

Bíoske retrieved a metal flask from his coat and gulped down a hard spirit from Keotagosdi. He passed the container to Syla, and she took a sip. Holding the bottle out to Brenko, the gruff soldier titled his head back and a mischievous smile emerged. "C'mon. Drink some."

"You know I don't drink that kíma. But if this goes well, then maybe I'll take one sip. Until then, let's stay focused."

They held each other's hands tightly and prayed. The magnitude of the moment was ineluctable. The outcome of the forthcoming battle would shape Qeauríyx for cycles to come, no matter who succeeded or failed.

It was 221 OGI, the fifteenth day of Opíz, an Oplé. Brenko, Syla, and Bíoske snuck into Phenplyacin as stowaways on a seacruiser three days prior and infiltrated three strategic points within the city. The city's southern edge was home to the still waters of the Lancryptox Ocean. From the shoreline, facing inland, one could witness the beautiful landscape of the metropolis. Large foothills to moderate mountains flanked every side, providing a semicircle of ridgelines in the background. The center of Phenplyacin had large, tall skyrises and three universities, celebrated throughout Damüda and Tannódin as the best schools on Qeauríyx. Phenplyacin was, without a doubt, the most technologically advanced city on the planet.

Subway systems, rail-lines, a skyport, electricity in every structure, and of course, Tannódin's major military installation—Phenplyacin was the platinum standard for Global Initiative. That was why the city was such an appealing target even though Megaphyx Bonicin, Tannódin's capital city, was only thirty lengths away. Though the capital was technologically advanced, its buildings were purposely kept in their olden glory for historical and symbolic purposes.

Civix Setrin, the city landmass of Tannódin, was covered by three distinct landmarks: mountains, rivers, and cities. The most densely populated region on Qeauríyx, over three hundred and fifty million people lived there. Cities sprawled to such an extent that only the mountains, rivers, and sea could contain their borders. The population and infrastructure explosion was only possible because of the labor, materials, and innovations that sprang forth out of Nez Spirita and Phmquedria. Miska Kea's attack would disrupt and hopefully sever that iniquitous relationship.

Brenko had placed a large explosive in the barracks of Blue Rapier, with the help of two Rapier soldiers who were unflinchingly loyal to Miska Kea.

Syla, who was Miska Kea's master of stealth, made her way to the major communication area and set up four small electrical charges and one large package that would cripple Tannódin's ability to send messages to its fleet and within the continent itself. At the time, Phenplyacin was responsible for all major radio transmissions between Zorét, Damüda, Tannódin, and Phmquedria.

Lastly, Bíoske, aided by three Miska Kea loyalists from White Scythe, hiked into the hills, forests, and high cliffs of the mountains that surrounded Phenplyacin and set an enormous amount of explosives and incendiary grenades in uninhabited, yet fire and rockslide prone areas.

All three of them had inside help in some way or another. To achieve so many high-risk objectives by themselves was impossible. The trio received valuable information concerning southern Tannódin's layout, terrain, and road systems from their contacts within the ranks of Global Initiative and civilian sympathizers. The plan was so surreptitious that only their most trustworthy of spies were alerted to the attack, and no one knew its full scope except for a select few. The entire strategy was based on completing multiple ends with variegated tactics.

For two cycles, Syla, Brenko, and Bíoske poured over every detail of the attack. The plan was risky, but every operative in Miska Kea—from the higher-ups to the informants—realized that while small-scale attacks against Tannódin and Damüda were a nuisance, they were hardly upsetting Global Initiative's long-term propagation. At some point, Miska Kea had to provide Qeauríyx an opportunity to redirect the course of history.

"Get ready," Bíoske said, referring to his explosives.

At once, a large detonation ripped through the northern hills of Phenplyacin. A fireball descended upon the forests. Within two minutes, a large section of the hills were conflagrated and the fire swept towards the city below.

"How many minutes?" Brenko asked.

"Three," Syla answered.

"The siren?"

Sure enough, a large siren blared from the communications area. The alarm signaled that the Blue Rapier barracks had been ordered to mobilize and help fight the fire.

"Blow it," Brenko ordered.

Syla clicked her detonator five times, and in response, the main communication towers were consumed in a fiery and smoky concussion accompanied by flashes of electrical discharge.

"Give the barracks another minute to empty," Bíoske said.

The three sat in the darkness and quietude of the eastern hills, as pandemonium ensued in the city of Phenplyacin.

"All right." Brenko flicked his detonator seven times.

In a catastrophic blast, the entire barracks became temporarily invisible to the naked eye.

"Let's go," Syla commanded.

"Right," the two men responded.

The three warriors entered a small motorized vehicle they had commandeered. It was time to head to their next destination, the imperial palace in Megaphyx Bonicin. Their final task was to eliminate Kaz Phenicia Supreme and her daughter, Késhal.

The Brycian tactician sat in the back seat, looked in the rear view mirror, and glanced at the destruction behind them. Checking his watch, Brenko gave his team another chronological update. "The témos should arrive within the hour. If they can take out enough ships in the docks, as well as the missile defense area, we should have a chance."

Starting the vehicle's engine, the half-breed commander from Keotagosdi fixed his head band. "If anyone can pull it off, it's the témos."

The Nez Spiritan veteran placed her sheathed sword in her lap and punched Bíoske in the shoulder. "You really admire those creatures, don't you?"

"You talk like they're distinct from us, Syla…" Bíoske responded. "They are us, and we are them."

"Shut up, both of you." Brenko smiled. "We can debate this later (and I am sure we will) but we need to get to the imperial palace. The plan is working so far. It should take us about a half hour to get there."

The témos were the next line of Miska Kea's attack. The winged felines were to embed themselves in Phenplyacin for a half hour. Then the naval force, consisting of battlecruisers and seawinders, would find their way to shore and attack, followed by an airlift assault. Miska Kea had gathered nearly eighty thousand troops for the battle, a number so large that it would force Tannódin to send aid from the next largest installation, the imperial capital, which was home to a large White Scythe contingent. Once

White Scythe sent reinforcements into Phenplyacin, Syla, Bíoske, and Brenko would have a greater probability of success.

On top of a ridge that strafed the southern coast of Tannódin, the three sped down an abandoned road towards the capital and arrived within forty minutes. From atop the hill, they beheld Megaphyx Bonicin, home of the House of Kaz. Sirens screamed, warning Megaphyx of the attack on Phenplyacin. The imperial palace was in full view, as all roads and lights pointed towards its architectural magnificence.

"The témos will be here in five minutes," Bíoske reported.

In order to assist the three Miska Kea operatives in their task, three témos were to break away from the main body of felines heading towards Phenplyacin. Brenko, Syla, and Bíoske would ride the témos into Megaphyx Bonicin, before White Scythe sent reinforcements to Phenplyacin. Once a sufficient number had dispersed, the Chénínqua of six would land on the top of the estate of Phenicia, descend, find and kill her. Next, they would search Késhal's wing and attempt the same. None of them were self-deceived. All of them would die during the assassination attempt. The imperial palace was home to one hundred and fifty guards at all times. Their hope was in the element of surprise, boldness, and luck.

Luck…

The témos landed. Before anyone could exchange pleasantries, the three sages saw dread in the felines' eyes.

"What?" Brenko asked nervously.

The leader of the témos, a large brown and orange feline, roared gravely, "Sczyphameks are here."

Bíoske could hardly enunciate. "Sczy—wait… what? Did you say *Sczyphameks*—like more than one?"

The other two témos nodded in quietude.

"Oh kíma!" Syla exclaimed. "They are not with us, so that means…"

The three stared into the eyes of the témos, whose eyes were looking towards the sky. The nel'asmív followed their gaze and saw a red aura streaking across the atmosphere, heading towards Phenplyacin.

"Call the attack off," the témo warned. Her hair stood on end and her ears perked in anticipation. "That was a Zananín… a *powerful* Zananín."

Bíoske was already shaking his head in the negative. "It's too late. We're out of radio range, and this is our only chance."

No sooner had he spoke those words, a sea of fire engulfed the imperial palace. The three nel'asmív were bereft of understanding.

"It is the other one," the témo purred emphatically. "She may be stronger than the first. If you all go, you will be destroyed."

"Why would someone destroy their own—" Syla was unable to finish her inquiry. She was still in shock.

Brenko patted Syla on the back and made eye contact with his friends and the témos. "Forget the palace, now. We have to fight. We have to try."

The Chénínqua looked at one another and nodded. They had to.

"Do as much damage as you can to the ships and facilities, and get out of there as if Qalfocx was chasing you," Brenko ordered the témos. "But, do not engage the Sczyphamek."

"We must," the lead témo intimated. "Or no one will survive."

With those words, the témos launched themselves into the heavens, heading in the direction of the red aura.

Bíoske, Brenko, and Syla were left in silence.

How did it go so bad so quickly?

The three comrades jumped into the automobile, said nothing, and raced back to Phenplyacin.

They had nearly arrived back to their original location when the ground rumbled barbarously, and a tree fell in front of the auto. Brenko swerved out of the way, but the vehicle slammed into another tree. The three emerged unhurt. Before they could collect themselves, another tremor forced them to the ground. Brenko grew unnerved. The enormity of their situation and the certainty of their utter defeat settled down on his reflective qanín.

Bíoske presciently observed his friend and calmly admonished him. "Come on, Brenko. It's too late for that now."

Suddenly, shots rang out. It was a small group of Blue Rapier. Brenko glanced at Syla knowingly. She had already tossed grenades in the air towards the direction of the discharges. Bíoske had fully cycled an AEAR and fired a massive round of suppression fire, while Brenko removed the rest of their supplies and arms from the vehicle. He set a grenade within the car and gave the signal to move. As the three friends ran down the hill, their previous location erupted in concussion and shrapnel, which caused them to tumble down the side of the ridge and into a brook that was on the extreme western side of the city of Phenplyacin.

Brenko's face emerged from the shallow water, but he could not stand due to the tremors. Something in the air felt so oppressive he could hardly breathe. His skin desired to retreat into his bones. His bone into the marrow. And the marrow into Kímaios'lo. In the northeast Firmament, the Brycian noticed a large aura spreading into the horizon. Energy discharges from Miska Kea's airlifts coalesced around the center of the aura, and a group of at least twenty témos were attacking the central figure.

"By the One!" he heard Syla say, "It *is* a Sczyphamek!"

"What in Qalfocx is that?" Bíoske's voice quivered for the first time. The man from Keotagosdi pointed to a black mass that was obfuscated by the nighttime darkness and energy bursts.

A large chunk of something had been torn off the apex of a small mountain, and within a second, the mass of earth swung in the direction of the témos and airlifts, killing all twenty of the felines and breaking the crafts into pieces. Limp bodies and shrapnel fell to the city below, only to be followed by the mass of earth, which indiscriminately smashed the buildings and people.

"Whose side is this Sczyphamek on?" Brenko wondered aloud. "Both sides were probably killed by that."

"Do not move!" a threatening voice shouted from the banks of the river. "Drop your weapons!"

Seven Blue Rapier soldiers strafed the one who had spoken. He had a noticeable scar on his right cheek. The three operatives prepared themselves for battle.

"Staxis," Bíoske cursed while attempting to light a drenched daggerweed cigarette. "You bastards are damn persistent... damn persistent."

Syla was as swift as the wind, and if it were not for Brenko gripping the barrel of her AEAR she would have killed two Blue Rapier troops before they felt their mortality slipping away.

"It's too late for this now," Brenko said to Syla. He faced the commanding officer of Blue Rapier and asked, "Can't you hear him?"

The Brycian closed his eyes and the commanding officer of Blue Rapier dropped his energy rifle. It was faint at first, but soon, it became unmistakable. The Sczyphamek's voice reverberated through the air.

"Ah... That voice belongs to Vincallous Fierce," one of the Rapier soldiers stammered.

"What?" Syla's face grew pale and her countenance was one of distress and dread. "*He is the Sczyphamek?* No..."

"I am guessing that if we can hear his voice, we must be in the range of his powers," Brenko reasoned. "He just dropped a mountain on both of our forces. I don't know why; but right now, he is not distinguishing between friend and foe. I think we—"

"Keh mányx phen da pet... *Keh mányx phen da pet!*"

Vincallous' voice boomed through the air and down into Phenplyacin and its vicinity. The treble and bass of his voice were perfectly equalized and chilling. Fierce's aura had become an even deeper red and pulsated vibrantly. The air around Vincallous destabilized.

The eleven nel'asmív in between the riverbanks could not bury their inclination to face his direction. His voice eliminated their antagonism. Though they were more than ten lengths from his position, all of them— Miska Kea and Blue Rapier—at the riverside felt as if they were face to face with the Elemental warrior.

Time and space shifted to allow an interpersonal relationship with the events of Phenplyacin, and for a moment, Brenko embraced the desperation of the témos; their terror of and disdain for Fierce frightened him all the more. Syla could feel the ground of Phenplyacin; it felt *hungry?* Bíoske encountered the screams of nel'asmív from all corners of Qeauríyx—screaming and pleading for such a fate to escape them. Yes, at that moment, the Cycle stood still. Lo, for a instant, in the stream of an unnamed brook, they saw Qalfocx in its enormity.

If only for a moment...

The suffered no chance to cope with the inanity. In an instant, the ground shook more viciously than before. And somehow, in the midst of their unholy epiphany, Bíoske noticed the mundane. The brook's flow had surged exponentially, and rocks and trees followed in its wake.

"Staxis!" he yelled. "Everybody, get to the banks!"

Their legs responded to the fear of Bíoske's voice, even though their minds did not have time to process the absurdity of their forthcoming struggle. However, two Blue Rapier soldiers hesitated. They were swept into the current, gnashed, and then crushed by the rocks, trees, and debris even as they drowned in the vitriolic rapid. Everyone else barely made it to the eastern banks of the riverside.

"What in Qalfocx is he doing, ah?" the commanding officer muttered. "He'll kill us all."

A Blue Rapier soldier, still viewing Miska Kea as her antithesis, aimed her gun at Syla. Within an instant the commanding officer shot a minimal discharge at his subordinate, striking her on the arm, which caused the grunt to drop her weapon and her comrades to stare in bewilderment.

"Stop!" the commanding officer yelled.

"Yerna!" his subordinate screamed. "You are siding with them, ah? You're a traitor!"

"Siding? Look around! Don't be foolish! There are no sides right now," Yerna explained. "Maybe never again… It's going to take all of us to live through this."

The ground cracked beneath their feet, and Syla would have nearly fallen into a crevice if Bíoske had not grabbed her hand. Yerna raced to Bíoske and helped him pull the woman up. She looked at the Damüdan in amazement, returning the same perplexed glance his subordinates just gave him.

Yerna grimaced and addressed Brenko. "It'll be a miracle if we escape this, ah."

Bíoske responded before Brenko could answer. "This planet doesn't need a kímaz miracle or a Sczyphamek. How could the Nameless One let this happen? Kíma!"

"Wha… what is that?" Syla asked. Incredulous tears gushed down her face as she gazed at the central area of Phenplyacin. "That can't be… this can't be right… That can't be happening."

No more energy bursts were fired. The fighters and inhabitants inside the city realized what Yerna and Brenko accepted. Qalfocx was taking no sides, and Vincallous was its agent. Or perhaps the roles were reversed. There was no time to reflect on a reason or purpose; there was no space to scrutinize meaninglessness and chance. The ground thundered, careened, and trembled to such an extent that Brenko and Yerna were unable to hear the desperate words Syla murmured anyway.

Phenplyacin—the city, the vicinity, the rivers, the land, the buildings, the people in its borders, the south-central coast of Tannódin—rocked back and forth, eerily, in the same manner a mother rocks her newborn to sleep. Yet, many would not awake from this slumber. The torment allowed no hiding place. There was no relief from the mangling and heavy arms of the Vicious Zananín and the violent contagion of death and misery he carried.

The steel skyrises of central Phenplyacin cracked underneath from the raw pressure of the trembling earth. Men, women, children, animals, plants, and trees—the living—were crushed by the collapsing structures. The sound was so terrible and loud, their shrieks were inaudible to Bíoske's ears. Syla, on the crumbling ridge, watched the chaos in dismay. Over eight million people inhabited the city. That did not include Miska Kea or the Blue Rapier and White Scythe members. A sea of nel'asmív was beneath them, but Yerna could not tell who was alive or who was dead. Brenko tried to find stable ground, but what did "stable" or "ground" mean now? There was so much debris; they did not know what was before, behind, above, or beneath them.

"Everyone hold hands," Yerna commanded. "Do not let go, no matter what."

Before Yerna exhaled from that statement, one of his comrades was sucked into a newly formed chasm, and within seconds, the Global Initiative soldier was catapulted out of the crevice choking and smoldering.

"Staxis!" Brenko yelled. He would not let himself grasp what that manner of death portended. "Run!"

Perishing. Living perished. The planet feasted. Qeauríyx chewed, crunched, and swallowed them, as if it had not eaten in millennia. With boulders, trees, and water chasing after them, Brenko and Yerna's group ran down the hill, towards the beach on the outskirts of Phenplyacin and stumbled upon a large group of nel'asmív who were no longer identifiable by cause, region, religion, or ideology.

They had no plan. They tried to stay clear of all structures, but some were unable to escape. The sound of crushed bones and cartilage under the weight of concrete became a common noise to Brenko's ringing ears. The reverberation of hopeless, violent death found its way into every secret space of Phenplyacin. Underneath piles of rubble, ravenous death searched endlessly for its prey.

Suddenly, the shaking and harmonic dissonance stopped, which caused the pack to slow down their scamper. And in the midst of the madness and herd of folk, Brenko reclaimed his senses.

He wasted no time. "We have to head back to the hills and cross over them! The beach is not safe."

But no one heeded his words.

Yerna, in a revelatory moment, spoke in agreement. "This man is right. The beach is the most dangerous place for us now. Fierce is sealing this location off. The further we are from his voice the better off we will be."

"You are siding with the enemy?" a Tannódin'é asked Yerna.

"Who is the enemy?" Bíoske yelled in poignant disgust. "Who is killing us or allowing us to be killed? That's our enemy."

"Come on," Syla said impatiently. "They can follow us if they want."

"This was your plan!" a Miska Kea fighter shouted after recognizing his three comrades. "We followed you into this! This is your fault."

Ashamed and guilty, Brenko pleaded, "We didn't know. You must believe us. We didn't know about this. But when it's this kímaz bad, even ignorance can't be excused.

"Please, follow us. You don't want to be here when it happens."

The four of them ran back towards the hills, but only a group of about thirty followed them. The rest headed to the beach, believing they could escape by boat.

"Dé'wa. Dé'wa. Fá'atoño má. Keh mányx! Keh mányx!" If it was at all possible for Vincallous' voice to grow louder and more maniacal, the possibility became reality.

"Whatever you do," Brenko warned the group following him. "Do not stop running."

"Vincallous... He went that deep, didn't he?" Yerna asked Brenko knowingly. "I saw what happened to my brother. He was burnt."

"That was your brother?" Brenko asked, speaking through huffs. "I'm sorry."

"By the end of this, he may have been one of the lucky ones."

Suddenly, holes in the surface opened in numerous locations, and some who were fleeing with them were siphoned in.

"Get to the high ground!" Yerna howled.

Seconds later, the remains of those sucked into the ground were sent flying into the air as steam and magma erupted from the same hole that ingested them, burning their broken bodies while they were still alive. The former adversaries heard screams of agony and pain that cried to the Firmament. They cried for answers to a question that should not have to be asked... ever.

Soon, molten rocks shot out of the holes, pelting the group with orange-white pellets that singed and burned their clothes, hair, and skin.

It was a hopeless attempt to live.

Behind him, Brenko witnessed a man and woman no longer capable of struggling against the inevitable. With somber smiles, the couple sat on the crumbling crust and held each other. A stream of lava rushed over them, incinerating them in seconds. To his right, a large chunk of flaming bedrock raced through the air and attacked a father carrying his helpless son, erasing them both from history. To his left, a young woman crawled on the que, mercilessly scorched and bloodied. He wanted to stop and assist her, but she would not survive anyway, and he would be killed trying to aid her. Self-preservation or selfishness? Was there actually a difference? Before he could ponder such asinine questions, a large tree fell on the woman, and a pile of flaming rocks crashed on top of the tree, setting the area ablaze.

"You won't kill me," Brenko heard Bíoske yell. Against all odds, Bíoske was near the top of the hill ahead of him, carrying Syla whose leg was broken. "I'm not afraid of something that doesn't exist! You won't kill me!"

And like a refrain sung by a bitter, crazed man whose vision of the cosmos was unjustly shattered by the intersection of random, intergroup, historical, divine, ecological, military, and interpersonal violence, Bíoske shouted between every breath: "You won't kill me! No. You won't! Worthless! You're kímaz worthless! *Worthless*! Damn worthless! Worthless! Bastards! You won't kill me!" Soon his words became nothing but painful groans and heartbreaking murmurs. "*Mmmmmmm... Mmmmmmm... Uuuuuunnnnnn... Mm... mmmmmm... Mmmppphhh...*"

Syla sobbed for the man she loved. Even though so many had perished, Bíoske's rage and broken qanín was the most unbearable sound and sight she had witnessed thus far.

Brenko and Yerna were side by side, running with all their might to the apex of the mount and past the brook—now waterless—where they had met at what seemed a lifetime ago. Only twelve remained. As his mind became desensitized to the murderous conditions, Brenko wondered how it was possible that Syla, Bíoske, and he had survived. If anyone should have died, it should have been them. Should they not be punished for this folly? Or was their punishment survival?

Soon, they could run no further. They had struggled their full measure as a nel'asmív; and collectively, one by one, they collapsed in a grassy field high above the city. Yerna listened intently. Fierce's voice was a soft evisceration in the air.

"I think..." Yerna coughed and wheezed, "I think we are safe, for now."

"No," Brenko was exhausted but frantic nonetheless. "We can't rest for long. You know what he is about to do. See! Do you see?"

Gazing to the northeast, Yerna witnessed magma erupting in a semicircle, strafing the hills that surrounded Phenplyacin. Steam ascended from the top of the ocean.

An anonymous woman trembled in impotence. "What is he doing?"

"He's gonna sever it. *Damn it!*" Brenko cried, unable to contain his emotional torment. "*He's gonna rip Phenplyacin off of Tannódin.*"

"That's impossible," a Tannódin'é survivor gasped. "Sczyphameks are potent, but he would have to be an elite Sczyphamek, on the level of Exceptional or the near the First, to do something like that. Even Imperial was not that powerful."

Syla shuddered when she remembered the words of the témo. The témo told them that the other Sczyphamek was more powerful than Vincallous. Brenko glanced at Syla and Bíoske and visually ordered them not to tell anyone about that information now, for it would surely crush the qaníns of the survived.

The ground shook, cracked, splintered, and disintegrated—the worst since the quakes commenced. Moving was pointless. Movement was no longer possible. The tactician understood exactly what was happening. The smaller tremors, although terrible, were deceptive. Vincallous was at work, deep beneath the crust of Tannódin, severing the earthen tie of Phenplyacin from its continental plate. The deeper an earthquake, the harder it was for the surface to feel its effects. The temblor they felt now was the final breakage.

"They're finished," Brenko said, thinking of those who ran towards the beach and those in the city. "They're kímaz dead."

The ground swayed and cracked at the seams of the magma vents. Vicious' hair flapped in the wind as he surgically altered the face of Qeauríyx. The land ripped and the ocean retracted, extending the southern shore of Phenplyacin ten lengths. Yet the ocean returned—as a tsunami whose height was two thousand feet—and rushed toward the shore of the soon-to-be-island of Phenplyacin. The battlecruisers belonging to Miska Kea were picked up and tossed in the sea of water, drowning countless victims in the process. Those who made it to the coast and had survived the magma runoff now faced an inescapable wall of water. The velocity of the ocean snapped bones, leveled what remaining buildings stood, and launched seawinders, shrapnel, and the living hundreds of feet in the air and inland. The sound was deafening.

Bíoske waited and watched. Waited and watched if they were far enough inland and high enough to escape the water. He waited. Waited to see if they would be on the new shoreline of Tannódin, or if they would fall into the Lancryptox Ocean.

The side of the foothill directly in front of him continued to erode and break apart.

The gestating cliff and bay edged its way towards their position.

Each time a slab of que crumbled into the ocean, Bíoske cursed the One with No Name, Qeauríyx, Sczyphameks, and Global Initiative with all his qanín. He would never wait for *It* again. And after that day, he never saw *It*, except in his waking nightmares and in the questions he would never be able to answer. But he wouldn't wait for a response.

"No." He smelled it. But he still said, "No." He happened as his kind; he knew how nel'asmív carried about their business.

His qanín would not accept the inevitable. He anticipated the spin, the megalomaniacal additions that Phenplyacin would accumulate. He smelled the myanála. It smelled like the dung of a jungle sloth that subsisted on the kíma clinging to a poor man's sandal. And nel'asmív were insects that flew about the shit, ready to dig into the feces of tragedy, parading the meal as the Firmament's ambrosia.

Kímaz myanálas.

His heart wanted none of it. One side would claim this moment of genocide and ecocide as a necessary evil to advance the cause of Global Initiative. The other would speak of it as a battlecry that symbolized the demonic nature of Qeauríyx and Global Initiative.

Nel'asmív would do anything to survive and make meaning, even if it meant lying, cheating, stealing, killing, obscuring, and/or grandstanding. They'd create or kill a god if need be. Qeauríyx drove his species to a rational madness.

He heard the longwinded speeches. He saw the deaths. He tasted the obscurity in which this moment would end. This lingering, precarious moment of real life was destined to die. Phenplyacin was destined to die in interpretation and reinterpretation, objective facts and subjective opinions. It was destined to no longer be experienced. And all those who didn't live through Phenplyacin, all those who didn't die from this moment, all those who would come after or who came before, would act as if they experienced this random, purposeless necessity. *This* moment would become *that* moment.

That was the way of history. Not written by the victors or the losers, just those who could not bring themselves to touch the ugly, raw truth. The word "Phenplyacin" would forever be linked to this moment even though it was destined to obscure and conceal, just as much as it revealed.

Undoubtedly, "Phenplyacin" would signal the beginning of Miska Kea's end. "Phenplyacin" would be used as a marker in time that would become sanitized by those who wished to continue or fight against Global Initiative. Even though the anger and the scars would be real, the eight million or more who died would be unable to tell their stories, bested by hyperbole and anecdote. And as a result, the sheer brutality of history and nel'asmív would have a chance to manipulate and silence them.

In order to survive, the dead must be buried or burned. History allowed no open graves. Open graves weren't *sanitary*.

He shook his head. The tears wouldn't fall. He clenched his teeth till the enamel chipped. His fist was so tight that his fingernails tore into his skin. He would have designed new curse words if Phenplyacin had not taken his breath away. His knees knocked, but his fear was no longer worldly or theological. It was cosmic.

Bíoske would be convinced forever. His enemy was this tragic satire, which paraded itself as lowbrow humor or epic drama.

The cliff neared their position and stopped. The shaking subsided, and the aura that had once covered the horizon retreated back to Vincallous.

"We are the Sczyphamek called Vicious," he boomed through the atmosphere, speaking to the remnant. "Kaz Késhal Supreme is a Sczyphamek and my consort. They are Pre-Eminent. Let it be known that Global Initiative will have no rival."

With that, the red aura streaked back toward Megaphyx Bonicin.

Syla was unsure, but it sounded as if the Sczyphamek was crying. If he was not crying, Qeauríyx did because it started to rain. Syla checked

Bíoske's timekeeper, which was miraculously undamaged. Only three hours had passed since the first explosion. But in those three hours, the world completely changed. In three hours, Qeauríyx revealed itself to happen how it always happened. In three hours, Syla had lost her faith, regained it, lost it, found it, and was now unsure of anything.

She grimaced and yelled when Bíoske set her broken left tibia in place and used a thick tree limb as a splint.

She still felt pain. She was still alive. She was relieved she was not dead. She was still alive. She was unsure of the future. She was still alive.

Chagrined and indignant, she beat her chest and muttered to the Nameless One, "This was more than we can bear. It's too much. But it could have been all of us. You did what you could…"

Syla unstrapped the sword and sheath that had been in her possession for cycles. The sword, "Harmony," represented her full measure as a nel'asmív and warrior. She tossed the weapon and her identity as a Cílal over the cliff and into the abyss.

In faithful protest, she wept. "Full strength" and absolute control had no place on Qeauríyx or in the universe. No entity possessed such stupidity. Did justice or mercy exist in the cosmos, or were they simply nel'asmív attempts to create order out of chaos, security out of primordial fear? No matter the answer, she could no longer embrace that "omnipotence," "justice," and "mercy" exhausted the Nameless Mystery, if they described the Happening at all.

She believed her faith was unshakeable, but in the wake of Phenplyacin, she was forced to reconsider the very meaning of faithfulness. Faith was no longer formulaic. The Divine was no longer bound by the categories of "cause," "good," "power," and "knowledge." Her theology was stripped of metaphors and symbols and became a theology groping clumsily in the dark for words to describe that which could not be grasped yet was still somehow tangible.

The deity was no longer a deity in the midst of harmony. If the One with No Name was indeed real, then It must also dwell in the dissonance and in the meantime.

Suddenly, her theological confusion vanished. The material gripped Syla as its prey. Her complicity swallowed her with contempt. In guilt and horror, her cry of protest became a mournful wail. Her life and death would never atone for this righteous folly. This was her, Brenko, and Bíoske's plan… Their lives would never find peace now.

Living was their punishment. And after they had endured the sentence of life, their deaths were sure to be violent and in defeat.

Yerna blinked and wiped the sweat from his brow. His hands, like his heart, trembled without ceasing. There was no metaphysical or theological confusion in his mind. The concrete facts before him cast aside all manner of cosmic and terrestrial speculation. It was a hard burden, but Yerna bore the weight of the real.

Bitterly, he asked questions, which, four hours prior, he never considered. Was that *the* Vincallous Fierce, the man all of his soldiers admired, and even he aspired to be? Was this the legacy of Global Initiative? Were the Southeast Damüdans right after all?

Yerna moved towards one of his wounded comrades. The Damüdan did not notice or feel the burns on his back from the hot pellets of molten rock. He was still in the grip of dismay. He was angry at Miska Kea for attacking. Their cause had set off the chain of events that transpired. But could there be an honest comparison between the terrorists' actions and Vincallous' eco-genocide?

Yerna—burned, bruised, and bloodied—crawled toward the cliff, which was only three hundred feet from their position, where a Blue Rapier soldier agonized in unquenchable misery.

The soldier squealed and beat her fists on the terra. "My mother! Kanoso! My consort... *My son and daughters*! That is my home... This was my home! He killed them! Why? He didn't even know them... *He didn't even know them*!" The female soldier, struck with a fathomless grief, shook and cried... with no comforter.

Yerna peered over the edge and saw Phenplyacin on fire, drifting out to sea. The waves had settled somewhat, but were still crashing against the new cliffs of south central Tannódin. Phenplyacin was over fifty-five square lengths, and yet Vincallous had dissolved the unity between the region and the continent. Small volcanic domes formed throughout the area, and quakes of different varieties shook the surrounding locale.

The Damüdan placed his arms around his *former* comrade and whispered impossible promises to ameliorate her. Perhaps if he spoke soft enough, the woman would feel his compassion and not the uselessness of his empty assurances. Yerna was ashamed of himself, but he knew no other words. "...be alright... get through this together... maybe they escaped... I'm sorry... shhhhhhh..."

Brenko crawled, stood, and hobbled to the other side of the hill to check his hypothesis.

He knew it.

Megaphyx Bonicin had only sustained minor damage, other than the destruction of the imperial palace, which took place before the tremors. Vincallous, the other Sczyphamek, or both of them, kept the catastrophe of Phenplyacin from spreading inland into the rest of Civix Setrin. However, the quakes were sure to produce tsunamis planet-wide.

The rain sprinkled and wetted the tactician's weary face. With a hewn qanín, Brenko surveyed the eleven survivors. He was sure that other pockets of folk had survived too. But what did that mean? Four or five thousand surviving out of nearly nine million?

Bíoske was right; the témos were more than commendable. Any nel'asmív who survived owed their thanks to them. By engaging Vincallous in mortal combat, the témos provided just enough time for the living to escape. In the fiery distance, Brenko counted only eight winged felines remaining. Two hundred and fifty participated in the attack. The remnant flew southwest, back to the Crossroad Islands, to tell their kind the oracle of doom they survived.

Only a Kylanín with strong abilities, faith, and determination could help the rebels now. An event like Phenplyacin happened once every other Cycle. Vincallous' actions were not random. The Sczyphamek sent a message to every sentient happening, animal, plant, and insect on the planet.

Weeping bitterly and wildly, Brenko stumbled toward his best friends. But before he could meet their consoling eyes and arms, he fell and thrashed about on the ground. If he could have entered back into his mother's womb he would have. He clawed at the ground, yelling and raving inaudible words.

He could not calculate. The outcomes. The minutia. The equation didn't lie. He tried to contort the variables; he used a different calculus, a different philosophy, a different folklore, a different theology, a different science, a different perspective. None availed. The outcome: the axe was at the root. The trunk was already reduced to cinders.

There was no hope.

The General Maximum, Commandant Feolenz, Isürus Tekil—three Wielders—and two Sczyphameks were under the same banner. The cycle was 221 OGI. There had not been a Sczyphamek in over eighty cycles, and the first Sczyphameks to appear were both Zananín. And *both* were on the level of the First and Exceptional. It had been *over* 1700 cycles since a Kylanín or Zephanín emerged, and there was no guarantee that another 1700 cycles would pass before another would.

Whether or not there was a Nameless One, the devilry of this Cycle was demented, spiteful, and uncanny. Metaphysics be damned. It was simple logic and mathematics. Hope and faith were negligible variables in this newfound equation.

How (or why) anyone would hope for something different, better, or greater than what they just lived through was beyond the tactician. Nameless One or not, hope and faith were no longer needed.

"Meaningless! Damn it! It's all kímaz pointless." Looking at Yerna, then Syla, and finally Bíoske, the tactician said with reddened eyes and quivering hands, "Staxis, give me that damn flask."

CHAPTER TWENTY-ONE: FOR THE GREATEST OF CAUSES...

Diplomacy

9 Opíz, 241 OGI
Kazlé

She intuited their combined exhaustion, a weariness so bottomless that Késhal became winded herself. It was not only because of the battles they had fought recently, or the fact that although Lywa and Cálo were deadly adversaries, they were now allies. No, their fatigue was longsuffering, as old as the Great Extinguishing. For that was the day, the tragic moment, that Anzél lost its chance to dislodge itself from Líachim and the Backbone Mountains became the permanent stern on the terra of Anzél. That event all but solidified Anzél's nearly ten thousand-cycle-old civil war, a war that should not have happened and was never "civil." That anyone remained alive after ten millennia of conflict and genocide was astonishing.

Pre-Eminent was convinced her presence had brought the opposing sides together and united them, before they destroyed themselves. Her cause was right. Even when Global Initiative was seen as the enemy, it still drew people closer.

They would not need much persuasion. They did not want to fight anymore.

Késhal arranged the meeting as soon as Lywa and Cálo were captured. Her orders to Feolenz were plain, and true to form, the Commandant carried them out with efficient prejudice. She wanted to lessen all deaths and casualties on both sides of the conflict. Each day, at dusk and at dawn, Blue Rapier would extend terms of peace and offer the folk of Anzél, Focalites and Anmetrians, a chance to surrender. And finally, after almost four durations of war, they accepted.

This was an important summit for the Empress. She had to persuade them, without the fear of annihilation or coercion, to join with her—no, to join something greater than she could ever hope to happen. She had been in this complex situation before, and she prevailed. She did it with Van, Damüda, Nez Spirita, Bryce, the Windward Isles, and with Reníz. She would do it again.

When she rose to power after Phenplyacin, Pre-Eminent did much to shore up relations with Damüda. Within the first five cycles of her ascendancy, the Tannódin'é/Damüdan alliance was unshakeable. She allowed the Damüdan Guild a freer reign with their people, and Vincallous became the symbolic head of state. Galís, a young politician at the time, was elected as the lord minister of Damüda and oversaw all executive and legislative duties on the continent. This pleased the majority of Damüdans, though those in the eastern regions would not trust Tannódin for many generations. Pre-Eminent had no quarrel with them. Their generational distrust was just another sign of her parent's failed policies.

In the first decade of her planetary stewardship, the empress took bold and silent steps to bolster Global Initiative's propagation. Her first move was to push for imperial advances so that an attack like Phenplyacin would never happen again. These advances would be accomplished in three steps.

The first step was obvious. If Tannódin'é technology had been sufficient her armed forces would have detected such a large fleet approaching Phenplyacin. Késhal asked Vincallous and Haptian Spiax to devise a method of detection from far distances. Using the Sczyphameks' powers as stepping-stones, Vincallous and Spiax developed a complex system of radar and sonar posts around Qeauríyx. High frequency communication was also set up across Tannódin, Damüda, Cometstone Island, Bryce, the Windward Isles, and Phmquedria, with future projects in Nez Spirita. Bryce also became the home to Global Initiative's budding space industry, and several rockets and satellite prototypes had been launched into the Firmament over the past six cycles.

The second shift in policy was towards the lands conquered by Tannódin and Damüda, namely Nez Spirita, Bryce, the Windward Isles, and parts of Phmquedria. She assembled a group, headed by her kin, Alzhexph ju Xaníz, to create and institute effective, transparent diplomatic solutions to quell many of the uprisings in those lands. And for the first time in ages, not only did Tannódin and Damüda draw up treaties, they also did not break them. As a matter of course, however, they demanded concessions from the indigenous populations, which, over time, granted the Tannódin'é a stronger presence and authority.

Her parents were too impatient and had forced Global Initiative onto the backs of millions who did not understand its true intent or principles. Unlike her predecessors, Késhal allowed the indigenous of every land the freedom to practice their religious and philosophical perspectives without the fear of imperial reprisal. The Tannódin'é/Damüdan alliance also integrated and/or curtailed their economic principles with local customs concerning trade and commerce. The same measures were taken for political structures; the empire reformed its colonial governmental systems in order to share power with the original inhabitants of every land.

Késhal's evangelical strategy was clear and uncompromising: imperial conversion was to be won by example not by compulsion. Pre-Eminent trusted that when nel'asmív saw the honest, meaningful purpose of Global Initiative, they would turn their backs on their archaic, divisive ways of the past.

And yet, Késhal was certain that some nel'asmív would never convert.

That led her to the third and final step, which was covert in nature. The facts were undeniable; Miska Kea was able to carry out such an impudent and costly attack precisely because they enjoyed an overwhelming advantage in espionage. Her parents underestimated their adversaries; they underestimated the rebellion's resourcefulness. Therefore, in 223 OGI, Késhal created a new military wing of Global Initiative to be created. This wing would focus exclusively on imperial security, intelligence gathering, clandestine operations, and the continued extermination of the témos. She named the wing the "Eradicate," the final chamber of the Daknín.

The House of Kaz had long possessed an imperial guard, but under Késhal's recalibration, the entity expanded its function and role within Global Initiative. During her mother and grandmother's lifetime, a member of the Tekil household, a prominent family within Tannódin, commanded the imperial guard. The head of the imperial guard also possessed the Violet Manacle. Isürus[1] Tekil was the last person to have a filial tie to the weapon.

In 224 OGI, Pre-Eminent stripped Isürus of his status and ordered the Violet Manacle and the newly formed Eradicate to be handed over to an unknown nineteen-cycle-old Tannódin'é assassin named Reníz Bläno.[2]

Bläno was an enigmatic, loyal, fiercely competitive, and violent woman from the Windward Isles.

A distant Tannódin'é colony in the Phyxtríalis Ocean, the Windward Isles were a logistical necessity if Global Initiative was to succeed against Líachim and Keotagosdi. Tannódin had forged an uneasy relationship with the natives when they arrived in 127 OGI, but within fifty cycles, both sides realized the unsurprising truth: the Tannódin'é wanted complete control of the area. But due to the region's great distance from supply lines, the Tannódin'é could not maintain an adequate hold on the Isles.

In the cycles leading up to Vincallous' decisive victory there, many of the Tannódin'é colonists were attacked and raided by the indigenous inhabitants of the Isles. Bläno was the daughter of Tannódin'é immigrants, who came to the Windward Isles to find work and possibly attain a name for themselves. But on Qeauríyx, names and titles are soon forgotten.

---

[1] Isürus (ih-soo-roos)
[2] Bläno (blahh-noh)

In the autumn of 213 OGI, the indigenous, along with hired mercenaries, destroyed Bläno's township. Most of the adults were murdered while the mercenaries took the children in order to train them as soldiers, using the fear of death or sexual exploitation as a catalyst for their service. Bläno was eight-cycles-old.

In 218 OGI, a White Scythe division, led by Vincallous Fierce, entered an enemy outpost and discovered all of their adversaries killed. The only survivor was an adolescent female pulling the trigger of a long emptied energy rifle. The second Vincallous encountered Reníz, a young girl with vacant eyes, the Damüdan was attached to her. They shared a kindred qanín: a robbed childhood. Anyone who drank from that cup of contagion easily recognized a fellow imbiber.

Her appetite for violence was nearly as insatiable as her want for sex. Both were products of her forced participation in war and from the sexual predation within her own ranks. Bläno had killed her first enemy and was raped before she entered puberty. Nothing could glamorize or lighten that reality. It was her reality. Each day brought her the silent loss of hope and change. Only the solidification of the antitheses remained: despair and monotony. As she grew older—twelve cycles of age—the Tannódin'é demanded sex. However, she would kill a man if he did not please her or if she felt violated. The line of such offense and vitiation was imperceptible, which left many injured or dead. Soon, no man dared to touch her adolescent body, for she had decapitated, castrated, and disemboweled (in that order) her commanding officer for blemishing her invisible halo.

Bläno fought against, murdered, and maimed her kind—the Tannódin'é—for five cycles. She outlived the other children from her township who were cut down by the energy bursts of their kindred. Yea, for five cycles, Bläno killed her ethnic brothers and sisters, amassing a body count higher than anyone else in her squad. The mercenaries who trained her nicknamed her "Violence," because she showed no mercy or self-preservation on the battlefield. Due to her perennial fighting skills, she came to be prized by her compatriots. But Reníz, unlike many in history, never forgot her real name. She remembered. And those who had done this to her would pay.

At the time, she did not believe in the Nameless One, nor did she believe in nel'asmív as a species. Why should she? What kind of world existed where children were killed and died in conflicts they did not create or understand? How could people create sadistic and pernicious relationships, yet rationalize them away with such ignorant animosity? Bläno comprehended little when she was little, except that adults were more capricious and self-deluding than children.

That initial encounter between Reníz and Vincallous was unnecessarily but inevitably violent. With open arms and unarmed, Van invited the girl to leave the camp with him. Mistaking his care for sexual advance and deception, she attempted to kill him, even as he stood in the midst of his troops with their AEARs fixed on her. Fierce ordered his subordinates to hold their fire. Brandishing a knife, Bläno swung the blade at Fénúra's throat, so that he would join the corpses of her former, murdered comrades who lay in ruin and righteous betrayal. Indeed, she had slit their throats while they slept and used their dead bodies as target practice, hours before Vincallous arrived to her outpost.

Reníz's countenance was feral; her body was soaked in blood and despondency. Her vacuous eyes were unforgettable. They were wholly apathetic and uncompromisingly helpless. She was begging to be put out of her misery.

Fierce had overtaken the Windward Isles without one Global Initiative casualty lost on the battlefield. In the anonymous Reníz, the man from Nosgüth saw himself. Her death would be a casualty for *his* side. Each time he knocked her down, she got up and continued to fight. He was forced to beat her unconscious and close to death. Vincallous had Reníz transported to eastern Damüda. Once he had completely secured the Windward Isles, he took a cycle's leave to her location, his first extended break in military duty. Reníz did not trust him for many weeks. After six durations, she finally accepted that Vicious had a genuine interest in her wellbeing.

Soon after Vincallous and Késhal learned of one another, Fierce informed the successor of Global Initiative about Bläno. Késhal was troubled that a young one endured such a terrible childhood. Pre-Eminent's attitude surprised Vincallous and made the Damüdan's love for the Tannódin'é swell to new proportions.

Much to her parent's dismay, Késhal brought Reníz into the royal palace to rehabilitate her. Vincallous' occupation as a soldier of White Scythe made it impossible for him to care for Bläno, for he was constantly on assignment, and the last thing the fourteen-cycle-old needed was to be near violent conflict.

Bläno enjoyed a relationship with Vincallous and Késhal unlike no other. No nel'asmív dared to be as close to the co-leaders of the House of Kaz. In fact, before Phenplyacin, Reníz Bläno was the only person who knew that both Fierce and Supreme were Sczyphameks. And in time, the former child-soldier, who neither cared for her life nor the life of others, was reeducated and given a new purpose and direction. However, her skills as an assassin and a plotter were undeniable. Késhal spent four long cycles, using every measure of her empathic abilities, to stabilize the adolescent who soon became like a daughter to the empress.

Késhal ordered Feolenz to personally instruct and tutor Reníz during his free time. After their confrontation with her mother, both she and Vincallous realized that Old Flint was probably their most trustworthy ally. He vehemently objected to Vincallous' use of power at Phenplyacin, which showed that he was more concerned about Global Initiative than his life or the feelings of the leaders of Kaz. In time, Reníz saw the Sczyphameks as the parents she lost and Feolenz as the grandparent she never had. Her loyalty to Késhal and Vincallous grew unwavering.

When Késhal ordered the Eradicate to be formed, Isürus Tekil was deposed of his title and rank as the leader of the imperial guard. Soon after, Bläno volunteered to lead the new wing of the Daknín. For obvious reasons, Vincallous and Késhal did not want their daughter near armed conflict. However, the nineteen-cycle-old was persuasive and qualified. Under the tutelage of Feolenz, she became quite proficient in all manners of leadership, learning, and fighting. The leaders of the Global Assembly (Global Initiative's legislative body) were reticent because of Bläno's age and questionable background, but under the testimony of Feolenz and Késhal, she was legally confirmed. It was one of Késhal's most vivid and proudest memories.

The Sczyphamek who happened as Pre-Eminent took a deep breath and petitioned her Elemental. Lywa and Cálo were capable of reason and would undoubtedly see the utility and scope of Global Initiative. They were tired. They had fought long enough. They were like Reníz.

Opening the door to the quarters where the two former leaders of enmity were housed, Sczyphamek Pre-Eminent stepped through the foyer with a smile and in brazen confidence. Lywa and Cálo could not look at her in the face. They felt fear, contempt, weariness, and shame. They were like so many she encountered.

They would convert.

Murder

5 Opíz, 241 OGI
Fürnlé

Kéma glanced right once more.

Kíma. No coincidence.

She was being followed.

She was wise enough to avoid the primary or secondary escape routes back to Líachim, her home. And her tertiary plan was only known by Bíoske. Who knew what, when, and how no longer mattered. They were not after *her* anyway. The *information* she carried was their quarry.

These were not the plans to some prototypical structure or weapon of doom. These were formations, personnel assignments, and reinforcement positions. Líachim was a continent, not a city. Only a masterful plan with warranted adjustments would give anyone the possibility of victory, even Sczyphameks.

Kéma had not been able to retrieve much data. The information was scattered, broken, and corrupted. She probably only retrieved a fourth of the original. It would take a military mind greater than hers to draw out any

407

real meaning. The chances of that were *slim*, but there was still a chance *at least*, and that was better than *no chance at all*.

Her seawinder would not arrive for another five hours. She could not risk being spotted when she boarded the vessel. The ship would be tracked, and in open water, she would be caught and murdered. But more than her death, the remains of the war plan would be lost, all but guaranteeing Líachim's defeat. And if Líachim fell, Global Initiative would claim its penultimate victim.

How would Keotagosdi fare if Líachim was struck down by the might of Tannódin? No, not just Tannódin, but Damüda, Phmquedria, Bryce, Zorét, Nez Spirita, and now the peninsula of Anzél. The entire world was truly against Líachim.

Just get the plans to Líachim, Kéma. Just make it home. One task at a time.

Kéma braved the entire winter of Nez Spirita. The Cílal crossed over the Gemansu Ranges and somehow made it to Nez Spirita's west-central shoreline, the only place on the continent in the winter daytime that consistently reached near freezing. She used the full extent of her training and abilities to traverse the mountain ranges in two weeks. The experience nearly took her life, but she had to leave Pike Metropolis as soon as possible in order to outrun the advance of winter. Had she stayed in the Infinite Circle, she surely would have been found and killed. It was common knowledge that everyone involved in the destruction of the Triple Skyrises was on their own after the attack. The owner of the Unseen Inn was unequivocal. There would be no vacancies.

The Cílal talked to no one, and in every village she tarried, she made it a habit to mind her business. Because the wintry weather was so arduous, she traveled only during the daytime hours—all five of them. As a result, it took her two and half durations to make it to Leel, a small, inconspicuous town on the western shore of central Nez Spirita. If she were a normal nel'asmív, Kéma would have died on numerous occasions. Too many nights she starved, and the Líachimian did not possess the proper attire to survive a Nez Spiritan winter.

Forced to use most of her energy at the beginning of her trek, Kéma tracked and killed the few wild animals that had not yet hibernated or migrated. Nothing was wasted. She ate every bit of flesh (sometimes raw) and used her game's fur for garments. Every moment in the wild was like the eight cycles she spent training at the Sacred Keep, but her situation was more desperate than anything she had prepared for.

She slept in the slain carcasses of windhorses and other wild beasts. She ate whatever she stumbled upon, from insects to grass to the occasional fish—when the weather permitted her to go on a beach to fish. She rested in caves, made small ice huts, and was given assistance by a few compassionate nel'asmív. Kéma'fém lost considerable weight, but her senses and skills had been sharpened fivefold. She went through Qalfocx and dwelled in gynix, all because of those corrupted, unintelligible plans.

And now, she had nearly crossed to the other side of a Cílal's potential.

She embraced it. She was almost a Premier: a Cílal unparalleled in speed, strength, durability, and skill, yet having no desire to fight. Legend held that a Premier developed a fighting ability on par with a Wielder. Few of her kind attained such a level, so there was no way to confirm such conjecture. Whether the legend was true or not, somehow she was drawing nigh unto the last stage of Cílal ju Néwan.

She arrived in Leel ten days before the boat was scheduled to dock. It was an inevitable consequence of Qeauríyx that she would encounter someone she did not need to. She did not know how many, but the odds were one or two agents at the most.

Think like Bíoske. I've got to assume the worst. They're Eradicate agents and they're not from the Assassin, Protectorate, or Espionage wings. Staxis. They're "Wind."

Wind was the most elite and clandestine wing of the Eradicate. Numbering around fifty, Wind agents were a dangerous combination of insightful violence and excessive detection. Unlike those belonging to the Assassin, Protectorate, and Espionage wings, members of Wind typically functioned without a team of subordinates and operated independently from the rest of the Eradicate. They were also tasked with the destruction of the témos. They could not be reasoned or negotiated with. Their mission was crystallized in an oath: "to jealously and efficiently defend and execute the cause of Global Initiative unto death."

Kéma was so tired of death.

Think like Bíoske, Kéma, she thought. *They must've discovered I'm a Cílal. If so, Tannódin sent either one of their best fighters or two exceptional killers. No more than two. Anymore than that, I'd have noticed right away. If these are Wind members, I've got to incapacitate or kill them. Kíma. Sorry, Nez.*

Sympathetic to Neztríanis' wish to not murder, the Líachimian's heart had grown heavy while traveling to Leel. Kéma had done her share of killing and now wondered if it actually accomplished anything other than awarding her a tainted piece of information that was only twenty-five percent complete.

But if these were Wind, she would have to use her real skills against them. She held back her destructive abilities during her fight at the Triple Skyrises because the task focused on stealth, not power and speed. But a few Wind agents were as formidable as a Cílal, and like them, they did not believe in using firearms unless absolutely necessary.

Affliction and Feather gave me away. Damn it.

Her sword and long knife never left her back or her side, and if Tannódin had collected any intelligence on her, those two features were surely included. Kéma'fém made sure she was cloaked throughout her journey, but she had been in Leel over a week. It was possible that someone had noticed her uncloaked, thereby exposing her, Feather, and Affliction. And since winter was over, one week was enough time to follow a lead and send agents to the area. Informants were everywhere, and the information she carried presented Tannódin with an enormous dilemma. The House of Kaz had no way to confirm if or how much of the data was stolen. They *had to assume* Kéma obtained all of it. They would risk all harm and false leads for those plans.

Let's get this over with.

Emerging from the mental milieu of context and decision, Kéma found herself on a bench one length from Leel's harbor. In five hours, a boat hailing from Keotagosdi would dock at the town's miniscule marina. The seawinder was on a strict schedule that had been agreed upon almost three durations ago. If she did not board the vessel within 40 minutes of docking, the boat would leave.

Her adversaries had to be dealt with before then. Mercy was not an option. Líachim was too important.

Kéma walked away from the docks, towards the town square, and into a clothing shop. The entire time, the agent following her kept a good distance behind her. He was good; if she was anyone else, she would not have noticed him. She hoped that her journey to the clothing shop would expose if the agent had an accomplice. If he did, his partner was an expert at concealing movement.

A hectic time of day, the locals were busy about their everyday routines, while would-be killers, imperialists and a liberator/"terrorist" were in their midst.

No one followed her into the bazaar. Scanning her surroundings, the Cílal spotted a Nez Spiritan woman her size and complexion. Kéma offered the woman fifty credits to leave the shop wearing the Cílal's cloak. The Líachimian explained that a man kept soliciting her and she wanted nothing to do with him. The woman agreed to Kéma's offer. She was heading to the docks anyway, and her family owned a local eatery there. If the man said or did anything unbecoming, he would pay for it. Kéma smiled and removed her cloak. Nez Spiritans from small towns reminded the Cílal of Neztríanis, trusting and helpful.

When the nameless woman saw Kéma's exposed weapons, she gave the Miska Kea operative an unsure glance. Kéma nodded in assurance, pleaded, and told the Nez Spiritan that "they" would do nothing to her if she walked to the eatery and removed her hood once she got there.

The woman gave a sign of affirmation. The Cílal saw no betrayal in the Nez Spiritan's eyes. Kéma bought a green cloak, placed it around herself, and stepped out of the back entrance while the Nez Spiritan walked out of the front. Kéma was certain the Eradicate agent(s) would do the woman no harm. Killing an innocent Nez Spiritan would not aid Tannódin'é/Nez Spiritan relations. The agents, even Wind, verified their targets before they struck.

As she had hoped, the agent following Kéma tailed the woman from the bazaar. However, the silent slayer felt neither accomplishment nor relief. A second agent, dressed in brown Nez Spiritan attire, *was* there, and now she was trailing the Cílal.

Kíma. They're good.

Sighing to herself, the slayer was left with little choice but to fight, even as she hated herself for coming to such a conclusion. In order to keep the agent from attacking preemptively, Kéma made sure she did not reveal her face and walked out of town and into the forest.

Once the warrior reached the forest, which was starting to show the signs of spring, she removed her cloak and pulled out Feather. The Eradicate agent exposed herself and stepped out of the shadows. She appeared to be Brycian.

Neither said anything. There was nothing to be said. One of them would fall.

No chances. I can allow for no chances. Death…

Reaching her left hand over her back, she unjacketed Affliction, and with her right, she unsheathed Feather and twirled the long knife between her fingers. In turn, the Eradicate agent pulled her coat back, revealing a sword casing of her own, and unsheathed her blade, examining Kéma'fém with quiet and discerning eyes.

Only three hours remained before the boat from Líachim arrived. The Yarníngas would be witnesses. The insects would provide commentary. In 241 OGI, sword duels rarely occurred. Was it the timeless anachronism between the adversaries, their weapons, and goals that contrasted against the background of the forest? Or did the forest only reveal its own anachronistic state and forced the adversaries to play along? The Yarníngas were pieces of Nez Spirita and Qeauríyx, which were quickly dissipating under the auspices of Global Initiative. Perhaps the Cílal and the Eradicate agent were merely pawns in a game of old.

No.

Depersonalizing murder was an abomination amongst evils. Murderous depersonalization should never be anachronistic, just as it should never happen…

But anachronistic, anonymous murderers/victims they were. They were both out of place and time…

Studying her opponent's face and person, Kéma saw no signs of a radio device. It was probably for their sake; a Cílal's high frequency hearing was nearly eight times keener than the sense perception of a normal nel'asmív. The two agents were not in communication; such a move would have given them away much sooner. Somehow, the Eradicate deduced that she was a Cílal.

The Wind agent slightly smirked and gave a visual sign that Kéma's interpretation was correct. Her adversary's stance, the way the agent gripped the blade, and her physique were all subtle indicators of the woman's mettle. Violent Fist had dispatched one of her better fighters to subdue Kéma'fém. *Better* fighters. But not her *best*.

Her stance is one clip too wide. She doesn't have enough scars. Her blade is too clean. She's an exceptional fighter, but she lacks experience. They sent an adolescent to an elder's game. No chance. She has no chance...

A strong ocean breeze blew Kéma's hair out a large, though loose knot. She had not cut her hair in nearly three durations, and it fell just below her shoulders.

Noiselessly, they rushed each other.

The agent, showing the signs of her talent, swung her blade at the Cílal's chest in a manner that required the perfect defense. Kéma blocked the attack with Feather. The imperial operative was powerful, but her two-handed attacks could not withstand the Líachimian's one-handed defense.

She's holding back. That's fine. So am I.

Within a second, the Brycian released her right hand from the grip, and attempted to punch Kéma in the face. Kéma'fém dodged and readied Affliction for a punishing blow, but the agent masterfully blocked the attack with her sword, using only her left hand. The Wind agent was a truly gifted fighter. The swordswomen sparred and parried for nearly a minute and backed away from one another.

They had gathered enough information on each other's fighting styles. Their eyes met once again and they resumed their battle.

The woman was no match for the Cílal. Kéma heightened her speed at a level beyond a normal nel'asmív, and to her anticipation, the woman blocked Feather's attack. Yet within the same moment, Kéma sliced the woman's chest and left arm with Affliction and stabbed her right shin with Feather, which caused the Brycian to drop her weapon. It was as the Miska Kea agent suspected. The Wind operative could make out one attack, but not two, especially when the second was more powerful and faster than the first.

Though in agony, the Wind agent did not scream. The Cílal was unsurprised.

Weary of life-taking, Kéma could not bring herself to deliver the final blow. The information was safe; that was all that mattered. With silent steps, Kéma sauntered past her fallen adversary. The Wind agent gazed at the Cílal's feet. Kéma rummaged through her adversary's few possessions, but just as she assumed, the Brycian possessed neither identification nor any sort of documentation, just an accurate description of her target and homing beacon. Wind agents were nameless and ruthless. They relinquished their identities the moment they stood before Violent Fist.

You won't die, but with those injuries, you'll never wield a sword again. You're the least of my worries now. That homing beacon means that you have armed support. And since they saw that she left Leel, they probably sent their main contingent to back her up.

The Cílal quieted her qanín and sensed her surroundings. She smelled them.

Fifteen. And they have AEARs. Staxis.

Looking down at her defeated foe, she knocked the woman unconscious and said, "Your friends won't be as lucky as you."

When the Wind agent came to, she gasped. The screams pulled her out of the coma. Thirteen corpses surrounded her. Every White Scythe soldier had been killed by either one blow or slice. Very few blast marks were found on the trees, suggesting that the Cílal was able to take out a large number of them before they had a chance to discharge a burst. In the near distance, the woman beheld two soldiers, writhing in pain without fingers, eyes, and feet. They were tortured for information, which meant that her partner and his support group were already dead. The Wind agent needed to report this to Violent Fist. The Cílal was as formidable as Syla.

"Lucky, eh?"

Kéma spotted him one hour before the boat arrived. He did not notice her. She could not make it to the boat without taking his life. The two White Scythe troops held out as long as they could, but eventually revealed the two possible locations of their remaining squad. Kéma made her way to them quickly and killed them without hesitation, though each subsequent kill made her wish she was never a Cílal. If it wasn't for Líachim, she would have thrown her sword away.

And so for half an hour she tried to think of a way to incapacitate her original pursuer, the Eradicate agent who followed Kéma's Nez Spiritan double. She tried to strategize a way to lure him away, but he was too close to the docks, and it was clear he was not moving.

This war has made life cheap and mathematical...

Amidst the crowd the Eradicate agent waited for her, certain she would reappear. He reasoned that the Cílal dispatched his fellow compatriot and the White Scythe contingent, since she had not returned to their rendezvous point and the soldiers had not contacted him in over an hour. Amidst the crowd, the man believed himself to be inconspicuous. But as he felt a cold sensation enter into his lumbar region, he realized he was mistaken.

"I'm sorry," he heard a somber voice whisper. And within three seconds, all of his motor abilities were silenced. He stumbled towards the shadowy figure that had attacked him, but he collapsed amidst the crowd. As he lay in his own constitution, heaving and splayed, Kéma quickly eyed her enemy and winced in horror. He was from Líachim. He was her countryman.

The townsfolk of Leel hovered over his bleeding, Líachimian body and tried to staunch the flow of blood. But it was to no avail. A death-strike by a Cílal was absolute.

Kéma boarded the boat with tears streaming down her face, beside herself for killing one of her own. Yet, deep in her qanín, her angst was not only caused by her murder of another Líachimian. All nel'asmív were her brothers and sisters. Every time she killed, she was killing her family and portions of herself.

I can't. I cant do this anymore. When I get home, I'm done...

The boat left the docks, bound for Aphaz, Líachim.

She was about to toss Feather and Affliction into the sea when her finger brushed against a small bump that should not have been there. Feeling around her armored pouch, which contained her minicomputer, Kéma'fém noticed a small device planted on the casing. After removing and throwing it in the water, she opened up the pouch and turned the computer on. The device had sent out a small, yet effective electrical charge that shorted out even more of the memory. The Cílal browsed through the data and realized she lost half of what she already had.

Thinking back, she retraced all of her steps, and she felt it. When she stabbed her brother from behind, he grabbed her pouch. She thought he was trying to right himself, but he placed the device on it. Even in his death, he managed to achieve some sort of victory. If it were not for the protective casing, the computer would have lost all of its information.

All of this kímaz murder and harm. And all I've got to show for it is twelve and a half percent of corrupted and fractured data, which hardly anyone can decipher.

Amidst the crowd of waves and water, the captain of the boat witnessed the Cílal shake, cry, then yell at the top of her lungs. The Cílal unstrapped her blades and readied them to toss in the sea. But before she could throw them, her hands gripped them tighter. She sobbed in helplessness. The plans were too damaged. Líachim needed her skill. Unfortunately, she would have to hold on to Affliction and Feather for a little while longer.

Survival

2 Opíz, 241 OGI
Myalé

In the distance, Anámn beheld countless volcanoes, smoke, ash, and lava.

"We gotta get through *that?*" Lénü asked Brenko. "Kíma."

"It's the only way to get into Damüda unnoticed," Brenko responded.

"Brenko." Anámn frowned in reticence. "I don't know about this... seems like a bad idea."

"Like I've ever had one of those," the mastermind joked.

The que shook even as they stood on Barrier Island, gazing at the immense Volcanic Line of Damüda, some seventy lengths away. The Volcanic Line was a true remnant of the Great Drift and the Extinguishing. Its soft thunder and tremble sounded a chord of instinctive remembrance for the three nel'asmív. Rational fear beset them.

Though annexed by Damüda and built for trade, Barrier Island was not inhabited by too many folk. It was an island with six skyports, where lifts refueled and restocked supplies and where business transactions were consummated. Military presence on the island was nonexistent. Since flying into Damüda unannounced was such a challenge—the continent possessed the best aviators and aerial defense force on the planet—the Damüdan Guild did not need to waste any resources policing a shipping colony. As long as he collected their tax revenue, Galís, the leader of the Guild, did not care what went on there.

The Dark Nimbus landed on an older airstrip on the eastern side of the island. There was not much there, just a fuel station, some old hangars, and well-worn lifts. The newer runways were on the western end of the island, further away from the black smoke and moderate tremors of the volcanoes.

Yerna's concern and pity almost convinced Brenko to go to Keotagosdi with him, but Brenko would not be deterred. His goal was southeast Damüda. Anámn was tempted to travel with Yerna; he did not see the advantage or point of willingly venturing into the same continent from which his vicious predecessor emerged.

"Remind me again… why're we doing this?"

"I told you Anámn; don't come if you don't want to. But Lénü and I are going to find a good piece of land, cultivate it, and live." The words sounded hollower with every repetition. Why should he even pretend?

"But this is Damüda."

"No, Kinesis." Brenko had been referring to Anámn by his Sczyphamek title more and more. "We're going to southeast Damüda. How many times do I need to say it?"

"'And southeast Damüda isn't like the other parts of the continent'," Anámn finished. "I know. I know."

"If you understand, then why are you scared?" Brenko asked.

"He ain't the only one scared, Kanoso." Lénü'íque shook her head and smacked her lips in displeasure. "This feels more an' more like a suicide mission… How are we gonna get through *that?*" The young woman repeated and nodded in the direction of the Volcanic Line.

"The Comphyx Cape is on the other side of those volcanoes. *When* we get there, we will meet an acquaintance of mine—"

"*Not Tarían,*"[3] Lénü said with disappointment.

"*Yes*, Tarían."

Unpleasant quietude set itself between the father and daughter.

"Who's Tarían?" the runaway asked.

"Brenko," Lénü said, "Yerna's still here; we can still leave."

"If Anámn can't survive here, he'll have no chance in gynix of winning against Pre-Eminent or Vicious. Keotagosdi would've been good for him two durations ago. But we're all out of time, even me."

Lénü and Anámn stared at Brenko, demanding an explanation.

---

[3] Tarían (tair-*ee*-uhn)

The coward grunted with grit. "Anámn, you feel it; don't you? I can't feel it, but I can guess and calculate it. It's only a matter of time for Líachim and this planet. If we go to Keotagosdi, you will be one continent away from Pre-Eminent. The Eradicate has a strong presence there already because Keotagosdi is the last piece of Qeauríyx Global Initiative hasn't completely claimed.

"On the other hand, the Eradicate has a minimal contingent in Damüda. The Interror handle pretty much everything here. Damüda is still in many ways feudal, so southeast Damüda is relatively autonomous and spacious. I can train you there without too much interference.

"Vicious won't be back this way for awhile. He and the General Maximum are in Nez Spirita trying to deal with that other Sczyphamek. Feolenz is with Pre-Eminent in Anzél, and they are not leaving the battlefield for you, unless you were in Líachim. That only leaves Violent Fist. No one knows where she is, but probability—as useless as that kíma is—states that she's in either Bryce or Keotagosdi. These are the only people who have the ability to defeat you as you are now. And I doubt they've guessed that Damüda is our destination.

"If we stayed in Phmquedria, the number of soldiers and agents of Global Initiative would've been too high and too many enemies are looking for us there. Even though you're stronger, I don't think you would last under an assault of hundreds of fighters. Damüda is our only choice.

"I was going to come here in order to live out the rest of my life; it's true. But something tells me that won't happen. It appears that Sczyphameks won't leave me alone."

Anámn was quiet. The man's mind exceeded the legend.

"Of course," Brenko continued, "this plan is bad too. Damüda is enemy territory, and until we reach our destination we will have a high chance of getting caught. The Interror is run by Fencero, a Miska Kea operative who went imperial. The man is resourceful and obsessive. If he's alerted to our presences then…" Brenko paused, shuddered, and nodded nervously. "You all must do precisely as I say."

Lénü and Anámn returned Brenko's nod with their own.

"Anámn, you are my slave that I purchased two cycles ago from Phmquedria. Lénü, you know the routine. Tarían believes that I am a sex-trader—"

"Don't you think he knows that you aren't a sex-trader now?" Anámn asked. "Lénü said that the Eradicate knows who you are; they must have tried to find out who you used to keep company with."

"Good point," the Brycian admitted. "He probably does know that I'm actually Brenko. But believe me when I tell you, Tarían is cut from the cloth of southeastern Damüda. He loathes the Damüdan Guild and the Tannódin'é. Staxis, he pretty much hates anything that has something to do with Global Initiative."

Lénü scowled. "Yeah, whatever. That kíma of a man hates Tannódin as much as he's arrogant and childish. An' if he looks at me like dat…"

"Taríán is very fond of Lénü," Brenko explained with a smile.

"The man can't keep his kímaz hands off me. Staxis." Lénü'íque cursed. Anámn could tell she was annoyed, which made him silently jealous.

"You know I don't like that, Kanoso. Bastard. I'll kill 'im this time. I'm tellin' ya. If he grazes me in an untoward manner, the man is dead."

"We just have to live long enough to see that, won't we?" Brenko asked. "We gotta get through *that* first."

"It'll be a miracle if we get through there," Lénü muttered.

Brenko frowned and brusquely blew air out his mouth. "Miracles only help if you already believe in something, otherwise no one'll acknowledge it or people will demand another sign. And even those who believe will start to believe in the miracle more than what the miracle points to. Trust me, in the grand design of things, miracles are pointless. Everyday reality is miraculous in itself. If this place can't get you to trust in or commit to something greater than yourself, nothing will."

Anámn looked at Brenko with a furrowed brow. *Something* sparked that aside.

The tactician returned Anámn's gaze. "We need you. We can't make it without your powers."

"I know," Matriester said warily. "I don't—"

"Don't say it," the Brycian commanded. "Do not. You can. And you will."

"Kanoso, I believe in Anámn's kinetic abilities as well, but what will be our mode of transport? A sea vessel is out of the question."

The tone, vocabulary, and enunciation of Lénü still baffled the runaway. She switched so effortlessly.

Brenko pointed to an old, small passenger aircraft, large enough to fit only four persons. "That."

"*That?*" Anámn and Lénü asked and scoffed at the vehicle.

"This is what I paid Yerna for, besides a small bit of credits for getting us here."

Lénü ran her fingers through her hair. The daughter's anxiety was plain. "How high can that thing fly?"

"Not high enough," her father answered. "I'm a good pilot, and I was sure I could navigate through the line by myself. I know the lift doesn't look like it, but it's nimble. But seeing the Volcanic Line up close, I can tell this would've been suicide." Placing his hand on Kinesis' shoulder, the veteran continued, "Legend has it that Vicious trained out there."

"Are you serious? Staxis," Anámn mumbled.

"Navigating through the Line should teach you how strong you aren't."

"I understand."

"Lénü, you don't have to come with us. Anámn may be able to survive even if the lift goes down, but we will die. No question."

Lénü'íque's smile was melancholy. "Kíma. That's kíma and you know it. I done told you; I'm goin' wherever you go, Kanoso. I trust you."

Within an instant, she embraced her adopted father. The moment caused Anámn to look away, but he forced himself to return his gaze to them. This was a scene that he would never obtain with his father, but that did not mean he could not appreciate the bond between those two. Brenko pulled the hood back on his daughter's cloak and looked at her with a parental love that made the three of them tear up for three different reasons.

"Thank you for staying all these cycles," he said warmly and hugged her. "I've been and I am a mean bastard. But I want you to know—because I may not have a chance to say it again—I want you to know that I love and appreciate you too."

He faced Anámn and gave him a look. Its meaning was plain. If the lift went down, and all options were exhausted, the Sczyphamek was to save Lénü and let him die. Anámn gave Brenko a beleaguered face and affirmed his visual request.

Brenko started up the engines to the craft; they nearly quit that moment. But after some cajoling, the lift grew in stature and in health. The engines hummed and Brenko checked all of his flight protocols.

He turned to Anámn. "Listen, Kinesis. Since you are in this lift, the first thing you may want to use to store power is this lift. You *cannot in any circumstances* do that. If you rob this lift of its energy, you'll cause it to drop."

Anámn laughed. "Damn. C'mon, Brenko. I ain't that bad."

The tactician grunted in amusement. "You're right. My mistake."

"Any other suggestions, teacher?"

"Don't try to beat back the lava or rocks with your power; try to relieve them of their motion, of their energy, and then store it. If there is a lava squall you can't handle that way, use the energy you've stored to beat it back. I'll try my best to fly around those areas, but the Volcanic Line is a large, unstable system of energy. Even you won't be able to predict and sense everything. If you can get us through this, I honestly feel that you will be close to your Awakening. But you have to concentrate."

"Got it." Anámn closed his eyes and recited, "Fá'atoño má. Fá'atoño má. Téza. É müz keh fíp Téza má."

He chanted those words softly and quietly while Lénü beamed in admiration. She turned and gazed out of the windshield. The airlift crawled to the runway and faced the southwest. To the lift's left were lines of volcanoes, with tops that reached as high as twenty thousand feet. Lénü had flown in all kinds of crafts. Their airlift would only attain fifteen thousand feet at best. Before Anámn disrupted his plans, the coward was going to leave her with Yerna and perish in the flames of obscurity. Brenko lied. He planned to die on this trip.

She sneered at Brenko in disgust. "Ya damn fool."

He was ashamed. He knew that she knew. However, circumstances had changed. For the moment, he no longer wanted to die. But, he had to negotiate with the strong possibility of death in order to ensure a better life in the future. They had to survive.

But the Volcanic Line was a masterful death-dealer.

On the other side of the Line lay the Comphyx Cape, a virtual wasteland. Volcanic fragments incessantly shot across the sky and deposited there, destroying the possibility of life-giving soil. The western shore of the cape was barren and rocky. Only after about thirty lengths inland could one encounter a single, small shrub. No Damüdan base, no outpost, and no radar area stood within seventy lengths of the western shore. Such infrastructure was a waste of resource and person-power.

From Barrier Island to the cape, it was a three hundred and fifty length trip. But two hundred of those lengths would be death-defying. Damüda possessed an unspoken rule: if someone entered the continent by way of the volcanic line and without perishing, then that person earned the right to step foot on Damüdan soil.

No one earned the right yet.

After chanting for twenty minutes, Anámn was lost in his Elemental. It was a strain, but he was able to differentiate the forty-three sources of potential and kinetic energy that allowed the air vessel to stay aloft. Téza was remarkable; the Elemental was holding back even more information. Téza was able to sift through and analyze much more than Anámn presently comprehended.

Little by little, the Sczyphamek siphoned the energy from the air molecules that were disrupted in the wake of the airlift. He also stored potential energy from the water below. Every fiber of his constitution was soaked in massive amounts of possibility, and Téza's amorphous and shifting qanín grew and contracted, repeatedly.

Anámn understood.

Every time Téza's qanín became filled with a certain sum of energy, the Elemental would transform into a smaller, more efficient shape, which stored the same amount of energy. After contracting into a smaller shape, Téza grew amorphous again and expanded, until the Elemental had its fill. Then, it would reduce once more; however, Téza's new shape was slightly larger than the one that preceded it.

The Elemental was not taxed, but the nel'asmív was.

With each successive cycle, a distorted melody reached the Sczyphamek's ears—a melody within the chant: "É müz keh fíp Téza má." He barely scratched the notes, but they were definitely there.

His forehead gushed sweat, and his fingernails dug deep into his hands, even as Téza prodded him to relax. His aura engulfed the cockpit and the front of the plane. Lénü and Brenko almost fainted when the aura emerged. Kinesis' power was unencumbered and unbelievably puissant.

"Brenko," Anámn murmured softly with closed eyes. "A large rock is on its way here from the northwest. I'll try to relieve it of its energy, but it's gonna be close."

Anámn's dark green aura extended nearly a length ahead of the craft. The tactician was awestruck and impressed by Anámn's maturation, but he focused his attention on the black horizon, which was ominously mute.

"Brenko," Lénü muttered.

"I see it."

When the airlift neared the massive rock, the projectile decelerated, which allowed Brenko to maneuver around it with little effort.

"Thanks," Brenko said to Anámn.

The sky was invisible. Only the haze of smoke and ash remained. The line of volcanoes roared vociferously, rattling the aircraft. Small pellets became visible, and Brenko gripped the controls of the plane and tried to fly over them. They were still fifty lengths before the major barrage would begin, and the tactician was already regretting his decision.

Lénü placed her loving hand on Brenko's back and rubbed it. The daughter turned around and gazed at Anámn, who was deep in methodical concentration. His words were nearly inaudible.

The Sczyphamek opened his eyes, and for a moment, the woman barely recognized him. His light brown pupils were golden crimson, vibrant, and intense. Lénü gasped, but Anámn looked past her, adroitly surveying the visible and invisible panorama of energy in the distance.

Fifteen minutes passed, and Anámn was no longer sweating. He was no longer in the aircraft. He was no longer in the air. He was meeting with Qeauríyx, particularly in the region of the Damüdan Volcanic Line. He had been chanting for over half an hour.

"Get ready," Anámn said calmly, although his serenity translated to intimidation for his friends.

"Lénü take the other set of controls, and follow my motion. It's gonna take both of us."

"Alright Kanoso," she replied steadily.

The woman clasped her hands on the controls. She blinked in rapid succession and hoped that what she witnessed was not reality. The volcanoes were tall, extremely tall and more massive than she ever believed possible. Three of the largest ones were less than fifty lengths away from the plane, and they were active. Smaller domed furnaces also spewed lava and ash into the heights of the sky.

"Anámn?" Brenko prompted.

"It doesn't matter," the Sczyphamek said. "Every path is just as dangerous."

"Kíma," he cursed and banked the lift to the right and down three thousand feet.

The radical explosion from the top of a volcano ten lengths to the north was senseless. A wave of smoke and debris speedily pursued an enormous shockwave. The entire horizon grew distorted by the unsettled and sizzling air.

"Fá'atoño má!" Anámn chanted in a forte voice. Within a split-second, his aura completely surrounded the plane, as the shockwave bolted towards the craft's location.

Lénü's eyes widened in disbelief. "By the One!"

"Hang on!" Brenko screamed.

The shockwave clashed into Anámn's aura. The Sczyphamek, as much as he could, drew off the energy from the wave, which put the plane in moderate turbulence. Both Brenko and Lénü breathed sighs of relief. If it were not for Kinesis, the lift would have folded, broken into pieces, and fell into the fiery ocean below.

The ordeal was not over. The debris followed directly behind the shockwave, carrying with it the velocity near the speed of sound.

"É fíp Téza," Anámn declared with crushing intent. "Keep it steady, Brenko."

"Lénü…" the Brycian responded, which caused the woman to hold the controls tighter, if that was indeed possible.

The aura on the left side of the craft erupted in a blast of energy that decimated every bit of debris, lava, smoke, and ash in its path. The air vessel careened to the right due to the whiplash, but the Sczyphamek lessened its impact significantly. The Kanoso and his daughter would have perished along with the aircraft had the backlash of the blast not been mitigated.

The sky and volcano, which moments ago were obfuscated and rendered invisible by the shockwave and debris, was now momentarily visible. In wonder and respect, the cowardly tactician shook his head. Lénü turned around; Anámn was no longer sitting. He was down on all fours breathing heavily. The last display of power greatly fatigued him, and he looked like he was about to collapse or perish.

Téza spoke to him inwardly: "You are only as tired as you believe yourself to be."

"But, did you see what we just did," he intimated.

"That was not with your energy, remember?" Téza's intimation penetrated the nel'asmív's qanín. "You are capable of so much more, Anámn, even at this non-Awakened state. Trust me; *we* are capable of much more. Recycle…"

Recycle…

Recycle?

ReCycle.

While Matriester gathered himself, Brenko used the time Kinesis had bought them to nimbly guide the plane through the remainder of the first spate of volcanoes. Moderate stones were hurled at the craft, almost as if the volcanoes were aiming at them, but Brenko dodged them with great agility. The eruptions, explosions, and trajectories of the projectiles were beginning to defy the law of probability. Something else was at work.

Kinesis was still siphoning energy and within ten minutes, he reconstituted himself. He had to trust and have faith. He had to hope...

There was only one line left, and every major volcano was active, launching molten rock and cinders in the air. Brenko could not keep himself from thinking about Phenplyacin no matter how hard he tried. The scenes were too similar. Little by little, his grip loosened the controls.

"Kanoso!" Lénü yelled. "*Kanoso*... I need you. We need you. I can't pilot this kímaz thing myself!"

Wiping the perspiration off his forehead, Brenko regained his composure and promised himself he would not let the controls go until he landed the craft or he was dead.

The tops of the tallest magma domes roared and erupted in anger with no sign of subsiding. The sky above was covered in red lava and/or enormous chunks of rock. Within seconds, Brenko ascertained the cyclical nature of the Volcanic Line. The volcanoes would erupt and destroy their tops, only for the magma to harden and rebuild the slopes again.

Brenko could not respond to the controls fast enough. The Sczyphamek simultaneously relieved one large rock of its energy and destroyed another via an energy blast from his aura. Both stones were only tens of feet away from the craft. If Brenko was correct, Anámn would need a few moments to recuperate from using his Elemental in those two separate and distinct ways. The three nel'asmív and the airlift had not a minutia of a moment, however, as lava spurted lengths from its home, stalking the plane with all possible speed.

"Lénü," the Brycian said, "let go of the controls, and hold on."

Lénü did as her father ordered and Anámn held on to the back of Lénü's seat.

"Kinesis, just keep your aura around this plane," he commanded, then added softly, "Remember, heat is generated by a lot of movement..."

Meditating, Anámn drew his aura in, around the plane, and thickened its density. Brenko executed a deep barrel roll to the left, descending nearly one thousand feet. Lénü almost lost consciousness. The radar had grown so noisy and relentless, the three of them had long become desensitized to its beeping and blinking, but the new repetition they now heard signaled an extreme danger. Suddenly, the cockpit became noticeably warmer.

"Staxis," Brenko grunted.

The lift was between two volcanoes thirty lengths apart, but both of them were gushing and spraying their fiery innards in every direction. Avenues to death and injury were now omnipresent and nearly omnipotent. The tactician beheld the western coast of Comphyx in the distance, and although only sixty lengths separated them from their destination, each second actually increased the space... Because time was just as prominent a factor. And they had stretched their relationship with time and chance to the breaking point.

Kinesis was in anguish; even Téza was fatigued. Lava lashed at the plane, but the Sczyphamek was able to absorb much of the lava's inner locomotion and turned the once hot liquid into a warm semisolid. Steam rose from Anámn's skin and clothes, and he moaned in terrible displeasure. "Brenko, Lénü," he gasped in duress but with a gravity that demanded attention. "Grab your stuff and come here."

The two hesitated, which caused Anámn to raise his voice. "If you don't you'll be killed! The volcano to the right is about to change the shape of this entire area. We don't have the ability to handle this kind of energy. It's Qeauríyx!"

In an instant, Anámn felt his two comrades crouching beside him, their supplies in hand. Brenko had engaged the autopilot.

"Hold me tight," the Sczyphamek ordered. "Hold me damn tight. And take a deep breath…"

Something stirred in Anámn. It was Téza. The intimation was clear, and Anámn could not afford to lose his trust in the Elemental now.

"Wait. Chant with me," he said. "É müz keh fíp Téza má. É müz keh fíp Téza má."

The father and daughter, scared beyond disbelief, complied, as the plane caught fire and rumbled toward the sea below.

"É müz keh fíp Téza má," all three of them chanted. With each repetition, Anámn's aura and power grew denser and more massive. They were completely enveloped by it. The aura's shape was spherical, and its discharge blew the front of the lift off. Brenko felt the potential energy collecting behind them. Lénü tasted the path Kinesis set before them.

"Don't let go.".

In an awesome explosion that swept aside all rock and lava, the sphere, which contained the trio, was catapulted towards the western shore of Comphyx at a speed that defied reason, but not possibility. Anámn had gathered as much potential energy as he was able, the way in which a firearm has a trigger, or a bow tightens before it launches an arrow, or the way that the fingers of Malchían held the rock.

Siphon. Convert. Release.

The sphere hurled toward the coast, at hundreds of lengths per hour. Behind the trio, the churning volcano erupted in a blast so savage that the smaller, adjacent volcanoes were destroyed. The reverberations were felt on Barrier Island, and those nel'asmív on the island stopped their activity to witness the spectacle.

Turning around, Lénü beheld the remnants hurtling in every direction, including theirs. Judging from the destructive power of the upsurge and the angle of some of the debris, they would have to contend with the shockwave and a large amount of the fallout once they landed. The Sczyphamek's speed was faster, but Lénü wondered how long Anámn's momentum would hold, or how in Qeauríyx they would survive the impact. Kinesis would have to slow the sphere down in order for Lénü and

Brenko to withstand the landing, but that would allow the fragments from the line to catch up to them. The fireballs would kill them by impact or incineration. And even if they endured that, the dusty fallout would undoubtedly choke them to death.

Too, too many *"woulds"*.

It *would* be a miracle if they survived, but Qeauríyx's laws of nature were as fluid and laughable as nel'asmív who thought they understood those said laws.

The sphere's trajectory leveled off, and its descent was now underway. Father and daughter held onto Kinesis with all their strength. Lénü'íque recalled her first flight with Anámn. The air around the Sczyphamek was so unstable that she had to hold her breath. This sphere, however, contained enough air for the father and daughter to breathe without incident. Anámn was truly stronger and more in tune with his surrounding environment.

The sphere raced over land, nearly eight thousand feet in the air, yet falling fast. The energy bubble began to decelerate; Anámn was converting its kinetic energy into potential energy.

"Anámn, I know you sense the rocks behind us," Brenko warned.

"When we touch the ground stand directly behind me," Kinesis said, sweating and bleeding from his nose. Then, he started humming a melody unknown to the Brycian.

Their speed had not slowed down to a point that would keep them uninjured, but Brenko trusted Anámn. They would not have made it this far without him. The tactician was astounded by the level of power the Phmquedrian had attained. At the same time, Anámn was only able to conjure such amounts of power, because he was near large and admittedly obvious energy sources. Indeed, his true power would only be unleashed in the most humble of surroundings. He was certain Anámn knew this too.

They should have made a crater; their incoming velocity was that fast. Yet, they landed uneventfully and stopped instantaneously. Their bodies should have broken under such stress. But Brenko and Lénü felt the energy that should have jarred and killed them, pass through them and into Anámn, who immediately turned around and faced the oncoming rain of volcanic remains. He was still humming.

Kinesis quickly removed his bag and jacket and handed them to Brenko.

"Stay back," he ordered and stopped the tune. "Or you won't survive us. We don't have the strength to relieve all of that..."

Within a flash, Anámn released a considerable yet considerate push of force that sent Lénü and Brenko hurtling to the east nearly a length away. Again, they landed without much fanfare.

"What is he going to do?" Lénü asked Brenko.

"I'm not sure, but we should get down." Brenko lay down on the rocky ground. "And don't look in his direction. If he can't relieve that, he must be planning on obliterating it."

Lénü did not want to know if that was possible; however, she was going to have to live through it or die.

Transferring and combining the energy that should have destroyed them when they hit the ground with the remaining potential energy he had stored within Téza, Anámn placed his palms together and pulled them apart slowly, revealing a greenish orange emanation of power. Next, he rotated his arms clockwise, so that on the other side of the emanation was the palm of his left hand, while the back of his right hand was directly before him. This expanded the dimensions of the force of energy into a cube-like structure, which crackled and hissed fiercely. The deluge of sizzling rocks was almost near his location.

"É müẑ keh fíp Téẑa má," he sang, in the same meter, melody, key, and tempo as the tune he had been humming.

Anámn placed his left hand within the cube of energy and it ripped the left sleeve of his shirt to shreds. Pulling his right hand back and curling his fingers down halfway, a dark green emanation emerged and flashed wickedly.

"Qeauríyx, I am Sczyphamek Kinesis, a Kylanín." Anámn's eyes were the picture of exhaustion and hope. "Please be enough. Fá'atoño má."

Ramming the two emanations together—the greenish orange cube meeting his glowing right hand—Sczyphamek Kinesis ignited a devastating wave of energy that ripped through the sky and the atmosphere. The cube flared, transformed and emitted a robust, sharp semicircle, whose dimensions and colors were incalculable. The shower of rocky fragments dissipated into nonexistence under the crushing force of the burst of energy. The smoky clouds of ash and soot were nearly vaporized. The ground shook with such vehemence that Lénü and Brenko were throttled about. Every color of the visible spectrum entered into the atmosphere. But within a few seconds, their surroundings grew eerily calm.

The genius and his learned daughter stood up. Their ears rang and their equilibrium was equally affected. They stumbled and crawled towards Anámn's prior location. Half of the way back, they came across the Phmquedrian. Comatose, he lay face down and was stark naked. The blast had hurled him backwards and disintegrated his clothes, even down to his shoes. His body smoked, and he groaned in pain. The beard and goatee that once covered his face was now singed and smoking, and the hair on top of his head was patchy, brittle, and sparse, so hot the blast was.

It was the first time Brenko beheld the whip scars on the Phmquedrian's back, which caused the tactician to recoil in shock and horror. Yet, he was also awestruck. Anámn's actual body suffered no burn marks. His Elemental aura protected him at the level of his skin, but that was all it could afford. That was probably why his clothes, shoes, and even his hair suffered the devastating effects of that blast.

The woman looked at Anámn with tears in her eyes and then towards the distance. She took silent steps toward the west. Her ears still rang. The volcanoes were still venting, but the sky temporarily opened up. It was nighttime, and the two moons shone brightly onto their location. The western Comphyx cape had not seen the moons in over ten millennia. Ironically, the cape could thank a Sczyphamek for the relentless clouds of smoke *and* the moonlight it now enjoyed.

Brenko covered Anámn with the jacket Nísyx had given him durations ago. The Brycian was ashamed of himself. If not for the Sczyphamek, he would have surely fallen. How could he have been so foolish and suicidal? The tactician knew better.

His death awaited him on the field of battle. And it would be gruesome and thankless. For he, Bíoske, and Syla, their suicide was in living and in the participation of hopeless causes.

He sauntered towards Lénü, who had retrieved the flask of spirits belonging to Yerna. She opened the cap and took two large gulps. Her hands trembled as much as her wild eyes.

Brenko rubbed her back, took the container, and threw it down on the rocks, spilling its contents.

"Come on," he said and hugged her. "Let's get him into some clothes and carry him out of here. We've got to move."

Trust

"That was notable, although he was desperate," Vincallous said to himself and Dé'wa, emerging from deep meditation. "That hatchling Phmquedrian may grow to be quite formidable."

The Sczyphamek known as Vicious had been chanting and meditating for three days. While doing so, he fell into the consciousness of the land. Vincallous had trained for many cycles in the Volcanic Line and had developed a longstanding connection with that particular piece of que within Qeauríyx. As a result, he perceived, somewhat, the exchange between the son of ju Xaníz and the Volcanic Line.

"Qeauríyx, you were trying to kill him, were you not? He must have failed the first encounter."

The potentate stood from his penitent sitting position and walked out of his quarters. The repairs to the Triple Skyrises had proceeded with all possible speed. The reconstructive effort was twenty five percent complete, and only three durations had passed since the attack. Vincallous stayed within Pike Metropolis the entire winter in order to oversee the project. When winter ended, he ordered Blue Rapier and White Scythe to patrol and search for the Nez Spiritan Sczyphamek in the Bitzroy Plains, the mountains of the Infinite Circle, and all adjacent areas with excessive fervor. The General Maximum personally oversaw this order, even though Blue Rapier was not his jurisdiction, but because of the rare occasion of combined forces, he was given command of Feolenz's troops. Vincallous also resumed the Auría expedition but as of yet, he was unable to locate the entrance to the temple.

Fierce walked down the hall of the 245th floor of Tower I, in contemporary Tannódin'é attire. It was late morning, and the Damüdan was hungry. He had not eaten in eighty-one hours—exactly three days. So, he stopped in the commissary to partake in a meal. When he entered, the room fell quiet, but Vincallous did not notice. He was too busy thinking about what he just partially witnessed.

He ordered juice, fruit, a hot cut of meat, and a warm piece of sweet bread from the cook. The meal was prepared quickly and handed to him on a tray. Normally, Vincallous ate his food in his quarters and was quite reclusive. Moreover, his subordinates were only used to seeing him when something was wrong or if something needed to be overseen. Watching the co-leader of Global Initiative eat amongst them was almost scandalous. Soon, noise and conversation returned to the eating area.

He sat down at a table near a window that faced to the north. It was a clear day, and Mt. Xarkim was losing some of its snow pack. Before long, the Xarkim River would thaw and water the southern Nez Spiritan countryside.

His mind wandered as he ate his meal. *There are so many loose ends*, he thought. *But Global Initiative needs to be* earned *not* stolen. *There is a fine line between the two.*

He finished his food, drank his juice, got up, and headed towards the communications room thirteen floors above. He entered an elevator already occupied by two passengers, a man and a woman. They immediately fell silent and stood nervously as the elevator doors shut.

"Is it out of fear or respect?" Vincallous asked with a smirk.

"Sir?" the woman responded cautiously.

"Are you silent because you fear me or because you respect me?" he clarified.

They glanced at each other, unsure of how to respond.

The woman responded first. "Both."

The man nodded then nervously added, "You are a Sczyphamek and you are our leader, along with Empress Késhal. Both of these things naturally inspire fear and respect."

"*Naturally*...? Fear deals with the unknown and negativity, while respect is based on merit or necessity," he quipped. "These reasons are good enough to be silent, but not to be a participant in Global Initiative."

The elevator slowed down, and the man and woman could not wait until the doors reopened.

"Do you trust me and the Empress? Fear and respect do not lead to trust. Ultimately, fear leads to distrust, and respect only means that you have warranted something as worthy of your full attention, not that you trust it. If Global Initiative is based on fear and respect alone, it will ultimately grow silent and gaunt in the face of history, just as you have before me."

The elevator doors opened and Vincallous stepped out.

His back to them, he turned his head and continued. "We need you to trust us and this process." The doors closed slowly while Vincallous finished, "Give what I said some consideration."

He sauntered down the hallway toward his destination, laughing to himself. He could only imagine Késhal's face if she saw him talking like that.

The moment he entered the recently repaired communications room, Vincallous commanded, "I want Reníz Bläno on a secure channel, now."

"Yes, sir," a technician responded and sent a signal to the leader of the Eradicate. "You are connected."

"Leave."

All of the workers exited the chamber. Fierce closed the door and approached the communications station.

"Reníz," Van said energetically, revealing a level of personality few were privileged to hear.

"Kanoso," she replied, gasping for air.

"How long are you going to train like that?"

"As long as it takes."

"I am sure you are keeping an eye on things," he prodded.

"Of course." Her Tannódin'é accent was mixed with the tones and choppy delivery of the natives of the Windward Isles. It was a distinct dialect that only she carried. "I've dispatched agents to Leel. Jennó's contacts placed the Cílal there."

"Good. Where is Jennó now?"

"On his way to Anzél."

"Are you planning on sending him to Aphaz this soon?"

"He wanted to go soon as his surgery was complete."

"Staxis," Vincallous cursed. "He is a good detective, but Zotham is no fool. If Jennó survives, he will be lucky."

"But if he can give us any information from the inside, our chances of victory will increase, 'gspecially if my agents fail to deal with the Cílal."

"Do you think they will fail?"

"Possibly, if the Cílal is of legendary caliber. We had to scramble a team on short notice. One of the agents is Assassin; the other is Wind. They were given twenty White Scythe troops as backup. The Wind agent's a second-tier fighter. If the Cílal's an average fighter, I got no doubt the information will be obtained and destroyed. But if she's highly skilled, both agents will probably be killed. But she will likely perish due to the combined forces of Eradicate and White Scythe. And who knows? The Cílal may not even have the plans."

"Maybe..." Vincallous' voice trailed.

"Kanoso," the woman probed. "What is it? I know you didn't open this channel just to talk about that…"

"Hmmph," he smiled. "No, I did not."

"What, then?"

"Though it truly pains me to break with Damüdan custom, I need you to contact Fencero and Galís. Tell them a Sczyphamek has entered their territory by way of the Comphyx coast."

"*The Comphyx coast?*" she gasped. "Vincallous, are you certain? That would mean that he was able to pass through the—"

"Ah. The Volcanic Line," he finished. "Yes, that is precisely what that means."

"I thought you were the only person who's ever survived out there."

"He was not alone," the Sczyphamek replied. "*He had help.*"

"Brenko?"

"It must be. The last Eradicate report out of Phmquedria had Anámn escaping our forces with his subordinate, a young woman. I am sure that the son of ju Xaníz was smart enough to stay with Brenko. Even though he is a Phmmy, he cannot be that dimwitted."

"I'll contact 'em soon as we're done," she replied. "Confidential, correct?"

"Yes. Nez Spirita is already abuzz because of the other Sczyphamek, Neztríanis. We cannot afford for word to leak out about another Sczyphamek. I am certain that he will do everything he can to keep his identity a secret."

"You been able to sense Phyxtríalis?"

"No…" he sighed.

"Do you think she's…"

"I hope not. She better not be dead. However, I have not been able to sense her presence at all. It would be almost impossible anyway because she has not Awakened; yet I cannot sense even a residual aura."

The daughter knew her father. "A chénala, ah? Kanoso, you seeking the fight and reasons to justify this."

The man gave no reply, but smiled smugly.

"I will do as commanded, Potentate," Reníz said with militaristic respect. "I trust you."

"Exceptional. And Reníz, I am sure Késhal would like to hear from you."

"I just want to be the best that I can be before I contact her," she said with a twinge of somberness.

"She treasures you just as you happen," Vincallous said warmly. "And so do I."

"Kanoso, you know I love you and Mamisí more than anything or anyone. I will notify you if anything important happens."

"Very well. And one last matter…"

"What is it?"

"Haptian."

"Spiax..." the leader of the Eradicate trailed in frustration. "He's definitely doing something behind our backs. My agents have had a hard time hacking into his files or finding any possible leads."

"Not surprising."

"Why don't you deal with him yourself?"

"He is too old to fear death, too detached to be moved by the death of an innocent, too smart to let his death be the end of his work, and too valuable to us to be killed... And he knows it. But, I am certain he is continuing his research on the témos even though I ordered him not to do so, which means..."

"Which means he has help and he can't be doing any of the research from Pike Metropolis," Bläno finished her father's statement.

"Have your agents check Keotagosdi, Bryce, Phmquedria, and the Windward Isles. The Synthesis must be stopped at all costs. I am relieving Spiax of his authority over the témo extermination program. They are under your jurisdiction now. Place all of your unassigned agents in the field to gather live intelligence on the témos. It has been cycles since we have done so. We have to try to eradicate them as soon as possible."

"Yes, Potentate," she responded. "It shall be done."

"Exceptional. And Reníz... do not overexert yourself."

Vincallous ended the transmission, left the communications room, and headed back to his quarters in order to resume his meditation and the heightening of his Elemental. After nearly half a day, he stopped. Sweating profusely and drawing his aura in, he collapsed on the floor, exhausted, yet grinning intently.

"She's not dead."

Flight

? 241 OGI

It was not snowing.

"Where are we?" the Sczyphamek asked.

"I do not know, Temperature," the témo answered. "Perhaps, the better question is 'when?'"

Neither of them were prepared for what they saw when they walked out of the opening to the cave. It was not winter. They were not inside the Infinite Circle, nor were they anywhere Neztríanis recognized. In front of them lay a vast plain of land that stretched for what appeared to be at least one reach. It was very probable that they were facing east, for the sun was setting behind them, over against the mountains. If the Plains of Bitzroy were in front of them, and they were looking east, then they were emerging from the eastern Gemansu Range. But how was that possible? And why was it no longer winter? Neztríanis doubted they had been in the passageways of the temple for two and a half durations... or were they? How long were those visions? How many reaches did they walk?

The book jostled about in her shoulderpack. The Auría granted her newfangled power, which left her baffled and self-assured. However, she understood little of the verses and oracles contained within the holy book. And the auditory pages contained at least four distinct voices at any given time. Yet, the verses spoke to her in ways that gave her confidence and warmed her qanín.

"This must be the Bitzroy Plains," she stated.

"The caverns of the temple appear to be loosed from time and space," Timura purred. The time spent in the tunnels provided them with an understanding, friendship, and rapport that defied explanation. Their teamwork would be legendary if Neztríanis Awakened. "What is the fastest and safest path to the North Country?"

Neztríanis blinked and hesitated. *That's right. The North Country... My mission...*

"Flight, I suppose," Nez answered, somewhat begrudgingly. "With this book, I should be able to sustain flight for a longer period of time, and it appears that your wings are completely healed..."

"They are," she replied confidently. "At maximum speed we should be able to—"

Timura needed no words to interject; her face was ashen, agape, and angry.

"He's on his way?"

"Y-Yes," the témo stammered in terrifying remembrance. "It is as I thought. The Auría is magnifying your powers, even though you have not Awakened. He either believes you have the book or that you have ascended to the title of Kylanín."

"How far?"

"He is far off; the only reason I can sense him is because he is emitting a powerful aura. He wants me to sense his presence."

"Why would he do that?" the Nez Spiritan wondered aloud. "One day, Timura, you must train me on how to detect a Sczyphamek's aura from great distances."

They both ascended into the sky and flew a few lengths, but within an instant, shots exploded behind them. Aircraft were gunning for them. Neztríanis created an extremely dense ice shield with ease, in order to give them some protection. The Myanín nodded to one another and hastily descended into the tree lines below. They detected a large number of lifts at various altitudes trying to detect their position.

"This is not good," Neztríanis remarked. "We may not be able to use the skies."

"Indeed," the témo scowled, her mind racing. "Temperature, hop on my back and ensconce your Elemental as much as you can. That should at least keep Vincallous from locating us with great accuracy. Now that I am healed, I can maintain my ground speed for many lengths."

"Why should you have to do that?" Neztríanis asked. "We have the Auría. I am much more powerful now. We can take them and—"

"We would leave a trail of destruction in our wake that would lead Vincallous directly to us," Timura warned and suspiciously eyed her partner. "Though you have become strong, understand this, even with the Auría, you are no match for Vincallous."

"Kíma!" Neztríanis cursed and hopped on the témo's back. "Timura run! Something is heading straight for us, and it has a lot of heat!"

With no hesitation, the témo ran with all her might, hearing the sound that Neztríanis sensed. It was a bomb. The témo would not look back. Vincallous was risking nothing. The témo was sure Neztríanis could survive the attack, but she would not. His goal was to extinguish the possibility of the Synthesis at all costs.

Blasts in the distance grew closer and closer, and the témo reached speeds above one hundred and fifty lengths per hour. The entire tree line was consumed by concussion and fire. They could outrun these attacks, but their journey was now complicated.

Chapter Twenty-Two: Galís

Anámn's body ached. His head hurt; his qanín, weakened. Moaning, he opened his eyes. A rush of disorientation beset him, and for a few moments, he was unsure of where and who he was. He barely sensed the presence of Téza.

It was dark. A fire crackled. Trees rustled. His head was cold. Apparently, he was bald again. His facial hair was also gone. He was not wearing the same clothes he wore the last time he was conscious.

The fire adjacent to him needed more wood. A few feet away lay a pile of kindling. Reaching towards the stack, he nearly fainted.

"Anámn!" Lénü gasped suddenly.

The Sczyphamek was just as startled. Grasping kinetic signatures was impossible at the moment, which left him entirely unaware of Lénü's presence.

The former sex slave placed more wood on the fire and asked with a stern tone, "Just what are you doin'? You can't be trying to move!"

"Lénü," Matriester mumbled. It was a strain even to talk. "Lénü... where..."

"'When?' is the question you should be askin'. Been five days since you passed out."

"*Five days?*" Was that true? Anámn examined the campsite with his eyes. "Where's Brenko?"

"He went out to survey the area in order to verify that no one is in our vicinity. We actually been able to make progress, e'en though we been carryin' the likes of you around."

Anámn smiled weakly.

"Kinesis, what ya did—that was amazing," she said quietly. "You saved our lives."

Lénü'íque did not know how truthful that statement was if she added another independent clause: Anámn endangered their lives just as much.

433

Qeauríyx would have killed them, and they had nothing and everything to do with the matter. He felt it as soon as the first large stone made its way toward the condemned craft. He did not have the heart to tell Brenko, because the tactician would have lost his nerve. But Anámn was certain that near the end of the ordeal, Brenko deduced exactly what was occurring. Luckily, Matriester had developed a more intimate relationship with Téza since his original meeting with the planet. Even so, the experience was more terrifying than the first encounter.

He actually believed he had *bested* Qeauríyx back in the jungles of Phmquedria. He was mistaken. And because he failed, the second coming of Qeauríyx was more horrific than the first. The planet required a Sczyphamek to pay heed to its reality in order to be able to wield its share of an Elemental. Anámn's myriad of failures piled ever higher. He felt stupid—lacking intelligence—and ignorant—lacking information.

Lack of food, lack of intelligence, lack of information, lack of love, lack of personhood…

He had to resist self-hate and the ever-present temptation to believe that he was nothing more than an inferior Phmmy bastard in a world of nel'asmív much smarter and more deserving than he. But the weariness…

"Lénü, I didn't save…"

"Anámn, I know what I saw—or what I didn't see. We would've died if you ain't done what you done."

The Sczyphamek was too tired to argue.

Lénü edged closer to Anámn and placed her hand on his head. The hood on her cloak was pulled back, and if Anámn did not know better, her scar was almost unnoticeable. Her dark hair was longer than when they first met each other, what now seemed lifetimes ago. The light of the fire illuminated her yellow face and made her deep, purple eyes that much more mysterious and gorgeous.

"Lénü'íque, what is your family name?"

The former sex-slave was unsure of the origin of the question or the response she should give. "I ain't used that name in a long time," she muttered.

"I'm sorry. I didn't mean to upset you. I just wanted to know more about you…"

"It's Jínwa."[1] Her vocal intonation revealed that she was about to switch into her formal dialect. "Jínwa is my family name. A sex slave was not allowed to speak of family. We were without family."

"It's a lovely name." Shifting the conversation's gravity, he inquired, "What happened to my hair?"

"We cut what was left of it off." Lénü's disposition altered to match the runaway's. "That blast left you stark naked, Anámn. Your hair was just as cooked as your disintegrated clothes."

---

[1] Jínwa (jeen-wah)

"Wait. Did you just say '*naked*'?" The night did not conceal Anámn's embarrassment. "You saw me naked?"

"Wasn't nothing special." She nonchalantly placed some wood on the fire then saw Anámn's agape face. "Oh. That is not what I meant. I mean that we had to get some clothes on you, and nothing was as impressive as the way you manipulated that potential and kinetic energy."

Anámn was as mystified with the woman's disregard for and love of grammar, pronunciation, and vocabulary as her dismissal of his nakedness.

"Plus," she said with a bit of awkwardness, "I tried to be respectful."

"*Tried?*"

"Anámn." She giggled and tried to steer the conversation away from an uncomfortable space. "Why did you ask us to chant with you and what were you humming?"

"Téza told me to ask you both to chant with me," he responded. "Somehow it made my powers grow beyond what I could do by myself..."

"Beyond your own capability," Lénü cleaned up his vocabulary.

"Yeah. My 'capability,'" Anámn smiled. "As far as me humming, I don't really know how to explain it. But the longer I chanted, the more I started to hear this tune. It matched the way I chanted..." He stopped because he knew it was coming.

"It matched the meter of your enunciation," she corrected once again, intrigued by this revelation. "You mean, ya ain't ever heard that melody 'fore?"

"Not that I can remember," Anámn said. "I think singing affects my powers too, although I have not quite grasped the full implications of such an observation yet."

Jínwa smirked then grinned at Anámn. He was trying to flaunt his own burgeoning lexicon vis-à-vis her constant nitpicking.

"I thought about everything you and Brenko have taught me over this past duration. And while I was humming, and Téza and I came up with an idea."

"Sounds like you learned an incantation. How crazy is that? Singing affects your powers. Corporate chanting affects your powers. Kíma... Sczyphameks are strange."

"Like you aren't." Anámn laughed feebly then coughed.

Lénü's face emoted romantic concern, and instinctively, she stroked his hairless head. Her eyes softened. Before Anámn stopped himself, his eyes returned her gaze with similar emotions. He was nervous and hoped Brenko would return that instant to break their visual communication, but he did not.

Anámn looked away first. Lénü, gaining control of her feelings, followed suit. She placed more wood on the fire and sat opposite Anámn.

"I don't think I'll be able to use my powers for awhile," the Phmquedrian commented. "Téza feels so distant."

"Then you're gonna have to be extra careful. Just focus on walking first;

the rest will come when it needs to."

They were silent for awhile, until Anámn asked curiously, "So you *tried* to be respectful huh?"

"What can I say?" Lénü smiled. "When a stark naked man who saved my life is in front of me—I guess I couldn't help myself."

The surrounding bushes rustled in a way that signaled approach. Instantaneously, Lénü's energy pistol was charged.

"It's me, Lénü," Brenko called out, appearing out of the darkness. He gave Anámn a sign of affirmation. "I see you regained consciousness. I doubt you can walk though..."

Anámn shook his head.

"I thought so," he sighed. "I wish I had some good news, but I don't. I climbed a tree about two lengths from here and saw some faint lights I should not have seen. They are about thirty lengths to our west, but they are moving this way."

"Anámn said he can't use his powers for awhile," Jínwa added. "So we're gonna have to be extra careful." She gave Anámn a heartfelt, attractive smile, which Anámn sheepishly returned.

"Fall in love when this is over," Brenko interjected wryly. "Right now, we gotta get moving. Lénü, let's clean this campsite up and cover our tracks. Anámn, we'll carry you, and don't even try to be recalcitrant..."

Anámn was unsure of the meaning of "recalcitrant," and he was embarrassed that Brenko called out he and Lénü's romantic uneasiness so brusquely.

The blushing woman rubbed Anámn's shoulder. "He means don't overdo it. If ya can't walk, you can't walk. Ain't nothing you can do now but get better. Let us do some of the hard work."

In ten or so minutes, the campsite appeared as if it never existed. Anámn was impressed, although it only showed the experience that the duo had attained throughout their cycles of travel and plotting. Hoisting Anámn up, the father and daughter propped the Sczyphamek between them and started walking with his feet dragging on the ground.

"You all carried me like this for five days?" he asked warmly with his arms on their shoulders.

"We'll carry you as long as it takes," Brenko said. "But, Kinesis, the sooner you can walk, the better. And the sooner you regain your powers, the better chance we'll have of surviving."

"Where are we?" Matriester asked. "It is so dark out here."

"Your eyes'll get used to it after 'while," Lénü said.

"Brenko, I'm crazy for even asking; but, do you know where we are or where we're going?"

The grunt of the tactician was without parallel. Anámn heard it before the man even made the sound. "We haven't been caught, have we?"

"What would you have done if the aircraft survived?"

"I would've flown under their radar for a hundred lengths or so, and then ditched the lift. Walking was always a part of the plan."

"*Right.*" Anámn sighed weakly. "I forgot you have an answer for everything."

"Not *everything.*" Brenko returned Anámn's sigh with his own. "And my family name is Zó'ethys.[2] My mother's family name was Zo'il and my father's family name was Ethysán."[3]

Lénü'íque Jínwa and Anámn Matriester grimaced. Obviously, Brenko had overheard their conversation more than either of them realized.

"Kanoso," Lénü said with contempt. "It ain't nice to eavesdrop, ya chunk o' kíma."

Anámn cackled at Lénü's proclamation. Brenko chuckled heartily and nearly dropped Anámn. The two men gathered themselves, and the trio resumed their walk in the dark forest of the Comphyx Cape.

"But seriously," Anámn repeated, nearly unconscious just from laughing, "do you know where we're going?"

"We are going to meet Tarían," Brenko responded.

"Does he even know you are looking for him?"

The tactician grew irritated. "Go to sleep, Anámn."

The Sczyphamek said nothing and within a few moments entered a deep slumber.

Anámn did not wake again for three more days. The father and daughter created a cot to transport Matriester, using his coat and two long, thick branches from the yardük trees, which were growing in number. The invention allowed them to move at a faster speed. They had not a moment to spare. Aerial patrols were now commonplace and more troops continued to enter the Comphyx Cape.

Qeauríyx allowed for very few coincidences, and their situation was clearly not one of those moments. They were found out. Either Yerna had been compromised or Damüda's surveillance was altogether beyond what Brenko imagined… or neither was true and something else happened. After all, their entrance into Damüda was heralded by the destruction of a volcano. No matter the reason, stopping for long stretches was not possible.

Making a fire was also ill-advised, though the temperatures were quite chilly at night. But it *was* Opíz, and they were in Damüda. The weather was autumnal, and in Damüda, autumn started early in the seventh duration. Travel during a Damüdan winter meant certain death. Only Nez Spiritan and Keotagosdian winters were worse, but that was not saying much.

Bad. Worse. Worst. Death. Death. Death.

---

[2] Zó'ethys (tz*oh*-eth-is)
[3] Ethysán (ey-thih-s*ah*n)

Brenko did not respond to the inquisitive Phmquedrian's question regarding Tarían, even though he actually had an answer. But after Phenplyacin, the Brycian tactician never liked to explain situations where and when the outcome was in serious doubt. Nor did he reveal his full hand to anyone. Lénü'íque had traveled with him so much that she naturally understood his patterns of behavior. And yet, even she had not seen all sides of him.

The coward had lost weight since he had the unfortunate pleasure of meeting Anámn, partially because he had stopped drinking, but also because of a lack of food and the constant exercise of navigating through the Damüdan woodlands. His belly still protruded, yet it was not as round as before. More than any area on his body, Brenko's face was not as chubby, and he appeared a bit more youthful.

Yerna, per Brenko's request, contacted Tarían indirectly before the pilot of the Dark Nimbus made his way to Minusía to pick up the tactician and his daughter. Brenko, Tarían and Yerna had developed a nearly unnoticeable and ingenious way to communicate through underground channels. They employed a system of code words and phrases, which were mediated by common acquaintances who had no idea they were being used. In all the cycles they had done business, Brenko never trusted Tarían. But he trusted Tarían's hatred of the Guild.

Even so, the tactician's plan was still exceptionally ignorant. Brenko, Lénü, and Anámn were in hostile territory. In their present situation, Keotagosdi was probably their best option, but Brenko allowed fear and pride to dominate his actions. How nel'asmív…

At the same time, what he said to Anámn and Lénü was true. Keotagosdi was swarming with Eradicate from all wings of the third chamber of the Daknín. They would not have lasted there for long either.

In truth, there were no good choices for his kind. Global Initiative garnered all preferential options. They should have gone to Líachim.

After one and a half weeks of eluding their would-be captors, Anámn was finally able to walk on his own accord. He could not wield his power at all and could barely summon his Elemental strength, speed, and durability. The trio covered much ground, but they also had to backtrack and find hiding places. Interror presence was now endemic. There were too many occasions where the forces of Damüda were seen by the trio; however, they had not been spotted yet.

Brenko used his full array of knowledge and experience to elude capture. Anámn's esteem of the Brycian climbed with each passing day. His esteem was also accompanied by a hunger for learning, and the Sczyphamek and Lénü soaked in as much knowledge as they could. However, Brenko's mind was constantly eight steps ahead of anything a normal nel'asmív could ponder.

Another week passed. The days were becoming gloomier and colder. Anámn, Lénü, and Brenko had managed to pry themselves away from the

Interror and were only a day away from meeting Taríen in the forests of west-central Damüda. Anámn was still incapable of using his Elemental, but his latent physical powers had halfway returned. Using them was taxing, and Brenko told him to conserve his strength because they would need it later.

Talking was at a minimum; so most days, Anámn silently chanted and sang to himself. He dialogued with Téza, whose exhaustion was unambiguous. The element of potential and kinetic energy was also proud of Anámn. Téza intimated that many Sczyphameks did not survive a second coming of Qeauríyx. And the recovery time from the first engagement was much shorter than the second. When Anámn asked if a Sczyphamek had ever failed the planetary encounter a second time *and* lived, Téza was mysteriously still.

"This place is familiar," Lénü said.

Brenko nodded. "This is it… We were here two cycles ago."

Anámn could not distinguish any markings, buildings, or running water that would grant any bearings in the stock forest.

"The position of the trees," Brenko answered.

"You can tell where we are based upon the position of the trees?" Anámn asked in disbelief.

"You can destroy a cloud of debris and magma by yourself?" Brenko responded.

Immediately, Anámn remembered Malchían's lecture to him four durations prior. *Power.* When he gave Anámn the ticket to Kamo, he told him that he had given him "power." An unyielding Anámn spurned the connection at the time, but not now. Power, at one of its most basic levels, was the ability to achieve outcomes. Different folk wielded it in different ways. Anámn's qanín was very close to *something*, but this thing(?) was still hidden from him. One thing was certain; if Taríen could find such an obscure place by memory and skill, he was clearly an intelligent man.

"Wake up, Anámn," Brenko said. "We aren't staying here tonight. Come on."

"Do you think he is going to show?" Anámn asked.

"He'll be here. Either to hand us over or for the best profit he's ever made."

"He will be *here?* Tomorrow of all days…? That is random. It isn't like you planned to meet him exactly tomorrow…"

Anámn was exasperated. No one should be able to plan something so *random.* But Brenko was confident. The slave was both jealous of and perturbed by the tactician. Something about the Brycian's exercise of power reminded Anámn of his father.

"How could you have set this up so well? That's impossible."

"Not impossible, just unlikely," Brenko answered with a smile. "And I've got a habit of making the unlikely likely."

The young man stood in place with Lénü by his side. She grabbed his hand and pulled him forward. Once Anámn complied, she attempted to let his hand go, but he would not let her do so. Turning around, she smiled at the Phmquedrian and held his hand tighter.

They settled at a location five lengths from the meeting place, Brenko gave orders while making a small fire.

"Do not speak unless spoken to, especially you, Lénü."

The woman frowned.

"Tarían possesses a strange sense of loyalty, but there's a good chance that he's going to betray us... Anámn, how are your powers?"

"I still can't use them for a long period of time."

"All I need you to do is scan for kinetic signatures once we get close to the meeting place. If you sense anybody besides Tarían, grab my shoulder."

Anámn nodded.

"We can't allow for any kind of kíma, so I'm going to be direct with Tarían and see if he can even halfway be trusted with this. I'll be gauging his facial expressions the whole time. I need you all to investigate everything else about him—like his hands. See if he has a radio, or if he is leaving marks on the ground with his boots. But if you address him, look him in the face.

"Anámn, Lénü will announce you as Huyé, but Tarían has got to know who you really are. The Interror and the sex traders have surely contacted him by now. So he's definitely found out that I'm not Plenz, and that you're the son of Alzhexph ju Xaníz. I doubt they told him that you're a Sczyphamek. It's disadvantageous to the House of Kaz and us if your identity was widely known."

"Yeah, I figured that."

"Tarían's not stupid though. You have to come up with your own reasoning as to why you are being hunted."

"It's the sex traders? Are they the one's you are most worried about?" Anámn asked.

"Who can tell? They are probably working with the Interror on this one. Both want me dead..." Brenko grew lost in the flames of the fire before them. Breaking his trance, he stared at the stars. He took a breath, which was visibly seen by his daughter and the Sczyphamek, and rubbed his cold hands together. "We can't stay out here much longer. A Damüdan winter will kill us. Even with your powers, Anámn, I doubt even you will last out here for long without shelter. We need Tarían. We need better clothes... Staxis... If it really starts to snow, they will be able to track us, without a doubt... Kíma..."

Lénü patted and rubbed Brenko's back. "Kanoso, you are doing the best you can. I'll take the first watch. Y'all get some sleep."

Brenko's face was weary and he complied without much complaint.

"One more thing," the Brycian said groggily. "This thing that's developing between you two... Don't act like that around Tarían. You know how he feels about you Lénü. There is no telling what anyone will do when romantic rejection is thrown into the equation. Staxis, a Sczyphamek and my daughter..."

He muttered inaudible words to himself. Before Jínwa and Matriester could translate, the man was already asleep. The past three and a half weeks had taxed Brenko beyond measure. The young man and woman were both embarrassed. Every time Brenko talked about their feelings reddened faces emerged.

"You too, Anámn. Go to sleep."

"Lénü'íque Jínwa," Anámn said. "If it goes bad tomorrow, I want you to know that I appreciate everything that you've done for me."

"Ana-"

Anámn leapt forward and kissed her passionately. At first Lénü's body was stiff and unsure, but when she felt and tasted his care for her, she wrapped her arms around his back and returned the sign of affection. The kiss lasted only for a half a minute, but it seemed like an eternity. They held each other silently for a few moments before Anámn loosened his hold on the woman. Lénü did the same, and the Sczyphamek lay down in front of the fire.

"I'll take the second watch." His heart was still beating fast from the kiss. "Let Brenko sleep. Since we can't act like this around Tarían, I had to tell you now."

Lénü nodded. She felt uncertain, enamored, and conflicted. She had not been touched like that since she was a sex slave. But Anámn happened differently. She wanted him to touch and kiss her. She looked at Anámn, who was smiling. She nudged closer to him and held out her hand, which he clasped fondly.

Tomorrow, they would happen as different people.

***

31 Opíz, 241 OGI
Nekolé

"Anámn?" Brenko muttered under his breath.

The Sczyphamek shook his head. He felt no trace of anyone other than the approaching figure within a three-length radius. If Anámn pushed himself further, he would have fainted.

The man grew into focus. He wore a long and deceptively dense jacket that fell down around his knees. The jacket was buttoned tightly. If the man packed any weapons, they were not visible. Tarían routinely carried combustible firearms, which reminded the tactician of Bíoske. He seemed ten cycles older than the Brycian remembered, and the large backpack he carried nearly dwarfed his tall frame.

"Tarían," Brenko greeted.

"Plenz," Tarían smiled and then looked at Lénü. "Lénü."

"Tarían." She frowned, grabbed Anámn's hand and pulled him forward. "This is Huyé."

"Tarían." Anámn's voice possessed a twinge of standoffishness.

"*Huyé*," the Damüdan said with jealous eyes.

Brenko interjected, "Tarían, I'm sure you know who I am, so let's not keep up this pretense."

"And to think, all these cycles, I was doing business with Brenko, the hero and coward." Tarían shook his head. "Lénü, I'm shocked you didn't tell me, ah. I thought we were closer than that."

"Yeah, right…" she trailed.

"Be nice," Brenko said to his daughter. "He hasn't even said anything crazy, yet."

"*Yet*," the woman repeated. "Only a matter o' time with that one…"

"What's the deal?" Tarían asked, ignoring Lénü'íque. "What do you need?"

"We need to get to southeast Damüda," the tactician responded.

"I figured. Always the hard requests…" Tarían paused, then stared at Anámn. "Huyé, who are you, really? The Interror's been hounding me for days and I doubt that it's just 'cause they're on the lookout for a washed up tactician. No offense, Brenko."

"None taken." Brenko rolled his eyes.

"So how about it, Huyé." The man smiled inquisitively. "Who in Qalfocx are you, ah?"

Lénü squeezed Anámn's hand warning him to lie, but Brenko gave the Sczyphamek no signal, signifying his willingness to let Matriester make the call.

"I am the son of Alzhexph ju Xaníz," he responded. "I ran away durations ago and somehow managed to run into these two."

"*Wait*. Did you just say that you are Alzhexph ju Xaníz's son? Are you kidding me?"

"No," Anámn stated matter-of-factly. *Technically*, he was not lying. He was just withholding the fullness of the truth. "He is my… he's my father," the runaway muttered with spite, not wanting to admit the relationship from the top-down.

"Well, that's not that bad…" Tarían said. "But I thought ju Xaníz's son's name was 'Anámn,' *ah*? At least, that is what the Interror told me, when they were looking for you, 'Huyé.'"

Brenko smiled. If anyone was going to lie or double-cross, it was going to be Tarían.

"You lied about your name, but not about who you were," Tarían mused. "Ah."

"What does a name mean anyway, especially my name?" Anámn retorted.

"Right. But still, happening as his son and running away—that doesn't seem like a good enough reason for the Interror to be hunting you, ah?"

Anámn was firm. "You don't want to know what I did; if you found out, you probably wouldn't help us. *And I don't feel like talking about it.*"

Which 'did' are you talking about, Anámn? Lénü thought to herself. *You're blurring the line between truth-telling and deception.*

"That bad, ah?" Tarían turned to Brenko with listlessly intent eyes. "This is gonna be tough. And I'm telling the truth. There's a good chance we're gonna get caught. The Interror is set on finding you all. And, by the way they've been tailing me and by their numbers, I gotta say, they know you're here."

"We figured that," Brenko said.

"A mark's on your head, Brenko. You basically killed the damn sex-trade when you and Lénü killed Gisé. Some folks aren't too happy about that, ah." He added in frustration, "You definitely put that part of my hustle out of business."

"Least we ain't kill you." Lénü's grin was ice cold.

"*Lénü...*" Brenko's warning to his daughter was the harshest Anámn had ever heard the man speak. "Tarían... you still have contraband and goods to exchange. You always made more credits that way, anyway."

"I made enough, ah..."

"*But...*" Brenko tapped his fingers on the trunk of a tree three times, signaling the possibility of betrayal. Anámn took notice of it all. Brenko was forcing Tarían's hand.

"*But* a little extra never hurt," the Damüdan finished.

Measuring every contortion and wrinkle on the Damüdan's face, Brenko spoke, "If you get caught helping us, you're either going to be killed or sent to The Gate. You know that, right?"

The peddler bowed his head for a moment and then looked back at the tactician. His face was nothing like they had seen previously.

"Ah." Tarían's voice was gentle and thoughtful. "You're an enemy of the highest kind around here. Galís or Fencero will probably torture you personally if we're caught."

No words were exchanged for a few minutes.

Brenko broke the silence. "All right. How many credits is this going to cost?"

"I'll tell you when we get there... *if we get there.*"

In all the cycles Brenko knew Tarían, he had never known him to *not* bargain for a price before an exchange was made. Brenko was unsure of what that portended. Tarían was the kind of hustler who would siphon off as much as he could from a person, before he betrayed that person for outside credits.

"Tarían," Lénü said with a level of true amicability that hitherto she was unable to display. "Why are ya doin' this?"

"Maybe you'll think better of me, then..." he replied solemnly. "Fact is,

I haven't done anything since I left home that wasn't selfish or questionable…" He chuckled to himself and grinned. "I probably won't ever change, ah. But I can't live my life knowing that I hadn't done a damn bit of good.

"Brenko, you stood up to those bastards and fought against everything I hate. At some point, my life's got to be more than thieving and hustling… Most good deeds go punished on Qeauríyx. And this is the worst time for me to grow a qanín.

"But then, there's that Sczyphamek that they're chasing down in Nez Spirita. That person's got it worse than all of us. Vicious and the General Maximum are there…"

Anámn's agnostic prayers went out to the mystery Sczyphamek. He or she did not know there was another. At least he knew someone else was like him.

Brenko looked directly in the Damüdan's eyes. "Tarían, can you can get us there without any interference from Galís, the Interror, and the Guild?"

"Ah, Galís and his kímaz Guild can go to Qalfocx," he spat out in such a strong Damüdan accent, that Anámn was more shocked by his dialect than his choice of words. "Damüda doesn't belong to anybody, ah. Damn sure doesn't belong to them or the House of Kaz. And the Interror can go drink piss!"

Brenko was right. The man's loathe for Global Initiative was impossible to conceal.

"I'd spit in that upright's face if I could, ah."

"*Upright?*" Anámn repeated with misunderstanding. "What's that?"

"Back before Damüda was a part of this farce, we were good friends with the témos, and that's what they called us nel'asmív." His nostalgia was strong, even though 700 cycles had passed since nary a témo stepped foot in Damüda. Their presence was still that deep in the consciousness of his kind. "Now we call lying and thieving cléths like Galís an 'upright.' It ain't a term of endearment."

Lénü, Brenko, and Anámn snickered at Tarían's talk and countenance. The hustler's expressions basted the listener in the words he spoke. His language, mixed with his facial expressions and hand gestures, made the meaning of his intimations unmistakable.

"Damn it, Brenko," he smirked. "You made me do that."

"I just wanted you to remember why you can't betray us."

"That was nasty, ah. I'd only betray you to somebody other than them, like those sex trader bounty hunters who've been following me for the past three durations."

"Where are they now?" Brenko pressed.

"Ah… I thought that'd interest you. They are about two hundred lengths east. Lost them about a week and a half ago. I didn't want to risk using a mechanized vehicle or a windhorse to get here. I figured they would be easier to track. And I've been on foot for the past four days.

"We're going to have to walk for at least a week until we can get faster transportation. Only Zénan knows how we're gonna make it home before it starts snowing. Mashé and Parce haven't been favorable to me the past few lunar cycles."

Anámn's face must have appeared puzzled because Tarían's smile turned into a laugh that boomed throughout the forest.

"Staxis, Huyé, or Anámn, or whatever… Why're you looking at me like that, ah?"

"*Zénan, Mashé, Parce.* Those are the names for the sun and the moons… Why do you talk about them like they matter?"

"*They matter.* The Firmament matters."

"*The Firmament?*" Anámn grew more perplexed than before.

"Don't you got any religion, Phm-" the man stopped himself before he called Anámn a "Phmmy." "Don't you believe in the Fragments?"

Brenko hoped the Sczyphamek would not lose his temper. He should not have worried; Anámn was changing.

"You must not be talking to me, because I don't see any Phmmys around here," Anámn quipped. "But the Fragments…" the runaway's voice trailed back into the stream of their original conversation. "The Fragments talk about the ancestors and the One with No Name. That's who we're supposed pray to."

"Your *ancestors?*"

"Yeah."

"Beliefs change from land to land," Brenko explained to both of them. "In most parts of Damüda, the heavenly bodies are the primary divine force. The One with No Name is important, but not active, and ancestors have never been worshipped."

"The Firmament contains all that we need," Tarían said with mischievous reverence.

"I didn't know you were such a believer," Lénü said to Tarían.

"There's a lot about me you don't know, Lénü'íque," Tarían responded with a flirtatious smile.

Anámn's countenance remained unchanged, *only* because he was in deep consideration of the variations in theological and religious beliefs. He surmised that other lands fared the same. "Brenko, is it like that on every continent? I mean, do those nel'asmív have different beliefs?"

Tarían was about to say something but paused. The rascal in him hushed. The Phmquedrian offered a question even the hustler had once pondered.

"I'll answer this, but then we have to move." The Brycian made sure to choose his words carefully. "I've been on every continent, except Meve, and everybody believes something different and something similar and some believe nothing at all. And the témos… their ideas of the Nameless One and Qeauríyx vary even more."

"So then is everybody wrong?" Tarían asked, with real interest, as if his own stake in the matter had been brought to bear.

"When has everybody been all wrong?" Brenko asked. "And when has everybody been completely right?"

"Then is one…" Anámn stopped himself. One person or group did not have all or the "best" answers. That was the iniquitous assumption of the House of Kaz.

Tarían understood Anámn's silence all too well. "Ah. The Guild is full of kíma."

Seizing the moment, Lénü'íque finally asked the question she had possessed for cycles. "Kanoso, what do you believe?"

Brenko saw all three of them gazing at him as if their own faiths were dependent upon his.

The tactician did not blink or flinch. "I believe that there is no point to any of this. It's all meaningless."

"Then why are we…" Lénü pressed.

"Because I could be wrong," the tactician finished. "Let's go."

***

The days were growing shorter, their steps more wearisome. For an additional two weeks, they used none of the main roads. Within days of their meeting with Tarían, the first snow fell. Providentially, Tarían was able to procure outerwear and two windhorses for the three imperial fugitives. They ate whatever they happened upon: insects, wild animals, leaves that were not yet been despoiled by the oncoming winter. The thickness of the snow stupefied Anámn. It rarely snowed in Euhilv, only at the top of the nameless mountain. His tropical constitution was unaccustomed to such weather, so the elements had an exaggerated effect on him.

Traveling under such strenuous conditions provided an opportunity for what began as an uneasy alliance to slowly turn into a group of four. Brenko was still surprised that Lénü would stay as long as she did or that the sex trade assassinations would place him on such a path. Lénü was still shocked that she befriended a Sczyphamek and that she enjoyed a familial relationship after her experience in the sex trade. Anámn was uncertain how he even made it to Damüda. It seemed like only days ago he was working in the mines or on his sister's roof. And now he was in the company of notoriety, loveliness, and an incorrigible rascal and hustler.

Tarían still found it hard to grasp that he was not going to betray them. But the past few durations had changed his perspective and his hustle. When the sex traders and the Guild approached him *together*, attempting to garner information about Brenko, he nearly distrusted his own eyes. Global Initiative was becoming all-consuming, which soon meant he would be out of a lucrative job. If those three could hurt the chances of that possibility, Tarían would do whatever he needed to do. And he perceived something strange about Anámn. Though unsure of what kind of strangeness, the hustler knew trouble when he saw it. Subversive behavior was not far from Anámn's plans.

In total, Anámn, Lénü, and Brenko had been in Damüda for a duration and a half. They had traveled nearly nine hundred and fifty lengths, and yet they were more than fifteen hundred lengths from their destination. Damüda was indeed an unforgiving continent. An unnamed mountain range stretched from its northwest corner and traveled down and across its midsection, only to rise back up the short eastern seaboard. The range's tallest peak, Mount Sunset, was at the northwesternmost point of the range, and its reputation was just as famous and indomitable as Sunrise Mountain and Edaw Peak. Those who traveled to those three mountains were labeled fools.

The quartet found themselves in extreme south-central Damüda. The terrain was a harsh reminder of life during The Drift. To their north lay the anonymous mountain range, which sent blast after blast of unfiltered arctic air, a gratuitous gift given by the northernmost continent of the eastern hemisphere. The southern edge of the mountain range was only one hundred and fifty lengths away from the shores of the Anplo Sea, so precipitation was guaranteed. There were nights when all four of them and the windhorses huddled together around a fire and still nearly froze. Villages were few and far between, and half of them housed informants or Interror within their limits. Therefore, only rare occasions allowed the quartet to have a roof over their heads at night. Circumstances grew direr by the day, and daylight grew sparser with each passing sunrise, signaling the proximity of the winter solstice.

"We've gotta get a vehicle, Brenko." Tarían proclaimed the obvious on some unknown day during some unknown hour. "The windhorses'll die if we don't. Qalfocx, we'll die if we don't get one. It means I got to do some business in the next town. But we can't go on like this."

There was no counterargument to give. Staying in a location to ride out the winter was not an option. The windhorses looked as if they would soon die from fatigue. Unless they were in southeast Damüda, they would never be safe, and even if they made it there, they would still have to keep to themselves.

"We haven't seen the Interror in over a week," Tarían added. "They may be done for the winter."

"Fencero is not Violent Fist and Galís is not Vincallous," Brenko reminded the Damüdan. "Those bastards will not be patient. Fencero won't stop, and Galís will order his soldiers to their deaths if it means capturing us."

"Ah…" the Damüdan agreed. "See, Anámn. I told you the moons haven't been on my side as of late."

Anámn's shivering body concealed his genuine worry. Even with adequate clothing, the Phmquedrian could not adjust to the weather. His discomfort also impeded Téza's recovery. The Elemental had reconstituted itself, but still had much more room to grow.

Unfortunately, however, his Elemental's recuperation was not his greatest trouble. One night, when Tarían and Lénü were asleep, Brenko woke Anámn and had a long conversation with the Sczyphamek. He told him that they would not be able to talk like this for a while or ever again. Brenko gave him one order and one piece of advice.

His order was that if they were captured and Anámn had not fully regained his powers, then he could not use them. When Anámn asked why, Brenko's stern face became tormented. He told Anámn that first impressions were everything for a Sczyphamek and for a battle. Brenko reminded the runaway of Phenplyacin and the statement it sent and the time it bought Pre-Eminent and Vicious. After such a horrendous defeat, Miska Kea dared not attack them. As a result, the House of Kaz was able to put in place policies and tactical programs that gave them an overwhelming advantage for cycles to come. If Anámn was able to do the same, that is, if he wielded his Elemental in an awesome, observable display of power—the enemy would be forced to retreat until they felt they were able to match that power. Anámn would then have adequate time to Awaken, because the only ones who could defeat him were the leaders of the Daknín and the Zananín.

Brenko made him promise. Anámn complied.

Then he gave Anámn advice. He told Anámn that they would be captured. It was inevitable. Their capture would not be due to betrayal but probability. If their apprehension happened before Anámn was at full power, then Anámn had his orders. If Anámn was at full power, then he should spare no expense to show his level of potency. However, the mastermind believed that probability demanded the former and not the latter possibility. His advice to Anámn was simple. He told the Phmquedrian to let himself, Lénü, and Tarían die. Galís was no doubt under orders to keep Anámn physically unharmed, so the Sczyphamek was not in any physical danger.

"You cannot jeopardize yourself for us," Brenko warned. "I know how you feel about Lénü. But it will not help her or Qeauríyx if you try to save us and end up dead."

"But I thought you said that only the Daknín…"

Brenko cut off Kinesis' obvious interjection. "True, in a heads up battle, you would only lose to the Daknín and the Zananín. But this wouldn't be a heads up battle. These troops can take one of us hostage and compromise your powers based on your concern and love for us. If Lénü had a gun to her head, you would hesitate."

Anámn could not argue against the rebuttal. "Why aren't you ordering me to do this?"

"Because if I did, then you wouldn't listen to me," the man smiled. He had indeed come to understand Matriester. "Your Awakening is all that matters now. If you don't attain that, Líachim will be lost and those bastards will probably have their way for another four or five hundred cycles. Staxis, even if you do Awaken there's no guarantee. But we're done for certain if you and that other Sczyphamek don't make it."

Five hundred cycles. Five hundred more cycles of Global Initiative. Five hundred more cycles of slavery. Anámn could not fathom it. He would not allow it.

Anámn emerged from the recollection of he and Brenko's conversation. The Sczyphamek quivered and huddled closer to the fire. "Tarían, how long would it take to get to southeast Damüda in a vehicle?"

"A week to a week and a half," Tarían said through misty breaths. "But we would need to use the main roads at some point, and they are sure to have an Interror presence. I'm familiar with some back roads and we can make our own paths, but we'll have to refuel at some point. The likelihood of us getting caught will get higher, ah."

"What would your grandfather do in a situation like this?" Lénü asked Tarían with great interest.

Tarían smacked the snow off his shoulders and sighed. "Ah, my Old One was a Mystic. He'd make the hard decision and take the risk. My folks would've done the same."

Anámn shuddered. Tarían told them what happened to his grandfather. He had been tortured and killed by Galís personally, and his dismembered, burnt body was sent back to his parents as a means of dissuasion of revolutionary activity. However, Tarían's "folks"—his mother and father—did the same as his grandfather and were killed during an assassination attempt on Galís, four durations after Phenplyacin. Tarían was sixteen.

From that moment onward, the hustler wanted nothing to do with overt resistance, but he would be damned to Qalfocx if he ever supported the regime that had taken his Old One, Mamisí, and Kanoso. And now he was following in their insurrectionary footsteps. The gates of Qalfocx were opening slowly…

Anámn looked at Brenko. Brenko's face was plain: "remember what I said."

What could they do? If they stayed out in the Damüdan winter with no real food or adequate shelter, they would certainly die. If they took a vehicle, they would most certainly be caught, but might survive.

Lénü broke the silence. "We don't have a choice."

All four of them nodded solemnly.

Though somber, Brenko playfully slapped Kinesis on the back. "See, Anámn? Even I make mistakes. Planning only gets you so far." Eyeing the hustler, the tactician outstretched his hand. "Tarían, you don't have to go any further. You've done enough."

"Shut it, coward," the Damüdan joked. "You think now is a good time to betray you, don't you? I know what you're thinking."

Anámn had to admit he was thinking the same thing.

"I mean to do this one thing right, ah. Zénan would strike me down if I turn back now."

"Ah," Brenko said in agreement.

"The nearest town is a day away. I'll go inside the city and sell the windhorses and use some credits. If I'm not out by nightfall with a vehicle, keep going."

The next day, Tarían traveled to the small town, while Lénü'íque, Anámn, and Brenko stayed on the outskirts. Anámn desperately—frenziedly and urgently—desired Téza's full return. He asked Brenko and Lénü to chant with him, remembering how corporate chanting and prayer had affected his powers nearly two durations ago. Lénü and Brenko complied; however, his Elemental was unaffected.

The Phmquedrian gazed at Brenko discerningly and realized that cajoling the tactician to chant with him was probably a once in a lifetime experience. Although the Brycian repeated the words and phrases he had said on the airlift, his disposition was anything but the same. Lénü also appeared markedly distracted. Anámn wondered if it was only chance and desperation that caused the three of them to pray together. Perhaps it was sheer coincidence that caused his powers to expand beyond their normal capacity. Or maybe his strategy was mistaken.

Within three hours, Tarían returned with a moderately sized land vehicle with large tires. He was alone, but his face was not the least bit congenial. He signaled them to get aboard and then sped off of the main road.

"The only good news is that I was able to get this mobile." His eyes and voice were without hope. The trio waited for the Damüdan to continue. "Ah. The folk back there told me that the Interror has been through the town on three or four occasions the past two weeks. Informants and undercover agents were probably there. I gotta say, we've been found out."

Brenko nodded. "They didn't capture you. That means they're following you. This vehicle will leave tracks, so the only thing we can hope for now is that we can outrun them."

"I bought some extra fuel," Tarían replied, a bit more encouragingly. "So we won't need to stop in any other town for at least eight hundred lengths."

"Tarían, Anámn is a Sczyphamek. A Kylanín," Brenko admitted to the Damüdan hustler.

Tarían nearly wrecked the mobile into a tree. "Still didn't trust me after all this Brenko," the Damüdan muttered. Tarían was genuinely hurt.

"No, that's not it," Brenko responded with a steady tone. "The more information you have that the rest of us don't, the more you are going to be tortured. And the information you don't know will also get you tortured because they'll assume you do know. So, I thought it was only fair that you know now."

"Why aren't you using your powers, Anámn?" Tarían pressed.

"He can't," Brenko replied. The tactician's answer was cryptic and to the point. "He's simply not strong enough to help us yet."

For one and a half days, the quartet traveled off the main roads. Tarían and Brenko exchanged driving duties and neither of them slept. But soon, something stirred within the Sczyphamek. Kinetic signatures. The signatures were legion. Anámn looked at Tarían and Brenko, then Lénü, who grimaced in return.

"We can't escape," Matriester reported. "They're too many."

"Stop the mobile," Brenko ordered.

Tarían complied.

"Everybody get out. Leave all your weapons in the auto."

The three did as commanded, and within seconds, they heard the sound of vehicles approaching from the air and ground.

"Make no movements. Don't say anything… Tarían, if you act like you've betrayed us they'll kill you here. It's too late for that now."

"It was too late a duration ago when I decided to help," he reminded Brenko somberly.

With fear in her eyes, Lénü reached toward Anámn and held his hand tightly.

Brenko looked at Kinesis and frowned. "Anámn, *remember what I said.* Let go of her hand. You're putting her in danger if you show how you really feel. Lénü, I know you don't want to go back there… but while we're imprisoned, you have to."

"Thanks for the consideration," Tarían said to Lénü'íque and Anámn. "That was respectful of you, ah. But I knew how you felt about each other the moment you introduced me to him, Lénü."

Lénü withdrew her hand from Anámn's. She hung her head, and when her face lifted, Anámn barely recognized the woman. Jinwa's face was ice cold, bereft of sentiment and gorged with apathy.

The tactician gave his final piece of advice. "Keep your hands above your head; do as you are ordered; and whatever you do, differentiate between violence that bloodies and violence that kills. We'll at least be kept alive to see Galís or Fencero. Even you, Tarían."

No sooner had Brenko finished his instructions, the entire area swarmed with Interror, clad in white and gray battle fatigues and aiming their energy rifles at the quartet.

Brenko glanced at Anámn for a final time. It was up to the Sczyphamek now. Whatever it took, Anámn had to regain his Elemental veracity.

"Identify yourselves." The charge was belted out of the sea of soldiers.

"I am Brenko; this is Lénü, Tarían, and Anámn. But I am sure you already know this."

"Search them," another unseen order was given.

Twelve soldiers descended upon the four and found no weapons on them. They were motioned to enter a large vehicle, where they were bound and transported to an airlift. Based on their handling and chaining of Anámn, the Interror soldiers were unaware he was a Sczyphamek. It did not matter. Their pain and troubles had not yet begun.

***

20 Ízneko, 241 OGI

"It is cold, is it not? Damüda happens frigidly during these late durations of the cycle, ah. When it is this cold, heat becomes a necessity. Do you not agree?"

His voice was so nurturing and calm. The questions were better to be left as rhetorical.

"This tea I am drinking…" The man paused and held a ceramic cup up to his lips and took a sip. "This cup of tea—it proves the point all too well. Who would want something cold to drink naked in the bite of winter? Handing some poor person in the frost of winter a cold glass of liquid would be mean and tortuous. Do you share the same sentiments?"

Placing the cup of tea on a table and rising from his chair, the muscular frame of his slender body told the sign of his true capability. His middle-aged fair face was unblemished and his gray-brown hair was cut perfectly. Perfection screamed from every precipice of the man's chiseled exterior. The creases on his dark brown pants were sharp. The ends of his black boots were parabolic and shiny. His long, gray jacket was iron-pressed to an unbelievable degree. There was not a wrinkle to be found, except on his body, especially his forehead. However, even those were perfectly symmetrical and equidistant.

"I asked you four questions. There are four of you. All of you had the ability to respond to at least one of my questions, yet you remained silent. You will find that one of my greatest irritations is when people refuse to answer my questions."

The man walked towards the four compatriots and stopped a few feet in front of them.

"Yet my greatest irritation yields my greatest joy. Ah, for I love to help those who find it hard to dialogue with me. Cajoling them to speak, and to speak truthfully… yes… *What pleasure!*"

Brenko wondered how such a nurturing and calm voice sounded so ecstatically eerie and sadistic.

"Tarían, the vagabond." The leader of the Damüdan Guild faced the hustler. "Are you not capable of answering my questions? Where is your gratitude? Where is your loyalty? I did not order your execution when your mother and father tried to avenge your grandfather's death, even though they should have thanked me for ridding this planet of another Mystic. Leaders and despots of the past would have murdered you as due course, but I allowed you to live. I even allowed you to do illegal business in my land. You have made quite a profit and were never taxed (although your illegitimate commerce has been good for the Damüdan economy). And this is how you show your thanks for my gracious mercy?"

The hustler was tempted to speak, but Brenko had told him there was no point in talking to someone who was going to torture you anyway.

"You have silenced them, Brenko?" Galís smiled. "Interesting."

The lord minister walked behind the four and nodded to nearly eighty of his underlings, who were ready to do and mediate their master's bidding. At once, twenty stepped forward and forced the rebels on their knees. Anámn did not resist.

Taking notice of Matriester's acquiescence, Galís inquired with curiosity, "Why do you not use your powers, Anámn? Why did you not use your powers when you were surrounded, bastard offspring of ju Xaníz? Are you *that* weak?"

Anámn did not respond, which prompted Galís to step directly in front of the Sczyphamek, kneel, and place his forehead on Anámn's forehead.

"What is the nature of your power, ah?"

His breath and bodily fragrance were exquisite.

Anámn remained quiet.

Moving to Lénü and stroking her hair gently and lasciviously, the man inquired, "Tell me whore, what is the nature of the bastard's power?"

Every strand of Anámn's qanín—even Téza—desired to strike Galís down, but the Sczy was only slightly above seven-tenths of his full capacity, and there were too many soldiers. If he attacked in his present state, it was more than likely that Brenko, Lénü, or Tarían would be killed.

Galís eyed the three men carefully, watching if they flinched. Leaning in close to Lénü, he licked the scar on her cheek.

Brenko's fist clenched first, but it was only to save Anámn. Lénü, however, *had* gone to the place she never wanted to return. Jínwa had prepared herself for the probable possibility that she would be raped repeatedly during their incarceration. Accordingly, she rediscovered the mental place of solitude she created during her cycles as a sex slave. The lord minister's misogynistic advance barely registered in her consciousness.

"Brenko, the coward, ah," the Damüdan vassal chuckled. "I doubt there is anything I can do to you that will equal the torture of Phenplyacin. *But I guarantee I will try.*"

Sighing, Galís' face became solemn and controlled. It reminded Anámn of his father's countenance, but something about Galís was much more disturbing. There was no telling what the man would do.

"You all have rendered my thesis ineffective. But a thesis can be proved in more than one way. Strip the vagabond," he commanded ominously.

Galís sauntered towards his chair, which was atop a raised wooden platform, varnished with a polish so translucent, the wood seemed like glass. Galís' wooden reflection promised a sinister end for Tarían.

In seconds, Tarían found himself stripped of clothes. The hustler prayed to the Firmament that he would survive his oncoming torture. Galís' personal force was as cruel and self-righteous as their leader. Preemptive mercy did not occur in the halls of Galís' castle of terror.

They arrived to The Gate within ten hours of their capture, unaccosted. The Gate was old, one of the first major cities in Damüda, nestled on the eastern side of the anonymous range in central northwest Damüda. Over fifteen million people lived in the metro area, and Galís chose it to be the capital of Damüda after he, the Guild, Pre-Eminent and Vicious signed a new treaty that put Damüda on par with Tannódin. Funds were appropriated to reinvigorate the city, and he personally oversaw its construction. Half of the city was architecturally antiquated, although all buildings possessed electricity and running water. The other half of the city was just as technologically advanced as Pike Metropolis or Kamo, replete with skyrises and a skyport. Galís' palace was a spectacle of beauty hiding a terrible secret. The grounds were built upon the old barracks and dungeons of feudal Damüda. Galís kept that throwback intact and constructed his citadel around and on top of the olden structures of death, decay, and imprisonment.

Tarían's naked body was hoisted up by soldiers and dropped near the platform where Galís sat.

"I am doing this to you first because your betrayal has wounded me the most," the torturer confessed sadly. "Bring the ice."

Anámn's eyes widened. Lénü tried to look away, but a soldier's iron grip on her face would not allow it.

"I asked if you thought it was cruel to give a poor lad a cold drink when it was already cold outside. Are you willing to respond now?"

"You're gonna do it anyway, you kímaz cléth," Tarían cursed. "Whether we talk or not."

"My first rule is that you only respond to the questions I ask. There is a penalty for adding your own commentary."

Galís nodded, and his underlings dumped four large barrels of ice on the stone floor. Though resisting with all his might, a naked Tarían could not overcome the combined power of Galís' subordinates. The soldiers thrust Tarían into the pool of ice, held him down, and poured more ice and cold water on top of him. The Damüdan hustler squawked in glacial discomfort; his nervous system erupted, and within twenty seconds he was pulled out of the pile, shivering and chattering. His back was pink and blue and even the soldiers who held the hustler shook from the chill.

"Does not my thesis gain more credibility now?" Galís asked.

"Go to Qalfocx," Tarían yelled.

"Anger often precipitates the violation of my first rule. Understandable.

But still penalized."

The lord minister arose from his chair and slapped Tarían with restraint. Even so, the hustler lost two teeth.

"Now, would it not be cruel to give someone a cold drink when they are in such a state? Is not giving them something hot the proper thing to do?" Galís picked up the pitcher of tea and seductively held the metal container in front of the hustler. "Would you like some of this tea, ah? See how the steam rises from it? Would you not feel better?"

The pitcher was two clips away from Tarían's cold, shuddering body. *It was so warm.* As much as Tarían tried not to give Galís the satisfaction, the instinct to draw near warmth when one was naked and freezing was overpowering.

Galís said to the three clothed compatriots, "Take note: at this moment heat and warmth is such a necessity, ah? Yet in a few seconds, he will be wishing he was cold again." With simple movement and nonchalance, the man opened the container of scalding hot tea and poured the tea on the head and down the back of Tarían.

The hustler's cry was horrid. Tarían was in such a shock that he threw himself out of the soldiers' grip and buried himself back in the ice, all the while cursing and yelping. The Sczyphamek could not let this happen. Brenko saw Matriester's mouth about to open, so he coughed and shook his head, sending Anámn a signal and reminding him of the promise he made.

"Don't you find it interesting?" Galís said gleefully. "It never grows old. That which you hate can become that which you love in an instant. That which is senseless, makes sense in a matter of seconds, once the right stimuli is applied." Galís laughed at Tarían, who had tears of pain streaming from his eyes. Finally, the lord minister of The Guild ordered his subordinates, "Get him out of the ice and back into his clothes. I do not wish him dead, yet. And send them all to the dungeons. Lock the bastard Phmmy up with three times the chains. Let the rest of them enjoy this one night unharmed."

Anámn did not sleep. He spent the whole night chanting, praying, and even inaudibly singing and humming. After Tarían's torture, he grasped Brenko's warning. Though the quartet had been in Galís' company for only a few hours, Anámn recognized too much of his father in the Damüdan vassal. Only a show of power, *real* power would give them the opportunity to escape, and in Anámn's present condition, he could only manage about ten minutes of sustained use of his Elemental. Even though his strength was returning, his stamina was still very weak. They were deep in enemy territory, and a partial escape or intervention was not going to be enough. His Elemental stamina had to be near its once amaranthine state. Anámn also realized that he was out of sync with the relationship between potential and kinetic energy. His battle with the planet disrupted and nearly maimed his connection with that aspect of reality.

They were put in different cells. The dungeon was dimly lit, and its vomit-inducing smell was something out of legend. None of them said a word to each other. Their only hope was in Anámn, and he knew it.

"Elemental warrior, why do you choose to remain mute?" an old voice boomed throughout the caverns of the cellblock.

"I wondered the same," another voice responded, a female this time.

Both sounded physically weak, but purpose buttressed their words.

"Kylanín," another said, "we do not need your title, but might we inquire about your silence. Will you not join us in our morning prayers? They will be good for you and your qanín."

Anámn was unsure of how to respond to the voices. He realized that he was waiting for Brenko to make the call, yet Brenko said nothing.

"Who's speaking?" Anámn asked.

"Some call us 'wise,' some call us 'Mystics'," the female voice said.

"Galís calls us 'useless relics'," another said.

"You're Mystics of the Aurías?" Anámn asked with wonder.

"That is correct, Kylanín Sczyphamek. Your Elemental is vast and perpetual. Yet you cannot sense it, unawakened warrior. An encounter with Qeauríyx perhaps?"

Their words were sharp, mysterious, and non-coincidental.

"Will you chant with us this morning? Galís tortures us for doing so, but we care not."

"Sometimes the spirit is more important than the body, and sometimes the body is more important than the spirit..." a Mystic answered Anámn's unspoken question. "Chant with us Sczyphamek."

"Yes, chant with them Sczyphamek." It was Galís. The door to the dungeon opened, and the lord minister stepped through the threshold with five underlings. "Chant those meaningless phrases."

The unseen Mystics grew quiet at the sound of Galís.

"Open the whore's cell," he ordered.

Anámn, still chained, walked gingerly to the door and tried to peer through the small opening near the top.

"Whore, I asked you a question yesterday, yet you did not answer. Now you shall tell me the truth regarding the bastard's powers."

Anámn was unable to contain himself and snapped his chains.

"Anámn!" Brenko yelled.

The young man came to his senses.

"So the coward speaks. Whore, please tell the coward that he is not allowed to speak."

For five seconds, Lénü's screams and yelps of affliction filled the dungeon.

"If you tell him not to speak, I will stop."

Lénü continued to shriek. Anámn was beside himself, and the fact he could not see what was being done to Jínwa made his torment all the more indescribable.

"Kanoso, do not speak," she moaned feebly. Anámn heard her voice. She said that to him and Tarían as well.

"Guards, take the whore to the platform."

"I'll tell you!" Anámn yelled. "Just leave her alone."

Brenko's unseen tears kept him from stopping Anámn. They truly were dealing with the heartlessness of nel'asmív.

"I did not speak to you," Galís replied. "Do you wish her to suffer more?"

"But you did," Anámn replied. "I am answering the question you asked me first yesterday."

"That is correct, bastard. I did ask you the nature of your powers before I asked the whore. But alas, I am afraid I will not and cannot believe a word you say now, ah. You might say anything to cause the punishment and purification to stop."

"But why? Are you saying that you would've believed me yesterday, even though you didn't hurt me like you are now? And now you don't believe me because I'm hurting? What sense does that make?"

His laugh was as cold as a Damüdan winter. "I cannot make sense to the unenlightened. If you had responded yesterday, I wouldn't have believed you, because truth is only learned through pain and suffering. So even if you were telling me the truth, I can only test that if I torture you."

"But you just said you don't believe me now that you have caused me pain."

"That is why I need the whore's pain to verify the truth," he responded with wicked righteousness and circular logic.

"You don't care what we say," Anámn muttered. Information and "truth" were only byproducts. Ultimately, Galís wished to cause injury. Even though he would be unsatisfied with the lord minister's answer, Anámn spoke and asked anyway. "You don't need to do this... This isn't necessary. So, what's to gain? Why're you doing this?"

"Enmity lives between us. You are my enemy. And my enemy possesses no rights I must respect. The only way for this enmity to cease is to admit that you are wrong and be purified. We need information and you deserve to be punished. Your confession of wrongdoing and spilled blood will make for the proper atonement. Only then can we be truly reconciled. Justice demands no less.

"Besides, the lesser have no reason to complain when the greater display their power, even if it seems unfair. Your inferior mind is incapable of seeing the larger canvass, ah. But do not worry, bastard. Your anguish will cause you to repent and your repentance will allow you to see and believe in the grandest of views."

The soldiers drug a limp and silent Lénü out of the barracks. The dungeon door slammed shut. Anámn leaned against the wall in his cell and cried for hours, pleading with himself and Téza to return to form.

An unknown length of time passed. The dungeon door opened, and Galís breathed in the dank air. "I do so love the smell down here. Don't you, *Sczyphamek Kinesis?*"

He had cracked Lénü'íque. Anámn was not upset with her.

"The whore was not sexually assaulted. I forbid the first round of interrogation to be sexual. But her right arm, hand, and fingers took some time to break.

"You manipulate potential and kinetic energy, ah? You were significantly weakened from your bout with the planet, but she cannot fathom as to why you do not utilize your powers now."

"It took some doing, but the whore confessed that she wished you would have saved her from my interrogation. I think she said this because she thought that was what I wanted to hear and that such a confession would end the punishment. Who knows?"

Galís looked in the direction of Brenko's cell. "Coward, do you know? *Ah?* There are some sex traders who will pay the Damüdan Guild handsomely for your capture. And once I collect their payment, I'll have those perverts executed, after much affliction. Global Initiative has no place for their kind."

The tactician would not give the lord minister the pleasure of hearing his embattled voice, so Galís tapped on the large metal door between he and Anámn. His voice would have been soothing if not for reality.

"Bas*tard*. Ah. This shall be marvelous. Though I have orders to keep you physically unharmed, I cannot help but think of some way to hurt you. So others must be harmed in your stead. I must find surrogates... *I must.* Someone must suffer. My desire is to hurt you. If my people knew about you, they would demand your death. Their demand must be satisfied.

"You bastard Phmmy. Your very happening has dishonored us. You, who dares to rise against a great man like your father. You backwards foreigner, one who has dared to immigrate to my land as if you belong here. You artificial Sczyphamek, one who dares to stand against the wisdom and power of Empress Pre-Eminent and the magnificent Kaz Vincallous Fierce.

"You are in *my* Damüda. And in Damüda, Global Initiative is Law, and laws do not apply when our sovereignty is threatened. My people elected me to do whatever it takes to protect them, and I will.

"I will hurt you Sczyphamek Kinesis. I will find a way. I will make you attack me."

He stepped away from Anámn's cell and left the dungeon.

Democratic or not, Anámn wondered what kind of place Damüda truly was, where the leader of the land openly and personally tortured and murdered his own citizens and foreigners for the sake of national security. Damüda was supposed to represent the ideals of Global Initiative. Yerna's words rang true. Most Damüdans did not care or ignored this portion of Damüdan reality.

"Lénü, are you alright?" Brenko asked.

"I'm sorry Kanoso, Anámn…" she muttered in distress. "I tried."

"Don't worry," Anámn's voice was reassuring, yet inwardly, he was raving mad.

"This is bad, ah?" Tarían added. "I see why you left me in the dark Brenko. Galís knows who has the information he wants, but he doesn't care about obtaining it as much as he cares about punishing us. At least Fencero isn't here. Then we'd really be…"

"Kinesis," a Mystic spoke loudly. "Chant with us, now! Now!"

"Fá'atoño má. Fá'atoño má," they chanted in a moderate tone.

The Sczyphamek felt Téza urging him to join, so he complied. Instantly, he felt the Elemental's vitality regenerate at a spectacular rate.

However, within a minute, Galís opened the dungeon's door and silence fell upon the room.

"I told you useless relics that your superstitious chanting is banned and that you do not control the meaning of the Auría anymore. *We do.*

"Guards, bring me the Líachimian relic."

A door was opened then closed, and the imprisoned heard a body dragged on the floor.

"Charge your weapon," he ordered one his subordinates, "and kill her."

The shot rang out and the remains of her body dispersed to the floor.

"Leave it to rot," he declared. "I have told you. I do not mind if you speak to one another when I am gone. But I forbid chanting. You should not take my mercy for granted."

A slammed door and administered locks signaled Galís' exit.

That bit of revelation cost someone their life. Anámn would not let it go to waste. When the moment came, he knew what to do. The petition behind the Mystic's chant was earnest and true just like in the airlift, even though Lénü and Brenko did not know what they were uttering.

Despite the revelation, Anámn continued to sink into the apparent absurdity of their situation and wondered where the *thing* was. How could something so wrong happen? Why did they go to Damüda in the first place?

Galís blurred the line between sadist and loyalist, protector and despot. Ends, means, and justification… Was there a difference between necessity, just desserts, and sadism when torture was involved?

"Doubt all you want now," a Mystic said. "But be ready to respond, embrace, and trust when the time comes."

CHAPTER TWENTY-THREE: AN ABILITY TO ACHIEVE
OUTCOMES

? 241 OGI

The days were growing warmer and longer. Neztríanis and Timura had journeyed in the Bitzroy Plains for nearly one duration. They found themselves straddling the plains east of the hills that strafed the Gemansu Desert. Considering the circumstances, the duo had made excellent progress on their travel to the Northern Country.

Neztríanis, although reluctant, had drawn in her Elemental quite considerably. It appeared that Vincallous had lost track of them, but the plains were still filled with Blue Rapier soldiers. The témo and Sczyphamek had grown desensitized to the sound of airlifts. When the Myanín did not hear their engines roaring, they thought something was out of the ordinary.

Because the plains possessed very few trees, they only traveled during the nighttime hours. However, the grass was extremely high and dense and small canyons were littered throughout the area, which aided their daytime attempts at camouflage. Neztríanis poured over the Auría daily, obsessing over its contents. And the daughter of Hopha's countenance grew more agitated and aggressive with each passing day. Timura grew concerned for her partner and friend.

Phyxtríalis mumbled in her sleep about finding the true meaning of its pages. She offered Timura a chance to look at its contents, but Timura only obliged her request a few times.

"I can almost distill it," the Sczyphamek said.

"Should it be distilled?" Timura asked pointedly. "Is it meant to be distilled?"

Neztríanis blew air out of her mouth in displeasure, although admittedly, she could not answer the question. However, she believed, *she knew* that something this wonderful should possess a *clear* purpose, an

460

essence. But at least four voices spoke/sang within the text at all times. And sometimes the text sang sweet melodies, while other times, Neztríanis read some of the driest passages of prose. Still on other occasions, the book chronicled the most wonderful of stories of divine and creaturely interaction.

Neztríanis had definitively gleaned two things, however. First, the mystical weapons of Qeauríyx were ancient, and there was no telling what their purpose was. Second, there were *too many* moments when the One with No Name appeared exceptionally *weak* in the course of the planet. And, a deity that was not omnipotent should not be a deity—at least, this is what Neztríanis believed. She must have been interpreting those passages incorrectly.

"Are you saying that this book has multiple meanings? That nothing is central to all the voices?" the daughter of Hopha asked, perplexed.

"Yes. No. Maybe," the témo intimated. "Maybe it has no meaning." Neztríanis Phyxtríalis gasped in anger.

"I do not mean to upset you, Temperature, but it seems that in order to have faith there would have to be such a possibility and risk, or else it is not faith."

Neztríanis had traveled with Timura so long that she began to see her as similar in species and cosmovision. She forgot that témos possessed a different religious and philosophical outlook on the world than nel'asmív. No matter how multivalent and varied a nel'asmív's faith was (or lack thereof), témos still managed a different interpretation.

Neztríanis often wondered if it was their unwillingness to change that caused them so much death and placed them on the brink of extinction.

"Maybe it is your kind's unwillingness to listen," Timura purred, perceiving her partner's thoughts. "Maybe it is neither... or both." Patting her paws on the ground, the témo intimated quietly, "Perhaps you are too near the words to glean the meaning."

"Perhaps." Neztríanis sighed. "The Auría seems to say everything, which is the problem. *Everything* cannot be true."

"It certainly can sing beautifully," Timura replied. "The harmony is at least four parts at all times."

"Yes, I have heard that as well. I wonder if that is why my powers are affected. Singing affects them, anyway; so maybe the added voices aid in the growth of Renzgé and Rai."

"When was the last time you spoke with them?"

"Huh?"

"The last time—when did you last commune with your Elemental?"

"Oh." Neztríanis scratched her head. "I do not recall."

"It seems strange that you would be growing more powerful, yet you have not dialogued with them in quite some time."

"But reading the book *is* talking to them."

"Talking to them *is* talking to them. And you must listen to them as well."

"*I know.*" Her face showed the visible signs of annoyance. Every syllable she spoke became more belligerent.

"Temp—Neztríanis." Not once had Timura called her "Neztríanis." "Neztríanis, I think I should hold that book for awhile. Your mood and qanín have changed since you have obtained it."

"You think the book has changed me, do you not?"

"No. *I think you have changed.* The book has not changed for it does what it exists to do: change. The transformation I am witnessing in you has everything to do with the way you are approaching the Auría, not the Auría as it happens."

Neztríanis looked down at the text and then at her partner. It was hard to lie to herself when a témo and a *friend* made such strong observations.

"Here," she mumbled begrudgingly and handed the Auría to Timura.

The témo grabbed the book with her mouth and set it down between her front paws. Neztríanis could have sworn the book's dimensions grew smaller under the feline's shadow.

"Thank you, Temperature."

The Nez Spiritan breathed slowly and readjusted her thoughts. "Timura, what are we going to do? Do you really think we can keep this up? How much longer will we avoid detection? Our enemies are in every direction."

"We just have to make it to the new moons," Timura replied.

"The new moons? That is in three days. What happens then?"

"I will be able to fly with no possibility of a shadow. I will simply fly below their radar system. If I push myself to the limit, we should be able to make it three quarters of the way there, well beyond their probable calculations for our location."

Neztríanis was impressed every time Timura discussed strategy.

"However, since Vincallous needs me dead and wants you alive, it is hard to guess what he will do or how far he has extended his reach in Nez Spirita. The General Maximum is also here, and I doubt that either of us would survive him, no matter what Vincallous ordered."

"Why do you call him 'Vincallous'?" Neztríanis probed.

Timura was plain. "He does not deserve to be acknowledged as a Sczyphamek. He is a monster, for that is how he sees me."

"You do not think that both of us can match White Scythe's power?"

Timura shook her head resolutely. "No. That blade has destroyed and consumed Awakened Sczyphameks. I have little information concerning the present wielder of the blade, but oracles have been passed down throughout the generations regarding the madness of the Generals."

"If those weapons correspond to the visions we had, then they are made of events that even pre-date the First Sczyphamek. Who knows how powerful they are," Neztríanis said. "And I have heard rumors that the present wielder of White Scythe is extremely masterful. Some say that he is nearly immune to the blade's overriding bloodlust."

"If that is true," Timura rasped, "then he would definitely kill us. White Scythe has a strange ability. The more powerful the enemy it perceives, the more powerful it becomes. And it has consumed countless victims for more than twenty-five hundred cycles. We must keep our distance from it and the wielder."

Neztríanis nodded and looked at the Auría once more before gazing into the sky. Every half hour they would use their own inherent gifts of perception in order to scan for their adversaries. The Myanín had been trading such responsibilities since they escaped capture near the Gemansu Range. It was Nez's turn.

The daughter of Hopha wondered what her detection halo might be now that she no longer possessed the Auría. "Fifty lengths, give or take, that is my limit," she stated, seconds before her Elemental would become visible and possibly detectable for another Sczyphamek.

"That does not give us much space for miscalculation," the témo responded. "When Vincallous captured me, he did so without arming his weapon until the last possible moment. He knows about a témo's sense of hearing and our ability to perceive high frequencies…"

"Which means?" Neztríanis prodded.

"Which means we would not detect our enemy until they crossed your four length radius," the feline answered. "I have become desensitized to their scent, and they have only been attempting high frequency communication in their flying crafts. And we have neither seen nor sensed them in four days…"

Neztríanis observed Timura's mind working in a fashion she had not seen since Bíoske's assault plan on the Triple Skyrises. The creature from the Crossroad Islands growled in a low, discontented tone.

"What is wrong?" Temperature inquired.

"We are surrounded. They are clever."

"Wait- *what*? Did you say *surrounded*?"

"Yes," the témo affirmed. "Four days have passed since we have seen anyone, and we have not heard an aircraft in half a day. How is it possible that after four days you have not felt a single heat signature? They are keeping their distance. The reason why I became desensitized to their smell is because they have surrounded us. If they had moved into your detection zone, this would be understandable."

The témo's ears perked up and her canines protruded. "The randomness of the search is ended. No perception of aircraft. No heat detection. No smell of scent. No hearing sound. It is unlikely that even the most efficient of troops were so silent in apperception. Such an absence can only mean that they are close…

"Chant with me, Neztríanis, but keep your concentration towards me. I wonder if the Auría can heighten my senses as it has your Elemental."

The Myanín chanted with solemn concentration. Timura was right; the

Auría augmented her sense of sound, as well as her other senses. At first, there were so many sounds that Timura became overwhelmed at the massive amount of sensory input.

She relaxed, focused on her heartbeat, and worked her way outside of herself. However, she heard/sensed *it*. It was weak, but it was not hers. A sound wave cycled, bounced off her heart, and headed towards the southeast. Making certain she was correct, the témo double-checked her senses and perceived it again.

"Im... Impossible," Timura rasped and broke her chant.

Using the Auría as a catalyst, Timura brought her innate ability to sense Elemental signatures forward and merged it with her sense of hearing. The miniscule sound wave, directed squarely on the feline's heart, contained an Elemental residue within it.

"Vincallous..." Timura muttered. "How could he become this powerful?"

Following the sonic Elemental back towards its source, the témo's canines emerged, and for the first time, Neztríanis heard the feline hiss. The sonic frequency nearly dissipated into hundreds, *no*, thousands of heartbeats. Losing her focus, Timura could no longer track the Elemental frequency responsible for the sound wave. Neztríanis stopped chanting when she saw Timura's head hang low and close her eyes in an almost defeated manner.

"Kíma," the témo cursed with a grave and resentful tone. "Temperature, let me tell you about the power of an elite Sczyphamek. The kind of power you do not possess, even with this book."

"What happened? What did you sense?" the daughter of Hopha pressed for an answer.

"*Listen to me*," Timura commanded, ignoring her question. "Whether you live or die now depends totally upon your ability to grasp what I am about to tell you."

Neztríanis was silent; her connection with the témo was nearly telepathic. Timura was intimating that they might not escape Sczyphamek Vicious or perhaps the General Maximum.

"Sczyphameks have at least three ways they can use their Elemental," Timura explained. "The first level, while destructive for most nel'asmív, is normally not strong enough to kill a témo, Sczyphamek, or a Wielder. This type of technique, whether for defense or attack, can be activated without incantation. A Sczyphamek can be completely mobile and in the heat of a fight. These techniques are as normal as striking, jumping, or running.

"The second kind of technique is even stronger. It can kill anyone depending on the faith, understanding, and stamina of a Sczyphamek. These displays of power *usually* require incantations and chanting; however, for elite Sczyphameks, it is possible for them to use these techniques without chanting. Also, these summonings involve not only the

Sczyphamek, but a significant manipulation of the properties of Qeauríyx itself. The range of these techniques can be local to regional. Phenplyacin was an instance of this. It is possible for a Sczyphamek to be mobile during these kinds of attacks, but their physical speed and strength will decrease during the wielding of this kind of power.

"The third and most potent level can only be used by elite Sczyphameks. The use of the Elemental is so powerful that most people mistake the instantiations to be weak."

"*Weak?*" Neztríanis interjected.

"Yes, *weak*," Timura replied. "This level is what Vincallous utilized to locate us. He is an elite Zananín of the worst kind."

"I do not understand."

"Vincallous used his Elemental of sound to locate us by sending out a frequency beyond my hearing range. He cannot draw near to us or I will sense him. In order to get around that, he embedded his Elemental signature in a pitch that was imperceptible to my ears. He remembered the distinct sound of my heart and searched for it with his Elemental. Once he found it, he used an echo system to measure our location.

"How he conjured such a technique is beyond me. He has improved his skill in the durations since I last encountered him…"

"I still do not understand," Neztríanis reiterated. "How is that attack— no, it is not even an attack—how is such a skill more powerful than Phenplyacin."

Timura had no more time to teach the Nez Spiritan and ordered sternly, "Locate Kéma, the Cílal."

"How can I do that? She is hundreds if not thousands of lengths from here by now. It is…"

"Impossible for you." Timura finished.

Neztríanis gasped in understanding. If Kéma was over a hundred lengths away she could not find her. She could extend her temperature detection no further even with the Auría. "Kíma. How did he do something like that?"

The témo's growl was disconsolate. "The third level technique requires a type of relationship that is beyond an Awakening. At this point, one's stamina, belief, and understanding must be at heights unknown. A nel'asmív's qanín becomes completely one with the Elemental's. That is to say, Vincallous became and did what sound is and does.

"*Vincallous happened as sound.*

"There was scarcely an Elemental signature because the Elemental became sound. This state requires so much concentration that it is impossible for a Sczyphamek to be mobile. His body is completely defenseless at this moment, which means he is hundreds of lengths from this location."

"If he is far away then why do you think we will be unable to escape?" the Nez Spiritan asked in exasperation and rose from her seated posture.

Why can Timura not see how strong I am now? It is not as though we are being chased by Vincallous. Neither White Scythe nor Blue Rapier soldiers pose us any threat, no matter the number. We can escape.

"When we chanted," Timura explained, "I sensed over a thousand soldiers to our southeast. They are only about sixty lengths away. I lost the echo in the midst of their distinct heart rhythms. There must be more behind those lines. Let's assume the worst; Vincallous amassed enough troops to make sure we do not escape, and the General Maximum is close by. They have not attacked yet, so their lines are not fully fortified. Since Vincallous knows where we are anyway, it does no good for you to ensconce your Elemental."

Neztríanis grunted in vindication.

Placing half of her right paw on the sacred text and cajoling Neztríanis to do the same with her left hand, Timura said, "I will use my hearing and you use your heat detection. Let's find the path of least resistance. The thinner the line, the better chance we have of escaping."

Neztríanis nodded, and as she touched the Auría, she smiled in anticipation of the oncoming battle.

"Fá'atoño má!" they both chanted.

Neztríanis' aura erupted with such force that the ground trembled. So did Timura. The feline looked at her partner with serious reservation. Yet, this was unavoidable. They had to make it to the Northern Country no matter the cost.

"You feel them too?" Neztríanis asked.

"Yes," the témo responded. "Seventy lengths to the northwest, a gap in their formation. Forty soldiers, with no one near their position for five or so lengths."

Suddenly the touch of death emerged within their qanín. Neztríanis shuddered, and Timura recoiled.

The General Maximum. *White Scythe.*

Sixty miles to the east, they felt the blade's bloodlust. The scythe was starving for and salivating over an Elemental encounter. It had not tasted such sweetness in millennia. It had not ripped, mangled, masticated, and digested témoic flesh and qanín in spans.

"Oh… staxis!" Neztríanis stammered, afraid for her life. "We must leave now. If Vincallous is far away, that means he cannot reach this area for awhile. We should be able to outrun the General Maximum."

The same feeling Timura felt on the rocky cliffs of Mt. Xarkim now crept back into her heart. A terrible danger approached, and this time she was certain. The danger was *Neztríanis.*

The daughter of Hopha was uncharacteristically erratic. One moment she was filled with arrogance and ready to fight. The next minute she was cowering in fear. If threatened, there was no guessing the measure of her response.

Grabbing the Auría and placing it in her shoulderpack, the Sczyphamek called Temperature glanced Timura's way. Her face was now steadfast. "We must get this book to Sunrise Mountain. This is all that matters now." Timura had no time to argue and nodded. No sooner had they set out, the Myanín sensed four aircraft barreling towards their position. The attack order must have been given at the sight of Temperature's aura. There was no shelter or cover from their aerial adversaries. Their only chance was to make it to the enemy line before the airlifts dropped their ordinance on them. The témo and Sczyphamek broke out in a full-fledged flight, yet stayed low to the ground, nearing speeds of three hundred lengths an hour. The entire time Neztríanis chanted to herself and petitioned her Elemental, readying her qanín for battle. They were minutes away from the enemy lines.

***

Galís was not one to mince words or time. Two days later, at dusk, Anámn, Brenko, Lénü, Tarían, and the remaining Mystics were taken out of their cells and escorted up the long steps of the castle by the Interror. They had not seen each other since Tarían's torture.

Lénü's right eye was black and swollen shut. Her right arm was fractured in multiple places. Every movement made her wince. Her mouth was puffed up, and a large bruise originated near her clavicle. Her injuries were so severe that her scar had become nearly invisible.

The four remaining Mystics were in even worse shape. The rags they wore no longer fit their emaciated frames adequately. They gazed upon the Sczyphamek with sunken eyes. And yet, they walked with a strength that reminded Anámn of Malchían.

Tarían hunched over. His scalp was burned, with patches of hair spattered across his head. His back was better left to imagination.

When Brenko saw his daughter, he nearly lost his wits, but he held his ire. He knew that Galís would soon pay. Anámn and the Mystics would put an end to him. During the brief moment they chanted and prayed, Brenko felt Anámn's inner aura—although he was uncertain how. Anámn was too close to Téza to notice, but the Sczyphamek's Elemental had grown at least ten to fifteen times its prior capacity. That was undoubtedly one of the reasons his recuperation had been so slow and complicated.

"Your na'ísa[1] is almost stabilized," one of the Mystics whispered to Anámn, as they walked up the staircase.

"Na'ísa?" Anámn asked. "What's that?"

"It means 'sustained force' in the Ancient Tongue. You probably think of it as your Elemental's stamina. This is incorrect. It is the meeting place between you, your physical constitution, your Elemental, your commitment, Qeauríyx, and the One with No Name, or in Its absence,

---

[1] Na'ísa (nah-*ee*-sah)

your greatest concern. At least, that is how it is described in the Keotagosdian Fragments. A Nez Spiritan Mystic once told me something similar, yet a bit different. Regardless, your equilibrium has almost returned. You are nearly ready."

Anámn nodded. If they chanted again, Sczyphamek Kinesis would be completely healed.

"Do not act out of vengeance, Kylanín. It will only limit your potential."

Anámn was a solemn kind of reticent. But, the Mystic was perceptive. Matriester wanted to kill Galís.

"Galís is weak, Kylanín. It is easy to kill and hurt those who are less powerful than you."

Kinesis' facial expression changed. He remembered the encounter with his father and the encounter with that *thing* when he was in the Valley of the Ancestors.

"Remember, happenings are rarely what they seem to be and do. But they are what they are and do what they do. Certainty and trust are not the same thing." The Mystic offered no other words.

Soon, they were led back into Galís' main chamber, where a large contraption and a host of Interror lay in wait.

"Wha- what is that?" Anámn could not stop himself from speaking.

Galís laughed in amusement. "Don't worry, bastard. I do not mind you voicing such an obvious question. Even as imbecilic as you certainly are, only a mind like the coward's and mine can truly comprehend such genius. Is that not correct, coward father of the whore?"

"It's a modified gallows, Anámn." Brenko ignored Galís and shook his head in disbelief. "It's a torture device for all of us, especially you."

In front of them was a large, raised platform that had a beam of reinforced wood hanging above it. On the platform were seven wooden, cross-shaped beams... *Balancing beams...* Brenko's heart faltered. He doubted Anámn could save them or himself from such a device.

"You are right," Galís replied. "It took me hours to conceive of this. My servants and I slaved two days and nights transforming this gallows into a torture rack..."

Noticing Anámn's posture and disposition, Galís clapped his hands twice. Immediately, Interror soldiers swooped upon all those in Anámn's company, except him, and placed the barrels of their energy rifles at the heads of his compatriots.

"*You are stronger than you were two days ago... Good...* But, if you make any movement, or if the hum of those rifles become silent, my soldiers will execute whomever they can."

Anámn took not a single step. He was unable to disarm all the weapons at once. Even though Téza was almost restored, his connection with potential and kinetic energy was still slightly vitiated. He was certain the connection would completely return once he and the Mystics chanted, but not until then.

But if the Mystics are gonna be killed if they start chanting, how can I be sure that me and Téza are gonna be back to normal any time soon? Anámn asked himself. *I can't risk them dying because of me...*

Anámn chanted silently and surveyed the technical dimensions of the torture device. Showing no signs of resistance, Matriester was directed to sit down and watch, while his friends and the sages were placed on their own respective wooden balancing beam. Nooses were tied around their necks, and their hands were bound behind their backs. The balancing beams were the amalgam of vertical and horizontal bars of wood. The bars were taut and sturdy, yet moveable.

Anámn soon realized why.

A cord entered every balance beam, through a hole in the middle of the vertical and horizontal bar's intersection. The cord allowed both the vertical and horizontal beams to move. Satchels containing unidentified substances hung on the cord between each cross-like balancing beam. The satchels were of equal spacing and weight. Anámn observed the nooses, and a similar configuration was also in operation. Each noose had its own cord and weight system as well as a shared system with the other nooses. Just like the balancing beam weights, reinforced steel cords connected and distributed the weight and energy. On top of this, each balance beam appeared to be capable of swiveling, through the use of a pulley system underneath the platform.

If any of the weights were disrupted on any of the balance beams, his comrades would have to compensate, because the beams would tilt. Tilting would also cause the nooses and the weights connected to them to move and place stress around the necks of his friends.

However, the disruption did not have to start with the balance beam. It might start with the nooses or the pulleys or the weights on the nooses. *And* there was one small, but exceptional detail about the modified gallows Anámn almost missed. The seven stilts that held up the platform could be raised and lowered at will, via hydraulic pumps, which would allow the entire platform to shift and tilt up, down, or diagonally.

Balance, weights, movement, hydraulics... The torture rack was a complex energy system. It *was* a torture device for *Sczyphamek* Kinesis.

Kinesis and his friends had taken in no food since they were captured, and were certain to be weak. The Mystics could barely carry their own weight. *Every one of them* would stand on the balance beam according to their *own* constitution. Because of Tarían's burned back, he was unable to stand completely upright; therefore, his balancing stance—if he could even manage one—would be different from Lénü, whose right arm, hand, and fingers were broken. The very fact that they bound her hands already placed her in considerable pain, and she would undoubtedly stand in a way as to minimize the discomfort. In short, beyond the mechanical and manipulative sources of potential instability, Sczyphamek Kinesis would have to contend with the imperfections and constant shifting of nel'asmív.

This test was in a different stratosphere than flying across the volcanic ridge. Anámn used very little nuance and control when he wielded his power back then. He relieved *all* of a cinder's energy or blasted an *entire* rock to bits. He could not do the same with the weights. If he removed all of a particular weight's potential or kinetic energy then more stress would be added to the system. So many weights, so many pulleys, so many stilts, so many cords, so many nel'asmív…

Anámn bit his lip. His qanín did not lie. He did not possess the knowledge and command necessary to simultaneously adjust and redirect every emanation of constitutive energy from the mechanical/existential torture device.

Sweat beads of nervousness and a gulp of unwanted anticipation signaled the Phmquedrian's distress. Anámn muttered inaudible curses upon himself and the lord minister.

"You understand, do you not?" Galís asked. "You will have to balance all of this in order to save your friends."

I don't think… I can't do this, he thought.

The Mystics gazed at the Sczyphamek and nodded. Brenko glanced away and then back at the Phmquedrian. Lénü could not bring herself to look in Anámn's direction. She did not want to add any unnecessary anguish to the son of ju Xaníz. Tarían grimaced and a scowl remained etched on his face. Anámn took a deep breath and tried to relax.

The nooses were fitted and tightened around his comrades' neck. Behind them, seven Interror soldiers pointed their energy rifles at the prisoners' kneecaps.

"I can't wield my powers if I don't chant," Anámn stated plainly. "Will I be penalized for that?"

"I will allow this concession," Galís answered.

"Will you penalize my friends and the Mystics if they do whatever they can to keep their balance?"

"No. Their penalty will be their death for opposing me and for believing that a wretch like you would ever be able to save them."

"I have one more question," Anámn prompted.

"What is it?"

"How long am I supposed to keep this balanced?"

"You are incapable of doing so, unawakened Sczyphamek. But if I must offer an answer, I would say until I feel you have suffered enough."

Anámn understood all too well. Galís would never let his friends go, and the torture would not stop until all of them died of asphyxiation.

"Fá'atoño má. Fá'atoño má. Fá'atoño má," the Mystics commenced chanting.

Galís stared at the Mystics with a hateful wrath that burned white and heavy. However, he stayed true to his word and did not harm them. Harm was the gallows' job. The lord minister gave the order, and the weight, which contained water, between Lénü and Brenko's balance beam was stabbed with a knife. Water dripped out slowly but surely. Anámn sensed the beams shifting due to the loss of weight.

In a loud, resolute voice, Anámn recited the ancient phrase himself. At first, a green haze flickered discordantly around Kinesis, but by his third repetition his aura blossomed in a flash of power and thickness. The Elemental warrior kept the force of the emanation from reaching the platform, which already signaled a greater control in exerting his power.

Galís became anxious, while the Interror soldiers unconsciously added distance between the Sczyphamek and them. The Mystics and his friends shifted on the beams, in order to attempt to right themselves. If Anámn was a telekinetic, he could have simply lifted his friends off the balance beams so that the nooses would not suffocate them, nor would they have to balance themselves. But, as he learned in the forests of northern Phmquedria, telekinesis was not his power. He could not "think" and make something move with his mind or use his brainpower to "make" kinetic energy. Potential energy was not in nor did it solely revolve around his mind.

He and Téza were a Sczyphamek whose ability was the manipulation of the dynamic relationship between potential and kinetic energy. Their location was everywhere. And once the torture rack's energy system was put in motion, Anámn could not simply exert his will as if he was some sort of outside, omnipotent force. Even if he lifted his comrades with controlled bursts of kinetic energy, he would probably need more energy than the energy system allowed. And if he made one mistake, their deaths would be assured.

"E müz keh fíp Téza má," Kinesis sang in a mezzo forte volume. In response, a Mystic sang the same phrase, but using different notes, which created a beautiful harmony.

As much as he could without creating a physical backlash, the Sczyphamek robbed the kinetic energy of the water droplets falling from the punctured bag, due to force of gravity. The water began to drip in a fashion that almost made it appear to be falling like a weightless feather. Converting half of the water's energy into potential energy and storing it, Kinesis transferred the other half of the water's kinetic energy into a sustained force that upheld the initial disruption between Lénü and Brenko's balancing beams. He was unable to use all of the energy because Brenko and Lénü had already shifted their weight to compensate for the loss of water, adding their own energy to the system.

One by one, Anámn searched the potential energy of his fellow prisoners. The Mystics were by far the weakest. Tarían and Lénü were nearly the same, and Brenko, who had hitherto remained physically unscathed, was the strongest. Anámn was shocked that he was now able to discern and interpret the potential energy of nel'asmív, of living creatures. His perception of kinetic and potential energy had mostly remained on the level of mechanical interaction, not the possibility or impossibility of inaction or action.

Galís signaled one of his subordinates at the bottom of the platform. In an instant, the platform shifted and declined to the back-left, which caused the tortured to instinctively lean forward-right. One of the Mystics lost her footing and nearly fell from the balancing beam. In response, Anámn robbed the woman of the force that would have killed her, and she was able to right herself with minimal use of energy. She responded by chanting louder and with more conviction. In turn, the Mystic, who spoke with Anámn, hummed and sang, with august precision and depth, the notes that corresponded to the phrase, "E müz keh fíp Téza má."

Anámn sensed both he and Téza's growth. The stature, grace, and will of the venerable Mystics nearly brought green tears to his face. Sczyphamek Kinesis moved his energy-gathering outside the walls of the castle and into the surrounding area. The wind was blowing, river water was running, people were walking, and an auto's engine was burning fuel... Never had the Phmquedrian Sczyphamek perceived, with such penetrating depth and clarity, the various complexities of energy. He nearly fainted from all of the information and was forced to pull back from the excavation. But, he was no longer scratching the surface. Yet there was so much he did not understand.

Once Galís saw that Anámn could sustain two mechanical energies and that nary a prisoner had yet suffered injury or death, he gave *the* order. Complying with the lord minister's bidding, the soldiers moved to the various weights and pulleys and manipulated the entire system.

One of the weights was barely sliced and sand sifted out of it. Another sack was ripped, and rocks spilled out. A soldier pulled the pulley controlling the balance beam Tarían was standing on, swiveling the hustler's beam to the left and forcing Tarían to compensate. Galís' subordinates also began to shift the platform's stilts ever so subtlety.

Anámn was overwhelmed and was forced to triage. He kept Tarían from hanging himself by robbing the energy of the falling rocks and applying a kinetic force to Tarían's back, which allowed him to stay upright. However, this move had the unintended consequence of placing new energy in the system, energy that caused the weight between Tarían and a Mystic's beam to bob up and down, destabilizing both of their beams.

Meanwhile, Lénü's noose weight was suddenly severed from the noose, which nearly sent her flying forward and off the beam. Anámn siphoned the kinetic energy of the falling weight, converted some of the potential energy he had been gathering, and applied both to keep Lénü from dying. Yet, this readjustment caused the cord between she an Brenko to jostle and twist. Brenko righted himself in a way to keep himself from strangling and to minimize the stress on Anámn.

Sweat gushed from the Sczyphamek's forehead. His inability to grasp all the nuances of the erratic system nearly caused him to succumb to the amount of energy, pressure, and information he was handling. The Mystics chanted to the best of their ability and kept Kinesis afloat, but the outcome became inevitable. Achieving a semi-stable system was beyond his present ability.

The Mystic, who was chanting the loudest, gazed keenly at Anámn. The Phmquedrian runaway grew weaker by the moment, and soon they would all die. Anámn's na'ísa, though potent, continued destabilize under the immense knowledge gap between Téza and Anámn. From the moment the Mystic saw the modified gallows, he, like Brenko, knew the type of power Galís required of Kinesis was beyond the Sczyphamek's present ability.

Anámn had not Awakened. Therefore, he naturally lacked a comprehensive understanding of his Elemental. He was compensating for that loss of power with his faith and na'ísa, and because the Mystics were chanting with him. However, the young man neared his limit with those two aspects of his power.

Examining his fellow prisoners, the Mystic made up his mind to commit suicide. He could think of no other solution. If Anámn saw Brenko or Lénü die, he would probably lose his wits and everyone would perish along with them. But if the Mystic sacrificed himself, he would be one less variable. Anámn needed more constants and fewer variables. Smiling at the Sczyphamek called Kinesis, the Mystic stepped off the balancing beam and into asphyxiation.

Anámn's eyes closed in horror. Galís clapped his hands with excitement. Brenko, while flabbergasted, focused on his own life and tried his best to keep his balance. He intuited the Mystic's intentions. Anámn would not be able to handle either he or Lénü's death.

Although Brenko told Anámn to let him die, Galís figured out that Brenko had given Anámn that command by way of Lénü's torture. Galís' cleverness was terrifying. If Lénü and Brenko died because Anámn could not or did not act, the Phmquedrian might have been able to move on from the loss eventually, since he would have been unable to help or he was under strict, well-meaning orders from Brenko. However, if Brenko and Lénü perished now, it would be *in spite of* Anámn's acting, trying, and suffering.

"You are a sadistic piece of kíma," Brenko said to Galís. The lord minister was trying to recreate a small-scale, yet no less damaging, Phenplyacin for Anámn. And Brenko was forced to participate. If the tactician absconded, his death would probably damn Anámn to a loss of purpose as much as Phenplyacin damned him. And just because the tactician found existence meaningless, he did not wish the disposition on anyone else.

Because of the Mystic's suicide, Anámn lost some of his power, although the loss of a nel'asmív did help him navigate the energy distribution a bit easier. His mind raced to find a solution to their torture. In the midst of his analysis, he lost concentration and heard a sickening snap. Another Mystic had lost her balance, and without Anámn's assistance, she fell victim to strangulation.

"Damn it, Galís!" Anámn yelled. "Stop this… you know I can't…"

Galís did not turn around to face Anámn, but replied, "Bastard, do not interrupt me. I am savoring these deaths at your weak expense."

Téza was tiring and Anámn was beyond fatigue. Both approached the point of no return. They were nearly spent of the energy required to keep the system from claiming the lives of his friends, *and* the Sczyphamek was just about depleted of the energy it would take to escape.

Brenko told me that if I use my power to escape it's gotta be so ridiculous that a cléth like Galís won't try to follow us… And he said to let him and Lénü die if it came to this…

But this is different. I can't… I can't let them die. I can't let them fall and die in front of me…

Fall… Buckle… Fold… Collapse… Collapse…

That's it.

Though unable to sustain the system, he could try to collapse it. He could rob the entire system of its potential energy and kinetic energy. This was dangerous and complicated, but Anámn remembered Yerna telling he and Lénü that it was easier to destroy something than to create and sustain. The Mystic told Anámn something similar; the verification, yet *limitation,* of the seemingly powerful was their ability and predilection to raze something weaker than they. Anámn realized that the oncoming moments would *seem* powerful, but in truth, the forthcoming display would only expose how weak he was. It was a brazen, lesser emanation of power that would momentarily save his friends' lives. Even if he was successful, he would be foolish to believe he had reached a new level of possibility. It was only because he recognized such folly that the possibility presented itself.

"*Fá'atoño má,*" Anámn sang with intention, determination, and defiance. The chant alone caused Galís to turn around.

Kinesis crooned a melody of melancholy fierceness, "*É müz keh fíp Téza má.*"

The stilts, the weights, the beams, the nooses, the platform, the pulleys—any mechanical object that exerted energy in the torture device— Anámn located the energy needed to keep the structure from collapsing and completely robbed all of those components of their energy. The wood and metal could no longer be held together in tension, for Anámn intentionally severed—in one act consisting of a hundred acts—all of the energy required to maintain the bonds of the device. The feat took all of Anámn's concentration, but he was aided by the fact he had been in dialogue with the gallows' energy for nearly twenty minutes.

Wood cracked, nooses snapped, metal tore, pulleys dismembered, and in one crashing cacophony, the platform imploded.

But that was not all.

Taking and converting all of the potential energy that Anámn collected from the gallows and adding it to the potential energy he had already stored within him, as well as stealing some of the energy emitted when the gallows collapsed (which caused his compatriots, the Interror, and the splintering gallows to fall slower)—Sczyphamek Kinesis created a violent, kinetic discharge, an explosion of force, that erupted from the immediate boundary of the imploded structure, in all directions.

In an apparitional instant, a momentary green hemisphere emerged around the rack and discharged a savage, incombustible pulse throughout the chamber. The soldiers and Galís were violently thrown into the air, and the walls and ceiling of the great hall were obliterated against the force of the blast. The lord minister was slammed against a statue and broke it in half.

Anámn's aura grew thick and his Elemental absorbed and recycled the fiery-less explosive force that directly came in his direction. The Phmquedrian stood up and raced to the fallen structure and dug the prisoners out, snapping their chains when he unearthed one. That a feat bought him a few minutes of time, and within a minute or so, he had freed his friends and the Mystics. Brenko was freed first and gathered energy rifles from the incapacitated Interror. Astonishingly, no one died from Anámn's attack, although some of his adversaries were critically injured.

The tactician glanced at Anámn and then at the chamber, which would soon be filled with Interror. "I hope you know what you're doing."

"You remember how to get to the airfield?" Anámn asked.

"Yes," Brenko responded. His memory was photographic.

"Good," the Sczyphamek replied. "Everybody, come close. Mystics if you can, please chant with me."

Although weakened, the remaining two Mystics nodded. And Tarían, Lénü, and Brenko huddled close to Anámn. The Sczyphamek's green aura flashed and turned into an orb that levitated and engulfed his comrades.

Amidst stone and wood, a woozy Galís was crouched on all fours and attempted to stand.

Staring down at his torturer, Kinesis growled, "If you follow me, I will kill you and whoever you send.

"Téza haito!" Anámn chanted without realizing he had learned a new incantation.

Forthwith, the sphere raced out of the chamber, creating a kinetic backlash so awesome that the castle itself began to cave in. Galís and those who could do so escaped from the disintegrating palace, while Kinesis, under the direction of Brenko headed towards the airfield. Anámn was exhausted, but he and Téza defied the obvious.

Sirens sounded as the escapees headed towards Galís' personal skyport. Once they landed, Anámn created energy bursts, without chanting, that destroyed every airlift in the field, with the exception of one. He also enlarged his aura so vociferously that those on patrol cowered in fear and ran away. For the first time in their lives, a Sczyphamek was *not* on their side.

"Anámn..." Brenko started.

"You can get them to southeastern Damüda," Anámn stated.

"We're gonna have to fly over Glacier Bay," Brenko replied. "No one flies over it this time of cycle because of the weather, but if we got through the volcanic line..."

Lénü was filled with amazement, confusion, and sadness. "Anámn."

"I'm sorry Lénü; we're out of time." Anámn breathed hard and almost fainted. "You have to go with your father." Gazing at Lénü'íque, Matriester embraced and kissed her on the forehead. Then he turned to Brenko. "I don't think you can help with what needs to happen next, and you're the only one who can fly and is in any condition to do so. The plane that's left had the most potential energy; I figured that meant that it had the most fuel and the best fuel management."

Brenko translated the Sczyphamek's statement and shook his head. Anámn determined the most potential energy for an *airplane*. In other words, he had advanced enough in his powers to discern and differentiate potential energies as they related to particular happenings. He ascertained that an airlift's potential for sustained flight was not determined by fuel alone. Fuel economy was equally important. This meant that at an intuitive level, Anámn was now able to sense the potential energy generated by the interconnected parts of engines, the weight of the lift, etc...

Kíma, Kinesis... Brenko thought. *What you have the* potential *to become....* *Staxis...* Turning to the Mystics, Lénü, and Tarían, the tactician stated, "Let's go."

"Give those bastards Qalfocx," Tarían grimaced and boarded the craft.

One of the Mystics went aboard the airlift, but the other did not move. "I am staying with you, Kinesis," he said.

"I know," Anámn nodded and glanced at Lénü who somberly boarded the lift. "Lénü, don't let Brenko stay here. Go to Líachim."

"Aye," she nodded. "Goodbye, Anámn."

Anámn and the Mystic backed away from the airlift as its engines engaged. The Sczyphamek detected no aircrafts within a twenty-length radius of the skyport. If Brenko could pilot them safely to that body of water, they would be free from hostile aircraft but not from the inclement conditions. The tactician guided the lift to a uneventful takeoff and headed due east.

As fires raged around him, Anámn extinguished all of them, converting their energy into his own potential. The Mystic drew close to Kinesis, hopped on his back, held on to his torso, and chanted. Anámn's power swelled ominously.

Ascending above the skyport they both chanted simultaneously, "É müz keh fíp Téza má."

Outstretching both hands, Anámn let out a flash of black and green energy that decimated the skyport's runways. Making sure that his aura was visible in the nighttime sky, the Sczyphamek's green illumination illuminated the horizon.

"Where are we going, Malchían?" Anámn asked the Mystic, for even though the man's features were different, the runaway from Euhilv always remembered the elder's kinetic signature or smell.

He realized the sage's identity the moment he finally and completely realized the paradox of power, the "obstacle" Malchían had told him about so many durations ago. True to his word, Malchían said he would not see Anámn until he confronted it. He met him in the jungles of Phmquedria after his confrontation with his father, when he first puzzled over the paradox. And he met him now that he realized it in all its mindboggling complexity.

The torture system completely shattered Anámn's obsession with brute omnipotence, and in so doing, he gained an even greater power. Brute omnipotence was too clumsy to handle and relate to the nuances and intricacies of indeterminate systems of energy in a sustainable way. His na'ísa, embrace, and will would have remained weak as long as he held omnipotence as his god.

"North," the Mystic answered. "Head out west first for a few lengths. Stay visible until you land, then we will go north."

"Will we survive this?" Anámn asked.

"I don't know that answer any more than you do," the old one responded.

The man was not lying. Malchían gambled that Anámn would realize the paradox while he was balancing on the gallows. The prior torture was not an act. Anámn felt the man's potential energy. He was not faking. Malchían almost died in the heat of Galís' torture and Anámn's inability, just like the other two Mystics.

The tears finally fell from his eyes. Anámn wrestled with the death of the Mystics. Even though he did not kill them, he felt responsible for their deaths. The more Anámn tried not to cry, the more he sobbed. Malchían, nearly comatose, said nothing. The suffering Anámn now encountered could not be rationalized away or made redemptive, not at the expense of the life and torture of their friends.

In a streak of dark green, the Sczyphamek who happened as Kinesis and a transfigured Malchían flew due west.

***

The Sczyphamek called Temperature and Timura the témo, the Myanín, approached the enemy lines at an intimidating velocity. The Blue Rapier soldiers they would soon encounter were almost caught by surprise. However, Neztríanis' aura was so fluorescent that the troops of Feolenz readied themselves with little time to spare. Within seconds of the Myanín setting their sights upon them, energy bursts blanketed the horizon.

Neztríanis lifted her head to the sky and said, "Timura."

"Understood," the témo responded, increased her altitude, and drew some of the fire.

"*Zí mányx que Rai,*" the daughter of Hopha sang.

Without the use of her hands, the Sczyphamek created a large, dense ice shield that emerged directly in front of the Blue Rapier soldiers. The shield was nearly half a length wide. The troops would have to flank the structure or cycle their energy cells to destroy it, granting the Myanín some time.

Yet, before she could make her next move, Neztríanis felt the heat from large, guided projectiles. She could outrun them, but Neztríanis was tired of running, especially when she knew how strong she was. If she displayed a violent eruption of her power, perhaps the agents of Global Initiative would be hesitant to follow them.

No...

Her weariness ran much deeper. The very fact that Neztríanis was being attacked by her adversaries when it was clear that the Auría had *chosen* her—this unassailable and uncontestable *fact* disgusted and annoyed the Nez Spiritan to no end.

I saw the First in all her glory!

Yet these were the same people who had taken over her land, dominated her people, and continuously mocked her culture and religion. And even when the most sacred of texts had validated *her* cause, Global Initiative still had the *audacity* to project its self-righteous, imperial arrogance upon her, as if their wicked ideals had actually been blessed by the First.

Why were they so obstinate? Why were they blind to the truth? They truly were the *savage animals* she had always believed them to be. Why should she withdraw when Vincallous was so far away?

She stopped her flight towards the enemy lines. Neztríanis faced the southeast, in the direction of the aircraft and the missiles, and whispered vexingly and recurrently, "Mona fla Renzgé ná."

She had no way of detecting the projectiles' payload, but she anticipated the worst. She did not think Blue Rapier would bomb their own soldiers. However, they might be desperate. So she decided to incinerate the missiles while they were still in the air. Concentrating, Neztríanis drew the Auría out of her shoulderpack and clutched it tightly. Locating the projectiles with her Elemental, the woman discharged an intense swath of blue flame in their direction, but she did not intimate this to Timura.

When the témo felt Neztríanis' aura swell, the feline turned around in mid-flight. The Myanín had discussed their strategy; they were supposed to barrel through enemy lines at an excessive speed and sustain their flight for at least two hours. Neztríanis was to make an ice shield so that the Rapier soldiers would be forced to flank or fully discharge their weapons. If they flanked, Neztríanis would melt the middle of the ice shield and the duo would pass through at their most blazing speed. If the troops discharged their weapons, then the Myanín would flank their position. They were not to deal with aircraft or an aircraft's weaponry until they had crossed that first hurdle. The less variegated their enemies were, the greater chance they would be successful.

Timura had no time to warn Neztríanis of the obvious. Just because the Sczyphamek was immune from the explosion's heat, that did not mean that she was impervious to the blast's kinetic expulsion. The témo dived towards the ground, since she would be hurled there anyway. Hopefully, she would minimize injury by doing so. Neztríanis, on the other hand, would take the brunt of the backlash.

What is she thinking? Timura thought.

In an instant, the sky flared in a horrible combustion and blinded any onlookers. The pilots of the aircrafts did not expect Neztríanis' attack and were too close to the explosion. All four lifts and pilots were obliterated in the fireball. Temperature, who had no time to react, ensconced herself in her aura, held the Auría ever tighter, and was hurled towards her ice shield at a cataclysmic velocity one length away.

Slamming and shattering the ice structure, the Sczyphamek hit the earth and created a small indentation on the surface. Timura reached the ground before the shockwave arrived at her position. The témo was able to absorb most of the blast with little to no damage. She felt no relief. Their troubles had only begun. It was imperative that she wrest the Auría from the clutches of her partner.

As soon as Neztríanis stood up, she felt forty guns trained at her position, *her entire position.* She was surrounded. Some Rapier soldiers aimed in the air, some at her flanks, and others directly at her. She was slightly injured, but her Elemental aura protected her from the brunt of the fall. The cells of every energy rifle were cycled to full power.

Apparently, the soldiers had chosen to destroy the ice shield. Now, they could destroy her.

The Ease of Calamity

Neztríanis encountered the Auría.

The book sang and recorded the events in its pages. The experience felt similar to her vision in the caves of the Infinite Circle, *except this story was about her.* The five-part harmony was remorseful, guilt-ridden, and tragic. Was it because the flame that Neztríanis conjured was so white hot, that even when the Rapiers' guns fired at full discharge, the energy bursts were negated and consumed by a heat twenty times greater?

The Elemental flare touched the skin of an older female Blue Rapier soldier, the commanding officer of the unit. She hailed from Bryce. A mother of three children, she had not seen her family in a cycle. She was miserably homesick. Neztríanis saw a tear emerge from her green, Brycian eyes. The tear evaporated before it fell, and her iris became smoke and ash. What was her name?

Did Neztríanis now perceive history and emotion in the manner by which she encountered Anplo? She was both witness and participant in this story. The two perspectives shattered her perspective and made the truth of this event real, inescapable, and indisputable. Time slowed, and the merging of Neztríanis' Elemental with the Auría made her take in the moment's entirety with painstaking clarity. As her first victim disintegrated into cinders—why could she not stop herself?—the blaze grew and claimed twenty more lives. Their lives were revealed to the consciousness of Neztríanis Phyxtríalis.

The twenty-second victim's name was Hyalál[1] from Civix Setrin, Tannódin. His family had served Tannódin for generations. He tried to scream but there was no more air to make a sound. The immediate atmosphere was devoid of life, save Neztríanis. The fire created its own wind, and it made Hyalál's long, dark brown hair gravitate towards the Sczyphamek. Each individual follicle became like a lit fuse, clamoring its way back to the main charge—his face. He was unable to exert audible horrification at such a nightmarish end. His eyes grew fearful and resigned. His mouth erupted in a silent scream. Beholding his contorted face, a face that became like the opening of a volcano, Neztríanis shuddered.

"What am I doing?" the daughter of Hopha asked herself, while time and space continued to move at a glacier's pace. "What was I thinking?"

Each millisecond felt like half an hour to the Sczyphamek. The thirty-fifth soldier to perish was from Damüda. He had idolized Kaz Vincallous his entire life. In his heart, he hated this Sczyphamek whom he only knew for a mere five seconds.

It is easy for Sczyphameks to kill.

Namí's words rang in Neztríanis' consciousness deeply. The Nez Spiritan did not bother to think before the conflagration began. The Auría would record this moment for all posterity: The moment when Sczyphamek Temperature wiped forty nel'asmív off the face of the planet in an instant. Hanging her head in shame, even as the bodies burned around her, the woman knew that she would now be counted in the ranks of Pre-Eminent and Vicious.

Millions, thousands, hundreds, or tens… Did it matter?

The remorse was *her* remorse. The guilt was *her* guilt. The tragedy was *her* tragedy. The Auría continued to chronicle in poetic verse, musical expression, historical reflection, and prose the power belonging to the Sczyphamek—a Kylanín(?) of *justice*.

Bíoske told her that she would *have* to kill before this was over. But that

---

[1] Hyalál (hahy-uh-*lahl*)

was no justification. She *did not have to kill* these people. Her life was not in danger; her mission was not overtly jeopardized. They could have been incapacitated; they could have—the thirty-ninth soldier's name was Zelá, a Tannódin'é woman from Loama Setrin, the farming landmass of Tannódin. She was secretly in love with a Nez Spiritan named Nezalé... Neztríanis cried... "Nezalé" meant "day of peace" in the Ancient Tongue... the same Ancient Tongue that recorded this act... Zelá did not want to fight for Blue Rapier anymore and had serious doubts concerning Global Initiative. Her experience with Nezalé opened her to a new point of view. So when the searing flames consumed her, she felt sorry for Neztríanis and forgave the Nez Spiritan Sczyphamek of the cyclical violence to which they were both ensnared.

Fenz was from Damüda. Neztríanis' capture was his first mission in the field. His squad placed him in the rear because he had the least experience and his comrades wanted to protect him from harm or becoming a liability.

He was the only one who had enough time to react. But he was frozen in the midst of the inferno.

His ankles felt cold and numb.

Gazing down, he saw a white, crystalline structure wrapped around his feet... the coldest ice the native of northern Damüda had ever felt.

Inexorable.

The blaze resembled Zénan in the middle of the summer.

Stretching out his hand, Fenz instinctively tried to protect himself. His fingertips flaked and crumbled. His blood soon wafted like dust. His metacarpals emerged. The sleeves of his jacket incinerated instantaneously. The fire crept up his arms and towards his trunk. The ice, like his face, melted, and the boiling water stung and smoldered his ankles and feet.

1) Fenz fell to the ground.

2) It was only a matter of milliseconds until Fenz combusted.

3) Fenz was sixteen cycles old.

4) Fenz lied about his age to join the military as a way out of an abusive household.

5) The cremated Blue Rapier squad was the only family Fenz possessed.

How the five-part harmony expressed such tragedy with such acoustic precision!

But compared to the total pages of the sacred text, this story was but an afterthought. Would the scandal of this moment be understood? There was no context given by which to understand her actions. Did the Auría record the stories of the victims?

The daughter of Hopha wept. The Auría's song-filled codification came to a close. Her folly and guilt in this death-dealing calamity were apparent, but what saddened her most deeply was that she knew this moment of tragedy might be made into a moment of triumph...

A triumphant display of newfound power...

...if this incident found its way into the Fragments...

...it was not necessary for an act of indiscriminate violence to be interpreted in such a victorious manner.

No; it was not necessary, but was it inevitable nonetheless?

***

Timura saw nothing except a blinding flash of light. She was two lengths away from Neztríanis' position, but when she felt the power of the Sczyphamek's Elemental, Timura retreated another length as a precautionary measure.

The témo's heart sank. Neztríanis lost her innocence much faster than the feline predicted. Regardless of the Sczyphamek's newfound disposition, the Nez Spiritan did not have the qanín for massive life-taking.

The flash only lasted for ten seconds before it suddenly disappeared. Once Timura regained her focus, she beheld a large, smoldering area. Though three lengths away, she still heard the wailing of Neztríanis. The témo reluctantly yet resolutely trotted to her partner's position. Temperature was surrounded by piles of ash amongst a charred terra.

Neztríanis shook her head. The tears kept falling. Her nose dripped. Her teeth chattered. Her grip upon the Auría gave way. The book fell on the blackened que.

The témo coughed and spoke as the cinders stung her eyes. "Temperature, we must keep moving. Neither of us can breathe in this area... Temperature?"

The yell of Neztríanis' shame and anguish was so great and her Aura blossomed so depressingly, that Timura herself was drawn back into her own loss.

Gathering what remaining resolve either of them had left, the winged feline said, "Neztríanis, though this matter is hard, we must keep moving."

Timura use of "Neztríanis" grasped the daughter of Hopha's attention.

"I am no better than they are!" She picked up the Auría and walked out of the ash. "*I'm no better...*"

Following Neztríanis out of the gray, Timura sensed their surroundings. No one, not even an airlift, neared their position. The Sczyphamek's white flare put the attack on pause, or...

"Timura." Neztríanis called to her friend in the key of apology. "You tried to stop me. I should have listened to you. I have jeopardized everything, and these deaths may yet become even more meaningless." The Nez Spiritan looked at the book and frowned. "I am *weak*. I used this book to cover up my weakness... my arrogance..."

The Sczyphamek beheld her hands. Her mission was to keep the book out of the wrong hands. Yes, even her hands were *wrong hands*. She never assumed that her hands were just as mistaken as a Zananín. A terrible folly. Neztríanis seriously wondered if a Sczyphamek, no matter their persuasion, should *ever* carry the Auría. The problem was not primarily the book in itself, but how her kind handled it.

Although she was exposed, her wrists and her beliefs still felt chained. The shackles were deteriorating. But at what cost?

"Being weak does not make you wrong or evil," Timura commented softly, her hair standing on end.

"Yes," the woman agreed and sniffed. She had to regain her composure. Time was running out. "Because being powerful does not make you right or good."

Taking off the large windhorse satchel Namí gave her, Neztríanis fastened it around Timura's trunk and placed the Auría inside. "This book does not belong in the hands of *any* Sczyphamek." Rubbing Timura's head somberly, Phyxtríalis stood beside the témo and continued, "You're faster than me. Go to the Crag Mountains at the southern edge of the North Country. Keep the Auría close to you; it will shield you from his Elemental. If you do not sense me in a week's time, take it as far as you can into the North Country, and bury it."

"You must survive this encounter, or he will eventually find it," the témo said earnestly. "Do not provoke him. Vincallous, although evil, is a peculiar Sczyphamek. Just because you cannot win, this does not mean that you cannot escape."

Both of them would not be able to outrun him now. He headed towards their position the moment he realized his Elemental echo had been sensed. That was fifteen minutes ago. But an elite Sczyphamek flew at speeds between five and six hundred lengths an hour: two to three times, Neztríanis' maximum speed, and nearly one and a half times the maximum velocity of Timura. Their only chance was for Neztríanis to confront Vincallous now, and hope that she could give her steadfast ally some time to put enough distance between them. Neztríanis felt his approach the moment her attack ended. If she carried the Auría, Vincallous would continue to sense her presence now that she wielded her Elemental so brazenly. *She had to stay behind.* If she would have kept to their plan, then perhaps...

"Spare no speed," Neztríanis stated imperatively.

Timura nodded, flapped her wings, and levitated. Within moments she was out of the Sczyphamek's sight, heading north. The daughter of Hopha sat on the ground, meditated and sang. Temperature petitioned the One with No Name and her ancestors for forgiveness, as well as the ancestors of those whose lives she had just taken. Phesiana's daughter clasped the grass with her hands, and tears once more streamed down her reddish-brown face. She also apologized to Rai and Renzgé for her attitude towards them. Their sorrow, however, extended into hers.

Why did calamity always seem to precipitate revelation? Why did it take so long for Temperature to understand that the Auría *did not want to be found?* At least, not yet...

A few minutes passed, and in the southeast horizon, Neztríanis detected a red streak in the sky bolting towards her. Wiping her face of tears, she stood up and continued to chant inwardly. She recalled all of the information she had gathered from Timura about the type of company and power that would soon enter her midst.

Neztríanis had forgotten the warmth and coolness of her Elemental. How amicable they were to her! The Auría offered her a chance to grow closer to them, but instead, her use of the text had driven them apart.

"*Zí mányx que Rai. Mona fla Renzgé ná.*" Neztríanis sang the melody she learned durations ago in Hero's Valley, when Qeauríyx attacked her. She felt no shame in singing, and as Vincallous drew closer and closer, the Nez Spiritan continued to hum and sing, all the while mentally chanting and humming the phrase of ages, "Fá'atoño má." She kept her Elemental aura to herself; she only wished to commune with Rai and Renzgé. If she was to perish, she would not do so alienated from her Elemental.

Gazing up at the horizon, Neztríanis saw Vincallous glaring down at her. He descended and touched the ground elegantly, in such a way that revealed only his profile. Turning his head towards the smoldering pile that was once nel'asmív, the Sczyphamek hung his head and sighed. Then, he faced Neztríanis.

The Damüdan Sczyphamek gave her an indescribable, curious look. It was filled with confusion, satisfaction, shame, sadness, eagerness, and hatred—in a word, imperceptibility.

CHAPTER TWENTY-FOUR: CONFRONTATIONS

The grassy plain seemed endless. The wind blew. A film, emanating from the piles of ash, blackened the sky. Neztríanis smelled the burning remnants of what were once Blue Rapier soldiers. She detected no aircraft or mechanized vehicles heading in their direction.

Apparently, he wanted the confrontation to be between them, and them only. A meeting with no witnesses.

She had nightmares of this event, and though stricken with fear, she knew in her heart this confrontation was inevitable. It was in her mind the moment the Great Mother told her about her quest. It chilled her body when she met Rydín and the survivors of Lozé. It crushed her spirit when she experienced the betrayal of Jennó. The vision of it nearly destroyed her qanín after Bíoske died and during Timura's retelling of her encounter with the Damüdan Sczyphamek, the one who happened as Vicious. The same man who twenty cycles ago killed over eight million nel'asmív in only a few hours. His presence had always loomed over her entire quest.

Before she even exchanged one word with him, her na'ísa, trust, and understanding were already fluctuating to such an extent that she wondered how much of her Elemental she could truly display. She tried to remain calm, but soon realized the impossibility of such a feat. Yet, fearful anxiety was not her only feeling; it was accompanied by a seething anger.

Should she not be afraid? Should she not be angry? Were great Sczyphameks the ones who controlled their emotions? Why did she feel so diminished by fear and anger? Why did these thoughts and emotions make her angrier? Was she wrong for fearing someone who was so much more powerful than her?

Neztríanis was not only victimized by her own powerlessness, but also by the fear emanating from her powerlessness. But again, was it *wrong* that she was angry with a man who killed countless of nel'asmív and acted as if he was the Nameless One Itself? Why was righteous indignation now such a hindrance? Why did it now feel like *weakness*? She felt trapped and mired in *something*...

She could not escape.

Taking deep breaths and unclenching her fists, Neztríanis gathered herself. Rai and Renzgé were with her. She was not alone.

Neither was Vicious.

There would be witnesses after all.

His palms were open and his face revealed nothing. No frown, no smile or smirk, no pursing of the lips. His unkempt hair and goatee added to Nez's baffling experience. There was a noticeable, though faint scar across his forehead and cheek, no doubt from the claw of a témo, probably Timura's. He sported no cape. Neither was he dressed in traditional Sczyphamek attire. He wore Tannódin'é gray slacks and a gray shirt that displayed the symbol of White Scythe across the front. A black jacket covered his shirt, and on its left sleeve was the insignia of Blue Rapier. Apparently, Vincallous was in such a rush that he did not have time to change into his traditional vestments. He was also unarmed, which confused Neztríanis even further, for Zananín routinely carried swords.

However, he was not defenseless.

She sensed his Elemental, and it was *frighteningly* reserved.

Vicious was taller than Temperature expected, although she always pictured him as tall. But since she was taller than most, she did not think he would still be about two clips taller than her. He was also muscular, but not ridiculously large. His stance was as loose as a feather in the wind. This was not how Neztríanis imagined the despicable Damüdan Sczyphamek, Kaz Vincallous Fierce.

He was completely unafraid of her. The feeling was not mutual.

"Neztríanis," he spoke softly. "That is your name, ah?"

Jennó probably relayed my name to him. Unsurprising. Neztríanis looked away and offered no direct reply to his inquiry.

She had questions of her own. Most urgently, the daughter of Hopha worried about her village and the possibility of its destruction. Secondly, both she and Timura were unable to assess *when* they were since they emerged from the caverns exactly twenty-six days prior.

"What is the date? And what did you do to Hopha?" she pressed, catching Vincallous off-guard.

"The *date?*" His face displayed confusion as he pondered her first interrogative. "You *have* been eluding us for awhile, have you not? It is Oplé, the Thirtieth day of Ízneko. And, we did nothing to Hopha. You are no longer a problem for Nez Spirita. You are a problem for Qeauríyx."

Neztríanis knew what he meant when he said "Qeauríyx." In his mind, he was *Qeauríyx*. She was a problem for him and Pre-Eminent. Hopefully, that meant Namí and Hafir were safe. And she was astounded that so much time had passed since her ascent of Mount Xarkim. It only felt as if one and a half durations had passed not *four*.

"Why did you kill my troops, Neztríanis?" he probed. "What changed?"
"*Changed?*" she asked, aghast that he seemed to be psychoanalyzing her.
"You did not kill Jennó. You killed no one in the Triple Skyrises. You evaded us for nearly half a cycle without direct confrontation. That bloodthirsty wretch of a témo traveled with you, and yet you kept that ill-begotten, kíma-ridden animal from killing once she was free of the Skyrises. So, I am asking you—why did you kill my troops? Do you honestly expect me to believe that they posed you a serious threat? You incinerated all forty of them in seconds, and they were only capable of one round of suppression fire."

"That is not so," Neztríanis muttered inaudibly, forgetting that Vicious' hearing was unparallel.

"Not so...?" Vincallous' mind raced for the answer. "I see... You negated their second volley so abruptly that I was unable to perceive the sonic disruption... *Astounding...* How astounding..."

The Zananín's eyes betrayed wonderment, but his countenance soon returned to its relaxed stoicism. "You still have not answered me; so I shall ask again. Why did you kill my subordinates?"

Why was he not trying to kill or capture her? Why was he talking to her? She expected a different kind of confrontation from Kaz Vincallous Fierce, the Zananín called Vicious.

"You do not wish to answer?" He nearly smiled. "Is it because you want to avoid the truth?"

"Did you come here to lecture me or to kill me?" Agitated, she frowned but quickly tried to right her face.

"I have not made up my mind yet," he replied. "Since you pose me no threat, I do not feel the need to kill you. Unlike you, I realize the difference between a life and death struggle and a time for restraint."

"*Did Phenplyacin teach you the difference?*" Neztríanis retorted before she could stop herself.

What was she doing? Timura warned her not to provoke him. But she was unable to control her anger towards the man who had come to represent all that was wrong with Nez Spirita and Qeauríyx.

Vincallous bit his lip and paused. He truly did not believe she would resort to that accusation... *so early.* Was that his legacy—no matter what he did before or after that event? Neztríanis, unawakened or not, was the first Sczyphamek to question his handling of Phenplyacin, and her words and emotion reminded him of his younger self. Both Dé'wa and his qanín shifted.

A minute passed, yet their eyes remained fixed on each other.

"Fá'atoño má," chanted Van. His red aura burst forth, pulsated, and shook the ground. His breaths were not hurried. He was not preparing for battle, *yet.* "You don't see how much we are alike, Kylanín."

Neztríanis was shaken by his response and his aura. *They were not alike.* They could not be. They happened on opposite ends of a spectrum. His

Elemental was stronger, and she was not a Zananín. If they were *so* alike, why was she so afraid and livid?

"Who says I'm a Kylanín?" Neztríanis asked.

"What? Are you saying you are one of *them?*"

Neztríanis offered no reply. She was unsure of how she happened, whether as a Kylanín or a Zephanín. But she was certain that she was not and would never happen as a Zananín.

"Hmmph," Vincallous grunted. "It matters little. You have yet to Awaken; you cannot predict how you will happen."

Again, Neztríanis glanced at the pyres of fiery cinders that were once nel'asmív. She blinked, and the moment she opened her eyes, Vincallous had closed more than half the distance between them. Gasping, Neztríanis automatically took a few steps back. So did Rai and Renzgé.

"You are different, ah. Something about your Elemental is altered. It does not feel quite as potent. I thought it was tripartite... And I cannot sense that animal either. It is as if she has obscured herself in the same manner as you..."

Vincallous' frowned and shook his head. He understood completely. "*Ah.* You did... you retrieved *it*, did you not? The Auría *was* in your possession. And now that kímaz témo has it." Vicious' aura flashed in discontent for a split second.

Neztríanis' heart jumped and her knees nearly buckled. The power behind the emanation was absurd. But the lesson she learned from the Auría was indisputable. Regaining the last remnant of her emaciated composure, the daughter of Hopha said without fear, "That book is not meant for Sczyphameks, whether one is a Kylanín, Zephanín, or Zananín."

Vincallous perceived the implications of the Nez Spiritan's words. "Really? Is that so?"

"You would have destroyed this continent and probably the planet." Neztríanis spoke not as an enemy, but as one Sczyphamek addressing another.

"I doubt that. But something just as... *unfortunate*... might have transpired..." The Zananín put his index finger to his lips. "So that is what changed, then, ah? You believe it was the Auría. Or rather, you *allowed* the Auría to change you."

Vincallous looked upon Neztríanis in disappointment. "You survived the heights of the Infinite Circle, but have fallen so low. You are *weak*... how pitiful..."

"Don't you think I know that by now?" Neztríanis countered in self-loath and frustration. "Of course I am weak."

"Yet, you do not realize *how weak*..."

Neztríanis felt the ground beneath her warm ever so slightly due to the friction of the soil. She jumped back twenty feet as a considerable chunk of earth was torn from the que of Qeauríyx. Vincallous did not chant. Recalling Timura's instruction, Neztríanis reasoned that this was an elementary attack of a Sczyphamek. Vincallous was testing her. If she could not dodge or protect herself from this minor display of power, she would not survive an intermediate instantiation of his Elemental.

The detritus raced towards her, but Neztríanis was no fool. Such an obvious exhibition of power was not his real attack. And Temperature realized something that she had not known before Timura's lecture and Fierce's own personal confirmation. Vincallous carried at least two elements, earth manipulation and sonic vibration.

Summoning the very best of her acumen, Sczyphamek Temperature released a thin, yet extremely condensed version of her orange-white aura, all the while dodging the slab of earth. At the same time, she analyzed and memorized Vincallous' distinct heat signature. As soon as she was clear of the earthen object, she heard a crumbling sound. The ground underneath her was giving way. Neztríanis levitated a few clips off the grassy plain and expulsed a beam of ice from her left hand that covered the faulty ground. With her right hand, she shot a saturnine mist towards the large piece of floating earth and froze it almost instantaneously. In addition, the mist gathered all of the surrounding water vapor and channeled it to the chunk, increasing its mass. The soil's weight nearly doubled, for Temperature had lodged a piece of her Elemental aura in the glacial burst.

Sensing if Vicious was strained or if his na'ísa had increased even slightly, Temperature scanned the Zananín's aura with auburn eyes. Instead of continuing his line of attack, Vincallous allowed the detritus to crack under its own weight. Gravity sent the icy mass crashing down, and it split into many pieces. Observing that the test was over, a slightly winded Neztríanis settled to the ground. Throughout the entire skirmish, she did not stop inwardly chanting.

Vincallous sighed in wonder. "*Elemental individuation...* Kíma... *and you did not even chant...* You did all this without its aid. And yet you relied on its power as if the Auría was the cause of your strength. As if the Auría had given you faith. Would I have been any different?"

Fierce moved though the ashes of the Blue Rapier troops, but kept his gaze upon Phyxtríalis. "If you thought that losing the Auría meant that you would lose your faith, that means you don't have any faith at all, and it certainly means you understand nothing about that book. As a fellow Sczyphamek, I pity you. But then, you are a Nez Spiritan Kylanín; I would expect nothing less from your narrow-mindedness.

"Do you honestly believe the Nameless One and Qeauríyx are confined to those pages? Do you think they are those pages? I cannot believe we are indebted to that wretched témo. She probably saved us all from you. She may have even saved me from using it..."

Even though she was intrigued by the phrase "Elemental individuation," Neztríanis' ire—no, her *hatred*—boiled (controllably) as the Agent of Global Initiative questioned her beliefs.

"You do not know what you are talking about," she sneered.

Vincallous ignored her. "We wanted that book because we knew it would help us to promulgate Global Initiative, not because we were bound to it absolutely. That book is powerful, and as a nel'asmív, I do not wish it to be destroyed. However, it cannot contain that which is uncontainable. At best, the Auría can only point to and at worst misrepresent our reality."

His movement escaped her. Before Nez could defend herself, Van was face to face with her and struck her in the stomach, knocking all breath out of her. The woman hunched over and coughed. Temperature's eyes dilated in fear and confusion. He was holding back ten—maybe twenty... maybe *fifty*—times his true power.

Bending over and speaking softly in her right ear, Vincallous orated, "I will say it again: *You are weak*. You used that book to hide your weakness, instead of letting it show you that you are weak. You used that book to kill others, when on some occasions you heard it tell you not to kill. You used that book to cover your ears and eyes to reality, when the book is a representation of how this planet and its people have coped with reality."

Neztríanis tried to catch her wind and petition her Elemental, but her focus was shattered, so vitiated was her na'ísa, understanding, and belief. His words assaulted her as much as his fist. How could a Zananín be "right"?

"This is why our cause is just. We do not need the Auría in order to believe there is a Nameless One or to—"

"Or to kill anyone, any family, any creature, any culture, any belief, any land, and any Sczyphamek that stands in your way or disagrees with your interpretation!" Neztríanis blurted out. She turned her head and looked directly at her assailant. Only two or three clips separated them. It took her entire qanín to keep from attacking him, and her Elemental drew noticeably close to her. The Nez Spiritan was near eruption.

Vincallous cautiously took two steps back and remained silent. Her interjection startled him.

Neztríanis did not yield her position. "If you possessed the Auría, it would only exacerbate the deaths of all forms of life."

"Was the First any different?" Vincallous inquired.

"You know nothing about the First!" the Nez Spiritan screamed, stood up and placed some distance between them.

Neztríanis could not hold back the outburst, even though she realized how reactionary it was. She did not even take Vincallous' query sincerely. She reacted before she let the question sink in. He did not announce the idea as if it were a statement of fact; he simply asked a question. His question was not innocent, but the daughter of Hopha wondered if his intentions mattered. Did she not react in the same manner when Namí said something similar? And Namí was not being shrewd or disingenuous.

Why was she so reactionary? Didn't she just tell Timura that she was no better than Vicious and Pre-Eminent? Why was she so intransigent? Did she believe that she and the First were actually synonymous? Her faith was wracked with frustration, confusion, and disillusionment.

Seizing the historical, philosophical, and theological confrontation, Vincallous raised his voice slightly. "How many perished during the Great Extinguishing? Do you have the exact number? Did the Auría tell you?" Neztríanis was quiet. That line of interrogation was unexpected.

Vicious stared at the ground, the Firmament, and finally gazed upon Neztríanis with hesitance. "If all Sczyphameks were truthful, we would have to admit that none of us truly understand why the First did what she did. And we would admit that we have never understood the ramifications of her actions.

"But that is only half of it. We also have learned things, real things, from those actions. Some happenings are true, like the fact that many people died along with her when she extinguished her qanín and the Sundry Elemental.

"Or do you really think that this entire world was saved at the cost of only one life?" The daughter of Qeauríyx offered no answer. Both Kylanín and Zananín earnestly believed they were continuing the path of the First. And the Zephanín… who knew what Exceptional actually believed…

Vincallous pressed his case further. "How many people, how many animals, how many plants, how many died—and not just died—but lived before her? Their lives made possible her life and her death. How many died when she died—swallowed up in valleys that no longer exist, submerged and drowned by waves that wiped out coastal towns, pierced by newly formed mountain ranges, incinerated by magma, starved and died of thirst as weather patterns became erratic?"

Neztríanis thought back to the final vision/revelation/experience she had in the caverns of the Infinite Circle.

"I cannot answer," Temperature responded gently yet antagonistically. "What I do know is that you and Pre-Eminent have no reason or right to subject Qeauríyx to your whims."

"Whims? *Whims!*" It was Vincallous' turn to sneer. "Is that how you think Global Initiative happens—*as a mere whim?*" The Damüdan Sczyphamek gave Neztríanis a visceral stare. *"Are they the same kind of 'whims' that caused you to kill forty of my soldiers?*

"Do not project your arrogance, guilt, and myanála onto me. You are too intelligent and twenty cycles too late for such a tepid comparison."

Neztríanis hung her head in humiliation and disgrace. Vincallous did not move and continued to fix his eyes upon the Nez Spiritan. Temperature struggled to keep the tears from returning. Vicious would not continue his attack until she gave a signal that she was ready to resume the confrontation. She knew from her studies and Elemental intimations that a battle between most Sczyphameks consisted in the complete exercise of Elemental power. Ideals and reality were just as much at stake as her life and her cause.

The First Sczyphamek gave them an example to live by. Her entire qanín was extinguished in the decimation of the Sundry. Her motives, her stamina, her ideals… Victory and defeat required nothing less than placing a Sczyphamek's na'ísa, faith, and understanding on the line.

Biting her lip and refusing to cry, the woman raised her head, faced her adversary with reddened eyes, and petitioned Rai and Renzgé for strength.

"Ah." Van remained steadfast. "These are not whims. We have worked and deliberated unceasingly with regard to our—no not ours, but the Nameless One's vision."

Jolted out of her depression, the Sczyphamek called Temperature gave Vicious a look of prophetic denunciation. His words were blasphemy and apotheosis to her ears. "How can anyone claim to fathom the will of the Nameless One?" she inquired.

"Did your ancestors ask that question when they sacrificed countless nel'asmív during your ancient Nez Spiritan religious ceremonies?"

The daughter of Hopha was silenced once again. Those practices were a mark of disgrace for all current Nez Spiritans who believed and prayed to the One with No Name and the ancestors.

"Your people claimed to be reenacting the sacrifice of the First and paying homage to the One with No Name," Fierce continued. "And if I am not mistaken, did not the témos call your beliefs into question? And was it not their guidance that changed your religious outlook?"

Neztríanis knew that Vincallous was comparing the role of the témos to the legitimacy of Global Initiative.

"You are a killer of témos and their unborn cubs." Neztríanis responded spitefully. "You are not the same as them."

"Thank the Nameless One I am not. You are upset that I killed an unborn cub? What about when Global Initiative saved the city of Nextu from starvation, when no one else in Nez Spirita could? Dying from starvation must be a lesser evil than killing a kíma of an unborn cub.

"What is it, Neztríanis? You care about the creation of a life, but not its sustenance? As long as the cub or baby is born, you will allow it to starve or destroy it later, if it poses you a threat? *Is that what you did when you murdered my subordinates?*

"Even in the randomness of this Cycle, some of those soldiers would have ended up in Blue Rapier, no matter what their own decisions were. If that is the case, some of them should not have been born if they were to face such a terrible end. Do you not feel the same way about how I handled Phenplyacin?"

The Zananín peered through Neztríanis and into her qanín. "Or are you so haughty that you honestly believe you can legitimately arbitrate life or death? Are *you* the Nameless One? Spare me your moral superiority… That is your myanála speaking—a myanála that traps your very progression."

Phyxtríalis was horrified, confused, and scandalized. Her horror stemmed from Vicious' unmitigated hatred of témos. The malice he had for the felines seemed to run deeper than the lengthy conflict between the Zananín and their species. Her confusion arose from Vincallous' ability to counter her every accusation—accusations she knew were valid. The scandal lay in the fact that Van Fénüra's responses were not an attempt to scapegoat some other party or to confuse Neztríanis. His questions were incisive, paradoxical queries.

Why did her kind treat some kinds of suffering and death worse than other kinds? Why were some moved by Timura's loss, but not by the loss of hunger and want? She was reminded of the hard decisions Hafir made and continued to make concerning Nextu. Had she learned so little as to still be caught in such a myanála? Her na'ísa was erratic, clamoring in all directions, which was no direction.

"Never again," he barked. "*Never again* will you claim that Késhal and I are whimsical, capricious taskmasters. Such an assertion is altogether false and insulting. You can judge us as evil and unforgiveable all you like, but do not act as if Global Initiative was achieved through happenstance, luck, or foolishness. And never again make the flagrantly baseless claim that this undertaking is not fueled by our utmost beliefs and knowledge.

"That is why I say you are weak. You are trapped in a myanála so large that you mistake it to be but a small thing. Do you actually believe us to be so aloof and removed? You will never defeat us if that is your disposition."

Recalling her exchange with Rydín, the daughter of Hopha shook her head with understanding. She had forgotten. Vincallous and Késhal were not removed from their policies. They rode into battle with their troops. Vincallous killed Timura's cub and mate personally. Her demonization of the House of Kaz allowed her to generate deep hate, shallow rationality, and violent reprisal. Yet these were no use to her now that she was face to face with Fierce.

Despite the immediate threat of Fierce, Neztríanis found herself in deep self-reflection. And for some reason, Vincallous did not seem to be in a hurry.

"You believe I am caught up in two points…? You are right. Maybe we are more alike than I realized." Neztríanis' orange-white aura emerged unconsciously.

"That's good, ah," Vicious commented in a low, anticipatory tone. "Keep it just like that."

"You say that I try to arbitrate life, as if I am morally superior…" Neztríanis said with a resurrected sense of cloudy perspective. "Then, am I the same as you when you killed Timura's cub and mate? Am I the same as your consort, Pre-Eminent, who killed over ten thousand because they were not fit for Global Initiative? That was not twenty cycles in the past. That was half a cycle ago."

Vincallous' face frowned briefly and his aura temporarily fluctuated. "You do not know me, and you underestimate the empathic abilities of Késhal."

"Does Késhal not make a mistake? Is *she* the Nameless One?"

"She is not, nor has she ever claimed to be. But, we are Its emissaries." The Damüdan stroked his goatee and picked up some grass with his hands. "We do not claim to be superior. We happened as superiority. But we are not masters nor are you servants. No master is greater than his servant. A leader should never ask a subordinate to do something she would never do."

Phyxtríalis' heart was cut because she was reared on similar words. She was truly amazed how similar phrases contained such completely different interpretations… Much like the First's Extinguishing…

"You cannot defeat me yet," he said plainly and without derision. "You know this."

"I know. But it has already begun, so I must try…" With reflective determination, Temperature rephrased her original assertion. "I do not know what chance of ultimate victory or defeat either of us have, but your kind must no longer influence this world."

"I agree," Vincallous stated without reservation. "I am doing this so that a Sczyphamek like me will never happen again. It appears we are fighting for the same goal."

Shocked, Temperature gawked at the Damüdan and her aura flickered, but Vincallous was unwilling to say more on the matter.

"Keh mányx phen da pet," the Sczyphamek called Vicious chanted.

"*Wha… what did you say?*" Neztríanis stammered and nearly fell to her knees in theological angst. Instantaneously, her aura dissipated. Temperature remembered the First had chanted similar words on the heights of Edaw Peak… Some words (she could not remember) were missing in Vicious' phrase… Yet, why were their chants so similar?

A large rock bashed her shoulder with excessive velocity before she could mount a defense, so distracted was the Nez Spiritan Sczyphamek. Neztríanis flew into the que some thirty feet away. Although the pain was intense, her shoulder did not feel broken.

Gathering herself, Temperature stood upright. She was about to call forth her Elemental, but Vicious was already behind her, pulling her hair. Within an instant, he kicked her in the spine with noticeable moderation. Even though the Damüdan held back, the Nez Spiritan was launched forward at a violent speed. Her back screamed in affliction. Once again, Neztríanis found herself on the ground. This time, it was harder to get up. She could not do this alone.

"Fá'atoño má!" she chanted.

The orange-white aura of Sczyphamek Temperature bloomed, and Rai and Renzgé readied themselves. They would stand by Neztríanis to whatever end.

Vincallous' heat signature rushed towards her.

"Fá'atoño mona," she whispered.

A fiery wall emerged five feet in front of her. Blinded by the fire's light, Vicious halted his pursuit. Neztríanis felt the friction of the soil and jumped towards the sky, placing her in Vincallous' line of sight. The Zananín was already in the air, anticipating Neztríanis' every move. When his fist met her face, both Sczyphameks grunted in pain. Temperature encased the right side of her head in the densest ice she could construct. Although the ice shattered and Neztríanis absorbed some of the impact, Vicious was unprepared for the defense and broke the knuckle on his left middle finger.

Putting some aerial distance between them, Vincallous gazed at his foe. Neztríanis expected a scowl or a smirk, but Fierce gave her neither. His eyes, mouth, and forehead remained tranquil and apathetic.

Trying to catch her nemesis off-guard, the daughter of Hopha went on the offensive. Holding out her left hand and bracing it with her right, Neztríanis' aura blazed dark orange. Vincallous did not know what to expect, nor could he believe that Temperature's stabilized na'ísa was so formidable.

Temperature's body soon grew obfuscated by the heat she emitted. The visible sign of oncoming offense caused Fierce to retreat a few feet and the surrounding air to ambiguate.

"Renzgé ná," Neztríanis chanted. The wind picked up, and the clouds dissipated. Temperature's hair lifted and swirled, and her chant changed into a melody. "*Renzgé ná. Renzgé ná.*"

The woman was consumed in a heat so blue-white, that the Damüdan was nearly blinded. However, Neztríanis was not burned.

"Fá'atoño má. Dé'wa," Vincallous muttered nervously. His red aura became dense and flashed with power.

Vicious' aura partially buckled and his eyes widened as Temperature discharged an orange-blue flame in a burst that devoured the air between and beyond them. The eruption's power jolted Neztríanis backwards, but she managed to maintain her balance. The calefaction was so hot that she lost Vicious' heat signature in the blast. The sky ruptured from the flame, and soldiers from lengths away felt the ambient temperature rise considerably. The ground beneath her was reduced to ash and the unsettled heavens above unleashed a torrent of wind.

She had not used that technique before and had only thought about it in her mediation and communication with Renzgé. However, the discharge drained her more than she foresaw. She *had* grown weaker during her *singular* reliance upon the Auría.

Searching for his heat signature, Neztríanis gazed down at the charred remains of the grassy field. A large burning, smoking, yet formidable earthen hemisphere emerged from the ground. Vincallous had encased himself in the que of Qeauríyx to protect his body from what would have undoubtedly been a punishing attack.

The speed and power of Vicious confounded Temperature. The earthen structure crumbled, and Vincallous raced skyward, back towards his original position and stopped ten feet away from the Nez Spiritan Sczyphamek. His right sleeve and pants leg was burned; the soles of his shoes appeared melted; and ash fell from his body.

"Staxis… You do have potential," Vicious remarked with interest, but showed no signs of fatigue. "However, the gap is larger than you understand and believe. Myanálas die hard, and yours will not be overcome in such a short time."

Neztríanis tried to regain her wind. She knew whatever attack or defense she used would require Rai primarily, for Renzgé was too weak for any sort of emanation.

"*Níyama Wanesé*," Vincallous sang slowly. Neztríanis despised admitting it, but the Zananín's singing voice was absolutely breathtaking.

"*Zí mányx—*" Phyxtríalis sang and attempted an ice-shield.

Before she even experienced what happened, Temperature was hurled towards the burning terra of Qeauríyx at a speed that defied sound. The friction between her body, the air, and whatever attack Vincallous conjured, ripped her shirt and pants and pulled her hair out of its braid. She closed her eyes in hellacious anticipation. The collision between her body and the terra created a crater at least one length in diameter. If she had not inwardly chanted while falling, she would have been critically injured. Dirt and large pieces of soil flew in the air and landed on the conflagrated ground, causing the majority of the fire Neztríanis created to choke.

Her nose and mouth were bloody, and her right shoulder, humerus, radius, ulna, wrist, and hand suffered multiple breakages. Her clothes were shredded and barely had enough stitching to cover her torso and thighs. Her body ached all over, and her left ankle was also fractured.

A sonic boom erupted. The vibration made her lose what balance she had just precariously obtained. The daughter of Hopha nearly fell on her face, and her Elemental intimated the severity of their plight and the challenge of their foe.

That was not an elementary attack. In the moment before Temperature was flung to the ground, she saw/felt it. It was at least a quarter of the Zananín's power and aura. For a brief moment, the aura nearly took up the entire horizon. *That attack was an explosive vibration that was faster than the speed of sound.* And tracking a supersonic technique was simply and realistically beyond her present ability.

She could not win. The outcome was self-evident before she even said a word to him. And the fact that she was completely at the *mercy* of Vincallous—a man who knew no mercy—collapsed her na'ísa, understanding, and faith/will.

"Staxis," she cursed feebly.

"Indeed," she heard his voice say in the air, even as a fallen Neztríanis looked at his feet.

The man had closed the distance between them again. This time Neztríanis was certain. Vincallous' Elemental transcended sonic vibration. His Elemental's power was *vibration itself*, which allowed him to move his physical body faster than the speed of sound. That was the only way he could have dodged her fiery attack.

Vincallous bent down and whispered, "If you had tried to escape this confrontation, I would have struck you down that very moment.

"Now then…"

Grabbing the Nez Spiritan by her tattered shirt and lifting her in the air, Vincallous drew his right hand back. His fist was lined with a crackling, red emanation. She barely saw his face through her undone, thick, and lengthy hair, so battered was she. Neztríanis, bruised and eyes half-open, tried to elicit her aura, but the Damüdan was too quick and too strong.

Her facial skin ripped and her left jaw shattered in the clash between two opposable masses. The weaker one lost.

Temperature was throttled headfirst into a pile of gravel. Dirt and rocks embedded into her forehead, skin, and frazzled tresses. A bloody and beaten Neztríanis screamed in agony, even as such an instinct caused her more anguish. Writhing in unmitigated suffering, the tears and blood of Temperature fell unreservedly. No matter how much she tried to stop crying, it was impossible to prevent. The last blow to her face was the greatest amount of physical pain she had experienced in her twenty-seven cycles of life. Her toes clenched as much as her teeth, and she spit two bloody, dislodged molars from her mouth.

Attempting to find some position that softened the agony, the trembling Nez Spiritan Sczyphamek soon relinquished hope and resistance, and with great fatigue, Neztríanis embraced the full measure of her wretched torment. Her cry was a mourning whimper, emanating from a nel'asmív bereft of personhood and dignity. The historical weight of her violent subjugation and abjection was undeniable and unfettered. Ineluctable. In the eyes of Global Initiative, she was truly an insignificant speck of kíma. She was a nonperson.

In dreadful injury and utter oppression, Neztríanis wept. Fierce turned his back to her while Neztríanis wailed. And although his adversary did not notice, Van Fénüra shuddered for the first time in cycles.

He was right. He knew it in his qanín.

It has caused too much pain to be won by crooked means, he thought.

"At this point in your development, you should probably heal from most of these injuries in about one to three weeks," Vincallous said and sat down beside her. Gazing at his routed opponent, he almost appeared remorseful. "You are still so ensnared in a myanála—this was the only way I knew you would listen. And I needed to see… Ah."

Seized with ache and defeat, Neztríanis knew it was impossible to run away. She could not even move. They were only two clips away from each other, and Vincallous directly faced her.

"Find that témo and take the Auría to a place where neither a nel'asmív nor Sczyphamek can survive or guess its whereabouts," he commanded her. "If a restrained person like you can kill so easily with that book, *the Auría might have been our undoing*. It might have caused Késhal and me to fall into another myanála, just like you.

"We had reservations about locating the Auría in the first place. Our fears were not unfounded after all. Galís should have listened to the Mystics... Perhaps it was providential that you were to find the Auría and keep it out of our hands. Perhaps the Nameless One commissioned this task to you because Késhal and I would have undone all the progress we have made with Global Initiative... That book seems to be able to expose anyone's weakness, especially our kind."

The daughter of Hopha's expression was one of distrust and incredulity.

"I mean what I say," he affirmed. "You are free to go. But before you do, I will tell you the other reason I am letting you limp away from here. You must have no illusions."

Neztríanis stared at the man she believed to be incapable of the principle of mercy.

"There is no arrogance in my statement: as it stands, you cannot defeat me and you certainly could not face Pre-Eminent.

"The truth is, I did not know what I should do if I encountered you, but now I do. If I kill you here, how would that serve Global Initiative? That is the easy road. We do not need the Auría to believe in Global Initiative any more than I need to kill an unawakened Sczyphamek. The Nameless One would not forgive me... And I am already beyond forgiveness."

Picking up some dirt with his fingers, Vincallous caused the soil to coalesce and form a miniature globe. "This planet of ours deserves something better than that. Qeauríyx has seen its share of useless battles. Killing you now would only add to this number." Metaphorically and artistically representing his point, the globe crumbled.

"Global Initiative is to be earned and legitimated, not stolen and coerced. Destroying you would be the latter, and two hundred cycles from now, when Pre-Eminent and I are no longer on this planet, someone will remember or think about this moment and believe that the only reason Global Initiative was successful was because the Sczyphamek known as Vicious killed a nameless Sczyphamek who had no possibility of defeating him."

Vincallous stopped his explanation suddenly. He remembered what Pre-Eminent's parents did to Nosgüth. "An incident like that would cause the cycles of violence to continue forever...

He stood and shook his head. "I refuse to participate in a farce such as that. Yes, I even hope you are able to achieve the Synthesis, as frightening as such a prospect is. Késhal and I have had it easy for too long, and Qeauríyx will not stand for a straight or narrow path to victory. There are times to wrestle with this place, but this is not one of those times…

"If we destroy you, that beast, and Anámn after your Awakenings, when you actually stand a chance against us, how much more legitimate will Global Initiative become? If we can do this without the aid of the Auría, how much more powerful would we have happened? Any attempt or thought of defeating Global Initiative would be accompanied by the actual fact that two Awakened Sczyphameks were killed by the hands of Pre-Eminent and Vicious. The institutional fear of such a feat would guarantee us the real possibility of at least four to five hundred cycles of global transformation. A transformation that would spread throughout this planet and silence all backwardness and futility…"

Vincallous was so deep in thought that he did not realize Neztríanis' eyes opened when he spoke the name "Anámn."

Fierce looked down at her mystified face. "Ah. I suppose you are the last to hear. Yes. Another Sczyphamek has appeared besides you, Késhal, and me. His name is Anámn. He is in Damüda as we speak. And if everything goes as planned, he should be close to his Awakening by now… *just like you…*"

Vincallous Fierce stood and sauntered away from Neztríanis Phyxtríalis, but turned around. "You do realize, do you not? Awakening is not enough to defeat us. Do you embrace this, Neztríanis?"

Neztríanis would not deceive herself. The woman nodded solemnly in teary affirmation. There was nothing to debate. Even if she Awakened, Vincallous' power was beyond that state. He was an elite Sczyphamek, of the same stature as the First or Exceptional. Yes, even if she Awakened, another journey lay ahead of her. And the longer it took her to become an elite Sczyphamek, the more the bodies of dead nel'asmív and témos would continue to accumulate.

Van Fénüra levitated and nodded. "I will call my troops off. We do not need any more pointless deaths. Do what you need to do, but do it fast. We will not stop to wait for you or him. And the témos are as good as extinct. Tell your partner that we are thankful for her intervention. And as a sign of our gratitude, we will not track her down and kill her. She will be the last of her kind, so it is only fitting that the Synthesis belongs to her. That beast is the final testimony to an obsolete species."

Flying away towards the southeast, the Sczyphamek stopped and added, "One last thing. In the unlikely event you decide to join us, you are most welcome. However, the next time you oppose either me or Késhal, neither of us will show any clemency. *None.*

"Regardless of your decision, we need you to be strong and formidable. Move past the myanála. They lead only to slumber. Késhal and I, Qeauríyx, the Nameless One, and all nel'asmív are counting on you."

Nodding to the northeast, the Zananín concluded ominously, "The General Maximum and I are forthwith departing to Líachim.

"Farewell, Sczyphamek Temperature. This was enjoyable. The fact that you were able to defend yourself at all, even while being so conflicted, is a testimony to your true power. I honestly cannot wait to face you for the first time…"

Holding her shattered shoulder, Neztríanis lay still and in shock. He spoke her title, and no one could have told him… no one except… yes, Rai and Renzgé intimated the information to his Elemental… Dénque and Wanesé… Those were the names of his Elemental. Even as the nel'asmív spoke to each other, the Elementals were engaged in their own kind of dialogue. They *were* once Sundry.

Staggering out of the crater, Temperature scanned her surroundings for heat signatures. Indeed, White Scythe and Blue Rapier were retreating from their original position. Neztríanis felt no relief, for she realized that Kaz Vincallous Fierce was not a maniacal, crazed killer. He was a thoughtful, cold, and peculiar kind of Sczyphamek. That scared her to the qanín. If Pre-Eminent was on the same level… how could they win?

They.

Anámn. She might have an Elemental ally.

And what did Vincallous mean about wrestling with Qeauríyx? Hadn't she already won the right to become a Sczyphamek? Or was Vicious mentioning something else? She could not even process the discouraging words Vincallous had spoken about the témos.

More than anything, Vincallous shattered her myanála into irreparable fragments. He outclassed her in na'ísa, understanding, and faith. But more than that, he was willing to see himself in Neztríanis. That was why he was able to let her go and why he accepted her advice concerning the Auría. Neztríanis started the confrontation unwilling to yield this: the fact that victimizers can be victims, and victims can be victimizers. This did not make things simple, however. This myanála was not easily resolved by treating the victims and victimizers the same. They were distinct, yet they were similar. Vincallous was able to realize the distinction and similarity. How much of the complexity he was willing to embrace was another matter. However, because Temperature refused to see herself in Vincallous, even when she committed a similarly violent act, she was hindered from learning that their true distinctions were not superficial. *They were deep.* And yet they were still related.

A definitive similarity existed between Kylanín and Zananín; both believed in intervening in the affairs of Qeauríyx. And because they chose to do so, life-taking became inevitable, if not necessary. That was undoubtedly what Vincallous meant when he asked her about the First *and* why he called her a Kylanín even when she said otherwise. For the first time, Neztríanis seriously considered the position of the Zephanín.

Walking towards the north, Neztrínis chanted to herself, her Elemental, *and* the Nameless One, petitioning for healing. Her thoughts were scattered, but one thought grew louder and louder. She needed to find Timura. As soon as she tried to levitate, she lost consciousness.

CHAPTER TWENTY-FIVE: MOUNT SUNSET

It was winter. Zénan nearly refused to rise, so close to the North Pole they were. And although moonlight was ample, that candescence did not translate into heat. To say that Anámn was cold was more than an understatement; it was comedic folly. All of his possessions lay in the hands of Galís.

Malchían was also subject to the elements. Yet, neither of them complained, nor had they spoken to one another since they departed from The Gate. Once Kinesis was clear of the city, the Mystic—if that was indeed what/who he actually was—nodded down towards the mountain range that traversed the entire Damüdan continent.

Anámn landed near the base of one of the foothills, and Malchían released his hold upon the neck, shoulders, and back of the runaway. Although certain the man before him was indeed Malchían, Matriester was still astonished. The man seemed a mix of Damüdan and some other kind of nel'asmív ethnicity. More noticeably, he exhibited no Phmquedrian features, and he was about twenty cycles younger than the Phmquedrian Malchían. The man appeared to be about sixty cycles old.

"Where are we going?" Anámn asked the man, once they landed safely on the ground. Anámn was exhausted, and Téza was nearly drained.

"To Mount Sunset." The Mystic(?) tilted his head towards the north.

"Mount Sunset..." Anámn murmured. Something about the place seemed familiar. "Is it far?"

"As far away as you believe it to be," Malchían answered.

Yes, this *was* Malchían, full of his double-meanings. Only this time, Sczyphamek Kinesis was not annoyed. It was as if double-meanings were a part of the man's qaníns.

"I see." Anámn grunted. Right and specific answers needed right and specific questions. "How many lengths from here?"

Smiling—the same smile Anámn had witnessed on so many occasions but now on a different face—Malchían responded, "About twelve hundred lengths."

"We need two railcruiser tickets," Anámn laughed. "I don't suppose you have any?"

"No," the man smirked. "I do not."

Matriester could hold the question back no longer. It was not going anywhere. So he might as well ask.

"Malchían… who… what are you?"

"If I answer your question now, it will only take longer for you to Awaken. And Anámn, believe me when I say, you *must* Awaken. We are already past the point of infinite outcomes."

"Awakening isn't enough, is it?" Kinesis asked somberly.

"No, it is not enough if your goal is to challenge them. Galís taught you that, didn't he?"

"Yeah, I don't have time for regret… but I could have learned it earlier if I would've listened to you or Nísyx all those durations ago." Matriester shivered in the cold wind. "Where is your cane?"

Walking over to a tree and placing his hand on its trunk, Malchían muttered indistinct words, and in the blink of an eye, the Blackwood cane emerged from the bark and shadow of the yardük.

"What in Qalfocx are you?" Anámn's question was instinctive. He expected no answer.

"I don't know how I happened," the man responded quietly. It sounded as if the Phmquedrian Malchían's voice was layered on top of the present voice and body. "We cannot remember… We don't think we've ever been sure. Can you trust us in spite of that?"

"Yes," Sczyphamek Kinesis, Téza and Anámn, affirmed. "Téza is telling me that the energy from that cane cannot be fathomed. That's not a walking stick, is it?"

"You have increased your vocabulary," he commented and then snickered tiredly as he tapped the staff on the ground. "This thing… doesn't it look like a cane?"

"Looks are deceiving," Anámn retorted. "I sense what I sense."

"I told you, if we go down this path, it will hinder your Awakening. In these many Cycles, you are one of the few Sczyphameks who has potential, and I don't mean your Elemental."

"You say that like you've seen a lot of Sczyphameks, but there are only three others besides me." Kinesis looked at the man as if it was the first time he had seen him. "How old are you?"

"I cannot remember."

"What's your real name?"

"I cannot remember the first name I was called…"

"Are you a Mystic?"

"I've been one on eight or nine occasions…"

"Staxis…" Anámn cursed, not wanting to deal with the ramifications of those answers. "North, right?"

"Right."

"How are we going to survive out here? We need clothes."

"There is a town thirty lengths to the west, in a valley on the other side of this mountain range. I'll obtain for us outerwear more suitable for this climate. But neither of us will survive out here much longer if we do not make a fire."

"I don't sense anyone around or any airlifts in the sky." Anámn frowned, thinking about Brenko, Lénü, Tarían, and the other Mystic.

"Don't worry about them." Malchían was ever intuitive. "That was Brenko, the famous tactician, wasn't it? I believe your friends will be safe."

"Ah," Anámn affirmed. He had appropriated the Damüdan colloquialism as a result of his friendship with Tarían. "You're right."

"Unlike before, you must worry about yourself now," the man said. "I fear the task is now harder for you and Neztríanis."

"'Neztríanis?'" Matriester quipped. "Who is that?"

"She is the Nez Spiritan Sczyphamek."

"I'm going to be quiet." Anámn sighed in agitation. Every answer Malchían provided sparked more questions.

"Ah," the man wearily agreed. "That would be best."

Anámn gathered some dead branches and other burnable material. When the youth had set brushwood down, Malchían struck his cane in the middle of the kindling, which caused a moderate black flame to spark and blaze. The fire was disproportionately warmer than the flame's size. Weirder than that fact was the apparent lack of smoke from the embers.

Anámn was too tired to think anymore. A journey with Malchían would provide more than enough opportunities to ask questions. The elder was already down on the snowy ground and fallen fast asleep. Anámn leaned his back against a yardük and jolted up. The yardük was *scorching* hot. His senses nearly deceived him; the bark on the tree gave off a dark red glow and emitted a strange kind of heat. Looking back in Malchían's direction, Matriester noticed that the snow was melting, and the entire campsite was warming to a most pleasant temperature.

Even though Anámn was mystified, something about Malchían and his cane and became inconspicuous to the Sczyphamek's Elemental perception. It/he was either wounded or dying. For although the energy was untranslatable, its potential was decreasing.

The next morning, they both awoke later than either anticipated. Already late in the morning, Zénan was nearly at its peak position. Matriester's stomach growled. He had not eaten in days, and Malchían(?) appeared as if he had not enjoyed a decent meal in months. Téza, on the other hand, was near its full state, so Anámn knew that they would be able to make it to the town Malchían(?) had spoken about the night prior.

The runaway asked no questions and scanned his surroundings. The Sczyphamek sensed no one approaching their whereabouts, whether in the sky or on the ground. His act of deterrence must have worked. Picking up the weakened Malchían(?) and placing him on his back, the Sczyphamek did not want to risk flying. Such a feat would tire him quicker than either of them could now afford. They needed adequate clothes, shelter, and food by night's end.

The elder held the cane tightly and drew close to Anámn. He uttered phrases unknown to Anámn, although occasionally "keh," "É," and the chant of ages emerged. Leaping and running, Kinesis followed the directions of Malchían and crossed over the snowcapped Damüdan range with fatigued vigor. Within five hours, the duo traversed the range and found themselves in a valley that stretched about one hundred and eighty lengths across. In the distance, electrical lights shone and revealed signs of life and community. Nearing the city, Matriester and the Mystic(?) quietly hummed an old tune from Euhilv, a song about the insect from another planet that desired more.

When they arrived at the village's outskirts, Malchían said to Anámn, "Stay here. I will obtain everything we need. This village is remote; I doubt we will find much trouble here.

"While I am away, I want you to think about something. When you chant 'É müz keh fíp Téza má,' do you realize what you are saying? You know what Téza and má mean, but do you understand anything else about the phrase?"

"You are asking me if I *know* the phrase, aren't you?" Anámn asked reminiscently.

"Very good. Back at the torture rack, you chanted the phrase with such faith, and your na'ísa was so strong, but I noticed you lacked understanding."

"All those durations ago, in the jungle… you told me that becoming a Sczyphamek requires faith, will, and embrace," Anámn recalled. "You were trying to tell me that 'Fá' relates to my na'ísa, and 'Toño' to my faith or belief. 'Mányx…' To embrace is another way of saying to know or to understand… Is that right?" the Sczyphamek asked, desperately trying to ascertain Malchían's words. "'Fá'atoño má' is the chant that incants the three aspects of a Sczyphamek's power."

"That is correct," the Mystic(?) replied.

"But that's not enough," Anámn continued. "The words exist in a relationship, so knowing what each one means individually will only help me so much…"

"You truly have grown." Malchían(?) had a proud smile etched on his face. "At least you have grown." The man walked towards the village then suddenly faced Anámn. "The same rule that applies to the sacred chant applies to your own special incantations, with slight variations."

"But I don't know the Ancient Tongue," Anámn explained.

"Maybe not, but Téza does," Malchían responded. "You have been with Téza this long and have not realized this. A great chasm exists between you two." Continuing to walk toward the settlement, the man said, "I'll be back soon. Give what I said some thought."

A cold wind blew onto the Phmquedrian's face, causing his lips to purse and his eyes to close. When he opened them, Malchían was already halfway to the town. Anámn leaned against a Yardük and chanted, attempting to dialogue with Téza.

The phrase "É müz keh fíp Téza má" first appeared when he was attacked by Qeauríyx. That seemed like lifetimes ago.

The next time he encountered the phrase in a new way was during his time in the Valley of the Ancestors, at the behest of Téza. Téza was the *water*, and they, Sczyphamek Kinesis, were *yet/not yet*.

The phrase exerted itself differently a third time during the second attack of Qeauríyx, when Anámn was at the mercy of Damüda's Volcanic Line. On that occasion, he *sang* the phrase, which caused his power to multiply exponentially.

The final memories he possessed of the words were only hours prior, at the torture rack, when he learned the paradox of power.

What did those experiences have to do with the phrase?

"Téza," the Sczyphamek intimated, "please help me. What does the phrase mean?"

"Your thinking is correct. The Ancient Tongue does not express meaning as much as it expresses relationship," the Elemental silently explained. "You must embrace this before all else."

"*Relationship?*" Anámn spoke aloud.

Sitting down, the man drew himself into deep concentration. What was the difference between relationship and meaning? Was there a difference? Anámn fell upon one word that might help him to discern Téza's insinuation: *love*. When he thought about how love actually happened or what it meant, there were no words he could give. When Anámn thought about his sister—how much he loved her and how much his actions scarred their bond—he had a hard time expressing any real meaning, other than misguided attempts to recount the story.

But was the story so misguided? Was it not the story or perhaps a song that expressed the relationship, better than any word or phrase hoped to suffice? Love meant nothing if it did not express or foster interconnection. Love was not only a place or a thing; it was also an action. Love happened.

In addition, the runaway *slave* thought about meaning and relationship in terms of his mother. During his most vulnerable and innermost moments, he craved the lost contact with her more than he craved meaning. *No.* This was not true. The search for meaning made him long for relationship. Or was it the other way around?

Reimagining life during the Great Drift, Anámn realized that such a transient and harsh existence was altogether different yet similar to his own. His species faced extinction every day, due to the Drift's cataclysmic nature. Happening as a nel'asmív in such conditions must have provoked questions concerning meaning. However, the language developed by his ancestors focused on interdependence first. Why?

Anámn thought of Brenko's words that day in the frigid forest of southern Damüda: "*I believe that there is no point to any of this. It's all meaningless.*" But he added something when Lénü challenged him… "*Because I could be wrong…*"

…Meaninglessness…

At times, life during the Drift had to seem pointless. But even as his ancestors questioned the meaninglessness of their existence, they developed a tongue of relationship. Relationships: contingent and necessary interconnectivities that helped them survive and sometimes triumph in the desolate lifescape of Qeauríyx. They had the audacity to admit and face meaninglessness even as they pursued wholeness.

The Ancient Tongue was not so much a search for meaning as it was a testimony to the (dis)unity of his species between themselves, the planet, and the One with No Name. The words were symbolic yet real. They did not attempt to "explain" anything in themselves. Their primary purpose was to express the connection and disconnection Nelon Ásmivü felt towards the cosmos. The meaninglessness was so apparent and ever-present that "meaning" shrouded all attempts at expression. Meaninglessness was intricately related to the injurious and death-dealing reality of living… To overcome meaninglessness was to simultaneously overcome damage and mortality…

Anámn's deliberation was so intense that beads of sweat condensed and descended from his brow.

"*Because I could be wrong…*"

The Ancient Tongue was a manifestation of such a possibility, that life was not meaningless… life was more than injury and death and absurdity… but those three remained as well…

Frustrated and unnerved by the implications of such thinking, Anámn watched the city gates to see if Malchían was on his way back, but he neither saw nor sensed any sign of the Mystic(?).

"Fá'atoño má," he chanted quietly.

His dark green aura gently shone forth, and Téza pulsated in slow rhythmic accompaniment.

"É," the Sczyphamek repeated the word over and over again, slowly and in tempo to Téza's meter. "É, É, É, É…"

Gradually, Anámn felt his movement. *His movement.* He moved because Qeauríyx moved. He felt the kinetic energy of Qeauríyx's rotation as the planet traversed its elliptical orbit around Zénan. Even while at rest, he felt the movement of Qeauríyx… even while at rest he was moving. Potential energy rested; kinetic energy moved.

Relationship, Anámn reminded himself. *This is not about meaning but about relationship.*

How could that which rested relate to that which moved? They appeared to be distinct, but both were a constitutive property of energy. Both were a constitutive property of life. They were distinct, yet they were not. They were distinct, yet they were not pure. They were distinct, yet they were not pure nor were they completely separable. They were distinct, yet they were not pure nor were they completely inseparable, but they were distinct nonetheless. The relationship was cyclical and linear and spiral. A solidarity existed between rest and movement previously undisclosed to Kinesis.

"Arrgh..." Anámn grunted. The weight of Qeauríyx was on him, and he was almost knocked unconscious by the amount of information and energy he was *relating* to.

"By the One!" he shouted, grasping the *meaning* behind the relationship. The more he thought about it, the more certain he became. "É" expressed the paradoxical reality of Qeauríyx. The phonic pronunciation and subtlety of "é" was still active in the spoken languages of Anámn's time. However, the accent was lost or softened on many occasions: Qeauríyx, nél'asmív, Chénínqua, Phmquedria, Zénan, Mashé; even Késhal ...

More than this, the Sczyphamek felt and theoretically encountered two dimensions/meanings of the word turned expression turned relationship. The first was clear: rest/movement. The second, Anámn almost missed: *chance/purpose*. At first glance, they appeared to be myanála; however, this was untrue. Chance did not obliterate or seek to subsume purpose, anymore than rest did movement, or vice versa. Neither were they completely complementary terms. They were both states and actions. The words existed because of the intermingling of some aspects of reality...

That was how Téza *found* Nísyx in Kamo and Lénü and Brenko in Minusía.

"Anámn!" he heard Malchían yell.

Awaking from his cosmic/religious/scientific haze, Kinesis' aura had blossomed to such an extent that the Yardüks careened and the snow on the ground lifted and swirled about him. Seconds later, the Elemental emanation retreated and Anámn gazed at—?—Malchían(?).

"'É' expresses the paradox of all of this, doesn't it?" Matriester breathed moderate inhalations. "Hamin and Kaimero... they talked about how the use of myanála can't express reality..."

Handing the Phmquedrian a shirt, trousers, and a long, heavy coat, an insulated Malchían(?) nodded, "That word means everything and nothing. Rather, it describes that relationship."

"I am trying to understand." Anámn put on the shirt, pants, and jacket. "Where did you get these clothes? You don't have any credits."

"No," Malchían(?) replied. "But I have..."

"Power," Anámn finished. "There's more than one way to get clothes. I don't need to know how you got them, but I do want to know how much food we've got 'cause I'm starving."

Malchían(?) placed his hand in a bag, pulled out some bread and some dried meat, and gave the food to Anámn who ate it ravenously. The spices used to season the meat reminded Anámn of Malchían's sauce.

"We don't have much," he said. "Only about a week and half's worth." Reaching into the sack again, Malchían retrieved a fur hat. "Here. This should keep you warm."

"Ah." Anámn affirmed and placed the hat on his head.

Before he asked, Malchían(?) already held the canteen in front of Anámn, who took two large gulps from the bottle. It was truly amazing that Malchían(?) retrieved all of the supplies with no money.

Anámn shook his head. "All right. I lied. I gotta know how you got all this stuff."

"My great, great-grandchildren live here." His answer was unflinching and somber.

How can a Phmquedrian have Damüdan great-grandkids? Anámn wondered. *And how old is this guy?*

"They were happy to see that I was alive, but sad that I had to go again." He looked the Blackwood cane. "It didn't take much for them to help me."

Anámn did not want the man to be more saddened than he already was, so the runaway tried to encourage him. "You can come back when you show me how to get to Mount Sunset."

For the first time, Malchían's(?) face was completely unmistakable to Anámn's eyes and perception. *Malchían(?) was not coming back.*

"How long can you fly, full speed?" the man asked the Sczyphamek.

"I can't say. I haven't tried to since my encounter with Qeauríyx. But Téza's much stronger now than back then. "

"Well, it's time to find out; ah?"

"Yeah…"

Strapping the bag around his waist and holding the cane in his left hand, Malchían(?) hopped on Anámn's back once more.

"That way." He pointed towards the north. "Stay within this valley, close to the base of these mountains. Mount Sunset is the source of this mountain chain."

"Why doesn't it have a name?" Anámn asked. "Tarían kept calling it anything but 'the mountains'."

"I don't know… maybe Anplo knew…"

Anámn was befuddled. "Anplo? Isn't that the name of a sea?"

"The sea was named after him."

"Who was he?"

Malchían(?) looked reticent, as if no words would suffice. But Anámn's face demanded an answer.

"Damüda," the Mystic(?) responded. "Some think he was Damüda, that he was Damüda's original name. But, I have heard Mystics claim that he was the first Mystic. And I remember hearing stories when I was young about Anplo, the one who made the weapons…"

"What do you mean 'the weapons'? You mean *the* weapons—White Scythe, Blue Rapier, and the Violet Manacle?"

"There are more mystical weapons than those three," the man added.

"*What? More…*" Anámn's voice quavered in fear and anticipation.

"Staxis. Are you serious?"

"Yes." The man tapped Anámn with his cane. "I am quite serious."

"Who are you?"

"My answer will make no sense if you don't embrace the phrase. What does *müz* mean?"

***

The flight to Mount Sunset was nearly eleven hundred lengths from their location, and during Anámn's third hour of flight, he grew winded. He had no idea of his speed, and Malchían(?) said nothing to him. Apparently the old one was waiting for Anámn to explain to him the meaning of *müz*. Anámn already knew it was a trick because *müz* was not primarily trying to convey meaning, but relationship. Therefore, while Anámn was flying, he concentrated on the word and simultaneously focused on the flight path in front of him.

No tree incidents.

Soon, he became exhausted and settled down near a cave in a larger-sized mountain of the unnamed chain. Malchían hopped off Anámn's back and sat down, still remaining hushed.

Müz.

Anámn asked Téza what the word expressed countless times, but the Elemental seemed baffled as to how to relate the relationship the word sought to signify. Apparently, there were occasions where and when Téza could be at a loss for words/intimations. Yet, such barriers would not discourage the Elemental.

After an hour or so, Anámn neared the relationship, and it was indeed a *relationship*. Téza plunged Anámn into an apparitional cloud of people, animals, plants, trees, oceans, and volcanoes. He stood in the midst of them, even as he saw the planet and the cosmos from the Firmament. He was *a part of* them not *apart from* them. There was not only connectivity but a sharing, an interdependency—a possession of many... *ours/ all of ours.*

"Malchían," Anámn called out in weariness. Searching for relationship was a thankless and tiresome practice. "Does 'müz' mean 'ours'? Like, 'this food is both of ours'?"

"Very good," the man responded. "But müz is more mundane than even that. At its deepest relational expression, the word brings to mind the kind of happenings endemic to our planet."

"'Endemic?'" Anámn's smile was weak. "Lénü'íque or Nísyx didn't teach me that one."

"Endemic is like a characteristic or temperament that is at the very heart of a matter or a happening. This cane is *müz*." Malchían held the Blackwood staff in front of him and towards Anámn. "No one can say this cane is theirs alone, even me. This cane acts like müz and is of keh."

Anámn knew that the old man was not attempting deception or

cloudiness. He told Anámn that all explanations regarding his identity would be misunderstood if the Phmquedrian did not embrace the phrase and Awaken. Therefore, Matriester said nothing to the Damüdan Mystic. Instead he chanted to himself and communed with Téza. "Keh" was next…

"We should be good for awhile," Anámn said, referring to his na'ísa. "I think I can make it another two or three hundred lengths now."

"Good."

Like an ancient ritual that lost none of its meaning, the old one hopped on the Sczyphamek's back and clutched everyone's cane. Anámn levitated and flew out of the cave, heading towards Mount Sunset.

***

Anámn was certain that "keh" was related to the words "Qeauríyx," "que," and "Phmquedria." It was one relationship that was not lost to him when he mulled over the words after his second encounter with Qeauríyx. Even though he knew this, an expanse lay between him and the meaningful relationship implied by the word. Téza expressed to the son of Nísephetsu that he had dropped the sharpness and ruggedness of the pronunciation.

It was nighttime. The Sczyphamek was flying with the aid of his Elemental. Matriester noticed that his na'ísa had grown since the exercise began, not just because of the revelations but also because he conversed with Téza nonstop. He truly felt the Elemental's ever-changing form and content. But feeling was not the same as understanding. Though intricately connected, feeling was only one part of embracing. And feeling something and being subsumed by something were two different things.

Instead of hurrying at great speeds at the sacrifice of duration, Kinesis flew at a moderate speed that would allow him to fly for hours, not an *hour*.

His thoughts were scattered, yet focused. Speed, distance, Téza, "keh," Mount Sunset, Awakening, Malchían, É, müz, fíp, mányx… He lost sight of none of these and grew more and more taken with the cane Malchían carried.

Again, Téza indicated that Anámn was pronouncing the word "keh" incorrectly. The vowel sound at the end of the consonant was nearly truncated and silent. The phonetic enunciation was as if one only pronounced the "k" in "keh." He repeated the sound over and over, audibly and mentally. The Sczyphamek attempted to place his qanín in the relationship…

Volcanic Darkness

It ripped through the Firmament.
Somehow, in the lifelessness of space…
It rips through the Firmament…
Lo'Ché and Kímaios'lo intersected there…
The eighth time they danced in such a manner.
It emerged from the disruption in fire and darkness.
The stars were aghast at its figure.
Rough edges.
Indentations…
It could hardly be considered a globe…
It would never be a life-giving planet…
It grimaced and scowled at such heavenly judgments…
If not by its power alone
If not by its might alone
If not by its will alone
If not by its anger alone
If not by its hope alone
If not by its understanding alone
The Dark would disprove the cynical Firmament…
In malice and hope, it screamed…
No matter how many arrived,
There would always be a deposit of it—
Ineradicable
Henceforth and forevermore…
Even as I am recorded in this
I happened before the Auría
I happened before Qe
What is my name Sczyphamek?

"Keh," Kinesis answered.

His eyes were golden-crimson. His green aura pulsated with vigor.

Where were the mountains? Where was Malchían? How could a sound
be made in the vacuum of the Firmament…?

"Anámn! *Anámn*!" the Phmquedrian heard the old man scream.

Why did he seem so far away?

"Sczyphamek Kinesis!"
Suddenly, Matriester saw the terrain in front of him and nearly crashed into the side of a mountain. Gaining control of his senses, the Phmquedrian descended to the ground and rested on the trunk of a Yardük. Malchían(?) dismounted from Anámn's back. Steam and flashes of energy erupted from the body of the Sczyphamek. The Mystic(?) gazed upon the runaway insightfully and retreated a few feet from Anámn's position.

"Keh, *keh*, keh, *keh*, keh," Anámn alternated between chanting and singing. "Keh, *keh*..."
Kinesis' body shuddered and his golden-crimson eyes streamed down the waters of disclosure and perplexity. The Blackwood cane in the nameless man's hand emitted a strange sort of blackness, which caused the Mystic(?) to clench the staff tighter. The Damüdan Mystic fell to his knees and recited, "Fá'atoño má" with compassion and intercessory groans.

Kinesis' green aura flickered and flared in a magnificent, silent eruption. He looked at the ground and touched its presence. He looked at the trees and tasted its presence. He looked at his hands and smelled its presence. He gazed at the sky and atmosphere and loved its presence. He looked at the nameless man and felt nothing but it, nothing but *keh*. And the staff the man was holding—Anámn witnessed within it an indescribable type of Darkness. The Darkness was extremely condensed and utterly potent. Everywhere Kinesis gazed keh was present to certain degrees, but in the nameless man and his staff... they were filled with keh, brimmed over with keh, nourished by keh...

"É müz keh..." the nearly Awakened Sczyphamek chanted. "Fá'atoño má."
In the blink of an eye, the once silent aura sonically reverberated through the area. Anámn and Téza felt innumerable pockets of potential and kinetic energy. The dark green aura surrounded his body in a thick, luminous shield. Holding his left hand out, Anámn drew on the potential energy of keh, and almost transformed it into an intermediate, indeterminate state of energy—one that was *nearly* between potential and kinetic.

While taking a deep breath, Kinesis' Elemental aura completely withdrew.

Both men sat down on the ground and were quiet for many minutes.
Finally Anámn spoke up. "What is the name of that sacred weapon?"
"Black Staff," the man with no name stated.
"I've never heard of it," Anámn responded.
"Only nel'asmív versed in the history of the planet and the Fragments would know about it. It has not been used overtly for thousands of cycles."

"It happens as keh," Anámn reasoned aloud. "It is müz. I am a part of that staff, but you're almost one with it." The Phmquedrian touched the end of the cane. "Is Malchían the same way?"

"Yes," the man answered.

"Keh is the name of this nameless planet... before they came... but something happened... I saw a vision... I saw, I experienced.... I can't describe it..."

"You fell into the Auría," he explained. "Its words have been following you since you left Nísyx."

Anámn thought about that *thing* that he tried to outrun but could not escape after his encounter with Qeauríyx.

"*That was the Auría?*"

"Not just the Auría," the man replied quietly.

"How many of you are happening?"

"Right now?"

"Yeah."

"Not enough..." the nameless man trailed. "Altogether, Malchían and I have carried this staff for over two hundred cycles, but as you have surely sensed, our time has grown short. Malchían, as you happened upon him, departed a few days ago."

"How is that possible? I don't understand," Anámn commented.

"You may never understand us," the man replied. "But that is not the point. I did not bring you out here so that you would find out about Black Staff. You came here to Awaken. What happens with this staff is our business."

"You know I'm gonna ask."

"I know," the man grunted solemnly. "Go ahead."

"Why haven't you fought against the other mystical weapons?"

"Who says I want to?"

"But aren't you keh? Weren't you here first?"

"You are still thinking linearly, and even if I was first, I am no longer the only one here..."

"I don't understand..."

"I know you don't; that's why I said you must Awaken," the man responded. "And even if you do that, there is no guarantee that you will be able to embrace everything. Can you go on in spite of this?"

Anámn, for the first time, seriously considered the old man's question. Every revelation brought answers that, in turn, only brought more questions. It was and would probably continue to be an infinite cycle. Malchían asked Anámn a similar question after his tragic encounter with Alzhexph.

"Staxis..." he muttered.

"Ah..." the man affirmed.

"I... I can't go back. I've come too far now..."

For a brief moment the sun broke through the clouds and Anámn looked to the north. He was unable to see it before because the panorama was so ridiculously gray and visibility was only a few lengths. But as Anámn gazed at the rock in front of him, some two hundred lengths away, he knew his eyes did not deceive him. It was Mount Sunset, and it's height was mythical. He could not see the top. Smaller, yet no less intimidating mountains spawned from its southwestern and southeastern slopes, creating the beginning of the nameless mountain chains. The snow was inescapable. The only thing that contrasted with the snow was the dark, gray rock of the crags. The elevation appeared to increase sharply about fifty lengths ahead.

"By the One!" he exclaimed. "How tall is that thing?"

"Around forty-two thousand feet," the man answered, with a smile. "Only Edaw Peak and Sunrise Mountain are taller."

A gust of cold air fell upon them, causing both men to shiver.

Facing the mountain, Anámn kneeled down. "Hop on. We need to find some shelter."

"A few caves should meet our needs." The Staff Wielder added with an impish grin, "And Anámn, wait until we get there before you start meditating on 'fíp.' Ah?"

The Sczyphamek chuckled. "All right."

Kinesis ascended out of the trees and made his way to the third highest mountain on Qeauríyx.

***

Once they found a suitable cave inside Mount Sunset, Anámn and the Damüdan made three trips into the tree line to gather wood. Their rations would only last for a week, but Anámn did not believe eight days was long enough for him to Awaken. If his memory was correct, it was the thirty-first day of Ízneko. In two days, the winter solstice would arrive. The days were only one to two hours in length, and the mountain would probably claim what little sunlight there was, for the sun set to the east northeast. Mount Sunset was named precisely for the fact that the Zénan appeared to set behind its rocky blanket.

The climate was already plenty cold. Another two or three weeks in the mountains of Damüda would kill him. But Anámn stopped worrying about such matters. The relationship "fíp" implied was much more important.

However, the runaway was no fool; he did not expect to Awaken once the last word in the phrase was revealed to him. The word was part of a phrase. And like the word, the phrase expressed relationship. It took him almost seven durations to understand what "Fá'atoño má" actually expressed. And he knew the phrase had even more "meaning" beyond and beneath its ancient terra.

As usual, the nameless Damüdan kept quiet. He folded his arms and sat with his legs crossed while Black Staff resided in his lap. Anámn had observed the cane on numerous occasions, but had yet determined its length. The Damüdan appeared asleep, but then, how could keh slumber?

What did "fíp" relate to? At first Téza showed Anámn a similar vision of the one he witnessed when *müz* was revealed/reasoned. However, Matriester could not shake the picture's original interpretation. Discouraged, Anámn had come to admit that one moment possessed multiple meanings and interpretations, just like the dynamic relationship between potential and kinetic energy.

Téza encouraged Anámn by intimating how complicated an Awakening was. Some Sczyphameks never actually Awoke, and those that did still had room to grow. Some Elemental warriors took numerous cycles to Awaken while others Arose in only a few durations. Before Anámn finished formulating the question, Téza answered it. Sczyphamek Exceptional held the mark for the fastest Awakening: one duration.

Anámn was flabbergasted. Other than Neztríanis, the present Zananín, Imperial, and the First, the only other Sczyphamek Anámn knew about was Exceptional. He possessed little information about him, only that he was believed to be the greatest Sczyphamek since the First. And none had surpassed him since, though Anámn wondered how adept Pre-Eminent and Vicious were. Exceptional's position might have been eclipsed now.

Concentrate, the Phmquedrian thought to himself.

Fíp, fíp, fíp, fíp, fíp, fíp, fíp, fíp, fíp, fíp, fíp, fíp, fíp, Téza... Keh fíp... müz... fíp... Téza fíp... The nameless Damüdan opened one eye, as Anámn's aura illumined. However, unlike previous occasions, the Sczyphamek controlled the emanation. Keh fíp Téza... Anámn fell into Téza. The Elemental contracted, enlarged, and contracted, discharging a force of kinesis that shoved Anámn into Qeauríyx. So much connectivity, diversity, paradox, and irrefutable reality. But something mysterious threaded the variegated phenomenon together. Thread... bind... connect... stitch... fíp... It was an action.

Fípy'skax... Y'skax... Y'skax... Elemental... Fípy'skax... to (elementally) thread/bind... Anámn was bound to Téza, bound to keh, bound to the Damüdan, bound to Qeauríyx, bound to...

"You understand it now, don't you?" the Damüdan inquired. "You were running from the inescapable."

Stubborn, Anámn would not let himself cry at the revelation.

"I am bound to you and you to me, and we... we are bound to all of this," the Mystic stated. "What you do with this knowledge is up to you."

Matriester almost ignored the Wielder's statement, for he had already translated the phrase. But something was wrong. He recited the phrase over and over in his head, but it made no sense. Finally, he attempted the incantation audibly.

"Paradox all of ours nameless planet bind Téza embrace?" Anámn questioned himself while uttering the phrase. It sounded like nonsense.

The Damüdan laughed so heartily at the runaway that he nearly came to tears. Kinesis' face was a thing of legend: righteous confusion mingled with an ignorant honesty. Even inwardly, Anámn sensed Téza reacting in what could only be related as humor.

Silencing his amusement, the old man closed his eyes and resumed his stoic look.

"Malchían… or Damüdan Mystic… whatever your name is," Matriester said with a twinge of spite. "I have a question about the way the Ancient Tongue speaks, not about the phrase itself."

The man's eyes opened.

"The order of the words—they don't make sense."

"Ah. Syntax—the structure of the sentence—and grammar," he said. "Is that what you mean?"

"Yeah," he replied. "I think so. Lénü was teaching me a lot of things and I remember Nísyx using that 'syntax' word."

"Yes, I would imagine that that would be difficult for you… I hadn't thought of that…" he murmured.

"We don't have time to go over the rules of sentence making, much less in the Ancient Tongue," Anámn stated. "But writing and talking are two different things. Nel'asmív can talk and learn different languages easily, but proper grammar is a completely different matter."

"Not *completely*," the Wielder responded mysteriously. Sitting up straight, the Damüdan instructed the Sczyphamek on the general rules of the Ancient Tongue. "The word that signifies the major action, this word is normally found at the end of the phrase. Of course, there are exceptions."

"Yeah, there always seems to be those," Anámn grinned.

"Indeed," the man agreed. "The second most important word, whether it is a thing or an action or something else, this word normally goes at the beginning of the sentence or phrase. Action words are context sensitive so they might be describing an action in the past, present, or future. The words that are in between are in no particular order and infer connection. There are no words like 'to' or 'from' or 'with' in the Ancient Tongue. These words are surmised through context and translation."

"Ah," the young man trailed, pondering the words of the Black Staff Wielder.

At this stage in his development, the Phmquedrian Sczyphamek should have known better. *Of course* the words were not in order.

The most important word was last. That was "má," which meant "embrace." The second most important word was "É," which meant chance/purpose and rest/movement.

"Embrace [the paradox of] chance/purpose [and] rest/movement…" Anámn muttered to himself in deep contemplation.

The words were like pieces of a puzzle. Anámn placed *miüz* "here," but then "over there" seemed to be a better place. *Fíp* was a tricky action word…

The Damüdan dozed off, leaning against the wall of the cave, while the fire lay in between them. For three hours Anámn wrestled with the incantation, chanting the various permutations, until he was sure of the phrase. Finally, the Sczyphamek called Kinesis was ready to audibly speak the incantation he learned so many durations ago, but did not understand.

"Téza embraces [the paradox of] the chance/purpose [and] rest/movement [that] binds/threads all of us [and] our nameless planet," the Kylanín recited confidently. "É müz keh fíp Téza má."

"Very good," the Damüdan smiled. "You never would have found this out until you learned what paradox truly does."

"Ah." Anámn's stomach growled. He was worn from travel and his qanín was nearly enervated from searching, thinking, and wrestling with his mind, body, and spirit. "Malchían, I am hungry."

Malchían(?) handed the Phmquedrian the bag of food, stood up, and headed to the cave's exit.

"Where are you going?" Matriester asked the Damüdan.

"Down a road you do not know to a place you cannot follow," the Mystic replied with a solemn smile.

"Why are you leaving?" the Sczyphamek nervously redirected.

"Because I have nothing more to teach you. I am a Wielder, not a Sczyphamek. And I must do something before I am taken."

Anámn was overcome with sentiment and gratefulness, and he could not help but wonder *why* the Black Staff Wielders put their lives at stake for him. "I can't ask you to stay. I don't have the right. But I have one question."

"When I leave there will be another," the old man anticipated Matriester's query. "That person must decide their own path. But the kindness we displayed to you, please return it."

"I will," he said. "Damüdan, what is your name?"

"Van," he replied. "My name is Van."

"Thank you, Van," Anámn stated with sincerity.

The young man stood up, stuck his right arm out, and turned his forearm parallel to his chest. Bracing the Staff against the wall, Van responded in kind. Walking towards one another, they bumped their fists and forearms together, while holding each other's right shoulder with their left hand. It was a standard Phmquedrian sign of affection and familiarity.

Tears welled in the eyes of Matriester. "You were the only family I had in Euhilv. I never appreciated how much I counted on you."

Van's countenance changed, and his voice had two layers, both his and Malchían's. "You were a stubborn child, a hardheaded adolescent, and an obstinate young man. But you have grown and stubbornness can become tenacity…

"Anámn, once you Awaken, you must return to Euhilv. Not as a leader or liberator, but as a brother-in-chains who desires freedom."

The Damüdan hesitated, but then reconsidered. His voice was uneasy. "I did not want to tell you this. But Malchían insisted... Your father invoked the runaway provision."

Anámn was agape in fear and guilt.

"It wasn't because of you directly. It was because of what you did to Héthyx and one of your father's mansions." The Damüdan Wielder of Black Staff looked out of the cave and into the nighttime, but soon returned his gaze to the waiting eyes of Anámn. "*This place... sometimes... Staxis...*

"The mineworkers were thrown into frenzy, and they openly talked of insurrection. As you know, slaves of Euhilv are not lazy or weak as much as they were demoralized. Given the right spark, Euhilv would revolt the same way it did all those cycles ago.

But your father is as ruthless as he is intelligent. That man happened as one of the most ruthlessly intelligent nel'asmív to ever walk this planet.

"Ju Xaníz announced that he would use the runaway provision as a means of control. Only this time, he ordered that even those who spoke of escape or insurrection would suffer its consequences."

Anámn did not want to hear anymore because he knew how the story was going to end. Even so, he had to hear it.

"Ah," the Mystic continued. "Malchían reappeared and told ju Xaníz that he was your family and that Alzhexph knew his life was more important than all the slaves that would be killed under the runaway provision—not in terms of significance or dignity, but in terms of utility."

The Sczyphamek was the son of Alzhexph ju Xaníz. His father did not respect life; his father respected utility. Utility granted him power. And Malchían's death would grant him the utilization and actualization of enormous power, for the entire metropolis of Euhilv knew of the wise elder.

A rapid of tears rained from Anámn's cheeks and collected into a lake of sorrowful anticipation, but he bade the Mystic to resume the story.

"Your father agreed. He publicly tortured and killed Malchían..." The Wielder's eyes reddened. Van shivered, and his voice lost its resolve. "He... he was... out of all of us... he was my best friend and a great nel'asmív."

Anámn braced his forehead on the rocky wall of the cave and sobbed. No aura. No flashes of power. No weather disturbances. No visceral reaction. No sign of grief other than a man hitting his fists against the immovable wall of stone and sediment.

"I do not have a father," Matriester said in a still, faint voice. "But if any man ever deserved to be called 'Kanoso,' it was Malchían."

"He loved you, Kinesis," the Mystic replied. "How could I have been or acted any different?"

"I know." He gave Van an amicable smile. "Have a safe and good journey."

"You too."

Matriester picked up the bag that contained their supplies. "You don't want to split what's left?"

"No. I have... *alternative* sources of food. But Kinesis, let me ask you something before I leave."

"What's that?"

"If you can make your own energy, why do you get hungry? After all, movement constitutes the cycles of life."

Anámn could not stretch his eyelids or mouth further apart than they were. Being hungry meant that his body *needed energy*.

Why am I so blind, he thought to himself.

"Stop being so hard on yourself," the Mystic stated in a manner that reminded Anámn of Brenko and Malchían. "You happened as a slave who was barely fed the overwhelming majority of his life. It is not a shortcoming to think of food as your concrete source of energy.

"But let me tell you—because I am not a Sczyphamek with your powers—while my mind can conceive of such a transfer of energy, this does not mean that it would be easy or even possible. It is what they call a 'hunch.' The wise ones of old called it a 'theory'."

Kinesis embraced his teacher's final instructions and insights. Anámn did not know what his body was made of, *actually*. He was and was not like wood, pulleys, engines, magma, and volcanoes. Those were mechanical and natural manipulations of energy, not biochemical ones.

Van broke through the Phmquedrian's thoughts. "Think of it more as a goal than as the moment of your Awakening. Staxis, if you *could* do that, there is no question you would be on Pre-Eminent and Vicious' level."

"Van, I have one last question. You don't have to answer. But how powerful is Neztríanis, assuming her na'ísa, belief, and understanding is steady?"

"Good qualification," the Mystic smiled. "She has, beyond a doubt, the potential to emerge as an elite Sczyphamek..."

"But..." Anámn anticipated the exception to the rule.

"*But* her path and yours are not going to be exactly the same," Van smirked. "You know, it is not that I possess foresight. I have simply forgotten my name because I have been here so long."

"And now you must go."

"Ah. I must."

"Goodbye, Kanoso."

"Goodbye, Anámn."

Walking to the cave's opening, which was actually a cliff at the twelve thousand foot mark of the mountain, the Mystic jumped out and off. Within an instant, Anámn no longer discerned Van's kinetic signature.

Sitting alone in the cavern, the young man felt a range of dispositions: turmoil, sadness, gratitude, and confidence. He took a small meat strip out of the bag and chewed it slowly. Vengeance was not on his mind, but Anámn was horrified at Malchían's decision and the unspeakable tragedy that was Euhilv. He had to go back.

In addition, Kinesis was awestruck that a Wielder had pitched his tent amongst the lowly of Qeauríyx. Not only that, but a Wielder and Mystic *personally* invested their lives to help and direct Anámn. Never in his wildest imagination did he think a Wielder could act in such a humble manner for such a sustained period of time. The runaway was unwilling to call such a commitment an act of divine favor, but he was growing to appreciate nel'asmív and the planet in a way he previously had not. Dealing with and confronting meaninglessness did not necessitate a belief in or action of a deity, however.

Throughout the entire exchange between Anámn and Van, Téza remained noticeably silent.

Chapter Twenty-Six: Sunrise Mountain

Wincing, Neztríanis continued to fly at a moderate speed to her north. Frequently, she stopped and rested. Her wounds ran deep—physically, religiously, theologically, philosophically, and emotionally. Her left ankle was undoubtedly broken, and her right arm hummed in excruciating torment. Because of her shattered jaw, grimacing caused even greater pain to overtake her expressions of discomfort. After about five hours of sustained flight, Temperature reached her limit. Falling unconscious while in mid-air, the Sczyphamek plummeted to the ground.

She awoke alone in the grassy Bitzroy Plains. She rolled over, faced the sky, and thought about Vicious' final words. He told her that he and the General Maximum were heading to Líachim. Pre-Eminent, Vicious, Commandant Feolenz, and the General Maximum would soon march against the continent of Líachim *together*. How could anyone stand up against such a force?

Neztríanis was too worn to move and too hungry to wander aimlessly. She did not know her exact location, just that she was in northern Bitzroy. Focusing with her entire qanín and with the aid of Renzgé, Neztríanis tried to locate the heat signature of her friend and ally, Timura. Overextending herself, the woman fell unconscious.

The next time she awoke, Neztríanis felt heat signatures to her east. Her Elemental, although weak itself, gave her notice. There were only three, and one was a windhorse. The woman could barely move—so spent was she—but with her remaining energy, she sat up. Something felt vaguely familiar...

Summoning all of her strength and ignoring the pain in her jaw, the Nez Spiritan yelled at the top of her lungs, "Help! Can anyone hear me? Please help me!"

The affliction of her broken jaw pounced on her. It was as if Vincallous had left a deposit of Dé'wa in her fractured bones.

The two nel'asmívs and windhorse changed direction. They were heading her way. The woman lay back down and waited.

Soon, she heard the sounds of what she sensed. They were Tannódin'é judging by their language and accents. However, their dialect was different than what Neztríanis was used to. They sounded almost Nez Spiritan. Five minutes later, she was face to face with a middle-aged Tannódin'é man and a young woman. The woman strongly resembled the man, but she also possessed undeniable Nez Spiritan features. The man appeared five to ten cycles older than Hafir, and both the father and daughter were wearing northern Nez Spiritan attire, brown cloaks with hoods, which provided protection from the constant wind that blew in from the coast and the mountain. The windhorse huffed as it came to a stop a few feet from her body. Various supplies were on its back.

The way the strangers gawked at Neztríanis only confirmed what her qanín knew, but had not accepted: Vincallous had physically beaten her to a most terrible and wicked extent.

The young woman was apprehensive and pulled her wind-blown black hair away from her face. "Kanoso, what should we do?"

"We cannot leave her here to die, or to be found, raped, or sold," the father commented. His maroon eyes softened. "Perhaps that was already her fate… Who knows how she came into such a happening, but injuries like these are not accidental."

The daughter stared at the nearly comatose Neztríanis and sighed in displeasure. "But we are a four day's journey from home."

"Please… please help me," the daughter of Hopha begged with quivering lips, ignoring the sting of her jaw. She was starving, dehydrated, and completely at the mercy of strangers. The chance of their departure was more agonizing than all the combined afflictions throughout her body.

"What will you think of yourself in the morning?" the elder sternly questioned his offspring. "Take some supplies off the windhorse and retrieve a canteen. *Now.*"

"Aye." Begrudgingly, the daughter complied and gave her father a jug of water.

Holding the jug above Neztríanis' head, the man let some drops fall out and into the Sczyphamek's mouth while the daughter set up camp. Next, they prepared a meal. When they finished, the daughter took the horse to nearby running waters. The father cut and mashed very small pieces of vegetables, fruit, and luku. Then, he sat Neztríanis up against a large supply bag. When he did so, the daughter of Hopha's shoulder audibly popped. She grunted in misery.

The man was dumbfounded. How was it possible that a nel'asmív so thoroughly wounded was not dead? Even though nel'asmív were exceptionally durable creatures, the damage sustained by Neztríanis was beyond what any*body* could handle.

Feeding her tiny portions so that Neztríanis did not have to chew, the man asked her, "How long have you been out here?"

Neztrίanis gave him a facial expression signifying her lack of temporal knowledge. After traveling the Infinite Circle, she realized that a Sczyphamek's conception and perception of time was quite different from a normal nel'asmίv.

"Where are you going?"

"North," she whispered nearly inaudibly and in such a way that minimized the pain.

"Who did this to you?" he asked probingly.

Neztrίanis wept in reply. She was overwhelmed by her lowly, eviscerated, and nearly naked condition. "Someone... someone so much stronger than I."

The man did not want to add any more burdens to the heavy ones she obviously carried, so he quieted himself and continued to feed her miniscule portions of food. The Nez Spiritan was famished and despite the discomfort, she ate every bit the man provided.

The Tannόdin'é introduced himself. "My name is Isürus. That well-meaning but sometimes selfish young lady is my daughter Crίna.[1] I am sure you have noticed that she is half-Nez Spiritan. Her mother, my consort, was from this lovely land. She has been gone now for six cycles." His eyes grew saddened yet resolute. "I guess that is part of the reason I am helping you. We were about your age when we met."

Neztrίanis could not keep her eyes open. Digestion took her remaining strength, and the man helped her lay down on the ground. Within moments, she was asleep.

***

"Who are you?" Isürus asked warily, as soon as Neztrίanis opened her eyes.

Her jaw was noticeably pain free, and her ankle was nearly healed. But her shoulder and arm still ached, although to a lesser degree. No doubt her Elemental recovery and healing factor emerged after she had taken in some food and water. Rai and Renzgé restored her by triage. By far, her jaw needed to be healed the fastest, due to her need to incant and sing. Her ankle allowed her to travel. Indeed, her shoulder was the last thing that needed to mend. She would have to deal with its soreness. Vincallous told her it would take two to three weeks to completely revivify, so she surmised that at least a week had passed since her encounter with the Zananίn.

Isürus witnessed her entire recovery. The daughter of Hopha had to say something. Crίna was a few paces behind her father, with an armed energy pistol.

---

[1] Crίna (kree-nuh)

"Crína," the Sczyphamek said amicably. "I promise that I will not do you or your father any harm; you can put the energy pistol away."

Isürus' eyes stared blankly and pithily at the Nez Spiritan.

"My name is Neztríanis," she continued. "I am a Sczyphamek."

At once, the perceptive Isürus stood up and backed away from Phyxtríalis.

"Only two people on this continent could have done that to you," he muttered.

"It was Vincallous," she replied.

"He let you live?" the man replied rhetorically. "In all these cycles, I will never come to understand that man..."

"You talk as if..."

"I knew him," Isürus replied nonchalantly. "I knew Késhal personally. That is, before I was forced to vacate the Imperial Guard."

Neztríanis gave the man a suspicious glare. Did she just make Crína a promise she could not keep? And what bedeviling sort of circumstances placed her in the company of someone who had personally kept company with the leaders of Global Initiative—in Nez Spirita of all places?

"That was nearly twenty cycles ago," he explained. "Many things have changed since then... Many things...

"Vincallous might not even know that I am still here. The Eradicate stopped their reconnaissance on me cycles ago, once they were certain that I truly was done."

"Done?" Neztríanis asked.

"I came here because I was done with Global Initiative, its purposes, its aims. Well, more like, they were done with me."

Neztríanis' face demanded that the man explain himself.

Isürus kicked the ground and sat down. "My family was aristocracy. We served Tannódin's aims even before Imperial. The Violet Manacle was in my family's possession for two centuries." Although he spoke with such short sentences, the words emanating from his mouth mixed with the countenances upon his face revealed so much with so little.

"You were a Wielder?" Temperature asked.

Pulling his cloak's left sleeve back, Isürus exposed his inner forearm. A conspicuous scar ran down the center, from his wrist to the groove in his elbow.

"Courtesy of the Manacle," he elucidated. Tekil stared at his arm reflectively. "All Wielders of the Violet Manacle carry this scar... This kímaz, damn scar... How many people did I kill for the House of Kaz? How many suffered senselessly because of Global Initiative...?

"I didn't realize it at the time, but losing the Manacle, my title, my family's honor, and coming to Nez Spirita—that was the best thing that ever happened to me. I have not been back to Tannódin since I left, and I do not plan on doing so. But I still keep myself abreast of the happenings of Qeauríyx." He turned and faced Neztríanis. "Search me, Sczyphamek;

search me and discern for yourself that this is not fabrication."

The Sczyphamek called Temperature did not need to search. She felt his passion-filled voice and saw it in his passion-filled daughter.

"I don't agree with them anymore, but I do understand them. If you are planning to fight against them then you better understand them," he warned. The man was quite the definition of pithy.

"I learned that the hard way," she responded. "I am curious. What do you do now?"

"Crína and I live in northern Bitzroy. We farm and trade the fruits and vegetables that grow on our land. I have tilled Nez Spiritan soil for nearly eighteen cycles."

"Have you met Jennó?" Temperature asked warily, for the spy claimed he was from the surrounding area.

"Jennó... the merchant?" he replied. "Of course. He was responsible for taking some of my dried fruit down to Nextu. It sells quite well there now."

"He is Eradicate. My race against Vicious was precipitated by him."

"He... he is? They use Nez Spiritans now? Staxis, Reníz you are ingenious. And they still don't trust me... exceptional..."

"Jennó is gone, or at least this version of him," the Sczyphamek explained. "And who is Reníz?"

"She is the current Wielder of the Violet Manacle and the head of the Eradicate. Even more, she is the adopted daughter of Késhal and Vincallous."

Phyxtríalis tried to stop her face from engaging in contortions of disbelief. But, it was still difficult for her to truly see her adversaries as anything but monsters.

"You underestimate them," he observed. "The General Maximum, Lo'Marc P'tan—you might as well call him Vincallous' son. Fierce trained and stood by that man even when he was just a young volunteer in Blue Rapier. And then there is Commandant Feolenz. He is like a grandfather to all four of them." The thought of Feolenz made Isürus sigh and shake his head. "*Do not underestimate that old man.* That man... That man is beyond description..."

Tekil gathered his things and placed them on the windhorse. Suddenly, he paused, looked Neztríanis in her eyes, and asked, "Do you see, Sczyphamek? Do you see how strong their alliance is?

"Pre-Eminent is a far greater leader than her mother, even greater than Imperial. She surpassed them both in only twenty cycles. What you hear in my voice is respect, not blind admiration. It is truly unfortunate that Késhal is unable to understand 'normal' families..."

The Sczyphamek was quiet while the father and daughter continued to pack their supplies. Once they finished, Neztríanis spoke up. "Isürus, thank you for your help."

Crína could no longer contain herself and blurted out, "You do not think this is coincidence? Kanoso, how likely is it that on all the days we take our cyclic journey to the coast before harvest season that we would meet this woman?"

"It is highly unlikely," the father responded. "But Crína, I have told you countless times. Who knows what truly happens when freedom and destiny intertwine. This is Qeauríyx, and sometimes things do not make any sense.

"Tell me, was it through coincidence or necessity that I was stripped of the Manacle and met your mother?"

"I do not know," she responded, pondering the (im)possibility of her own (non)existence.

"Neither do I. But meeting your mother and living here means more to me than thirty-four cycles of service to Késhal and the House of Kaz." Walking over to Neztríanis, Isürus handed her a cloak and small bag with some food inside. "I hope you make good use of it."

"Thank you," the Sczyphamek repeated, wrapped the cloak around her half naked body, and gazed upon his daughter reminiscently.

"What?" Crína asked.

"You remind me of myself," Neztríanis replied. "Your father is a wise man, and I am sure your mother matched his intelligence. Even when you disagree with him, remember that, Crína. Because a day is coming when his wisdom must live on in you."

"Aye," she said sheepishly.

Returning her gaze to the former Wielder, Temperature nodded in affirmation. "I have another question."

"What is it?"

"Vicious told me that he and the General Maximum were heading to Líachim. How long do you think Líachim will be able to hold?"

"They are…? Staxis… Késhal and A'reznu are already there… " He thought to himself for a few seconds then expounded, "If Zotham (that's the leader of Aphaz, the largest city on Líachim) planned well, he should at least be able to hold for nearly a cycle, two at best." Isürus paused in meaningful silence. "But that is Pre-Eminent and Vicious. That is Feolenz and P'tan. They will not withdraw under any circumstances. And I do not know the strategy of either side. So much depends on the war plan. Even if Líachim has planned well, if the House of Kaz's plan is better, Líachim will fall much sooner."

"I see," she replied somberly. One cycle was not long enough to become an elite Sczyphamek, even if she Awakened within the next duration or two. Neztríanis hoped Kéma had made it to Aphaz and that the stolen data would yield Líachim an advantage.

"Best of fortune," the Tannódin'é said, hitching the last of his things on the windhorse.

"I pray that you all fare well," she replied, and then asked three departing queries. "How far are the Crag Mountains from here? Is the water safe to drink? And what is the date?"

"The Crags are about four to five hundred lengths north, northeast of here," Crína responded. "The water here is pretty clean, but you should boil it to be safe. And it is Kazlé, the ninth day of Janíz."

"I am grateful. Farewell."

"You too," Crína said. "Our village won't believe it when I tell them that I met the Nez Spiritan Sczyphamek…"

"You aren't saying anything about this to anyone," Isürus warned. "This woman is already wanted for damaging the Triple Skyrises. And apparently, I'm still under surveillance. You will not speak of this day until Nez Spirita is out of Tannódin'é control."

"Yes, Kanoso."

"You can make that happen, can't you?" Isürus asked Neztríanis with a grin.

Neztríanis smiled back. "Not without some help."

"Aye. Very good."

"Fá'atoño má," the Sczyphamek chanted and her orange-white aura emerged. She levitated off the ground, and in an instant, she streaked towards the north, in search of Timura.

Crína and Isürus gazed in wonderment, until they lost the daughter of Hopha in the horizon.

"What do we do now?" the daughter asked her father.

"The same thing we do before every harvest," he replied. "We go to the coast and fish."

"And then what," she pressed, longing for an answer.

"The same thing we always do. We hope, trust, and keep living."

***

Neztríanis did not want to overexert herself. It was a hot summer day, and the fact that she *felt* hot meant that she had not regained her Elemental equilibrium. Therefore, she did not fly at her maximum sustained speed. Every hour or so, she stopped, rested, and dialogued with Rai and Renzgé by meditating on the sacred chant and her own personal incantations.

"*Zí mányx que Rai,*" she sang, while sitting in the grass. Rubbing her hand in the soil, she translated, "Rai embraced, embraces, and will embrace the frigidity/emptiness of the emerging-land."

"Mona fla Renzgé ná," she chanted, then converted the phrase into her present language. "Renzgé lives and ignites presence."

"Nányx" related to the mystery of sustained living in the Ancient Tongue, while "mona" signified the mysterious and tenuous reality of "presence/existence/journey" in the lives of nel'asmív and of all animate creatures. "Flanyx…" Neztríanis encountered the word on numerous occasions when she read the Auría. The word lingered in her mind from the moment she met Qeauríyx. Flanyx implied the action of "ignition or kindling." Its presence in the Auría's creation stories and descriptions concerning the processes of life were prolific. Neztríanis had long semi-translated both of the phrases, during her journey to Nextu. And once the Elemental revealed their names to her, during her sojourn in the visions from Qeauríyx, she completed the phrases' relationship. She pondered the phrases during the Cycle(?) she and Timura spent with young Anplo. (And she was still unsure *what* Anplo actually was and what he saw in the water…)

Even still, there were deeper meanings and significances to the expressions.

However, Neztríanis, with a grave heart, had come to understand that embracing the relationship and meaning of her powers was not her most significant challenge. Nor was it her na'ísa. She would have preferred those battles compared to the one she now faced.

Her belief/faith was her most glaring issue. Even though she believed in the Nameless One, her belief only scratched the surface. Belief in the Nameless One was neither a *cause* nor a *disposition*. Neither was belief *only and merely* a *personal* relationship.

Vincallous exposed something much deeper in her *Toño*: Prior to their confrontation, Temperature had come to believe that the Auría was *her* cause. *That was false*. Locating the Auría and transporting it was only the beginning of her journey. The daughter of Hopha had forgotten what the Great Mother told her. Her mission was a *task* not a cause. Neztríanis disastrously confused the two. She turned her task into an idol and worshipped it and the Auría.

No matter how much the Auría chronicled the Nameless One, it was not, could never be, did not, and could never do what the One with No Name is and does. Though interconnected, the Nameless One and the Auría happened differently.

In addition, the First Sczyphamek now fell under the same critical gaze of Neztríanis.

After she was beaten and Kaz Fierce sat beside her, she experienced it. But the seed had already sprouted deep within her. The seed was planted by Namí and Bíoske, fertilized by Hafir and Rydín, and watered by her murderous actions and her encounter with Vincallous.

The roots were numerous. The soil was settling. The ground was now firm, yet still permeable. Soon the stalk would emerge from the dirt. Neztríanis felt the stem burrowing through the topsoil, ready for the rays of the sun. She was venturing up a new and unpredicted way.

She was becoming a Zephanín.

The more she reflected on matters, the more she could not deny her rationale, her emotions, or her body. Neztríanis Phyxtríalis took a deep breath and confirmed it. *Both* the Kylanín *and* Zananín positions were *idolatrous*. Both parties made the First's *task* their *cause*. Such confusion could only lead to the inevitable: Global Initiative.

However, Neztríanis was not foolish. She needed help. Anámn, the other Sczyphamek, was more than likely a Kylanín, but at least he was not a Zananín.

And throughout all she encountered, she never believed in her wildest imagination that *both* Vincallous and the Great Mother would have validated her task. She was afraid to know what that meant...

The Sczyphamek called Temperature quieted her thoughts, squinted, and beheld the outlines of the Crag mountain range. She was not close enough to sense Timura's signature and held back the temptation to try. She told Timura to wait a week for her, but more than a week had passed since she last saw the témo. Did Timura heed her advice and take the Auría into the Northern Country? If she did, the témo might already be dead. The Northern Country's conditions were legendarily inclement.

Worried and alarmed, Neztríanis called upon Rai and Renzgé. "Please help me. Please lend me your strength."

By the time Neztríanis made it to the Crags, she could sense Timura's heat signature. It was faint, but it was hers. The témo was nearly fifty lengths into the North Country. The woman kneeled on the northern face of one of the mountains and gazed ahead. Within a few lengths, the daughter of Hopha observed snow. Within tens of lengths, the Sczyphamek witnessed blizzard-like conditions. And if her eyes deceived her, Neztríanis' qanín was none the wiser. She was certain she saw *Sunrise Mountain*. It was a jagged, majestic triangular amalgamation of que, in dimensions beyond the planes of imagination.

There were no adjacent mountains, just hills. Or were six thousand foot mounds only foothills compared the heights of Sunrise Mountain? Perspective was challenged and shattered next to such a behemoth. The hills appeared drawn in and submerged by the gravitational pull of the mountain's base. The mountain was over five hundred lengths away and blizzards were rampant throughout. And even though such low visibility should make the conclusion seem utterly preposterous, Neztríanis beheld the mountain where Zénan's rose.

Fear settled into her heart. She recalled her ascent of Mount Xarkim, which nearly claimed the Myanín's lives. And Sunrise Mountain was nearly *twice* the height and size of Xarkim. Only Edaw peak was taller, but such a comparison seemed useless.

Forty-two of the nearly forty-eight thousand feet of altitude Mount Sunrise occupied were uncontested by any other mountain. No one could explain its dominance and happenstance. Though covered in snow, legend held that the base of the mountain was only four hundred feet above sea level. The coast of the North Country was straddled by icebergs, dangerous winds, and persistent snow, making sea travel inadvisable. And since Sunrise sat in the center of the North Country, any approach would contain at least three hundred lengths of land travel.

Neztríanis was about to undertake a mission in a land that less than a hundred ever dared to wander. And as far as she knew, none who journeyed one hundred lengths past the Crags ever returned.

"Timura and we will be the first," she promised Rai and Renzgé. "Fá'atoño má."

She raced towards her partner's position. The témo's pace slowed. Timura must have felt her by now.

Tears froze against Neztríanis' face. There were moments during her fight against Vincallous, when she thought she would never see her friend again.

The Nez Spiritan Sczyphamek settled down in the snow. Her pace quickened when she saw the feline, and a smile emerged on her face. The témo trotted in the direction of Neztríanis, slowly and deliberately, purring cautiously. The two met in the snow; only a few feet separated them.

Neztríanis sobbed with no shame or reservation. For cycles, she did not know what meant to have a friend—one who was not her mother. The majority of her life was nothing more than a constant struggle with loneliness and the sting of depression. But Timura, out of all the people she had encountered on her journey, was unparallel in friendship and camaraderie.

"Timura." Neztríanis laughed, sniffled, and wept. "I am so happy to see you."

The feline was hesitant, baffled that her complement appeared alive and well. Her mate was destroyed at the hands of Vincallous, and despite her best attempts, Timura did not believe Neztríanis' could survive the Damüdan. The témo's hope soon ran out, and she accepted Neztríanis' demise as reality. There were moments when her partner's Elemental signature flickered, but then three days passed and Timura sensed nothing.

"Temperature," the témo rasped in amicable bewilderment. Her qanín wanted to trust her eyes, but experience had taught her the benefits of skepticism: the avoidance of disappointment. "You... you are alive...?"

The nel'asmív could not restrain the instinct any longer and threw her arms around the témo's neck. Neztríanis buried her head in the black, blue, and white coat of Timura.

The témo had wrestled with and knew nothing but loss and extinction her entire life. She had become almost desensitized to it. She did not know why she even joined Neztríanis. She used the Auría retrieval as an excuse. In retrospect, she must have done so out of hope—hope she thought her canines and claws had relinquished durations ago. Neztríanis provided her something to believe in again, and that was enough for her.

This woman seemed like Neztríanis. She smelled like Neztríanis. She emitted Neztríanis' aura... *It must be Neztríanis.* For the first time in ages, the témo cried tears of joy.

"Temperature, *you are alive!*" Timura claimed reality and batted her tail on the frosty ground in excitement.

"Yes. Yes, my friend, I am… but only because of mercy and aid."

"*He let you live?*"

"Not without punishing me most severely. If I had not run into some helpful strangers, I do not know if I would have made it here. Let's head back to the Crags and come up with a plan. We need to gather a large portion of supplies. I am sure you have enough for yourself, but…"

"I agree," the témo replied. "You must tell me everything."

Everything… Neztríanis thought.

How would Timura take the news of her partner's ongoing conversion to the ranks of Zephanín?

The Sczyphamek turned around and faced the Crag Mountains. "How cold are you right now?"

"This was not so bad…" Timura replied. "But, I am under no illusions. I have heard that after one hundred lengths, the temperature plummets five degrees every ten to twenty lengths. It is believed that the temperature surrounding Sunrise Mountain is nearly two hundred degrees below freezing. It would have been and will be impossible for me to survive here without you."

Temperature nodded her head in nervous affirmation. *Two hundred degrees below freezing…?* How was such a temperate degradation possible? Such a climate was mythical or legendary. However, Sunrise Mountain was a natural phenomena that spawned myth and legend.

Once they arrived back to the southern side of the Crags (where the temperature was markedly scorching), the daughter of Hopha briefed the témo on the majority of her story, including all the details of her exchange with Vincallous and her encounter with Isürus, whom the témo could not help but snarl and gnash her teeth against. The Imperial Guard, long before they were converted into the Eradicate, had hunted the winged felines for Tannódin.

So much misery…

"Timura…" Neztríanis' tone and cadence became reflective and mysterious. "I have something to tell you…" The woman anxiously fidgeted about and ran her fingers through her hair. "The path of Kylanín is not for me."

The témo bade her partner to carry on.

"I can see how the Kylanín position seems credible, but it is no longer convincing… And the Zananín position is absolutely deplorable, even though I now understand the motivation behind it… I…" She took a deep breath, nodded her head, and would never flinch on the matter again. "I cannot hold to either of their positions…They both feel blasphemous to me…"

"So, then are you saying…"

"I am not there yet, but yes, I am happening as a Zephanín."

The témo recalled how the rift between the Kylanín and Zephanín Sczyphameks inevitably plunged her kind into a civil war. But truthfully, the conflict started before then.

We should have never agreed to partake in the Black Staff Incident, thought Timura.

"I understand if you no longer want to be joined with me," Temperature said. "I know the history of the conflict that led to the Bitter War."

"Then you also know that many témos Synthesized with Zephanín Sczyphameks?" Timura probed.

"I know," she replied. "But I also know that officially, Zephanín remain condemned by The Keep."

"What does 'The Keep' mean now?" Timura queried. "So few of us are left now. Such terms are almost meaningless…

"My species may not survive Global Initiative, and if Vincallous is 'letting' us reach the Synthesis, that truly means that my entire kind will probably be killed off…" The témo hung her head. "I might be the last the témo left on Qeauríyx by this time next cycle… and even I may be taken before then…" The feline flapped her wings and ascended in the direction of Sunrise Mountain. "This North Country is unforgiving. I might die here…"

Neztríanis did not respond and awaited the decision of her partner and friend.

"They might have been right," the témo growled in deep, historical contemplation, returning to the ground. "Perhaps Exceptional was right…"

"I would be honored if we could earn the title Myanín together," said the Sczyphamek called Temperature.

"I will join you," the feline purred quietly. "But I must warn you. As of this moment, I do not fully agree with the Zephanín position. Maybe you will convince me otherwise. But, a moment may arise where and when I cannot follow you. Please do not take that to mean…"

"I never would and I never will," she interrupted. "Your friendship is unquestionable."

"What is your birth date?"

Startled by such a mundane question, Neztríanis blinked rapidly. "Huh?"

"When I was awaiting your return, I realized that after all we discussed in the caves of the Infinite Circle, you never told me the day you were born."

"It is because I do not know… well, not really," she explained. "Since I was an orphan, I never knew. Neither did the Great Mother. However, she gave me a birthday, the third of Kazíz, in the 11,211th cycle after the Great Extinguishing. That was the day I entered into her household."

The daughter of Hopha used the traditional dating she was reared upon instead of the imperial time of "BGI" and "OGI." Global Initiative actually began in the 10,997th cycle post-Extinguishing. In Tannódin'é count,

Neztríanis was born in 214 OGI.

"Thank you," the témo rasped.

"Timura," the Sczyphamek redirected, "you do not have to come with me."

"I know," she purred. "I *must* come with you. I have been reading the pages of the Auría and it is imperative that I at least attempt this."

"I will not reach Sunrise Mountain without a strategy, and—*oh, I almost forgot*," Neztríanis interrupted herself suddenly. "Vincallous commented upon one of the techniques I used. He mentioned something about 'Elemental Individuation'..."

The ears of the témo perked. "You individuated your Elemental without the Auría?"

"I do not know what the term signifies, but according to Vicious, I did. And I did not chant."

"Yet, you have not Awakened..." the Orator became still and contemplative. "Elemental Individuation is a necessity for the Synthesis, and normally, only Awakened Sczyphameks are able to actualize such a variation in power. That's why I never mentioned it directly."

"The third level of power?" Temperature inquired, thinking back to Timura's lecture. "*That* requires Elemental Individuation, does it not?"

"Correct," the Orator nodded, still in shock. In all the chronicles of Sczyphameks from all factions, there were no accounts of an unawakened Sczyphamek achieving individuation, not even Exceptional. "*Elemental Individuation* implies that you successfully discharged a portion of your Elemental and it maintained the symbiotic sentience that you, Rai, and Renzgé share. Especially since your Elemental is bipartite, it seems unimaginable for you to have done such a thing...

"But now I understand why Fierce let you live. He is accurate; if you reach an elite level and he and Késhal defeats us and that other Sczyphamek, no one will stand against them. Such an opportunity, as risky as it is, would be too good to pass.

"Mína, one of the greatest leaders of the Keep, once told a story about a similar occasion. His daughter had come of age and wished to leave the Crossroad Islands. She was born of the same mettle and tooth as her father, and many believed she would find herself as a member of the Principle. However, she wanted to emigrate to the Phmquedrian Den. This was two cycles before the rise of Imperial.

"Mína was wise. He perceived Tannódin's aims. Phmquedria was more than likely Tannódin's next target. Should he stop her or should he let her go...?"

"What did he decide?" Neztríanis prompted with anticipation. She forgot how well the Orator narrated stories.

"He retained her," she replied darkly. "And though he soon realized his decision saved her from betrayal and treachery at the hands of the Phmquedrians, there was no telling what her presence might have accomplished had he not barred her from going. Not only that, but the decision caused a rift in Mína's household that festered until his death.

"'And therein lies the trap,' he would always say. The trap of false inevitability. And those who believe in it completely are doomed to extinction. Because Mína believed Phmquedria was already lost, he tried to protect his own. But the very act of protecting his daughter possibly led to the destruction of the témos at the hands of the Phmquedrians and Tannódin'é.

"There are *moments* of inevitability, but not *Cycles*..." Timura said this as much to herself as she did to Neztríanis. "Vincallous does not view Global Initiative as inevitable even though he believes it to be necessary..."

"But could Mína's daughter have made that much of a difference?" the daughter of Hopha asked.

"Mína believed so, and so do I. She was my mate's grandmother," the témo rasped in fond reminiscence. "And you know this as well as I. The difference would not have been because of her alone, but through the uprights and témos she would have undoubtedly influenced.

"Of course, we could have been mistaken. But if Phmquedria had taken ten cycles to fall instead of two... who knows what the future could have been? Who knows how different Global Initiative would have been today?"

"Phmquedria..." Neztríanis murmured.

"A land of treacherous, parasitic dogs," the témo spat out. The hurt of their betrayal was still fresh in her qanín. "Nothing worth mentioning can come out of that land... *Nothing*."

So much hatred...

"Did you not just speak of inevitability and the folly of remaining etched in its wake?" the neoteric Zephanín commented.

"Perhaps," the témo smiled with irritation. "But until I am proven wrong, my declaration stands. You will not find a single témo sympathetic to the plight of Phmquedrians. After all we did with them and for them. They are without honor and without shame. Their kind is wiped from our remembrance."

Neztríanis was shocked by the témo's display of antagonism but she remained silent. Her mind anticipated their immediate future. She was just thankful that the témo decided to join her on this quest, even if it was a tentative agreement.

However, the daughter of Hopha was still unsettled. Looking to the northeast, she said, "We must come up with a plan."

"If Vincallous is no longer pursuing us, then why do I detect such haste in your voice?"

"The haste is in my qanín. The longer it takes for us to go to Sunrise Mountain and for me to Awaken, the worse it will be for Líachim.

"My mother instructed me to take the Auría to Sunrise Mountain. She did not say that I would Awaken before or after then..." Neztríanis paused. The Great Mother *did* tell her where she would Awaken. "Mamisí told me that I would Awaken if I continued on this path. She told me to *take* the Auría to Sunrise, *not* to leave it there…" She gasped in disbelief. Her mother's foresight was incredible. "I won't be able to Awaken here at the Crag Mountains; it must happen at Sunrise Mountain or along the way. I do not know why it should take place there, but I must finish this part of the journey as soon as possible.

"Even if Kéma's stolen plans are decipherable, I cannot imagine a circumstance whereby Líachim can stand against two Sczyphameks; two, maybe three Wielders; and a host of Global Initiative troops. The odds are…"

"Staggering," Timura finished. "If Líachim falls, Qeauríyx as we know it will probably be lost… Lost to the Zananín. Even though Keotagosdi is a large continent, there is not a large upright population within its shores. Líachim is the third most populated continent on the planet. I suspect that this is the reason why the House of Kaz has been so deliberate in its destruction. After all, the Zananín did not want to go to war with them at first."

"How do you know that?" Phyxtríalis asked. "If you have been on the run, how did you hear of this?"

The témo appeared sorrowful and reticent to answer, but forced herself to speak. "Zotham, the leader of Aphaz, was counseled by us in exchange for solace and protection. That was where I—where all of us were supposed to deliver…" The témo cast her head down and muttered, "We left a few durations before the Tannódin'é arrived on Anzél…"

"Why did you not tell me?"

Tears fell from her mournful eyes. "The pain and imprudence of our decision is still too much to bear," she whispered. "We should have stayed there… I could have… Did we learn nothing from Mína?" Stopping herself from embarking on the road of infinite regret, the winged feline silenced herself.

So much despair…

"I am sorry," the Sczyphamek apologized. "I should have known that you had your reasons…"

Instead of responding, the témo walked down the hill and into the plains of Bitzroy. Neztríanis understood. Timura needed time to gather herself. The loss of the témos was unlike any other on Qeauríyx. The daughter of Phesiana wondered how she would react if she had to walk the Orator's journey. How could the native of the Crossroad Islands even summon a reason or illusion to go on? Neztríanis was fighting for her cultural, religious, and philosophical well-being and life, but her kind still roamed the planet in large numbers. It did not lessen the tragedy of the Solemn War or Nez Spirita's subsequent subjection; however, the Sczyphamek could still see a Nez Spiritan or a nel'asmív for that matter… what would she do if she would never see her people again… and she knew it?

Timura's tears rained down from Neztríanis' eyes. If Timura could not cry them, then the daughter of Hopha would. Tears of loss, tears of grief, tears of hope.

They chanted and exercised for a week and a half, fourteen hours a day. The Sczyphamek alternated her use of the Auría every six hours, in order to dialogue with Rai, Renzgé, and Timura. Near sundown, the Myanín searched for food of any kind; they were certain they would find none in the permafrost of the North Country.

Neztríanis still wore the clothes supplied by Hafir. The same clothes she wore when she fought Vincallous. However, they could hardly be called clothes now. They were torn asunder, mangled, and useless. She had practically been training naked, but felt no shame around Timura. Only her boots maintained their utility. Luckily, she removed her jacket and placed it in her shoulderpack before she confronted Vincallous; otherwise, it too would have been destroyed. Rummaging through her bag, she smiled to herself. She laid her hands upon the attire she wore at her journey's genesis, almost one cycle prior: her tan shawl and dark brown animal-skin pants, with a hint of blue and burn mark. Underneath them lay the outfit Bíoske had given her nearly six durations ago.

Had her journey been so short?

The duo had located a river near one of the taller mountains in the Crags. Although the water was close to freezing, Neztríanis easily warmed the stream and took a much-needed bath. So much of her vanity was lost on the journey. But once she washed herself, her old habits and dispositions returned like the scent of her trusted enormous bar of soap. Neztríanis could not recall the last time she bathed. Layers of dirt and que were embedded in her skin. Her hair was longer, more entangled than ever with innumerable specks of indiscriminate particles clinging tightly to every follicle. But the woman did not linger in the water. She quickly cleaned herself and her hair and laundered all of her clothes in the river.

Once she finished, Temperature clothed herself in her original attire. Then she put on the outfit from Bíoske over those. She did not tie her hair back into a tail. Instead, she completely brushed and combed it out and down, letting it fall past her shoulders, mid-back, and breasts. She did not realize how much her hair had actually grown since she started her quest. It would definitely help keep her warm. Finally, the woman covered herself with Isürus' cloak, Hafir's coat, and Bíoske's hat.

Try as she might, the Nez Spiritan could not help but think of their ascent of Mount Xarkim. After that hellacious climb and her savage defeat at the hands of Vicious, Sczyphamek Temperature recognized her mortality more than ever. She hoped her na'ísa, faith, and embrace had stabilized.

The daughter of Hopha picked up the Auría with a remorseful and reflective qanín. She felt no angst or self-aggrandizement. She *would* give the book up or *die* trying. Placing the sacred text and her remaining possessions in her shoulderpack and closing the bag, the woman flung the satchel across her back. Speedily climbing the mountain, the Myanín looked north and into the icy void. Snares and temptations of epic design awaited them.

Neztríanis' aura bloomed and Timura's emerging Elemental aura flickered. They exchanged no words. Neither did they nod or give any visual sign of affirmation; yet, they moved as one body. Casting themselves forward, the Myanín entered the realm of Sunrise Mountain's North Country, *together.*

***

20 Janíz, 241 OGI
Gamlé

They were both sure of it. By the ninetieth length, the temperature was that of the heights of Mount Xarkim. Snow swirled and cascaded about them. Neztríanis' aura was thick and surrounded both she and the témo. Luckily, Timura could generate at least a fourth of her own aura now. They agreed the best strategy was to move at a deliberate yet moderate pace toward the mountain, and they would only use the Auría as a measure of last resort.

At times the blizzard was so thick that loss of direction became commonplace. Zénan was lost in the gray sky.

The thought was in both of their minds, although they would not speak of it. After enduring nights on the cliffs of Mount Xarkim, both the Orator and Sczyphamek dreaded sundown and the unmitigated temperature degradation that was sure to follow.

It was the wind. It was cold. A zephyr. An arctic zephyr. The Arctic Zephyr.

The Arctic Zephyr was like a large bird of prey, with powerful, sharp, gripping talons—talons that seized the Myanín with polar precision.

Nez's theory was confirmed. No one, not even the other Sczyphameks could survive out there. Survival was not just a matter of faith, will, and understanding... It was about Qeauríyx. And Neztríanis had come to embrace that one's Elemental power would never fully succeed against the conditions of the planet or its *precipitation.*

The precipitation danced in mad arrhythmia. Snowflakes, snowballs, hail, and even ice chunks fell from the sky. *No,* not just fell; they also *shot* sideways like projectiles. An unexpected occurrence. But then no one had ventured this far, had they?

Visibility would only grow worse, which meant the precipitation would soon become a threat to their very livelihood. Neztríanis expanded her aura to one length in diameter, in order to warn the Myanín of any large, threatening icicles. Such Elemental usage was unforeseen, yet not altogether unanticipated. No one truly knew the meteorological patterns and conditions of the North Country.

Soon the sun became dimmer than normal. Out of all the strategies they discussed, they both agreed on one condition unanimously: *nighttime travel was forbidden.*

Kneeling down and stopping while Timura drew close, Temperature chanted with firm conviction, "Zí mányx que Rai."

Within seconds, an ice hemisphere of moderate dimensions formed. Miniscule openings emerged peppered the structure. The holes were large enough for air to circulate, yet tiny enough so that the wind would not be able to penetrate the structure. In order to protect the hemisphere and themselves from possible projectiles, Neztríanis conjured stout and multilayered ice. The Sczyphamek would perish if she had to continuously maintain the structural integrity with her Elemental. Though mundane, that sort of maintenance would not allow her or her Elemental to rest.

Once the ice dome was finished, the Sczyphamek stood still in contemplation. How was such destructive precipitation possible? Normally, the colder the temperature, the harder it was for precipitation to fall. Water vapor had to rise in order to make clouds. And for that to occur, sufficient and sustainable warmth was necessary… was it not?

Neztríanis diminished her reliance on Renzgé for heat and sat down on the frozen ground. Without the wind caustically brandishing its frigid desires upon her, the Nez Spiritan was actually not that cold. Timura crouched down on all fours and yawned. Then she shook her body to remove the liquid residue from her fur.

The wind howled outside the barrier. Taking off her shoulderpack and retrieving her incomparable water jug, Neztríanis warmed the container with a moderate heat in order to unfreeze the water inside. She unstrapped the windhorse hide water canteen around the témo's midsection and did the same. Both of them gulped the heated water with unrestraint.

Another condition of their journey was that no words were to be spoken, except for audible incantations. Otherwise, each creature was to inwardly petition, pray, and chant unceasingly, unless spoken communication was absolutely necessary. True to their promise, the Myanín remained silent for over ten hours.

Reaching into the shoulderpack, Neztríanis procured some dried meat and handed it to Timura while she snacked on Yarninga berries and nuts. Snuggling next to one another, the daughter of Hopha lay on the témo's stomach and drowned herself in the feline's coat. Neztríanis whispered and the témo quietly rasped "Fá'atoño mona" and "Fá'atoño má" alternately until they both fell fast asleep under the cover of an orange-white blanket.

When they awoke the next morning, they found the sky completely cloud-free. Rai informed the Myanín that the temperature was colder than the previous night. The hemisphere held up nicely, and the temperature inside settled to a few degrees below freezing, easily manageable for them. Yet, Timura dreaded Neztríanis' retraction and deconstruction of the ice dome.

They ate with speed. They had to take advantage of the weather. Even though it was colder, they could cover more ground during a hiatus of the wintry precipitation in the middle of summer. Neztríanis refilled their containers with fresh, newly unfrozen water, and melted a hole in the side of the structure. When the Myanín emerged they were assaulted by the Arctic Zephyr and the specter of the second tallest mountain on the planet, Sunrise Mountain. The sky was clear and aquamarine; the only obscuration in sight was the failing of the eye against the horizon.

Drawing close to her partner, the woman did not need to ask. Timura's sight was beyond the nel'asmív's.

"Unless my eyes deceive me, we are a little less than four hundred lengths from the base," the témo relayed. "Can you feel the cold fifty lengths ahead?"

"Yes," the woman affirmed.

"They are pure ice glaciers, two or three of them, and they are unlike anything I have seen. They are at least six thousand feet in height. We cannot go around them; they are too wide, and the path would lead us to the coast and lengthen the journey..."

"Then we must," she said.

"Yes, we must," the témo agreed solemnly.

"Can you see the top?" the woman asked, referring to Sunrise.

"Impossible," the feline answered. "Too much cloud cover. And the mountain is beyond dimensions my eyes can grasp at the moment."

"We will soon grasp it personally," the woman said encouragingly. "Let's quicken our pace, but we will stay within our means. I cannot fathom that we will have another day such as this."

"Agreed."

They raised their auras and flew towards the large chunk of icy que in front of them at speeds of sixty lengths an hour. Staying close to the ground in order to avoid the insufferable wind, the duo arrived at the glaciers within an hour and halted.

This will not be easy, Nez thought.

There were three of them. And each glaciers' temperature was erratic and stable depending on the sections she scanned. Without warning, a large chunk of ice broke away from the glacier directly in front of them. Timura and Neztríanis backed away and levitated off the permafrost in anticipation. The debris crashed into the ground, shook the entire area, and sent out a sonic yelp that made the other glaciers careen and crack.

Timura observed the heights of the coagulated ice and then nudged Neztríanis. The daughter of Hopha shook her head in the negative. They could not go over the structure. Neztríanis had scanned the water vapor and ice flecks at the top of the glaciers, and the molecules were consistently traveling at speeds in excess of one hundred lengths per hour. Not only was the wind speed intense, the direction of the gusts was equally perplexing.

The North Country's ecosystem generated some of the worst gales on Qeauríyx. Flying at high altitudes with such enigmatic head, side, and tailwinds was out of the question. They would expend too much energy that way, and the Myanín did not want to use the Auría unless they were left with no other choice. While the Auría granted a temporary increase in power, the text also demanded nothing less than the consumption of one's qanín, leaving a considerable recovery time in its wake.

The glaciers possessed three openings, but after their transit through the Infinite Circle, the woman knew that all three of the openings could be dead ends. One was a natural opening between the westernmost glacier and middle one. The middle glacier appeared to be split, granting access to its cavernous belly. The easternmost glacier also had a noticeable, yet smaller opening.

Placing her hand gently upon the spine of the témo, Neztríanis audibly chanted, and Timura joined her. In an instant, three separate emanations of her Elemental sprouted forth and raced towards the three passageways. The center passage was found to be blocked the first few lengths. However, the left and right passages had currents of air passing through them beyond twenty lengths. Neztríanis anticipated fatigue approaching after the fifth minute of chanting, so they stopped. Both the left and right walkways stretched at least fifty lengths, with no determinable terminus.

One guess was as good as another.

The témo trudged to the right entrance and the nel'asmív followed. What else could they do? An intense feeling of familiarity beset the feline and the woman, but they continued forward. The height of the walls was impressive, but soon, the glacier closed its rooftop and plunged them into darkness. They did not hesitate and cautiously trotted ahead.

Time soon became lost…

The ice that fell from the ceiling was massive and unavoidable. The Sczyphamek could not release a large discharge of heat. Such an offensive action would destabilize the ice cavern even further.

Concentrating with intense fortitude, Nez lifted her hands up and sang emotionally, "*Renzgé ná. Fá'atoño mona.*"

Her hands became consumed in a white heat that stayed extremely local, and she created a small canopy for the Myanín, which stretched six feet above them. She moved her hands towards the ground and the white heat responded in kind and fell just above her ankles. Meanwhile, Timura chanted phrases that partially incanted Rai to simultaneously keep them from conflagrating inside the fiery wall and to reinforce the frigidity of the surrounding icy walls of the glacier. Had Neztríanis attempted such a double display of power, she would have surely spent herself and fainted.

The falling ice encountered the dense heat canopy and became water and steam. However, because Timura incanted a small yet indomitable portion of Neztríanis' frigid Elemental, the steam was rapidly chilled to a tepid gaseous state. The arctic slab was enormous, and the force it placed on the canopy was excessive, which caused the Sczyphamek to grunt in displeasure and kneel on one knee. She could have expended less energy if she destroyed it, but that might have set off a chain reaction that would have ended in their deaths.

The ordeal was over in a manner of seconds but the fatigue-inducing setback left its mark. The Myanín were forced to halve their traveling speed. Neither muttered or bemoaned. *Such* a task in *such* an environment was bound to elicit *such* a potential hindrance. Neztríanis, with Timura beside her, pressed on towards an opening that might not even exist. However, after about what the Myanín could only speculate was a half an hour (how easily did the sense of time evaporate due to the expanse of space), the daughter of Hopha perceived the exit.

By the time they emerged from the glacial cavern, the gray clouds had assumed their rightful place in the late afternoon sky. A blustery current of air swooped upon them and nearly dislodged Neztríanis' hat from her head. The témo dug her claws into the ground, and the Sczyphamek struggled to keep from falling. The Zephyr was so loud and diverse, it sounded as if it were singing… lamentations.

They walked until they could walk no further. The sun had almost set, the end of the second day.

"Zí…" Neztríanis struggled to chant. "Zí mányx…"

"Zí mányx que Rai," the témo rasped, joining in with Neztríanis.

Within seconds, an ice hemisphere of moderate dimensions formed. It was smaller than the previous day, yet no less thick. The woman unstrapped her shoulderpack, and it crashed to the ground. Sitting down and maneuvering her body towards Timura, the woman unfastened the windhorse container with noticeable weariness. Breathing hard and lightheaded, the woman warmed the water to a lukewarm temperature. She handed the shoulderpack to Timura, who dug some meat out with her paws. The woman grabbed a few nuts and a meat strip of her own, downed them and the water, and passed out on the ground. Timura drew close to her, and tugged her collar in order to place the woman on her abdomen.

The témo was impressed by her partner's resolve and strength. She knew that Neztríanis perceived it, but did not say a word. The temperature had decreased nearly seventy degrees throughout the day's journey, which taxed the Nez Spiritan Sczyphamek to no end. However, her aura did not waver, and they consistently maintained the same ambient temperature the entire day.

The témo yawned and, while falling asleep, reflected on the implications of their journey thus far. *Exceptional. This environment, like Mount Xarkim, will hasten her Awakening... Or kill her... Her mother knew this and sent her on this journey anyway. For her to risk her own daughter... It can only mean that Temperature has the potential to become an elite Sczyphamek and that Global Initiative is nearly irreversible...*

They awoke to the sound of large hailstones banging and rattling against the ice hemisphere. Instinctively, Neztríanis jumped to her feet and ran to the inner wall of the sanctum. Night still reigned. They could not have been asleep any longer than a few hours. Unconsciously extending her aura into the structure, the woman assessed the integrity of the dome. She surmised that it had sustained little to minor damage and should hold if the precipitation become more violent. Just in case, she added an extra five feet of ice to the outside of the structure. Lying back down, the témo and nel'asmív grew desensitized to the sound.

They awoke to the sound of a precipitous chunk destroying the wall of the ice hemisphere. Shards of the stuff flew everywhere. Neztríanis barely had time to release a fiery blast that decimated a large mass of hail streaking their way. The combustion also obliterated the hemisphere. The Arctic Zephyr descended upon them, salaciously groping and harassing what little warmth they could contain.

The sun had not risen and Neztríanis beheld a void of gray.

"Get down!" the témo growled with eyes of terror.

Within a moment's disappearance, a floe-covered rock grazed the head of a ducking Neztríanis, nearly decapitating her.

"Fá'atoño má!" Neztríanis chanted with controlled excitement.

The radiant blossom that was her aura shone forth in a burst of orange-white luminescence, and for a moment, no wind, precipitation, or temperature dared to touch the Zephanín. In a force that erupted with aggressive resilience, the Sczyphamek's aura enveloped a half-length radius.

Turning and facing Timura with auburn eyes, the daughter of Hopha said, "We cannot stay here. Our strategy must change. Four large ice formations are heading this way. They will be here in minutes..."

The témo nodded in agreement, while Neztríanis' aura retracted yet covered them both.

"I need your eyes too," Temperature said to the Orator. "I will focus on the ice."

"Visibility is only tens of feet," the témo commented. "We must be cautious."

They walked slowly towards the northeast in order to avoid the massive particulates racing their way. The climate felt nothing like the daytime. It was a nightmarish comparison to an already terrifying reality. With intense concentration, she kept her na'ísa stabilized enough to generate a consistent aura. Luckily, they were able to outflank the ice formations.

However, for eight consecutive hours, the woman and témo battled the uncompromising element of the North Country. It was a reconfirmation of a fact she long knew was true. It was the quivering of her knees when her mother told her of her destination. The North Country was of the same ilk as the Desert of Woe in Líachim, the Volcanic Line in Damüda, and the Infinite Deep off the shores of Meve. They were self-sustaining Phenplyacins, inhospitable remnants of ancient Qeauríyx. The weather, erratic as it was, made sense, *even in its senselessness.*

Late summer occasioned the hottest days in Nez Spirita, and the calendar did not lie. It was the third week of Janíz. If Neztríanis was back in Hopha, she would be wearing that seasonal short skirt of hers that made the men of her village stare at her legs.

How absurd... Hopha was closer to the South Pole than the *North Country*, yet Hopha was warmer. And what should have been a lie truly reflected reality: the temperature around Sunrise Mountain was colder than the North and South Poles. Logic stated that the climate during the late summer season should be hot and humid, but the *Presence* of Sunrise Mountain categorically denied such a rationale.

Did Zénan truly rise there?

Sensing the air in the upper-atmosphere, Neztríanis was shocked. The air was *warmer, warm as summer.* But locally, the air was absolutely frigid. The clash of air temperatures was unlike anything she could fathom; it made her think back to her training in the Windhorse Peninsula all those durations ago. She started a local thunderstorm due to a similar yet infinitely smaller set of circumstances, did she not?

"By the One," she muttered. "It might have been better to come during the winter."

Her calculations were completely off. In the summer, the weather was better if one were closer to the Crags, in the same manner as Hafir, when he painted the picture hanging in his home. But that was an illusion. Hafir must have traveled and painted the work of art on a day like the Myanín's yesterday, the calm before the storm.

For eight hours, lo, for six hundred and forty minutes, the Orator and her partner gave their full measure. At some unidentified moment, neither of them could move nor find their bearings amidst the deluge of wind, snow, sleet, hail, and ice-stones. They ducked and dodged. Neztríanis blasted, deflected, and smashed. Timura sliced and roared. Unceasingly... infinitely...

By the eighth hour, however, Neztríanis' aura finally started to flicker in dissonance. Breathing in the cold air, which almost cryogenically paralyzed their lungs, the Myanín attempted to catch their wind, during a short lull in the onslaught. How much longer could an unawakened Sczyphamek and her steadfast ally struggle unaccompanied?

She did not hesitate, but retrieved the Auría out of her shoulderpack. Three minutes had passed since her aura waned, and her fingers were already frostbitten. The daughter of Hopha nearly dropped the book out of her hands. Nervously flipping to the section that chronicled their ongoing journey, the Elemental warrior placed her index finger in between the pages and closed the book.

Nearing Timura, she chanted, "Fá'atoño má."

The rush of power and vitality she felt was like none other, but she had no time to waste or marvel.

Rising a few feet off of the ground, the woman and témo recited together, "Renzgé. Mona fla Renzgé ná. Renzgé ná. Fá'atoño mona."

The aura that surrounded them became a fiery combustion, blazing in orange-red savagery. The surrounding ice immediately melted, creating a steaming lake beneath them. Timura expanded and flapped her wings, expulsing a scorching-hot flame in her wake. The témo roared, and the interior of her mouth became volcanic. The North Country was just given ample notice.

"Hold nothing back," the Sczyphamek warmly bade her comrade. "Do not stop. We cannot stop until we get there."

"I will not stop, no matter what," the Orator responded.

"*Fá'atoño má!*" they sang majestically.

For a split-second, the space that surrounded them seemed to warp and fold upon itself. And within that moment, two red-hot creatures from Qeauríyx bolted towards the obfuscated Sunrise Mountain at a speed unknown, a velocity Vincallous had already mastered.

Although the mountain was nearly three hundred lengths away, the Myanín reached the base of the mount in about a half hour. They arrived, steaming and emitting a heat so intense that it caused the ambient snow to sizzle and nearby rocks to become white-hot and liquefy. The ice pack beneath them also thawed, which created a chasm and exposed the rocky dead ground. It was still dark, and the weather was as irascible as ever.

Ravenously, the Auría drained Phyxtríalis' qanín. Timura was emptied faster than the nel'asmív. Not only had they used the Auría to travel at a high velocity, they also used the sacred scripture to keep themselves warm, for the temperature was now the coldest it had ever been, an untold number of degrees below freezing.

"We need to find some shelter," she commented and scanned the *entire* mountain in two minutes. "Follow me. I found a suitable location. Timura, you will not believe this, but the northern side of Sunrise is much warmer than this side."

"Let us go," the témo wheezed. Her breathing was stressed, and the Orator could only open one eye. "I cannot maintain this form much longer."

The base of the peak was over six hundred lengths in circumference. Although it would have been shorter to circumvent the mountain by increasing their altitude, Neztríanis ascertained that they would be battling the wind the entire time, which would decrease their speed and increase their reliance upon the Auría and its accompanying taxation. They had to stay close to the base.

But within ten minutes of circumvention, the Myanín's velocity decelerated quickly. Luckily, the precipitation was subsiding. Neztríanis sighed in relief. She did not want to trade a nightmare for a daymare.

Suddenly, Timura's na'ísa waned and altogether dissipated. The Orator could no longer sustain her aura. Comatose, the témo fell from her flight and crashed into the snow.

"*Timura!*" Temperature yelled in alarm and frantically raced to her partner's body.

The nel'asmív landed, searched for, and found Timura's heat signature and dug in the general area.

Why did I continue this pace? She thought to herself. *Why did I not slow down?*

The témo's aura was non-existent. Seeing this as a harbinger of her own fate, Neztríanis placed the Auría in her shoulderpack and dialogued with Rai and Renzgé. Indeed, her Elemental had expended the majority of their present ability. After unearthing Timura, the woman firmly rubbed the témo's face.

"Tem… Neztríanis," the témo moaned then passed out.

The Synthesis was still beyond their reach. Timura had been under great distress, more so than Neztríanis realized. After all, the Elemental was at least müz to the daughter of Hopha.

Hoisting and placing the Orator upon her shoulders, Neztríanis nearly collapsed from the weight. Temperature was always impressed by the size of the témo. But impression now became unwanted appreciation. The Crossroad Islander was heavy beyond belief. The Sczyphamek had not trained her physical body in durations, since her time in the Windhorse Peninsula. And it showed. Her reliance upon her "higher" gifts had been to the detriment of her "mundane" powers, powers that were not "mundane" at all.

Laboriously, the Sczyphamek took measured steps in the cold, wet snow. It took all her faith to carry on. It took her entire will to tread through the thick stuff. It took every bit of her embrace to make sure she was walking on ice that could support their weight. But where could she hope to go? She was still a hundred lengths from the northern side of the mountain. Discharging her aura around both she and the témo, her heart palpitated in radical fashion and the Sczyphamek nearly died.

Did her eyes and body just deceive her? It felt and seemed as if Zénan rose and set, within a matter of minutes…

Even after all she experienced thus far, she could not help but cry. How many insurmountable odds must she surmount? How many hills did she have to climb? How many Zananín did she have to encounter and defeat? When was it going to stop? When would it end? She had had her fill of abandonment.

"Where are you?" she asked the Nameless One, who appeared so radically absent. "I need you. I haven't Awakened. Don't you see us? We cannot do this alone... Why did you give me this task?"

No answer. No answer in the cold snow. No answer in the ice. No answer in the wind, the horrifically cold wind—just a faint, nearly inaudible whisper.

It could not be for the sake of endurance.

"Fá'atoño má. Fá'atoño má..." She repeated the phrase of petition, the phrase of her ancestors, the phrase of faith, the phrase of angst... She repeated the phrase twenty-seven times, and every repetition grew more endeared, disconsolate, and weary.

She cried to the Firmament. She heard the témo purring, clinging to life.

Yes, there were times of celebration and joy. But this was not one of those times... Times such as these could not be made for endurance. It could not be that they were made only to endure. What did it mean to endure Qalfocx?

"Fá'atoño má. Fá'atoño má. Fá'atoño má. Fá'atoño má. Fá'atoño má. Fá'atoño má. Fá'atoño má. Fá'atoño má. Fá'atoño má. Fá'atoño má. Fá'atoño má."

This journey could not be for strength. It could not be to make her and her faith strong. Her Awakening could not be contingent upon this path. Too many had perished. Timura could die from this. Did a témo's death justify her growth? Unacceptable... *Unacceptable*... That was not the One With No Name she believed in...

"*Fá'atoño má. Fá'atoño má. Fá'atoño má. Fá'atoño má. Fá'atoño má. Fá'atoño má. Fá'atoño má. Fá'atoño má. Fá'atoño má. Fá'atoño má.*" Neztrĭanis sang out of key, with melancholy emotion and through short breaths.

This could not be a test to prove her worth. How many tests had she passed and failed since she left the Great Mother? Surely the One with No Name knew where she stood by now.

A test? A test to endure and to be strong?

This was a test?

This was a test that had an unawakened Sczyphamek carry her best friend—a best friend that weighed four to five times her own weight—in an environment that would have killed any normal nel'asmív... *After* she accepted this quest, *after* Rai, Renzgé, and Qeauríyx had confirmed her, *after* she had helped Rydín, *after* her betrayal by Jennó, *after* she fought and bled with Miska Kea, *after* she climbed the heights of Mount Xarkim, *after* she spent Cycles journeying through Qeauríyx, *after* she had found the Auría, *after* she had killed—*murdered*—Blue Rapier soldiers in violent excess, *after* the brutalization, humiliation, and excoriating rebuke she received at the hands of Vincallous—was she still... *still* being tested?

This *could not be* a test... De*test*able... *utterly detestable...*

"Fá... Fá'atoño... Fá... Fá..."

It could not be for goodness... It could not be... Were all the deaths for the good? Were the ashen corpses of those she murdered for the "good?" How many evils, how many injuries, deaths, and absurdities would it take until one could no longer state such an obvious inaccuracy and...

"*I am afraid!*" she cried, shivered, and sobbed in spiritual torment *and* because of the weather. "I do not know what to do. I don't understand what this means! What are we doing? How did we happen like this? I don't know... Staxis... This... this... This is so wrong... Senseless... *This is so kímaz meaningless!*"

She finally allowed herself to say it, after all the cycles she kept it buried. It was not a disbelief in the Nameless One; it was a disbelief in purpose, a disbelief in complete and total meaning; it was the recognition of a kind of absurdity that could not be explained away. The tension between her belief in the Nameless One and the recognition of the absurd was finally allowed to emerge.

What did it mean to believe in the Nameless One and acknowledge meaninglessness, the senselessly empty events and sagas that comprised the cycles of Qeauríyx?

But it was more than the absurdity... It was the randomness. It was the planet's erratic precipitation and attitude. It was the wicked and finite pettiness of nel'asmív as a species... the abysmal pain of being a dominated people... The many faces of affliction and suffering... and the millennial absence of *It.* The ancestors, by and large, had not prepared her for such a quandary.

What was this she was feeling...? It felt cold and warm... It felt amaranthine in its weakness and power... it felt like... It could not be... it could not *do*... everything...? what was Power? Was it the Nameless Ineffable Thing(s)?

She did not realize she had closed her eyes. She opened them, and the aura was hers, not the Auría. It was hers and *Its*. Were they struggling together? It made no sense... Levitating and racing forward in confusion and frustration, yet with a goal in mind, the Sczyphamek flew towards the north with the témo on her shoulders.

Her breaths were spastic and the weight of the témo felt as if it had doubled, but the only thing that she would let stop her would be her death or loss of consciousness. She would drag Timura by the tail if need be. The content of her hope was a nondescript flux. She wondered why she cared anymore. Why had she remained faithful to such a senseless task in such a ridiculous environment this absurdly long?

Did It feel the same way? Could It actually feel...?

"Renzgé," she stammered through painstaking breaths. "Please, please help me. We must not... Rai, do not leave me... Nameless One..."

She was hallucinating. The elements and theological confusion must have driven her insane. That could not be Zénan. It could not be Zénan. That could not be Zénan. That could not be a warm sunray. That could not justify what she just went through... *and she was not ungrateful for the assistance...*

The clouds were breaking. The woman stepped on... *rocks?* Gravel... dirt? Where in Qalfocx was she? Squinting her eyes and blinking rapidly, she gasped. It was an oasis in the middle of a winter hellhole. For a stretch of about twenty miles, Neztríanis could actually see the que of Qeauríyx. Beyond the oasis was an icy wasteland, with mountainous glaciers over ten thousand feet sprawling to the coastline. Yet in between the mountain and the fjords, there was a space. There was grass. There was running water... There it was...

"Timura," she said to her comatose friend. "We are here. We made it."

Walking to a grassy(?) knoll, the Sczyphamek sensed the temperature. She had used Rai so much to ascertain the subzero climate that she grew unnerved when she realized that the temperature required Renzgé. No... It required them both. The temperature was in a state of consistent motion, moving between one degree below and one degree above freezing. Neztríanis shook her head in amazement. The very fact that she could (in such a decrepit state) discriminate temperatures that easily could only mean that she was near her Awakening.

Near, but not there...

The woman collapsed on the grass on both knees, set Timura down, crawled towards the feline's furry belly and cared for nothing but rest...

Chapter Twenty-Seven: [Temperature]

and [Kinesis]

Anámn and Neztríanis awoke with gravel clinging to their lips. The Phmquedrian looked towards the entrance of the cave. The Nez Spiritan sat up and gazed at Timura. The témo was asleep and thankfully did not appear to be comatose. After checking Timura's core temperature, the Sczyphamek assessed the physical condition of the Crossroad Islander. Anámn brushed the residue off his face.

Untold intervals passed before either of them opened their eyes. There was no wind. Zénan was visible, hoisted and pulled by the mast of Sunrise Mountain. Yet this area of the North Country would put no air in the sails. The Myanín were in the doldrums. And it suited them both just fine. No wind, no windchill.

"Neztríanis," the témo prodded softly, still exhausted from the Auría and the trek. "Temperature?"

"I must Awaken," the woman moaned. "I must."

"How did we get here?"

"I carried you… with a little help from a friend…"

The feline's ears perked in curiosity. "*It* helped you?"

"I am unsure if 'help' is the correct word. I do not know if I will ever possess the words to explain that which is unexplainable. To do so will only cause violence and destruction." The Sczyphamek paused. The metamorphosis was complete. She was happening as a Zephanín. "Never have I felt so terrified, yet comforted. It destroyed a myanála through paradox."

"Yes, paradox is but one way to topple myanála."

They were quiet for many more hours, chanting to themselves and eating the remainder of their food. The témo sat on her hind legs while Neztríanis leaned against Timura's trunk, sitting with her knees drawn close to her chest. The Nez Spiritan lifted her head toward the mountain and could not ascertain its apex. They were too close, and it was too big.

"You cannot assist me, can you?" Neztríanis' question was barely audible. She already knew the answer.

"No," the témo affirmed. "No, I cannot. I can chant and pray with you. But the Awakening is yours not mine."

"I heard that Exceptional Awakened one duration after his powers emerged."

"Actually, the Orators recorded forty days; one duration and one week."

"Nine durations have passed since my powers emerged... almost one cycle," the Nez Spiritan replied. "Yet I have not Awakened. I believe I am close. However, proximity means nothing if I do not know what I am searching for."

"Have you spoken to Rai and Renzgé?"

"Their words grow foreign to my qanín when they attempt to speak at such a level of understanding, faith, and strength." The woman stood up, stretched, and knelt beside her partner. "Keep your distance from me. I do not know what I might do or how far this might go."

"Understood," the témo said. "Before you begin, can you make an ice hemisphere fifteen lengths from this location? Judging from sight, this area seems to have a diameter of about twenty to thirty lengths."

Timura gazed around the oasis once more. "Hopefully, we can find food because we have no chance of leaving until you Awaken. We cannot overeat or overhunt here. We will not destroy the ecosystem of such an obscure environment."

The woman grinned. "Témos are truly remarkable. Only your kind would worry about this area's local environment."

"It is what we do," Timura replied in a low tone. "We happened this way."

The feline expanded her wings and stretched them wide—wider than Neztríanis had ever witnessed them stretched before. The very size of them caused a shadow to form over the body of the Sczyphamek and nearly removed Zénan from her sight. Perhaps it was because she carried Timura for over a hundred lengths that she now realized how large her best friend truly was.

"Best friend..." How had this creature—no, this *person*, whom, in Nez's most magnificent of imaginations, would have never dreamed of encountering a cycle ago—earned the title "best friend?" Was the daughter of Hopha so alone the past twenty-seven cycles that she never had a "best friend?" The more she reflected, the more she accepted that the only thing she *missed* about Hopha was the Great Mother and the space Hopha occupied.

There were no friends to return to.

Rydín started it. Hafir and Namí provided the solid foundation. Jennó, Kéma, and Bíoske forced her to reconsider the contents of it. And Timura...

"Timura," a teary-eyed Neztríanis cried with deep appreciation. "Since I was a little one... I—I've always wished for a friend like you. I did not even know what it meant to have friends until this cycle. Even if you will be unable to follow me one day, I want you to know..." She wiped her crumpled face with the back of her shaking hand. "I want you to know that you are my greatest friend. I have traveled Cycles with you. You are my sister... I, I cannot replace what you have lost, and I would never try..."

The témo pulled her wings in, sauntered towards the woman, and brushed Neztríanis with her coat. "Temperature, we carry heavy burdens. But we should not carry them alone. From here until we can go no further, we will carry our burdens together." Moving her tail around on the ground, the Orator quietly continued. "My mate's name was T'Kly, and my cub... if it was a boy, we were to name him Mina. And if it was a girl, she would carry the title Kíaerna..."

The entire time the nel'asmív and témo had journeyed together, not once did Timura utter the names of her loved ones, anymore than she talked about her own personal story. Neztríanis had spoken to Timura the Orator more than she had the témo who happened as Timura.

"When you Awaken, I will tell you more," the Crossroad Islander promised as incentive.

The feline rubbed her whiskers and cheeks across the face of the nel'asmív. Témo's truly possessed luxurious fur. Neztríanis smiled through her tears. Rai and Renzgé—in the form of her aura—sprouted forth. Yes, *they were her friends too.* The four of them embraced each other under the gaze of Sunrise Mountain. For a moment, to a keen observer's eye, it appeared as if there was but one discernible presence amidst the mass of elements, nel'asmív, and témo. In a silent spark of light, the quartet that comprised the Myanín shared in each other's qanín, past, present, and future.

Qeauríyx trembled.

The aura retreated. Nez and Timura backed away from each other. The témo looked at Sczyphamek Temperature and nodded. Turning around, flapping her wings, and ascending, the Crossroad Islander bade the Nez Spiritan to follow. Timura found a suitable location, and Neztríanis fashioned an ice structure. The temperature was so erratically constant— tenths of a degree below or above freezing at any given moment. They had to assume that the hemisphere would maintain its structural integrity. For the first time, Phyxtríalis made the structure from the outside and left an opening large enough for Timura to traverse.

Once she finished the abode, Neztríanis knelt down, stared at her hands, and then at the témo. She was not winded. She had traveled as far as she could in her slumbering, half-cognizant state.

"Farewell," the Sczyphamek said. "My aim is for you to never see me again."

"This *will* be the last time I will embrace you *this* way," the témo smiled. "Do not worry about food; I will leave whatever I can find near your position once you lose consciousness…"

"*Lose consciousness?*"

"You always push yourself beyond what you should… You won't stop that habit until you are forced to…"

Neztríanis recounted the many times she passed out during her journey. Smiling to herself and then snickering, she whispered, "Perhaps you have a point."

The témo laughed and purred heartily. The Sczyphamek arose and ran towards her own campsite, where her shoulderpack, water jug, and the Auría lay. After a few strides, her orange-white aura took shape. She jumped in the air, and as she straightened out her body, she was completely covered with its luster. Flying back towards the mountain, Temperature chanted and sang with a *loud* voice, completely unashamed. She had no time for shame. Kéma, Líachim, and Qeauríyx could not suffer it.

***

Anámn arose the next morning expecting to see Van or Malchían, but instead he heard and felt the falling snow outside his cave. In his right hand was the bag of food and looking inside of it, the man counted six pieces of meat, one loaf of bread, and something wrapped in special packing paper. Holding the mystery item to his nose, Anámn sniffed in order to ascertain its contents. The smell was sweet, but there was another intriguing fragrance subtly underneath the sweetness. Even though he had been blessed by the cooking of his mother and Nísyx, Anámn believed that the bread under his nose was the best food he had ever smelled in his twenty-nine cycles of living.

It took his entire qanín to hold back the temptation to tear into it and wolf it down. However, he knew he might need to save such a savory treat on a day when his training would yield him nothing but defeat. A time like that occasioned some comfort food.

Standing up and yawning, the young man felt an anticipatory liveliness undergirded by a layer of sadness. The sadness was not due to the loneliness caused by missing his friends. It was the loneliness of being an *other*. An outsider. Though unawakened, the Phmquedrian runaway had already experienced the pain of "otherness." He could not bring himself to imagine the solitary path of an Awakened Sczyphamek. There were four of them, and two were certain to be his adversaries.

"Téza, what should I do?" he asked.

"Be still," the Elemental intimated.

Anámn complied.

"Discernment," Téza resounded. "Discernment. You take too long to wield me. You must feel what I feel, sense what I sense; move, exist, and embrace like I do. You must happen like me."

"*Like you...*" the nel'asmív said in deep thought. "You told me that we are 'yet and not yet'."

His mind raced to the lecture Malchían gave him. He remembered the old man picking up the stone. He held it. Let it go. "...tied to this thing..." No, that was not what he said. Anámn saw the elder's lips moving but he could not make out the words. "...tied to this phenomenon..."

"Your Elemental is tied to this phenomenon." That is what the Phmquedrian Black Staff Wielder told him.

The water. Téza said that it was the water, that it was in the water. *No.* They—*Anámn and Téza*—were the water. They were in the water.

"We are yet/not yet," the nel'asmív murmured reflectively. "Yet/not yet, yet/not yet, Fá'atoño má...

"I wield you too slowly... no, you are saying that *we* are too slow. Discernment...."

What did it mean to discern...? No, what did discernment relate to? É má Téza. Téza embraces the paradox. Malchían held the stone... it was so small... "potential energy," he said... "Kinetic energy is this 'falling to the ground'..." "Know the words." "Relationship between them."

Unreservedly, Anámn thought and remembered. Unrepentantly, Anámn thought and remembered. With all of his intention, Anámn thought and remembered. He *remembered*... the relationship between yet and not yet, kinetic and potential energy.

"We are related to this relationship. I must happen like you..." Sczyphamek Kinesis muttered. "Why am I so slow to wield...?"

He wielded nothing in the jungles of Kamo after his betrayal of Nísyx. The tree incident at the beginning of his journey was sheer desperation. Anámn had no faith and very little embrace. The Elemental was forced to embrace his misery. He simply did not want to die before he killed his father. However, "not wanting to die" meant absolutely nothing against Pre-Eminent and Vicious. Against a more powerful opponent or even one that was more skilled, he would die.

He only began to use his powers after he embraced Téza, on his way to Minusía. Brenko and Lénü helped him. The Volcanic Line of Damüda. The information nearly overwhelmed him. Galís' torture rack. The system broke him.

They were too slow.

Neztríanis sat down with her legs folded, her hands on her knees, and her head bowed. Nighttime had taken hold; yet, the temperature remained unaffected. What kind of atmospheric conditions led to such a phenomenon? Through the cloudy sky, Neztríanis observed the moons shining.

She knew what she had to do. Renzgé told her near the very genesis of her journey.

The Firmament.

The path to her Awakening was above and beyond, beneath and within her. Even the pain Vincallous rained upon her did not come close to matching the terror she felt when the starry hosts unleashed their indefatigable fire upon her. The moment was so terrifying, she buried it within her subconscious the second after its happening. Her qanín was almost burned alive.

The daughter of Hopha did not realize it at the time, but through her journey, she now understood. Her powers could easily happen as myanála. She was the very definition of two points: *hot and cold.* The opposite ends of a spectrum. Other than the ice hemisphere, she never consciously combined her powers. Did Vincallous perceive that during their fight? Was that why he was able to defend himself from the hottest attack she could muster?

She was wrong… There was one other time she consciously conjured both Rai and Renzgé… The Nez Spiritan dropped her head in guiltiness and clenched her fists.

Fenz was the young volunteer's name. Neztríanis would always remember him. He was the only soldier aware of her two-pronged attack. How did she possess such diabolical creativity? She froze the Blue Rapier soldiers' feet to the ground, so that they could not escape, *even* as she generated a heat so flagrant, it consumed the energy bursts of the Blue Rapier soldiers. That event would forever tarnish her Awakening and her path.

"Fenz, please forgive me," she pleaded. *I will atone for that folly one day.*

No matter that they were at war with her. "War" was an illusion once power-gaps were calculated. Her opponents never stood a chance. And her primary victim was the One with No Name. She maimed and murdered nel'asmív. Repentance without such remembrance was no repentance at all. True repentance consisted of conceding the irrevocability and irrecoverability of events and life.

Taking a deep inhalation while clearing her thoughts, the Sczyphamek called Temperature refocused her attention.

The stars in the Firmament boiled her qanín. *However*, the stars were not the only thing present in the Firmament.

"Kímaios'lo," the woman muttered. "Nothingness, no happenings, the [unimaginable] void," she translated.

"Lo'Ché," the woman spoke softly. "The Infinite [Place]…"

According to the Fragments, the ancestors, and the discernible verses within the Auría, the Firmament was produced by Lo'Ché and Kímaios'lo. A backdrop of indeterminable consequence, their meeting spawned the possibility of life. Life emerged somewhere between infinite possibility and nothing at all. The Firmament was Elemental and contained fathomless temperatures. The hottest and the coldest, right beside each other, next to each other, within each other, within Rai and Renzgé, *within* Neztríanis.

"Th- That's... I- I do not know if I can do... if I can be... I do not think I am capable of happening like that..." she stammered to Rai and Renzgé.

"You must," the elements replied.

In order to Awaken, she would have to resist and overcome the myanála of her own power.

The chants must be combined, she thought. Either that or a new incantation that I have yet to learn.

She happened as Neztríanis. She happened as a Sczyphamek and Nelon Ásmivü. She was a happening on Qeauríyx. Qeauríyx was but a speck on the Firmament's parchment. Zénan, Mashé, Parce... they were irreplaceable crumbs too. The Firmament was the backdrop of Lo'Ché and Kímaios'lo... Kímaios'lo and Lo'Ché were...?

Unbeknownst to Temperature, her aura materialized with unassuming boldness. In the distance, Timura watched her complement. It was the first time she could visibly see Neztríanis' Elemental illumination.

Standing up, Sczyphamek Temperature assessed the temperature surrounding her. She had to be able to identify multiple temperatures with relative ease if she were to Awaken. She could not house a range of temperatures without encountering them first.

She felt the temperature of Timura. She felt the temperature of a water droplet in a cloud. She examined the temperature of a rock on the slopes of Sunrise Mountain. She leapt into the temperature of a blade of grass...

Falling down on one knee, the daughter of Hopha would not be deterred and finally chanted, "Fá'atoño má." Quickly, she moved from chant to song. "Fá'atoño má."

Her aura grew in density and length and pressed forward in every direction, even underneath the ground she stood on, which caused some soil, dirt, and rocks to lift.

Her dark brown eyes grew auburn. Passing out would take away precious time, time that could be spent in reflection.

"Only as far as we can go," she reminded herself.

The ground beneath her was warmer than anything she presently sensed. She sensed there. And there. And there. And here...

Within a half-hour, she was dialoguing with fourteen different sources of temperate emanation. Pushing herself beyond fourteen was not her goal. She needed to discern the temperate constitution of each phenomenon with second-nature precision. She not only analyzed the ambient temperature, but also the internal dynamics of each particular object.

The woman perspired, so she took sips from her water jug. Her mind and body grew taxed. Fourteen encounters in the same moment was beyond her ability as a nel'asmív. At that moment, she finally embraced the difference between her and the rest of her species. The power-gap was more than might; it was also knowledge-based, a particular kind of knowledge, which did not necessarily mean it was belief-based as well...

"Fá'atoño má."

Neztríanis' hair lifted and hovered. For two hours she dialogued with the fourteen specks on the speck of Qeauríyx. She needed to anchor herself to the planet before she attempted the next step of her growth. Though drenched in sweat, she refused to sit down. She stood; she knelt; she paced; she did everything she could other than giving in or passing out.

Anámn stood near the cave's exit, which was also its entrance, and watched the snow fall to the ground. Chanting inaudibly, his dark green aura emerged and his eyes became golden crimson. The Phmquedrian sat down and meditated. His Elemental was connected to rest and movement, chance and purpose. These were relationships, but they were also systems of energy. Systems of energy... systems... Systems implied context, constants, variables, means, ends, and indeterminacy... Kinetic and potential energy were dependent upon such pieces.

"If I wield you too slow, that means that I'm not able to understand the major things that allow things to happen..." he muttered to himself and Téza. He smiled at both his insight and the vagueness of his own statement. *As long as it made sense to him.* "Because I can't make things move or happen just by thinking about moving them."

There were both filled with dread and anticipation. Awakening would bring closure while thrusting them farther into the uncharted. It seemed counterintuitive that Anámn and Neztríanis would be afraid of succeeding. However, if they Awakened, even greater challenges awaited them— challenges like the Zananín and the Daknín, and challenges that were either completely unforeseeable or only vaguely discernible. As beads of sweat fell from their foreheads and their auras' radiance became more developed and controlled, the Zephanín and Kylanín embraced the possibility of their deaths at the hands of their adversaries.

The Nez Spiritan, although confused and beleaguered by the persona of the Damüdan Sczyphamek, could not amend herself to the destruction and havoc wrought by the hands of the House of Kaz. *And they would have no rival.* Their myanála was deep.

The Phmquedrian breathed hard, recounting the past cycle and the things he had learned. Those who allied themselves with sadistic and reprehensible characters, like Galís and his father, could not be accepted as legitimate. Anámn embraced the implications of his encounter with the Damüdan vassal. Galís was not "an exception to the rule." In fact, the statement, "exception to the rule," was a lie. Global Initiative made its own rules and hid behind deity and ideology in order to justify their arbitrariness. The only concept that appeared absolute to them, Matriester surmised, was *victory*. Anything else was transient.

Neztríanis sat down on the gray, grassy tundra of the Nez Spiritan North Country, while Anámn leaned back against the wall of the cavern. They wondered about each other. They wondered if they could be allies.

Both of their journeys had revealed the precariousness of friendship and antipathy. What kind of power did the other possess? What was the name of his/her Elemental?

Despite their differences, they held in common a deep concern for Líachim. It pained Anámn to not go back to Phmquedria, but the truth was that if Líachim fell, there would be little chance that the tide of Global Initiative could be stemmed. Indeed, once they Awakened, the call of that continent would have to be answered.

"Once I Awaken?" Neztríanis asked herself, with a smile. "I am going ahead of myself. I must Awaken first before I take any other course of action."

On her third day of training, the woman was able to sense over twenty-five different sources of temperate emanation with ease. Neztríanis' Elemental had multiplied exponentially. She was able to locate water, ice, and water vapor in virtually no time. Her skills of discerning atmospheric gases that would allow Renzgé to burn at even greater temperatures had also become much more honed. She was able to ignite blue fires from over five lengths away; in addition she was able to create ice hemispheres at a distance of ten lengths. Most importantly, she could now anchor herself to Qeauríyx. Although the temperature constantly varied, the planet had a particular scent to its temperate signature. Neztríanis could smell and taste it.

Yet something was missing. Although her abilities increased and she wielded Rai and Renzgé with ease, she was still far from her Awakening. The distance was not measured in time, but in revelatory and rational knowledge and radical interconnection. Each time she dialogued with the Firmament, the Nez Spiritan was subject to the same treatment that she received almost one cycle prior.

They *still* overwhelmed her. She could not cool herself enough to withstand the heat of the stars, and she could not sufficiently warm herself to exist in the vacuum of outer space.

Timura had placed food near her campsite every day. It was not much. Just a few insects, small animals, and edible grass. They could not stay there much longer. The woman stared at the impenetrable mass that was Sunrise Mountain and discerned the temperature of its apex. It was impossibly two hundred and seventy-five degrees below freezing.

Neztríanis shivered and instinctively drew on Renzgé to warm her. And suddenly, she realized her impediment. And she understood why they could not tell her. She could not hear and receive it.

How did Vincallous know?

She was woefully trapped in *her* myanála.

When she grew cold she used Renzgé to warm herself. When she was nearly burned alive, she incanted Rai to cool herself. When hot, she used cold. When cold, she used heat. But, why? Why did she use opposites? Why did she utilize the two points to balance herself when she was immersed in *both* hot *and* cold? If she truly embraced Rai, then she would no longer be/do cold, her qanín would happen as/with the Elemental. Likewise, if she fully embraced Renzgé, of course she would be hot—for a moment—but she would soon be beyond "hot." The Sczyphamek called *Temperature* should happen beyond "hot;" she would happen as the conditions that gave "hot" the possibility of acting and being.

In other words, she had to plunge her qanín into the Firmament's vacuum and trust that Rai could sustain her. She would have to baptize her spirit, body, heart, and mind into the very heart of a starry blaze and trust that Renzgé would not be consumed.

It was revealed to her even as she reasoned it within her mind: Neztríanis' Elemental could only protect her based on the extent of her na'ísa, faith, and embrace. Because Neztríanis could not conceive or *trust* that Renzgé would guide, protect, and never leave her side when she discharged a fiery combustion, Rai came to her aid, so that she would not be consumed. But that was a waste, *such a waste of energy.* Renzgé had never been nor could it ever be "consumed" by eternal fire and presence. The same was true of Rai in relationship to eternal emptiness and frigidity.

In effect, she used unnecessary energy to shield herself. But against Lo'Ché and Kímaios'lo, she had *no chance* of protection. She now realized that her powers could not exceed their intersection. Their intersection gave her powers the possibility of happening. And if she could not best their power, then she would have to surrender hers. The statement worked both ways, for there would be times where and when surrender would not be an option. And during this exercise, she could not surrender her surrender...

Awakening meant that she would have to withhold her Nez Spiritan birthright: *Resistance.* Neztríanis never considered relinquishing that, even temporarily.

Yet, this was *her* path to Awakening. Vincallous and Pre-Eminent must have faced different, yet no less challenging sets of circumstances. And Anámn would not take her path either.

Her instinct and experience as a nel'asmív had guided her wielding of Rai and Renzgé. However, she was no longer *just* a Nelon Ásmivü. She happened as a Sczyphamek. She was part of a community, an aggregate. Awakening meant that she truly embraced that concept.

She was not an individual who easily *controlled* some sort of power. That type of thinking led towards the myanála, the myanála that inhibited *all* Sczyphameks from Awakening.

"*Fá'atoño má,*" she sang with a newfound understanding and faith.

When her aura exploded in power, Neztríanis was unafraid. Timura backed away in respect and anticipation. The témo sensed her partner's Elemental. Neztríanis was on the precipice. The Sczyphamek called Temperature—Neztríanis, Rai, and Renzgé—*their* aura was completely visible over thirty lengths away.

Timura's ears perked, and a little over a minute later, Temperature was before her and held the Auría before the témo.

"Hold on to this," she murmured. Her gaze was directed both within and beyond the Crossroad Islander.

"Y-yes," the témo stammered. *Temperature... if you continue this... You will happen like Exceptional and the Zananín... Vincallous knows this too. He is taking an unbelievable gamble...*

Timura clasped the Auría in her mouth, placed it on the terra of the North Country, and soon felt Neztríanis' hand on her head, between her ears. The Nez Spiritan scratched her partner's neck and smiled.

"I know I made a promise that you would not see me again until I Awakened, but I want to give you this. I do not want the Auría to chronicle this moment from such a close perspective. Future readers might misinterpret... because even I do not know to what this all portends. I cannot control the potential for misinterpretation entirely, but that which I can mitigate, I will."

"You have not used the Auría since the first day of your training," the témo commented.

"As far as we know, I am the only Sczyphamek who ever possessed the Auría during her Awakening. I do not wish to be the first one to use the Auría as a guide.

"It is not due to pride or humility. Vicious and Pre-Eminent Awakened without the Auría. And I am certain that Anámn is under the same conditions. I do not wish to be 'special' or 'chosen,' or thought of in such a misleading way. I will not be able to defeat the Zananín nor partially understand Anámn's challenges if I use this book, this most wonderful and confusing book..."

The témo nodded quickly, but by the time her head rose, the Sczyphamek called Temperature was nearly halfway back to her campsite.

"Exceptional," the témo commented.

Neztríanis stood still and relaxed her shoulders, arms, and hands. Flying at such a high velocity was no longer instantly taxing, although it did slowly drain her energy.

Anámn neared twenty hours of vigorous dialogue with Téza concerning the nuances of potential and kinetic energy. They did this while hovering outside of the cave. The aggregate stayed afloat by converting some of the precipitation's energy into theirs—Téza and Anámn, the Sczyphamek known as Kinesis. The Sczyphamek could not control the temperature, but he had learned early on that when energy was excited, it created heat. Therefore, he also used his Elemental to convert the surrounding area's ambient potential energy into heat, by accelerating the conversion within his aura, which kept him warm. Two days prior he could not imagine such a feat.

It was truly amazing what dialogue could inspire if one was willing to listen, trust, and admit the possibility that one could be wrong and did not have all the answers. Neztríanis was told this by the Great Mother and Timura; yet, neither of them possessed an Elemental. Brenko had lectured Anámn about potential and kinetic energy, but the Phmquedrian was too ashamed. His self-esteem was too low to listen.

However, the runaway had listened to Brenko on one occasion: "*Because I could be wrong.*" That was undoubtedly why the Brycian tactician was one of the most keen and resourceful nel'asmívs ever to roam Qeauríyx. He truly entertained the possible, even in the midst of his cynicism. Anámn wondered if he could accomplish and hold the tension that Brenko maintained. That tension was like a symbol for the relationship between potential and kinetic energy.

Anámn bit into the sweet bread. The taste was exquisite. Abandoning the temptation to tear into it with savage craving, the Phmquedrian Sczyphamek wrapped the bread and placed it back in the bag. At some unknown hour on some unknown day in the duration of Janíz 221 OGI, he stood up and walked to the entrance of the cavern that was in the third highest mount on the face of Qeauríyx.

As he exited, he said with a robust tone, "Fá... Toño... Mányx... Fá'atoño má. É müz keh fíp Téza má."

He leapt out of the cave, and as he did, his aura burst forth.

Energy carried no essence. It happened as a constant state of motion. Anámn understood. He took too long to wield Téza because he was searching for an inextinguishable constant for all energy.

Impossible.

Energy flowed. Energy shook. Energy rested. Energy *did* more than it *was*. And more than doing and being, energy *happened*.

Anámn did not know the names of *them*, but he perceived the two of them. By themselves, they were so ethereal and ephemeral that their existence would be unnoticeable. But something happened when they related to one another. Yet/not yet emerged. The very possibility/happening of energy lied in the midst of absolute impossibility and unconditional certainty.

Téza did not embrace the inextinguishable constants, but the variables and the dissonance. It was through the Elemental's embrace of such paradox that it was able to access the constants, and they were few, yet immense in meaning.

Téza was counterintuitive, but no less meaningful. Sifting through energy, relating to energy, and wielding it, Anámn had to trust, understand, and believe that Téza would not lead him into a fragmented place, but through the fragments, they would be able to scratch the inextinguishable.

Anámn cried to himself as he settled down on the snowy ground. He did not want access to *the* inextinguishable.

He hated It. He despised the One with No Name. But in his anger, in his hate, he could not escape the "ultimate." Even if he did not believe in the Nameless One, even if he did not trust in It, something else would take Its place, would it not? As a Nelon Ásmivü, Anámn could not escape his utter contingency and his awareness of a larger reality beyond him. Whether he admitted it or not, he filled in the gap of the ultimate when he focused on revenge. Revenge became his Nameless One. Knowledge had become his Nameless One. Fear had become his Nameless One.

Malchían's words were so clear in his remembrance, it was as if he could see their conversation before his very eyes. The Damüdan snowland became the jungles of Phmquedria.

"The most cunning and perceptive Sczyphameks, whether they were Benevolent or Malevolent, or even somewhere in between—Apathetic, they were reckoned—they embraced their faith and practice; however, they also embraced something more. This step challenges one mentally and physically. You see, a Malevolent Sczyphamek believes and is embraced just as much as a Benevolent; for idolatry is still belief, and it causes people to do anything if they truly believe in it. Truthfully, most Malevolent Sczyphameks do not see themselves as 'evil.' Even apathy is a belief, and its effects are just as reverberating. You must train your mind, body, spirit and Elemental in relation to each other, for there is no difference in them, and yet, they are distinctly important. This will allow you to heighten your Elemental..."

Faith was more than belief. Anámn fell into the revelation even as his mind processed through his memory. Faith was more than belief; it was trust.

The Zananín did not just believe their cause was right; they trusted; they *hoped* it was right. They staked their very lives and legacy on its "rightness." This was why they could not see themselves as evil. *That was why Malchían hated those kinds of stories.*

The Black Staff Mystic even said that "Apathy" was belief... but Anámn did not think he meant "indifference." He had asked Lénü what "apathy" meant, and she said it meant not caring about anything. But Anámn doubted that the Zephanín had such a belief. In his dreams, he had recollections of the great Sczyphamek war, although he knew not the name of the battle. But it was clear to him that all the Sczyphameks trusted in something.

Beyond this initial observation, there was a word Malchían used that Anámn had forgotten but now recalled: "idolatry."

Idols were not only problematic for those who believed in a deity. Kinesis now realized that idols, to a certain extent, had nothing to do with the Nameless One. They were about control. *Ultimate control.* They enforced a false presence and concealed a real absence. Such a cosmic and/or theological configuration led to the sacrificing of countless victims in order to placate an illegitimate order. All the while, the *real and definite* absence of the Nameless One, justice, life, mercy, peace, and love grew more and more concealed.

Something burned within Anámn at this disclosure. A deep, deep disturbance that would not be silent... *Idols had no place on Qeauríyx.*

"I... I..." Kinesis whispered and felt himself standing in a long line of Elemental ancestry whose names had not yet reached his memory. "I'm happening as a Kylanín... I will do what Kylaníns did. I will expose and crush all idols. Fá'atoño má."

Because I could be wrong.

Idols could not allow for such a statement. Their rule was absolute and unbelievers would have to perish at their uncompromising feet. And Anámn realized the paradox of his angst over idolatry and their absolute rule. He heard Brenko say it many times and Anámn himself believed it: *some kíma on Qeauríyx was not right.* His slavery, those deaths, the sex trade... *that kíma was wrong.* He would have to crush all idols but make sure he would not place new ones in their stead. Such a task was easier said than done.

Anámn placed his palms together while humming the chant endemic to Téza. Spreading them apart, Anámn released what could only be called a visible emanation of potential energy. He had long recognized that he used his hands too much when he displayed his powers. If he could surround an enemy with tens, maybe hundreds of such emanations...

It was the seventh day of Neztríanis' sojourn in the tundra north of Sunrise Mountain. She was able to discern over fifty sources of temperature with little to no strain.

It was time to try.

The Nez Spiritan Sczyphamek was methodical. She did not attempt to Awaken once she left the témo. She had to reach a place of trust first. The relationship between her, the elements, the planet, and her unyielding hope in the Nameless One allowed her to bind herself to an even greater community of things, animals, reality, yea, even the Firmament. She gave herself a full night's slumber and woke up early, just before sunrise.

Although Neztríanis possessed a habitual disdain of ultimatums, the day in which she now dwelled—this day *had to be* the day she Awakened. Supplies were scarce, and the Zephanín's strength would only decline from this point forward. Undoubtedly, achieving an Awakening would tax all parts of her qanín.

Rai and Renzgé seeped out of her heels and into the ground. The woman responded by taking off her shoes and letting her feet touch the que. She removed her outer layer of clothes and found herself wearing her sleeping attire and little else. She did not feel... no... she *could not feel*—differentiate—her toes, soles, and heels from the que.

Qeauríyx was her anchor. Her Elements were the vehicle. She had to trust that no matter the sway, the jostling, the turbulence... *she would not capsize.* They would not capsize.

Timura's hairs stood on end and her tail thrashed against the ground. The témo nearly lost her wits and consciousness. Neztríanis' aura was graciously unrelenting. Judging by outer appearance alone, an superficial onlooker might believe that the Zephanín had not increased in Elemental stature to any large degree. Such a judgment was folly. Rai, Renzgé, and Neztríanis Phyxtríalis were approaching a holy symbiosis.

Marveling at her partner's progression, the Orator recorded the witness of her own eyes, in témoic purr, verse, and meter:

"And in the Shadow of Sunrise
Descending from the home of Peace
The Sczyphamek, Happening as Temperature
Her portion was double—Two within the Sundry
Rai and Renzgé merged with the one I embrace as a Sister
Neztríanis... her Awakening...
I witnessed. I am witnessing. I will witness.
I dare not look upon her.
Such a fascinating and fearful sight...
I am overwhelmed by this Mystery..."

Neztríanis trained her eyes to the Firmament and murmured, "Rai mányx Renzgé monazí. Fá'atoño ma..."

Instantaneously, she was ripped through the Firmament in what seemed to be irreparable splinters. Parts of her burned, smoldering in the unquenchable fire of the stars. Other sections of her qanín were nearly broken to pieces by the empty cold vacuum of space.

Lo'Ché and Kímaios'lo were such tricksters.

Instead of attempting to pull herself together, Neztríanis let the gravitational wells of the stars and the emptiness of space draw her into their qaníns, holding ever tightly to Rai and Renzgé while chanting and singing to herself.

The ground beneath her split open and a sizeable earthquake echoed throughout the North Country. Timura had to ascend in order to not be swallowed up, for various crevices and cracks became enfleshed on the terra. Neztríanis levitated.

A star incinerated her. But it could not consume her. The more it tried to burn her, the more she was drawn into its temperature, the more Renzgé was there with her. In a flash from the heavens, Neztríanis was accosted with a primordial burst of heat from Lo'Ché... She felt it coming. She could not best it. She had to trust... she had to...

She was so afraid. But all she could do was surrender...

"Arrggghhh!" she screamed, burdened-down.

She understood. It was not done to hurt her. It was not even done to test her. What else could she feel the first time she felt something completely beyond her, but terror...? No... it was not *just* terror... Renzgé... *Renzgé was there.*

"Mona... Mona fla Renzgé ná. *Mona fla Renzgé ná. Mona fla Renzgé—*"

The emptiness maneuvered into the experience unexpectedly. But what did she/they expect? Her existence was due to their intersection.

"Zí mányx... Rai... I trust you... I... *I...*"

The extremities, the elemental, cosmic myanála was now upon her, beyond her, within her.

The atmosphere precipitated and rent itself asunder in lightning and thunder. Timura could not believe her senses. At times that Neztríanis' body evaporated away from the témo's keen eyes, only to be suddenly reconstituted.

In her heart, body, mind, and spirit—in her qanín, Neztríanis was immersed with primordial energies. Her hands(?) shook and uncontrollable tears fell. "Rai... Renzgé... Rai mányx Renzgé monazí. *Rai mányx Renzgé monazí. Rai mányx Renzgé monazí...*"

Cycles passed. Visions amassed. History came, went, and cycled again.

In their intersection, she could feel her connection with the Sundry. In their dance, she met Rai and Renzgé. In their dance, she saw how lovely they were. And how much love they had for her.

They loved her? They *could* love... themselves, each other, and her...

She did not surrender her surrender. In a moment she would never be prepared for, Lo'Ché and Kímaios'lo brandished upon her the full extent of hot and cold, Renzgé and Rai, presence and absence.

Could she handle them? Could she handle the very happenings that had chosen her as worthy though she felt so *unworthy*?

Falling to one knee, she nearly ------ in the revelation and evolution of herself/themselves.

They did not have to happen as myanála.

"If you love me this much... If you trust me this much... If you hope in me this much... Let me see you as you happen, please. Let me see myself with you..."

No one was able to witness them, except for Neztríanis and the First and whoever else had carried a Fragment of them... However, something was different. She was not carrying shards of Rai and Renzgé... Neztríanis was the first Sczyphamek to carry them in their rawest and most chaotic state.

She saw them... She saw them in a way that the First may not have even been able to witness. Within the follicles of her hair and down to the tingling of her feet, the Elemental embraced her. *Both* of it.

Though the experience bucked description, the woman became a kind of heat that would reduce any piece of matter into cosmic nothingness and vapor. At the same time, she held inside her the kind of cold that would solidify gas within the blink of an eye.

She was so *mild*. She was filled with a crushing presence so vast and overwhelming; it felt as if it would obliterate all dimensions, even *time*. Simultaneously, a void happened so expansive that no dimension could be given it. There was neither an *inside* nor *outside* of it. Yet, anything it touched would utterly collapse. And yet somehow they touched and did not negate each other.

Neztríanis, although a Nelon Ásmivü, now embraced a reality that was beyond what was signified in the name for her species, even as she was most certainly still a nel'asmív.

She was almost Awake. She could feel her pupils ready to take in the new light and darkness that was sure to await her… infinitely.

Her aura disambiguated into two, fluctuating colors, a dark bluish orange and a blackish white. Although one might be able to describe the former color with incredible hardship, words were absolutely abysmal in describing the latter color. It seemed visible while simultaneously distorting the entire background so that whatever was behind her was no longer visible. Symmetrically, the auras zigzagged and swirled across her body, yet they did not lose their balance. They became like helices, spiraling and growing around her. Soon, her aura reached five lengths in diameter.

"*Fá atoño má. Zí mányx que Rai. Mona fla Renzgé ná. Rai mányx Renzgé monazí.*" Suddenly, she stopped singing and whispered in a faint boom, "Fá atoño ma."

Qeauríyx anchored the woman as she traversed in the vehicle of Rai/Renzgé in order to meet Lo'Ché and Kímaios'lo; yet in meeting them she met herself and Rai/Renzgé while being throttled back to Qeauríyx. Directional thinking was preposterous.

Pulsating slowly in a low tone, while soon accompanied by another complementary melody, she grew concerted. A concerted melody of the Sundry filled her and her Elemental. Its percussion was timely and timeless. Its hum was profound and mysterious. The instrumentation of this newfound reality was beyond her reckoning. Who could have written such a sweet, tempestuous composition? In her left ear(?) Neztríanis heard the sound of ominous, melancholy horns. In her right(?) strings of rapture. The tempo's pace was gradually quickening… She was gradually quickening.

There they were.

They were two of the many melodies found within the Sundry.

Silence.

Stretching her qanín out, she became the melodies. She happened as the melodies.

Her eyes were open, just like always. She happened as the Sczyphamek known as Temperature, but she was given a new name, a new title by the elements, a title she had always possessed. But only now could she finally hear her name…

The inclement weather ceased. The wind abandoned its domineering ways. Soon, the ground settled and closed, and Sunrise Mountain moved closer to its original position.

Timura landed on the ground, completely exhausted. In the distance, Neztríanis fell to her hands and knees. The area around her was frostbitten and steaming. Slowly trotting her way, the témo drew in her wings and chanted. Although the aura was drawn in, the merged qaníns of Neztríanis, Rai, and Renzgé were oppressive in their intimacy. Timura grew milder and more invigorated with every step; Rai, Renzgé, and Neztríanis were calling for her. They—she was altogether different.

By the time the témo reached her complement's position, the Nez Spiritan Sczyphamek was laying face-down on the ground. Her head was turned to her left, with her eyes gazing towards Sunrise Mountain. Timura walked in front of her and sat down, looking intently in her partner's eyes.

The Myanín's faces met each other.

"Who are you?" Timura asked. "What is your title?"

"I happened as a Sczyphamek," the woman-Elemental answered. "The Sczyphamek embraced as Ambivalent."

"Ambivalent [Temperature]," the témo repeated. "By the One…"

"I wonder…" the nel'asmív said falling asleep. "I wonder what their original titles were… since they are now called by their Awakened names."

Neztríanis entered into a deep slumber, and the témo looked upon her in stupefaction. However, she understood her partner's last statement. Ambivalent was speaking about Késhal and Vincallous, Pre-Eminent [?] and Vicious [?]. The second names were descriptions of their first title just as much as they were symbols for their relationship to the entire cosmos.

He *felt* her. She and her Elemental were completely discernible to him, for only a moment. But he was sure, and Téza confirmed it. She *Awakened*. If Anámn intuited it, Vincallous and Késhal recognized it too.

"You're gonna feel us before this day is over," Anámn declared.

For the majority of his life, the Phmquedrian Sczyphamek believed that staying below the surface was his daily, infinite lot. Yet, when his powers emerged, he felt a new sense of urgency. Perhaps, maybe, he could *ride the surface*. But, riding the surface only brought him face to face with his own reflection, his father's mirror-image. Riding the surface could no longer be his goal. Nor was ascending above it in self-righteous idolatry. In order to Awaken, he had to *break the surface*.

He had been hanging in the pit too long. It was not enough to climb out of the pit. It was not enough to be on top of the pit. It was not enough to be at the pit's edge. *The pit must be demolished.* Yet Anámn was not deceived. Even as he disintegrated *that* pit, *another* one was sure to emerge. Sighing heavily and swallowing confidently, yet nervously, Anámn affirmed this Infinite Cycle.

He was outside, near the base of Mount Sunset. The snow fell so mightily that ocular visibility was unsustainable. But there was more than one way to see. The Yardük tree that Kinesis leaned upon gave him some energy; so did the raining snow. The wind lent him some of their motion. The melodies grew closer to his qanín every day. One of them was his; one of them was Téza. But the composition would not allow him to join in its recitation just yet.

Anámn had been training for two weeks. His supplies were diminished. The sweet bread was gone. His stomach began to remember what true hunger was. But Anámn would not surrender. His path to Awakening had to be in the embrace of perpetual motion, rest, chance, and purpose. He could not "control" any of these things, yet neither could they completely "control" him. They had to meet each other freely, openly, yea, even amicably in order for Anámn to Awaken.

Kinesis summoned potential energy for two days without sleeping, and he was famished. Although he could not convert the energy into food, he could use it to lessen the load of his own personal energy consumption. For fifty-four hours, Anámn marshaled rest and chance. He talked with it/them intently, in all their various configurations. Not all chance was the same. Some was more probable than others. Not all rest was the same. Some rest was completely still and uninhibited; it would take a great deal of energy to draw it/them out of slumber. While for others, rest was more precarious; nudge them just a little and things would be set in motion.

He was finally ready.

Sweating, hungry, and full of embrace, faith, and na'ísa, Sczyphamek Kinesis spoke in a soft, actionable tone, "Fá'atoño má."

Before his aura even emerged, the Yardüks and snow tried to clear out of his path, for they knew not their fate if they grew entangled in such a happening as Anámn's Awakening. The aura's bloom was so massive, it reached halfway up the heights of Mount Sunset, an altitude easily above twenty thousand feet. Yet there was no movement. No force was released. There was nothing palpable, only visible.

Indeed, Kinesis only made observable what was already present: amaranthine instantiations of potential energy. The dark green aura was noticeable for over two hundred lengths away. Anyone who was in that radius was sure to see the illumination. No wind, no rumble, no hum, nothing. It was all left up to chance and to rest.

He could feel them barreling towards his position. They were in and beyond the Firmament, but they still had to *move*... well, at least *one* of them.

The potential energy that Anámn assembled was enough to obliterate Mount Sunset and probably the entire nameless mountain range of Damüda... *if* Anámn's embrace was cogent enough. Just because the potential was large, that did *not guarantee* that Anámn would be able to harness it to its maximal kinetic discharge. In order for such a kinetic discharge to occur on such a large scale, Anámn's precision would have to be exceptional.

And one implication of this realization unnerved him: *Vincallous held back during Phenplyacin.* If he wanted to, Vicious could have possibly sunk half of Civix Setrin. Anámn was certain that the Damüdan was capable of such a feat. But he chose not to… *So what did that mean?* Did the reprehensible actually possess mercy and restraint?

The thought vanished as soon as the visitors arrived.

He deserved to live. He deserved to happen. Both of them—whoever, *what*ever they were—could not take that from him. They were larger and obviously more significant. He was minute and barely noticeable within the Infinite Cycles. It did not matter; even in recognizing his insignificance, *they only existed because of happenings like him and vice versa.* They needed and tolerated him just as much as he needed and tolerated them.

His aura flashed in steadfastness, not in arrogance or despotism. Anámn's aura cried to the Firmament. All the pain, all the suffering, all the unanswered questions, all the oppression, all the paradox felt by him, his people, *nel'asmív*, keh, and Qeauríyx, they filled his aura. The pain, suffering, questions, oppression, and paradox—he had the power to redeem their misbegotten potential. He could convert it into energy.

But Anámn was steadfast.

The suffering was not meant to—it was not *given* to redeem him. *The suffering was meant to crush him and others like him.* He would not automatically treat the injury, death, and meaningless suffered by his species as tests from some deity. Such logic was idolatrous. Furthermore, the questions, induced by suffering and misery, were not the sole or primary path to enlightenment.

No. Anámn had learned.

There was more than *one way* to convert potential energy into kinetic and back into potential…

No, he was steadfast.

It was his calling, his duty—his qanín would not be deterred. The wretched of Qeauríyx had surrendered too much already. They had been pained too much already. They had been wrongfully questioned too much already. The cosmic accuser(s) had prosecuted long enough. It was time for the accused to speak. The speck of dust that belonged to the Firmament hushed the heavenly ensemble.

A whirlwind whisked around Kinesis. Téza was so close to Anámn's qanín. The barrier was nearly eviscerated.

They revealed their names to him, at least, the only names his tongue could pronounce and his mind could comprehend.

"Lo'Ché and Kímaios'lo."

Other utterances, groans, and hums trailed and surrounded them in identification, but Anámn could not fathom them.

At that moment, the potential that Anámn carried within and about him, magnified and under control, could collapse half of Qeauríyx into nothingness. It could also grant a creative use. Energy was partial to neither creation nor destruction. It could be used for both.

Out of negative potential, creative forces could be at work.

Out of positive potential, destructive forces could be at work.

Out of negative potential, destructive forces could be at work.

Out of positive potential, creative forces could be at work.

Out of negative potential, creative and destructive forces could be at work.

Out of positive potential, creative and destructive forces could be at work.

Out of positive and negative potential, creative forces could be at work.

Out of positive and negative potential, destructive forces could be at work.

Out of positive and negative potential, destructive and creative forces could be at work.

Out of any kind of potential, *nothing happening was also possible.*

Out of no potential, *something happening was also possible.*

No rule, no inextinguishable law or principle could calculate something so dependent on chance *and* purpose, rest *and* movement. The cosmic and planetary crime was to preclude these *possibilities* and permutations to silence, as if one or two of them were the only ways things and energy could happen.

Lo'Ché could only be approximated to "positivity"—but, in reality, it was beyond such a designation.

Kímaios'lo could only be approximated to "negativity"—but in Anámn's qanín, he could feel that it was so much more.

They were on *both sides* of the equation because energy was cyclical. Time became irrelevant in the midst of these Happenings.

The "positive" and "negative" potential both created and destroyed… *Infinitely.* This meant that something about existence was both permanent and transitory.

That was no consolation.

"We don't have those ways of thinking," Anámn retorted. "I was in the mines every day. And not just me. Do Phmquedrians have to be transitory so that the Tannódin'é…" Anámn stopped himself in mid-thought. "Wait…"

Kinesis thought about Nísyx, Lénü and Brenko and Tarían, Van and Malchían, and all he had come to embrace. The testimony of nel'asmív surrounded him. "*Do some of us have to be destroyed so that others can have life?* …They don't want life; they want *everything.*"

The concerted melody continued to crescendo.

"Everything and enough are not the same."

The potential was converting into something. Its character was yet to be determined. Like an amorphous hourglass slowly sifting its grains, the energy was like a formless mass. Anámn was weighted down by personal choice and outside influences.

Kímaios'lo and Lo'Ché did not retreat. They pressed Anámn. "We can't be just a game, just an example of you. You all don't end, while many of us don't even die regular deaths. *We get killed.* And even those who die old, some of them die better deaths than others.

"Can you even understand what I am saying?" he asked. "You all are so big and beyond, can you even relate to us? Or would it have to be on your terms? Can you be just as powerless as I am, as we are?

"I can't beat you," he said. "I'm a part of you. And you're a part of me." Anámn's countenance changed and became earnest—the most serious he had ever been in his life. "But I will crush *anything* that makes it seem like things *have to be* this way. I and whoever will join me—we'll change this, we will create something different down here, over and over again. If it's big enough and infinite enough, maybe then you will understand."

Téza was so raw, *so* full. Anámn's qanín held the possibility of life, death, space, and time. This uninhibited side of Téza was unknown to Anámn. It was frightening, yet seductive. Téza withdrew no longer. The Elemental was ready to fully embrace Anámn, and Anámn found its melody ringing in his qanín. Henceforth, Anámn would be the first Sczyphamek since maybe the First to experience Téza in all its potential and power.

Lo'Ché and Kímaios'lo were not "amused." They "listened" intently to the molecule named Anámn Matriester, the Phmquedrian nel'asmív.

The chord struck Anámn hard. If it were not for *them*, he would not have been able to speak. And he was too ashamed, too full of potential and power, too full of righteous indignation—he had to admit the uncompromising Truth. *He did not want to die. He wanted to live.*

No.

There was *more.*

He was *afraid.* He was not prideful. He was scared.

That was why he wanted to know everything. That was why he wanted to live forever. He was afraid of his condition and the unknown beyond it.

This fear, this *xenophobia* of his own condition, he felt it like cool waters dripping over his head and down his spine. The water collected and soon found itself pooling with the water of his own kind.

They were all terrified.

He could feel their terror expressed in the potential. Some trained themselves, sedated themselves, *did something* to themselves so that they would no longer be afraid. Such effort, such energy, Anámn felt it. But those were actions, whatever his kind did to cover the fear, they were all actions. Before those actions was the potential, and to those who had seemingly thwarted the fear, the potential had to exist in order for them to even overcome it. It was almost endemic to his species...

"Fá'atoño má," he chanted. "É müz keh fíp Téza má. Téza...

"*É müz keh fíp Téza ma,*" he sang. "*Fá'atoño má.*"

More and more, the potential energy drew in. More fuel to the fire, more combustion to the engine, more tension to the string, more heat to the blade, more pressure to the nel'asmív…

Téza's melody was so nigh to the Sczyphamek that it drowned out the hum, volume, and meter of his chant.

Freely and without precondition, Kímaios'lo and Lo'Ché met Anámn Matriester, the Sczyphamek known as Kinesis, under the shadow of Mount Sunset. But more than anything, Anámn met Téza.

"I don't need to," Anámn said to himself. "We don't have to do it that way."

The potential energy vanished, yet there was no discharge, no sign of any release of energy. That was because Anámn did not have to release anything. He was between gathering potential and releasing kinesis.

In a power that was not from neither potential nor kinetic energy, but from somewhere else, Anámn's aura erupted in a brilliance and power that defied cataclysm. Snow lifted; trees rattled; Mount Sunset braced itself; the clouds vanished; Zénan shone, the Sczyphamek breathed hard and opened his palms.

Within moments, nothing happened. There was no observable data to imply what just happened. But it happened. Anámn Awakened with the smallest fanfare ever known to a Sczyphamek.

What's the point of wasting energy? he thought.

Gripping his sides in exhaustion, sweating profusely, breathing softly, and murmuring endlessly, the Sczyphamek gazed at his surroundings. Staring ahead, the Sczyphamek's golden crimson eyes were fixed upon the nameless mountain range. Within seconds thousands of green energy spheres emerged within the air and slightly above the ground, scintillating with a different kind of energy, a state, a moment, a happening of energy, *between* potential and kinetic. But just as soon as they appeared, they vanished.

"You are a wonderful friend," Anámn said to Téza. "A new name… Another name… my real name… I happened as Sczyphamek Latent. Latent [Kinesis].

"I wielded you too slowly… We really happen as yet/not yet."

It was only when Kímaios'lo and Lo'Ché met Anámn, did the Sczyphamek realize that he was focusing too much on the potential and kinetic sides of energy. Something about Téza was both/and and neither/nor. In fact, Téza happened more in the latter than the former. In the fraction of the smallest increment of time, an *intermediate* space occurred where potential and kinetic energy became inexorably entangled. However fleeting the moment, the actuality was real, and this was where Téza dwelled, at the "zero" point of energy, after the potential energy had begun to transfer, yet before the kinetic energy fully discharged. It was in that space, where infinite impossibility and possibility truly resided.

He fractured the myanála of his power by finding an in-between moment. Téza's power stemmed precisely from its "in-between" nature. Of all the ways to disentangle the two points within his own power, Kinesis could not imagine that such a path was possible. But Latent [Kinesis] could. "Yet/not yet" did not refer to him embracing both sides of the myanála in order to overcome it; on the other hand, dwelling fully in neither placed him squarely in both of them.

Turning energy into food was still beyond him, but that was not the point. He would be unable to achieve such a feat without Awakening. If he could not embrace Téza in all its fullness, any technique he produced would be wanton, because they would be *his* techniques and not *theirs*. Sczyphamek Latent [Kinesis], his title mischievously suggested the ever-changing middle of energy.

"Thank you," the man said to the Firmament and to the two grand elders of the beyond, Lo'Ché and Kímaios'lo. How could such grandiose things know humility?

However, Anámn felt no presence of anything close to resembling a Nameless One or Spirit. The Awakening was too revelatory and evolutionary for Anámn to deny the implications of the energetic system he now found himself so bound to. Just because he did not feel It, that did not mean It did not exist. Instead of denying Its existence, Anámn modified his belief. He was uncertain, unsure of Its existence, but that did not mean that It did not exist. Neither did it mean that It did exist. But as a matter of practice, he would operate as if It did not.

Any nel'asmív that believed the cosmos was limited to their experience and their investigation no matter how thoughtful and rigorous, Anámn deemed them fools. And he, like many in his species, used to be a chief amongst fools.

Neztríanis awoke from her sleep and looked at Timura in excitement.

"He did it!" she rejoiced. "Thank the Nameless One. On the same day…That is…"

"Improbable, yet not impossible," the témo said guardedly.

Neztríanis, noticing her partner's demeanor asked, "What is wrong? Why are you troubled?"

The témo shook her head. "No Orator has recorded a Cycle such as this."

Timura's tone conveyed that she was not speaking of the simultaneous Awakenings.

"Record of what?"

"You all. *All four of you*," the témo paused, unwilling to even admit the reality. "No Orator has ever reported such dispensations…"

"What do you mean…?"

"I have sensed you and Vincallous personally. Pre-Eminent and Vincallous are thought to be at nearly the same level. Honestly, I was hoping that Anámn would not be…"

"But?" the woman intuitively felt the qualifier coming.

"But he is on your level…" the témo whispered.

"I don't understand. Is that not a good thing?"

"There have been some great Sczyphameks of the past, but for the most powerful, adept, and mysterious, we always refer back to Exceptional and the First. And those two were separated by nearly nine thousand five hundred cycles! Now, four Sczyphameks are each other's contemporary, and all of you have the potential to be on the level of the First and Exceptional. In all my recollection, this has not happened before."

"When you say the level of Exceptional, you mean Elemental Individuation and a masterful use of the third level technique that Vincallous used, do you not?"

"Yes. Very few Sczyphameks achieve such a level, and only two were able to use them repeatedly and successfully, Exceptional and the First."

The Nez Spiritan considered the meaning of this newfound information. She felt Anámn's Awakening, but it did not feel as *potent* as hers.

"Do not take that feeling as a sign of less strength," the témo said instinctively. "That Sczyphamek is unbelievably strong, just like you." The Orator looked up towards the apex of Sunrise Mountain and then back at Ambivalent.

Ambivalent [Temperature] stood up and asked, "How long was I asleep?"

"Six hours or so."

Picking up the Auría next to the témo, the woman flipped to the tentative final page, and it read, "Thus concludes this cycle of the Sczyphamek once known as [Temperature], who Awakened Ambivalent. These pages shall soon rest in the heights of Zénan's rising." Moving back two pages, Neztríanis sighed in relief. The book did not chronicle her Awakening to any significant degree. The last thing Phyxtríalis wanted was to be heralded as the second coming of the First or Exceptional.

The ground still showed the signs of its movement and unsettling, but fortunately, Neztríanis did not lose her shoulderpack or water jug in the newly formed crevices of the North Country. Walking over to her disheveled campsite, the woman dressed herself, although the action was only for cosmetic purposes. In truth, Neztríanis was neither hot nor cold.

Lacing up her boots, Ambivalent beckoned the témo to her position. "I will return shortly. But I must ask you now, before this new journey even begins: will you join me for as long as you can, Timura? I am not the same person that you made that promise to two weeks ago. So I will not hold you to that pledge."

Timura drew near the Nez Spiritan. "We will probably be the last Myanín on Qeauríyx. I have to at least see where we are going." Nodding her head solemnly, she rasped, "Yes, I will join you, sister."

"We needed to know," the Sczyphamek said. The woman placed her hand on her friend's head, and her aura sprang forth. Ambivalent's illumination enclosed the témo and wrapped around her gently, infusing her with Elemental power. Timura could feel that the tax on Neztríanis was nearly negligible. Her abilities took only a slight, nearly unnoticeable drop.

"Rai and Renzgé intimated that once we achieve the Synthesis, I will not lose any of my ability. Apparently, you will wield them in a different way."

The témo gasped in wonderment. She could not believe how clearly she perceived Rai and Renzgé. And in hearing Rai and Renzgé, she also heard Neztríanis. Their bond was at the level of the qanín. Timura smiled and was disconcerted. A feeling such as this... It would be difficult to part from this sort of mutual interrelationship.

Timura wondered if Vincallous realized what he was doing when he let Neztríanis embark on this path.

"Yes," the Daughter of Qeauríyx answered. "He understands the risk. Which means that he must have a counterstrategy."

"If we are defeated..."

"We cannot lose... if we lose..."

Neither of them would even utter the obvious implication for Qeauríyx or their ancestry and lineage if such an outcome transpired.

"I hate to say it," the témo scowled, "but Sczyphamek Vicious is as remarkable as they come. We cannot underestimate either of them."

Neztríanis gave Timura a piercing glance. She perceived the témo's withdrawal as much as she realized *it* in her mind. Timura turned away in unmistakable shame.

"*Timura...*"

The témo faced her partner with disgrace in her eyes and unwilling to yield the information.

"You know what I am going to say. You know what I am going to ask."

"Yes. I do..." the témo trailed.

"You knew about them, didn't you? You knew Vincallous and Késhal were Sczyphameks? Or at least, you knew that there were at least two Sczyphameks before Phenplyacin. You—*the témos*—you all knew this because your species can sense the Awakenings of Sczyphameks."

Timura was condemningly quiet.

"I only realized this now... because Anámn and I just Awakened. I did not know témos had such ability or that your ability to sense Elementals was that strong. I honestly thought that Awakenings were for Sczyphameks and Sczyphameks alone."

The nel'asmív pressed her complement with unrelenting eyes.

"We helped train Vincallous," she said softly.

"*What?*" Neztríanis spat. "*Kíma.* That is kíma, Timura. Tell me you are lying."

"No. It happened."

A strong wind blew on their spot as Neztríanis' aura flashed in horrible discontent.

"You must understand; Vincallous was not like he is today. He is from eastern Damüda, an area long sympathetic to the témos."

The témo scratched the ground with her front paws, unearthing small rocks and dead grass. "Vincallous Awakened first. After he Awakened, the Den was perplexed. Témos can only sense the Awakening, not the exact location or the particular person. Not long after, Vincallous sought us out. He was forthright."

"Forthright?"

"Global Initiative, in the form of Blue Rapier, had destroyed his hometown and tortured and killed his parents before his eyes."

Neztríanis' mouth dropped before her aura waned.

"He was a member of Blue Rapier when he approached us, but he was soon to be promoted to the ranks of White Scythe. He wanted our help. He asked if we would grace him with a témo so that he could attain the Synthesis, but our numbers were so few that we were unable to lend him physical assistance. But we trained him to the best of our knowledge, for he needed it."

"What do you mean?" the Nez Spiritan asked.

"You felt White Scythe. It senses the qaníns of all living things. A Sczyphamek's qanín is a bit different though. We informed Vincallous that General Maximum would be able to sense an Awakened Sczyphamek with ease; therefore, we taught him how to suppress his Elemental in a way that would avoid detection to everyone except a témo and a Sczyphamek. We also taught him how to completely ensconce his Elemental…" Timura hung her head and shook it regrettably.

"Wait. Why? Why did you teach him these things? If he was against Global Initiative then why…"

"Why did he go back?" Timura finished her question. "He was a member of Blue Rapier. He planned to destroy Global Initiative from the inside. His plan was to kill the parents of Késhal, *personally*. Few had tried to assassinate the leaders of Global Initiative, but they all failed. None could get close enough to them. The Daknín was too swift and potent. And only an elite Sczyphamek could defeat three of them."

Seeing that Neztríanis was quieted, the témo continued the tale. "We trained him whenever we could, for he still had to participate in Global Initiative. We acknowledged the risks, but we had to try. And it was obvious that Vincallous' hate for Global Initiative was ineradicable. Neztríanis believe me when I say this: It was stronger than yours."

The woman sat down on the ground and Timura followed suit. "Two cycles after Vincallous Awakened, in 217 OGI, we felt another Awakening.

As you know, it was Késhal. But at the time, neither Vincallous nor we knew who it was. We were all concerned because Vincallous would soon be at a level where he would be able to destroy the Wielders and the House of Kaz. We waited for some sign of the Elemental warrior, but nothing happened, which meant one of two things: either that person was in Tannódin and was in all likelihood a Zananín or they were a Zephanín and would not participate in the affairs of Qeauríyx."

Timura's hair stood on end, her canines protruded, and her tail slapped the tundra, signaling the turning point of the narrative. "Vincallous scored a major victory in 218 OGI, crushing the insurrection at the Windward Isles with no casualties for White Scythe and very few for the insurrectionists. Because of this, he was to be awarded the Medal of Kaz, the highest military award in Global Initiative. After consulting with us in the Windward Isles, Vincallous set off to Tannódin. He told us not to interfere, in case his plan went awry. He did not want my species to face virtual extinction. We honestly believed that he had enough mastery and power to topple the Daknín and the House of Kaz. But then he encountered *her*."

"Késhal?"

"Yes. Vincallous sensed her the moment he arrived in Tannódin. Unfortunately for us all, he put his plans on hold... Vincallous is a masterful tactician. He could not defeat the Daknín and an Awakened Sczyphamek whose powers he had no way of ascertaining."

"But did Késhal not sense him?"

"She did, but she never told her parents that Vincallous was a Sczyphamek."

"*What?*" Neztríanis asked in disbelief. "That seems impossible. What possessed her to do such a thing? She is staunchly loyal to Global Initiative."

"Her motivations on the matter have remained unclear. But she did not tell anyone that Vincallous was a Sczyphamek, although she knew nothing of Van's history."

"*Van?*"

"That is Vincallous' real name: Van Fénüra."

"By the One." Neztríanis grew unnerved at the story's direction.

"Yes... I suppose we lost him then... He returned back to us and told us about his encounter. It was obvious to us all that he was attracted to her, but his hate for Global Initiative had never been stronger. After having her parents pin that medal on him, he was full of vengeance and wrath. He told us that Késhal was much more powerful than he, and he requested the Synthesis once more..."

"You refused, didn't you?"

"Yes. He was quite disappointed. He firmly believed that he could not defeat her without the aid of it. However, we gave him other news. Miska Kea had a plan in the works, which at that time was only one cycle old.

They were going to strike Tannódin on their own soil. Vincallous could not believe it, but we assured him this was so…"

Neztríanis exploded in disdain. "*Timura… Don't tell me you all had contacts in Miska Kea and did not them about Vincallous or Késhal…?*"

"Our kind was trapped in a myanála of our own," the Orator replied solemnly. "Remember what I told you about Mina?"

The Nez Spiritan nodded.

"We felt like this was an opportunity that we could not pass up again. But in our caution, we overreacted."

"What do you mean?"

"We were too withdrawn with Phmquedria, but we did not want to be overly aggressive either. In trying to stay out of that myanála we fell into another one."

The silence did the prompting.

"Fear of our extinction and hope for the planet," she answered. "Though it seems terrible to say, but as far as not telling the Miska Kea about Vincallous and Késhal, I do not regret that decision of the elders."

"How can you say that? Phenplyacin would not have happened!"

"*Exactly*," Timura said. "Whether utter victory or utter defeat, Phenplyacin would have never happened if nel'asmív loyal to Miska Kea had known that a Sczyphamek on the level of the First or Exceptional was next in line to lead it. Do you truly believe your species would have stood up to them, knowing that Pre-Eminent and the Daknín were together? And do you honestly believe that nel'asmív could have kept secret Vincallous' true identity for almost six cycles?"

Neztríanis looked away. She knew the truth in her qanín.

"Although we did not allow the Synthesis to take place, we gruesomely trained Vincallous to the best of our ability, and his power rivaled that of Késhal's. We were unsure of who would win their battle, the victor would be undoubtedly drained. Our hope was that at best Vincallous would defeat Késhal or at worst she would be critically wounded and we would be able to finish her.

"We kept Vincallous abreast of the developments for Phenplyacin, but he was being sent on increasingly desolate and death-defying missions, with little support from White Scythe.

"It was only a matter of time. Késhal's parents wanted Vincallous dead because of their relationship. They sent him on témo extermination missions and remote suicide missions of espionage even though those kinds of missions were out of White Scythe's normal jurisdiction. Many in his company died during those military engagements… But Vincallous was so patient, so methodical. He never complained. His countenance never wavered…"

"Until?" Neztríanis could sense it coming.

"Until Késhal's father died and he missed his opportunity to kill him. He grew impatient with the plans for Phenplyacin, and it was then that we became wary. He pressed us for the Synthesis one last time, but we rejected his request and called attention to his insatiable quest for vengeance. He was neither a Kylanín, Zephanín, nor Zananín. But we had come so far, and the battle was only six durations away. His hate for Global Initiative was the only thing we could actually count on. Even though he possessed a great love for Késhal, we never expected those feelings would win out…"

"I did not take part in the battle. I do not know what changed him in those final six durations. He knew the plan and was at the imperial palace that night to kill Késhal's mother and Késhal.

"But something happened… When my brothers and sisters arrived, they intuited that matters had gone wrong. The majority of them tried to stave off Vincallous' wrath. However… you know the rest…"

Neztríanis was so beset by Timura's confession that she trembled. She revisited their confrontation. The thoughts she had of him were placed in even greater flux. Right before their second Elemental exchange, he told her that he was "doing this so that a Sczyphamek like [him would] never exist again…"

She downplayed his statement. She barely remembered those words. What did he mean?

"Before he killed my mate, T'Kly, Vincallous stared at us with hatred in his eyes," Timura said in traumatic recollection. "I still remember his words:

'What gave you the right to judge us malevolent? Who appointed you judge of our cause? Why were we denied The Synthesis?'"

Neztríanis shook her head. "He was not saying 'us' as a Zananín—he was questioning you all about himself and Késhal, wasn't he?"

"No," the témo replied darkly. "It was the three of them. Van Fénúra and the Elemental, Wanesé and Dénque. Dé'wa they are called. The three qaníns that make up the Sczyphamek known as Vicious, that was who questioned us. They truly despise the témos now.

"Ambivalent, when témos reject a Sczyphamek, we are rejecting the Elemental too. In your case, we would reject Renzgé and Rai, as well as Neztríanis. This is what makes the Synthesis so powerful, coveted, and also so dangerously partial.

"Dénque, for instance, is deeply tied to Qeauríyx, and the rejection of that particular Elemental was undoubtedly felt by the planet itself…"

Neztríanis put her hand up and signaled that she could take no more. These revelations alone destroyed her cosmovision.

After a stretch of quietude, the woman said with no pretense, "He is beyond me and both of us. He would still crush me. Even now. I wonder if Pre-Eminent knows how strong he really is…"

Neztríanis threw the shoulderpack over her torso and grasped the Auría in her left hand. "There is much more for us to do… But right now, I have a task to finish. You can stay here."

"Yes, Ambivalent [Temperature], I will stay here. Your mother gave you this task. See it through."

"Fá'atoño má."

With little effort the Awakened Sczyphamek flew towards the second highest mountain on Qeauríyx. The temperature was ludicrously cold. But [Temperature] embraced Rai ever tighter, trusting that she would not be bested. The winds were murderous, and twenty thousand feet up, the Sczyphamek asserted her Elemental aura. The wind hushed. Neztríanis had stabilized the erratic atmospheric conditions in seconds.

Racing higher and higher, breathable air soon grew scant. Neztríanis compensated by using Renzgé to draw in the breathable gases in the lower elevation. Soon, Ambivalent broke through the clouds and reached four thousand feet below the apex. The view was absolutely stunning.

The Sczyphamek's eyes discerned warm and cold air currents; atmospheric ice, liquid, and gas; and the warmth emanating from Zénan. Setting down on a cliff, two thousand feet from the top, Neztríanis found the small crease she had scanned for some thirty-nine thousand feet below.

She was about to create an opening to the mountain, when her qanín was thrust into a vision—a vision not of her own choosing.

"Sczyphameks... Awakened Sczyphameks..." the voice resounded.

"What in the..." Anámn was completely taken aback. Somehow, he felt the other newly Awakened Sczyphamek's presence—hers and *someone else's*. However, it was not Vicious or Pre-Eminent.

"Anámn?" Neztríanis asked incredulously. "Is that really you?"

"How do you know my—"

"There is no time for this!" It was a man. "She will detect my location if this goes on too long." The voice possessed a clear sense of purpose. "Now chant the phrase!"

"Fá'atoño má," Neztríanis and Anámn chanted inwardly, the former in the heights of Sunrise Mountain, the latter walking along the base of the nameless Damüdan mountain range.

Instantly, they were drawn into a momentary rip in the intersection of space and time. And beyond their understanding, Anámn Matriester and Neztríanis Phyxtríalis, Latent and Ambivalent, stood face to face with each other, although they were continents and reaches apart.

"You *must* come to Líachim," the voice said with urgency. "Make your way here as quickly as possible."

"That was my plan all along," Anámn said. "*Who's this?*"

"Mine as well," the daughter of Hopha chimed. "And yes, who is speaking?"

"No time!" the man yelled then chuckled. "No time. Kíma... There's never enough time..."

Neztríanis and Anámn looked at one another in the temporal and spatial rift with eyes of confusion.

The daughter of Hopha's qanín fell. Anámn was Phmquedrian.

"You must come to me. Not to Aphaz or to Dynasty. Come to the Desert of Woe."

"*The Desert of Woe?*" Neztríanis was rattled out of her thoughts. Nothing was said to live in that desolate area.

"Where is that?" Anámn asked. "And why should we?"

"Because you will be defeated if you face them as you are now. Both of you should have embraced this by now." The words were so unguarded, clear, and concise; neither of them could argue the point. "I am located in the Temple of the Flowering Spirit. Together, you both should be able to find me."

"You cannot expect either of us to—" Neztríanis said.

"My name is Sczyphamek [Solstice]," the man interrupted.

"A Sczyphamek!" the Phmquedrian nearly fainted in disbelief. "Other than me, this woman—"

"Ambivalent," Phyxtríalis interjected. "My nel'asmív name is Neztríanis."

"Yeah, well, other than me (I'm Latent by the way), Ambivalent, Pre-Eminent and Vicious, there hasn't been a Sczyphamek in almost eighteen hundred cycles, except for Imperial."

"Eighteen hundred cycles," the voice trailed in near disbelief. "*By the One*, has it been that long?"

"[Solstice]?" Neztríanis inquired. She was ready to ask a host of questions.

"No more! The decision is yours to make. But if you are serious, you will come to me. I await both of your presences."

Neztríanis was back in front of the cavern. Anámn was still walking. They almost second-guessed the event's occurrence until Rai, Renzgé, and Téza confirmed that there was a residual Elemental aura present in the spatiotemporal rift. Whoever that man was, he had mastered a tertiary Sczyphamek technique.

The woman placed her palm on the rocky surface and chanted, "Mona fla Renzgé ná." The rock soon turned white hot and melted. She extended her aura and moved closer to the stone, and Renzgé continued to gorge and gouge the rock in calefaction. Before too long, an oozing opening formed. Using Rai to cool the surrounding area, the Sczyphamek carved a deep cavern within the outer wall of Sunrise Mountain. After about a hundred feet or so, the woman stopped. Her aura was bright and she set her eyes on the Auría one last time. She would have cried if she did not laugh. Before she was even able to finish this task, another one already presented itself.

Kneeling down in a reverential posture the woman prayed, "Nameless One, thank you for this day. Thank you for accompanying my sister and me this far.

"I do not understand everything about You; I do not know why You appear to be so 'weak;' I do not know why You happen so wonderfully; but I would rather have you loving than powerful, 'weak' than evil. I understand now that 'power' and You should not be equated, at least in the ways in which we nel'asmív conceive it.

"Help me on this journey, this infinite journey, O Nameless and Ineffable Happening(s), whose touch is as comforting as any I have known. Lead and guide me…"

The moment she placed the Auría on the newly formed cavern floor, the tears began to well. She would not hold them back. She missed her mother to the point of despair, but there was no chance she would see her now or maybe ever again.

Her purpose, at least its rough edges and outline, began to take shape. She had no time to rest. Her journey required movement. She was already cycles too late.

"I do not know how or why such madness and suffering entered into our planet," she resumed. "But our kind must no longer add to the madness. Suffering caused by the hands of *any* Sczyphamek must be put to an end. *And I will end it.*"

She wiped the tears from her face and gazed beyond the cavern's walls. "Will You help me? Will You remain silent? I do not have all the answers, but I understand enough now to know that if faith in You means absolute certainty, then it would not be faith at all. Fá'atoño má."

Upon exiting the cavern, the woman created a frozen cover to the entrance. The ice was so thick and so cold, and the location so terrible, that only a person deserving and able to survive would be able to find it. That was, if the Auría did not choose to move. However, Neztríanis could feel at least that much of its qanín. It still *did not want to be found.*

The woman descended hurriedly and found Timura stretching her wings, legs, and back. The témo was ready to leave, but a question lingered.

"What happened up there? It was almost as if I felt another Sczyphamek."

"You did."

"That is not possible. Témos are masters of tracking and analyzing Elemental auras."

"What if the Elemental displaces space and time?" the woman asked.

"I… I do not know…"

"We must go to Líachim. We must wait for Anámn though. He is to journey with us."

"You saw him?"

"Something like that." The woman shrugged and looked to the southeast. "It's time to leave. We will go south of the Crags first and get some real food. And, I need a bath… staxis…"

The témo and the woman laughed heartily as their auras erupted. They darted south, southeastward. Flying at such a speed with such an Elemental discharge would take some acclimation.

The daughter of Hopha was secretly vexed. Although the Myanín's link was nearly telepathic, they did have the ability to keep information from one another. Neztríanis did not want to tell the témo Anámn was Phmquedrian. The témos looked upon them with disgust and wrath. She only hoped that Anámn's disposition and Elemental were amicable.

"Kíma," Anámn spat. "We're supposed to go to Líachim, ah? Téza, what do you think?"

The Elemental gave Anámn a nudge of confidence. Téza had the ability to discern space and time. Space-time was linked to chance and purpose, rest and movement. And something about [Solstice] seemed familiar.

Anámn did not think he could fly to Líachim on his own. He had no idea how far away it was. He just knew it was far. His best bet was to go to southeast Damüda. Even if Brenko and Lénü were gone, the people there might be able to help him out. Knowing Brenko, the tactician had probably left some way for Anámn to follow them. The Sczyphamek missed his friends, even though his appreciation and awe of Téza was profound.

But the person he thought about the most was Nísyx Tekil. He cried unashamedly when he thought about her and the faith she had in him. She pressed him to leave Phmquedria and Awaken. She admonished him to be like the Kylanín of old. She saw the best in him.

His longing for her was like a dry lake before the commencing of the rainy season. His heart also longed for his people, the Phmquedrians. But even as a Sczyphamek, he was not omnipotent. He could only triage. His return to Euhilv would have to wait. Even so, he hated himself for coming to such a conclusion.

The nel'asmív was famished. If he was lucky, he could make it to Van's village in half a day, flying at a moderate speed. Maybe a loaf of sweet bread lay baking in someone's oven.

His thoughts shifted to the mystery person Van referred to as one of the next Wielders of the Black Staff. Anámn would not forget the promise he made to the Damüdan Wielder. He owed Malchían too much. Perhaps the new Wielder would seek to join he and Neztríanis. The newly Awakened Sczyphameks could use all the help they could get. After all, the Zananín were accompanied by the Daknín, and White Scythe, Blue Rapier, and the Violet Manacle were sure to be formidable.

However, gazing upon Neztríanis with his own qanín—if only for an ephemeral moment—gave Matriester some hope. He was comforted that there was another like him and that he was not alone. They had each other.

Two Kylanín against two Zananín. Anámn could think of no better way to crush the myanála of Global Initiative.

Téza seemed unnerved, although humorously so, when it listened to Anámn's musings.

"What?" he asked. "What's so funny?

"...Oh... Right... *Kíma*... I almost forgot... They're infinite."

Acknowledgements

Special thanks to Keedra Sales (I love you), Malcolm Sales, Matthia Sales, and all extended family; Jonathan Moody, Steven Battin, Rufus Burnett, Janeare Ashley, Jordan Clark, Kelvin Black, David Friend, Eric Gerlach, Michelle Milam, Marion Grau, Phillip Linden, St. Paul AME Church, the Graduate Theological Union, 3935, and so many others. A special shout out to my eldest bro and the creator of Type Illy Press and Southside Nefertiti, the one and only Michael T. Sales! Thank you for the cover art!!! And I thank the One and the many who inspired me to write and gave me the strength to carry on. To the Mystery that only metaphor can grasp in limp frailty... Thank You.

CPSIA information can be obtained at www.ICGtesting.com
Printed in the USA
LVOW04s2152201114

414859LV00014B/357/P

1837005